GHOST LIGHTS

GHOST LIGHTS

* * * * * * * * * * * * * *a novel*

LYDIA MILLET

W. W. Norton & Company
New York • London

The author thanks Maria Massie, Tom Mayer, Denise Scarfi, Amy
Robbins, Nancy Palmquist, Don Rifkin, Tara Powers, Anna Oler,
Ingsu Liu, and David High for all that they have done.

For information about permission to reproduce
selections from this book,
write to Permissions, W. W. Norton & Company, Inc.,
500 Fifth Avenue, New York, NY 10110

For information about special discounts for bulk purchases, please
contact W. W. Norton Special Sales at specialsales@wwnorton.
com or 800-233-4830

Manufacturing by Courier Westford
Book design by Chris Welch
Production manager: Anna Oler

Library of Congress Cataloging-in-Publication Data

Millet, Lydia, 1968–
Ghost lights : a novel / Lydia Millet. — 1st ed.
p. cm.
ISBN 978-0-393-08171-8 (hardcover)
I. Title.
PS3563.I42175G49 2011
813'.54—dc23

2011026502

W. W. Norton & Company, Inc.
500 Fifth Avenue, New York, N.Y. 10110
www.wwnorton.com

W. W. Norton & Company Ltd.
Castle House, 75/76 Wells Street, London W1T 3QT

1 2 3 4 5 6 7 8 9 0

GHOST LIGHTS

1

The walls were kittens and puppies. Like other pet facilities he had seen—even the Humane Society, where he had taken Casey when she was six to pick out a kitten—the kennel trafficked in a brand of cuteness he could not endorse. He had nothing against pets; in theory, the more pets the better, although he personally did not own one. Not in the sense of unchecked proliferation, feral cats mating all over the place, etc., but in the sense that cats were good, dogs were good. No argument there.

But he did not see why this high regard for pets, his or anyone else's, should be represented by photographs of puppies with word balloons emerging from their mouths—balloons that contained supposedly witty sayings that were, in fact, stupid. There was no call for dachshunds dressed up as the Blues Brothers.

Susan's name had been on the list of emergency contacts for

this particular dog. When its owner failed to pick it up after several weeks the kennel had finally called her. Instantly she felt guilty; she should have thought about the dog far sooner, she told Hal. She had forgotten the dog, forgotten all about it.

What was *wrong* with her? she asked him insistently.

Now here they were, come to pick up her missing boss's dog—the dog of a man who had vanished many weeks ago into a tropical jungle—and the woman at the front desk was worried for the dog. Not for the absent owner, no. She was interested only in the dog's situation.

Hal glanced over—surreptitiously, he hoped. She was a heavy, lank person with bleached hair showing black at the roots and a kind of jowly gray pallor that bespoke ill health. Neither dog kennels nor the Humane Society were typically staffed by so-called beautiful people, in his experience. They were staffed by committed pet lovers, and frankly these committed pet lovers put less than average value on appealing physically to their fellow men.

Or maybe they sought out the company of pets in the first place because they did not enjoy the company of said fellow men. It was understandable—a form of relaxation, perhaps. Even if he himself was not a committed pet lover per se, a committed a.k.a. professional pet lover, he could appreciate that. As to the lank half-dyed hair, greasy pallor, etc., they were probably caused by a philosophy. Hygiene and style were aimed at winning the favor of others, after all, and the committed pet lovers already had the respect, or at least the gratitude—which might even be preferable, in the eyes of a committed pet lover—of peers and strangers alike. They were monks and nuns, in a sense. Monks and nuns of the pets.

The dog woman held up a rubber banana printed with a smiley face and squeezed it. It squeaked.

"She's not eating well. I recommend a chew toy. It could ease the transition."

Susan, on the other hand, was worried not about the dog but for the dog's owner, her boss. She was fond of this employer far beyond the livelihood he provided, which might no longer be forthcoming since he was gone from the United States and possibly also dead.

She had confessed she was afraid of this. She had leaned over in bed and whispered her fear in the small hours of the morning. She was afraid her employer, to whom she had grown close—in the kind of unequal, crypto-friendship for which such relations occasionally allowed—would never return from the tropics, where he had disappeared some weeks ago while ostensibly conducting some routine business.

Hal was strongly ambivalent about the employer, known for some no-doubt-pretentious reason simply as T. For starters, he refused to refer to the guy using a single letter. He called him by his last name Stern, though seldom to his face. But Susan would brook no criticism. Ever since the boss guy's girlfriend died—for which Hal had sympathy, of course, but which still did not sanctify him—he could do no wrong in her eyes. To her he had become almost a son surrogate.

"Just sign these and we'll release her into your custody," said the dog woman abruptly, and shuffled papers. Susan was shaky, emotional, and clearly the dog woman was uncomfortable with this display. She handed Susan a clipboard and a pen. "She's all up to date on her shots, see? Two months ago, 08-05-94 it says here. And the leg's healed pretty well where it was amputated. The name and number of the vet he uses are on the card here. Wait a minute and I'll make you a copy."

She turned and disappeared through a doorway.

"It's a *three*-legged dog?" he asked Susan.

"She was run over."

"I didn't know it was a dog amputee."

Susan seemed to be trembling. He pulled her closer and held her. First the man let his dog run around in the street till she was hit by a car, then he flew off to Central America and left her in a kennel.

Quite nice.

After a minute Susan pulled away. While she busied herself rummaging around in her purse he wandered over to a door marked RESTROOM. He often escaped to bathrooms when he was in public, stood at sinks and gazed into mirrors. Bathrooms were the respite. What would he do without them? From when he was a boy, gangly and shy, he had found comfort here.

Slowly he washed his hands, let the warm water run. On the wall behind him was a mural of clouds, with stylized dogs and cats jumping among them. In the mirror he saw himself with a flying poodle over his head.

The three-legged dog deserved to be happy, as did they all. But a three-legged dog was not a four-legged dog. A three-legged dog had to mean more upkeep, with the addition of pathos . . . of course, this right here was the kind of impulse Casey despised. She hated pity and railed against it, in particular the presumption that pity implied and the way it had of raising one person above another, subjugating the injured and then elevating them to make up for it. Injury is not a moral state, she had said to him once when she was angry. People think disability makes you a better person—on the inside you must be some kind of martyr, they figure, since on the outside you're wrecked. But losing the use of your legs does not make you the Dalai Lama, she said. So the pity, which people usually reserve for things that don't threaten them, is bullshit.

He accepted this, from her perspective, but pity was a fact of life when it came to dogs with amputations and when it came to the paraplegic. There was nothing in his life that had hurt him more than what happened to Casey, the shock of which would never fully recede; so he and Susan already had, occupying the central space in their lives, a victim—the only victim, the closest victim possible. They did not need a canine victim too. They were decent people but they were not cut from the same cloth as the kennel employee. They were not caregivers first and foremost; they didn't wake up in the morning and say, "Hey! Let's go nurture something."

They were only parents.

Other parents, whose children had not been hurt, could never know how parenthood could be extended infinitely on the heels of such an event and become a domed universe, a closed universe beneath the opaque dome of the accident. Even the stars were not visible anymore.

The Milky Way, he thought suddenly. The Milky Way was out there. Not only that—a hundred billion galaxies, some with a trillion stars.

Shifting away from the blurry spiral arms that could not be fathomed, he gazed at the tiles on the wall beside him, their creamy blandness. At a certain moment—oftentimes at the crossroads between youth and adulthood—a change of position occurred between the self and the world. As a child and even a teenager he had felt small, looking up at the rest of it all as a monument, but then suddenly he was older and part of the architecture, its tangibility and the impulse behind it, its failings and its strengths. The heavy installations had lost their majesty and seemed temporary, even shoddy, with a propensity for decline.

At the same time he had felt himself fading in and out of the installations like patterns of sunlight or lines of insects; according to his mood he might be a partner in their solidity, a detractor or an opponent, but he had passed from outside to inside and become culpable for the world.

That was the price you paid for the feeling of inclusion: the buildings, the grids of cities with their roads and subways, their storefronts and systems turned approachable, even trivial. The two of you were locked in an interdependence in which you were both always decaying . . .

He had been bred to feel like an insider, no doubt—had grown up in an affluent Southern California suburb in the wake of the war, though the fifties and sixties were the time he remembered. It had been a pleasant blur of a youth. Sun on the lawns, his mother and father sitting at a thick pine table in the evening by lamplight. Braided placemats, soft butter in a dish and green beans in a bowl. The gentle sheen of the wood.

Time was like the table when he tried to recollect his childhood—vague but solid, fingerprinted and warm.

"Hal?"

It was Susan, on the other side of the door. She often lost him in bathrooms.

"Coming. Just a second," he said, and dried his hands on a soft paper towel. He had read a pamphlet that said the softest and thickest towels and toilet rolls were made not from woodchips but from the ancient giants: you wiped your ass with the history of the world . . . what was different for him and for Susan too, for anyone whose life had been interrupted, was that after that ascension to the citadel he had suddenly been ejected again. He'd been ejected from that communal life of achievers, the life of regularity. He had found himself there, in the span of the arches and the rise of the walls—that quick belonging, those years of lockstep—and then, with the accident, he was outside again forever. His own childhood and Casey's merged in his recall, encased in a golden glow; at the moment of her paralysis the childhood turned into a lost paradise, and so it would remain—for as long as he lived he would not be able to shrug off the sense of this loss. It left him with the sear of heartbreak and the pressure of resentment.

You worked, of course, to get clear of that resentment, to give it up like an offering. But it was a struggle that did not end. One day you felt it rise from you and disperse, you felt an upsurge of freedom, but the next day it settled on you again.

He existed, in fact, half in the moment of her childhood, suspended for all time. The memory dogged him with such persistence that he wished he could replace it with one that was less glowing, more tarnished and scuffed. The shine of her lost joy was blinding.

Of course the memory was not the childhood itself but a

vision of it he had created without wishing or trying to—a memory as unchanging as the accident itself, formed almost at the same moment, or at least at the moment when he was told, in the hospital, that the damage was permanent. At that instant a barrier was thrown up between what was and what should have been, a future for his little girl that had never been permitted. The childhood memory was a bridge between them, between then and now, which had to stay separate to be bearable. But there it shimmered, with a deceitful, sly nostalgia.

The dog woman came out from the back office trailing the dog on a sturdy brown-leather lead. No cheap and functional nylon for Thomas Stern. But Hal had to admit he took to the animal right away. She walked gamely, hopping with her hindquarters; she wore an attentive expression and wagged her tail.

He glanced at Susan: her eyes were filling with tears.

"Let me," he said softly, and reached out to hold the leash.

Susan knelt down and petted the dog, put her arms around it.

It was all Stern's fault. Stern had been an imposition on the family from start to finish. First he was an imposition on Susan, demanding her full-time loyalty as the caretaker of all the most trivial details of his gainful enterprise; into their quiet home had come long discussions of his youth and conscientiousness, even his overpriced wardrobe and alleged charisma. The latter of which was a myth Hal saw no reason to believe.

As a husband he had been forced to endure this intruder in his house constantly—not his physical presence but the daily, dull news of him. Many times he had wished that Susan was employed in an office with more personnel, for the sake of a little variation in her bulletins from the workplace. He himself was stationed in an office whose very size kept him from getting on oppressively intimate terms with any of his colleagues.

Then he had imposed himself on Casey—who knew how, Hal did not open his mind to the permutations, but he and Casey had been close, briefly—and now, missing, possibly even deceased, he was imposing on all of them.

．．．．．

The mutt sat in the back seat of the car, her ears forward, watching and listening. Hal drove.

"If she sheds a lot we can spread out a blanket back there," he said.

Susan gazed out the windshield.

"Casey might want her," she offered after a few minutes.

"Maybe she could have the dog some days but not all the time. That would be easier."

But strangers might laugh at them. Someone might laugh to see the girl in the wheelchair, walking a tripod dog.

He did not say this, of course.

They lapsed into silence until he turned into the grocery-store parking lot. They had to buy dishes and dog food.

"I'll stay with her," said Susan, so he rolled down the windows, crossed the lake of pavement and went into the store alone.

In the dry-goods aisle, where he gazed at brands of dog food, hypnotized and vacant, he felt himself floating back. It was the chief pitfall of any time he spent alone, anywhere from minutes to long hours. At work he did not drift so easily, because work occupied him. It commandeered his attention in a way that offered relief.

Casey had picked out a white kitten at the Humane Society and that was the last time he remembered being in a pet food aisle—although he must have bought cat food in the succeeding years, of course, after the kitten had grown into a cat, but he did not recall this. The cat had finally died shortly before the accident, of a kidney infection. But the first day of the kitten, with his six-year-old Casey in her blond ponytail, he had walked up and down an aisle indistinguishable from this one—it might even have *been* this one; they might have walked here together—holding her small hand.

He looked down at his own hand, which had flexed suddenly as though feeling the imprint.

Casey had gazed up at him and asked him why kittens didn't eat people food. His thoughts flicking briefly over slaughterhouse by-products and rendering and bone meal and carbolic acid and what "gourmet lamb entree" was code for, he told her smiling that kittens just liked cat food better.

Such was the duty of fatherhood, he had thought to himself, neatly satisfied at a simple task well accomplished, and reached for a bag of Purina.

Standing in front of the bags again, red backgrounds with head shots of golden retrievers, cocker spaniels, he wished it had all been so easy, even if it was a lie and a facile one too. What he would give now to be able to hand her such a lie in place of the life she had. Anything. He would have no qualms at all, not one.

He would lie through his teeth if it would do any good. If only lies would suffice.

* * * * *

There was a libertarian in his office. It happened fairly often.

This one believed carmakers should pay for all roads. He was a hefty man in his thirties and his face was red with anger as he sat in the seat across from Hal's desk; understandably, in a way, since his house had been seized by a revenue officer.

The case was closed, but he had hammered on the bullet-proof glass door.

Hal made a gentle case for public roads—a gentle and inoffensive case, he felt—but still the libertarian looked at him through narrowed eyes as though he were a damnable liar.

"The way I see it, the tax system is what *gives* us our freedoms. The freedom to move, for starters. I mean, what would happen if every man had to build his own roads? Or if every single mile of road was a toll? You could try looking at it that way."

The libertarian's narrowed eyes were already glazing over. Tax protesters liked to talk, often, but once someone else took a turn at talking they felt a nap coming on.

Roads were easy as a soapbox because no citizen could cling to the belief that roads were built for free. On the roads where they drove they *felt* free, of course—they drew in a sweet breath of independence and let it out again happily. Americans loved to drive, discovered in driving both a splendid isolation and the shimmering mirage of connectedness.

But how did they come to drive on those roads, those slick long roads that gave a view of mountains or valleys, of suburbs or cities? They paid for their vehicles, of course. Hal had never yet met a protester who believed the cars themselves should be free, handed out like candy at Halloween to all and sundry from a benevolent car-giving source. A typical protester did not blame car manufacturers for charging money, for he held private enterprise in high esteem. He blamed the government for charging for its myriad services, but private operators could rob him blind in broad daylight, all in the name of liberty.

Hal's own father had been wary of government programs. Possibly this was why Hal had an affection for libertarians, albeit patronizing. Most of them had a chip on their shoulders, a heavy chip. It was as though, when they were young, a schoolyard bully had terrorized them, and in the memory of that bully an idea of Big Government had come to be encoded.

But government is only a bully, he liked to tell them, when it needs to be for the common welfare . . . crime was another arena where government took a stern and paternal hand, and most tax protesters did not mind this a bit. When it came to crime—a matter far more serious, in the eyes of your average protester, than say education or poverty—protesters were all about government. Also they had no argument with the government when it came to the commissioning, manufacture and deployment of vast arrays of weapons, both conventional and nuclear.

According to your typical tax protester the potential oblivion of all things living was rightly the province of government, but not so a measly ten- or fifteen-percent garnishment of their salary.

It was not the mandate of the Service, of course, to psychoanalyze or proselytize. It was not the purview of the Service to take taxpayers under its wing and baby them. It was the task of the Service simply to evaluate, assess and finally collect. But Hal often chose to engage personally despite the fact that, under the law, he was not required to do so or even, frankly, encouraged.

In truth, no matter what facts and figures he marshaled to defend government, the protesters were never converted. Simply, they cherished their right to direct fear and loathing at government bureaucracy. It was a God-given right, and one they insisted on exercising to the fullest. All he could give them, in the end, was an impression of having been listened to and reasoned with. Though they stoutly resisted reason—it was another God-given right to be unreasonable, indeed to hate reason almost as much as they despised government—they might not forget that he had made them a cup of coffee.

"Let me get you some coffee," he said to the libertarian, who was jiggling one foot. "Milk? All we have is that powdered dairy creamer."

While he was in the hallway pouring the coffee the libertarian might notice the pictures on his desk, of Susan in a dress and Casey in her wheelchair. Casey hated the picture and accused him of pandering, but he genuinely loved it and in any case could not bear to have earlier pictures of her around.

His coworker Linda came up behind him at the coffeemaker.

Her large round earrings were like Christmas tree ornaments. "Hal," she said, reaching for a tea bag, "the papers room is a mess. Where are the 433-D's?"

"New stack," he said. "Beside the obsolete forms? Second shelf. On your left."

Protesters often rejected reason without even pinning down what it was they rejected, he thought as he tapped in the dairy creamer. They understood in the most nebulous terms the difference between argument and debate, or even raw unquestioning instinct and rigorous logic. Finally what they cherished most, he thought—and he made these generalizations only after decades of service—was their relationship not to morality or individualism but to symbols.

The symbols had about them an aura of immanence, and to the symbols many protesters cleaved. It was often not one symbol for them but many—say a flag, say an eagle, say a cross; say a pair of crossed swords. The symbols were richly pregnant, pregnant with a meaning that would never be born.

It never needed to be.

Against a symbol there could be no argument.

"Here you go," he said, in his office again, and handed over the coffee mug.

His colleagues in general were not believers like him but cynics. They were cynical about their jobs and cynical about the tax code; they were cynics about human nature and about civil service. Indeed his own deep convictions on the subject of taxes and government would likely have been objects of their ridicule if not for the fact that, due to Casey's paralysis, he often got a free pass on everything.

And it wasn't simple pity either. Everyone came to know illness in the course of their lives, everyone came to know death, and somewhere within this grim terrain was the situation of Casey, Susan and him—a situation in which people beheld the inverse of their own good fortune. In Casey they saw a lamb on the altar: there others suffered for their sin. If they did not believe in sin they tended to be superstitious at least, believing her affliction filled some kind of ambient bad-luck quota that might otherwise have to be filled by them.

He reorganized a taxpayer file idly. The dog had slept at the foot of the bed last night, where she'd whined until lifted, and left short white hairs all over the red quilt. He did not like these hairs but he had liked the feel of the dog on his feet while he was falling asleep. In the morning, as he was pouring coffee into his travel mug before leaving, Susan had called Casey from the wall phone in the kitchen. "We have his dog," he heard his wife say, watching the dog lap at her new water bowl, and then, "No. Still nothing."

A knock on his office door.

"Come in," he said.

It was Rodriguez, who wore his pants belted high.

"Hey, man," said Rodriguez.

"Hey."

Often a single habit of an otherwise unremarkable person, such as wearing high-waisted pants, struck Hal as tragic.

"So you coming to lunch? It's Linda's fiftieth."

"Fiftieth," said Hal. "Whoa."

With the pants tightly cinched right below his rib cage, Rodriguez limited his options. Figuratively speaking, Rodriguez shot himself in the foot every time he got dressed.

"Who woulda known, right? She doesn't look a day over sixty-five," said Rodriguez, and laughed nervously.

"Thanks for thinking of me. I have an appointment with my daughter at lunchtime, though," said Hal regretfully. It was his standard excuse, but in this case a lie and thus in need of fleshing out to have the ring of truth. "She's in the market for a new car. I have to go with her to a dealership to talk about conversion. You know—hand controls, wheelchair loader. You'd be surprised how many of those mobility-equipment folks try to rip off paraplegics."

"Oh man," said Rodriguez, looking pained. "You kidding?"

"Yeah," said Hal. "I am. They're all right. But she needs help with the process."

Rodriguez was not a real cynic but wore the guise of cynicism to fit in. His attempts at sarcasm had the air of a strained joke, and from the rare moments when he allowed his actual persona to reveal itself Hal suspected he was secretly and painfully earnest. The earnestness and the high-waisted pants were connected, of course. Intimately. Anyone could tell from looking at his beltline that the cynicism was a juvenile posturing. But Rodriguez was a guy who could watch comedians on TV make fun of nerds simply by wearing their pants belted high and laugh heartily along with the crowd, never suspecting that their target was him. Essentially he had a blind spot—as everyone did—but Rodriguez's blind spot was in the public domain, like Casey's paralysis.

"Sure, man. Too bad though. We're going to that place with the kickass enchiladas."

Hal had a weakness for Rodriguez. And he presumed that his own sincerity—mainly his devotion, which had become known to his colleagues only by dint of their collective involvement in taxation, to the quaint idea of a wise and kindly government—would look practically jaded next to the near-cretinous gullibility of Rodriguez.

But this genuine, earnest persona of Rodriguez, being kept in lockdown, was never allowed into Gen Pop long enough for Hal to be certain.

"Eat one for me, OK?" he said in what he hoped was a tone of finality. "With New Mexican green chiles."

"No way," said Rodriguez. "Those chiles'd be repeating on me."

"Jesus," said Hal, and waved him away. "Enough said then."

Rodriguez retreated with a swaggering manner, as though his remark about vomiting into his mouth placed him firmly within the pantheon of the suave.

At one o'clock Hal drove west, partly because he was committed to his fabrication and partly because he wanted to pay his daughter a visit. Casey had recently relocated from her Soviet-style tenement in the Marina to a pleasant building dating from the thirties or forties, rare for Santa Monica, with large, airy rooms and arched doorways. He was delighted with the move, which signaled a rise out of apathy. Calla lilies grew in profusion beneath the front windows.

She had a new job in telemarketing. Difficult to see how selling timeshares in Jamaica could satisfy her in the long run, but for now at least she had a steady income. He should have called before he left but if she wasn't home, fine: he had to get out of the office anyway.

The freeways were open and before long he had parked on the street and was walking around to the back door. Through an open window he heard her voice—"Uh huh. And what do you want me to do then?"

The tone struck him as wrong for telemarketing. Of course she was a novice, she might not have it down yet. Casey had a nice voice, low and husky, which to him had always seemed tomboyish. It occurred to him she was probably, in fact, talking to her new boyfriend, a man from the support group, and he felt sheepish. For the so-called differently abled, privacy was a chronic problem.

He rapped on the window and waved to her inside; she turned, wearing a telephone headset, smiled, and mouthed at him to wait. He nodded as she rolled into the next room and out of earshot.

He was used to waiting: he waited for her often. Sitting down on the ramp, he gazed out at the backyard. Behind a small patch of grass, the usual deep and lush L.A. green that looked fake but in fact merely represented an extravagant level of water use . . . but here she was, already.

"I hear you got yourself a new cripple," said Casey from the back door. It was automatic and had swung open silently. "I'm so jealous!"

"Hi, sweetie. Hey, you meet any of the neighbors yet?" he asked, and stood.

Good if someone close by was looking out for her.

"Dad, please. I mean I know your little girl is coming out of her shell finally, every day is a blessing, rise and shine and like that, hell, I'm full-barrel on the positive attitude. But I didn't get a lobotomy. I don't roll around to the neighbors smiling and doing the meet and greet."

"A lobotomy wouldn't have that effect," he said, and went up the ramp and inside.

"So the three-legged dog thing, it's like a classic empty-nest syndrome, child-surrogate deal. Am I right?"

She went ahead of him through the kitchen, where an electric teakettle was whining. She switched it off and poured.

"You want a cup of tea? I'm having peppermint."

"Thanks. I'll just get a glass of water I think," he said, and moved around her.

"I knew this couple that when their basketball-playing kid went away to college—and this guy was like seven feet tall— they went out and got a dog two days later. Thing was though, the dog was a hundred-and-sixty-pound English mastiff. Came up to their chest level. True story. Remember Cal Shepard? From Samo?"

"The kid that drooled," he said, nodding.

"Cal Shepard did not drool. He was a popular jock. That was Jon Spisiak."

"A kid that drools in high school," he mused, shaking his head. He stood at the open refrigerator looking in. It was almost empty. "You don't have bottled water?"

"And I wouldn't even say Jon drooled per se," she said, and gestured at a white watercooler in the corner. "It was more like he had extra saliva. Oh. So Sal's coming over, by the way."

"The new boyfriend from group? This is great. I can submit him to the rigorous screening process."

"He'll fail. I have to warn you."

"Of course. They always do."

"But more than usual. Trust me."

"What. Is he a protester? A militia member?"

"He used to be a cop. Now he wears fatigues and sometimes a balaclava."

"Guy wears a balaclava in L.A.?"

"He took me up to Tahoe once. He wore it then. A black one. He looked like a paraplegic ninja."

He was following her into the living room, where a leather couch and chairs surrounded a low glass table.

"What, he wants to keep his face hidden?"

"I dunno, Dad. Ask him yourself."

"I can't ask him about the balaclava if he's not wearing it."

"OK. I'm like officially tired of this subject."

"Touchy!"

She spun her chair slowly and stopped, picked her mug out of the cup holder. He sat down opposite.

"I'm sorry," she said.

"Anyway. I look forward to meeting him."

"So T. still hasn't been heard from."

"No. And I think it's time your mother moved on."

Casey blew across the surface of her tea.

"I realize she's loyal," he went on. "But who knows what's happening with him. You know? It could be anything. Maybe he had legal trouble she never knew about and a secret account in the Caymans. Right? Change will be good for her. Something new."

Casey nodded and sipped.

"It'll be hard," he went on, and drank his water, "for her to know how long to wait before she makes key decisions, lets people go. There's that young guy that works there, that she hired a while back. And then the financial situation. I say find a good lawyer and pass the buck."

"She filed a missing persons report," said Casey softly. "And she's been calling the embassy every day."

"The U.S. embassy? In Belize?"

He heard the front doorbell ring.

"That'll be him. The father of your grandchild."

"What?"

"Kidding."

"I'll get it," he said, and rose.

As usual she was right; as soon as he pushed the button to open the door he knew the guy was a loser. Tamped-down anger, free-floating rage.

"Hey, welcome," he said affably, and stood back.

"Who are *you*?" asked the guy.

"My father," called Casey from within. "Hal, meet Sal."

"We rhyming," said Sal flatly, and rolled past him with no gesture of greeting. Hal had seen his share of bitter disabled guys and was inured to it—more or less preoccupied with this new information about Susan, he realized, turning from the door as it closed. His wife who was consumed with anxiety about the real-estate guy. The extent of her affection for Stern, the transparently maternal attachment, if examined by a professional, would likely prove rooted in some psychopathology related to the accident.

"I should get back to the office," he told Casey, and extended a hand to Sal. "It was nice to meet you."

Sal did something with his own hand that looked like a gang sign. A poser, thought Hal, as he stooped to kiss Casey's cheek. Understandable, but hardly deserving of respect. Before he was paralyzed he had been a cop, likely a swaggerer and a bully since almost all of them were, but now that he was spinal-cord injured he identified with the same underclass he used to dream of bludgeoning.

Outside Hal passed the suitor's conveyance, a battered hatchback in gunmetal gray that featured a bumper sticker calling for the rescue of POW/MIAs. It was parked half on the driveway and half on the lawn, and the right-side tires had ripped up a fresh track in the turf.

Law-enforcement officers were not his favorites among the varied ranks of persons who chose a career in public service. He recognized that the job carried with it certain personality requisites, such as a predisposition to violence, and that the demand for violent enforcers was embedded in the system, as was the supply of violent offenders. By some estimates, one out of twenty-five Americans was a sociopath.

And that was higher than anywhere else on the globe: this great nation was a fertile breeding ground for psychos. Or rather, as the economists would put it, the U.S. of A. had a comparative advantage in antisocial personality disorder.

And hey: these guys had to have incomes, just like everyone else.

At the very least one in fifty.

Casey, of course, could not be dissuaded from her choices,

having become stubborn and intractable after the accident—a development he had come to accept for the strength it lent her. This boyfriend choice, like the others, had to be left to play out. Still it was difficult to believe she had been on the telephone with the cop-turned-homeboy using that tender voice. Slipping behind the steering wheel, Hal repressed a shudder.

Remember: she is grown up. He often had to remind himself.

Also, she carried pepper spray when she went out at night. She had taken a course in disability martial arts.

Susan had to be frustrated, he reflected, driving. She likely felt responsible for what had happened to Stern. This feeling of responsibility was completely irrational, of course, but he knew it well. When regret was strong enough, guilt rose up to greet it. Maybe she thought she should have kept Stern from traveling alone; maybe she thought she should have persuaded him into therapy or grief counseling. Not that this would even have been possible.

They should talk more, Hal and Susan. They lay down to sleep at different hours, they rarely went out, lately there had been more distance between them than he wanted.

An old lady with a walker stepped out in front of his car; he swerved and hit the curb hard.

· · · · ·

The car had to be towed. He called Casey, and Sal came to get him.

"I appreciate this," he told Sal, mildly humiliated.

Sometimes a sociopath helped you out.

They drove together to a rental car agency, Hal shooting side-long glances at Sal's hands on the controls. The fingers bore small tattoos between the knuckles, which he was relieved to see were small plantlike designs rather than, say, LOVE and HATE. Looked like pot, possibly. There was a stale smell in the car—sweat, grease and cigarettes. He cracked the window, then rolled it all the way down. The dash was covered in stickers: rock bands, possibly, to judge by the graphics. Of course the names were unfamiliar to him. Blood, skulls in cowboy hats, sheriff's badges and guns, tigers and poppies and roses and faux-Gothic lettering.

Some of the paraphernalia was Mexican, some American, but all of it was equally encoded. Loud music played, a polka beat with electric guitar and an accordion. A *narcocorrido* if he was not mistaken: he had learned about these on National Public Radio. They celebrated drug kingpins.

Sal was moving his head to the beat and seemed to be muttering the lyrics.

"So your Spanish is fluent?" Hal said loudly, and smiled.

Sal nodded and flicked his fingers against the wheel, still mouthing.

"You grow up in L.A.?"

"East. I used to be police," said Sal. "L.A.P.D."

"Casey told me."

"She tell you I got shot by a friendly?"

"She didn't tell me that part."

"Yeah. This little kid, his first day on the job."

"Jesus," said Hal, shaking his head. "That's . . ."

"Fucked-up shit," said Sal, and went back to hitting the steering wheel and jutting his head forward in an embarrassing rhythm. Thankfully they had already reached the car place.

She has to be kidding, thought Hal as Sal screeched out of the lot touching his forehead in a mock salute.

He called the office from the car-rental counter. He had to take the rest of the day off, he said: car accident, and half the afternoon was already gone. Then he tried Susan's office and got the answering machine.

He wished he could go back to Casey's apartment, but that was inappropriate and would come off tedious and doting. Also very possibly Sal had gone back there also. No, he had to make his own entertainment. He would drive home in the rental and relax, take the dog for a walk.

His street was silent —neighbors dispersed to other parts of the city, in their compartments of earning. The branches of trees were still, there was no breeze at all, and pulling into the drive-way in the rental car he had a curious impression: nothing was moving.

The car shifted into park, he sat beneath a giant maple. The leaves had turned red. After he turned the key to shut off the engine, even he was still. He concurred in the stillness of the scene, half by choice, half by temperament. There was a kind of soft suffocation in it . . . time, he thought, passing forever in front of him and not passing at all.

A young man was coming out the front door. It was Robert, who worked with Susan, shrugging on a jacket as he closed the door behind him.

"Robert!" he said, but since he was inside the car the sound of his voice was trapped. He opened the car door and Robert glanced up from his feet, startled briefly before he smiled. Hal stepped up and shook his hand.

"Hey," said Robert. He was handsome—far nearer to what Casey should have for a boyfriend than, say, Sal was. Although Robert, like Tom Stern, erred on the side of a prep-school caricature. No doubt he had rowed for Yale. "Hey! Yeah! So how you doing, man? I'm here on courier duty. Susan's working at home today."

"You looking for a new job yet?"

"I am. I wish I wasn't."

"I know. Unfortunate."

"It's a tragedy, is what it is."

"You don't think maybe he, you know, chose to leave? Numbered accounts, like that?"

"Hey, you gotta think that way. Right? Being the IRS and all."

"Occupational hazard, I guess."

"Seriously, I considered it for a minute or two. But nah. He's basically a good guy. And I mean there are projects we're right in the middle of. I'm talking, with him not being here? Like literally millions of dollars are getting washed down the drain."

"Have you met my daughter?" asked Hal, aware this was a non sequitur. When he hit the curb something had jarred him—he thought the shock of the crumpling fender had torqued his neck, possibly. Suddenly he was feeling lightheaded.

"Casey? Sure. Why?"

"Oh, I don't know . . . ," said Hal vaguely, and all at once they were awkward. "Anyway. Good luck with the job search."

Inside he heard the shower running. A sealed manila envelope lay on the dining room table, along with the mail. The dog must be upstairs with Susan. But climbing to the second floor, he shivered with a passing chill—the house felt wrong. He and Susan needed to go away somewhere, he thought: since the accident they never traveled much, fearing Casey would suddenly need them.

"Susan?" he called, and the dog came galumphing out of the bedroom.

"In here," came her voice, and he went into the bathroom, where the mirrors were steamed.

"Ran into Robert on his way out," he said to the shower curtain.

"Uh huh? What are you doing home, honey?"

"Car accident."

She pulled back the shower curtain. Her face was flushed; she looked lovely.

"You OK?"

"Maybe a little headache. No big deal. But I have a rental."

"No one was hurt though?"

"Zero casualties." He reached out and kissed her. "You smell so good."

"It's the shampoo."

He wanted to go to bed with her. He held her and kissed her more, water falling on both of them.

"Oh, Hal, not this second," she said. "I'm all wet."

"That's fine with me."

"Later. I promise."

He let her go and stepped back, his hair plastered.

"You look cute," she said, and swatted the wet mat of it before she pulled the curtain closed again. He gazed at the blur of her form through the blue plastic, which was covered in raised dots. He could barely tell what she was doing. One of her arms stretched up and back again. Had she put a hand up to adjust the nozzle? Her movements were shrouded. Equally she could have been reaching for a razor. She could be anyone, seen through this filter, doing almost anything. She was unknown to him.

"So what happened, exactly?" she asked through the curtain.

"I swerved to avoid a pedestrian."

He turned around and went into the bedroom, sat down on his side of the bed. The stillness from outside was with him here, ongoing. In the doorway stood the dog, watching. Their bed linens were still wrinkled and mounded from the morning; the triangle of sheet he sat on was warm. She must have been napping. But then, when Robert arrived, she would have risen. Why was it still warm now?

Maybe the dog had been sleeping there.

Hal's stomach felt nervous.

In a minor panic he pulled back the coverlet, checked the sheets. Nothing, of course. Paranoid.

Usually—only on weekends of course—she took a brief afternoon nap on her own side of the bed, just as they kept to their own sides at nighttime, but it was warm on his side today. Still, it was a trivial anomaly. A young man coming out of his house at midday and for this he was suspicious? He had turned into a middle-aged cliché. Suddenly a blip in the routine had become a conjugal violation.

He stood and began to straighten the blankets, unthinking.

The dog lay down, head on paws, in the hallway. He finished with the coverlet and the pillows, hospital corners because he kept on perfecting them mechanically, at the same time struck by the phrase: *cuckold*. But someone had to do it. The bed had to be made. A bed unmade in the afternoon seemed decadent, even ugly.

When it was accomplished he turned toward his nightstand. The alarm clock had fallen on its face; he set it upright again. Otherwise the order was usual—all of it familiar except for, wait, a very small piece of plastic.

It was minuscule, a triangle maybe three millimeters long with a couple of scallops along the edge, and shiny black or maybe even dark green. It could be anything. He thought about this, his heart racing. He held the dark piece of plastic between thumb and forefinger. A small scallop, a small serration.

He was paranoid. He should seek help.

In the meantime, it was an itch that had to be scratched.

With difficulty he deposited the fragment on the nightstand again, careful not to drop it on the carpet and thereby lose it, and went back to the bathroom, to the nearest trash can. Susan had the shower radio on—a song about coming to a window, which he seemed to recall was sung by an annoying yet strangely popular lesbian.

The air was hot and moist and heavy and he couldn't see even her blur through the curtain now. Good, for his purposes.

Quickly and furtively he pulled the can from beneath the counter and looked inside. Balled-up tissue, mostly; a Q-tip was visible. To stick his hands in the trash can would be openly desperate. Yet he did so.

Nothing hidden in the wads of tissue but an empty aspirin bottle. He put it down and washed his hands, let his breath out softly.

Still.

He went back to the bedside table and carefully picked up the fragment. He did not let it go.

"Going out for a soda, back in five," he called out.

He stepped over the dog and took the stairs two at a time. There was a drugstore on Wilshire. He kept the fragment pressed between the pads of his fingers, pressing it hard even as he grabbed his keys with the other hand, strode out the front door and got into the rental car. He pressed it hard all the way there, strode purposefully to the back and was face-to-face with a wall of condoms.

But his findings were inconclusive. The piece was small, its color indeterminate. It might be one brand with certain specifications or it might be another. He held it up next to the packages and leaned in close, squinting despite the fluorescents in the hope of seeing more precisely. It might be none of them. Plainly. Abruptly he smelled something familiar from antiquity—what was it? Yes: benzoyl peroxide.

A pimply boy leaned past him and grabbed a single Trojan.

Science, he scolded irritably as he made his way up the aisle, could easily discern the answer, with a microscope and maybe one or two more instruments. Science could plumb the mystery, could discern, for example, whether this had been part of a foil packet or simply plastic.

He was not a scientist, unfortunately.

What other form of packaging would there likely have been, in that location on the nightstand? Kleenex? It was not a piece of a Kleenex packet, though. Too thick, too solid. Crackers? No. Also no. The fact that she had been taking a shower right then, the warmth of the sheets . . . he could ask her himself, but regardless of the answer it would be humiliating. Even the suspicion was destructive. He knew this. Better simply, on his own recognizance, to know. One way or the other. Robert: maybe he would test him. Go into the office tomorrow. Find a pretext to discuss marriage? Casually, in passing. Few specifics. Confide in Robert, ostensibly, about the pluses and minuses of marriage? The costs and benefits it might bring? On Robert's face, as he listened, he would catch any sign of shame.

But this would not happen.

When he first met Susan, he remembered, stepping through the metal detectors and out into the parking lot, she was almost a hippie. The year was 1966. She was a teacher back then. Though she did not engage in politics much or smoke marijuana she had honey-colored long hair, wore all-natural fabrics and believed in free love. Shortly after they met she announced a plan to move into an intentional community called "The Eden Project" up in Mendocino. He had to work hard to dissuade her. She was young and idealistic and more than that she was romantically inclined, with a tableau in her mind of fresh air and fields of strawberries. A pure life, etc. He was idealistic too, but wary of stereotype and quite certain of what he wanted, namely for her not to move into an intentional community with a lute player named Rom.

In the end he won her over by arguing that the intentional

community was elitist. He added to this an insinuation that it was also racist.

He smiled ruefully at the memory, recalling his earnest youthful idiocy and the forcefulness with which he had prosecuted his aims. He could still hear the discussion, at a party on the beach. She wore faded cutoff jean shorts and her legs were tan and slim. He had held her wrists in his hands and argued passionately that for her to move with the other well-meaning hippies to Mendocino would mean a "renunciation of society" that would lock her into a "white, upper-middle-class cultural ghetto" and ultimately augur "an abdication of personal responsibility."

After that they had moved into a one-bedroom together—in a white, upper-middle-class neighborhood, of course. She cut her hair and he finished his accounting degree. Eventually the free-love notion faded.

Possibly now, however, the free love had made a resurgence.

He tried to remember how the free love had ended. They had argued about it on and off, but not with great engagement; Susan had always believed it more in theory than practice. She was shy by inclination and reluctant to let others see her naked. But she said the usual things the hippies liked to say back then about the limits of monogamy, such as "Why should the intimacy and joy of sex be reserved for one relationship?" and "People are not property." Once, almost to prove her point it seemed, she kissed another man at a foreign movie—an individual she barely knew who was French, had body odor and smoked cloying cigarettes. This had provoked a minor drama in the relationship. But in due time the Frenchman retreated, as they were wont to do.

Still, he had never, he reflected, actually asked her formally to renounce the free-love idea. There was nothing contractual, there were no stipulations. He had merely assumed she had grown out of it. In a certain sense it seemed ridiculous now that the matter was unclear to him; most marriages did not allow for such ambiguity. Did they? On the other hand this was not ambiguity, exactly, rather it was an element they had forgotten, a corner left untucked . . . it was like a religion that receded, leaving a vague memory of faith but few practical details. The religion had been overtaken by the day-to-day.

He had to admit: there was the possibility that quietly, in a private realm, she was still a believer.

The fragment was imprinted into the pad of his right thumb. He stood beside the rental car and flicked it off with his forefinger. It disappeared instantly; it was too small even to watch flitter down . . . to tell the truth, he thought, unlocking the car door, Susan was probably right, or at least had been more honest back then than he had. He had been looking out for himself, frankly. He had known she was too good for him, but also felt that, having attracted her, it was more or less his sovereign right to retain her. Like a lost-and-found coin.

They got married, had Casey and were happy, the three of them. Time passed; the events were not important, only the feel of it. Then the accident happened. Somehow after the accident he had assumed they would always stay as they were, exactly.

In his own case he loved Susan steadily and took for granted that he always would. He had believed until now that she felt the same way. Also, when couples lost a child they frequently divorced, but something like the accident tended to lock you together like clenched teeth. At least that was what he observed in the parents' groups. Sitting in pairs around the circle, on those hard, awkward chairs, many wives and husbands seemed to share nothing more than a sloping and gray defeat.

When he considered it, though: since the boss man went missing her interest had been diminishing. He had not taken it personally. He had believed she was preoccupied, and this, he thought, was still true. For whatever reason, he had seen, he was currently on the periphery of her life, or at least at the periphery of her attention. By itself this was not a problem; he was comfortable in the background. He often thought of himself on the sidelines, not at the center of the action, and the image was not unpleasant. For a long time there had been more pressing matters than his own needs or preferences; there was Casey first and always and then there was Susan's job, where she considered her boss a virtual prodigy, a kind of urgent cause that required service.

Why the cause of real-estate profit should now command her fealty, when it had never before done so, he had not seriously questioned. Her sense of professional obligation seemed grounded in the personal, chiefly.

Backing up in the rental car—careful now, careful; he could easily have two accidents in one day—he considered the possibility that her preoccupation had been due not to Stern's absence, as he had previously reasoned, but to the new chemistry of her small office in the awareness of that absence, a small office now inhabited solely by her and Robert.

2

The mother lived in a small townhouse not far from their own near the Venice–Santa Monica boundary, connected to other units around an open yard. She was not much older than Susan or Hal but apparently somewhat *non compos mentis*, since she required a live-in attendant. He was not clear whether she suffered from early-onset Alzheimer's, presenile dementia or some other condition, and Susan did not enlighten him.

They met to visit her at lunchtime, pulling up to the curb at the same time from different directions. Susan had spent the morning at her office, of course, no doubt closeted with Robert, whereas he himself had spent the morning at his office closeted with Rodriguez, who picked his teeth with a plastic cocktail sword. When they stepped out of their cars Hal leaned in to kiss her and breathed in her sweet smell; he also scrutinized her face closely, trying to detect the vestigial presence of the free love.

But there was nothing out of the ordinary. Still his suspicions hovered as he followed her up the front path.

A busty, squarish woman opened the door, a woman with a large mouth and bulbous nose. She had a thick accent, possibly from eastern Europe. She led them in and seated them on a sofa, where a large china cabinet dominated the view.

"You're lucky. It's a very good day for her. Clear, you know?"

As they waited Hal gazed through the glass diamonds of the breakfront at a large, Asian-looking soup tureen in faded pink and green, trying to discern what scenes it depicted. He was deciding whether to rise and inspect it more closely when Susan grasped his hand with a sudden fierce need.

"I'm not sure how to tell her," she whispered. "Even though I practiced."

He leaned his shoulder against her, but before he could say anything Mrs. Stern came in smiling, wearing white slacks and a linen blazer. A good-looking woman, if a little weak-chinned— thin and pale-blond and somewhat patrician, as though born into wealth and then faded from it.

"Susan," she said warmly. "It's so good to see you again."

"Angela," said Susan, and rose to embrace her. "This is my husband Hal."

"A pleasure. And what a wonderful daughter you both have."

"We think so," said Hal.

"We used to do jigsaw puzzles, the two of us. I had to give it up though. It's my vision—I need cataract surgery. Can I get you a drink? Iced tea or coffee? I have a fresh pot brewing."

"Oh. Sure. Thank you."

"Yes," said Hal. "That would be nice. Thanks."

Roses and leaves and very small Chinamen.

The term was out of favor.

"So what's the latest," she said, as she moved into the kitchen. They were separated by an island with barstools. Susan got up nervously, followed her and leaned against it.

"We—we still haven't been able to establish contact," she told the mother with some hesitation, and he felt certain that only he could hear her voice waver.

"Milk?" asked Angela. "Or sugar?"

"Just a little milk, please," said Susan, and nodded distractedly.

"No thanks, not for me."

"I check in with the embassy on a daily basis," went on Susan. "But there's nothing they can do, on the active side. It's quite a small facility. They don't have resources. All they can do is relay any reports that come in."

"Oh, yes," said Angela, nodding as she poured milk into both of their cups. Hal considered waving a hand to prevent her, but then gave up. "The boat man worked for them, didn't he."

"Pardon?"

"I think the man who called about the boat worked for the embassy."

She put Susan's cup in front of her on the counter and walked around the island toward Hal. At the same time Susan turned to both of them, wide-eyed and deliberate. He accepted his cup and smiled gratefully.

"What boat?" asked Susan, with a hint of alarm. "What do you mean?"

"The man called about a boat he was in."

"I had no idea," said Susan. "Oh my God."

She wandered back to the couch and sat down heavily. Angela glided back to the kitchen, oblivious, and poured her own coffee.

"Oh yes. The little white motorboat. They found it."

Susan gazed at her agape as she came back in, holding her cup delicately, and perched in a chair opposite.

"Tell us the details," said Hal carefully. "Won't you? Susan has been very, very worried."

"There was a little white motorboat he was in? With a native guide, you know, a tour guide doing the driving. Then the other day they found the boat, but there was no one in it. It floated back down to the beach, and there were some people fishing just then, or someone there was a fisherman . . . ? Anyway. Do they fish there? Something about fishing."

"Just the boat?" asked Susan.

She seemed to him to be entranced, breathless and possibly fearful. He reached out and rested his hand on her shoulder.

"A man from the embassy called me, I thought he said. Or wait. Maybe it was the United Nations. Don't they also have policemen?"

Angela crossed her legs gracefully and cocked her head, as though idly wondering.

"Uh," said Hal slowly. "Are you sure they called you?" She was beginning to show her lack of acuity; for all they knew the boat story was a full-fledged delusion. "Did you, for instance, get a name from this informant?"

"It was the hotel where Thomas was staying," said the attendant from the doorway, and Angela sipped her tea. "The resort hotel. They made an inquiry and then they called us."

"Of course," said Susan faintly. Her cheeks were flushed, Hal noticed, but he could not tell whether she was upset or excited at the news, whether it chilled or encouraged her.

"They have not seen Thomas yet," said the attendant.

"No," agreed Susan, and shook her head. "I do know that much." She went to pick up her coffee cup—for something to occupy her, Hal guessed—and gulped from it thirstily, looking away from them.

"You take care of his business," said the attendant, and smiled at Susan. "I know because of the paychecks!"

"Yes, I do," said Susan. "But we may need to change that. It's one reason I came. Mrs. Stern? If you have the means, you may find it easier to pay Vera's wages out of your own accounts for a while. T.'s finances are in transition. With all this confusion. Will that be a problem?"

"Oh? Oh. No," said Angela, and waved a hand dismissively at Vera. "My checkbook is in there," and she gestured toward a small writing desk.

"I am already paid for last week," said Vera. "No problem. OK. Excuse me."

"I would also like," said Susan slowly, as Vera disappeared down a corridor, "to hire someone. I want to take *action*, I want to step in. I owe it to him. We all do. And to his business, which needs him. We're losing money daily."

"Someone?"

"A private security firm. To investigate what happened down

there. I can handle it out of our petty cash fund at first, and draw on his other accounts later, if it starts to drag out."

Angela nodded but Hal thought she was hardly listening.

"You know, to fly down and be in-country. Have a team on the ground. A search party actively looking for him. I would do it myself, but I have to handle things at this end."

"Whatever you think, dear," said Angela. "But don't worry too much. He doesn't really need them."

"Them?"

"You know. Policemen."

There was a pause, during which Angela recrossed her legs and smoothed her slacks over one thin thigh. From the apartment above them Hal could hear a bass line thudding. The rhythm was powerful but the melody indistinct. He tried to attune himself to the music, in case of recognition. In the meantime he was conscious of the quietness in the room, the soup tureen with its outdated homunculi in their robes and black topknots.

He had a sense of the rapidly cooling coffee in his cup, which he could not drink because he did not like coffee with milk, and the uncanny calm of the mother, which settled on her like a soporific . . . was she indifferent to her son, his well-being? Or was she absent?

"I hope you're right," said Susan to Angela, and smiled tightly.

"That boy has always landed on his feet."

"But this is . . ."

"Trust me."

After a few moments Susan consulted her watch.

"Well. I should probably be getting back," she said, and Hal placed his coffee cup on the end table, relieved to be rid of it, and rose. "Do you have a couple of photographs I could take with me? To give them for the investigation?"

"Oh!" said Angela. "Certainly."

She handed Susan a white and gold album off a shelf, and Hal waited impatiently while Susan paged through it, slipping snapshots from beneath plastic.

"It was good to see you," said Angela when Susan gave it back. "Thank you for visiting me."

She stood beside them at the door, benign and passive as they filed out. Susan was agitated, almost distraught. For his own part, all he was thinking as they left was: So, about the free love.

He wanted to ask her but he knew the question would seem irrelevant, pathetic in its smallness and its self-interest. There was a man's life at stake. She was thinking only of that. The specter of death trumped the free-love worry.

"I should have done it before," she said, shaking her head as she strode ahead of him toward the street. "I should have followed my instincts."

For him, however, there was no specter of death, frankly. For one of them, there was the specter of death; for the other, only the specter of free love.

"I should have hired someone right away, but it's not the kind of . . . I mean who thinks of that? You know?"

"I do know," he said, with what he hoped was solemnity.

"I'm going to call them today. All it takes is picking up the phone and a credit card. A couple of photos . . . but why would they call *her*?"

"I'm sorry?"

They were standing at her car, facing each other.

"That hotel. They had explicit instructions to call *me*. I had to authorize the charges to his card, finally . . . she can't do anything with the information, you saw how she is."

"I did. It's just she *is* his mother."

"Still. It's unprofessional that they didn't call *me*."

"Maybe the language barrier. A misunderstanding."

He wondered if she was close to discerning his near-complete indifference to these questions, if she could discern the fact that he was hiding the real worry. What about the free love.

"OK. Anyway. Thank you for being here, honey. Sorry I'm so scattered," she said, and opened her car door.

He was due back immediately—it had been two days now of distraction and not attending to his workload—but he did not go back. Instead he let her car disappear down the street and then drove toward her office himself.

He pulled into a parking structure close to the Promenade, from which, if he went to the third floor and gazed southward, he could see through the windows of her suite. She had pointed out this feature to him when she first began working for Stern—how from the west windows of the office you could look over a few white rooftops to the Pacific Ocean, and from the east you had almost nothing in view save the hulking gray levels of the parking complex.

He made a few circuits before a space opened up in the right location. He wanted to be able to stay in the car as he watched, unseen. He had become a stalker.

He was almost sure he had the right window, and gazed at it expectantly, but the rectangle stayed dark.

For a few minutes, idle and slightly anxious, he listened to the squeak of tires as cars rounded corners in the structure behind him. He tried to rethink his position. Give this up, this adolescent fixation; return to doing your duty.

He was not quite willing to leave, but still he had his hand on the keys in the rental car's ignition—disappointed but also a little relieved—when the light in the rectangle flicked on. He saw Susan. She leaned over a cabinet. He could not make out her facial expression or even her features, only the lines of her silhouette. He wished he had a pair of high-end binoculars. She could be a bird, he thought, and he could be a birdwatcher. He had always thought there was something furtive about birdwatchers, mainly the ones who kept "life lists"—something voyeuristic and calculating in how they observed and catalogued their quarry.

The young man Robert stood in the room also, further away. His head moved slightly: he must be talking, Hal thought. He turned and opened a file cabinet. The free love. The free love.

But no: the free love was not yet in evidence. Wait, he told himself. Only wait. The free love was bound to rear its head. Eavesdroppers heard no good, or something. Almost because he was here, his wife had to be guilty.

Susan and Robert were currently in Stern's office, which was large and stretched from the east, or back, side of the building to the west. The main window in that office was the ocean window, a large picture window, he thought. He had been in the office several times, though rarely when Stern was. The large metal cabinet backed up beneath this eastern window, out of which Stern had probably seldom deigned to look, was a little lower than shoulder-height. It contained large flat drawers for large maps and the like. Hal felt he was fortunate the vertical blinds were not down; they might be, so easily. No one needed to look out this eastern window. And yet if Susan did so now, she might see him watching, if she could make him out in the dimness behind his windshield.

The young man was behind Susan now as she looked down at something, possibly something in a drawer she'd pulled out. Look up, thought Hal, but she would not—there it was. The young man Robert was facing the window as Susan turned; their heads were aligned. Hal could see the back of her head and this obscured the young man Robert's face completely. Jesus Christ. Were they kissing?

He had asked for it—at this point he believed he deserved it, even—but still he resisted. He sat there feeling a scream rise in him, trying to suppress it. Robert's hands were up on either side of Susan's head, blurs, moving. His own hands shook. He waited for Susan to turn, to adjust how she stood. They could be conversing face-to-face, having a close discussion. It was by no means a foregone conclusion. . . .

Suddenly their heads went lower. He could barely see them beneath the upper edge of the cabinet. Robert's head, of which chiefly a sweep of dark hair was visible, seemed to be gobbling, aggressively gobbling up his wife's lighter-brown head; the two blurred ovals, conjoined, sank even further as he sat without taking a breath—not believing, refusing to credit the sight. He could barely move. Now they sank down below the cabinet edge and were gone.

He felt queasy. He touched the steering wheel: his fingers were clammy on its grainy plastic. It traveled his mind that he had wanted to set up Robert with Casey. Sickening.

Guy rowed for Yale, went through his head, though it was a phrase he had constructed himself in the first place and had no concrete relevance. For all he knew Robert had attended community college. He was a paralegal, after all, not a lawyer, barely even a white-collar professional. He must be a faux-preppy, come to think of it: an impostor. A guy who rowed for Yale would not end up as a paralegal. Likely he *aspired* to be seen as Hal saw him. Hal had given him the benefit of the doubt, WASP-wise.

He had never read Robert's résumé, of course. It struck him now that he should have insisted on seeing it. There must be something there he could wield against him, some indication that he was wrong for the job, that he was far, far from qualified.

On the other hand it might be better to be cuckolded by a Yale guy, in a sense. A level of exclusivity, at least. Better a Yalie than a guy off the street. Wasn't it?

The paralegal got up again, was standing looking down, then turned to walk away from the window. His torso was all pale now; his jacket must have come off. Then the yellow rectangle of the room disappeared. He had flipped the switch.

Hal felt a stab of outrage. Susan was doing this right when she pretended to be so concerned about the specter of death. Here she was simulating an oppressive, pervasive concern, going to great lengths to demonstrate her worry about her possibly deceased employer—crying at dog kennels and getting choked up in the homes of Alzheimer's ladies, when really all she wanted was to sink down on her back and get it on with a good-looking guy in his twenties. It was the duplicity that gnawed at Hal. Because it was not free love anyway, was it, if you hid it, if you went around sneaking and concealing, if you lied and lied and covered up and were devious about it. It was not the hippie style of free love then, but something sleazy.

He could drive right to Casey's and tell her what he had seen. Right? Right? And how would Susan feel then?

But no, of course. Never. Not ever in this world.

He needed to get away: in place of the prurient need to know he felt only a disgusted, almost frightened proximity.

He backed up the car and found himself in a contest with Robert, a contest for Susan's loyalty—actually priding himself on the fact that it was still he who had been chosen to go to Angela Stern's house, that it was still he, the husband, the worn shoe, the swaybacked old mule, who fulfilled this supportive function— who had, in fact, been expressly chosen for it. Since Robert worked in the office with Susan she could easily have asked him to go with her to see Mrs. Stern: it would not, by itself, have been inappropriate.

But no: she had asked *him*. Him Hal, husband. The sacred trust was still there in these small gestures . . . he had been with her to hold her hand when she was nervous, hold it without saying anything (and while holding it to gaze steadily in front of him at the Chinese soup tureen, in tacit understanding). What *was* the understanding, exactly?

The strength you had when you sat there, a couple for many years now with all the landscape of a shared history, predictable glances, your own language sewn together of habits and tics and old jokes . . . it was the strength you had of knowing that you were not alone—the solid, indestructible knowledge of the other-ness of others.

And come on. Please. Robert the Paralegal was, after all, what pop culture referred to as a *boy toy*.

Then again, it was always said, wasn't it?—that women were incapable of sex without emotional involvement. This was held up as common knowledge. It relied on a conception of the weakness of women, that much was obvious, how they needed soft sentiment over the hardness of gratification, and further how childish and self-indulgent this was on their part. Women, you were led to believe, were seldom inclined toward physical intimacy without a projection of attachment—some association of their partner with an ideal or a fantasy of escape.

Was this empty? Or was there a core of truth to it?

He almost lost his grip on the wheel as he rounded a sharp corner, descending through the levels of the parking complex in a giddy spiral. There was the whole of life between him and Susan, the familiarity with each other that gave them meaning through time, but of course that whole life—that very same shared life and shared history—had removed his candidacy for objectification. At first the removal was slow, he might even have lost track of it, but now it was complete. He was not Robert and Robert was not him; she chose Robert, she wanted to fuck Robert.

What weighed him down, what was a heavy, awkward knowledge, was that it was exactly the quality of being known, of being yourself, that desexualized a person. It was time that all of them—all of them! In their millions!—stopped deceiving themselves and openly admitted what they knew: Love was not sex, sex was not love. They went together out of convention only, because the best sex came mostly before knowing, before real love was even possible.

He was angry as the yellow arm raised at the parking structure exit, as he drove beneath and made his right turn into traffic. A history of losing, he thought: he and Susan knew all about each other's defeats and defects, the rifts and cracks, the craters—and understanding those losses, they had realized long ago, was not erotic. Not the kind of loss they knew, anyway, of atrophy and defeat. Still, he thought they had put it aside, or put it aside enough. Hadn't they?

But for his *loss* to be held against him, he thought—cruel. He couldn't help that loss.

They had gone on anyway, they still had sex fairly often, and it was decent. Tender, familiar. He liked it. But it was not glamorous, that much he had to admit, not epic, not breathtaking.

He was the third man, pathetic—a paper-pusher, a dim gray shade. Faded from relevance.

Heading in a dull haze back toward the freeway entrance off Lincoln—he had directed the rental car back toward his office without thinking—it dawned on him that he could not confront her, that all he had of his own was the secret of this knowledge; that he would have to take a new road, strike out and away, and like his wife command a private dominion.

Of course it hurt him. It was a cut, and sitting behind the wheel, staring ahead, he felt the lips of the cut stretch open.

3

They were due at Casey's apartment for dinner that night. She cooked once a month for them and a few of her friends, a new routine since she'd moved into the place with the wheelchair-adapted kitchen. Sal the sociopath would be in attendance this particular evening, among more seasoned guests.

Before the incident with the paralegal Hal had considered the prospect and winced; it would be awkward and tedious to sit next to the guy for a whole long meal, the cop turned homeboy with his finger tattoos and his bogus argot of the ghetto. But now he felt relieved at the idea of Sal. To sit next to Sal instead of Susan would be liberating. He was more or less neutral when it came to Sal: Sal was impersonal, Sal had nothing on him. He was distaste-ful, sure, but distaste was such a trivial emotion—superficial, even. Hal could be generous to Sal, if only because Sal was not Susan. In his distance from Sal there was a beautiful freedom.

It was Susan's betrayal that occupied his full attention now, from which tense attention he needed a break. It was keeping him anxious; the tendons in his neck hurt. He was worried by how different she might look to him in the light of his discovery, and by exactly how he might go about concealing this silent revolution. Because she knew him. He was not a cipher to her. And without concealment he would have nothing left.

He would be late, first off, he would be late because he would go to a bar beforehand. He seldom entered such establishments, seldom drank much at all, but the occasion called for it. She had momentum, she had velocity, she *did*. He did nothing. He existed, simply, going along as always. He had to keep pace with her, had to seek out events.

He found a place that was dark and mostly empty and quaffed two whiskeys in a short time, watching a television screen where a colorful cartoon raged of a fat, bulgy-eyed family with strange hairdos. He watched TV only at Casey's instigation—always it was her choice what they watched and she did not watch this particular show—but he knew the program was popular. The sound was not on, which was frustrating at first but finally just as well. He watched slack-jawed, the whiskey dispersing in his bloodstream. Colors in my eyes, he thought, fields and fields . . .

He let the picture blur and then sharpen again, blur and sharpen.

Did this mean he was getting cross-eyed? He tried to see his own eyes in the mirror behind the bar, but there was no room for his reflection between the bright libations.

He did not want to be stumbling drunk at Casey's so he downed two large glasses of water in a row and drove slowly and carefully the few blocks to her house.

"Sorry. Office birthday party," he said, when she ushered him in. This would explain his buzz, if it was even noticed. Others sat around in the living room, he saw, but Susan was not among them.

"Where's your mother?"

"Bathroom," said Casey, and went into the kitchen.

Of course she might be engaged in a devious activity there—the removal of a diaphragm, say.

Such thoughts were unworthy.

And anyway, they used condoms.

"We're having a Thai soup," said Casey. "Chicken coconut. Tom Ka Gai."

"Sounds delicious."

"I don't know. Wait until you taste it."

While she hovered at the stove he wandered into her living room, greeted her friends. There was a woman named Nancy who was also in a wheelchair and a tall man Casey knew from a class she'd taken at Santa Monica College, thick glasses and a receding hairline though he was only in his mid-twenties. Hal forgot his name every time: Adam? Andy?

"Addison," said the man, obliging, and shook his hand.

"Can I get you a drink?" asked a voice behind him.

Susan.

Turning to look at her, he was surprised: she looked the same in her features but invisibly separate, as though she was cut off from him by a membrane. Instantly he superimposed the figure

of Robert the Paralegal on her image—it happened without pre-
meditation, almost violently, as though the guy had burst into
the room.

Then the picture was gone, thankfully.

"Sure," he said, and cleared his throat. "Just a beer. Already
had a double at the office, so—thank you."

"What was the occasion?"

Behind her Sal was in the doorway in his chair, chewing gum.
He blew a large bubble and popped it.

"Linda's birthday," mumbled Hal, as Susan turned.

"Sal!" she said warmly, and Hal had a vision of her strad-
dling him.

"Oh," he said aloud, inadvertently. "Excuse me."

He went to the bathroom, locked the door and sat down
hard on the toilet seat. Grabbed the cool rail next to him and
breathed deeply. Ridiculous. He was seeing her everywhere
with spread legs. It had to be the whiskey. He was not used to
drinking.

When he ventured out again the guests were gathering around
the table, pulling chairs out, organizing. Susan was standing near
the head of the table—the dark angle of her black sweater, the
rusty, autumnal orange of her slacks. He recalled how they clung
to the backs of her thighs, which had always had a nice slim
curve of muscle . . . it shocked him to think of someone else
clutching at them. He was still shocked, when he thought about
it—as though surfaces were falsehoods and the vigor inside them,
which could never be seen, had a purpose to it, a purpose that
was slyly hostile or at least secretive.

It could take a while for the dinner guests to get settled at the table, since several of them were in wheelchairs. The shifting of chairs, the discussion of positions . . . he shrank back past the doorjamb. He could not show Susan he did not wish to sit beside her. On the other hand, he did not wish to sit beside her. It was too soon and too public. He would hang back until others seemed to make the choice for him.

Casey was still in the kitchen; he could help her bring the food in. A pretext. But he would keep hidden till the last moment, even from her, in case the whole crowd had not taken their seats yet.

Lingering in the hallway next to the kitchen, he heard Casey talking to someone and hung back again: the food was not ready. There would be nothing to occupy him. He did not want to hover awkwardly; he would hide here, safely unseen.

He glanced down and picked a framed photograph from a bookshelf, to be doing something in case someone saw him. It was Casey with Stern's dog, when the dog still had four legs. Must have been taken by Stern, thought Hal, when the two of them were spending time . . . Casey was sitting on the beach in her chair, smiling, and the dog was standing up, her front paws on Casey's knees. Mostly the dog was featured: you could barely make the person out behind her. Casey did not like pictures of herself.

Nancy was in the kitchen with his daughter. From his hidden position against the wall he could see one of Nancy's bony shoulders and part of the back of her chair; its netting contained knitting needles and several large, bright skeins of yarn—red, orange, yellow, pink and purple.

A garment fashioned of those colors could only be an abomination.

"You told them tele*marketing?*" asked Nancy in a stage whisper, and then chortled.

"What else? They know it's a phone job."

"But I mean what if they ask you about it? The timeshare thing?"

"I have a spiel. I once actually did try selling timeshares, for like three days. It was hell on earth, I'm not even kidding."

"And this isn't?"

"You know what? I kind of like it. I do. Maybe it's still the novelty, but I like it, Nance. That's my dirty secret."

"You *slut!*"

"I'm a ho. Hand me the oven mitt, would you?"

"I'll take the rice. I can get it."

"You sure it's not too heavy?"

He could not enter the kitchen at all now. He could not present himself. He was falling apart. He crept back to the bathroom. Familiar refuge.

Did she mean what he thought? He tried to recall what she had said on the telephone yesterday, not knowing he was there: "What can I do for you," or words to that effect. But the tone had been sultry. He shivered.

1-900. Phone sex.

This was his family. Susan on the carpet. Casey in the chair. Doing that.

He breathed deeply in and out for a minute, bent over the sink and splashed cold water on his face. When he straightened he reached for a washcloth and then stared at his reflection in the bathroom mirror. He had once possessed a certain angular handsomeness, or at least he had been told this once or twice—a lean, affable appeal. Then again, most people received compliments on their appearances now and then, even those most egregiously victimized by genetics. It was standard. If he allowed for the margin of error created by social niceties, he would have to guess he was average-looking.

His eyes were blue but it seemed to him now they had faded, were more and more watery. He half-expected himself to start crying just looking into them—he was on the brink of tears already. Did he look like this all the time? He saw the parallel horizontal lines on his forehead, deeply etched, and thought the eyes disappeared beneath them. He had a full head of hair, small mercies. But he looked unremarkable.

He disappeared, he thought, against any background; he blended, he faded in.

How she and Susan must see him: an old man. But he was not old. He was only fifty.

"Daddy? Are you OK in there?"

"Yeah. Headache is all. Be out in a minute."

"There's ibuprofen in the first cabinet. Also acetaminophen with codeine."

"Thank you, sweetie."

The phone-sex men probably called her that. And far worse.

•

At the table, where he was seated between her and the four-eyes named Addison, topics of conversation included Rwanda and a dead rock star in Portland. Or Seattle. Some rainy city. Casey had played a few songs for him once by the rock star in question.

There was something to it, something genuinely interesting in the tone, he had thought at the time—he never liked to be dismissive of Casey's taste in music, about which she was painfully sincere and impassioned—but the vocal track was a problem for him. Frankly the guy sang like he was trying to force a B.M.

He was distant, nursing his beer, vision grown hazy. He did not attend closely to the chitchat. Something about the angle of a shotgun and whether the dead rock star had in fact been murdered by his rock-star wife, who was widely disliked as a loudmouth attention-seeker though as far as Hal could tell this was her legitimate job description. Then someone said primly that the shotgun angle was not dinner talk, was it now.

Across from him Sal ate his soup quickly and noisily—it was spicy—and wiped his running nose on his sleeve. Hal averted his eyes at this revolting display. The man was rudimentary. Nor was he well-liked, it seemed, by Casey's other friends: most of them avoided even looking at him, much less stooping to conversation. Even for Casey, he was a departure. It was difficult to imagine them together. Little affection seemed to pass between them. Luckily.

During the main course, yellow curry with rice, Hal noticed Susan and Casey were talking in lowered voices about the visit to Angela Stern—a good, safe subject for them, he decided, as Susan would probably not choose to discuss other elements of her workday with her daughter, such as fucking the paralegal on the office floor.

". . . they give an opinion?" asked Casey. "I mean what does it mean, I mean, did they analyze the boat or anything?"

"Analyze it?"

"Forensics. Were there blood traces?"

"You been watching too much TV, babe," said Sal.

"I don't think so, honey," said Susan, compounding Sal's offense against Casey with her own patronizing tone. "I mean first of all it's a small village in Central America. They're poor. And they just got hit by a tornado."

"Hurricane," mumbled Hal, correcting. "Different. Very."

An image came to him: an old motorboat, paint peeling, beached on the sand, listing. Seagulls cawing and swooping. He saw the silver braids of a river delta fan out in brown sand far beneath him, as though he were high up in the air. Susan had mentioned a tropical rainforest—that when Stern disappeared he had been headed upriver into the jungle.

Mistah Kurtz, he dead.

He could barely stand to hear Susan talking, he had to admit it. Every word had a tinge of disingenuousness, as though she could say nothing that was honest.

"Did you hire them?"

"First thing tomorrow," said Susan. "It's just, you know, I don't exactly—I just don't know anything about security. Private investigators? I don't know how to screen them, how to check their references. It's a big blank to me. For some reason I have a block around it."

"I'll do it," said Hal.

It came out abruptly. Around the table faces turned toward him, and the guests were waiting expectantly. Except Sal, who went right on eating. Hal gazed at him blurrily as he slid a whole wet bay leaf out of his open mouth, tongue lolling, and dropped it on his placemat.

"You'll research investigators for me?" said Susan.

"No. I'll go to Belize," he said. He picked up his beer bottle and took a deep swig. It was warm now, and now it was gone. Yes. He saw a chance and he took it.

Change. Freedom.

Robert the Paralegal would not do this.

"What?" said Casey.

"You'll—what are you *talking* about, Hal?" asked Susan, and smiled uncertainly.

"I'm going," he said. "I'll fly out as soon as you can book me a flight. Don't have to speak Spanish—see—English is the official language there. Former crown colony. British Honduras. Used to be called. As I'm sure you all know."

He had weeks of vacation days coming to him—months, very likely. He could use all of it if need be. He risked a brief glance at Susan's face: astounded. Almost stricken. He had blindsided her. He felt a surge of elation.

"Hal, that's . . ."

"Come on, Dad," said Casey. "What do you know about missing persons?"

"Actually a fair amount," said Hal. His eyes were dry and his head was almost spinning—or would be if he lay down—so he was gratified at his own lucidness. "I've been tracking down delinquent taxpayers for years. It's part of my job."

He mainly supervised the process these days, of course. A technicality.

Sal was picking all of the bay leaves out of his leftover soup and placing them one by one, with a wiping motion, on his placemat. Hal found himself captivated by the process. Its repugnance was bold. Practically courageous.

Was Sal insane, actually?

"Honey, we should talk about this," said Susan.

"You need someone you can trust," said Hal, a bit severely. He knew himself for a liar, because she could not trust him now, not when he was angry. Not at all. But *honey*? The nerve of the woman. "You need a known quantity. There's nothing more to discuss."

There was a silence, the guests chewing their food. Possibly they were simply bored. Hal noticed again that his beer bottle was empty; at the same time Nancy reached for a saltshaker and knocked her wineglass over. Red wine flowed and then dripped over the edge of the table.

"I'm getting up anyway. I'll get something to clean that with," said Hal.

"Daddy, I think it's brave of you," said Casey softly. "I do. Volunteering like that."

He felt a rush of tenderness toward her as he rounded the end of the table behind her chair and looked down at the golden cap of hair on her head, neat and small and shining—but then she too was deceiving him, albeit to a lesser degree. From now on, in his nightmares, she would say "I'm a slut" . . .

Not words to reassure a parent. No indeed.

It was settled: he would fly away from all of it and that would leave the field wide open, he reflected as he went into the kitchen. He had already forgotten what he came for . . . a rag? A rag for cleaning up the spilt wine. And a beer for drinking. He didn't care if he drove home at all; he would be happy to fall asleep here. Too drunk to drive would be, the more he thought about it, a very neat solution . . . of course Susan had her own car, but he could claim he did not want to leave his here, didn't want to have to come back for it in the morning. He would get so goddamn drunk no one could reason with him.

Then he would get into a plane and leave the field wide open; the field was crammed with paralegals, all of them stoutly armed with condoms.

Possibly, he reflected, Susan and Robert had an Oedipal relationship. She was, after all, twice his age.

Here also he would leave the fat, ugly men on phone-sex lines, grunting and jerking off as they listened to his baby girl.

It was all crumbling. No one had his back anymore, no one was with him. Not a single person. All he felt at his back was a cold wind, a falling-off into nothing. As he left, an abyss yawned behind him. He'd nearly been swept in.

Before him, the ground would be more solid. Anyway there was nothing more Susan could do to him once he was far away—nothing she wasn't already doing.

His own bed, slow and lavish afternoons.

· · · · ·

Although she made the arrangements for him dutifully he could feel Susan's shock reverberate throughout the day. It was gratifying, in a minor way. She had not let him pass out alone at Casey's as he preferred to, had insisted on sleeping alongside him in the guest room. But still he had crept away from the dinner early, three glasses of wine and two rapidly quaffed beers under his belt behind the two whiskeys, and collapsed on the edge of the bumpy futon. He slept so heavily he did not even register her

presence when she came in later, and in the morning he got up
stealthily, leaving her fast asleep with her back turned to him. He
rinsed his face, brushed his teeth with toothpaste on a finger, and
kissed Casey's forehead before he left, stopping at a gas station to
chase three aspirin with a can of V8.

He was glad of the shock. He would not like to see Susan get
comfortable with his gesture, adjust to it easily. He wanted her
to recognize this as a private venture whose meaning was locked
up to her and out of sight, a gesture belonging solely to him.

He drove home and packed a suitcase with a few changes of
casual clothing, a shaving kit and some work boots. All he had
for sneakers were worn-out Converse hightops, probably fifteen
years old. He packed his passport, which he was relieved to see
was still good, a phone card, a cheap camera. The dog regarded
him patiently as he ordered the items in the case; he felt a stab of
affection or regret, hard to say which.

But Susan would take good care of the dog, he did not need
to worry. In fact the dog would probably be right here, watching calmly and every so often blinking, as she and her boyfriend
thrashed and moaned on the bed.

Would the dog observe a moving tableau, slow and graceful
with soft shadows and a gentle light—and therefore chilling to
Hal if he saw it himself? With the dog as his proxy, would he
have a connection to this? Or maybe the dog would see a labored,
awkward contact, something Hal could watch with contempt or
disgust, almost entirely unmoved. Would a dog perceive any
difference?

Dogs had the habit of watching when you did it. Cats, not so
much. Dogs were bigger perverts.

Foraging in the hall closet, he found outdoor supplies left over from camping trips taken in the seventies: a windbreaker, a small bottle of iodine, a safety blanket, a bandage and a lighter. Who knew where he would have to go? It could be anywhere. And he could buy what he needed when he knew what that was, but it pleased him to think he might have an urgent need for these simple objects—objects that in his house, in his disused closet, seemed both commonplace and completely irrelevant. It signaled the possibility of a great departure from his life's routine.

After that he drank water and black coffee, popped some more aspirin, pet the dog on the head once or twice, heaved the suitcase into the back seat of the rental car and drove to work.

He was standing over his deck, parceling out files into separate piles, when Rodriguez came in and asked him where he was going.

"It's so sudden," said Rodriguez. "Like, ¿qué pasa, hombre?"

"Family matter. Helping my wife with a problem," said Hal.

"But like where you headed?"

"Central America. Her employer went down there and now no one can find him. I'm going down to see if I can suss out what happened."

"Holy shit," said Rodriguez.

"Yeah well," said Hal, and picked up a pile. "Here you go. And this stack here is Linda's. Can you ask her to come in and see me?"

"Oh, man. You gave me all the TDAs, didn't you."

"Do your worst."

"Huh. Going down *south*," said Rodriguez, lingering. "You da *man*."

"The man. Yes."

"Palm trees, margaritas, all the sexy señoritas . . . you need a sidekick? Hey! I got vacation days coming too."

"Thanks for the offer. Think I'll try flying solo this time."

"Send us a postcard, homes."

"Will do."

He called Casey to say goodbye. He would not talk to her about what he had overheard. She said again that she was glad he was going, that she admired him for following through on what was clearly an irrational impulse.

"I just wouldn't have thought it," she said, and he felt a twinge. It occurred to him that she had, for a long dreary time, basically been bored of him, her *boring old father*, and that this unexpected and sudden turn was possibly a rare opportunity for redemption. Spark-of-life-in-the-old-geezer-yet. "I never would have thought you would take it on. Like, I couldn't personally do this. I mean, even if I could, I couldn't. But you know what? I'm glad that you're stepping up. I'm glad one of us is looking out for him."

He almost asked why she and Stern were not close anymore. There was a time the two of them had got together almost every weekend. He had assumed the relationship was purely platonic, but that assumption was rooted in fatherhood and, if he had to be honest, also her condition. She would not appreciate a question on the subject. Not in the least.

Anyway he thought of her in the kitchen with Nancy and did not wish to know the details.

After they hung up he was torn: possibly she attributed noble motives to him where there were none, maybe he was lying to her by letting her think this was some kind of generous act. Then again she was not too interested in nobility, as a rule. She was interested in honesty, and also some other quality that sometimes seemed like courage and other times bravado, but she was not interested in altruism; she thought it was beside the point. Maybe she was just relieved to discover he could be spontaneous.

He had to talk to Susan next, there was no helping it. He had to get information from her: contact numbers, addresses, copies of photographs to show around, his travel itinerary. Reluctantly he called her office, praying Robert would not pick up instead.

"I got you a flight out this evening, believe it or not," she told him, a bit breathless. "The travel agent's next door. You know, Pam? It was either tonight or early next week."

"Fine with me," he said, and waved in Linda, who stood hesitating in his open door. Her frizzy hair descended from her head like a flying buttress, or a wedge not unlike the headdress of the Giza Sphinx.

The effect, sadly, was less regal.

Then he felt a stab of guilt, or sympathy. Both. Linda was a self-effacing, kindly woman. He picked at the flaws of his coworkers because he could never get at his own, he knew they were there but could not easily identify them—save for one, which opened before him like a hole in the very fabric of space, bristling with static. Bad father, father who let them hurt his baby.

It was transparent, but no less a habit for being so obvious.

He felt sorry for all of them, the coworkers and himself. He barely listened to Susan, who seemed to be nattering on about logistics. This lack of attention was a victory of a sort, a victory over her. Or his love for her anyway.

Meanwhile Linda sat down self-consciously in his guest chair, shifting in the seat as she crossed her wide legs.

"Is there a copy of his passport? With the number on it?" he asked Susan, mostly to sound official.

"I'll look."

"That would be helpful. Other than that, the hotel, his own itinerary, flights, cars, whatever records you have of the travel. His Social Security, just in case. Business credit-card numbers. All that."

Linda shuffled her feet back and forth in their sturdy brown shoes and fiddled with her watchband, waiting. He caught her eye and mouthed that he was sorry. The gesture was too intimate for her, however. She looked down, embarrassed.

"I'll have it ready in a few minutes. You fly out around six, so you should leave the office by four," said Susan. "You'll be staying the night in Houston before you do the international leg in the morning. I got you an airport hotel."

"And you'll need to return the rental car for me. It's parked in my space. Linda will have the key."

"I'll send a runner over with the documents. And your ticket. And whatever."

"Excellent."

"But Hal? You were drunk, honey. OK? You really don't have to do this."

"I want to."

"You don't realize how much this means to me. At least to know, finally. But I worry."

No doubt.

"Last-minute things to work out here, sorry. Gotta go."

He was relieved to have Linda with him, grateful her presence had given him an excuse to say nothing personal.

"I'm sorry to keep you waiting, but there's good news. At least, I hope you think so. You'll be Acting while I'm gone," he said, and saw her face light up.

•

When he left the office at four, slumped in the soft vinyl seat of the taxi and watching the buildings float past, he was by turns worn and eager—sunk by the loneliness of his position and then, as he let the defeat dwindle behind him and rushed onward, almost exhilarated. He sensed a kind of freedom and looseness in the air—in the things of the world around him, in the long low land and the height of the sky. It was a dream of running, running away.

It *was* running away. But he was not ashamed. He could not care less. It was what he wanted.

4

He had to hire a car from the airport, a four-wheel-drive taxi in the form of a mud-spattered jeep. When he got in, vaguely remembering film-noir detectives, he rummaged around in his case and brought out a picture of Stern to show the driver. This opened the floodgates, apparently, and whenever he was beginning to drift off in his seat, whenever he thought that maybe, by dint of the long moments of contemplation and engrossment, he was on the edge of coming to a new pass—a discovery or at least a mental accommodation about him and Susan, or more specifically him and Susan and Robert the Paralegal—the driver would interrupt his train of thought with a question of triumphant banality. Then when Hal grunted out a minimal acknowledgment he would offer up a few words about his country, words so flat and devoid of content that Hal drew a blank when called upon to answer. "Beautiful." "Nice weather, you know?" "We got beaches. You like the beach?"

There was nothing to say to any of this, though each remark seemed tinged with the expectation that Hal would answer with great and sudden enthusiasm.

Susan was a natural at responding to empty phrases, though she did not enjoy it either. He had watched her on occasion, dealing with, say, a person in a service transaction who was inclined to chitchat. She made soft murmurs of assent, often, nodding her head and smiling as she listened and, in a gesture of fellowship, asking questions so minute and tailored to the other person's mundane interests that he could barely believe she was expending the calories to produce them. It was an exhausting effort for no clear payoff.

Casey, on the other hand, never did this. She would go so far as to rudely announce that she didn't do small talk. And because of the chair, would be his own guess, she got away with this without blame or comment.

Twice the car stopped unexpectedly at a gas station and the driver got out, then loitered talking to other loiterers with no apparent purpose. Meanwhile Hal waited in the car, impatient and unmoving, full of rising resentment, until ten minutes later the driver got in again without bothering to proffer an explanation. A Caribbean cultural practice, possibly. Possibly Hal would be rewarded one day for broadening his cultural horizons.

It was three or four hours at least to the resort where Stern had been staying—first on a two-lane highway that meandered up and down hills with a view of the sea, then on a long red-dirt road down a narrow peninsula. Most people flew directly to one of the resorts on the coast and landed on a private airstrip, skipping the inland road where barren fields and dirty urchins with stick-legs would dampen the holiday mood.

Whenever settlement hove into view it was shacks with graffiti on them, snarled wire and molding, flimsy pieces of particleboard in place of fences and walls. There were fields of dirt where nothing grew but bald tires and garbage, smoke rising from ashcan fires, and no cars or trees or vegetation outside the hovels either, only bare expanses of soil with an occasional weed. Sometimes a woman or child or dog could be seen wandering through, emaciated; one old woman he saw through a fence with a ragged, open sore on her calf. He caught a glimpse of some skinny kids playing soccer outside what was probably a schoolhouse, which cheered him a bit until he also noticed, beside the stretch of baked earth where the boys were playing, a corrugated-metal rooftop. Underneath it two other boys were carving up a dead animal. He could not tell what it was.

Here and there a bedraggled brown palm tree struggled to look exotic. Forests must have been felled, for sometimes he caught sight of a clump of shiny-leafed bushes and trees in brief straggles of green against the backdrop of dirt and rust, with stumps around them that looked like they'd been hacked at with machetes. Once he saw a column of smoke on a low hill in the distance.

"When will we get to Placencia?" he asked the driver.

"Not too long, not too long," said the driver unhelpfully.

The peninsula had been hit hard by the storm. There were still power lines down, and here and there a telephone pole lay tumbled in wire beside the road. It was strange to him, the poles left where they fell—as though there was no machine here to move them and make the roads safe again, no vigilant authority.

The sky faded into a velvety dusk as he watched it through the window, thinking: I came here to escape my wife. My wife who may not love me after a quarter of a century.

Now he was far away from her, in a strange place. He was almost nonexistent; he was nowhere and known by no one.

· · · · ·

It was only the next morning that he got a look at the hotel grounds. Out his window he could see the ocean, a few small boats without sails, and near the dock white-skinned guests sitting atop the glittering water in colorful kayaks. The water, he thought, was gray-blue, not what they led you to expect in commercials for Hawaii or the Bahamas—not the emerald or turquoise transparence of a kidney-shaped pool. The color was less stunning, more familiar. Crews worked in the gardens, making flowerbeds, laying turf and digging. There were many of them, men in straw hats with shovels and wheelbarrows.

He would eat, take a walk. It was safe to admit it, since no one was listening: he was not here to find anyone. Not here to exert himself, but rather here to melt down, settle, coalesce, and rise in a new form . . . still he could occupy himself a few hours a day with a search of some kind. That was fine. It would give him something to do.

At his table in the restaurant, which overlooked the pool and beyond it the sea again, he gazed out the window. Children played in the pool, spitting long gouts of water out of their gap-toothed mouths. He watched a little boy bounce on the diving board and could not help seeing the boy's head split open as it connected with the concrete bottom, spinal trauma and then, as usual, Casey. It was a sign of his partial recovery that he was falling back into his old habits of thought again, the worn ruts of his neural circuitry—back to Casey and her injury instead of Susan.

But then even this flicker of Susan opened up the whole scene again. She and Robert in the bedroom or on the floor of the office; himself, papery and sad in the blurry distance.

So there was no recovery yet, after all.

He should not think too much. As a rule he set too much store by thinking. Or at least, complacent in the knowledge that thought was the most useful tool available to men—and one so often neglected by his fellow Americans—he relied on it to the exclusion of other ways of filtering information. Thought was the act of conscious cognition but there were alternative processes of the mind that could work around or alongside it, processes of slow and growing awareness that did not register until they were complete, or the accretion of vague ideas that suddenly produced a form.

Thinking alone had not given him an answer to Casey's situation and it would not give him an answer to his and Susan's either. That was his prediction. He should walk on through his day and let the passing of time mold him; time would go by and he would see what to do. This was a vacation—and after the four

long years of aggravation that Stern had given him, all the grating secondhand descriptions of his mini-malls and cookie-cutter
subdivisions, it was right that Stern should receive the final bill.

Eggs arrived, with a slice of papaya to remind him of his
location. Lest he mistake them for Hackensack eggs or eggs in
Topeka, the papaya came along to announce they were tropical
eggs, to remind him that congratulations!—he was on a tropical
vacation.

He ate the eggs and even the papaya, which had an overly
luscious, sweaty taste. He went to a rack and picked out a newspaper, then came back to read and drink his coffee. It was a day-
old copy of *USA Today*. This was not a newspaper he chose to
read at home—too many colors on the front page, for starters—
but it was nice to let his eyes rest.

Sometimes he glanced out the window, past the pool at the
stretch of beach: a few of the ubiquitous palms, a hammock,
some beach chairs and umbrellas, flapping a bit in the breeze,
a pile of upside-down red and purple kayaks and a man raking
sand. This was less opportunity, he thought, than the simple end
of something. Pebbles and sand and waves softly lapping. For
their vacations, people liked to arrive at the end.

He himself would have chosen something with height, cliffs
or mountains—something with grandeur and scale. Sure, the
water was mild here, and there had to be a coral reef or two. But
he saw mostly a blankness, a place that was less a place than an
erosion into nothing. That was what he had seen when he stood
on the shore that morning—the flat ocean lapping, the flat sand
beneath his feet. Maybe tourists came here because they actually missed flat blankness in their daily lives. The flat blankness

was possibly a reminder that there was an end to everything, a reminder they lacked while they were going to work and running errands in their suburbs and cities, where they were constantly required to answer the stimuli. Maybe they yearned to be in a place where there was little to see but a line between water and air.

He went back to the paper and listened to a conversation behind him as he scanned the headlines. He could not see the speakers, a man and a woman, could not turn to look at them without being noticed, but he could tell they were young.

"You can do the scuba class but I'm not doing it. No way."

"Come on! Come *on*. Do scuba by myself?"

"This one guy I read about who's a diver in the Marines or something? He got the bends and he ended up with these little pockmarks all over his face. Like bad acne. Plus he got double vision."

"You won't get the bends, OK? This would be at maybe twenty feet deep. They call it, like, a resort dive or something. To show that it's basically for wusses that would sue them if anything happened. The risk is like *nothing*."

"It can also hurt your brain. Or you can choke on your own vomit. You know who choked on their own vomit?"

"I'm getting the Belgian waffle. What are you getting?"

"Hermann Goering. Little-known fact."

"What are you *talking* about? The guy took a pill! Believe me. I saw it on the Hitler Channel. He was going to be executed like a few minutes later."

"May I take your order?"

"I'd like the egg-white omelet? With mushroom and tomato?"

"And I'd like the Belgian waffle."

"Very good, sir. Coffee?"

"Wait. Does that come with like just regular fruit or that jelly-ish, bright-red fake-strawberry stuff? Know what I mean?"

"Seasonal fruit, sir. Today it is fresh blueberries."

"OK. Yeah. OK then, I guess I'll get the waffle."

The woman addressed the waiter.

"Sorry. We're on our honeymoon. He's not usually so picky."

"Are you kidding me? Picky? That stuff is like fluorescent. It's full of Red Dye Number Three. Erythrosine. Heard of it? It's a known carcinogen. It causes cancer in mice. They feed it to those little tiny white mice and then the mice sprout tumors the size of a cantaloupe. Man. They can barely even walk lugging those things around."

When Hal got up to leave he saw they were pale and thin and black-haired—out of place in the resort, where most of the families were blond, overweight and Midwestern-seeming. Temporary refugees from SoHo, possibly. In fact he had not been to SoHo since the early 1970s but he imagined young people there might resemble these two.

"Excuse me," he said to the clerk at the front desk. "You have a Xerox machine, right? I'd like twenty copies of this, if possible."

He passed across Stern's photo.

"One moment, sir," said the clerk, a lofty woman with prominent cheekbones and beads in her hair, and went through a door. He would be expected to check in periodically with Susan— every couple of days, he thought, and wondered how he could get around it. He would fax her reports, that was it. Cheaper than

international calls, was how he could justify it, and people liked
to receive or send a fax. They liked to say the word *fax*, said it
with abandon. No doubt its moment would be brief.

Personally he preferred telegrams and mourned their passing.
He could remember getting one from his father when as a college
student, traveling in Italy, he had called his parents in a panic and
asked for money. His father had wired it to an American Express
office and sent a telegram to Hal's youth hostel to tell him this.
It contained only the AmEx address and the words *Next time beg
sooner.*

"There you go," said the clerk, and smiled with white straight
teeth. "Twenty."

"Bill it to my room, would you? Thanks. 202," he said, and as
he went out thought she resembled an African queen.

It flashed through his mind that he, too, should have an affair,
if only to prove he could, but then he knew this for a juvenile
impulse.

He stopped in at the manager's office and left a message with
the secretary. He wanted to hear what the hotel knew about
Stern's trip up the river and what had become of the belongings
from his room. He handed his business card to the secretary as
he was leaving and she smiled at him sweetly.

At home the card struck fear, or if not fear a kind of casual
contempt.

In the hotel gift shop he bought a local map, a baseball cap
against the noonday sun, and what appeared to be a child's
backpack—they had none for adults and damned if he was going
to carry his briefcase like a stodgy old fucker. The backpack was
emerald green, festooned with frogs and lizards. He slid the

photographs into the pack and ordered a taxi at the front desk, where the queenly woman had been replaced by a thin man with a pencil mustache. He had the address of Stern's foreman in the papers Susan had given him and he gave this to the driver when he stepped in.

The road was deeply rutted and the jeep had no suspension, so he bounced on the hard seat as they drove. Out the window he could see restaurants in rickety buildings on stilts, named after animals and painted in pastel colors. They had a temporary, slipshod appearance and were often combined with homes or small convenience stores; faded soda logos graced the storefronts and fluttering laundry hung on clotheslines out back. The thin walls would only suffice in this warm, mild place, where no protection from the cold was needed.

There was a garish, yellow-green color to the palms and other trees, gaudy and somehow translucent. He did not believe in the permanence of the trees any more than the buildings. He had read that many of the trees and flowers here had been shipped in from far away—Tahiti and Australia.

The peninsula was a glorified sandbar, he thought, waiting to be washed away by a towering swell.

As the jeep jerked along in the ruts he saw debris collected against the base of palms, clustered along hedges—food trash mostly, cardboard and plastic, but also netting and newspaper and old shoes and wrinkled pieces of mildewed rug or fabric. They turned left at what seemed like a construction site, many small shacks going up all over the place on the slick, muddy ground.

It was like a minefield of outhouses, he thought.

"Seine Bight," said the driver.

"This?" asked Hal, before he could stop himself.

"Rebuilding," said the driver, nodding. "You know: it was all knocked down. In the big storm last month."

They drove between the shacks, not on a road at all as far as Hal could tell—bumping over the corrugated curves of culvert pipes, weaving and tipping sideways. A white bird, duck or goose maybe, flapped out of the way and children ran alongside the car. He was enraptured by this, stared out the window at the flashes of light on skin, the kids' stretched and laughing faces. Then quickly the field of shacks was behind them again, the beach and ocean not so far ahead, and on their right in a grove of palms was a colorful small house with a nice garden.

"Here you go," said the driver.

"Please wait," said Hal, even though they had it all pre-arranged. "I won't be long. Maybe fifteen minutes." He recalled the driver from the airport, how he had randomly stopped at service stations and once leaned against a wall, doing nothing but gazing at the ground. The driver had kept up the pose so long that it seemed he was dutifully observing an officially appointed function.

The contract between driver and passenger here was a loose one.

He walked up to the house and knocked on the door, thinking he wished they had a telephone so that he could have called to warn them, but god*dammit*, while he was standing there wait-ing he heard engine noise and turned and sure enough there was the taxi pulling away again. He had the urge to run after it screaming—half-turned from the front door to do this, even—but then figured maybe the driver needed to use the toilet or some other mild embarrassment. Surely he would be back in fifteen.

Still. Couldn't he have said something? What was it with these people?

Impatient and a little anxious, Hal waited until the door opened. It was a short woman, her black hair tied back with a red ribbon. She was dull-eyed and barely looked up at him.

"Excuse the interruption," he said. "I'm looking for Marlo?"

"He is out working," said the woman.

"Can you tell me where I can find him, then? It's about Thomas Stern. His disappearance."

The woman nodded vaguely. "He's at the big hotel. The Grove."

"Oh you're *kidding*," he said, exasperated. "I just came from there. It's where I'm staying."

She nodded again, unsmiling.

"All right," he said lamely, and turned to go. Then turned back. She was already shutting the door. "Listen, could you tell him I'm looking for him? If we miss each other again? My name is Hal Lindley. Here, here's my card. Wait, let me write my room number on it. He can stop by whenever. Room 202." She had to open it wider again for him to stick the card into her fingers. "Thank you."

After she closed the door on him he stood there for a long moment letting the foreignness absorb him. He had an impression of being out of place: that was what it was, ever since he got here. Even more now, near the village that was in ruins, than at the hotel, of course, since the resort was populated by people he could just as easily have run into on the streets of Westwood.

He looked down at the details of the doorknob—a cheap brassy color—and the frame, which was painted purple. Marlo's house was not an American house: nowhere in America would you find a house like this. The difference might be in the physicality of the doorframe, the stucco, he couldn't put a finger on it. Possibly it was more asymmetrical than he was used to, or the lumber was a tree species unknown to him. But somehow there was an irregularity, a foreignness. It seemed to discourage him, imply he was not natural here. He was an intrusion.

Or maybe he had forgotten, over time, how familiar elements everywhere had a steadying influence. At home there was the security of known formulations and structures all over the place, in window fastenings, in the door handles of cars, gas pumps, faucets, sidewalks, restaurants, shoes. Products and habits were so deeply linked it was hard to separate them. And their reliable similarity helped keep him on an even keel, apparently, had given the world a predictable quality that made passage through daily life calm and easy: he glanced around when he was out in the world and he recognized everything. There was almost nothing that jolted him, almost nothing in the landscape that broke him out of his reverie of being.

He had not considered it before, this effect of mass production. Could it be that the very sameness of these commodities, these structures both small and large that gave the physical world its character, afforded a certain freedom from distraction? The ill effects of their sameness, of this standardization and repetition were talked about and studied—how their homogeneity devolved the world and denuded it of forests and native peoples and clean water and difference. But now that he was far from all the standard objects and dimensions what he noticed was how they also gave a feeling of civilization. In their reassurance they conferred strength on the walking man—strength and the illusion of autonomy.

On his way down the garden path he noticed the skull of an animal. It was stuck on a fencepost among flowers—a goat, he guessed from the horns. It still had a little meat on it.

His taxi was nowhere in sight. He stood for a few seconds, waiting, and then started walking back along the troughs of baked road-mud to the village.

• • • • •

He could not find Marlo on the hotel grounds and soon he gave up looking, found a lounge chair beside the pool and ordered a midday beer. He planned to sleep afterward, and was looking forward to it with a kind of greedy anticipation, when the manager of the resort bent over to talk to him. Hal blinked at the blinding light of the sun, saw the man's broad face recede as he sat up.

There was a small valise of Stern's clothes, the manager said, which he would have brought up to Hal's room. Beyond that he feared he could not be helpful; he knew nothing but the name of the town where Stern had rented his boat, and what he had already told Mrs. Stern. It was a very small village at the mouth of the Monkey River, so small it made Seine Bight look like a crowded metropolis. You could only reach the town by water, said the manager, which was why it was so small. There were no roads overland.

The boat itself, said the manager, had come floating back downriver to Monkey River Town during the night. He had told Mrs. Stern all of this. The boat had struck a dock and become wedged underneath, and kids had found it in the morning. They had noticed nothing out of the ordinary. It had been cleaned and tied up but that was all that the manager could tell him. If he wished to learn more Hal could visit the tour guide's brother, who was not reachable by telephone.

Hal nodded, drained his beer glass and hoped the manager would give up. The double bed was calling, with its bleach-smelling sheets and blessed privacy.

But the manager persevered. "There is a family," he said. "Other guests. They are from Germany. They are renting a boat to go on a day trip up the river."

To get to the river Hal would first have to take another, larger boat to the town, he went on. You took one kind of boat to travel down the coast over the ocean, to reach the river delta; then you disembarked and walked to a smaller dock, where you took a different boat to go up the river. Hal could tag along with the Germans if he liked, said the manager, as far as the delta town where the guide's brother lived. The Germans were taking an afternoon cruise up the river themselves, however; he would have to wait a few hours for the return trip.

So without his rest in the double bed, and slightly disgruntled, Hal met the German family on the dock where they were waiting for the first boat. He shook hands with them and smiled quickly. There were four of them, a mother and father and two young boys, all tall and tanned and lovely, with shining hair in shades of blond and golden-brown and perfectly molded biceps visible where their short, well-ironed cotton shirtsleeves ended. To make matters worse they seemed resolutely cheerful. They radiated something akin to joy. Such Germans were irritating.

On the one hand they were an unpleasant reminder of Vikings and Nazis, on the other hand you envied them.

He, by contrast to the Germans, was a low creature. He was not sleek and limber as a tree, but hunched and preoccupied; he was not shining and tanned, but dim and pale despite the fact that he hailed from Southern California, where movie stars and surfers reigned. He wore a baggy windbreaker and clutched his green-reptile backpack; he was a tired assemblage of imperfect elements. Protruding from his jeans pocket was a wallet messily stuffed with small bills and old receipts.

He watched the Germans file into the powerboat ahead of him, and in particular the two blue-eyed, tow-headed boys, who reminded him of a horror movie he had watched with Casey called *Children of the Corn*. It struck him that he had been picturing himself in a movie ever since his arrival. It was a movie of his life, which had suddenly become interesting in the way only a story could be, with hills and valleys of plot like a rollercoaster. There was much to laugh at in this posture, certainly, but the feeling of cinematography lingered. He was still half-dazzled by the warm beer.

All of them sat on a bench at the prow, touched by the clean spray as the boat thumped over the waves. No one spoke, though they were all quite close together, perfect strangers, side by side. The Germans, he sensed, felt no awkwardness at this. Probably they were content just to Be.

Though the kids, at least, were now rummaging impatiently in their bags.

"My wife's employer disappeared on one of the Monkey River boat tours, just a few weeks ago," he announced.

The boys ignored both him and the scenery. They had found what they were looking for; frantically they pressed buttons on their handheld video games. Beadily concentrating. This was a comfort since it showed they were as venal as regular U.S. children.

"We think he's probably dead," he went on.

There was something about the Germans and their seamless tans. He felt like shocking them.

"Oh my God," said the German woman.

She seemed earnestly concerned. The husband held her hand and nodded, also looking worried. Not only were the Germans beautiful and cheerful, they were also capable of empathy.

"What do they think happened?" asked the husband.

Hal was faintly gratified to note he had the typical German accent, endearing because it was also quite foolish-sounding. A slight but recognizable z sound on his *th*'s.

"No idea," said Hal, a little too breezily perhaps. "The boat came floating back empty." He turned and dipped into the backpack, handing over one of the photographs.

"When was this?" asked the husband, studying it.

"A few weeks ago. I'm here looking for him," said Hal.

"But there aren't any rapids," said the woman, peering over

her husband's shoulder at the picture. "It couldn't have been a drowning accident, or?"

"Maybe there were mechanical problems," said the husband. "If you are going to see this boat, you should check the outboard motor."

"Cannibals," said Hal.

They looked at him blankly. No doubt alarmed at his callousness. But they had a point. It wasn't witty.

"The truth is, we don't know what happened," he went on quickly, to cover up his inane remark. "That's what I'm here for. I'm here to find out."

He caught himself wanting to mollify them. The Germans should not think ill of him, after all. They were not unlike superheroes. You might mock them for their stolid, self-righteous attitudes and overly muscled chests, but still you wanted to remain in their good graces.

The three of them sat in an ambiguous silence for a few moments until the Germans turned and said something to each other in discreet, low tones in their guttural language. He imagined it was along the lines of "What a pig this guy is," or "Americans are stupid." He faced into the spray and closed his eyes, but then he felt a soft hand on his arm.

"Let us know," said the German woman gently, "if there is anything we can do to help you."

He found he was blinking back tears. It came on him without warning. He tried to smile at her, at the same time turning away a little to disguise his emotion. Ahead of them there were a few boats out on the water, and to the east a low, blurry line of trees on a far-out island.

What about him and Susan? Once, when they were young, they could have passed for Germans. Couldn't they? He was unable to look at the Germans to verify it. They might see the tears that stood on his lower lids. But if he could look at them, he would see statuesque beauty. See what humans could be: weightless and straight, beautiful in their purpose and their autonomy. The sun shone down on them and the breeze whipped back their light clothing.

But he and Susan had both aged out of that splendid independence, or the illusion of it. Whatever it was that young, beautiful people had—people who were young and strong, who could scale cliffs and toss their heads back in laughter, whose cheekbones caught the sun. Their own outlines were not so fine, their shoulders and profiles not so elegant.

Was it worse to have been beautiful once and not be beautiful anymore? Or to never have been beautiful at all?

Because he had never been a German.

And poor Casey had never been the blond boys.

She was better, his love said—better! She was everything.

But briefly it twisted him with sadness, this matter of never having been German.

It took a long, dull while to find the man he was looking for once he and the Germans parted company. He sat in a small restaurant with wooden floors, where they served nothing but fish with too many small bones in it and no discernible seasoning and rice and beans and warm soda. He waited. These were his instructions; another man had told him the first man, the tour guide's brother, was on the water and would come in later.

He had tried waiting outside the brother's house for a while but there was nowhere to sit, only a patch of dirt beside a screen door hanging off a single hinge, and eventually he had wandered back to the restaurant and told the hostess he would like to wait at a table, please.

Once or twice he got up and walked around, stretching his legs. In the back of the restaurant, on a small, dusty table, they sold folk art of a heartrending ugliness.

The Germans were coming back at four-thirty, when he was due to meet them at the ocean pier again for the ride back to the hotel. He consulted his watch frequently and worried that the brother wouldn't show up by then, that he'd come all this way for nothing. Finally he fell asleep with his head on his arms on the table, and a man came and tapped his elbow. He jerked his head up in startlement.

It was an older man, dark-skinned with thinning hair cropped close to his head.

"Mr. Lindley?" he asked, and Hal nodded, still sleep-addled, and gestured at him to please sit down, and could he get him something to eat or drink.

When they both had grape sodas in front of them—the only thing available in a bottle besides beer—Hal said he understood the man's brother had taken Stern on the boat, and only the boat had come back. The man said it was his half-brother Dylan, and that yes, the boat had come back but not the men.

At first, when the boat was discovered, no one was sure whether to do anything. After all the men had been headed out on a cross-country backpacking trip. The loss of their boat would be a handicap, but only when they returned to the trail-

head at the river and found it missing. No one knew when to
send another boat looking for them. They had taken enough
supplies for a couple of weeks, and Dylan knew the braids of
the river well and could bring them back down without the
boat. On the other hand, if their food was entirely depleted by
the time they discovered the boat was missing, that could be a
problem.

Hal remembered what the German had said and asked about
the boat's outboard motor. The brother said it was broken, one
of the blades had snapped, but it was not clear when this had
occurred, whether it was before or after the boat had been separated from the men. It was more likely, said the brother, that it
had happened when the motor was running. But this made little
sense, because Dylan would not have abandoned the boat. Under
no circumstances. He had bought it himself and rebuilt it with
his own hands.

In any case, said the brother, they had to assume, at this point,
weeks later, that the men were not returning.

He would never have thought it could happen. The Monkey
was a slow, muddy river; the only possible human predators in the
rainforest were jaguars, and in many generations none of these
had harmed anyone. There were venomous snakes like the fer-
de-lance, but it was unlikely a snake would have bitten both men.
Possibly they had been attacked by thieves or guerrillas wandering the jungle, but that too was extremely far-fetched.

He was confused. He was mourning his brother but it was an
odd, uncertain mourning.

"If I needed to find out more," said Hal, "what could I do?"

"I don't know," said the man, and finished his grape soda. His way of speaking had a kind of Creole lilt, or maybe Caribbean generally. It was melodious.

"Should I go up the river myself? Pay an outfitter or another guide to cover it, take along some rescue workers? I have a budget."

"The problem is," said the brother, shrugging, "there's too much ground up there. It's only jungle and mountains. We don't know where they went. One day I looked around where my brother used to go, this one place where there is a hiking trail, but you know, the rains already came then. There were no tracks or anything. I did a couple of walks with some guys from the village here, you know, but we never found anything. None of us."

"So it's a dead end," said Hal.

Then the Germans were at the screen door, looking fresh and invigorated with wet hair. Hal was surprised to see them until he recalled this was the only eating establishment in the town. Before he could say anything the man and woman were sitting on the rough bench on either side of him, their kids standing in the middle of the room toweling off their blond heads and then snapping the towels at each other.

"Did you find out good information?" asked the husband.

"There isn't any," said Hal.

"You know where the boat came from?" asked the German woman, looking at the brother.

"I know the trail he used," said the brother, and shrugged.

"Here, look," said the husband eagerly, and pulled a map out of a clear-plastic sheath. It was a topographical map, Hal saw, far better than anything he had. Trust the Germans. "Where is this? Show me, if you please."

The husband and the brother bent over the map, tracing their fingers up the line of the river. Their heads blocked the view and after a few moments Hal sat back, feeling superfluous.

The wife reached out and took his hand, squeezed it briefly and let go.

"We went swimming in the river," she said, smiling. He noticed her white teeth and the youthful, sun-kissed sheen of her skin. Her hair was caught back in a golden-brown braid. He could picture her in a blue and white dirndl, gaily performing a folk dance.

Too bad he couldn't have sex with her. But he was not an old lech. Not quite yet. He wouldn't wish himself on her even if she would have him.

"Aren't there caymen? Or piranhas or something?"

"Sure, crocodiles," she said, and laughed lightly. "But you know, very small. The water was so refreshing! We didn't see the crocodiles. Too bad. But we saw beautiful herons."

Germans always thought water was refreshing. They ran down to the water and plunged in boldly, welcoming the bracing shock of it as some kind of annoying proxy for life.

"Here, see here, Mr. Lindley?" asked the husband. Hal was surprised his name had been remembered. He leaned over the map, obliging. "Here is where Mr. Palacio says his brother would usually start the hikes. You see? There. I marked it with the pencil. Back at the Grove you can make a copy of this."

"Thank you," said Hal a little faintly.

Once they were back on the powerboat, the boys hunched over and pushing buttons on their handheld games again and the German couple became caught up in the momentum. They were enthusiastic.

"You must contact your embassy in Belmopan," said the husband. "They have military forces! Maybe they would help you."

Germans. They thought you could just call in the army.

"My understanding is, the U.S. embassy there is a very small facility," protested Hal, but they were already shaking their heads at this trifling objection.

"This is what they are here for," said the wife. "To help the citizens!"

"Technically I think they're here to prop up the Belize Defence Force," said Hal. He had skimmed a passage on the local military in his guidebook. "Which boasts about six soldiers."

"But also humanitarian assistance," said the husband, and the wife nodded in affirmation. They believed in the logic of cooperation, the good intentions of everyone. That was clear.

"They must have, what do you call it, Coast Guard," said the wife. "To do rescues in the ocean. Like *Baywatch*."

"*Baywatch*," said the husband gravely.

"Exactly," said the wife.

He had no idea what they were talking about. Possibly it was some kind of wholesome Krautish neighborhood-watch thing. He nodded politely.

Would he like part of a granola bar, asked the wife, with peanut butter in it? She divided one into three parts and they shared it.

The husband was some kind of electrical engineer, he learned, and the wife was a kindergarten teacher. They were living in the U.S. recently for some job of his. Their names were Hans and Gretel. He hadn't caught that at first. He asked if they were joking and they gazed at him with wide eyes and shook their heads.

He told them he worked for the IRS and they were practically admiring. That was a new one on him.

· · · · ·

In the hotel business office, his third whiskey in hand, he composed a fax for the clerk to send to Susan. It was in telegram style, though he had a whole blank sheet to write on.

RAISING AN ARMY WITH GERMANS.

5

He woke up in the morning with a splitting headache once again. Thankfully the drapes were closed and he was safe in dimness.

His bedside telephone was blinking, a red message light. He did not want to reach out and touch it so he lay there, long and heavy on the hotel bed. Susan and Casey had both visited him. He hadn't dreamt much but he remembered them both spinning around him like tops or bottles, either angry or worried, with white and yellow ribbons streaming from their hands. Now he had the taste of peanut butter and iron in his mouth . . . the peanut butter he could remember from yesterday, when Gretel had made him eat granola, but where did the iron come from?

When a woman like Gretel offered you a piece of something to eat, you took it. You put it in your mouth. You barely noticed what it was. Personally, he never chose to eat granola, in bars or other formats. He banished granola from his sphere. But when Gretel broke off a piece and handed it to him, he ate the granola. Readily.

He had almost no memory of lying down. It could be he'd put his mouth on the bathroom tap, though you were cautioned not to drink the water. That could account for the iron. Or blood. Had he bitten his tongue? He stuck a finger into his mouth but it did not come out red.

Was it Susan who had called the room? Probably. Few others had any interest in him. He lived a life that was neither broad nor open. Only a few days ago he had ascribed this narrowness to the committed pet lovers, but like all of his nitpicking criticisms it was, in reality, merely his own view of himself. Projection or whatever. You didn't have to be a Sigmund Freud to see that.

He had believed, once, that somewhere outside in posterity was an impression of him—the collected opinion of the rest of the world, in a sense. The way he was seen by others was out there like a double, not his real self but a view of him that might have more truth, or more style at least, than his own. But now he knew there was nothing like that at all. You did not exist in the mind of the world as a whole person, there was nothing out there that represented you. There was no outside ambassador.

All you were to the rest of the human race was a flash or a glint, a passing moment in the field of the perceived. Parts of you struck them, parts of you did not; the parts formed no coherent image. People had few coherent images of anything. Even simple concepts, small words like *dog* or *tree*, were confusing to them: a thousand trees might pass through their memories in the split second of invocation—the white of birch or red maple or palms or small pines with golden angels holding Styrofoam trumpets.

Or all the dogs in the world. What room was there for you in this panoply?

People were like dogs and this was why they took pity on them—dogs alone all the hours of their days and always waiting. Always waiting for company. Dogs who, for all of their devotion, knew only the love of one or two or three people from the beginning of their lives till the end—dogs who, once those one or two had dwindled and vanished from the rooms they lived in, were never to be known again.

You passed like a dog through those empty houses, you passed through empty rooms . . . there was always the possibility of companionship but rarely the real event. For most of the hours of your life no one knew or observed you at all. You did what you thought you had to; you went on eating, sleeping, raising your voice at intruders out of a sense of duty. But all the while you were hoping, faithfully but with no evidence, that it turned out, in the end, you were a prince among men.

•

Someone was knocking on the room door—knocking persistently. He had dozed off again, a glass of water on the nightstand beside him. The red light was still blinking. The knocking would not let up.

"Hold on. Hold your horses," he struggled to say, resenting the interruption. "I'm coming, dammit."

He stood at the door in his skivvies. He opened it, realizing in the same instant that he had powerful morning breath.

In front of him were Hans and Gretel in skimpy trunks and a

flowery bikini, showing their tan, smooth bodies and cornflower-blue eyes as they smiled at him.

"I have contacted the Coast Guard," said Hans proudly.

"Sure, right," said Hal. "Right. Sure."

"Good news!" said Gretel. "They will send a task force."

"Very funny," said Hal, and wondered if they would allow him to go brush his teeth. From the second he met them, he had basically been their captive. Even in his own room he could not get away from these eager Germans.

"No, but seriously," said Hans. "The Coast Guard has a boat in these waters currently. I was put through to them. Also there are some local cadets they are helping, a mentoring exercise. The Americans are training them in search-and-rescue, so it will be like a practice."

"I don't . . . give me a second, I have to splash some . . ." He was mumbling as he retreated, but still they stepped into the room after him.

Gretel pulled open the drapes with a certain exuberance.

"You need some fresh air in here, Hal Lindley!" she said.

Probably to let out the morning breath.

Germans were not known for their sense of humor, he reflected as he brushed his teeth, the flimsy bathroom door shut carefully behind him. Their idea of a joke was not his own, that was all. Cultural barrier. Not uncommon. But he could have used another hour of sleep.

Let them stand there in all their terrible beauty. He was secure here in the bathroom, with a toothbrush and a tap and a clean toilet. In the end there was not much more a man truly needed.

But it could not last forever. Breath freshened, head aching, he stepped out again. There was no helping it.

"They will arrive tomorrow," said Hans. "The Coast Guard and also the cadets. All of them."

"Ha . . . it isn't that funny, though," said Hal. He hoped the fly on his boxers was not gaping. Couldn't risk a downward glance, however. He was already playing the buffoon in this particular comedy. Where were yesterday's pants?

He bent down and grappled with the bedcovers.

"No, but really, really," said Gretel, and smiled again. "It is a special task force! There will be approximately twenty persons."

"That's impossible," said Hal flatly.

He felt around under the bed for the pants, found them collapsed in a heap.

"Hans was just talking to his friends," said Gretel. "It's not a problem."

"Hans has friends in the Coast Guard?"

"Actually they are working for NATO," said Hans, nodding. "The Supreme Allied Command Atlantic. In Virginia?"

"He consults for them on the avionics systems," said Gretel.

"I called in a small favor," said Hans.

Hal shuffled away from them to pull the pants on. When he zipped up and turned back, their heads were backlit by the window and their faces indistinct; he saw them for a second as leviathans. They might be slim and standing there in their G-string swimwear, which had an all-too-floral tendency and made them look far more naked, even, than him. But in the strength of their Teutonic conviction he put his finger on what it was about them.

They were machines of efficiency, purposeful. Even in the

simple act of unwrapping a granola bar there was the sense of a necessary fueling.

"I'm afraid you may be drinking too much," said Susan.

She had him paged in the dining room while he was eating his breakfast. Because the Germans were sitting at the table with him, believing him to be a family man who was close to his loving wife, he could hardly refuse to take the call. Reluctantly he had followed the waiter to a telephone at the end of the front desk.

"Not at all," he said.

"What was that fax about, then?"

"It was accurate. There's a task force involved. Something to do with NATO."

"Come on, Hal. I don't get how you're acting, these last few days. I'm asking you please just to be serious."

He had brought his coffee cup to the phone with him and took the opportunity to sip from it with a certain poised nonchalance, his telephone elbow braced on the high, polished wood of the counter.

Robert the Paralegal could not raise a task force. A Trojan perhaps, but not a task force. None.

"What can I say? I met Germans with connections. Germans who refuse to take no for an answer, I'm guessing."

"See? This is what I mean, Hal. You just don't make that much sense right now."

"I'm telling you, Susan. Either there's a twenty-man task force trained in search-and-rescue that's arriving tomorrow to look for your friend Stern, or the Germans are conning me. It's possible. As history has taught us, Germans are capable of anything."

She was silent for a few static beats. He sipped his coffee again.

"Really, Hal? Honestly?"

"So they tell me. We'll see."

"But that's amazing, Hal. Amazing!"

"The jury's still out on it. OK? Keep you posted. I was right in the middle of a hot breakfast, though. Do you mind if I get back to it?"

More static. He had hurt her feelings.

"Not that I don't want to talk. Just a rush here—hectic. Wreckage, repairs. Aftermath. Hurricane. You wouldn't believe the scene."

He gazed out over the tranquil dining room, where lilies stood in tall vases on the white tabletops. Hans waved out the window to the boys in the pool, and Gretel, her long, languid legs crossed, was peeling an orange and licking the juice off the tips of her elegantly tapered fingers.

"OK. But keep me informed, OK Hal? Tell me everything that happens."

"I always do. We've always told each other everything, haven't we?" He was feeling a pinch of malice. Speaking with a dangerous transparency. He told her goodbye, hung up and downed the tepid dregs of his coffee.

 · · · · ·

There was no reason, he found himself deciding, not to enjoy himself while he waited for the armed forces. The day was still

young, he had hours to kill before the night came on, and Hans
and Gretel had invited him to go scuba diving.

Fortunately the children of the corn were too young to qual-
ify for the scuba course and had resigned themselves to playing
ping-pong.

"For the whole boat trip? They're going to play ping-pong for
five straight hours?" he asked Hans, when he saw the boys hitting
the ball back and forth at the table beside the pool. They were
steadfast and tightly wound, their lips compressed, eyes darting
only a fraction to the left or right with a predatory glint as they
followed the bouncing ball.

"At least," said Hans.

"One time they played for two days, stopping only to sleep,"
said Gretel. "Of course it was a weekend."

They said goodbye to the boys, who ignored them studiously.
Then a resort employee led them down to the dive shop, a kind
of bunker with wet sand and footprints crisscrossing the rough
concrete floor. There were wetsuits hanging on a rack and fins
and masks arrayed in wooden cubbies along the wall; the ceiling
was low and the walls were painted a deep, gloomy blue inside,
maybe to simulate the ocean. The divemaster shook their hands
and welcomed them.

Before they went out they had to sit through a safety lecture.
Hal tried to listen attentively but was distracted by the presence
of half-naked Gretel in her bikini, smelling delicately of coconut
oil, and also by the belated arrival of the young bohemian couple
hailing presumably from lower Manhattan.

The bohemian couple appeared skeptical of the lecture by
the divemaster, bored and skeptical despite the fact that they
had never been diving before and, if their breakfast exchange of

the previous day was any indication, were also hypochondriacs. When the lecture ended and the divemaster began to choose gear for each of them, asking shoe sizes and moving along the row of cubbyholes searching, the bohemians raised an objection.

"This says we don't have the right to sue if we suffer injuries on the dive, up to and including death," said the man.

"Yes," said the divemaster politely. "It is a required legal waiver. I am very sorry but it is not possible to go out on the resort dive if you do not sign it."

"I don't know about this," said the woman, shaking her head. "I don't do waivers, normally."

"It says you can't go if you've ever had a lung collapse," said the man.

"I've never had a lung collapse," said the woman. "Have you had a lung collapse?"

"Not that I *know* of."

"It's something you would probably notice," said Hal.

The bohemian man ignored him.

"I had bronchitis one time in college," said the woman. "Is that a risk factor?"

"Or smoking. It says here you can't be a smoker."

"I did have that one clove cigarette at Dinty's. At that New Year's thing?"

"It was clove? Clove cigarettes are the equivalent of seven regular cigarettes."

The rest of the group stood waiting for them to sign or not sign the waivers, gear slung over their shoulders, fins hanging by the heels off two crooked fingers.

Hal felt impatient. He was irked by the bohemians. Previously he had been irked by the Germans, now it was the bohemians who irked him. Although the Germans had become his allies. What if the bohemians fell into line also? Would the bohemians also befriend him?

No. A bohemian was not a German. Socially speaking a German turned outward, like a sunflower toward the sun; a bohemian turned inward like a rotting pumpkin.

"Why don't the rest of you go ahead and get into your wetsuits," said the divemaster, and smiled affably.

When they came out of the restrooms the bohemians were also wetsuited. All of them stuffed their clothes and shoes into cubbies and walked barefoot down the beach toward the dock, the bohemians broadcasting a sense of glum foreboding. Or perhaps it was terror. Hal hypothesized that one bohemian had blackmailed the other into the scuba diving excursion, possibly with threats of poisoning via Red Dye Number Three.

Hans and the divemaster walked at the head of the pack discussing reef fish and Hal listened to Gretel tell him about swimming with stingrays in the Grand Cayman, how she had gently stroked their soft pectoral wings. He nodded without saying much, smiling in what he hoped was a beatific fashion and meanwhile wondering if, in the black wetsuit, he in any way resembled Batman. Was his torso, for example, slightly triangular? Just slightly, he didn't mean any big bodybuilder-type-deal. Did it descend just a bit from broad shoulders to a narrow waist, creating an impression of virility?

Squinting down at himself he noticed the wetsuit was in fact a very dark green. He was disappointed. In the shade of the dive shop he had thought it was black. Gretel's was black, as was Hans's. They gave the Germans the black wetsuits; him they gave the dark-green, the color of spinach slime. He suspected he most resembled the animated character Gumby, which as a child Casey had watched on TV with barely suppressed delight.

"Out at the caye," the divemaster was telling Hans, "where we will stop between dives for a late lunch and snorkeling, you will see lemon sharks. Some people feed them, although it is technically forbidden. Small sharks. Pretty. They swim around at your feet."

In the boat Gretel sat beside him and asked him about Stern.

"This is the man who is the boss of your wife?" she asked.

"The boss of my wife. Yes."

"And he is a seller of real estate, you said before. Like a small Donald Trump."

"Better hair, though."

"That is very funny."

"I notice you're laughing hard."

"But you must be very close to him, yes? To come all the way here looking. He is a friend of the family, maybe."

He considered telling the truth but dismissed this as rash. And in fact Stern was a friend of his family, both his wife and his daughter, though not him personally.

"It's difficult," he said, but nodded.

She reached over and squeezed his wrist in sympathy. So easily misled.

.

He would not have come scuba diving if Gretel had not lured him with her kindness and beauty, he thought resentfully as he sat on the edge of the boat, his tank hanging heavily off his back,

waiting to roll over backward into the ocean. He did not want to
roll over backward into the ocean. Who was he? He was a middle-
aged IRS employee, a father and a cuckold. He was an idiot.

He had let Hans and Gretel go before him so they would
not witness his tomfoolery. He anticipated some kind of choking, spasming incident. But it was time. He had to follow Hans
and Gretel, for they were his dive buddies. If he waited too long
he might lose them. The pressure was on. This was it. The divemaster was staring at him expectantly. The neurotic bohemians
were also watching. Their scrutiny was a grudging challenge.

He had hoped the neurotic bohemians would go before him,
but they had found reasons to fiddle with valves and masks almost
endlessly. Now there was no more excuse for delay. He could
not see the expressions of the neurotic bohemians through their
masks, but he imagined they were white-faced and trembling.

Middle-aged employee, or tax man? It was all in the wording.
He was the tax man, by God.

He felt off slowly, even limply. He grappled. Then he was in.
Sinking. For a second he panicked. Then: breathe only with the
mouth. It was OK. He was doing it.

He heard his breath, the slow in-and-out like Darth Vader.
There were white bubbles around him as he sank, a screen across
everything, and then they cleared and it was light blue and placid.
He looked down: beneath the black fins on his feet were rocks
and yellow- and gray-striped small fish. He raised his head again
and saw Gretel ahead of him, moving toward a wall of coral. She
was lithe and graceful with her fins moving back and forth; her
long hair floated behind her and caught the light, a stream of
warmth in the cold water. It rippled.

Off to the right at a slight distance was Hans, at greater depth. He had announced on the boat that he had two goals: sea cucumbers and moray eels.

Hal did not share his goals.

The fins felt good, powerful. He propelled himself forward, hastening to get close to Gretel. It was nice down here, lovely. It was a cathedral of light and softness. Down here you probably couldn't even tell the difference between a black wetsuit and a dark-green one.

The dive would last about a half-hour, they had told him. He would stay close by her. She would point at things.

As they held steady side by side about fifteen feet beneath the surface he found himself entranced, not only by her but by the corals and the fishes. Beneath them and around them—he had to be careful not to brush up against the coral, hit a sharp urchin or a stinging anemone—there were formations like brains and antlers, sponges and intestinal tubes and lace and leaves of lettuce. Among them the fish swam, some hunkering low and inside, others flittering lightly along edges. Gretel touched his shoulder and they looked down together at a speckled, dun-colored fish on the bottom half covered in sand, bloated and with spikes on it. Some kind of blowfish or puffer, he guessed. They ate them in Japan. Flat, tall fish that were a deep purple-blue with a line of bright yellow moved past him in stately elegance.

He thought how Casey would love all this. He would describe it to her when he got home. She had seen photographs, had watched Jacques Cousteau and the like, but she would never know how it felt to be here, the buoyancy. How everything seemed to move slower, with a silence that changed the world. Time, even. He felt a quick wrench of longing, worry and regret—what he always felt, when he recalled her and was not in her company. The guilt for not being there, actually, among other impulses . . . not that she wanted him there. He was only a father.

When they were small you were everything to them, then they grew up and you dwindled into next to nothing . . . she liked underwater scenes, had drawn them often when she was a little girl. He remembered her pictures in felt-tip pen: mermaids hovering beside straggly green seaweeds, mermaids with dots for breasts and large scales along their tails and yellow hair. She had believed that underwater was a kingdom where she would be welcome—where she could move like a fish, move like fluid itself.

She would have seen Gretel back then, when she was six years old, and thought she was beholding a mermaid.

Hans was also still in view, though just barely. He was always diving, scouting, always searching for something. Hans was not content to float and look, unlike Hal and Gretel.

Hal was watching a fish nibble at the coral, listening to the sound of many of them eating, like the *pop-pop-pop* of milk in rice cereal, all over in the background, when she suddenly grabbed him by the upper arm and turned him. They were surrounded by silver, or at least there was nothing but silver in front of them. It was a vast school, thousands. Small, moving in silver flickers, hundreds of them switching angles in the same pulse of motion, instantly. He was astonished by it, how hundreds or thousands moved in a flash, as one body. It seemed impossible.

Then he was startled, almost breathed through his nose feeling Gretel's hand move over the arm of his wetsuit with something akin to tenderness—was there intent in the touch? He could almost believe it. But it was through the wetsuit. Most likely she had just forgotten to let go. Both of them gazed at the flanks of the fish—the gleaming, moving-as-one legions. He thought they could never be like this, people. Never. Was she thinking it too? With her hand on his arm. It was the two of them, suspended, the rest of the world far above and in the dryness of air—nothing like this below, these silver thousands.

Finally the school thinned and dispersed, left them gazing out into a fading blue abyss. At some point her hand was gone from his arm, which he also regretted. He felt cold despite the wetsuit.

It was not their place, after all. They were here only by the grace of machines.

He had forgotten to check his tank and lost track of his oxygen, but luckily she was on top of it. She showed him her gauge and made a thumbs-up signal, which he thought at first meant everything was OK. In fact it was the signal to return to the surface, which he recalled a second later from their safety lesson. She was already rising slowly, and he watched her for a while before he went up too.

On the island where they went to eat lunch there were too many tourists crowded onto a slight, barren finger of sand. Many small boats were anchored, wave-slapped and bobbing, on the windward side, while on the lee side all he could see was a field of snorkels sticking out of the shallow water, black and day-glo yellow and fluorescent pink. Seagulls had splattered white onto the rocks and benches all around; there were bathrooms and some low shelters over picnic tables. On one end of the island were a few tall, thin palms, scraping and flapping their dried fronds in the breeze.

The neurotic bohemians found the last empty picnic table in the shade, unwrapped the packed lunches the divemaster handed them from a plastic cooler, then talked in low voices about how there was nothing in them they could stand to eat. The woman was a vegetarian, the man was lactose-intolerant.

Hal sat at the other end of the table with Hans and Gretel. He was ravenous. He wanted to order the neurotic bohemians to hand over their portions; he wanted to tower over them and scoop up their sandwiches into his gaping maw. Instead he quietly ate his own ham-and-cheese and listened to Hans enthuse to the divemaster about a sea cucumber.

Apparently, when alarmed, they could extrude their intestines.

Gretel was impatient to see lemon sharks so after a minute Hal got up from the table, left the neurotic bohemians and Hans and the divemaster and followed her with the final crust of his sandwich in hand as she walked along the lapping edge of the water. You could walk from one end of the island to the other in five minutes and soon they found the sharks, circling again and again in less than a foot of water. They were small, just a couple of feet long, and being fed by tourists, who tossed in fragments from their own bagged lunches.

Gretel shook her head, worried.

"It is not natural," she said.

Germans hated it when things were not natural. Hal remembered this from college philosophy. Heidegger or something.

"Sharks have strong stomachs," he improvised, straining to recall any actual facts. Natural history was not a strong suit, despite his years of watching *Nature* with Casey. "Great whites have been found with oil barrels in their digestive tracts. Rusty engines. I doubt a few Fig Newtons are going to hurt them."

"But these are not great whites," said Gretel, and squatted down on her haunches to see them more closely. "Look! They are like little babies."

A few paces away the divemaster was already gesturing at them: it was time to head back to the boat. Gretel left the so-called baby sharks reluctantly.

On the windward beach again, lagging behind the rest of the group, Hal looked out beyond the boats and saw a small skiff cruise by, a thin, bearded man standing in the front of the boat leaning into the wind with raised binoculars, one bent leg braced against the prow like a sea captain in books of yore. Hal tried to recall where in the hotel he'd run into him. Then the bohemian woman screeched. She was barefoot and had stepped on a bottle cap.

"You could get lockjaw," said the bohemian man.

· · · · ·

Back at the hotel the Germans pressed him into service for dinner also, as though he could not be trusted to be left on his own. Their two boys left the table in a rush once they had bolted their kiddie menus, running outside to continue the ping-pong tournament.

"We must get organized for tomorrow," said Hans. "We have the map. I have made many copies. We have many copies also of the photograph of Mr. Stern. The hotel is having them laminated."

"Nothing left for me to do then, really," said Hal. "Is there."

He had a cavalier attitude; he was drinking a margarita, which Gretel had encouraged him to order. She drank one also and her bright-blue eyes were shining.

"Does Mr. Stern have any medical conditions?" asked Hans.

"Not that I know of," said Hal.

"You should find out the blood type, in case he is located and is injured and requires a transfusion. Also a medical history."

"Huh," said Hal, nodding vaguely. "My wife would probably know." He had ordered the snapper, which was overcooked and too fishy. He decided to leave it mostly uneaten. The margarita tasted far better.

"Also, does his insurance cover helicopter evacuation," Hans was saying.

Hal was already at the bottom of his glass, and at the far end of the dining room a band was setting up. He was thinking how pleasant it was to be drunk, that he had been missing out all these years in not being drunk far, far more often.

Couples gathered at the edge of a dance floor. There was a drum flourish, bah-da bum. A woman singer in an evening gown said something husky and incomprehensible into a microphone.

Lights sparkled. Yellow and golden in the dining room, now a ballroom. Beyond the large windows, the pool, the chairs, the deep-black sky, the ocean. A room full of people and golden lights, and outside the whole dark world.

Tequila, he thought, made him sad—was it sad, though? Anyway, melancholy. Youth had flown. It wasn't all bad, though. You couldn't move as well as you used to, you didn't look as good, you had either forgotten the dreams of youth or resigned yourself to their disappointment.

But at least you could see more from your new position. You had a longer view.

"Come on, Hal. Why don't we go dance a little?" asked Gretel, smiling, and cha-cha-cha'd her shoulders. Hans was pushing buttons on a calculator, which seemed to have appeared from nowhere. He waved them to go dance, got up and headed off. Hal watched him buttonhole the maître d', nod briskly and start dialing the restaurant phone.

"He's really taken this on, hasn't he," said Hal. "This whole search-and-rescue thing."

"Hans does not like vacations," said Gretel. "He gets bored. He always needs to have something to do. He's some kind of genius, people tell me. With his electronics. You know, and he talks to me about his work? But actually I don't understand it. But always he likes to keep busy."

"I noticed," said Hal.

"Dance with me," said Gretel. It was cheerfully platonic, but he took what he was offered.

"With pleasure," he said, and set down his margarita glass. The stem of the glass was green and in the shape of a large cactus, the kind you saw in cartoons and Arizona. A margarita was not a manly drink. But more so than a daiquiri.

Heading for the dance floor, he was recalled to reality—the reality that he was a flat-out embarrassing dancer. Among the worst. He had almost forgotten. He was a finger-snapper and a head-nodder. He had no other moves.

"Wait. Only if it's a slow song," he added, and hung back. "I'm really bad."

"What's important is to have fun," said Gretel, taking him by the arm. "*Express* yourself."

"You don't want to see that, believe me," said Hal, feeling the silkiness of her fingers. "Self-expression is a young man's game."

"Oh, come on," she said.

They were on the dance floor, other people around them. She started to move, a couple of feet away. Lithe and elegant, as would be expected. He could not do anything. He was stuck. Then desperation washed over him. He had to cling to some self-respect. He reached out and grabbed her, clamped her to his person.

"Sorry," he said into her ear. "This is all I can stand to do."

She drew back, a bit confused, and then smiled. After a few seconds she balanced her arms on his shoulders and let him hold her and sway.

Leaning into her he let himself believe, for a moment, that others caught sight of them and assumed they were a couple. Yes: he was a party to this assumption, he welcomed it. Possibly they surmised he was some kind of businessman and Gretel was his trophy wife. Only for a moment of course, for a fraction of a second. As he felt her back under his hands, the swell of breasts on his front. Then the gazes passed over them and fastened elsewhere. But it was better than nothing.

Hans was tapping his shoulder officiously.

"Susan wishes to speak to you," he said. "She is waiting on the telephone. But do not worry, I have the blood type. Fortunately, Mr. Stern is O-positive."

Gretel stepped back from him and took Hans's hand with a light, casual gesture, twirled herself around as she held it. Hans danced with her, stepping primly back and forth; plainly his heart was not in it. Hal's own heart had been in it, very much so.

As he wandered listlessly toward the phone, which the maître d' was holding out to him, he could not recall ever resenting Susan like this. Not when he had seen her in the office with the paralegal; not even when they were young and interrupted by Frenchmen.

"So it's really happening," she said, when he picked up the receiver. "You're going to find him. I know you are."

"Maybe," he said. "Don't get your hopes up, though."

"Casey sends her love," she said. "She's here with me."

He softened, feeling homesick.

"Can I talk to her?"

"Daddy."

"Case. How are you, sweetheart?"

"An army? The Coast Guard or something?"

"Apparently."

"You're my hero."

·

Later the cornboys came running in from ping-pong, the smaller one bleeding from the head. In a doubles game with two other kids the wooden edge of a paddle had cut him upside the eye socket. Hans and Gretel were not overly worried, but Hans plied a white linen napkin to the wound, filled it full of ice from a nearby table's champagne bucket. He got the kid to hold the ice against his temple and then announced it was the boys' bedtime. Putting his hands on their shoulders to steer them to the room, he looked back at Gretel, but she shook her head and grabbed Hal's arm. She would be there in a few minutes, she said, but she was going to take a walk on the beach before bed, and Hal would escort her.

Hal was tired and ready for bed himself: he felt slack and let down. After the last drink he had turned a corner. There was an art to drinking and he had not mastered it. But Gretel was determined; she tugged at his hand, so he shrugged and agreed to go along. After all, due to the Germanness there would likely be a midnight swim, a shucking of clothes and plunging into the waves. It would not surprise him.

A vicarious thrill in it anyway, or at least a view of her naked ass. He could pretend there was more, that it was for his benefit.

"Leave your shoes," she urged, when she took off her own. Obediently he discarded them, balled up the socks inside the shoes and left them beside her sandals underneath a hammock. She walked a few paces ahead of him.

There were few stars—no visible cloud cover, but still the stars were obscured and the moon was high but not bright. He followed her, hearing the wash of the tide as the small waves curled in and feeling the water on his feet. They passed a dock and left it behind, passed a row of canoes on the sand. His jeans got wet at the hems and he bent over and rolled them up. If Susan could see him, walking by moonlight with a lovely young woman. Along a seam of the Caribbean.

"Look out for jellyfish," he said. "Washed up I mean. You wouldn't see them."

"I'm going to go swimming. It is so beautiful!" she cried, and idly he gave himself points for predicting.

"Of course," he said.

"You have to come in with me!"

He was flatly opposed to this. He would be cold and wet. He had no interest in it.

"OK," he said.

Wearily and without haste he took off his clothes. Who cared, after all, who would ever notice or give a shit? No one. Gretel herself wasn't even looking. The air was black around them and the blackness gave them a loose kind of privacy. She stepped out of her own skirt as though it was nothing, pulled her shirt over her head and dropped it on the sand too. No brassiere. He had a glimpse of pertness, the sheen of skin.

She left the clothes in a pile without casting a glance at them, bounded forward into the surf and dove. Submerged.

He watched the water, holding his breath. Shivering. Now he had to go in after her. That was how he was with the Germans— he acceded to their demands and then he had to summon the wherewithal. When in fact he did not have it. He was afraid of dark things in the water, surging up from the deep.

Where was she? She should have resurfaced by now. He waded out, up to his knees, up to his waist. Where was she?

She came up with a splash, laughing and shaking the water off her head.

"I love it!" she cried.

"Nice," he agreed, nodding, and dropped in up to his shoulders, dog-paddling. She went under again.

He remembered a scene from one of the British nature shows featuring famous, avuncular naturalists—wry, witty men who casually stepped down from helicopters in the African veldt and talked companionably to the camera in their Oxbridge accents as they walked through the tall, waving grass in their safari outfits. Such men were at home with the animals, picked them up and showed them to the camera as though there was no trick to it. They said *this little fella* as they described a mating behavior or trotted out a surprising factoid. But the scene he remembered had been part of an episode devoted to bioluminescence. They had shown deep-sea fishes that looked like spaceships, myriad lights rimming their graceful, pulsing bodies. Marine biologists had descended in a bathysphere like something out of Jules Verne. In the depths near the Mid-Atlantic Ridge, in the bathysphere's headlights, they caught luminous creatures undescribed by science.

Casey had cried when she saw that. But she hid it from him. She pretended she was crying for another reason, pain probably. She was embarrassed to be seen crying out of sheer emotion.

In the dark he saw mostly the glitter of the waves, Gretel, porpoise-like, diving and coming up again. For a few seconds she stood on her hands in the shallows, her legs and feet sticking out straight, toes pointed like a ballerina's. There was a breeze across his chest and shoulders and he threw his weight backward and floated on his back, water skirting his bare chest. He could not help but think of sharks and other predators, sluggish and ominous beneath him. Awakening. Tendrils or tentacles or rows of sharp teeth . . .

Above him he saw the moon, but not with clarity; just a blurred scoop of white. He closed his eyes. It was reassuring to have Gretel nearby. Nothing would befall her. No shark would dare. By extension he was also safer. Wasn't he?

Something brushed against his back from beneath and at the same time he panicked and he knew it was her. Her sleek, wet head emerged beside his own and she was spitting seawater on him and laughing. He sank down a little, coughed and sputtered and righted himself, feet searching for the sandy bottom and sinking in.

Without warning she kissed him. Their bodies were touching all over, under the water and above it, solid and inflaming. Her nipples were against his chest. At once he was both frozen and pulsing with current. Even as it happened, and then continued to happen, it was completely impossible.

He would have to pay for this, he was thinking. And he would pay. He would pay. Gratefully.

6

They were clean-looking guys with brush cuts, looking intently
ahead of them and carrying the smell of fresh sweat and what
he suspected was pine-scent deodorant. The armed forces weren't
as Caucasian as he'd imagined them, more Latino and black, but
just as muscular and young. He stood in the sand beside the
dock watching as they filed past, he in his shorts and tattered old
sneakers, they in stiff uniforms and bulky black boots. He felt
unarmored, a tiny pale civilian.

They dismounted from the dock in rapid succession, boots
thumping into the sand, and ran past him and up the beach, leaving their two powerboats tied to the dock. A few hundred yards
out on the water the mother ship was anchored, a line of flapping
flags flying over her gleaming white bulk. He recognized only the
Stars and Stripes.

"*Nantucket*," he read, off the side. "Wow. She's big."

Hans, a few paces off with his hands clasped behind his back, shook his head with a *tut-tut* noise. "Smallest patrol boat in the fleet, except for the Barracudas," he said. "A 110. Island class. 155 tons full load. Two diesels, two shafts, 5,820 bhp and about 30 knots. For guns, a 25-millimeter Bushmaster low-angle and two 7.62-millimeter MGs."

"I have no idea what you're talking about," said Hal.

Hans laughed joyously, as though Hal had told a good joke.

"I thought you did airplanes," Hal added.

"Tactical sensor networks," said Hans. "I like boats though. Kind of like a hobby." He waved at a man standing on the power-boat's massive bridge. Hal squinted to see him better; he was a small stick figure.

"I don't get it," said Hal. "How did you manage this?"

"They were already here. Humanitarian assistance," said Hans. "This mission falls in the category of hurricane casualties. Even though technically it was only a tropical storm. Your friend is an American citizen, no? And an important businessman also. An asset. I impressed them with this. They are based in an operations center in Miami. The ones in light-brown are the Belize Defence Force cadets. They are just here to learn."

"I didn't think anyone would show up," said Hal, still stunned and failing to adjust. "I really didn't."

"Of course," said Hans, and grinned. He put his hand up for a high-five.

Dazed, Hal slapped it compliantly and then felt stupid.

Hans consulted his waterproof digital watch, which he had worn diving the day before and of which he seemed to be quite proud. "We weigh anchor at 10:00 hours," he said. "So you have exactly ten minutes for preparation."

"Oh. I'll go get my shit, then," said Hal after a few seconds, and struck out for his room at a jog.

He was dizzy and almost trembling from too little sleep and too many margaritas and lying awake in disbelief remembering the recent past—Gretel's mouth, thighs, and hands all over him. They lay on their shucked clothes on the sand; they had to be careful not to get sand inside her, between them where it counted. He brushed it off her thighs and stomach, off himself . . . but she was lighthearted and playful so he had tried to seem lighthearted too, though he was dead serious.

After they finished he had walked her to the flight of stairs outside the room she was sharing with Hans and the cornboys. Salt-encrusted and shivering, he had gazed up at her back and legs, flashes in the dark as she went up. Probably he had been beaming the whole time, he thought. He had felt like beaming. The room door had closed softly behind her and he had almost run back to his own room, bounding forward giddily. Like a kid.

He was not without pride, lying there, he had to admit it. He even fell asleep proud.

Then first thing in the morning Hans found him at the lobby coffeemaker and rushed him outside to watch the patrol boat cruise in.

Back in his room he drank thirstily, a whole bottle of water he found standing on the dusty metal lid of his air-conditioning unit. He grabbed his green backpack and a baseball cap, filled the water bottle again from the sink and took a fresh one from the shelf. You weren't supposed to drink the water here but there were filters on the taps in the rooms . . . he should feel guilty in the company of Hans, he thought, but curiously he discovered his conscience was more or less clear. Maybe it was Hans's automaton quality.

The armed forces were present; he had flown down here on a whim and somehow now there were armed forces to do his bidding. Fortunately Hans would lead them, Hans would manfully take the reins. Hans would assume the armed-forces leadership. He, Hal, had no interest in armed-forces leadership.

He checked himself in the mirror. He had a tan, he noticed. Would Gretel come with them today? Would she see him by daylight and cringe?

He could hardly blame her. He had seen her as in control, seamless and perfect, mostly because she looked that way. But in fact she had been as drunk as he was, if not more, and she had the upper hand—laughably so. She was far younger, far better-looking, and married to a kind of Germanic Apollo who also happened to be an avionics genius. She must be regretting her rash act, her fleeting impulse. He could almost imagine the knot of remorse in her stomach.

He would respect that remorse. He would comport himself with discretion. Lowered eyes, deference.

But she was not there. It was only Hans, the armed forces, and him. The two of them stood with an officer on the forward deck of the *Nantucket*.

"Gretel is spending time with the boys today," said Hans when Hal asked. "They are going to see manatees. In the lagoon."

"Manatees," said Hal, and nodded.

"It is also possible to observe dolphins, crocodiles and sea tur-tles," recited Hans dutifully, as though from a brochure. "There are hawksbills, green sea turtles and loggerheads."

It was high above the water, which Hal was not used to since the few boats in which he had been a passenger before this were small boats. Except for a ferry once, past the Statue of Liberty. In the ferry there had been kids running and eating hotdogs, gum stuck on the undersides of benches and vomit in the bath-rooms. Overall it was none too clean. The *Nantucket*, by contrast, smelled only of bleach. And she was moving fast. Easy to see how in the armed forces, wearing a clean authoritative uniform with a machine like this beneath you, you might come to believe you ruled the seas.

On Hans's other side was someone named Roger, who was apparently in charge.

"Now in the event we get a Medevac situation," Roger told Hans, "that's going to be at least an hour out for the Dolphin. Minimum. Sorry we couldn't bring reconnaissance airpower on this one. Woulda been nice to have all the new toys to play with. But you know how it is. All dollars and cents. With UAVs, too much bureaucracy."

Hal moved away from them, stood at the portside rail and gazed out over the ocean, the white-blue curl of froth rolling away from the ship. He could see fishing boats dotting the waves out toward the atolls, though they were too far away for him to make out the fishermen. But he imagined all their faces were turned toward him, in awe of the leviathan. Or resentment, if the engine noise was driving off the fish.

He was finding it hard to relinquish his doubt. To get past his

own skepticism that this was real—the vast boat, the gunmen—
he had to remind himself he did not need it to be real. Accord-
ingly he could take it lightly, as though it might easily be nothing
more than a drunk or a delusion . . . if the hurricane had brought
humanitarian relief, for instance, in the form of these men, such
relief seemed to have missed Seine Bight with its muddy field of
shanties. He recalled the light-brown earth dried in right angles
where it had flowed around the corners of buildings that were
now gone. He thought of sheds the size of closets whose particleboard walls were held to the plastic roofs with what looked like
duct tape—sheds that apparently housed whole families, because
half-naked kids were running in and out of them in every appearance of actually living there.

He had not seen any sign of officials or their vehicles, a vast
white prow looming on the water or brand-new supplies being
offloaded into eager hands. Maybe the humanitarian assistance
had gone to settlements up the coast. Or maybe the humanitarian assistance had been the duct tape.

But clearly his information was incomplete. He glanced over
his shoulder at Roger, who was nodding, close-mouthed and san-
guine, at something Hans was saying. He had a humble, sun-
chapped face with a beaklike nose. Such a face was homely and
workmanlike. It seemed trustworthy.

Appearances were often deceiving.

The engines thrummed beneath Hal's feet. Their noise was
deep and steady, their vibration relentless. He was silenced. He
felt he had left his personality on dry land. He should ask Hans
how to address the men; their uniforms flummoxed him. When
he felt the urge to ask a question his instinct was to preface it

with "Officer," timidly and with a sycophantic tone, as on the rare occasion when he had been pulled over for speeding. He did not like policemen; neither did he enjoy the company of soldiers, but he felt more respect for them. Many came from poor backgrounds and were lured by the GI Bill.

Safer to say nothing.

When one of them walked past him he received an impression, in the quickness of the step and the forward-looking, dogged progress, that the walking itself was in the service of a greater business; the detail, the formality of personal transit was a small machination for the sake of general welfare.

And the bodies of the men were budding, strong, confident.

Yet Gretel. Gretel had picked *him*.

Maybe she was simply unaware that there were other options. Much could be ascribed to ignorance, in the world.

And anyway the fitness of these bodies was only partly a reflection on the men themselves. It was a fitness achieved by the state, in a sense, or at least the cost of the fitness was borne by the state. Also the state-sanctioned deployment of the fit and muscular bodies (which were in no way similar to Hal's body, sadly for him) was further augmented by a wide variety of complex and powerful weapons, explosives, and multimillion-dollar, high-tech delivery systems for same. When the state chose to spend roughly the same on its military as on all other things combined, the owners of these now-fit and muscular bodies were the beneficiaries.

True, their occupation could also bring sudden death. But so could many occupations. Sewage work, for instance. No one wept for the sewage workers. Or the electric-light-and-power men. Life insurance companies hated them. Were they needed? They were. Were they acclaimed as heroes when they died? They were not. Same with miners, truck drivers, roofers, all the guys with high premature mortality rates, or PMRs, as the insurance industry called them. Even doctors had a high PMR, the cause being suicide.

In Hal's line of work, which was also conducted in defense of the state, a fit, muscular body was not required. As a result employees of the Internal Revenue Service often suffered from a wide range of their own work-related ailments, including migraines, coronary artery disease, chronic obesity, and carpal tunnel syndrome. These were admittedly less glamorous than battleground injuries. Yet the discomfort was real. And like the sewage workers and the electricity guys, if Hal were to be killed in the line of duty he would not be mourned as a fallen hero. Despite the fact that he had toiled not for private industry but in the unflagging service of his country and all that it stood for, no Taps would play for him.

IRS service did not, however, happen to carry a high PMR.

But finally it was hard to sustain resentment toward the Coast Guarders. Armed forces personnel were not as bad as cops, when it came to the aggregate probability of antisocial personality disorder. They had a different makeup. They were not homicidal so much as Freudian; they liked to feel the presence of a constant father. And their fringe benefits included fit and muscular bodies.

Still, one or two might be behind on their taxes.

He smiled privately at the horizon, a hair-thin line between two shades of blue.

The armed forces took small powerboats from Monkey River Town, loaded with personnel so that they lay low in the water. Roger was not coming with them. There was a Coast Guard guy of lower rank, in blue, whose name Hal did not catch at first. Hans told him he could call the guy "Lieutenant."

There were others in camouflage, some in berets, all wearing mirrored sunglasses through which it was impossible to establish eye contact. His fellow Americans were bedecked in chunky black equipment, belts and holsters and field packs and canteens and knives; they wore headsets and spoke to each other in clipped undertones, as though everything they said was both highly confidential and extremely important.

The sheer weight of their accessories, Hal thought, could capsize the boat if they all moved at once.

The local cadets had no veneer of soldiery and hardly any gear either. Their beige uniforms hung loosely on them and Hal thought they looked eighteen or younger, thin and lost.

"How come they need all those guns? We're just looking for someone in the jungle," he whispered to Hans.

They rounded a curve in the river, which was so brown it looked more like mud than water.

"They are active-duty military. Of course they have guns."

"What are they going to do? Shoot the trees?"

"They're treating it like an extraction. For training purposes."

"Uh huh."

"By the way," said Hans, close to his ear, "no photographs are permitted. This is an unofficial mission."

"I didn't bring a camera," Hal protested, though at the same time it occurred to him that he probably should have. Documentation; proof. For Casey and Susan. "Are you kidding?"

Then the men hunched around maps, Hans among them. They appeared to be tracing routes on the maps with markers and pushing buttons on their watches. The Americans took a paternal air with the local cadets, who nodded eagerly at every directive. Hal tuned them out and gazed into the foliage growing over the stream banks. It was bushy and disordered, thick, unruly—it could hide anything. A wave of dismay rolled over him. There was no way they would find Stern.

That was all right though, in the end. Wasn't it? He would have made an unimpeachable showing. If these Rambos could not locate Stern, Susan and Casey would never think to be disappointed in little old him.

•

After a while they tied the boats to some trees at a place in the river where there was a muddy embankment. It looked like a dirt path of some kind, mostly overgrown.

"This is the trailhead," said Hans, and pointed at a place on the map. It was where Dylan's brother had directed them.

"So we're all getting out here?" asked Hal.

"There are several groups," said Hans, as the Coast Guarders surged around him off the boats. "You will go with the BDF group. The trainees. It will be less strenuous."

"Oh, good," said Hal. He was being babied, but he could care less. "Little hungover, sorry to say."

The Americans were using their black radios, or walkie-talkies, or whatever they were. Static squawked out of them, and nasal tinny voices. All of them huddled on the bank, nodding and talking; Hal grabbed his pack and stepped off the boat with barely room to walk between the broad impervious backs and the hem of reeds and bushes along the water. He stepped too far into these and soaked a foot, swearing, then skirted the crowd.

He felt lost.

"Mr. Lindley?" called one of the young cadets. He had a scar from a harelip. "Right here, sir. Just a moment, then we're going."

The cadet had an accent, but what kind Hal couldn't say. Maybe he was a native Garifuna. Light-brown skin, dark hair, like all of them. Hal didn't feel like getting to know anyone. Small talk, names and places, details. He wanted to trudge in peace, passively. Just let them do their duty. Whatever the hell that might be.

He found a low flat rock in the shade and sat down. It was all shade, just a few feet from the riverbank it was all trees, tall and thin-trunked, most of them. Underfoot was mud and tree roots, a few dead leaves. Young backs were turned to him, blue and beige and camouflage shoulder blades. He let his head flop back and stared into the green overhead, barely moving except for his toes in the clammy, wet shoes.

No sky through the treetops to speak of, only leaves. Strange how the green of these tropical places seemed so unvarying—as though every tree had the same color leaves. Was it the brilliance of the sun, washing out their difference? The quality of the light as it beat down on them? But in the shade they were all the same too, the same bright yet curiously flat green.

Then the men broke their huddle and were jogging past him down the path, a group cutting off along a trail to the right, another group getting into a boat again and gunning the engine upstream. The lieutenant was in charge of the cadets, apparently—the once-harelip motioned to Hal and they were striding after him up the trail.

Hal hoisted himself off the rock and followed.

"We got monkeys," said the once-harelip kid, turning back to him and grinning. "You might see some of the howlers. Way up. Black things. They're not so cute monkeys. They got big teeth. Kinda ugly."

Hal nodded and smiled.

It was a long march, a long, hot, wet, relentless, rapid march, it seemed to him, and three hours in he was bleary with exhaustion. He couldn't believe he was there, couldn't believe that no one had warned him. Hard to keep up—more than hard, actually painful: a form of torture. Long time since he'd had this much exercise and it was practically killing him. It was all he could do to stay in earshot behind them. He was far past embarrassment; he was past even humiliation. He had no pride left at all, nothing left but the strain. He had to struggle just to put one foot in front of the other. Every now and then, from in front, came the sound of voices or a branch snapping. Sweat had wet his shirt through and through, and it was making him cold in the shade of the trees; his water bottles were almost empty.

Take pity on me, he thought, and shortly afterward they stopped for lunch.

They had reached a rough campsite, he saw, coming up behind them, a small muddy clearing. The lieutenant knelt at a fire pit ringed with rocks, touching the ashes or some shit. Sniffing them? Hal wiped his dripping brow with the back of his hand

and sat down heavily on a log. Not watching. All he wanted was rest. He had no interest in them or what they were doing, except insofar as it caused him direct physical distress.

Maybe if he asked they would just let him rest here, let him lie down in the mud and sleep, sleep, sleep while they kept on marching.

He put his head on his arms.

"A watch," said someone.

Hal raised his head. It was the lieutenant, holding out a wristwatch.

"Do you recognize this?"

Hal took it, flipped it over. It was a cheap, bulky digital with a plastic band—no brand name, even. Dried mud between the black plastic links.

"No," he said. "He wouldn't wear one like this. He's more of a Rolex type."

"Could belong to the guide," said the lieutenant, and turned back to the others.

They were passing around sandwiches, eating them standing up. Hal's damp log was the only seat in the house. Someone offered him a sandwich, the cadet with the harelip scar, and he took it gratefully. Maybe after he ate he would be stronger, maybe it would invigorate him. He wolfed it down inside a minute, barely registering the contents. He drank the rest of his water and someone gave him a can of juice. It was quiet for a while as they all ate, hardly any birdsong, until a radio squawked and a low murmur of conversation started.

He got up to pee in the woods, picked his way over tree roots and ferns for privacy. Staring at a thin, light tree trunk with thorns up and down the trunk, ants traveling up and down between the thorns, he noticed movement far off, in the shadows—what? A dark shape—a long, low animal, roughly the size of a dog. Were there dogs in the jungle? It moved more like a cat, though. Jumped from a stand of bamboo to some trees and was gone. He wiped his eyes, which ached from tiredness or dryness or something. Hallucinations, now. He should go back to the boat. He was sick, possibly. In the tropics, viruses thrived.

He was no better than the neurotic bohemians.

•

The trail continued on the other side of the campsite but it was more overgrown. There were vines, and now and then a cadet took out a machete and hacked at one.

Hal dragged after the column, defeated. Sometimes he had to climb over a down log, encrusted with fungus, and pieces of rotting bark got into his shoes and irritated his ankles and heels. He had to stop to pull them out and then catch up to the others, who waited for him. There were biting insects, so he slathered on some bug juice a cadet handed back. He did not bother trying to hear their exchanges; anyway they were mostly lost up ahead.

After a while a light rain began to patter on the leaves and his shoulders. The cadets had ponchos on now. He had nothing. But his shirt was already soaked and he found he didn't mind the rain; the insects bit less. Not too much rain hit the ground, anyway, it seemed to him, much of it trapped above them in the canopy.

It was late afternoon when they turned around. Hal wasn't sure how it happened, but they turned, and he was so grateful he smiled as he stood watching them file past, waiting to bring up the rear again. The lieutenant told him they were headed back to the boats.

"That's it?" said Hal.

"We've been walking six hours give or take," said the lieutenant, nodding. "We got no sign since the campsite. We're tracking thin air. We got a timepiece, that's it. Plus there's a storm moving in. And we don't want you collapsing on us."

"Me?" asked Hal weakly, and as he fell into step behind them wondered if they were turning around for his sake. He wanted to weep with gratitude.

It was night when they got back to the boats, dark and raining. Hal could barely see—was so blurry with fatigue he blundered along the trail, slipping, with his eyes on nothing but the back of the man in front of him. That was his fixed point, that was his everything. He heard greetings in front of him, saw the shine of water beyond the light of the boats, but registered nothing more in the dark except the fact that he could sit down now, he could sit down. His legs shook violently as he sat and someone put something on his back, a blanket, then put a hot drink in his hands—a hot drink. How? But he did not think, he only drank and rested his bones. It was hot chocolate, possibly. Sweet and thick.

Hans was beside him, sitting in the boat, a clap on the back.

". . . sorry," said Hans. "But C Team believes it located a guerrilla training camp. In that sense the mission has been an exceptional success. And they have you to thank."

"Gorilla?" asked Hal, barely above a whisper.

"Guerrilla. Guatemalan guerrillas. Possibly Mayan."

"I see," said Hal, and something vague went through his mind about Rigoberta Menchú and the Peace Prize. The killing of civilians; the Guatemalan refugees, straggling to Mexico . . . but he was tired, too tired. He couldn't think of it now. He drank, half-dropped the empty cup at his feet. He wanted to slide down, lie down on Hans's lap. Maybe he could. But no. Other side: a clean slate.

Fumbling, he spread out the blanket on the seat beside him, where Hans was not.

". . . in troops," Hans was saying. "Possibly airpower."

"Humanitarian?" asked Hal weakly, but he was already lying down, arranging the side of his face on the blanket. He felt the hardness beneath it against his cheek, but it did not stop him.

* * * * *

As he trudged up the dock to the hotel he had the dawn at his back, bands of pale pink over the sea. Exhaustion was making him woozy, unsure of himself; it took over everything. He might still be dreaming. There was a crick in his neck. *Old man.* The palm fronds dipped a little in the breeze off the ocean, almost bowing . . . he and the palms deferred together, it seemed to him, his bent neck and their dipping fronds.

The beach was deserted except for a short wide guy in a baseball cap, raking sand. Hal went by him and pushed up the hill, passing beneath a coconut palm. A falling coconut could kill you if it hit you on the head. The neurotic bohemians had said so. Everywhere there were hazards, waiting.

He turned and looked back at the sea but there was a mist above the surface and he could barely make out the powerboat anymore. Was he losing his vision? A ridiculous thought. But there was something unreal about all of it. As though eyesight could be stolen, like an object . . . he felt a sudden panic and rubbed his eyes. It was a mist, that was all. Fuzzy whiteness.

He kept going toward the buildings. He'd been jolted awake a couple of minutes before by the harelip cadet, who put a small, hesitant hand on his shoulder as the engine throttled down in the shallows. He was groggy, having slept, almost reeling from it, but at the same time there was an edge of anxiety. If he lay down in the hotel bed he was afraid he would toss and turn and have to get up again. The morning light might seep in.

He wanted to talk to Casey, but what would he say to her? His exhaustion, the blur of it . . . first he needed more sleep.

Passing a fence he heard the light, plastic *tic tic tic* of a ping-pong ball hitting the table. He knew who it was. The cornboys were early risers, and this did not surprise him. He would not talk to them, though, he would avoid them neatly. No question. Their English was limited to single words they pushed out with a kind of belligerence. The last time he'd encountered them all they did was jab their fingers at items they were holding or wearing and assert the brand name. "Coca-Cola." "Swatch." "Nikes."

The more he pondered it the eerier it got.

He brushed past clusters of pink flowers on vines growing over a white trellis—*stapled* there. Wait: he leaned in close and saw the tendril of vine was *stapled* to the wood. Was it plastic? He had the suspicion the whole place was fake, was a façade—now that he thought about it, the cornboys in their eeriness were a little unreal, as all of it was turning . . .

The *tic tic tic* of the ping-pong ball, no one at all on the beach but the man raking sand, *scritch scritch scritch*. If not fake, the place must be abandoned. There was only a silence behind those faint sounds—like everyone had filed out of here in the night, faded away and left it empty in the gray of early morning.

Even Gretel was fading from him, the best part of it by far, by far . . . receding already like smoke, a wishful invention. But he would always have the shine of the memory. And a shine was all it was, a glow. No one could see it but him.

Still it shone.

At the moment he would actually be comforted, he realized, to run into the bohemians. He knew they were real. The way they got on his nerves would be a reassurance at this point, make the world more solid. With the bohemians complaining and bickering he was not, finally, far from all that he knew. It was too early for them now, however. Unlike the Germans they did not rise with the sun. But later they would be up, drinking their black coffee or espresso or whatever it was they drank . . . it would be good to see them. Ground him. Something like that.

Until then, pass the time—past the dreaminess, how it unsettled him—maybe he should lie down by the pool.

There were clean white towels in a cart on the deck, beneath a blue-and-white-striped awning. He helped himself to two, then another. He lay down on a chaise and covered himself with them.

"Excuse me. Sir?"

Coming awake again he realized the sun was higher in the sky but hidden, shedding a cold metallic light from behind the grayness. It was overcast. The towels had fallen off him and he was shivering. He sat up, dizzy. Wretched.

"Sorry, sir."

"Sleeping."

"I apologize. But they said you are looking for me."

Hal stared at the interloper. It was the man raking sand. The unreality . . . as though he would look for this man, as though he went around looking for sand-rakers.

"Who?"

"The manager. Mr. Lindley, right? My name is Marlo."

It was a fog. He sat tiredly on the side of the lounger. Marlo. Yes.

"Right! I was looking for you. Before the armed forces."

He leaned down, wanted to touch the water in the pool and splash it on his heavy face, but then the edge was further than he could reach. He let the arm fall, defeated.

"He said you wished to talk to me?"

"I was trying to find Thomas Stern. You worked for him."

"You are his lawyer?"

"Lawyer? Never. Friend—friend of the family."

"Please. Come with me."

Hal stood up unsteadily.

"Please. This way."

He was missing his belongings. What had he done with them? Wallet in the back pocket. Otherwise . . . he felt unmoored. He was floating. Why not: follow some guy named Marlo.

They went down a path from the pool, through a gate and a yard where the sand-raker said something to another yard guy, an unshaven youth in overalls with a lawnmower. They trudged on through the service area, where guests were not usually welcome, past bags of fertilizer on a pallet, ladders against a wall, rusty tools on a bench, boats turned upside-down and equipment under a tarp. Maybe it was the lack of sleep, but he had to watch his feet to keep from stumbling. Needed something.

A Bull Shot, was what came to him—he needed a Bull Shot, beef broth, vodka and a shot of Tabasco. His mother used to drink them. During a certain era she drank Bull Shots and served cocktail sausages.

"Here. It takes ten minutes, maybe fifteen. OK?"

He must have nodded because now Marlo wanted him to help push the boat off the sand, a small boat with an outboard motor. The man was already wading out, the bottom of his white pants swirling around his legs in the water. In the boat, nothing but wooden benches—no padding and no shade.

He didn't have it in him to object, so he bent down and grabbed the back of the boat and heaved. Then he took his shoes off and stepped into the water after it—his pant legs were soaked right away and he sat down heavily on the back bench, feeling the wet material and the grains of sand against the skin of his calves. Marlo was beside him, pulling the cord, so he groped his way to the center bench.

Head spinning, he was on the water. Again.

Neither of them said anything over the noise of the motor and the thump of the prow against the waves. Hal felt thirsty— a throat-cracking thirst came on him in an instant. Afraid his throat would crack he found himself looking under the rough benches for water bottles—anything!—and seeing nothing but an oar and a plastic bucket, he closed his eyes.

His mother stood at the corner of a bar they had in the rec room in the basement, a basement that opened with sliding doors onto the backyard patio. He remembered trays of the miniature sausages in pastry wrappings, toothpicks stuck in them with colored flags of cellophane, flags of yellow and orange. But something thirsty about it—the dry air . . . his father in a Hawaiian shirt, standing over the barbecue.

"Nadine, dear. Here. Have a Bull Shot," he heard his mother say. Nadine was the lady from across the street. She was getting a divorce, he had heard his parents whispering about it. She wore bright, aqua-colored eyeshadow, far too much all the way up to her eyebrows, which Hal, nine at the time, fixated on until his mother told him to stop staring. Hal had firmly believed the eyeshadow was the reason for the divorce. He remembered his conviction on this point, asking his mother why Nadine didn't just stop wearing it.

Even now he recalled the texture of the eyeshadow, how it made him notice the lines beneath the turquoise sheen on the lady's skin, their fine cross-hatchings.

Susan had gone with him to the funeral—his mother's, not the eyeshadow lady's—shortly after their own wedding, twenty years later. He had held her hand at the side of the grave, which was surrounded by a carpet of something like AstroTurf. He held her hand and felt this contact was the armor worn by the two of them. Armor was what it was, the pair bond, marriage: something enclosing them that offered protection. But it was not metal, finally, it was far too flimsy . . . at different moments in a life you had these companions, blurring around you like figures in stop-motion photography: mother, father, friends of his youth, wife, daughter. Gone.

Not one of them forever.

He was riveted by the pain of this flashing away, this dimming. He would die from it, die from being alone.

He opened his eyes.

"I am so thirsty," he said to Marlo over the engine noise, in the vain hope he might be able to help. But the man only nodded and smiled, probably no idea.

Then they were sputtering to a slow glide. Glancing down he saw the boat was over the shallows again, simple sand beneath them through the light water. No coral, no seaweed. He turned around—he had spent the whole ride facing backward, facing where they'd come from. There was a small beach, some trees— an island, he guessed. A small island.

"Where are we?" he asked Marlo.

"Mr. Tomás's property," said Marlo, as the boat cruised in and the hull scratched over the bottom.

Hal looked up the beach. He could make out what seemed to be piles—piles of what he did not know.

"You go," said Marlo, and gestured.

He had no idea what he was doing here but got out of the boat anyway, waded up the slope of the beach still clutching his shoes. He tried to cross the sand barefoot but there were sharp things in it, little sticks or twigs or something, that hurt him. He had to stop, wavering, hopping to keep his balance as he put the shoes on. Off balance, he almost toppled. The sensation of his wet feet inside the shoes was unpleasant: cold toes and gritty sand.

All he could do was walk toward the piles. Nowhere else to go; there was nothing else here. He felt a prick of fear. Maybe Marlo had brought him out here to kill him. Why? A good question. Still. Hal was middle-aged, exhausted and weak—a natural victim. It was just the two of them.

He turned around and gazed back at the boat, where Marlo stood cupping his mouth with his hands. He was lighting a cigarette.

Up the beach a little further were the collapsed walls of a building, its concrete foundation. What was Hal supposed to be noticing, for chrissake? He was too tired for games. Tired and stupid. He wasn't a forensics investigator. He was no Sherlock Holmes. He noticed nothing, did not even want to have to pay attention. Splintered plywood, chunks of plaster, waterlogged Sheetrock with yellow stains browning at the edges. That was it.

Then someone came out of the trees, a man zipping his fly. A dark, lean man with a full beard, shirtless and half-emaciated, his ribs showing over a concave stomach. A mountain man or hippie. His white painter pants were filthy.

"Who the hell?" said Hal, not meaning to. Then it struck him: this was the man on the boat, the bearded man on the boat he had seen from the scuba island.

"Wait," said the man. He was American. Small mercies. "God! I know *you*."

Hal gazed at him. His eyes were a startling blue against the brown of his face. The beard was brown but blond strands were woven through it; the nose was straight and peeling across the bridge from the sun.

He heard himself laugh nervously. He clutched his arms around himself, then let go.

Yes: he had seen this man standing up in a boat, the day of the scuba dive. It was him.

"T.," said the man, stating the obvious, and stuck out a brown hand. "You're Casey's father, aren't you? The tax man!"

Hal hesitated to take the hand, recalling how it had recently zipped the fly, and was startled when Stern clasped him into a warm embrace.

He felt a tinge of hysteria, then confusion.

"I'm tired," he said, drawing back. "But I'm really thirsty. Do you have some water?"

"Sure, come with me," said the newly brown, bearded Stern.

Wary of where he put his feet—there were rusty nails in the disintegrating Sheetrock—Hal followed droopily over the piles of debris, back through the trees. A sandy trail had been cleared, just wide enough for single file. Thin trees on each side, shiny miniature leaves. A minute later they were in a small clearing. Ahead of them was an unfinished structure of wood built around a tree; Hal saw a camp stove, a tent, a dark-green metal tank. PROPANE, read a red label on the side. There was a folding chair and he sank down into it. Stern was already handing him a cup.

He drank it down, all of it, with closed eyes. His blood was rushing in his ears.

"Have more," said Stern. He took the cup from Hal, filled it and handed it back.

Hal drank the second cup and realized his head was aching again but that he felt better. It was water he had needed, water and sleep.

"Is your head hurting? Your eyes?" asked Stern.

"Yes," nodded Hal. "Yes."

"You're dehydrated. It's a dangerous condition. Just keep drinking, small sips but steadily."

"They're afraid you're dead," said Hal, after a few seconds sitting there nodding and dazed, stroking the near-empty cup with a thumb.

"Dead? Oh," said Stern. "I kept planning to call. I needed someone to look after my dog for a while. I was just about to call."

"We picked her up. She's OK," said Hal.

"I knew the kennel would take good care of her. Place costs a king's ransom."

"She's at my house," said Hal.

"Oh, good," said Stern. "That's great."

"But they've been really worried," said Hal.

It was a letdown after everything to be sitting with Stern, the plastic water cup in his hand. Stern took it to fill it again, leaned over to a jug, a five-gallon plastic jug with a spout. Water gurgled as Stern tipped it forward.

Hal sipped and felt himself shiver and then laughed, a bit wildly. He could hear it but not stop it.

"We had the armed forces looking for you," he said. "It was a search-and-rescue. Organized by Germans."

Stern looked surprised and then barked out a laugh of his own. Hal laughed harder. They were fools, laughing. Uncontrol-

lable, stupid laughter. Hal bent forward, tears running from his
eyes. He shook his head to stop himself laughing. Eventually it
petered out.

"I miss them. I miss Casey," said Stern, nodding to himself.
"Susan too."

"She's having an affair," said Hal. It slipped out.

"Casey?" asked Stern.

"Susan!"

"I see," said Stern, and glanced at him sidelong.

"With that paralegal who works in your office. That young,
preppy guy named Robert."

"Robert? Huh," said Stern, shifting in his seat and turning
his face upward. He squinted a little at the sky. "Well. I never
liked him."

Hal felt a surge of gratitude.

"You know, it wasn't so long ago that your daughter told me,"
said Stern, "that I should avoid wearing those shirts with the blue
pinstripes on them and the solid white collars. You know the
kind I mean?"

"Those are bad," agreed Hal. "She was right about that."

They sat quietly, Stern gazing into the distance with a kind of
enraptured tenderness.

"And here you are," said Hal. "You're not wearing one.
Are you."

They smiled at each other again. A bird squawked.

"I do need a shirt, though," said Stern, musing. "I ran out of
them."

"I see that."

"I've been working," said Stern, almost apologetic.

"But," said Hal, "I mean—what happened to you?"

"I'll tell you," said Stern. "You should rest first, though. I'm serious, I think you're pretty dehydrated. Come with me."

He got up, gesturing for Hal to follow him. At the wooden hut built on the tree—a kind of tree-house, Hal guessed—he lifted a piece of coarse cloth that was serving as a door and put his hand on Hal's shoulder, guiding him through. Hal saw a sleeping bag on the rough floor.

"Lie down there for a while," said Stern. "You need to be out of the sun. It's cooler than the tent. I'll get you something for the headache."

Hal did what he said, lay down on the sleeping bag, which smelled a little of mildew but not bad, exactly. A few seconds later Stern was back with two small pills in his dark hand. Hal took them.

"Thank you," he said, and slowly crumpled sideways.

· · · · ·

When he woke it was dark out again. He had slept through the morning, slept through the afternoon. He could barely believe it. Time was wrong for him now, out of kilter since the invasion of the armed forces.

He scrambled to his feet. He felt better, almost normal, though there was still a dull throb at his temples. The ache was less urgent. Through a window in the tree-house, if you could call it that—a gap between the planks—he saw the glow of a campfire

in the dark and the silhouetted figure of Stern standing a few feet
off, back turned.

He lifted the cloth and went out.

"Thomas," he said. "Did the boat go? Marlo?"

"Call me T.," said Stern, turning. He was standing in front of
his camp stove, a two-burner thing, Hal noticed, connected to
the propane tank by a thin tube that snaked out of it, curling . . .
it was balanced on an empty crate. T. held a large spoon, with
which he was stirring something in a saucepan.

"T. OK then," said Hal, reluctant. "I didn't mean to sleep the
whole day. I can't believe it."

"You needed it," said T.

"So where's my, uh—Marlo?"

"Marlo left."

"He left? He stranded me?"

"I wouldn't put it that way," said T. "You're with me. He had
to get back to work. We thought you needed the rest. Dehydration, if it lasts long enough, you know—it can have serious consequences. How'd you get that far gone?"

"I don't know," said Hal. "I think—I wasn't paying attention.
Basically."

"Making chili," said T. "From a can, but it'll do. Got a kick to
it. Want any?"

"Sure. Thank you," said Hal, and made his way around the
fire to the folding chair. He was starving, he realized. Also thirsty
again. He looked for his plastic cup. It was back in the tree-house,
so he went to get it.

"Make yourself comfortable. There's a bottle of wine sitting
on the cooler," called T. as Hal came out again. "Cheap and red.

Probably not the best idea if you're still feeling the dehydration, though."

"I've been drinking too much lately," said Hal. He downed another two cups of water before he reached for the wine.

Slopping cup in one hand, the folding chair in the other, he went around the propane tank and the cooler and plopped the chair down in the sand to sit facing T. It seemed polite, though awkward.

In the trees around them there were the slight sounds of birds, maybe crickets. An insect landed on Hal's arm, a mosquito, possibly, and he slapped at it. He could hear the faint plash of waves through the screen of trees. They were low, scrubby trees not much taller than he was—more like overgrown bushes, really. He let his head fall back on his neck: above him the sky was huge. The stars were more visible tonight. They went on and on.

"So how did you end up down here?" asked T. He was slicing an onion.

"I should be asking you the questions," said Hal. "Are you kidding? I came looking for you, of course. To help Susan. And Casey. You vanished into thin air. Your business, you know—it's not doing so well. You're losing money. For starters. What gives?"

"You know," said T., and shrugged, "the usual."

"The *usual?*"

"Change of priorities. I went on a river trip."

"I know all that, the Monkey River. That guy who you were with? The guide or whatever? Dylan? His brother is worried sick about him. We found his watch at your campsite, maybe."

"Delonn. Not Dylan. But yeah. That's—I need to talk to his family about it, sooner or later. I've been keeping myself to myself. Marlo's brought me some food and supplies while I lay low. Maybe not the best idea. Tactically. It looks bad, if anyone's looking. But what happened was, our first night out, he was in his tent, I was in mine—we each had our own tent, you know?—and I must have been asleep when it happened."

"What happened?"

"He died."

"He *died?*"

T.'s face was in shadow. Hal tried to make out its emotion.

"A heart attack, I think. A stroke, maybe an aneurysm. Something quiet, while he was sleeping. He was an older guy, Delonn. Maybe in his sixties. Still. There'd been this—earlier he had problems breathing, but he didn't seem worried about it."

"Jesus!"

"He was a tough guy, you know, pretty rugged. Carried more weight in his pack than I did. I found him in the morning and what I ended up doing was, I dragged the body back to the boat. I was in shock, I think. I panicked. The boat's propeller broke after that and I ditched the boat. And the body with it. I tried to hike out on foot. Stupid, but that's what happened. I got lost for a while. Finally I made it down to the coast. I don't know if it was days or weeks, honestly. From there I hitched a ride to Marlo's place and he brought me here. Short version."

"It wasn't in the boat, though. I mean, the body."

"I know," said T., a little vaguely. "I noticed that. Yeah. That's a complication."

Hal sat for a second, waiting. He wondered if T. was lying to him. Here, though, he seemed better than he had before. Hal liked him more. Maybe only because he was familiar—after all, Hal had practically even been willing, just a few hours back, to cozy up to the bohemians.

In a strange land you found yourself seeking. Afloat among the aliens, your standards were relaxed.

Anyway, like him or not, T. could still be a liar.

"Shouldn't you probably tell someone?"

"Marlo was going to meet with whoever there was," said T. "He was going to say I was recovering, that I would talk to them soon. I didn't know . . . anyway, but. It should be me. I should go talk to them, I should face the music. You're right. Of course."

"And you didn't call anyone. How come you didn't at least call Susan?"

There was a pause. T. seemed distracted, pondering.

"You like onion? Because I can chop it fine or leave it in these big chunks."

"Whatever."

Hal watched as he tossed the onion into the tin frying pan, pushed it around with the spoon.

"My wife," said Hal a bit stiffly, "is devoted to you."

"I'm sorry for letting her down. Hard to explain. Call it a mid-life crisis."

"But you're what," said Hal. "All of, like, twenty-six?"

He took a slug of his wine. It was nice. The guy looked older at the moment, that was true, with the deep tan, the crow's feet at the corners of his eyes and the uneven beard that gave him the look of a homeless individual. He could pass for forty, if you didn't know.

"I've always done things too early," said T. "When I was seven I was already thirteen. When I was in college I was already in my thirties. Youth passed me by."

"Please," scoffed Hal. "Give me a break."

"It's a mind-set, is all I mean. Partly."

"My age, now," said Hal, "that's when you have a mid-life crisis. Fact I may be having one as we speak."

T. poured the chili out of the pan, dividing it between a bowl and a can marked CHILI.

"I only have the one bowl," he said apologetically, and held it out. "Here."

Hal took it gratefully. He was ravenous. T. was eating too but more slowly, spooning his chili out of the can with a deliberation that seemed incongruous to Hal—almost graceful, even. He looked underfed but apparently was in no hurry to remedy the situation.

Gnats landed on Hal's neck, or maybe they were sandflies— they bit lightly—but they were nothing to the hunger. He polished off the bowlful inside a minute.

"Bit more left, if you like," said T., and handed over the frying pan.

"So what are you, uh, actually doing here?" asked Hal, after he'd scraped it up. "On the island?"

"I was having a hotel built," said T., putting down his can and crossing his legs, leaning back. He held a scratched plastic mug with a coat of arms and some writing on it; Hal squinted to read it in the light of the lantern. There were four yellow lions on a red background. Faded words read CAMBRIDGE UNIVERSITY LIGHT-WEIGHT ROWING CLUB.

He rowed for Yale.

"You didn't row for Cambridge, did you?" Hal asked him after a few seconds, and quaffed.

"What? Row?—Oh, this? This isn't mine. This, actually, was Delonn's. It was in our camping stuff. I ended up with it. I didn't really mean to."

Hal was feeling the wine already.

"You go to Yale?" he asked.

"I went to a state school. Where my father went before me."

A relief. Somehow it had seemed to Hal, back in L.A., that Robert the Paralegal was a pale imitation of T.—that maybe Susan saw in him a reflection of her employer, to whom she gave such fealty. Maybe Robert was only a stand-in for T., had hovered at the far edge of his suspicion. Now he found out even T.'s WASP credentials were nothing much. Somehow it was consoling.

In point of fact he himself was a WASP, if he wanted to be literal about it, and specifically a WASP with some recent German background. His mother, long ago, had flirted with genealogical research and once told him the branches of their family tree sprouted nothing but Englishmen, Germans and a few glum, dead Swedes.

Still, it was the WASPs and the Germans that most alarmed him.

"Sorry," he said, "digression. You had a hotel here?"

"It was under construction. The storm destroyed it, though."

"Oh, wow."

"Half-destroyed it, technically, but it was totaled. So I've been demolishing it."

Hal watched as T. poured wine into his plastic mug, emptying the bottle. Luckily Hal's own vessel was still nearly full.

"Didn't know you were quite so hands-on," he said jokily. "What Susan said, you were mostly the brain trust. Not so much on the brawn side of things."

"I've been giving it to the ocean. Piece by piece. I figure it could be an artificial reef. You know, like the old tires they sink in some places, or the wrecks, and then the fish come and inhabit them."

Hal looked at him. He seemed sincere, but maybe there was something absent about him. Maybe he wasn't all there. Like mother, like son, finally. It made perfect sense, of course, with the sunburnt castaway look and the whole tropical island, spurning-society deal.

"Wait. So this is why you haven't called anyone? This is what you're—you know, with your business losing money and all that this whole time? So you can personally, like, lug the wreckage of your hotel into the water?"

"Well, when you put it that way," said T. lightly, smiling, and then gazed past him. "I mean, losing money—so yeah. It's OK, finally. All my life I thought that was the worst thing that could happen to you."

"Uh huh," said Hal. He waited.

"I thought money was real."

Poor guy.

"Well, I tell you," said Hal mildly, as though speaking to an infant. "Admittedly I'm biased, being an IRS man. But I can't think of a lot of things realer than money. I mean, to most people money is life and death."

"So that's two things right away. Life. And death."

"I don't really follow you."

"They're both more real. Living for money is like living for, I don't know, a socket wrench. Unless you're going to do something specific with it, it's a complete waste of time. Obvious to some people, I realize. But I just now figured it out."

"Sure. Hey, I get it. You're talking to a civil servant here. So obviously I'm no high-earning capitalist. I've seen what money can do, though. Take income tax revenues. Social programs."

"That's not what income tax revenues do," said T. softly. "Social Security has its own—"

"Not primarily, maybe—"

"Primarily, taxes pay for weapons. Weapons and war. Always have, always will."

A straw man. Statistically, it was far more complicated than that. Hal could break it down for him. Basic protester stuff.

"Well, tech—"

"I know. Weapons, war, and please don't forget the D.O.T."

"As a percentage of—" started Hal, but the guy was shaking his head.

"Hey. Can I show you something?" he asked. "I've also been building the tree-house. I'm using some of the hotel materials for that. This is an island caye, palm trees and sand, which is what made it buildable in the first place. You know, some of the cayes around here are only mangrove, no real ground to build on. Mostly water. This one is island but it has a lot of mangrove vegetation too, kind of a mangrove-swamp thing on the east side, and the west side is solid ground. Right here we're phasing into mangrove, and those are mostly scrubby. But I found one tree that was tall enough, that was it. Come here," and he rose and Hal followed him, both with their cups of wine in hand.

There were rough steps up the tree with the lean-to beside it, pieces of wood hammered clumsily onto the narrow trunk. Whatever else the guy was, he was no carpenter.

At the top there was a platform, several layers of plywood with holes cut in them for the topmost limbs, which stuck out like grasping arms. Hal pulled himself up behind T., unsteady.

"Is this thing safe?" he asked.

T. shrugged. "Enough."

They both stood looking out over the mangroves, over the low tangle of vegetation eastward to the open ocean. Nothing around them but air; at only twenty feet up they were the highest point for miles.

Hal saw a huge ship far out on the water, dazzling with light.

"Cruise ship, huh," he said.

"You can see from here to the utter east," said T. softly. "All the world ends in sea."

The wind picked up the branches of the trees that ringed their clearing, swept through and subsided again.

"Right," said Hal.

So the guy was maybe not doing too well, mental-wise. It happened. He had been in an extreme situation—lost in the jungle, pretty much. He had a little breakdown, or maybe an epiphany; he found God, he saw the error of his ways, he renounced the accumulation of capital. Good, fine, and even excellent. More power to him. Let him become ascetic, live in a small hut with zero Armanis. At last Susan could stop working for him.

Hal's new fondness was a pleasant enough sensation. The man

who used to be Stern had a gentle demeanor now, or that was what it felt like. Maybe Hal could even serve as his advocate with the Belize authorities, if it turned out he had committed a crime. If he had, for instance, murdered the tour guide, say, and that was why he had spiraled out of control and was building tree-houses and forgoing personal grooming. Hal could stand beside him like a brother.

He drank his wine and felt the cool breeze on his face and the warmth in his throat.

"Not a bad place to be," said T. "Is it?"

But wait, maybe this was why Marlo had asked if he was a lawyer. When he first woke him up by the pool, Marlo had asked if he was a lawyer. Maybe the guy knew he needed a lawyer. Maybe Marlo had already called for one.

"Not at all," he concurred, and looked up into the dark blue. It was light up here, the wind lifted you as though you could soar or fall, and let it, you wouldn't mind. Stars were visible, but soft and washed out by the water in the air, not like infinite separate pinpoints he'd seen once in the desert.

They had gone camping in Joshua Tree one weekend, Susan and he, not so long after the accident, because they had to get out, they had to go anywhere, they had to escape, and it was the clos- est empty place they'd heard of. Casey was in rehab then—the physical therapy kind, not the drug-using. They'd driven east on the interstate out of L.A., through the miles and miles of indus- trial sprawl and car dealerships flying their advertising blimps in the gray, smoggy sky along the crowded freeway. Finally they pulled up outside the visitors' center and sure, there was con- crete, just like at home, the concrete parking lot; but beyond it there was sand and sand and mountains and sky, and there was air all around them, plenty of room to breathe. The spiky cactus-trees were everywhere, the low mountains, the campsites with gigantic boulders.

What he remembered now from that trip, besides the stars, was how they hardly spoke, he and Susan, they hardly talked at all. But it was not bad, it was not a measure of distance, or it hadn't been back then. It was restful and good, peace in the wake of a long struggle.

Their borrowed tent had a transparent window in the top of it. He had lain there on his back at night, on top of his sleeping bag, and gazed out at the stars while Susan slept beside him. He thought they'd never looked so clear, and there had never been so many.

Casey would like this tree-house, he thought; Casey would love it here. She had looked into flying, flying in a glider. There was a program that could take her up in the sky. She hadn't done it yet, but she still could. He would call her and say do it, do it. To know that lightness . . . it was not the running, not a vision of her once in a race, say, her slim young legs flying, though there had been times like that and he remembered them well enough. Field Day at school, when she was in the hundred-yard dash: he loved to watch her but she complained both before and after the race, even holding her purple ribbon. She did not like run-ning. Hard to believe while he was watching her go, it so closely resembled joy . . . or flying a kite once, on a beach in Cape Cod, her feet kicking up sand on him. There were cliffs near them and the water was far too cold for swimming.

But that was not what distressed him, the memories of run-

ning. Only the simple memory of her face—her face without tension, without strain or grief.

"My daughter would like this," he said.

"She would," nodded T.

"I wish I could just take her—take her anywhere," said Hal,
with a rush of agitation. He saw Casey in flight, swooping. "Anywhere she wanted to be."

He was staring out at the cruise ship. Its lights were like the
lights of the ballroom in the resort—was it last night? No, the
night before—dancing with Gretel. The nearness to the water
made the lights blur and shimmy, part of the very same liquid.

"You know," said T., and Hal realized T. was looking at him,
reaching out to rest a thin hand on his arm, "she's going to be all
right."

"I don't know," said Hal, but it came out like a sigh. Something about the guy's bearing reassured him—his confidence, his
certainty. He said Casey would be all right. So she must be.

"I promise."

No need to move.

Only around the cruise ship was the water dappled with light;
other than that it was blackness. Hal did not want to take a step,
in case the platform broke beneath him or he fell off the edge,
but this was fine for the moment. This was where he was now.

7

The boat was anchored on the east side, where no one would see it coming from the mainland. There was no dock there, only a narrow sandy path through the tangles of mangrove.

After a breakfast of instant oatmeal and water Hal followed T. along the path, ducking between branches. T. carried a canvas sack of his belongings slung over one shoulder. They had swum in the shallows on the other side of the island but the saltwater bath had not made T. seem any cleaner. He was still wearing the filthy painter pants, on which the pockets bulged.

"I have a razor, you can shave at the hotel," said Hal to his back. "Before you get in touch with anyone. Because the cops, I mean if they see you like this, you know, the credibility issue."

"You have to wade out," said T. over his shoulder. "I recommend just leaving your shoes on. There are branches just beneath the surface, things that can cut."

They emerged from the bushes with their feet already in the silty water; the roots of the scrub reached below the surface, long, thin vertical brown lines like wooden drips. Hal felt their knobbiness through the soles of his shoes. The cool water was around his knees now and his feet slipped in the mud beneath. He could see the boat ahead, a long, simple white shape with peeling paint.

"Here we go," said T., and dropped his sack in. He climbed over the side and held a hand out to Hal. "Help?"

"I'm fine," said Hal, and stepped in awkwardly, the boat rocking.

As the motorboat throttled down, nearing the beach, Hal realized they had an audience: Gretel. Gretel and the cornboys.

She was watching them from the swimming dock a few hundred yards away, standing on the sand in her blue bikini and shading her eyes as she looked out over the ocean toward them.

The cornboys, in overlarge sunglasses and a hot-pink double kayak, were paddling toward Hal and T.

Gretel raised her arm and waved.

"One of the Germans," he told T., who was easing them into a slip. He waved back at her, trying to seem casual, which luckily was not difficult in the wave format.

Did she regret it? How deeply? Was she kicking herself? Seeing him now she would probably feel repulsed. Then again, maybe she would not notice him: he had T. in his company, the prodigal son. T. would demand her attention by not being dead.

"The Germans?"

"With the whole Coast Guard search thing? Looking for you? Her name is Gretel. The pink kayak? Those are her kids."

The cornboys were bearing down. They paddled fiercely, their small mouths clamped into grimaces that indicated they were trying desperately to win. Yet there was no competition.

"Hey, guys," called T., throwing his rope over the piling. "How's it going?"

"Their English is rudimentary," said Hal.

"My father went to get the airplanes," called one of the cornboys proudly, slowing the kayak with his paddle.

"Yes," nodded the other. Hal was still unclear as to whether in fact they were twins.

"Sounds pretty good to me," said T., bent to his knot-tying. "The English."

"I never heard them say that much before," admitted Hal.

"Airplanes!" repeated the second cornboy.

"Gotcha," said Hal. "He went to get the airplanes. Good to know." No idea what the kid was talking about, but who cared. Wanted a shower, actually; wished he could have had one before he ran into Gretel. Not that it mattered: he expected nothing, or less than nothing. But just for the dignity.

T. was climbing up onto the dock; Hal followed him. The cornboys were staring at them in that way children had—staring with no goal in mind, just like it was normal.

"This is the man your father was helping me look for," said Hal.

"The dead one?" asked the first cornboy. He tended to speak first; probably the Alpha. Possibly he was older, but they both looked the same.

"Exactly," said Hal, and hoisted himself onto the dock after T. He wanted clean, dry clothes, and the sun was making him squint.

Gretel stood at the end of the dock now, one hand on a hip, smiling quizzically; she was curious about T. already.

"Hi there," she said as they approached.

"This is the guy," said Hal. "This is him. Thomas Stern."

"No way!" said Gretel, and leapt into T.'s arms, hugging him. "Oh my God! You're alive!"

"I feel bad to have caused all this trouble," said T., and pulled away gently.

"*Doch,* the important thing is that you are *safe,*" said Gretel, beaming joy as though he was a long-lost friend. Hal stood by with his arms dangling, awkward.

"Well, thank you," said T. "I am. Thank you."

"I'm going to get him cleaned up," said Hal apologetically. "We'll see you a little later?"

"Yes, please," said Gretel. "I want to hear the whole story!"

"Of course," said Hal.

"OK," said T., and they left her smiling at their backs.

"She actually means it, I think," said Hal.

"I can tell," said T.

Hal lay down on the hotel bed while T. took a shower. The sound of its steady falling was a hello from the civilized world. *Welcome home.* He listened with his head on the soft pillow, his body on the long, solid bed. What a relief. It was so good to have them. The pillow and the bed. The lights, the air-conditioning, and the running water. He was no nature boy. T. could keep his tree-house, no matter how good the view. There was a reason their hominid ancestors first stood upright and started beating smaller creatures to death with cudgels. It was better than what came before, that was why.

The whole atavistic thing was overrated at best.

There had been a shaving kit in T.'s suitcase, which the manager had handed over to Hal several days ago now—a shaving kit and clean clothes, and T. had taken them both into the bathroom with him. But still Hal worried he had failed to impress upon his new friend the importance of a mainstream appearance, when dealing with authorities in a third-world country, and when there was the corpse of a local involved.

Sure: in the past the guy had been Mr. Mainstream. In the past the guy wore Armanis and refused to get behind the wheel of anything but a Mercedes. Once Susan had been forced to rent him a Lexus, when his Mercedes was at the shop for service. To hear her tell it the guy had suffered a martyr's holy torments.

But he was not that guy anymore. No indeed. Now he was a guy who ate chili from a can, had long toenails and a wiry beard that almost grazed his nipples, and apparently sported a well-worn, formerly white baseball cap—now sitting humped on the nightstand next to Hal's bed—whose inside rim was ringed with a crust of brown stain best regarded as a potential disease vector.

He had to call Susan, of course. He was still tired, felt almost waterlogged with a fatigue that wouldn't lift off, but he had to call her. Duty.

He raised the receiver, then remembered he needed the phone card from his wallet and rolled slowly off the bed to reach for it. As he typed the digits, it occurred to him that she might be in flagrante with Robert the Paralegal—she might not deserve this prompt, nay servile attention. Then the telephone rang on her end, rang and rang until he hung up before the answering machine clicked in. He had to tell her this himself, wanted the clamor of it in person—his reward in the form of her stunned amazement, her astonished gratitude at the good news.

He tried Casey's number next, but the line was busy.

She was probably working.

Lying flat on his back, waiting for the shower to cut off, he considered the likelihood the authorities could be bribed to overlook the problem of a dead tour guide. Of course, to offer a bribe would imply guilt. Were they corrupt? Were they righteous? And where were they, in the first place?

He called the front desk to ask. The nearest police station, said the receptionist, was twenty miles up the peninsula to the north. It was connected to an outpost of the Belize Defence Force, apparently. The cops and the military, in an ominous conjunction. But maybe the young harelip cadet would be there, take pity on them, and intercede with his superiors on T.'s behalf.

Was there a problem? asked the receptionist, still on the line. "No," said Hal, "none at all, thanks." He hung up.

Possibly they would be ill-advised to contact the police after all. Asking for trouble. If T. told Delonn's brother how the guide had had a heart attack, probably the brother would not bring charges. He wasn't the suspicious type. And anyway what motive could T. have for murder?

He must have dozed off then, because when he woke up T.

was standing over him with light around his thin, nut-brown face. The eyes were a piercing blue. Cleaner, wearing a white collar shirt and gazing down at Hal with what appeared to be compassion, he also seemed sanctified. Beneficent.

But he had omitted to shave, just as Hal feared. The long beard still stuck out stiffly from his chin like a useless appendage. He looked like one of the Hasidim. Or even a saint or Jesus.

Although Jesus was seldom pictured in collar shirts. They had not been popular at the time.

"Sorry," said the Jesus-T. softly. "I didn't mean to wake you. You can go back to sleep. I'm taking off for a while."

Hal sat up, jolted.

"Taking off? Taking off where?"

"Headed to Monkey River Town. With Marlo. Sit down and talk to Delonn's brother."

"Good, right," mumbled Hal, rubbing his eyes. "You're coming back here after, right?"

"Should be back by sometime around dinner," said the Jesus-T., nodding. "Don't wait on me though. Time runs slow in these parts."

"All right then," said Hal weakly, and lay back as the Jesus-T. receded. The room door closed softly.

The Jesus-T. left the scent of soap and toothpaste. At least he had used them.

•

A short time later Hal made his way to the hotel restaurant for lunch, himself freshly washed. He was spooning up soup and halfheartedly reading the paper when someone jostled his elbow: a cornboy, probably the Alpha.

Both of them were hovering, shirtless and dripping, in wet shorts. They held fluorescent boogie boards under their arms.

"Hey," said Hal, wiping his mouth with a napkin.

"Where's the dead guy?"

"He went to a meeting."

"You finished?"

"You mean—my lunch? No," said Hal, mildly astonished. "I just started it."

"My mother wants to see you."

"Uh . . ."

"You talk to her. OK? Then we go snorkel."

The waiter leaned down and removed his soup plate.

"She gets bored. She likes friends. You talk to her."

"Where's your father?"

"In the airplane."

"*Im Hubschrauber,*" intervened the Beta, shaking his head.

"Yeah, right. A helicopter," said the Alpha. "He took a helicopter to get to the airplane."

"Dolphin HH-65A," nodded the Beta, enunciating perfectly.

"I'll be happy to talk to her," said Hal. His club sandwich had come. He took a sip of iced tea. "Right after I eat. OK?"

"We are in front. We are by the ocean."

"OK," said Hal. "I'll come find you. Promise."

He watched them jog away, picking up a fry and dangling it over the small paper cup of ketchup. Were they actually concerned for their mother? Or was the snorkeling more the point? Or had Gretel sent them? Hal thought not. Their expedition had seemed self-directed. Gretel would have come to talk to him herself, if she wanted to. He might go over to her and then she might not be glad to see him. She might not want to talk to him at all, at least without T. in the mix. Possibly he could tell her T.'s story to cover up the awkwardness.

When he finished he took a chocolate-mint from the dish next to the cash register, popped it in his mouth and made a side trip to the bathroom in the lobby, where he splashed cold water on his face and combed his hair with his fingers. Nothing between them, in a linear sense: no future, no expectation. But still.

And he should call Susan again. Soon.

In the sun his eyes smarted. He had left his sunglasses in the room. He walked through canvas beach chairs, umbrellas, both with white and blue stripes, matching; hammocks were strung between tree trunks, his fellow hotel guests lying on them unmoving, fleshy and naked like human sacrifices. Mostly fat. Or fattish. He saw brown bottles of lotion with palm trees on them, dog-eared paperbacks splayed open on towels. One man had on a Walkman, and a tinny beat issued forth.

Shading his eyes, he looked for the cornboys. They were easy to spot in a crowd, typically.

"Hal!" cried Gretel. She was still excited, apparently, about the nondeath of T. She smiled happily.

She wore an orange and brown sarong below her floral bikini top and looked beautiful, though maybe a little older, he was noticing, or more tired than he had thought previously. Her face was shaded by a straw hat. She held her arms open. He leaned into them. She reminded him, suddenly, of people who mourned celebrities—celebrities they never knew, of course, people who were nothing but symbols to them. Fans at Elvis's grave, for instance. People swaying with candles, or gathered at mono-grammed gates holding armfuls of flowers. He had never under-stood it. The mourners had not even met the celebrities, never seen anything of them but a constructed public image, yet they wept, they swayed, some did violence to themselves.

Clearly the celebrities were symbols to them, and these sym-bols carried weight. He knew about symbols and their weight, their mystical eminence and power to enthrall. But that did not explain it. If the famous people were symbols, why did it matter when they died? Symbols went on forever.

Gretel had not known T., did not know Susan. How could she care, really? Her beaming happiness. For all she knew T. was a swine, yet she was visibly rejoicing.

"Tell me how you found your friend!" she exhorted, and pulled him underneath her umbrella. The cornboys were in the water. He plumped down on the canvas beach chair beside her, which turned out to be wet. The seat of his pants was instantly soaked and clammy.

"I went to an island," he said, wondering how much credit to take. "An island he owns. He was building a hotel there, before the storm hit."

As he told the story she gazed at his face attentively, nodding and smiling eagerly as though he, too, must feel overjoyed and brimming with triumph. In fact he felt unsurprised, he reflected; T. being dead had never been a foregone conclusion to him. It was Susan who had been so convinced of the worst-case scenario. To him the question of T.'s deadness had been, in fact, basically a matter of indifference—which shocked him, now that he thought of it. His former indifference rattled him slightly, he realized.

Now that he liked T., now that he had appointed himself T.'s protector and ally, how automatic, how thoughtlessly callous the former indifference seemed.

At the same time he was noticing Gretel's breasts, a caramel, tanned color, the scoops of them smooth and perfect where they emerged from the fabric of the bikini. He regretted his former indifference to whether T. was alive or dead; he was mildly astonished to recognize it. But he was more astonished at the beauty of the breasts, barely covered. They hid their light under a bushel. Men were not queued up beside Gretel's beach umbrella, for instance, rubbernecking for a gander. The breasts were here, and yet their presence had not been widely broadcast, though it would clearly be of interest to the general public. He thought of crowds along city streets, waving and straining for a look at the Pope in his Popemobile.

Not so in this case. The breasts were unsung heroes.

Incredible that his own hands and mouth had been on them such a short while ago—a few hours, a couple of days' worth of hours, anyway, many of them passed quickly in sleep. In geological time, it was a second ago—an instant. The sense memory of it . . . no one was mentioning this. Neither he nor Gretel said to each other, right away, we are people who fucked, you fucked me and I fucked you, or made-fucking-love, or whatever. Instead it was as though this fucking had never taken place, and here they were discussing the status of a third party, one basically irrelevant to the fucking and its memory, in a separate compartment. Neither of them was bringing up her tits, her ass, how he had been all over all of them and also in the deep interior of her personal and individually owned body, to which he had no right at all but had been granted, for a few fleeting minutes, a provisional entry.

Neither of them was bringing up this list of items, these glaringly real items whose reality was greater, in fact, than most other realities, at the moment. At least for him. While genuinely regretting his callousness—which no one else knew of, and which was therefore a secret even more than what had passed between him and Gretel was a secret, because in that case she, at least, knew of it also, whereas no one at all knew how indifferent he had been to the alive- or deadness of T. (he was so grateful, as always, for the privacy of the mind)—he was far more interested in the fact that he did not want to escape from any of them, Gretel's tits, her ass, even the softness and sweet, almost babyish smell of her inner-thigh skin. He wished it had not all happened in the dark, so he could have better recall, could see things as well as remember the feel of them . . . but now the tits and the ass, the soft, musky thighs with their hideaway—or at least the darkness that had surrounded all of these during his only contact with them—were added to his list of regrets. Which was ridiculous. Regretting his indifference, which had actually hurt no one, and now regretting the darkness, which he had not chosen.

"I hope you don't think badly of me," he blurted, interrupting his own droning and semi-vacant narration of the events associated with T. He was bored of it.

"Of course not!" said Gretel. "What do you mean?"

He shrugged, awkward. Maybe there had been a tacit pact between them never to mention the sex, the adultery, whatever you wanted to call it. Now broken.

"Your friendship is important to me," he said, lying. It was a lie, and yet not in spirit, because *she* was important to him—just not her friendship, per se, which was, given the logistics of their situation as well as the marital pairings, unlikely to the point of sheer impossibility. Could they be friends in theory, separate but aware? And what would be the point? "That's all."

"You don't have to be embarrassed," she said, and put her hand on his knee.

"It's not a problem, then?"

"No problem," she said, and smiled. She squeezed the knee lightly. It was as though she had nothing to hide, and nothing immoral or illicit had ever passed between them.

But the touch of her hand made him want to have sex again, with sudden desperation.

"*Mutti! Mutti!*" called a cornboy, and the two of them were running toward the umbrella, kicking up sand.

Gretel removed her hand, but not too hastily. Somehow her every movement was both graceful and casual. He wondered how she managed it.

"*Der hat eine grosse Qualle gefunden!*"

"A jellyfish," she explained to Hal, and turned back to the boys. "Use your English! Did it sting anyone?"

"No." They shook their heads.

"Good."

"Coke please."

"Me too."

"How many Cokes have you already had today, Stefan?"

"Two."

"Three," tattled the Beta.

"That's enough, then."

"Please?"

"Please?"

She sighed.

"Look in my bag, then."

They rummaged for money in her purse while she laid her head back and stretched her gleaming legs out beyond the umbrella's shadow. "We haven't lived in the States for that long, you know? They are still learning."

"T. thought their English was very impressive," said Hal, as the cornboys ran uphill again toward the poolside bistro. As he said it he felt the dynamic between them returning to normalcy, to the politeness of regular behavior. In the shift whatever had been intimate was lost, the raw, open thing between them was covered up and buried.

Which was an ending, but also a relief.

. . . . .

He tried Susan again from the telephone in his room, and she picked up on the third ring.

"Susan? I found him," he told her, in a voice that was carefully solemn. Suspense.

"Oh my God," said Susan, low. He heard her fear and felt a remorseful pang.

"He's fine," he said quickly.

"What?"

"He's fine. He's grown a beard."

"You're kidding."

"No. Really."

She screamed on the other end. It sounded like she'd dropped the phone. It was a minute before she came back.

"I can't believe it," she said breathlessly. "Hal! I can't believe you found him!"

"Seems he had an experience," said Hal. "He has a new opinion about capitalism. He's a changed man."

"But he's in one piece. He's all there?"

"He's physically fine. Thin though. You can see his ribs sticking out."

"But so, so why didn't he call me? What is he *doing*?"

"I think he had a breakdown, or something. He may need help. In the readjustment process. He's been living in the middle of nowhere like a hermit. No running water. Or electricity."

"*T.?* My God. I can't believe this. So when is he—is he coming home soon?"

"We haven't got it worked out yet. His tour guide died—"

"My God!"

"—is what happened. He was on a backpacking trip and he had to hike out alone. He got lost. It was a near miss, sounds like."

"God! Get him to call me, then, Hal. Get him to call me right away. There are things I can still salvage, if he calls me now. I mean finances, legal situations. He would want me to, I know it. If I still can. I should try. Would you please?"

"I'll try. But he's not all there, Susan."

"Just get him back here then. Get him back here. We'll take care of him."

It irritated him somehow, the assumption that T. would prove malleable in her hands and she could automatically mold him into his former shape.

"Who will? You will? You and Robert?"

There was a pause.

"I'm saying we need to have him taken care of, Hal. With access to services. Expertise and—and medication, if he needs it. It wasn't so long ago he had his loss, you know. This is still fallout from that, I'm guessing. You know, his girlfriend—her dying was out of the blue. But he never did any bereavement counseling. None."

He felt resistant to answering.

"Hal?"

"I'll do what I can," he said finally.

Selfishly she dwelled only on the functioning of her office, the linear track of returning to normal. As though normal was all she wished, all anyone would ever want to secure. It did not occur to her that normal might be flawed, might be wrong through and through—that maybe T., unbalanced or not, did not wish to be normal, did not want to go back to the steady state she apparently required for him.

"When you get back we should have a talk," she said, softening. "I know you're not happy right now. And it means so much to me that you did this."

"I saw you," he said. "On the floor of the office. In front of the file cabinet."

Silence.

He hung up.

●

Lying on the bed with the television on in front of him, not watching it exactly (it was not in English anyway and seemed to be a Mexican game show involving a tacky, glaring set and flashing lights, whose sound he had muted), he mulled over the various possible effects of his words. She might be considering the option of divorce, whether he wanted it, whether she did, whether this constituted, for the two of them, a divorceable offense; she might be cold to the very core or gleeful and exhilarated, terrified or relieved. She might already have called Robert the Paralegal with the news of their discovery, might have told him what Hal had said, or might never have thought to call him. Among all these, what were his own feelings?

It came to him gradually that he was not angry. His anger had dissipated. He had told her what he knew, and now he was not angry. There was still a sense of disappointment, of letdown—maybe for the unchangeableness of the past, the stubbornness of his unpleasant memories, which were now implanted within him permanently. Maybe for the fact that their marriage had been, in his mind, a pure union, and now it was adulterated. That was what adultery did.

He had wanted it perfect, he thought, but wasn't that a false want? What was perfect anyway? Possibly this new, sullied marriage was in fact more perfect than the previous innocent one, more perfectly expressed the state of lifelong union or the weather of affection. Possibly the previous, innocent marriage, uncomplicated by disloyalty, had in fact been inferior to this one, more superficial. Maybe they were achieving maturity.

On the other hand, it could be simply that the thrill was gone, that it had been eradicated and would never return.

Then again, he was assuming that, just because this was the first time he had caught her in an act of unfaithfulness, this was the first time such acts had occurred. But what if she had been practicing free love down through the years, ever since the Frenchman? (And Casey not his biological—paranoid crap.) What if the marriage had in fact never been what he thought it was? The real instability, real liquid . . .

Someone was knocking; someone looked in the window, through the crack between the frame and the curtain. Gretel.

He had forgotten about his own infidelity in all this. But his own infidelity was of a lower order, or a higher order, depending how you organized your judgment hierarchy. He would never have slept with Gretel were it not for the condom wrapper fragment on his own bedside table, the bad lesbian song playing on the shower radio, Susan and Robert on the floor of the office and his subsequent unmooring. It was a kind of post-traumatic stress disorder that gave him permission for misbehavior—even a broad series of permissions, airy and limitless as the sky.

It was second-order adultery. That was it.

He opened the door.

"Come for a paddle with me and the boys. Won't you?" asked Gretel, cocking her head and smiling.

It was late afternoon. Hans had not come back yet and neither had T., clearly: and Hal was sick of the silence of the hotel room, the static of his own body laid out on the bed.

He turned around, grabbed his sunglasses and bottled water, and followed her out of the room, down the stairs and onto the beach to where the hotel's bright kayaks were arrayed on the sand. They pushed two of them into the placid water, the corn-boys in a double kayak ahead of them, and scrambled in.

They were going to head out toward a mangrove caye, said Gretel, and pointed to it. A quick trip before sunset. It was about a half-hour's paddle to the southeast, and on the other side there was supposed to be a small reef. She had extra snorkeling gear, if Hal wanted to use it. She handed him a hat to wear—one of Hans's, no doubt. It was emblazoned with the single word BOEING.

The two of them lagged contentedly behind the boys, who raced ahead, locked into their perpetual battle of speed and strength. Once more they fought an imaginary opponent. Hal paddled at a leisurely pace.

"They have found some kind of rebel camp," said Gretel after a while. "Hans did what they call a flyover. In a plane with some-one from the Marines, or something."

"Rebel camp?" asked Hal.

"Guatemalans, I think."

"Correct me if I'm wrong," said Hal, mildly alarmed. "Isn't the army the bad guy, over there? Doesn't it do genocide?"

"I don't know about the politics," said Gretel apologetically. "Hans just said they were guerrillas. He said it was an armed camp of guerrillas that came from over the border."

"Over the border is Guatemala, right? And if it's the Mayans, they're probably escaping a fucking massacre! I mean there are official refugee camps for them in Mexico. You haven't read about this? There was a genocide going on, a couple of years ago. Civil war. All this shit with the CIA propping up the military there, the generals that are smuggling cocaine through to the U.S. from Colombia or somewhere—remember that woman who won the Nobel Peace Prize? Rigoberta Menchú?"

Gretel shook her head.

"What the hell," said Hal, and mulled it over, making deep, slow strokes with the paddle. What were they up to after all, those toy soldiers? Rigoberta Menchú: in all the pictures she wore bright, printed clothing. Cloth tied around her head, typically, and she had a brown, broad face, smiling. The smiling face was at odds with the reports of various family members of hers, shot dead or burned alive. He only half-remembered.

The Marines, or the Coast Guard, whichever branch of the armed forces they had been: while he was with them he had been pathetic, reduced to childishness. They were strongmen; he was nothing but a victim. What felt like a death march to him had been a pleasant day hike for them. You could be brought down to that—to contests of strength, to the brute force of physical superiority, if you put yourself into the situation. And it was a plain situation, a simple one, the situation of survival. That day, on that walk, nothing but the basic, primitive unit of the body had mattered. His unit had failed him.

But now he was thinking of those same Marines with condescension, as they must have thought of him, because their subjugation was permanent and far worse than it had been, briefly, for him. They were muscular windup dolls, forced to do the bidding of men of greater ambition. It was their job description.

The cornboys pulled ahead, further and further away from Gretel and him. There were powerboats on the water, though none were close at the moment. He thought of the jellyfish the boys had seen, the sharks, the rays—a great sea beast rising from the depths and lifting their kayak from below, capsizing it. Their small bodies splayed and sinking . . . but Gretel was relaxed. He looked over and saw her bronzed limbs, lazy but perfect in the sun, as she lifted and tipped her paddle. She looked up and smiled at him. He felt lulled, the awkwardness between them evaporated. They had started in water, in the cool blue, and here they were on the water again. It was all right. Gretel had her boys up ahead of her and him by her side—a temporary companion, sure. But then they all were.

That was it: that was it. She let her sons go ahead, and she was not worrying. He too had freedom, a strange freedom in this adultery, this strange and half-lonely honeymoon. The dissolution of everything. Because he had forgotten Casey this trip, he had been emancipated from her—Casey, who since he arrived in this foreign place had not, for the first time in years, guided his every impulse. For a time he had left her behind; the weight of carrying her had been released.

But for the years before that, what had he been doing? He felt a sudden panic. Wasted. He had wasted them.

He had lost them, and only realized the loss now, like a bolt, shocking. Like a nightmare: time shifted and the years of your life were gone. The light shimmered sideways over the water.

He had forgotten his wife, mostly. He loved her, but all this time he'd practically forgotten she was there. Susan had been left to her own devices, alone and in the cold while he dreamed his soft dreams of regret. That was what had happened to the two of them, nothing mysterious. He had drifted away to his memories of his daughter as she had been, the cycles of blame, remorse, longing. He had been somewhere else all the time, in spirit if not body—not with his actual daughter, for the time he spent with her in the course of a day or a week was normal, regular time, not a nightmare or dream, but the daughter he once had, or the daughter who might have been. He was like an enchanted man. That was who he had been, all these years, a man under a spell, a man absent without knowing his own absence. He had been gone, but he had not noticed. He had not noticed himself or Susan, had noticed neither of them. All he had known was remorse. He spent his life knowing it.

And so Susan had disappeared too. Of course. Even her job was a form of her disappearance. The job, her allegiance to it, the affair—it was all the stuff of her life, while he was not.

Susan had vanished for a simple reason: she had nothing better to do.

It was his fault. And here on the long, blind road he had been blaming her.

*   *   *   *   *

He used Hans's snorkeling equipment, his blue mask and fins. Putting them on he thought fleetingly that he was borrowing everything from Hans.

But Hans did not register its absence.

The corals were not so bright here as they were further out, toward the barrier reef—dying, he suspected, some of them dead already. He had read at the hotel that this year, suddenly, corals were quickly bleaching in Belize. But fish still moved among them, their bright bodies flashing among the worn gray humps like the Mohawks of teenage punks drinking in a graveyard. He saw small fish, mostly, but it felt good to follow them for a while and watch them disappear.

Gretel decided they should go up when the sun began to sink

and the water was darkening around them. It grew harder to see. After they surfaced he held her kayak steady for her while she clambered in, treading water with his free hand, and then she leaned over and held his.

The cornboys, blue-lipped, were already waiting, eating half-unwrapped chocolate bars and jiggling their legs, feet braced against the footrests. Without a wetsuit the coldness of the water had sunk in; Gretel's golden skin was goosebumped. The end of day cast violet shadows on her, on all of them. Quickly the surface seemed almost black.

When they put in at the hotel beach again people were eating dinner at the outdoor tables, beneath the bistro's palm-thatch awning. Citronella candles were burning on the tables and Hal could smell their bitter lemon edge as he walked up the beach.

"Bring T. and join us for dinner, won't you?" urged Gretel, and he said he would, as soon as he showered and changed.

But T. was not in the room, and there was no message light blinking on the telephone. He took his shower quickly, anxious, and was bent over his open suitcase with a towel around his waist when Marlo knocked at the door.

"Mr. Tomás had to go with the police," said Marlo. "He wanted me to tell you."

"Go with them?" asked Hal. "What do you mean?"

The towel fell as he lurched forward. He grabbed it and held it up tightly.

"They took him to detention," said Marlo solemnly.

"Detention? They arrested him?"

"First to Dangriga, then Belize City."

"I mean—why? Is it serious?"

"Because of the death. You know?"

"But it was an accident!"

Guests passed behind Marlo, a family with long-haired young girls. Self-conscious, Hal stepped back and waved him in.

"The brother, you know? He did not want to press charges. But then there was a neighbor who asked them to come. This lady—she does not like Americans. The soldiers, the other day, I think one of them was rude to her daughter, you know? So then they came. There will be an investigation."

"Jesus!"

Central American jails did not boast a good reputation for client services. He would have to leave right away for the city.

"I'll go up there. I'll pay his bail, or whatever. I'll get him a lawyer. Can you get me a car to the capital? Or a plane?"

"Tonight?"

"Tonight. Right now. I mean he's in jail, right?"

"They are taking him there."

"Then I need to go right now. I have to get him out."

"The flights from the airport in Placencia? They go in the daytime."

"Can't I charter one or something? It's what, to Belize City—a half-hour flight?"

"I will see. I can see."

He dressed in a hurry after Marlo left, stuffed his clothes messily into the suitcase with a sense of growing urgency. Anything could happen. The guy was *non compos mentis*, and they had arrested him. It often happened to the mentally ill, even in the U.S.—since Reagan anyway. They were let out onto the streets, wandered there, and were promptly arrested for the crime of existing. Then jail, insult added to injury. He would not let prison violence happen to T. Just when the guy was acting human for the first time in his life and abandoning his Mercedes-Benz fixation, they went and arrested him.

A man turned away from the path of Mamm on and that was what he got—thrown into the hoosegow.

In the lobby Marlo was talking to someone in Spanish, a bald guy in a satiny red windbreaker. The guy was shaking his head—a bad sign, surely.

"Is it going to happen?" asked Hal, and thankfully Marlo nodded, consulting his watch.

"He will drive you to the airfield," he said. "Five minutes."

He had to say goodbye to Gretel before then. Who knew if he would ever be back. He headed to the restaurant and stood in the doorway looking, but could not see her at the tables. No cornboys either. Their white-blond hair was a beacon. He would have to go to the room. It disturbed him, but it could not be avoided. Up the sandy cement of the stairs—was it 323? 325? He knocked at the first one. He had three minutes left. He hoped Hans was not there. He had no time for avionics experts.

A cornboy opened the door, video game in hand.

"Your mother in?"

The door opened further and the cornboy faded. Gretel had her hair twisted up in a towel but was fully dressed. Thankfully.

"Listen, I have to go," he said. "They arrested T. The local authorities. They took him to Belize City. I have to go get him out. I'm flying."

"My God," said Gretel. "Arrested? Him?"

"Because of the tour guide dying. The heart attack. Remember? But now they want to investigate it, apparently. I have to fly to the city, try to meet them. Post his bail or bribe someone. We can't have him in there."

"Yes!" said Gretel, nodding hastily. "Of course. You should go."

"So," he said. "I guess, goodbye?"

He leaned forward to embrace her, awkward as usual.

"You'll get him out. I know you will. You are a good friend," said Gretel with her arms around him. She smelled like cinnamon.

"Thank you," he said. He was late now, for the driver.

He smiled at her again. Should he ask for her phone number, or something? Cheesy.

"Wait," he said. "In case you ever come to Los Angeles." He slid his messy wallet out of his back pocket, slipped out a business card. "This is me."

"Thank you, Hal," said Gretel softly.

He backed out of the room, turned and took the stairs two at a time. When he glanced over his shoulder she was braced against the railing of the balcony gazing down at him, face in shadow, the towel standing tall on her head like a crown.

The airport was a small trailer with a dirty linoleum floor, fluorescent lights overhead and a desk at one end with a few papers piled on it, an olive-colored metal lamp on a bendable arm and a stained paper coffee cup. The lights were on but no one was around, yet Hal was supposed to meet his pilot. He went to the bathroom, the size of an airplane toilet, and when he came out he saw a light through the building's glass door.

On the airfield—all grass and weeds with a single thin, short runway that looked more like a driveway—sat a small plane. He pushed the back door open and walked over the grass toward it, suitcase in hand, slapping against his leg. It was almost completely dark out; a couple of lights on the runway had halos around them, and then there were the small lights of the plane itself and the squares of yellow that were its windows. The plane was small and white with a blue stripe on the side—a four-seater, he saw when he got close.

Its propeller was already whirring, there was a door open, and the pilot was seated, wearing a bulky headset. Hal put a foot up on the rim of the door to step in.

"Here, here," said the pilot, and gestured for him to sit up front. It was tight, barely room to move.

"This?" asked Hal, raising his suitcase.

"Back there," said the pilot.

Hal was sure they would skim the trees on takeoff. The night outside was daunting from the tiny cabin of the plane, its bottomless dark; he wore the headset the pilot had given him, but they hardly spoke. He recalled a phrase an FAA guy had once used with him on a commercial flight, discussing Cessnas just like this one: *single-point failure*. No backup systems in case of malfunction. As they taxied and rose up above the runway he willed himself beyond the plane, out of the frail and shaking capsule into the rest of his life.

L.A. was spread out far to the north, gray and blond and spidering everywhere—its fastness, its familiar blocky strip malls and wide boulevards with their unceasing traffic and smog and the glamorous jungly hills that rose above and housed the royalty. Everything was the same; his house was the same, even, full of the mundane objects he knew so well . . . by now Susan had told Casey T. was alive. They would both know by now, and Casey, at least, would feel affectionate and grateful. But Susan's gratitude he had foolishly squandered. By accusing her at the very moment of triumph, the moment of revelation, he had squandered all his credit. Such as it was. It should have been a pure gift, the culmination of a gesture that quietly knighted him; instead he had revealed his petty nature, his real motivation for leaving and coming here, thus giving the lie to any idea she might have had about his minor effort at heroism.

He had to get T. out of the hands of the Belizean cops. It was imperative. Both for Susan and Casey and for him, T. himself, because actually he did not deserve it.

A short time ago, before he went to the island, if someone had told him Stern was in jail Hal would not have objected too strongly. Only mildly, for the sake of politeness. He might have held the private opinion, in fact, that a few nights in a Central American hellhole could benefit the Armani-wearing shithead. But not anymore. Now he wanted to get the guy out, partly because he seemed a painfully easy mark, now that he had gone hippie. Hal had always had a weakness for hippies, despite their free-love tendencies. Between them and the libertarians, he'd take hippies. Now—a benevolent-seeming, almost submissive individual—T. was without defenses. He would be instantly victimized, by either the thugs in the police force or his fellow inmates. It was ugly to contemplate.

Often people prefaced a stupid remark with the words "There are two kinds of people in the world," and Hal had always been annoyed by this. The words tended to introduce a false dichotomy, an infantile reduction. At the same time he, too, felt the urge to divide and categorize, the satisfaction of separating the world into discrete parts that could be identified. If T. had once been a person who thought chiefly of himself and his shining Mercedes, he was now something else—if only on a temporary basis.

For it was entirely possible, as Susan had suggested, that he would revert to his usual form once the trauma of the hiking misadventure was past. People tended to settle back into their old routines. Returns to form were standard. Fundamental character change was all but impossible.

Still, for now he more closely resembled the pet lovers, for instance, than Donald Trump or Leona Helmsley. He was like the post-hippie nomads that drove around in painted vans, let their children grow dreadlocks and lived on pennies. He had the beard and the hygiene, anyway. But the key distinction was this: he had gone from being consumed with his own life and advance-ment to looking outward. Whereas Hal himself, once youth had passed, had gone the other way.

For there had been an interval, while he and Susan were both young, when he too had thought of the rest of the world quite often. He had often thought of justice and liberation, of the good of mankind, etc. But then he had forgotten it.

Except for his job, he had argued to himself over the years, but he had to admit it: even the job had become little more than a sinecure. He could not argue that in going to work every day he made a sacrifice of himself. It was more like a well-fitting shoe that was worn all the time but was never noticed.

If there were in fact two kinds of people in the world, those

who faced inward and those who looked out, he had been the latter and turned into the former, whereas Stern, or T., had been the
former and turned into the latter. It was T. who was taking the
road less traveled, whereas Hal, with all his ideas about a government that protected and sheltered the people, with his lifetime
of civil service, had in fact become a typical domestic drone, a
man wrapped up in the details of his own life and only his own.

He had acquired the habit of blaming the accident for this.
And yes, the accident had made it easier to shelve the concerns
of the world, to relegate them to the back burner. But if he was
honest, the patterns had been worn into him years before the
accident, possibly even from the time when he manipulated
Susan into abandoning her commune. He had manipulated her
away from her youthful Eden Project ideal out of a sense of desperation, true, but that did not excuse his cynical calculation. He
had been desperate to keep her and had reassured himself that
love was enough reason for manipulation. But it was selfish and
nothing else. Love had been an excuse, more than anything, for
greediness. Love and self-interest had coalesced.

And separated from her Mendocino ideal—from the future of
fresh air and the fields of organic strawberries—in time she had
given up public high-school teaching, with its long hours and low
pay and frequent disappointments, and become an assistant to a
real-estate guy. This was after the accident, of course . . . she had
taken an office job, become an office worker. He himself was an
office worker too, nothing more than a glorified clerk, really, but
still: who knew what she might have become if, back in 1967,
instead of manipulating her he had just let her go?

And it might still have worked out between them. In due

course he might have sought her out again, might have followed her to the commune, gotten down on one knee, and humbly asked Rom to give him a free lute lesson. After a potluck dinner, around a bonfire, Susan might have played the tambourine and sung songs about the giving spirit of trees while he and Rom accompanied her on twin lutes.

And Casey: Casey might have been born in a yurt with a midwife attending, instead of by emergency C-section at the UCLA Medical Center. When she was seventeen she might not have gone driving at all, in that snowstorm in the suburbs of Denver. She might have had different friends, might not have even have decided impulsively that she wanted to learn to ski, wanted to take her turn on the baby slopes, and therefore never have asked Hal and Susan if she could go on a Colorado ski trip with her L.A. friends, who in addition to skiing enjoyed drinking games and fast driving. She might have been, say, more of a horseback-rider type, competed in horse-riding meets in a black velvet cap and tall boots, and had different friends entirely, who knew, friends who did Outward Bound courses or line dancing, friends who won prizes at the county fair for growing outsize tomatoes.

But instead he had followed one urge, a single urge. What was an urge but a quick pulse of energy through the brain? He had followed a jealous, self-protective urge and consecrated his behavior to persuasion. For two or three weeks his attention had been focused entirely on preventing Susan from leaving—on preventing his future wife from realizing her dream.

And that petty urge of self-protection, that small urge that passed through him in seconds, had determined the future for all three of them.

6

As soon as his taxi pulled up alongside the curb outside the small police station he saw the building was locked up tight as a drum, lights off. He got out to check the sign on the door—a paper clock with the hands stuck at seven and twelve—while a streetlight above him flickered and buzzed.

"I don't understand," he said to the driver as he got back in. "What about the jail, then? There has to be some kind of holding cells, at least. Supervised by police. Do you know where that would be?"

The driver shrugged and shook his head.

"But what if there are crimes committed? And someone, you know, a criminal does something and needs to be arrested? I mean, no one commits crimes after the end of the workday?"

"You come back in the morning," said the driver, nodding. He had an accent like the harelip cadet: maybe Garifuna. "I take you to a nice hotel. Your friend be OK. Don't worry."

The hotel had iron gates and a fountain playing in the front garden; its lobby was empty save for a clerk at the long counter, who found him a room right away.

"Maybe you can tell me," said Hal. "The police. What do you do if you have to call the police in the middle of the night?"

"We've never had to call the police," said the night clerk, smiling. "We have a quality clientele."

"I'm sure you do. But let's say something happened—a break-in. Something like that."

"Yes sir, I would report it first thing in the morning," said the desk clerk.

Hal was exasperated. There was no way. Was the man ill-informed, or was it Hal who was wrong? There was no way to know.

In his room, which was small and so cloying he had to open a window immediately, the clock radio read 1:15. He sat down on the bed and took his phone card out of his wallet, keyed in the long sequence.

She picked up after a single ring.

"Hal?"

"Sorry to wake you."

"Actually I couldn't sleep. I called the resort and they said you guys were gone, both of you."

"I had to charter a flight to the city. They arrested him."

While he explained what he thought had happened he was preoccupied with himself—himself and the free love. What to say next, about the rest of it, the rest of their lives and whether there was a future? He was bound up in the saga, his own concerns.

"Suze," he said suddenly. "I know it's my fault. I don't blame you."

"Your fault?"

"I realized, this trip, how I've been preoccupied for so long. I'm always feeling regret. I go around in a daze . . . years now, Suze. For years. But I know it at least. I've seen it now. I mean I already knew it, rationally, but I hadn't . . ."

"It's all right, Hal. You don't have to apologize. Please."

"But you've been . . . I mean, I think somewhere in there I may have left you alone."

She was quiet. He had the window open, and a palm was waving. Outside he heard a car swish down the empty street. Had it rained? They were both alone now. She was alone because years ago he had left her for an idea of loss; he was alone because he had chosen it, without even knowing. He was afloat in the world, its vast and empty spaces . . . far away from his wife and his little girl, in a foreign city where not one person knew him. A silent, sweltering city in a subtropical country, toward the equator, toward the South Pole, toward the black place in the sky around which all the stars seemed to spin.

He was awake in the warm night, alone, while everyone else was sleeping.

The walls of the room felt closer than they were, covered in a dark-red-and-white-striped wallpaper like Christmas wrapping. Beneath his legs, the bed's coverlet was scratchy. Susan always stripped the coverlets off hotel beds as soon as she got into the hotel room. She said they were unhygienic—that hotels never washed them and they were the repositories of bodily secretions and pathogens. In the main she was not too uptight about germs, but when it came to hotel coverlets she made no exceptions.

"We'll talk about it when you get back," she said gently, after a while. "OK? I mean the phone isn't the best for this, you know. This kind of conversation."

"I just want to know if we're going to be all right. If we're going to get through it." He waited for a second, then got up restlessly, holding the receiver. The red wallpaper was closing in.

The cord barely stretched but he made it to the window, gazed through the silhouettes of fronds onto the dark street. She was not answering. The silence was ominous. His stomach turned. "Or if you want to, you know, leave me. And be with that . . ."

He let it trail off. Damned if he would say more.

The wait made his stomach lurch again.

"Be with—? Oh. No, no, no, it's nothing like that, sweetheart. It's not, you know. Anything important."

"I see," he said, nodding invisibly.

He felt lighter, though at the same time his skin prickled with a faint annoyance. It was not important to her, yet for it she risked everything: for a trivial fuck, or series of fucks, she had done this to him. But he should count his blessings. They were still married. It seemed they would probably continue to be. His home was still his home, his wife was still his wife. She was not trying to get away from him. On and on, as always, it would keep being the three of them, him and her and Casey.

"I mean, that's a relief to me. Of course."

He felt almost off the hook, now that he knew. Now that he knew, the familiar was coming back. Already—he felt it— already the strangeness of life was receding. He heard something in the background—was it here or in the background in L.A., across the many miles? No; it was here, it was outside the window. A siren, but different from the sirens he was used to, slower and tinnier. No surprise: in a foreign country the sound of a siren was bound to be a variation on the familiar theme, not an exact replica.

It was amazing, astounding, come to think of it, that even the idea *siren* was replicated throughout the world—and the idea *traffic lights*, for instance, wherever you went: red, yellow and green. (Although in the United States officials insisted on calling the yellow lights "amber," for some consistently aggravating nonreason—like a tic, like an officially sanctioned form of Tourette's. If you had to go to traffic school, say, or take a test for your driver's license at the Department of Motor Vehicles, it was a sure bet the yellow lights would be referred to as "amber," as though the word *yellow*, in this official setting, was somehow regarded as obscene and therefore required a euphemism. It made him glad he did not work for the Department of Transportation, which needless to say had a checkered past anyway. For while the Service was guilty of many things—many bureaucratic complications of a Kafkaesque nature all too easily lampoonable by opportunistic politicians who irresponsibly advocated for harebrained schemes like the flat tax—at least it had the cojones to call yellow yellow.)

The world seemed to be in opposition and even turmoil on many subjects—who would claim the rights to its riches, for instance, who would hold sway from year to year or decade to decade when it came to the rule of law, dominance and extraction, trade or sales or production. On the other hand it presented a more or less united front on who should do the fighting and dying, whose children should starve or die of malaria by the tens of millions. In these matters there was the polite appearance of dispute, in diplomatic and academic circles, but in fact a stasis of hardship on a massive scale that could only reflect, in the end, a kind of global consensus.

And when it came to details like traffic signals and sirens the human population might even look, from outer space, like a single race of peaceful, compliant men.

At first he did not register the siren's significance. Susan was saying something about *emotional rollercoasters*, a term he flatly, privately rejected.

You had aversions, in this life, aversions to foods like granola and terms like *emotional rollercoaster*. You wished to excise these items and the terms for them. But a woman like Susan, despite being highly intelligent, did not know that intuitively nor, if she did, would she necessarily respect the aversions. Instead she ran roughshod over them. In fact, few women respected his aversions.

Men also failed to respect them. People, you could almost say, did not respect the aversions.

Maybe, when all this was behind Susan and him—call it the free love, call it adultery—they could sit down and have a conversation on the subject. He could talk about the importance of aversions, and why the term *emotional rollercoaster* should be, as the Germans said, verboten.

Then the car went by, a light-colored car, its red lights flashing. A squad car, surely.

He should go! He should follow it. Sooner or later it had to take him to some outpost of the police, to what he needed to know.

"I was, at first I was so excited," Susan was saying. "When you told me it was like the best gift I'd ever had, but that, you know, that euphoria of relief—it passes so quickly and regular life comes back. With its own kind of normal and boring pace. You know?"

He had his eyes on the police car's taillights as the car made its way up the street. It had slowed down, it wasn't going that fast. If he ran, he could catch it. Maybe it was right nearby, the police emergency. He should drop the phone and run. He should run up the dark street after it.

Now. Now. Go.

"And now it's just like, I take for granted he's alive and I'm back to worrying about these petty details . . ."

He stayed where he was. It seemed unrealistic, impossible to catch the car. Of course, he would never know.

Standing there, watching the taillights disappear and holding the phone, he felt this had happened to him over and over. He never jumped out windows, never moved suddenly, with a jolt. The lights faded as he stood still and looked at them. He did not leap, did not give chase. It always seemed unfeasible and rash. But there was a defeatism in that, clearly, a submission to ease, a cowardly risk avoidance. The same force that had bound Susan to him through manipulation rather than honesty.

T. would have his night in jail, that was clear. He would spend the whole night in a cell while Hal lay sleeping in the soft hotel bed. Albeit with scratchy coverlet. He pictured a medieval torture chamber, the rack, a rusting Iron Maiden. Then burly sailors.

"You'll find him in the morning. Make sure you get a good night's rest," said Susan.

She did not know, of course, about Gretel, spinning now in a topless dirndl in his memory, German and gold forever.

There was no need for her to know. He could tell her, but it would be selfish, a small and petty revenge.

The private sanctum of the mind . . . he fell back on it gratefully. What a freedom it was, what a perfect freedom. In the future, if he felt lonely, he would have to remember this, remind himself of its benefits—the unending and sweet privacy of thinking. How no one else, no matter how great or powerful, could ever enter here. This place was truly his.

Because if it was painful to be alone, not being alone would be torment. A mind that was invaded by other minds could be nothing more than prison. And yet there were people out there who wanted to believe in ESP, who fantasized telepathy. Maybe what they had in mind was a kind of selective mind-reading? No one sane would want to walk around reading minds in some kind of flowing, open exchange.

Did an ant have a mind of its own? A bee? Uncertain. They seemed to operate differently, dying by the thousands for the sake of a queen and all the time never stopping their work. An ant, a bee, neither seemed gripped by doubt, typically. Doubt had to be a requisite of the private mind. It was a perk of being human: your mind was your own, always and forever a secret territory.

"You too," he echoed softly. "You too."

* * * * *

In the morning he walked out in front of the hotel and got a car to Belmopan, about an hour away.

It was a small town, the capital, and nothing else—grass, palms, scattered pastel-colored buildings. Less slumlike than the city, but with a feeling of vacancy. The embassy was a two-story white, wooden edifice with a porch all around, columns in front, palm trees, a flag and a bright-green, well-kept lawn.

Inside a woman rose from her desk when he came through the door.

"There's an American citizen who was arrested," he told her without preamble. "A businessman. Down in Placencia, but they brought him up to Belize City last night. I have to find him. Get him immediate legal aid. He shouldn't be in there."

"Give me his name," she said. "I'll make some calls."

The secretary went into another room. While he waited he sat in a teak chair and jiggled his leg. The floor was wood and a wooden fan turned on the ceiling; beside him sat a shiny, tall plant whose leaves brushed against his shoulder. He heard the sound of a fax machine dialing. Then the front door opened and two red-faced men came in wearing loud, floral-print shirts. They seemed to be familiar with the premises and moved past him into a back room, talking about sportfishing. One said he'd caught a wahoo, the other a snook.

After a while the secretary came back. She had a man with her, thin and balding, with glasses.

"Jeff Brady," he said. "Public affairs section chief. We don't have staff attorneys, but we do refer out. Not clear yet whether we need a lawyer though. Need to appraise the situation, put out feelers. Be on our way?"

"You found him?"

"We know where they're holding him, yes. Taking my own car, Sarah. Binadu's got the VW. Later."

He drove a small, open jeep, making swift, jerky turns until they got out onto the highway. Hal held onto the door handle. The exhaust of other cars made him cough.

He resolved to act as T.'s staunchest ally. He would tell the diplomat a story that would raise his sympathies.

"He was obviously deeply affected by the death of his girl-friend. I'm not saying he's in great shape emotionally. But he has no history of violence or anything like that. Not even a mis-demeanor or an unpaid parking ticket."

"Uh huh?"

"He's a conscientious boss-type guy, my wife's devoted to him. Right now, you'll see, he's unshaven, he looks like a moun-tain man, but the guy I know wears three-thousand-dollar suits and drives a high-end Mercedes. So yeah, was he depressed when he came down here? Sure. Anyone would be. But that's it. He needed a change. Decided to do some backpacking, so he hired a local guide to take him up the river. I think they were headed for some trailhead near the jaguar preserve."

"Ways up there. Cockscomb? Past the confluence with the Swasey Branch? You can drive there in an hour. Tourists don't tend to take the river route."

"Their first night out the guide apparently died. Out of the blue. He suffered a heart attack or something. Stern said he found out in the morning, because they were each sleeping in their own tents. He went into shock or something, the death of the guide really threw him."

"I bet."

With his left hand on the wheel, Brady fumbled with his right to shake a cigarette from his pack and light it off the dash. He seemed distracted. Hal needed to get his attention.

"I mean here he was, this young guy from L.A., up a jungle river with just this one person who was his lifeline. And that lifeline suddenly disappears. Plus the fact, this guy Stern, over the past few months, is like a death magnet. Everyone close to him dies. Or gets debilitated. My wife told me the father left the mother—this aging frat boy left the mother, you know, his wife of so many years, to be a gay stripper in Key West. Then the girlfriend dies, of some heart condition he didn't even know she had. This woman, by the way, was twenty-three and ran marathons. His mother tried to O.D. but ended up losing her mind. She's got dementia or something. His dog gets hit by a car. Even his business partner ditched him."

"Rough year."

A spark of interest. Either the cigarette or the drama was putting Brady in a better mood.

"So anyway, after he found the guide dead Stern went into shock I guess, and eventually he dragged the body back down to the boat. We're talking, for miles. I did that hike, looking for him. It was exhausting even without a 200-pound dead weight to haul. I guess he wrapped it up in the tent and got it all the way down to the river, where he put it back in the boat. But then later the boat's propeller snapped and he ditched it against the bank, body and all, and tried to hike out. He almost died too. It was a close call for him."

Brady nodded, negotiated a pothole. The car jumped.

"The guide was older, in his sixties I guess? It was a freak thing, but there's no way it was anything other than natural causes. A couple days later the boat floated down to the ocean, but by then there was no body in it."

"No body," said Brady. "At all? Huh. Problematic."

"The guide's brother, I met him, I mean he isn't bringing charges or anything. It was called in by some neighbor lady or something who has a beef with Americans. I don't even know what they're holding him on."

"We'll find out. Don't worry."

They drove in silence for a minute or two. Cars were smaller here than at home, smaller, older, more banged-up. The road was called a highway, but as in Mexico there was no fencing alongside to keep out stray animals. The corpses of roadkill appeared every few hundred yards, here a dog, there what seemed to be a raccoon.

"You know anything about a military incursion into the jungle down there, by the way?" he asked Brady.

"Come again?"

"A military incursion."

"Whose military?"

"Ours."

"When?"

"I think maybe yesterday. Or the day before."

Brady laughed abruptly.

"Uh, that'd be a no."

"I think there was one, though."

"I'd know. Trust me. This is a very small country."

"I heard they were doing a flyover. Some alleged guerrilla camp of Mayans, from over the border."

"There's no such thing."

"If you say so."

"Who told you this, anyway?"

Hal looked away from him to his own side of the road. There

were flat, ugly fields stretching out beside him to the east, while to the west rose the low mountains.

"A German schoolteacher," he said slowly.

"What?"

"Long story."

"I'm all ears. We still got half an hour to go."

Hal told him about the armed forces, the boat trip, the hike. He told him what Hans had said as he lay down on the boat's bench at the end, his stomach full of warm liquid.

"Aural hallucinations. Fatigue can do that to you."

"You think so?"

"I know so."

"But then what about what his wife said? Yesterday?"

"Guy sounds like a weapons hobbyist. Maybe he likes to spin tales to impress the little lady."

"Huh," said Hal. "I don't know, Jeff. I mean he did bring the Marines to me."

Then it struck him that this discussion might be impairing his credibility. He should change the subject.

But Brady did it for him.

"What do you do, anyway? Stateside?"

Hal was surprised. He was sure he had mentioned it.

"IRS."

"Kidding."

"Why, you delinquent?"

"My brother works at the Service Center in Austin."

"Government service runs in your family, huh?"

"That and gallbladder problems."

"Sorry to hear it."

By the time they got off the highway and headed into Belize

City he felt reasonably confident that Brady was won over. He had recognized, in Brady, the cynical posture of high-waisted Rodriguez. And by treating Brady essentially as he treated Rodriguez—as though they were brothers-in-arms, jaded yet hearty mercenaries in civil service's trench warfare—he was in the process of securing Brady's confidence.

He coughed, breathing exhaust fumes as they made their way down a narrow street behind a rickety pickup full of bags of garbage.

"No unleaded gas around here," said Brady. "Not yet. Pity. OK. Not far now." He pulled into a parking space abruptly and braked. "Here we go. Follow me, and don't speak unless you're spoken to."

"Draconian."

"Only because I've been in the situation. Trust me."

As it happened Hal was made to wait in the lobby, near a uniformed guard standing beside a young woman's desk, while Brady was ushered into the interior. The chairs were uncomfortable, the walls gray and the ceilings low. On a bulletin board was a picture of a wanted man with a banner above his head: FBI TEN MOST WANTED FUGITIVE. Beneath, three headings: DESCRIPTION. CAUTION. REWARD.

For a second it seemed to Hal that Belize was an outpost of America. It had been British Honduras, previously. But the British were nowhere.

An overhead fan whirred, the blades ticking monotonously against the dangling chain, but did little to aerate the room.

He wished he had a glass of ice water.

Finally Brady came out again, a portly man in shirtsleeves beside him, sweat stains under his arms.

"Hal, Jorge Luis. Hal Lindley, U.S. Internal Revenue Service."

They shook. The man's hand was faintly greasy. Hal's own was probably just as bad.

"Mr. Stern is not here yet," said Jorge, in English that was unaccented and fluent. "He's being transported overland. They should be getting in a little later."

"We can come back," said Brady. "We'll have our interview then, and talk to the detective."

"Do we know—"

"We'll get the details then," said Brady, smiling. "No problem." He turned and shook Jorge's hand.

Out on the street he told Hal not to seem overeager, that a casual attitude was best. Hal stopped on the sidewalk and turned to him, incredulous.

"Casual? Casual attitude? An innocent man's languishing in prison! Who knows if the rule of law even holds? I mean do we even know if they have grounds for arresting him?"

Brady took him by the shoulder.

"The key is not to get overwrought. Trust me. Keep things low-key, unless we get indications there's a hidden agenda. In that case, we'll go in from a whole different angle. But there's no sign of that yet. Best way to get him out quickly is to act like the stakes are low, like there's no official anxiety. Act like we're all on the same side. Because we are, basically. Walk softly, carry a big stick. Trust me."

"Poker face. That's what you're saying?"

"More or less. Let's go get some lunch. I know a nice little place right around the corner. Family runs it. Shall we?"

•

Lunch was jerk chicken they ate off paper plates on cheery red and green vinyl tablecloths. They washed down the chicken with tepid half-pints of watery beer, and afterward Hal retired to his hotel room, a relief. In the thick air the beer was making him feel heavy, his limbs difficult to lift.

He lay down on the coverlet, then thought of the bacteria Susan would assure him were writhing there—possibly even parasites such as crabs, which would take up residence in his pubic hair.

All right! Jesus.

He stood, pulled the coverlet off and lay down again on the cool top sheet. He was logy, but he was also restless. He missed Casey.

When she picked up the phone he felt drunker, suddenly, than he had since Gretel. It seemed all things were transparent, and who was he to pretend otherwise?

"I know about the phone sex," he said.

"Shit," said Casey.

"Yep. I do."

"Huh," said Casey. "What can I say. Sorry?"

"You're not sorry," he said. He was curious, actually. "You said you liked it. In the kitchen, to what's her name. Who crochets the hideous multicolored afghans. And the baby booties."

"Nancy."

"You don't have to lie to me, is my point. I'm your father."

"Come on, Dad. You don't want to know stuff like that. I mean really. Do you?"

He felt clean, miraculous. As though the details had no power over him. Everything was the idea of itself; everything was the shape of itself, not the texture—the shadow it threw or the light it cast, the arc of its traveling. Not the trivia, not the variables, no: the great sweep of feeling, the adventurous gesture.

"If it makes you happy, that's good enough for me. Whatever. I mean not everyone wants to work for the IRS, either."

"Nice try, Daddy. IRS, phone porn, same thing."

"Anyway, sweetheart, I don't need to know the details. But that doesn't mean I need to be lied to. I'd rather get the respect of hearing the truth and having to deal with it."

"I thought, you know, no one wants to think of their crippled kid doing phone porn for a living. Sordid. You know—do you really need the ideation? It's like seeing your parents have sex. Right? Pretty disgusting. No offense, but who wants that? Come on!"

"The truth will set us free."

"Speak for yourself."

"OK, the truth will set me free. That's what I'm seeing, since I've been down here. Or wait. What I'm seeing is more: I want to know the truth, but I don't want to have to *tell* the truth. See? You want to have the truth available to you, but then you also want the freedom of never having to tell it yourself. That's the deal with truth. It sets you free when you hear it, but if you have to tell it, that's pretty much a non-freedom situation. Get it? People should tell the truth to me, if I ask them for it. But I should be able to hide the truth whenever I want to."

"Are you drunk?"

"I resent the implication."

"Uh huh. Mom said you'd been hitting the sauce. It's not like you. So what is this? A mid-life-crisis thing?"

"I did have two beers with lunch. With the guy from the embassy. Beer in the middle of the day knocks me out, though. It's humid here."

"She also said T.'s in jail."

"It's more of a holding facility. Don't worry. We're gonna spring him. We'll bust him out. I'm working closely with the U.S. embassy."

"He killed someone?"

"Of course not, honey. A guy just happened to, you know, die next to him."

"Just die?"

"Hey. It happens."

"And there's no, they don't have any evidence against him, or whatever?"

"There's no body, even. Don't worry, Case. Hey, listen. What about Sal? How's it going with him?"

"Oh, you know. It's not anything, really."

"Good to hear."

"I bet."

"Hey. Case."

"Uh huh."

"So I've been wondering. What happened with you and T.?"

She was silent. He was overstepping, but he couldn't help it—there was a carelessness to him. Or he was carefree.

"In a nutshell? He condescended, Dad."

"He condescended?"

"He condescended to me."

There was nothing more. Casey was not one to step into an

awkward pause, to take up the slack. The static buzzed between them. He let it rest.

"That's all?"

"That's all, Daddy. So when are you guys coming home?"

After they hung up he lay back on the sheet, content. It always made him feel good to talk to her. She always sounded like herself, whole, confident, abrupt. Her matter-of-factness was comforting, her cheery pugnacity. When he went to see her, or even heard her speaking to him on the phone, it reminded him that she was not gone at all—not gone at all and not miserable, at least no more so than the rest of the humans. She was warm, she was there, she was not the specter of a miserable daughter that lived alongside him. That specter could be dismissed.

It was irrelevant.

•

When he met Brady outside the jail there was another man with him, a younger Anglo in a seersucker suit. It turned out he was a lawyer.

"You said there was nothing to worry about," said Hal, alarmed. It was beyond his control after all. It had run away on him. "You said walk lightly, not to show we're worried!"

"A basic precaution. Cleve's an old friend of mine from Miami. Jorge knows him too. He met him last year at a pool party. Remember that, Cleve? After the ribbon-cutting? At the new youth hostel?"

"With the—that woman with the grass skirt? The super-numerary nipple?"

"Right. Right! Who kept showing it to everyone."

"Jesus," said the lawyer, and shook his head. He turned to Hal. "She was an entertainer I guess? Something to do with the music? But she had this extra nipple. It was, like, right under her clavicle." He tugged his shirt collar down to display the area in question.

"It was weird, though," said Brady. "It was little."

"Almost like a big wart."

"But with an areola."

"So this won't, this won't make the cops think we're adversarial?" asked Hal. "Marching back in there with an attorney?"

"It's just a formality. Don't worry. After you, gentlemen."

Brady opened the door for him.

"She kept going, 'my supernumerary nipple,'" said the lawyer. "That's what she called it. I never forgot. 'Supernumerary.'"

"Made it sound official," said Brady.

"Bureaucratic," said Cleve.

After a few minutes' wait, with Brady and the lawyer still talking about the pool party—apparently a man had walked through a plate-glass door and been airlifted to a hospital in Mexico City—the stocky, sweat-stained man from before came out and ushered them in. It seemed to Hal that the security guard looked askance at him as they passed, as though Hal posed a security risk.

Inside they went down a brightly lit corridor and the stocky man opened the door to an interrogation room.

There was T., seated at a Formica table. At his elbow was a bottle of water.

Hal bent down and held his shoulders, then stepped back. He did not look upset.

"Are you OK? How are you holding up?"

"Fine, thank you," said T., and smiled.

"Where were you sleeping last night?"

"We were driving for some of it. There was a rest stop. I didn't get that much sleep."

"Man. I'm so sorry. This is wrong, T."

T. patted him on the arm and then looked past him, polite. "Tom Stern. Please call me T. And you are?"

Hal introduced Brady and the lawyer. On the other side of the table the stocky man arranged chairs.

"One moment," said Jorge the stocky, and left them.

"Have they accused you of anything?" asked Hal impatiently.

"No, nothing," said T. pleasantly.

"But so—on what grounds are they keeping you?"

"They have some questions, is what I've been told. They want to know what happened. Get it into the record."

"You haven't been interviewed officially, I assume," said the lawyer.

"No one's really asked me anything," said T. "We were in a car, then a transport van with a couple of prisoners, then we stopped at a rest stop . . . I'm tired. But nothing's happened."

"They'll be taping this now, then," said the lawyer. "Wish we had more time to prepare. Key is, you don't want to disclose more than the basic facts. You ever been deposed?"

T. shook his head.

"You have nothing to hide here, I'm sure. But keep it brief. We want to avoid even the suggestion there's anything you could have done to stop this man from dying."

"If I had EMT training, maybe . . . ," said T. pensively.

"That kind of speculation is exactly what we don't want. Just the basic facts. No emotional statements, for instance. You think you can do that?"

Then Jorge was back, and a woman with glossy lipstick and a tape recorder.

"Excuse me," said Jorge. "This is our stenographer. Could she—?"

There was little room. Hal saw he was motioning to the chair beside Hal, in which he had not yet sat down.

"Sure, sure," said Hal, but then, in the ensuing arrangement of persons as they settled, was left with nowhere to sit. He leaned against the wall, arms folded.

"You can just tell us what happened, your version of the events," said Jorge, and T. nodded. Jorge narrated some protocol in the direction of the tape recorder—who was present, the date, the date of the guide's demise. T. began to tell his story, which Hal had heard before, in an even, pleasant tone. It was as though he was unaffected by stress.

Hal himself was sweating. There was no air in the room, no windows and no air. Not even a ventilation grid, he saw, looking around. Maybe if he could crack the door open? Even a few inches would offer relief. But then there would be background noise, he guessed. Ambient sound on the tape recorder, compromising its integrity.

He was wet beneath the arms. Disgusting. And the ceiling, it seemed, was perilously low, pocked with little pinpricks in what looked like white cardboard.

Yet none of the others seemed to be noticing. They were not bothered by any of it. Except for Jorge they were not even perspiring, as far as he could see. He felt a tenuous bond with Jorge. They were the only ones with armpit stains.

Possibly he was slightly claustrophobic. Before his venture into this small, subtropical and foreign country, he had never thought of himself as a wimp. Yet it seemed he was often in discomfort since he got here, uncomfortable, exhausted, or alarmed. He had turned out to be a hothouse flower—a hothouse flower from the first world that wilted in the third. An American hothouse flower, adapted only to the United States. And within the U.S. only to Southern California, or more restricted still— adapted to the unchanging mildness of West L.A., where the worst weather you encountered was gray.

"By the time I dragged myself back down to the coast," T. was saying, in his low, well-modulated voice, "I was in a state of exhaustion. My body weight had dropped. I went to my foreman, Marlo. Later he said I was starving. But my own worry had been thirst, you know, potable water. The river water I'd been avoiding as much as I could. I was afraid of illness. Possibly giardia. Delonn had told me there were cattle upstream. So I used the filter, but I didn't trust myself. I was afraid I was using it wrong. By the time I saw the tourists—it was a family taking pictures of a toucan—I wasn't thinking clearly. And the recovery was slow. This is what accounts for my delay in contacting Delonn's family. I regret . . ."

The lawyer shook his head in a small, tight movement, but T. ignored him. Neither Jorge nor the stenographer, who seemed to be doing nothing other than keeping one hand on the tape recorder, noticed either.

"I regret that my recovery prevented me from contacting them earlier," he went on. "I do think Delonn's problem on the boat, the possible arm pain and mild distress he appeared to be having as we came up the river, were an early warning signal."

The lawyer shook his head again, but T. was not looking at him.

"But he chose not to turn back. At that time, as I said, I asked him if he was OK. He was an older man, but he seemed to be in good physical shape. He was active. My recollection is, he said it was probably heartburn. He had no interest in turning back, so he dismissed my concern."

The lawyer nodded, as though to affirm: good. Good. Blame the victim.

"Mr. Stern. What is your opinion," asked Jorge, tipping his chair back onto two legs, "about what happened to the body? Go over that one more time, please."

T. was drinking water from his bottle. He recapped it and set it down carefully.

"A couple of days after I abandoned the boat," he went on, "I was at my campsite at night. I saw the boat drifting downriver. I ran into the river and tried to climb over the side, but I was too slow. I slipped off and the boat kept going. But while I was still hanging on I saw the inside of the boat, and the body wasn't there. The tent, you know, that it was wrapped in?—was that bright yellow of raincoats. Even at night I would have been able to make it out. But there was nothing."

"You're sure?"

"He already said so," said the lawyer.

"My guess was—"

"You don't have to guess," said the lawyer. "That's all you saw."

Hal felt heat rush to his face, and a suffocation. He closed his eyes and lights pricked at the darkness.

"Excuse me," he said.

The hallway was slightly less stifling but not enough, and he kept going past the security guard and the reception desk, out the front door. The sky had clouded over and a cool breeze was up, and he relaxed instantly.

The guard would probably not let him back in by himself, but he was indifferent. The lawyer was his watchdog. The lawyer was being a lawyer. There was nothing Hal could do to help, past the fact of having brought him in, Brady and him. He was unsure of their competence, but what could he do? Nothing. These were guys who spent their spare time discussing women with extra nipples.

He sat down on a deep window ledge, feet planted far apart on the sidewalk, and raised his face to the sky. He took a deep breath and then looked level again, gazed in front of him. A car or two passed. Across the street there was a store that seemed to sell things made of ugly plastic. The objects festooned the windows brightly but their nature was unclear . . . he had always thought of himself as competent, but then he came down here and had to do everything through proxies—all he did was delegate tasks to those who were more qualified. His own qualifications, it turned out, were limited to Service business. He had no qualifications outside those narrow parameters.

And yet back home, day in, day out, he walked around like a competent man.

That was what his country did for people like him. It specialized them. They knew how to live, day in, day out, in one highly specific undertaking. They thrived in their tunnels, however narrow. Manual laborers knew more. Manual laborers, many of them, could perform myriad tasks if called upon to do so, but white collars like himself knew only one thing.

He was a surplus human, a product of a swollen civilization. He was a widget among men.

When civilization fell and government went with it, his people would die off, replaced by bricklayers, plumbers and mechanics—replaced by farmers, weavers, and electricians who could forage through the ruins for generators and fuse boxes and wire. There would be no more use for his kind.

Could he adapt, given time? Possibly. Although with some difficulty. His former mantle of confidence would fall away; losing authority, he would become a kind of beggar. He and the bohemians. Clearly they were even more useless than he was. This was why, no doubt, he partly identified with them. The presence of other broadly useless humans offered a certain comfort . . . more comfort even than Gretel, in fact, who had been so kind to him, because the young and beautiful were in their own privileged category. They would always be needed, or wanted, at least. The young and beautiful were an end in themselves. Even in the postscript to civilization, the young and beautiful would seldom be forced to beg. Plus they were good breeding stock.

In any case civilization was not quite falling at the moment. It was on its way down, collapsing in slow motion, but it had some good years left in it yet. Chances were he would continue to be what he was, live out his life as a widget, and never be called upon to learn to, say, butcher a calf.

There was Brady, coming out the front door. He nodded briskly at Hal, shook a cigarette out of a packet and lit it.

Brady, too, was a human widget.

"My prediction," said Brady, after a first inhale, "is they keep him in overnight. Maybe one more night for good measure. I don't think we're looking at a serious situation."

"Jesus," said Hal. "That's great to hear."

He didn't quite trust Brady. Brady was not smart enough, he suspected. But still it offered some relief.

"Can I talk to him by myself? Or do the cops always have to be there?"

"Give 'em another five minutes," said Brady. "You should be able to get some face time then."

·

Bail was not an option, apparently. T. had not been arrested, he told Hal, sitting in the interview room again with the door wide open. He was being detained, but no charges had been brought. He was staying on a voluntary basis, until they were satisfied he was not a flight risk.

"As a courtesy," he explained.

"You're staying in prison as a courtesy? Why be courteous? I don't get it. They have no right to keep you."

"It's all right, Hal," said T. calmly. "Really. They're doing a search for the body, just in case. Mostly the riverbanks, is all they can manage. Manpower issue I guess. But if they don't find anything in the next twenty-four hours, the lawyer said, I'll be free to leave. And if they do find it, they'll conduct an autopsy. Verify my story."

"That's bullshit," said Hal.

"It's OK. Really. It's not a problem for me."

"Do you even know the, you know, the conditions? Have you gone to where they're going to keep you?"

"Not yet. It's just down the street."

"And the lawyer advised you to go along with this? I mean we have money. You know. There's plenty of it. We should be able to post a bond. You could stay at my hotel while they do their search. Their autopsy."

"I don't think they'll find the body," said T. "I think the animals got to it."

He seemed matter-of-fact about the prospect.

"Listen. T. Why not stay in my hotel? You want to—I don't know—have to use the toilet in front of perfect strangers? Eat gruel?"

"My own cell, they said. It's not a high-security thing. There are private showers. And it's just for one night."

"I don't know," said Hal, shaking his head. He felt fretful. T. was not practical; in his new form he had become irresponsible, flaky. Could he be trusted even with self-preservation? "Maybe we should call a lawyer in the U.S. Someone famous. Get a referral, at least. I don't know about this."

"You know how you could help?"

"Just tell me."

"If you could arrange for the flight out, a couple days down the road, that'd be great. I was thinking of walking, but now I have other plans."

"Ha ha."

"No, really. I was going to try to walk home, at one point."

"In delirium, I assume."

"I just wanted to do it. But now I think we should maybe go ahead and get back, if that works for you."

"Good thinking."

"Mr. Stern?"

Jorge was at the door.

"We can move you on now, sir."

Hal stood, scraping his chair back.

"I'll keep close tabs on you," he told T. "That's for sure."

"I appreciate your concern, Hal. I do."

"Tomorrow," he said.

"See you," said T.

9

The young lawyer had told Brady about a party, and Brady told Hal. There was always a party, apparently.

Brady called the hotel room and invited Hal to join them. He himself was not driving back to Belmopan, but staying overnight in Belize City. It was a party held by a company, a company that had just opened a Belize location and was looking to make friends.

This meant, Brady explained, there would be ample libations. Hal was welcome to come with them.

Could they promise, asked Hal, a supernumerary nipple?

But he had nothing better to do. He was waiting for them in his room, bored, freshly showered, flipping through channels, when the telephone rang.

"I talked to T.," said Susan breathlessly.

"They're letting him make calls, then," said Hal. "Good sign. Glad to hear it."

"Hal, he's crazy. Do you know what he said to me? He wants to dissolve the corporation. He wants to give away everything."

"I told you he would need some adjustment time. Didn't I?"

"*Adjustment* time? He's delusional. Hal! I don't know what to do!"

"Just wait till he gets back. There's nothing you can do till then anyway."

"He wants me to start right away. He wants us to pull out of everything. I mean it's crazy. I don't even know if it's going to be possible. Or legal. Seriously."

"Just sit tight till we get back, OK? He's being detained. He needs to get home and get his bearings. Regroup. I warned you about this, honey. Right? Just try to be patient. I have us on a return flight the day after tomorrow."

"You do? When?"

"We get in late. Evening."

"I can't believe this. Hal, he's raving."

"Actually, he seems fairly rational to me."

"Are you kidding? Hal! Seriously. Are you *kidding?*"

"Different, but rational. In his way. I mean, he can still string a sentence together. He doesn't foam at the mouth or anything."

"Well, but you don't even know him. I mean, from before. Hardly. You wouldn't know the difference. You said yourself, he had a breakdown. He had a near-death experience!"

Someone was knocking at the room door.

"Just a second."

Brady, holding car keys.

"Phone with my wife. Give me a minute," said Hal, and stood back to let him in. "Susan? I should go. The, uh, the man from the embassy is here. I need to talk to him."

"He was going on about *animals*, Hal. Wild animals dying? I'm worried. What if he does something to himself before we can get help for him?"

"He won't, Susan. It's OK. Just sit tight. Can you try to do that for me?"

Brady patrolled the hotel room, picked up the remote and flicked off the TV. There was something overbearing about him, it seemed to Hal. He carried himself as though it was his own hotel room.

"I'm worried. He just doesn't sound like the same person."

"Maybe he's not, Suze. Maybe he's not. But does that have to be so threatening?"

"I'm talking about mental instability. You remember Eloise? Her son went down to the Amazon on a photo safari and took some malaria drug? He was like twenty-five and getting a Ph.D. in biology. Anyway the drug or the sickness drove him crazy. Forever, Hal. *Forever*. He had a psychotic break. He dropped out of grad school and his girlfriend left him. Now he wanders around Malibu carrying sand in his pockets and calling people 'nigger.'"

"In Malibu?"

"White people."

"You should chill out, honey. Stop worrying. There's nothing you can do, he's safe and sound, we're both coming home soon. And listen, I promise. He's not going to call anybody 'nigger.' I'll go out on a limb and guarantee that."

Brady was impatient. He was not paying attention. He stood with the room door half-open.

"OK," said Susan, in a dissatisfied tone.

"OK. I'll call you in the morning."

.

As they drove to the party, Hal in the passenger seat wrestling with a broken seatbelt, it became clear that Brady had an agenda for the evening. It was unclear to Hal what that agenda was, but clearly there was one. He was purposeful in his movements. He drove fast. He was out for more than just a good time; he had a mission.

"You think T.'s doing OK in that place?" he asked, as Brady lit a cigarette at a stoplight.

It was already dark and the streetlights were on, surrounded by circling insects. Staring at a single light, he could see hundreds of them, possibly thousands.

His eyes smarted with the brightness. He turned away, blinking, and saw stubborn afterimages.

"He'll be fine, he'll be fine," said Brady dismissively.

Hal found him irksome. Most of his smoke went out the window, but not all of it.

The afterimages of the streetlights were fading slowly.

"You ever spent the night in a jail around here?" he asked.

"It's a holding facility," said Brady, accelerating with a jerk.

"But how can we know what the conditions are? There's no transparency! What if it's a whole, you know, bitches-and-shivs kind of situation? Bend-over, rusty-razorblades-in-the-shower-type scene?"

Brady looked at him sidelong, one eyebrow raised.

"Relax. He's going to be fine. You know, you seem a lot more uptight about it than he was, you realize that? Guy didn't seem that worried to me."

The cigarette dangled and jumped precariously as his lips moved.

But it was true, seemingly. No argument there.

Hal should have had something to drink before he met up with Brady. He didn't like him, he realized. There was something sharp about Brady, something sharp and rancid.

Suddenly he longed for the company of Gretel. He liked Gretel. She was nice.

Germans, he reflected, were possibly not so bad. Even if they were a super-race, maybe they didn't mean to be. After all, as national arrogance went, in his recollection from traveling, the French were far worse. And people often forgot that it was the Frogs, not the Krauts, who invented fascists. When people thought about the French, they thought of wine, the Eiffel Tower, the fatuous berets and painters on streets. They forgot these were the same guys who invented the whole fascist deal in the nineteenth century, then let the Germans run with it.

It was easy to be sucked into the thrall of a European. That much was true. German or French, English or Italian, even quaint, poor and Irish, there was something superior about all of them. They valued education, for one thing, which gave them a bit of a head start. They did not cherish ignorance like his own countrymen. For that reason—recently, at least—they were less destructive, megalomaniacal and brutal, for instance. Which might be seen as an advantage for them. On the other hand, their maturity could also be somewhat boring. In America adults acted like children; in Europe the children acted like small adults. Even the cornboys, though boyish enough in their activities, were more like miniature engineering students than carefree ten-year-olds.

Also, the lack of childish, wanton destructiveness failed to stand the Europeans in good stead when it came to world domination. Being smart, educated and civilized, and having learned some fairly significant lessons from their history, they had pretty much retreated from the world-domination forum over the past half-century and now were like a small band of AARP members watching the carnival from a distance and drinking nonalcoholic beer.

But as far as super-races went, the German women, at least, were warm and generous. He liked them.

The one he knew, anyway.

"Here we go. Bit of a walk. Nice beach house. No parking any closer."

"Your friend Cleve coming?" asked Hal to fill the space as they got out of the car.

"Should be. Yeah. You know, see most of the same people at these things. Whole city's what, sixty thousand bodies. You got a small expat community, you got your local figures. Same old. Except for the help. The help changes."

Ahead of them was a large, white, blocky house surrounded by waving palms. A nice breeze had sprung up off the ocean. It was good to be here, after all, Hal thought with relief, if only for the breeze. There were people milling on a second-floor terrace, which was strung with lights.

"Pool, too," said Brady. "Jacuzzi."

"I didn't bring my suit," said Hal.

"No worries," said Brady.

He followed Brady into the house, through an atrium full of waxy-leaved plants with huge flowers, up tiled stairs onto the terrace, where the drinks were. There was music, but he could not tell where it was coming from. People around, most of them tanned and quite young. Where were all the geriatric expats? They had to be around somewhere. People retired here, after all. There should be plenty of wrinkled old crones smeared with Coppertone. But instead there were only models and athletic types. Among them Hal would not shine.

A bartender, tables with candles in the center, and there: a topless woman in the hot tub. Already. She was on the other side of the pool, down off the terrace on the first floor, but he saw her. Her shoulders were brown but her breasts floated whitely on the water like twin buoys.

He encountered a lot of nudity, in this tropical location. For years, in his life, almost no nudity, only clothing. Clothing, clothing, clothing. Wherever he went, there seemed to be apparel. Although he lived in Southern California, and not far from the beach either, somehow he did not frequent the nude locations.

Then he came here and suddenly: nude. Nude nude nude.

"Here, have this one," said Brady, and put a drink in his hand. Out of it stuck a parrot fashioned from colored pipe-cleaners: red, blue, yellow.

"So who's our host?" asked Hal, lifting the drink to his lips. As he raised it the parrot swiveled and hit him on the nose.

"The folks throwing this shindig," said Brady, whose own

drink featured no parrot, "are ethanol. They just inked some kind of deal with BSI. The sugar monopoly."

"Huh," said Hal. If he took the parrot out it would stop falling on him when he drank. But in his pocket it would be crushed. He liked the parrot. He could give it to Casey. She enjoyed souvenirs, especially if tacky.

He held the parrot with one crooked finger while he raised his glass. That was the trick: restrain the parrot. Keep the parrot captive.

"Toucan's giving you a tough time, huh," said Brady.

"Oh. I thought it was a parrot."

"Hey! Jeff!"

There was the lawyer, lifting himself out of the pool. He wore a Speedo. He reached out and grabbed a silky bathrobe, mounted the stairs and came up to them, nodding and waving at others he passed.

"Let me introduce you around," he said.

They walked down the far stairs to the pool area again, where there was another bar. Beyond a wall lined with flowering vines were the beach and the ocean. A DJ played music on a stereo and people danced. They stood next to the dance floor, watching.

"Thanks for inviting me," said Hal.

"Marcella. Marcella, this is Jeff Brady. The U.S. embassy. The one I told you about? The racquetball story?"

A passing woman shook Brady's hand. Hal noticed long fingernails, shining silver.

"Hal Lindley," he said, because the lawyer seemed to have forgotten his name. "Just visiting. Tourist."

A guy on the dance floor bumped into him, sloshing his drink.

"Marcella handles the Canadians," Cleve was telling Brady.

A server brought up an hors d'oeuvres tray. Brady picked up a small food item and shoved it into his mouth.

"What are they?" asked Hal, peering down.

"Sribuffs," said the server, a dark young woman.

"Sribuffs?" repeated Hal. "I'm not . . ."

"Shrimbuffs," she said again, nodding anxiously.

"Shrimbuffs. Huh," said Hal.

"*Shrimp* puffs," said Brady, impatient.

"Oh. Oh, I see," said Hal, and took one, smiling sheepishly at the server. He tried to seem obliging.

"Why they can't hire fucking English speakers," said Cleve, shaking his head. "When the official language is fucking English."

The woman moved off, her head down.

"You'd like her better if she had three nipples, you're saying," said Brady.

"Shit yeah. I would."

Hal wanted another drink. Not to be critical; to suspend his judgment. The second thing he had learned, on this trip—after the fact that he liked knowing the truth about other people and at the same time keeping his own truth to himself—drink more. He should drink more, in general. Not to the point of alcoholism, but enough to float, in the waning part of the day, in a kind of pleasant and light liquid, a beery amber light. Life was better that way. People were softer around the edges, their conversation less grating.

"Excuse me. Making a bathroom run, then a drink. Get anyone anything?" he asked, raising his near-empty glass.

"G&T," said Brady.

"Cognac," said Cleve.

"OK," he said, and moved off. See what the house held. He would have to find a way to keep the toucan in shape . . . on his way in he took it carefully off the straw it was impaled on and slipped it into the loose pocket of his shirt. It should be safe there, unless he crushed someone against him. Manfully.

But that was unlikely. Gretel was absent.

•

In the bathroom there were seashells of all shapes and sizes. They were made by something, seashells. Various organisms. Were they some animals' excreta? He could not remember. He had seen a show on shell-forming animals with Casey. The term *calcium carbonate* came to mind. The animals formed the shells slowly, but how did they do it?

Possibly the shells were like fingernails, protruding suddenly from the skin.

It was strange, come to think of it. He looked down at the back of his hand. Fingernails. They just started up.

They were made of keratin, he remembered that.

They were a form of hair.

He had read this, but frankly he did not believe it. Or simply, he did not agree. They might be made of similar proteins, he accepted that readily, but still they were not a *form* of *hair.* Any idiot could see that.

He finished peeing, washed his hands and picked up a shell that looked like a snail shell, except huge and spotted. There were also stripes. It was attractive. Inside, it was shiny.

He placed it back on the shelf.

The drink was treating him well. No doubt it had been mixed quite strong. They fooled you with the toucan. You thought: child's play, and swigged heartily. Then you were drunk. But he should not complain, not even to himself. It was what he had intended, after all. He had already made the decision. From now on he would be a man who drank. He would stop short of chronic impairment, though. That was the trick; you had to learn to drink the correct amount. It was said two glasses of wine a day improved your health. Surely three could not do it too much harm, in that case. He could become an oenophile. That was the name, if he recalled correctly, for wine lovers.

Wine-loving assholes. Because let's face it, a wine lover was basically an asshole. Like a cigar lover. The word *connoisseur*, in general, was a synonym for asshole.

If it was up to him, connoisseurs of all kinds would be audited on a regular basis, their files tagged and them personally harassed by the Service until forced to surrender their assets. They would be targeted for audits on a non-random basis, if it was up to him. Wine, cigars, old cars, all pastimes of the genus *Assholus*.

It wouldn't be wine, not for him. The point was, he could have three drinks a day and cultivate new fields of knowledge. He could keep more secrets, possibly lead a secret life with secret leisure pursuits. But what kind of secret life could he lead?

Before, when he found out about Susan, he had wanted to lead a secret life to get back at her. Now he wanted one for a different reason: his own pleasure. Excitement.

He picked up his glass. He still had to get drinks.

Because the life he had currently, he reflected, climbing the stairs, was insufficient. It was quite simply inadequate. At a certain point, you had to insist on quality.

A woman he once knew, who lived down the street from them, had said frequently, "I'm going to exercise my rights as a consumer." She had said this often. Then she would call a mail-order catalog, for instance, and complain about a substandard product she had purchased therefrom. She would receive bulk samples of things, or luxury items free of charge—bribes from companies in exchange for refraining from litigation, which she threatened often.

When she was his neighbor he had frowned on this behavior of hers, which seemed cynical and opportunistic. Susan had thought it was funny, but he had frowned upon it. Now, however, he felt a certain grudging admiration.

"Cognac," he said to the bartender beside the pool. He could barely hear his own voice. It was loud now. There was music, coming from who knows where. He did not see Brady or Cleve. There were more people now also. It was as though, alone in the bathroom, he had slept for hours by himself while on the other side of the wall the crowd swelled and gained momentum. Kind of a Sleeping Beauty thing. "G&T."

"What's your gin, sir?"

"Oh, I don't know. It's not for me. Whatever you want to give him."

Two women dancing near him wore hairy coconut-shell bikini tops. He had never thought he would see that, outside a movie context. The shells did not look comfortable. They had to be chafing. Your average breast was not a good fit for half a coconut shell. The breasts would have red circle marks on them, like glass rings on a coffee table.

Maybe he should work on Casey, with regard to the phone-sex problem. Sure, she was an adult, but adults made poor choices all the time and she was no exception. Maybe he should press her harder to go to college. She was still young enough. Was it wrong of him to let her choose her own path? She was his daughter. And she was only in her twenties. And she was doing phone sex. She was going down the old phone-sex road. Where did that road lead? That road was a dead end.

It was all very well to be accepting. Acceptance had its place. But maybe he was shirking his duty. Maybe he should plead with her, or threaten. Did Susan know? She did not, was his suspicion. Maybe he should talk about it with Susan. Maybe they should formulate policy. Of course, he had just told Casey he was fine with it. The downside of drunkenness. But it was true, in a way. That is, he was fine with the sex aspect, in a sense. What sense? Well, in the sense that he could admit his daughter was a female, and—

OK, so he was fine with it in the sense that he could ignore it, if he tried, or maybe chock it up to youthful mischief, risk-taking, or perversity, or also possibly a nihilistic, self-abnegating impulse Casey had been known at times to embrace. But he was not fine with the whole career dead-end thing. Would she feel amused and fulfilled doing phone sex at fifty? No she would not.

When he got home he would hunker down with Susan. They would devise a phone-sex strategy.

·

"What the hell happened to you?" asked Brady, when Hal approached with drinks in hand, finally. He already had a new one, and was talking to a pretty girl. Cleve the lawyer was not around. "You fall in?"

Brady's sharpness and his focus were on Hal, yet Hal sensed it was for the benefit of the pretty girl. She was half Brady's age at the most and quite elegant, with her black hair swept up on top of her head in a chignon style Hal's mother had favored. This, he realized, was why Brady had driven fast to the party.

He put down the cognac and G&T on a table, the better to drink his own whiskey. Behind Brady, against a vine-covered wall, people in skimpy bathing suits were blindfolded and playing Pin the Tail on the Donkey, shrieking with laughter. He drank the whiskey; Brady was leaning in close to the girl, plying her. He was trying to get her to sleep with him. Hal could not hear what he was saying, nor did he want to.

But his whiskey was already gone.

He grabbed up the extra G&T surreptitiously, without Brady noticing, and moved away from the two of them, toward the taped-up banner of the donkey. Tails hung all over it, willy-nilly. He stood there sipping and watching as a plump woman in a tiny, ill-advised purple thong approached, giggling. She was being roughly steered, almost pushed in fact, by a large man behind her who held onto her shoulders. She raised a braided donkey tail, her arm wavering.

"Colder, colder, warmer, colder," chanted other men in the crowd. But they were toying with the woman. They misdirected her and then they laughed.

Abruptly the large man turned her toward the pool, and she stepped forward. She screamed as she fell. But then seconds later she resurfaced, sputtering and annoyed, tugging at her blindfold as laughter resounded. Hal stepped away, thinking maybe she had let it happen—there was something about her, something irritating—but also touched by sadness.

At his elbow was a young man with a brush cut in wet swimming trunks, toweling his buff body.

"Pathetic, isn't it," said the young man.

Hal felt called upon to defend the woman.

"She's the victim," he said. Possibly slurring.

"That's what I mean," said the young man, and shrugged on a T-shirt. "They're pathetic. Not her."

"Oh. Yeah," said Hal, though in fact it was all of them.

"You know anyone here?" asked the young man.

"No one I want to talk to," said Hal. "You?"

"Same," said the young man. "I'm on leave, I don't live around here."

"You in the army or something?"

"Air Force."

"I was just with some Marines," said Hal. "Or something like that. Coast Guard. Green Berets. Shit, military-type guys, what the hell do I know. In the jungle."

"Yeah?"

"Down south, on the Monkey River," said Hal, nodding.

"No shit," said the Air Force guy. "Me too!"

"Get out," said Hal. Was the guy playing him?

"Serious," said the Air Force guy. "We did a raid on a guerrilla camp."

"A raid? You mean like—"

"I'm a pilot."

"So you mean like a bombing raid? A—dropping bombs on them?"

"Limited airstrike. Yeah. Cluster bombs."

"Cluster bombs?"

"CBUs."

"Don't we—I mean don't we have to declare war or something?"

"Hey. Just following orders. My understanding through the grapevine, this was a War on Drugs operation."

Hal felt dazzled. Water splashed up from the pool onto his back, and people were still shrieking. He thought for a second he was back by the river, exhausted. Was it his fault? Bombing Mayans . . . but maybe they weren't Mayans at all, maybe they were drug kingpins. He gazed down at the drink in his hand; he had mixed tequila, whiskey and now vodka. It was dizzying.

"There you go," said the pilot, putting a hand on his back and moving him. "Guy was about to stick a tail on you."

"You mean on this side of the border, right?" asked Hal.

"Wanna get some food? I'm starving."

"Sure," said Hal, but he felt unsteady. "They have shrimp puffs."

"There's a whole table. Follow me."

At the table there was a surfeit of food. The pilot picked up what looked like a kebab.

"Is that meat? Does that look like meat to you?"

"I think so," said Hal, bending to look at it.

"I think so too."

He put it back.

"What," said Hal, "you don't eat meat?"

"Vegan," said the pilot.

"A vegan bomb-dropper," said Hal. He drank from his glass. It was almost empty. He put it down on the table.

"Best thing for you," said the pilot. "Too much dairy clogs the arteries."

"You don't get anemic or anything?" asked Hal.

The pilot was piling fruit onto a plate, fruit and corn-on-the-cob and bread.

"You should eat too," he said to Hal. "You look like you need it."

"I'm not used to drinking," admitted Hal.

"Here, take that," said the pilot, and handed Hal his plate. "Sit down. Dig in."

The vegan pilot was looking out for him. Why? It was a mystery. Kindly people were crawling out of the woodwork, lately—vegan pilots and German women. Nice people and nude people. In fact there was definite overlap. Did being nude make people nicer? Quite possibly. The inverse was certainly true: putting on Kevlar vests, body armor, etc., made you more willing to go around shooting people. It might also be the case that nice people were more willing to be nude. Chicken or egg question, really.

But then technically the vegan pilot had just been on a cluster-bombing sortie, so maybe he was not so nice. A wolf in vegan's clothing.

Hal carried the plate to a table and sat. The bread was good, though there was no butter on it. He would prefer it with a pat of butter. He took a bite of the corn, also. Then the vegan cluster-bomber was back with him.

"So this bombing, did it, you know, kill people?"

"The bombs were anti-personnel, so yeah, that would have been an objective. I didn't do any follow-up though, I was in and out, that was it."

"You don't feel bad about that? Killing?"

"It's not ideal. But we all kill," said the vegan, and forked up a piece of roasted red pepper.

"Not *people*," said Hal.

"Of course we do," said the vegan.

"Me personally?"

"You eat other people's food."

"Not following you."

"People who need it more than you do and die for lack of a pound of corn. It's what we all are, isn't it? Killers. I mean, all that life *is* is energy. The conversion of fuel. And we take it all. A quarter of the world's resources for what, five percent of its population," said the vegan. "That's us."

He patted his mouth carefully with a paper napkin and raised a glass to his lips. It looked like bubbly water.

"That's ridiculous," said Hal. "Talk about oversimplified." He should drink water too, to clear his head. He looked around for a dispenser.

"Yeah well," said the vegan. "Arithmetic is simple. That doesn't make it wrong."

This kind of discussion was pleasing only in a work environment, and only when it dealt directly with taxation. In a party setting it was unwelcome. Hal had the feeling of being caught in a trap by the vegan. Maybe you had to be careful of vegans. The vegan menace.

Although the vegan still seemed friendly. He spoke in a soft, moderate tone.

"Come on," said Hal weakly. "You're talking about what, middle-class lifestyle? At worst it's manslaughter. It's not murder. It's not like flying over a jungle and cluster-bombing Mayans."

But the buttery corn was slipping out of his grasp. It was devious and slippery.

"Manslaughter or murder, the guy still ends up dead," said the vegan. "Does it matter to him how the killer rationalized?"

"Where'd you get that water?" asked Hal. He also needed a napkin.

"Right over there," said the vegan, pointing.

Hal made his way to the table with the water. He was leaning over an array of light-blue bottles when an elbow struck his ribcage.

"You're married, right?"

It was Cleve, with a woman hanging onto his arm.

"Oh hey, I got you that cognac," said Hal, nodding confusedly, and looked around for where he'd set it down.

"Because the guy you're talking to?"

"He claims to be a pilot," said Hal. "With the Air Force. He talks like an earnest grad student though. Do you know him?"

"He's a pilot. Yeah. But he's also a flaming faggot," said Cleve. "What, you didn't notice? He's probably hitting on you."

"I'm old enough to be his father," protested Hal weakly, but Cleve was already clapping him on the back with a smirk.

"Just a babe in the woods," he said, and moved off.

There was still butter on Hal's fingers, or maybe vegetable oil.

He reached for the top of a stack of paper napkins and wiped his fingers, then picked up a bottle.

When he sat down again beside the vegan he looked at him differently, applying a This Man Is Gay filter. He remained unsure, though. The vegan was buff, clean, and ate politely, but there were straight men like that.

"You know Cleve?" asked the vegan.

"Not really," said Hal. "I know someone who knows him, a guy at the embassy. I don't really like either of them. Just between you and me. But he told me you're gay."

The vegan laughed easily.

"Guilty," he said. "Though I doubt he put it that way. Cleve's got issues."

"They let gay guys fly fighter planes?"

"Don't ask, don't tell. Hey, it's not like we're color-blind. Or women."

"Ha," said Hal. He had finished the whole bottle of water. He felt almost sober. "My daughter always wanted to fly," he said.

"She should take lessons," said the vegan, and set his plate down on the table.

"Paralyzed," said Hal.

"I'm sorry."

"Me too."

He was far soberer, yes, but the food was making him drowsy, the food on top of the alcohol.

"I need to lie down, I think," he said to the vegan.

"There's a hammock," said the vegan. "I'll show you."

They walked down the stairs, past the pool, past the crowds

and onto the beach, where there was a small stand of palm trees. A string hammock swung there. Someone had just vacated it. There was a breeze off the ocean.

"Perfect," said Hal, grateful.

Cluster-bomber or not, the vegan had been good to him.

After he settled down in the hammock the vegan patted him on the shoulder.

"Good talking to you," said the vegan, and moved off.

"You too," said Hal.

When he woke up he would tell Brady: You were wrong. The kindergarten teacher was right.

They cluster-bombed and cluster-bombed and told the diplomats nothing.

· · · · ·

What woke him up was not the flying dinosaurs but their calls. The calls of the pterodactyls were the same as the hoarse, throaty cries of young men.

He heard them and shifted in the hammock, registering the way the strings were cutting into his back. He was sore along the lines the strings had etched. White light made him cover his eyes.

Struggling awake he saw it was morning—no, midday; the sun was high in the sky—and the monsters were in the sky too but shockingly close to him, red and green dinosaurs with spread wings. He was back with them. Prehistoric. He could smell the salt of the sea and the freshness of morning air. Dinosaurs had been birds, many of them, and birds were their descendants . . . they skimmed along the ocean, over the waves. It must be high tide, because the water was not far away. It lapped at the sand just a few feet downhill. He was between palm trees, so the dinosaurs were only partly visible.

One landed. It had feet rather than claws. It was running.

It was actually a young man holding onto a glider thing. Was it parasailing? No . . . kitesurfers, that was it. He'd seen them before, on Venice Beach. The man hit the sand running, calling out again hoarsely, a cry of triumph. The others were behind him, still over the water. The young man let his red wings go, his red apparatus on its metal struts, or maybe they were fiberglass. It tumbled behind him. How had he taken off? How did they do it?

Another one alit on the water.

Hal struggled out of the hammock as the fliers landed, rubbing his eyes, bleary: the party would have ended long ago. The party had continued without him, leaving him behind. When he was a young man, in high school and college, he had been almost frightened to miss a party, at least any party his friends were attending. He had thought that everything would happen there, at that precise moment, that on that one occasion all friendships, all bonds would be cemented without him. In his absence, he had feared, the best times would be had and he would have missed them.

He did not have that feeling now. Sleep was a good way to leave a party.

His neck was stiff, though.

He patted his pockets. Wallet, check. Something in his breast pocket; he extracted it. It was a mass of tangled pipe-cleaner. Formerly a toucan. He pulled at it, trying to get it back into shape, but no dice. He must have lain on it.

He left the shouting men behind him, the ones landing with hoarse cries of victory. There were more of them coming, more red and green shapes over the horizon. Best to leave before the full-scale invasion. Recover in the hotel room; possibly sleep more there. But first he needed to rinse his mouth.

He walked over the sand to the water, where waves were curling. The wind was up. Behind him the first man landed was grappling with his sail apparatus; ahead, beyond the break, another man was surfing. Hal bent and scooped water into his mouth, jumped back from the edge, gargled and spat. He did it again until his mouth felt salty but clean.

Around him the red gliders were landing. They made him nervous, as though they might land on him. Were they members of a club? They all bore the same pattern, like a squadron of fighter planes. Panels of red, green, orange. The men who held them were euphoric. Their muscles and the wind alone had carried them. Hal felt envious. Yes: when he got home he would enroll in a class, learn to do this. Or windsurfing. To be one of the blown ones, carried.

Today was the day; this very afternoon he would liberate T. He would hustle him onto a plane and take him back to Susan like a trophy.

Slightly dinged, admittedly. Luster dimmed, in her eyes. But still a trophy.

On his return, he would see Susan in a softer light. He owed it to her. And he would be with Casey again.

Climbing the steps to the pool, he looked across its breeze-rippled surface to the aftermath of the party—glasses still on tables, white tablecloths with edges flying up in the wind, flapping across leftover, greasy dishes. No one was around, not even cleaning staff. It was deserted.

Maybe, he thought, he could salvage a replacement toucan from the ruins. He wove through the tables, scouting. Toucan, toucan! He would score one for Casey. He swore to get one for her. It was his duty. Yet there were no toucans.

Still, as he rounded the last dirty table, where a bowl of floating flowers had been used as an ashtray, he saw what seemed to be a green pipe-cleaner turtle sticking out of a margarita glass. They swam thousands of miles to build nests in the sand a few miles south of here, the divemaster had told him, but after they laid their eggs had to return to the water, and poachers tore up their nests and stole the eggs. They had lived 200 million years, maybe more. Maybe even 400. They had outlived the dinosaurs. But now a few beachfront resorts, a few hungry poachers and they were on their way out.

He would accept the turtle, though it lacked the kitsch value of the toucan.

He snatched it out of its empty glass.

10

It was time. At the holding facility T. would be waiting for him. Turned out the place was an easy ten-minute walk from the hotel: the receptionist drew a crude street map on the back of a piece of stationery.

The humid air of the streets was heavy with a gray smog; cars here still ran on leaded gasoline. Simply because no one had yet passed a law to prevent it. As a result children breathed in the toxic fumes every day and gradually lost brain function.

It came to Hal—a curious thought, because he was not given to theories of the supernatural—that their ghosts must linger here, the ghosts of those children before they were impaired. Even as the living children went on, growing into adults of limited intelligence, so must the ghosts linger beside them, pale images of what they might have become.

How wrong Tom Paine had been. Not overall, but in the sound bites. "That government is best which governs least." If only.

Ahead of him a thin boy stepped out of the darkened doorway of a building. Hal felt an impulse to apologize to this boy in case he was one of the retarded ones. Not that Hal himself was personally responsible for the lead in the gasoline of this foreign country, but in the sense that they all were, that individuals were culpable, especially individuals like him, secure and comfortable and well-educated, for all of the rest of them . . . but now the boy must be confused, because he was not moving out of the way. Hal would have to step around him, down over the curb, onto the street and up again.

He moved to step into the street, smiling apologetically in case—since after all he was the interloper here, not the boy—it had been rude on his part not to do so in the first place. He noticed, in the boy's rising hand, something thin and gray. Then the boy stepped up to him, and the boy's hand was on his pocket; at the same time he felt a pain in his side, and was already on his way down to the dirty sidewalk before he could say anything. Falling into sharpness, or the sharpness was crumpling him. It happened so smoothly that as the boy ran away, a small bundle in his hand—a wallet?—Hal was still feeling beholden, as though he owed him an apology.

He was a child, after all. You wanted to protect them despite the bad behavior, knowing that all hurt animals had to flail . . . it was bad, it was surprisingly bad, but the sharpness faded, actually washed itself out a bit. It softened and covered him as he lay, doubtful, stricken by confusion. Was he supposed to be doing something? Was there something he could do about his situation?

He was part of the world's momentum, part of its on-and-on functioning, its inertia that was neverending. The pilot had said it, and it was true, finally. He himself was responsible for the boy, and by extension for this, for the sharpness and the spreading bewilderment. He had played by the rules—he had always played by the rules, even when, for a second, he considered breaking them and then decided not to. His life had been bracketed by rules, enclosed by their tidy parentheses; he had gone along in the forward motion, he had done nothing to stop it.

Warmth flowed over the sidewalk—his own, he felt in a wave of dismay. Had he disgraced himself? But it was thick—blood, not urine.

The sidewalk heated under his side and his arm but he himself grew colder despite the weather, his legs and stomach icy. He had thought it was so cloying in this place, so humid. Just a minute ago . . . how quickly it all flickered. Time was not in step with humans, in the end. It went too fast and too slow: and yet people expected it to guide them and shelter them.

And the boy was gone. Hal was alone and he almost missed him: come back, he thought. Boy? Anyone?

He tried calling out, but lacked the force or the breath. His voice dwindled.

His face against the sidewalk, then turning to lie on his back while the snake twisted in him—he saw the pain that way, an image vaguely inherited somewhere: a black and white snake with a diamond pattern—or no, the diamonds were not white but a sickly yellow. The image flicked past him, a snake slithering through his own blood. He felt a lick of panic, but then he was calm. It wasn't real, after all.

He would have to wait till someone came to help him. That was what happened, with these incidents. People came to help you. All life was based on this, the social compact. It would not let him down, would it? He himself had held up his end. Not that he was a saint. But he was not a bad guy. It was fair to say that, more or less, he had held up his end.

Sometimes you had to wait first. That was all. T. would be fine without him; there was no bail, so all he had to do was walk out. Possibly, even, he would walk out and find Hal. Rescue him, in a role reversal. At this point he was only a few blocks away.

But the flow—he was soaking. Could he stop the flow while he was waiting?

He felt around with his hand, felt his side where the heat was coming from. He tried to block it, pressing his hand against the wet slick, but his arm was so weak.

The boy might even *be* retarded. One way or another damage had been done to him, that was certain. If it was the wallet he'd wanted all he had to do was ask. No show of force was needed. It was Hal's official policy to give up money quickly whenever mugged. He had never had to invoke the policy, however.

If only the boy had asked . . . he felt a twinge of self-pity. Casey would poke at him with affection, needling. He had it all: he had legs. What right did he have to pity?

Above him a streetlamp winked on. He could not tell if the moon was out. When the moon was full you could not see the stars. Once he had seen the Milky Way. When was that? Long ago, he thought, before he got old . . . there was paradise in the Milky Way, in its seeming infinity.

When they came to move him, loading him onto a stretcher,

he would make sure he got a look at the sky beyond the buildings. The stars would be even better, but in a city there was too much ambient light to see the stars clearly.

He heard sniffing. There was a dog next to him, nuzzling his face. The way it tossed its head slightly, nudging with the long wet nose, was endearing. He had to squeeze his eyes closed against the tongue and at the same time he tried to reach out to pet it, but his arm was shaking too much . . . a black dog, a mutt in the Labrador family. Now it had moved down from his face and was lapping at something. He was afraid—yes. Lapping up his blood. He did not blame it for this, though it was a strange sensation: the dog bore him no ill will. We lick what we can, was the motto of dogs. Was it any different from when they licked the salt off your hands or your face?

He recalled T.'s dog, dog on three legs. This one was here, the other was back at home waiting. Dogs all over the world.

It was a comfort. He might be gone, he himself might be gone, but everywhere were the dogs, with their faithful dispositions. It seemed you could rely on them. The dogs were a kind of love, given freely to men. Their existence meant you did not have to be alone. For if, in the end, you found yourself alone, completely alone, and it was chilling, you could look for a dog. And there, in the dog, would be love. You did not have to deserve a dog. Rather a dog was a gift, a gift and a representative. What a dog was was simple: the ambient love of the world.

The dog moved off after a while—or rather, at a certain point it was not there anymore. Hal thought he might have fainted and missed it leaving.

If he still could, he decided, he would get his own dog. When he got home he would go out and get a dog of his own. A dog from a shelter, a dog that needed someone.

He could hear people laughing, possibly in a nearby bar or restaurant. He had always liked going to bars and restaurants; he should go to more of them. Take Susan along with him. Although he might be dying. If so, he couldn't take her to any more restaurants. But he was sorry for his behavior, so trivial and selfish. Whatever made her happy . . . have some paralegals. There, there. Have yourself a paralegal or two.

Really, I mean it, he told her. He would pass out the paralegals like cigars at a birth.

He was so sorry now that he had left her alone, left her alone years ago and never looked back, when all he thought of was Casey, worrying. He had never intended to leave anyone, it was the last thing he would ever have intended, but it turned out he was the abandoner.

This was shocking. It was just like the wound. It was a wound in himself, like the hole from stabbing. Only now did he look down and notice it: he himself did the abandoning.

Of course poor Susan needed company. She should never have been abandoned.

He hoped the laughing people were in a restaurant, celebrating something with lanterns strung up and deep warm colors that were welcoming. He was almost—almost—at the table himself. There were reflections of lanterns on his own glass, which he would raise to the crowd. If they could see him.

He was sorry for the boy, the stabbing boy, but then the boy, he recognized, was also his daughter. Not that Casey had ever stabbed him. He corrected himself, as though someone was listening. It was his feeling he meant, his feeling . . . as soon as they were past, perceptions took on a transparency. There was an impulse, it fled, and then he saw what the impulse meant. He saw through the obfuscations of his own mind, through the dodges of his remorse and his wishful thinking, and behind it all was a vision of his daughter.

It was Casey he wanted to apologize to, not the boy, and it always would be. When you were born, he could say to her, I was born too.

This appeared to him in the light of a new idea, though it was not. I was born then because it was true, as soon as you existed, that I only existed to care about you. From then on I myself was nothing.

And you know what, sweet girl?

I was happy that way.

"It was you who made me necessary," he said.

It came out as a mumble. He wished he could hold her close in perpetuity, as he had wished so often when she was small. He was astonished, when he thought about it, that every man was not a criminal before he was graced with a child, astonished that any man was good at all before that. Many of them were not, actually. Statistics told the story: most vicious criminals, the warriors and ax murderers and gangbangers, were young men. Except for the rare among them who were born nice, they needed a child to civilize them.

And yet, of course, they should not be granted the privilege.

He would tell her: It was you who gave me the reason for my life. Before you I was proud—proud and empty. I had no idea what it was like to beg the world for mercy and not be heard, never be heard at all. But still to go on begging, unheard. I knew nothing.

And then I failed you.

He would say this clearly, making sure she understood how fully, fully acquainted he was with his failure. He had failed to protect her, failed in his one genuine calling, being her father. He did not accept this, in the sense that he repudiated it, but he knew it all the same. You could know something and at the same time reject it, no contradiction there. I failed, he would say to her, I failed at the moment when you were hit and after that moment I would never stop failing.

And it was you who suffered for my failings.

That was the problem of the religion he'd been born into. Christians, he thought: his parents had been two of them, but he could never bring himself. He had lived and now was dying an un-Christian, quite pleasantly godless . . . for the problem with the story of Jesus was simply this: it was a reversal, it was a perfectly backward version of the story of humankind, a mirror image of the world. For in reality itself, as opposed to the holy script, it was not one man who suffered and the rest of the world that was saved. It was the whole world that suffered for the sake of one man.

He could make the stipulation now, he could indulge in bombast now that he was, so unexpectedly, becoming dead. The whole world suffered and bled for all eternity, through all of human history, so that a minuscule, paltry few could have leisure and joy and the liberty of wealth for as long as they each should live. There is no doubt, the poor are the sacrifice, he thought, and he remembered this knowledge like a sight he had seen—all the poor and the untended and powerless. Together they are Jesus on the cross, bleeding so openly, bleeding for all to see, and thin like Jesus too, their arms and veins opened.

And yet the rich, especially the very, grotesquely rich, that fraction of a percent that make up the one man that is saved, blithely deny the truth of this, though it is perfectly obvious and as transparently clear as glass. The rich may worship God or they may pretend to but they are kicking Jesus to the floor daily, kicking him viciously and stepping on his face.

Because the poor are Jesus, in their billions. Plain as the nose on his face . . . and he himself, neither Jesus nor Judas but some-one in between, was dying.

But maybe it would be all right in the end, or in the end beyond the end. Maybe somehow a second chance would come for him. And next time he would make sure she was not injured at all. He would take her away to a safe place and there she would be kept separate from accidents . . . there had to be a shelter like that for her, even for both of them. As simple as that bar at the end of the street, beaming its warmth. Was it so much to ask? A safe place for his little girl. If bargains were possible he would give himself up a thousand times before he would let them hurt her. Let them accept him, let them accept his pathetic, meaningless sacrifice. It was paltry. He knew that, for chrissake. But what else did he have, what else could he bargain with?

And this was melodrama, he knew that too, so sue him, who cared, he was dying. And anyway the melodrama did not make it less true . . . all he wanted was to hear the word *yes*. Yes: we will accept it. We will accept what you offer, be it ever so puny. In exchange we will give life back to your girl.

So she will always be young. And she will always be beautiful.

Whatever he did or could never do, in the end it was she who had formed whatever he was that was worth being. It is the child who makes the parent on this earth, he would say to her if she was here to listen, not the other way round. The child was more than father to the man; children were father and mother to the soul, whatever that might be. He did not pretend to know much about souls, or the idea of them. He never had. But once or twice he had thought he could hear a sound, a faint music. The spirit moves around us, falls past us invisible like air through air . . . all we are sure we have, all that we know, is the suspicion of its presence.

And if he did ever see it, if he ever caught a glimpse of this passing soul, it was because she let him: she let him see the world was full of hurt things. The world was made up of these shifting beings, of glancing pain between them as they moved—these solitary worlds that inhabited the total, the millions of small worlds that made up the host. That was where the pain came from, he thought, it came from the friction between worlds, the brushing past, the shiver of contact—the touch of feeling and unfeeling. The pain and grace of the temporary.

She showed him and he got to see, but by then it was already too late. By then his own world had become very small, and in his own world only the one hurt thing mattered.

He had forgotten all the rest. He never even saw them.

Small, my girl, oh small, small, small. You see? The world shrinks around us: we give it all up for you. We close our eyes to it, we shutter them, we give it away though it is not ours to give.

For you we give up the world.

THE
DANCER
UPSTAIRS

By Nicholas Shakespeare

THE VISION OF ELENA SILVES

THE DANCER UPSTAIRS

Nicholas Shakespeare

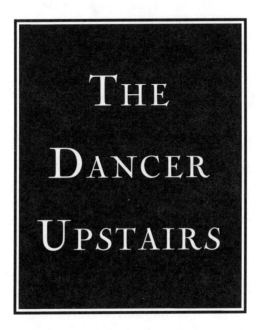

The Dancer Upstairs

Nan A. Talese

DOUBLEDAY

New York   London

Toronto   Sydney   Auckland

PUBLISHED BY NAN A. TALESE
an imprint of Doubleday
a division of Bantam Doubleday Dell
Publishing Group, Inc.
1540 Broadway, New York,
New York 10036

DOUBLEDAY is a trademark of Doubleday,
a division of Bantam Doubleday Dell
Publishing Group, Inc.

All of the characters in this book are
fictitious, and any resemblance to actual
persons, living or dead, is purely
coincidental.

First published in the U.K. by The Harvill
Press, London.

The words of "I'll Remember April" are
reproduced by kind permission of MCA
Music Ltd.

Library of Congress Cataloging-in-
Publication Data
Shakespeare, Nicholas, 1957–
The dancer upstairs / Nicholas
Shakespeare. — 1st ed. in the U.S.A.
p.   cm.
Sequel to: The vision of Elena Silves.
1. Revolutionaries—South America—
Fiction.   2. Guerrillas—South America—
Fiction.   I. Title.
PR6069.H286D36   1997
823′.914—dc20   96-15219
                                    CIP
ISBN 0-385-48513-1

Printed in the United States of America
January 1997

1   3   5   7   9   10   8   6   4   2

First Edition in the United States of
America

For Ruth Shakespeare and Donna Tartt

This novel may be read on its own or as a sequel to *The Vision of Elena Silves*. Like that book, it is a work of fiction. Although it is inspired by the capture of Abimael Guzmán in September 1992, none of the characters are based on anyone involved in that operation, or drawn from anyone in life.

I am indebted to many people for their help and generosity, including Patricia Awapara, Sally Bowen, Toby Buchan, Richard Clutterbuck, Frederick Cooper, David and Jane Cornwall, Iva Fereira, Celso Garrido-Lecca, Nigel Horne, Adam Low, Christopher McLehose, Juan Ossio, Christina Parker, Roger Scruton, Angela Serota, Mary Siepmann, Vera Stastny, Cecilia Valenzuela, Antonio Ketín Vidal and Alice Welsh.

"I have always thought that if we began for one minute to say what we thought, society would collapse."

—ALBERT CAMUS, quoting Sainte-Beuve

THE

DANCER

UPSTAIRS

Night was swallowing the square. The cobbles glistened with river mist and it was impossible to see more than a few steps ahead. Strange screams—he couldn't tell if they were human—penetrated the fog, and from the old fortress at the end of the quay came the thump of a samba rhythm.

Dyer remembered the restaurant being on the waterfront, at the corner of the square. He knew that he was close, for he could hear the river slapping against the steps. Then the wind picked up and through the parting mist he recognized the sign swaying beneath a wrought-iron balcony above him: CANTINA DA LUA. Light streamed down from the dining room on the first floor and one of the shutters crashed against the tiles.

Later, when he thought of those evenings and his walks across the square, there would come back to him nights which smelled of mango rinds and woodsmoke and charred fish. But mostly he remembered that wind, leaping in warm gusts over the waterfront, rattling branches on the rooftops, banging the shutter.

A waiter squeezed onto the balcony, secured the shutter with a loop of wire and stepped back inside. That was when Dyer saw the man for the first time, an outline defined by the overhead bulb. Dyer was struck by the stillness with which he held himself. How could he not have been distracted by the shutter's banging? But the man stared at the river pouring into the night as if nothing else existed.

Dyer passed beneath the balcony, through a doorway and up a stone staircase. At the head of the stairs a bead curtain stood guard over the entrance to a whitewashed room; burgundy-colored table-cloths, bentwood chairs, an old-fashioned till on a bar. Each table had a tiny vase and a flower. The restaurant was empty save for the waiter and the man at the window.

Straight-backed and attentive, wearing a navy blue polo shirt, he was talking to the waiter in Spanish. A book lay open on the table.

Dyer heard the waiter say, "How is the señora today?"

"She's better. Thank you." In that moment he looked up, took in Dyer, and then his eyes dropped back to the book.

Dyer saw a man a year or two older than himself: early forties, middle height, short black hair, clean-shaven. And, in that brief glance, eyes whose intelligence had been tempered by extremes of suffering seen and suffering borne.

Dyer could not have said from where, but he recognized him.

When the ultimatum came, Dyer was on the point of leaving for Ecuador to cover the flare-up on the border.

> I do wish we had the chance to talk this through. It's much easier across a desk than across the Atlantic. Long story short, the cutbacks we've got to make are so draconian that I can't see us maintaining the Rio bureau. I gave it my best shot with the proprietor. He said he didn't know why I bothered. The accountants want him to shut down three offices—and yours is first on his list, John. If there's another Falklands, we can always fly you out.

Everyone agreed, Dyer was the doyen of Latin American correspondents. No one more richly deserved another big challenge, etc., which was why the editor could make the following proposal:

> You can have either Moscow or the Middle East.

The only other question he needed to address was the date of his return.

The receipt of this rapid, handwritten note from his editor did not keep Dyer from flying north, but in the jungle it pressed on him. He spent four days and nights with units of the Ecuadorian army. Once, wading across a stream, he was fired on by a man leaning out of a helicopter. Throughout these days he felt a weight on his heart and behind his eyes, like mountain sickness. He could muster not one iota of enthusiasm for Moscow or the Middle East. This was the region which had formed and blooded him. Anywhere else he would be out of his depth.

He returned to Rio and the office on Joaquim Nabuco, from where he sent nine hundred words describing the dispute. Twenty minutes later the telephone rang. The foreign desk, no doubt, to suggest cuts. Anxious about his fate—the imminent parting from friends, from his wife's family, from his whole geography—he had overwritten.

The voice belonged to his editor, booming into a car phone. "If you won't get in touch, John, I'll have to give it to you straight. The accountants have decreed: Shut Latin America. Full stop. So which is it to be: Moscow or Jerusalem?"

Dyer walked to the window. He held the receiver an inch from his ear to distinguish the voice from the catarrhal crackle. "That's it?"

He stared down the street toward Ipanema beach. A paper kite had caught in telegraph wires and a white-skinned boy looked up at it.

"Believe me, this is the last thing I want," said the editor, overly sympathetic now. "But I speak after another bruising meeting with the proprietor. It's down to this price war. We haven't any money. If you were in my seat, what would you do?"

Dyer kept his eyes on the kite. "We're talking about fifteen years."

"Look, I know how good you are," said the voice across the sea, probably on its way to its club. "But our C2 readers aren't switched on to your neck of the woods."

"Twenty-one countries?"

"I can't hear what you're saying. Are you there? John? John?"

Dyer last heard a long, bracing obscenity and the line went dead.

He put down the receiver and leaned against the desk, waiting.

On the wall hung a watercolor he had painted of Astrud. His eyes fastened on her face while he toyed with the alternatives. The BBC had last month replaced their bureau chief in Buenos Aires. *Le Monde* needed him, God knows, but would probably not appoint an Englishman. The *New York Times*? A long shot, and the present incumbent was a friend.

The telephone rang.

Astrud smiled at him from beneath a green beach umbrella.

"There you are. These things are hopeless for abroad. I was about to say, can we look for you at the end of April?"

"I really can't. There's a book I'm supposed to be writing. I do have to finish it before I leave."

"How long do you need?"

"To assemble the bits—four, five weeks."

"Fine. Then next month is holiday. In June I want to see you here."

"All right," Dyer said rapturelessly.

"I give you this time-off on one condition. You write me a major piece. We can run it Saturday and Sunday. Allow yourself twelve thousand words, but give Nigel plenty of warning about pics. You have the background taped. There must be a story you really want to do? Something we can syndicate?"

Always Dyer had cherished the idea that if ever the time came to leave this continent, he would go out on one wonderful note. His book was to be an introduction to the cultural and social history of the Amazon Basin. But he thought of it as a task he had to complete. It was not a grace note on which to end his South American career.

On the other hand, the editor's valedictory commission did at least give Dyer the freedom to pull off an interview which every journalist down here would be envious to see in print, and which would be the logical climax of the story he had been tracking for a decade.

"There is something I'd like to write," he said. "Do you remember the terrorist Ezequiel?"

"The chappie in the cage?"

Ezequiel was a revolutionary leader who had been caught after a twelve-year hunt. His guerrilla war against the institutions of his Andean country had resulted in thirty thousand deaths and countless tortures and mutilations. Ezequiel's public humiliation—he was indeed shown to the international press from inside a cage—had captured headlines across the world a year before.

"You can get him?" It showed the editor's lack of awareness that he could ask such a question.

"It's not Ezequiel. No one's allowed to see him." After being paraded through the streets under military escort, Ezequiel had been kept underground in a lightless cell. He had not spoken a word to the press.

"It's the person who put Ezequiel in the cage."

"What's he called?"

"Tristan Calderón."

"And who is he?"

"On the face of it, a humble Intelligence captain. In fact, he's the President's right-hand man. He runs the country."

"Has he been interviewed ever?"

"Never."

"What makes you sure you can crack it?"

"I have a good contact."

The contact was truly a good one. Calderón was infatuated with Vivien Vallejo, an Englishwoman who had given up her career as a prima ballerina with the Royal Ballet to marry a South American diplomat. Calderón called her the whole time and sent presents, much to the annoyance of her husband. Vivien was Dyer's aunt.

"Why haven't you suggested it before?"

"I have. Twice." The foreign desk, under pressure to reduce expenses, had judged it too obscure.

While it was nowhere in his nature to shelve a story which excited him, he was aware of his aunt's hostility to the press: gossip-column pieces, photographs of Vivien on the arm of someone not Hugo, had jeopardized her marriage more than once. For this reason Dyer had not wished to enlist her support until he could be one hundred percent sure of an appropriate space in the paper.

"That's it, then," said the editor, sounding pleased. "You get me the Calderón interview and you have a month off. Nothing would make me happier than for you to come out with all guns blazing."

Dyer looked down the beach to where he had painted Astrud. The kite was still there, but the boy had gone.

When, two days later, he saw the gray-tiled turret above the jacaranda, he felt he was coming home.

The garden walls of Vivien's house on the seafront had grown since the summers he had lived here as a child. Topped with broken brown glass and electrified wire, they surrounded a building conceived in imitation of a Gascon manoir. The effect was wide of the mark it aimed at. The house resembled nothing so much as a subtropical folly, crammed, because of Hugo's profession, with objects of little beauty but plenty of nostalgia.

It was to this address on the Malecón that Dyer had sent his fax. He was coming to stay, he informed Vivien. He hoped this wouldn't be an inconvenience, but he found himself in desperate straits. He begged for her help in fixing an interview with Calderón—on or off the record. He had signed the faxed letter, perfectly honestly, with his love. Vivien, his top card, happened also to be the person he most wanted to say goodbye to before he was made to depart South America.

Until the last, when the taxi turned into her street, he had forgotten how much he missed his aunt. He had first driven up this road as a six-year-old, after his mother died. In that doorway had stood a small, vivacious woman. By the way she held herself, he had thought she waited to greet him, but she was saying goodbye to a neat bald man who soon excused himself. Catching sight of the boy, she had run out, flung open the car door, plucked him into the sunlight. Her understanding hands caressed his face, looking for her sister. Then she hugged him to her neck and laughed.

The sound of Vivien's throaty laugh was among his earliest memories. Her bold blue eyes would bewitch anyone they looked on. Unlike most charmers, she had known suffering of her own, so that those same eyes also shone with the pale brightness of someone who has peeked over the rim. As a young girl, she had been wasted by a rheumatic fever which no doctor, and certainly no one in her family, expected her to survive. Recovering, she had taken up ballet in order to develop her weakened muscles. "No miracle, my dear, I just decided one day that every hour was a gift and I liked being alive." It was not long before she had become famous as a classical dancer—and for renouncing everything the moment it came within her grasp.

She had been in her tenth season with London's Royal Ballet when she met Hugo Vallejo after a performance of *Giselle* in Lisbon. Hugo, at that time an attaché at his country's embassy, told her: Did she know? It was incredible, but in shape and color the birthmark on her right cheek matched exactly the drop of tea he had splashed that afternoon onto a tablecloth at his ambassador's residence.

"It was the corniest shit, and I told him so." That night they dined at Tavares. A month later she exchanged Covent Garden for South America.

Her body had thickened since Dyer had lived with them. In those days she attracted to the house a corps of dedicated admirers. Gossip accused her of reserving her most accomplished steps for the dance she led her husband. "I married Hugo," she told Dyer in one of those phrases of hers he never forgot, "because he didn't put his hand on my knee after dinner and say, 'What do you want to do now?' He put it here, on my hip, where it mattered." And if she had disengaged those fingers once or twice to indulge a passionate life behind Hugo's back, their marriage had still endured. Now approaching seventy, she remained devoted, balanced and worldly; and, despite her accent, modulated like that of a 1950s radio announcer, very un-English.

Neither the excitement he felt in Vivien's presence nor the fact she was his aunt did anything to conceal from Dyer her essential toughness. She was an effective figure in her adopted country and skilled at getting things done, something she ascribed to her Covent Garden training. "All ballet dancers are made of iron, my dear. If you work nine hours a day, your life is regimented, orderly and extremely strict. You can't have an ounce of woolliness." And it was true. When Vivien said, albeit with perfect grace, "This is what I want," people by God jumped.

Greatly loved, she was also well aware, not least through friends like Calderón, of the political processes of the country. Too wise to take sides, although her opinion and her company were deliberately courted, she acted as a sort of "ambassador without portfolio"—and at one stage was invited to be special envoy to UNESCO. She declined, offering as an excuse her worry that she might lose her British passport. Besides, diplomacy was Hugo's bag.

For Hugo she might have given up dancing, but she did not sever links with the world of ballet. As Principal of the Metropolitan, she had kept her name prominent—if not sanctified—in that milieu. Of late, though, she was more associated in the public mind with the Vallejo Orphanage.

The story was famous, how Vivien, driving through the outskirts of the capital, spotted some children playing beneath a water tower. She assumed the creature they were teasing as it thrashed on the ground was an animal. Then, through the circle of legs, she saw a boy. Telling Hugo to stop the car, she had pummeled her way past the children. Their victim was no older than five or six. His mouth was locked open in a spasm and his moans bubbled through saliva trails flecked with sand. One of the boy's tormentors lifted a foot and wiggled his toes between the caked lips.

Vivien had pushed him aside, gathered the boy in her arms and made Hugo drive to the hospital in Miraflores, where she had agreed to meet the medical expenses.

The boy spoke almost no Spanish, but phrase by incomplete phrase she had pieced together his history. He came from near Sierra de Pruna. His father had been executed by Ezequiel. His mother had fled. He had contracted meningitis. Such handicaps are a stigma in the highlands. His mother set out for the capital, and when she got there, she abandoned her son by the roadside.

"It changed my life. It would have changed anybody's life. What else could I have done? Left him there? Just be thankful you didn't find him, my dear."

In the weeks ahead Vivien learned of other cases. Two sisters from Lepe, alone in the city, their parents victims of the military. A girl, her family destroyed by a car bomb. A two-year-old, his mother seized by three men disguised as policemen.

"For every child I found, another two popped up—dazed, hungry, sick. My heart wrinkled to see them, but we simply didn't have room."

She began to call in favors.

Vivien's international status as a dancer had always endowed her with a snobbish appeal for a certain kind of powerful person. Now she sought their patronage. She cajoled and bullied friends for donations, rented a house in San Isidro and, before quite realizing it, had set up an institution for the orphans of the violence. Within eight weeks she found herself responsible for sixty children. Dyer would hear them during rehearsals at the Metropolitan, hiding under the seats, hitting each other, bawling. Once the music started, they shut up.

Among the influential people whom Vivien had badgered was the sometime lawyer Tristan Calderón. He was now a director of the orphanage.

On a silver tray in the hallway, under an authentic, moss-colored ballet slipper, an envelope waited for Dyer. The letter was on stiff cream paper. Vivien had flown the coop.

J—Paths have crossed/Must fly to Brazil, organizing charity gala at the Pará opera house/Can't wriggle out since it was *my* idea in first place/Meanwhile you're here/*Too* maddening.

Got your message/But Darling, I *can't*/For one thing, T's not doing *any* interviews/As you are *perfectly* well aware/For another, how can you possibly expect me to help after what happened last time with the President/What you wrote was most unkind/It was unworthy of you.

I feel badly about your job/But I'm an Old Lady and suddenly I cannot face one more of my friends saying to me: "Your Bloody Nephew, I only agreed to see him for *your* sake—and now he's revealed this Appalling Secret/ Did he think we lived so far away we'd never find out?/etc. etc."

You know I love you, Johnny/It's your profession I

can't stand/Do remember: Hugo and I have to live here/So while part of me is on your side and hopes you get your story, this time you are going to have to do it all on your own/Sorry.

Your birthday card was sweet/Tell your father Thank You for the lovely umbrella/By the way, could you take this ballet slipper back when you leave/The shop's somewhere behind Copacabana/I've taped the address inside/Ask Hugo—he knows/It's so bloody frustrating/I keep writing to them to say it's *this* kind of leather I like and they send me some other kind/I want them actually to see the shoe/ And, Darling, do make sure it's the Emerald—not the Forest.

Make yourself at home etc./Hugo is looking forward to your visit/You'll find him much better.

Love—V.

PS It is your home, whenever you need it/Do come back soon/Don't wait until there's another war.

PPS There is no such thing as off the record/As you jolly well know.

Dyer reacted with panic. When you sit in an office a thousand miles away, it is easy to make rash promises. Vivien's advocacy had been crucial to his getting the interview. Without her, he couldn't hope to track down Calderón.

He tried the obvious sources. There was a Deputy to whom Vivien had introduced him two years ago. He left three messages on an answering machine. Either the man was away—or had no desire to renew acquaintance.

Nor did the local press, commonly a rich seam of unexplored leads, prove useful. His buddies on Caretas and La República were happy to see him, but as soon as he mentioned Calderón's name, they became guarded in a way they had never been about Ezequiel. Not even in the days when his organization was killing them.

Dyer resorted to the official channels, but the people he had known at the Palace had been replaced. Captain Calderón was a functionary of average rank, nothing more; and it was not government policy to grant interviews to the media.

—————

On the second evening, he took Hugo out to dinner at the Costa Verde.

"How's that pretty girlfriend of yours?" This was the first time he had seen his nephew on his own.

"She's been gone for ages," said Dyer.

Hugo, humbled, shook his head. "I shouldn't ask so many questions."

His uncle had been with him in the Rio clinic when Astrud died. Vivien was touring Argentina with her dance company. Hugo flew over after things took a turn for the worse. Astrud had gone into labor prematurely. Dyer and Hugo sat outside the operating theater. Winter sunlight spreading lozenge shapes on the lino; down the corridor a man selling magazines; the doctor taking off his glasses to wipe the bridge of his nose.

The amniotic fluid had entered her bloodstream. She died giving birth to a stillborn girl.

Hugo took control. He dealt with the hospital, the burial, the foreign desk in London. He spoke with Astrud's parents in São Paulo and her grandmother in Petrópolis. Then he brought Dyer home to Miraflores.

That was eleven years ago. Since when, Hugo and Vivien always welcomed him with an unwavering warmth. "This is your home, Johnny." He must invite anyone he wanted to. So the house on the Malecón became the place where Dyer brought his new girlfriends.

"I'll get Mona over tomorrow night." Hugo mentioned the name of a dull cousin, recently divorced.

"I'm here to work," said Dyer.

Hugo nodded. He didn't ask about the nature of this work, nor did Dyer tell him. He had no wish to involve his uncle in his quest for Calderón. Hugo had not been well of late, and in any case had always preferred to turn a blind eye to Vivien's adventures.

While they ate, Hugo discoursed about Vivien's orphanage, to which Dyer supposed she would be donating the proceeds of the Pará gala. He ran through the membership of the Jockey Club, where he was now Secretary; and when conversation petered out over coffee, he turned to the subject of genetically modified vegetables, in which, since his stroke, he had developed an interest. About the civil war which had disemboweled his country, he said not a word.

"What are things like here now?" Dyer inquired at last.

"There's an uneasy peace," said Hugo cagily. "It's real because it's happening, but maybe something more is going to happen."

"You were brave to go on living here. Why in heaven's name didn't you leave?"

"It's not me. It's Vivien," said Hugo, and not for the first time Dyer was conscious that few conversations he conducted with Vivien's husband ever hit the nub of the matter.

"When is she coming back?"

Hugo had been adroit so far in steering away from this subject, and he remained vague. "I was expecting her home by the weekend. Or maybe she'll stay in Pará some more."

"I forgot Pará had an opera house."

Hugo raised what had once been an eyebrow. The stroke had removed both brows and given to his features, already bald, an unprotected air. "Pavlova danced there."

By Sunday there was still no sign of Vivien. "She's bound to be back tonight," said Hugo, who had spent all day at the racetrack. But she did not reappear.

Nor did she turn up on Monday.

On Wednesday morning Dyer joined Hugo for breakfast in the conservatory. Before going to bed, he had been rereading Vivien's letter.

"Hugo, what is it with this slipper?"

"Is that the shoemaker in Rio? She swears by his shoes. I discovered him by chance when I was staying with you that time."

Hugo accepted the letter from Dyer and studied it. His face was normally difficult to read, but not on this occasion. "If you ask me—and this is just a hunch—it's Vivien's way of saying she's not going to come back until she is sure you're gone."

"Why would she behave like that?"

Dyer sensed his uncle's reluctance to hurt him. "I didn't want to tell you," said Hugo. "But perhaps it's not such a bad thing, you know." The truth was, his last article had made Dyer persona non grata in one or two circles. "It frightened Vivien quite a lot. I've also had my share of barbed remarks at the club."

"About what?"

"Something you wrote upset Calderón. From what I understand, he intimated to Vivien that there might come a time when she is going to have to stop talking to you. He finds it disconcerting to have people around who are so well informed."

"I was hoping to get an interview with him."

"Well, exactly, but you can put that out of your mind. You're a good journalist, Johnny, and that's what makes you dangerous. For some people in our society, the whole practice of journalism menaces their peace of mind. Half the dinner parties Vivien goes to, she's terribly proud to be your aunt. The other half, she keeps very, very quiet about it."

There followed two fraught days. Dyer, his options running out, spent his time in the library of the Catholic University, using the opportunity to read early explorers' accounts of the Amazon. By Thursday it was obvious that Vivien was going to stay on in Brazil. Hugo spent conspicuously more time at the Jockey Club, but continued to behave with unflagging hospitality on the few occasions they met.

Unwilling to be more of a headache to him, Dyer announced his intention to go upriver. There was research on the Ashaninkas he needed for his book. Not to alert Vivien, he told Hugo he would be spending a few days among an Indian tribe near Satipo. But he had decided to smoke out his aunt in Pará.

The Pará opera house is a coral-pink building across the Praça da República from the Hotel Madrid. On the morning of his arrival Dyer walked down an avenue bright with mango trees to an entrance swathed in scaffolding.

The young woman in the administration office confessed herself perplexed. She had, of course, heard of Senhora Vallejo, but did not believe the Metropolitan was dancing in Pará. Besides, no performance would be possible until the municipality had completed the work of restoration. She suggested Dyer try the Teatro Amazonas in Manaus.

He telephoned Manaus and drew another blank. Six hundred miles upriver and no Vivien, no ballet. He contacted theaters in Santarém and Macapá. By midafternoon he knew he was wasting his time. The ballet story was a ruse. His aunt had left home because she knew he was coming.

He walked down to the river, then back through the bird market to his hotel. The air was humid, sweetened overripely with mangoes; beads of sweat tickled his neck and he wanted a shower. Afterward he lay down on a hard bed under the window, unable to sleep. He squeezed a hand over his eyes, but with each mango-laden breath the sensation increased. It was four in the afternoon in a place where he didn't want to be, and he was furious.

He was stuck. He saw that now. He had bought a fixed-date ticket; the return flight another week away. He was loath to give up the chase on Calderón. He thought it yet possible to snare his aunt with a last-ditch appeal. But what could he do in the meantime? It was pointless to fly back to keep Hugo company. The most sensible course would be to take a leaf from Vivien's book. Lie low for a few days, then surprise her.

Next morning he moved into a hotel close to the British-built port; a plaster-fronted building with white shutters and a veranda perched over the immense river. This was the old quarter, built during the rubber boom. Once prosperous, it had grown decrepit. Many of the houses were boarded up, with trees bursting out of the roofs. Others, like the building opposite, stood no deeper than their façade. To Dyer, the emptiness behind the preserved frontage mimicked one of Vivien's stage sets. Standing on his veranda, he could see the cloudless sky beyond the windows, the slanting drift of vultures between the architraves and, every now and then, the agitated flight of a black and yellow bird, the bem-te-vi.

Bem-te-vi, bem-te-vi—"I've seen you, I've seen you."

Frustrated, lethargic, crushed by the heat, Dyer could not hear that call without thinking of the slave hunters who trained the bird to hunt down fugitives. Catching sight of those yellow wings hovering in the sickly sweet air, he wanted to shout out, "Go and find her, you stupid bird."

Bem-te-vi, bem-te-vi.

He tried to be calm about his fate. He had been given free run of the world he cared about, the fount of his stories, and he had failed to deliver. If he telephoned Hugo, that would blow the whistle on Vivien. If he telephoned his editor, he ran the risk of having to return to London immediately. What could he find to do in Pará—except what he ought to be doing anyway?

The proposal of a book on the Amazon Basin had interested him when originally he was approached by a London publishing house. He had long been fascinated by the area and had no doubt that he was qualified to write an introduction—although, in the absence of any reminders, it did cross his mind that his publishers might have gone the way of his newspaper. Vivien's vanishing act gave him an excuse. He had the notes he had made in the Catholic University library, and had had the foresight to bring with him several learned works. And hadn't this wild-goose chase landed him by sheer chance in a seaport which he needed to write about? Rather than cooling his heels for a week, he would spend the time sketching out captions for as yet imaginary photos, studying texts, gathering information.

No sooner had he switched hotels than he began to enjoy Pará more. Due to its position on the equator, it was a place which lived obstinately in its own time. Pará time never altered. And then there were the hours kept by the rest of the world.

He liked the fact that the sun rose and set at the same time each day. He liked the unforgettable smells of the port, and the torpor of the riverside, which met a commensurate emotion in him. Something having snapped in his bond to the newspaper, he suddenly looked forward to this time on his hands, time to reflect on the future, time to lay to rest one or two hungry ghosts, time to plot his book. There was nothing and no one to distract him, he remembered thinking, as he walked toward a restaurant he had marked out earlier in the day.

Only Euclides da Cunha, whose *Rebellion in the Backlands* he was thankful he had brought with him.

2

Dyer sat down at a table and at once began reading. He had read a chapter by the time the man at the window called for the bill. Dyer smiled, trying to remember where they could have met. The man responded with the unfavoring half-smile people reserve for helpful shopkeepers. Dyer looked away.

The pattern repeated itself the following night. The two diners sat together in that room for no longer than twenty minutes before, punctual as the last ferry, the man called for his bill. They read and ate their meals in silence. It must have confounded the waiter to watch his only clients sitting like that, not exchanging a word.

Dyer would have taken the man for a fellow stranger to Pará had not the waiter treated him so respectfully. Emilio hurried for no one, yet when signaled by the man at table 17, he stopped whatever he was doing and directed himself between the straw-seated chairs, clasping his black folder as though it contained not a bill for a grilled fish but the freedom of the city. A moment later, walking like someone out of uniform, his other customer brushed past Dyer's table.

But Emilio could not satisfy Dyer's curiosity. The courtesy with which he brought and removed plates concealed a splendid disdain. Emilio, if Dyer was reading, was not above lifting both book and plate and dusting away the crumbs, all the while smiling apologetically, as though he were somehow to blame for their presence on the table. His manner seemed determined by the assumption that Dyer would leave no tip. Emilio would call at his back as he left, "Good evening, senhor," as if he didn't mean it. These words, spoken in correct Portuguese but with the trace of a Spanish accent, were the only three he addressed to Dyer. When asked about the person at the window, he shrugged.

Not until the third night did the man pause at Dyer's table.

Dyer was so engrossed in *Rebellion in the Backlands* that several seconds passed before he became aware of someone looking over his shoulder.

The man held out his own cloth-bound volume. They were reading the same book.

"I don't believe it. Extraordinary!" Dyer got to his feet. The coincidence was not so extraordinary, at least not in Brazil. But in that scarcely patronized restaurant it was strange indeed.

Dyer gestured at the chair opposite. The man checked his watch.

"I cannot stay long," he said, in Spanish. He drew the chair to him and sat on the edge of the seat, facing away. "I am expected at home."

Dyer sought Emilio, but observant as ever, he was already advancing.

"Beer?"

"A coffee, I'd prefer."

The man placed his book, the Spanish edition, on the table. "If only the author could see!"

Dyer said, "You know how people go on about a book, then you are disappointed. But it's as good as I hoped."

"I've come to reading late." His face had a preoccupied look. "My father had a library, but I never made use of it. At last I have time."

"Then we're in the same boat."

The eyes which inspected Dyer were brown and steady. He was neither good-looking nor ugly, and while he would not have turned a young girl's head, someone older might have been struck by his face and the evidence of a passion which had left its traces.

"Don't you think that each time a good book is written it's a triumph for everyone?" said the man. "The same each time someone is cured of a disease or a criminal is caught. It's one more tiny victory against the darkness." It was touching, this faith in books. He'd only just discovered them and now he had discovered them terribly.

"But da Cunha and his kind," said Dyer, "aren't they practitioners of a dying art? The public want to watch videos. They don't want to read *Rebellion in the Backlands.*"

He chose not to answer. "You're not Brazilian?"

"I'm English."

"You are here on business?"

Dyer found it sensible all over South America to avoid telling people he was a journalist. "I'm finishing a book."

"About Pará?" He gazed steadily at Dyer.

"I mean to concentrate more on the Indians."

The man sighed. "When we go to Europe, we're looking for civilization. Yet when you come here, you are seeking for the primitive."

Dyer said awkwardly, "And you, what do you do?"

Nothing in the eyes hinted at what the man was thinking. His gaze rested on the books which had brought them together.

"I used to be a policeman."

"Used to be? At your age? You mean you've retired?"

"Not exactly. But I am required to do less and less."

Family matters had brought him to Pará. He was spending some time with his sister, who was ill, taking turns with her Brazilian husband to sit by her bed. .

"You don't come from Brazil either?"

"No," and he picked up Dyer's book, keeping the place with a finger. "Tell me, where have you got to?"

Dyer had been reading an ode celebrating the death of a soldier who, kneeling beside his commander's dead body, fought on until the ammunition ran out. On the day after the battle, the leading Rio newspaper had devoted the lion's share of their front page to this poem. Dyer had been musing over the likelihood of the foreign subs in Canary Wharf being able to coax iambic pentameters to bed.

"I'm a little further on than you." He looked at Dyer over the book. "May I see—to test my English?"

"Please do."

He peered at the type. "You write in the margin." Then, twisting the book, "But I can't read your hand."

"It's a habit," said Dyer.

"I share it. I went through my law books the other day. All those illegible scribbles. Like a different person."

In that second the man's face relaxed and Dyer remembered who he was.

He was aware of palpitations in his chest. His breaths came fast. He watched the bubbles rising in his beer, calculating his next move.

"The most wanted man in the world." Headlines had debased the phrase, but for twelve years it might have applied to the philosophy professor, Edgardo Vilas—or, as he became known, President Ezequiel. Sitting less than three feet away, so near that Dyer could, if he wanted, touch his sleeve, was the man who had captured the Chairman of the World Revolution.

No one knew the story. The policeman had been forbidden to speak. He had defied his orders; had not immediately handed Ezequiel over to Calderón, who would certainly have executed him. Everyone had expected the revolutionary to be shot, to fight his way out, to take his own life. Only this man could say how Ezequiel had been arrested without a struggle.

His name was Agustín Rejas. For years he had worked undercover to capture the Public Enemy Number One. For years he had been an unknown police colonel. Then, suddenly, his name was on the lips of a whole population. Within a few days he was being touted as a presidential candidate. The following week he had vanished. Which is how things were in his country.

All Dyer knew of Colonel Rejas was that he was forty-four, that he came from a village north of Cajamarca. For twenty years he had served as a policeman and for twelve of those years he had been responsible for one case. It was about this case that Dyer had been trying, a week earlier, to contact him, though not with any expectation of success. His pretext had been to gather background material for the Calderón profile. Had he had the spectacular good fortune to meet Rejas, he would have wanted to discuss a great many other things as well. But this was a man nobody met. People said he was out of the country. He was unfindable.

"Apparently he's in a witness protection program," Dyer had been told by the BBC stringer. She was the most reliable of the local foreign correspondents. "Although I have also heard that he's abroad, talking to the Americans."

They were drinking chocolate in the Café Haiti. Dyer told her of the call from the editor.

"Maybe the fellow up there's telling you something." She blew her nose. "Maybe it is time to get out."

Lonely, in need of a companion, he would have asked her out to dinner, but she was taking her younger lover to a Brahms concert in the Teatro Americano. A year ago, with Ezequiel still at large, such an event would have been unthinkable.

"Has Calderón come to terms with Rejas?" Dyer had asked.

"I doubt it. I'm sure Calderón wanted to snuff out Ezequiel there and then. My contact in the Palace says that when he saw Rejas presenting Ezequiel to journalists, Calderón was so enraged that he put a whisky decanter through the television screen."

One year before, from a friend at Canal 7, Dyer had borrowed a videotape of Rejas reading aloud his prepared statement. On the tape, the policeman stood outside the Anti-Terrorist Headquarters in Vía Expreso. He held himself erect, hardly moving. The speech was impressive for its modesty. Thanks to the hard work, patience and discipline of his men during twelve years, the man styling himself President Ezequiel had been taken into custody at eight-forty the night before. Rejas said that he had not completed the process of interrogation. He concluded by speaking of his hope for the country; his belief in the institutions of justice and democracy. He would donate any reward to charities for children orphaned by the violence.

The camera had been jostled frequently. For a second it had focused on Rejas as he read, his chin caught in the same position as Dyer would see it in the restaurant. And here was the extraordinary thing: he betrayed not a trace of exultation.

Two days later a curt bulletin from the Palace announced that Ezequiel had been removed from Colonel Rejas's charge.

"There's a widespread feeling that Rejas has been treated extremely shabbily," said Dyer's BBC contact.

"So he's not given his version of events?"

"Apparently not. After they robbed him of his spoil, there was a quiet promotion. He serves as Quartermaster of the National Police, a post having no executive responsibility whatever. And it means that Calderón can keep tabs on Rejas. I can't tell you how much this sudden popularity unnerved the Palace." She took Dyer's *Spectator* and slipped it into her basket. "But Calderón must have some hold over him—or else why hasn't Rejas spoken out? Everyone would have listened. The people here worship him."

"Are the rumors true?"

"That he will run for President? All I know, there's a group of Deputies, quite influential. They've been to see him."

She gave the names. An impressive list.

"What chance he'll accept the nomination?"

"The people badly want someone of his caliber, a truly heroic person who is also a modest man. But who knows? Since the blaze of publicity, he's disappeared off the scene."

When Dyer's plan to interview Calderón was scuppered by Vivien's defection, he did not want to think about such characters again. Now, in a seaport on the Amazon, fate had thrown him a bigger prize, a man who could help incidentally over Calderón, but who knew more about Ezequiel's organization than anyone alive.

Dyer knew he had to suppress his excitement. He had this astonishing and wonderful catch. He must not scare him off. If he tried for too much, he might wreck everything—but there was no time for an elegant, oblique approach.

Rejas was still reading when Dyer said, "So, a policeman. Did you have anything to do with that terrorist who was captured?"

Rejas raised his eyes from the book. "Which terrorist?"

"The President Ezequiel."

Rejas threw back his head and laughed. The laugh was not unpleasant or cruel. An outsider might have taken it for an amused laugh, one that said, How could you imagine such a thing? But to

Dyer, the laughter contained the sound of hatches being closed, of shutters going up, of a man protecting himself. It declared that Rejas wouldn't tell Dyer a thing, that if he made an attempt to pry, he would be steered from the subject and the policeman would leave the restaurant, and once the beads had settled behind him, he would not be returning to that table by the window and Dyer would never see him again.

"It's another interesting coincidence," said Dyer, "but I believe my aunt is a good friend of an associate of yours."

Rejas lowered the book. "An associate?"

"Tristan Calderón."

Too late he saw that he had alerted Rejas, had shown him that he knew who he was.

Rejas replaced the book behind the paper tulip.

"Who is your aunt?"

"Actually, I believe she's quite well known in your country. Vivien Vallejo."

"The dancer?"

"That's right."

"The ballerina"—as if he wanted to be certain—"who runs the Metropolitan?"

"Yes."

Dyer watched him roll the thought in his head, approving it. "Do you have an interest in the ballet?"

"My daughter has a picture of your aunt on her wall. A great admirer. And there are others I know . . ." When he spoke again, he was looking not at Dyer but at the river. "Her philanthropy is very much appreciated."

"I would be honored to give your daughter an introduction."

"That's very kind, but . . ." Rejas didn't finish his sentence. A light moved across the black backcloth beyond the window, one of the palm-thatched boats puttering upriver.

"Naturally, if she knew it was your daughter . . ." Dyer said, seizing on the slenderest excuse to keep Rejas at his table. At the same time, why would such a rigorously secret man speak to him? This was not an Ancient Mariner. He was here to get away from his country, not to talk about it.

Rejas did not answer. And there was not a thing more Dyer

could think of to say. Here he sat, helpless, tired, a bit drunk, watching his thoughts flow out through that window with Rejas's gaze, unable to stop them.

At last, turning back into the room, Rejas said, "Did you know that we caught Ezequiel above a ballet studio?"

D id you know that we caught Ezequiel above a ballet studio?"
"No."

Rejas considered this lie.

"Have you seen a man with his head cut off?"

"No."

"Once I saw a man with his head cut off," said Rejas. "The body remembers what it used to do, what it was told to do seconds before, and it just keeps on going, shrugging blood, shuffling forward. It's a little while before it gets the message the boss man isn't there."

"Where was this?"

"A tiny hamlet. Jaci. Way up in the—hills. You wouldn't have heard of it. I was trapped there on the morning Ezequiel's people invaded. I watched the execution through an earth wall, on my stomach. The man was ordered to kneel and come forward on his knees. After the machete struck, he continued several paces as if at the end of a long day's pilgrimage to Fátima. My nights are still haunted by that rippling body. He jerked about on the ground, spraying up dirt, quivering, not dead at all. Then his executioner, a girl about seventeen, picked up his head and swung it like a lantern across his chest, yelling, 'Look, pig! Look!'

"That was the most extraordinary thing. The reaction of the face, I mean. Try to imagine the expression of a man's face staring at his own body. You see, the head goes on working too. For a few seconds he is still capable of registering sight and sound and thought. The eyes blink open, the lips pucker. He can even mouth a sentence or two. Well, almost. The words bubble to the lips, but you can't hear them because the vocal cords have been sliced. When I told our pathologist, he dismissed it. Muscle contraction, he said. But that's not what I saw.

"The man they'd executed was the sacristan: they'd discovered he was my informer. I think of the sacristan's face when I remember the situation in my country after May 1980. Ezequiel, when he declared his revolution, intended to slice off the state's head. He intended to swing us by the hair, force down our eyes, shout in our ears. He wanted us to recognize our past vileness.

"But perhaps you have no idea what I'm talking about."

Rejas leaned back, dug a hand into his jeans and produced a wallet from which he drew a small wrinkled photograph.

"Why I keep this, I don't know." His eyes flickered over the image, his expression neutral. With a forefinger he slid it across the table.

Dyer picked up the photograph, taken head-on in black and white, and held it to the light of the overhead bulb. It showed, patterned by finger marks, a handsome, clean-shaven man in his early thirties with mixed-race features similar to Rejas's own: dark eyebrows, a nose broadening at the base, narrow eyes. The eyes stared at the photographer, but telling nothing. It was a face from which all emotion had been extinguished.

"You know who that is?"

Dyer nodded. How many posters of it had he not seen, with details of a million-dollar reward across the top. It was for ten years the only known photograph of Ezequiel.

"It was taken at twelve-fifteen in the morning, the seventeenth of May, 1980. That is," Rejas said, "on the day he vanished."

Dyer looked at the well-remembered features. The chin raised defiantly. The thick black hair, swept back in iron waves from a high forehead. The unreflecting eyes. The dark scarf around his neck. No one visiting Rejas's country in the past decade could have failed to see this face.

"He's sitting on an empty beer crate."

Dyer looked closer. "Really? How can you be sure?"

"I took the photograph."

I met Ezequiel only twice. The first time I was thirty-one. I was coming to the end of my stint in Sierra de Pruna, a small town north of Villoria. Sylvina hated it, called it the Styx. "I didn't marry you for this," she said. But after the election we would be moving to the capital. I'd been promoted to a unit protecting foreign diplomats. Soon Sylvina would be among friends. Laura would be able to play with their daughters.

This was the first democratic election since the coup. Twelve years ago now. We'd forgotten what to do, although we anticipated trouble. My job was to set up roadblocks outside the villages and check documents. Very tedious work, like sentry duty at the Tomb of the Unknown Soldier: six months of vigilance in case someone blew out the flame! It did fail once, during a gas workers' strike; I had to use our Primus stove. Roadblock duty was like that. After three years in Sierra de Pruna I'd reached a point where I wasn't doing my job well. The routine was wearing me out. Just as much as Sylvina, I looked forward to a new start under a government elected by the people.

Hardly any traffic passed the police post on that morning. Then at eleven-thirty I stopped a red Ford pickup heading toward town. In the front, staring intently at the hot hood where I'd rested my hand, was the man in that photograph; next to him, bolt upright, both hands gripping the wheel, sat a long-nosed mestiza of about twenty. Three Indians were standing in the back, their hair snagged with bark and grass. Probably they had slept outside.

"Documents," I said.

They produced identity cards, all except the man in the passenger seat, who patted his pockets as if his card was there somewhere.

I was about to raise the barrier when my eyes ranged over the pickup and I see, lying in an odd sort of heap, a large jute sack. An animal's tail, the black and white fur clotted with blood, poked from the sack's mouth.

The girl, slender, wearing a loose-fitting skirt, got out of the car. "We ran it over."

She leaned over the back. "It came from nowhere onto the road."

I peeled back the sack to the tail's puckered pink base.

"A dalmation, it looks like," she said.

Who is the owner? Why did you pick it up? What are you going to do with a dead dog? But I didn't ask these questions. I didn't even bother to check the bumper for dents.

"We're going to a funeral." She pushed back her hair and the sun lit up a pulse on her temple. "My uncle—he's being buried this afternoon."

"Where?"

"Pelas." Twenty miles east. "He was a machine operator. All his life he sits on the same chair, then he drops dead." She clicked her long fingers, the sound cracking in the dry air.

I walked around to the passenger window. "Found it?"

The man inside shook his head. It was a scalding day, but he had tucked in at his throat a brown alpaca scarf. He was wearing a red shirt, collar up.

"Got to be somewhere." The girl had followed me. Her face in the side mirror looked anxious. "Come on, you must have it."

"Guess I left it at home," he muttered. He picked a packet of cigarettes off the dashboard, tapped one out, lit it. Behind his ears on his neck he had a skin rash.

"Where do you fit in?" I asked.

"He's family," said the girl.

I asked Sergeant Pisac to cover me and opened the door. "I'll need to take your details."

I typed out the notes in the small office, the man sitting opposite; a basic description to pin to a photograph:

Name: Melquiades Artemio Durán
Sex: male
Age: 34
Race: mestizo
Profession: laborer
Height: 5 feet 8 inches
Build: thin
Eyes: brown
Dental state: 5 fillings in lower jaw
Distinguishing marks: skin rash—possibly eczema

"Where were you born?"
"Galiteo."
"On the Marañón?"
"Yes."
"Then you know La Posta?"
He nodded.
"That's where I come from," I said.
"Really?" He lit another cigarette, a Winston, and blew out two smooth trails of smoke.

That's it. That's all there is. You cannot imagine the number of times I raked over that scene. The whole conversation, according to my notes, lasted seventeen minutes. From what he said it would have been impossible to believe this man was a philosopher who, twelve and half hours later, would initiate a world revolution.

Hindsight is like using powerful binoculars. I should have detained him. I should have waited, sent the woman back for his documents. I should have asked a lot more questions. But next day I was leaving Sierra de Pruna. I was not going to pay over-much attention to mislaid identity papers. And I was sentimental. We came from neighboring valleys, the man in the alpaca scarf and I, and he was going to a funeral.

At five minutes to twelve I escorted Melquiades Durán into the backyard, sat him on a crate and took his photograph using a police-issue Nikon on a tripod.

Probably he moved, because the contours of his chin are blurred. See? He's not well lit either. At the lab they thought the camera might have had a light leak. But that shaft of light is there because the sun was coming up over the roof. I didn't have much experience with a camera. He looks like a figure from a medieval painting, don't you think?

At twelve twenty-four we came back inside the police post, where the woman driver and the three Indian men waited under guard. I handed her the keys.

"Go to your funeral."

They went out. The engine didn't start immediately. The three Indians looked at me with accusing faces. Beneath them the pickup rocked back and forth.

"Wait. Give it a rest," I called. She had flooded the ignition.

She waited, then brushed back a strand of hair and turned the key, eager to be on her way. This time it fired.

I leaned against the barrier, watching the truck pull away. I expected the woman to wave, but she didn't. The man I had photographed stared at me from his side mirror. The pickup turned the corner, the sun flashed on the roof and they faded into a trumpet of dust.

The next time I met Ezequiel I found him alive, on a sofa, in an upstairs room in the capital. He had altered beyond recognition, only his scarf the same. But that was thirty thousand deaths, two thousand car bombs and twelve years later.

I now know that when I stopped him at the roadblock, Ezequiel was driving with his wife and his three bodyguards to a safe house in Sierra de Pruna. If I had dismantled the truck, I would have found explosives stolen from a tungsten mine concealed beneath the seats. I should have realized that there was something odd about a dog being in a sack, about the dog being in the truck at all.

That night Ezequiel would address a group of comrades packed into a storeroom behind Calle Junín. The meeting was tense. To fortify their spirits, he read aloud passages from Mao, Kant, Marx and *The Tempest,* including the line "No tongue! all eyes! be silent." At one minute after midnight, speaking in a low, precise voice, occasionally sipping from a glass of mineral water, he called for the armed struggle to begin. One by one he embraced his audience, kissing each person on both cheeks. He would not see them again until the revolution succeeded. After he walked through that door, he would be going underground, with another identity.

At twenty minutes past midnight, having been told that the road was clear, he left.

For me, though, the story of Ezequiel really begins seven months later, with another dead dog.

I am standing on a bridge in the capital, staring up at a streetlight. It is two o'clock in the morning of the twenty-seventh of December. Suspended in the dark, the orange capsule of the lamp is surrounded by a yellow haze. But there's something wrong. A black weight dangles beneath the bright artificial light. It has torn ears and a wedge-shaped mess across its neck.

I will never find a better allegory of the horror prepared for us.

"Why have they cut his throat?" whispers Sucre.

"So the soul can't escape through the mouth."

In my village, when you died, your dog was hanged from a tree. Dogs, my mother instructed us, were good at crossing rivers in the underworld. But we didn't slit their throats.

"Christ," says Sucre, who is going to be a policeman only until he inherits his father's fruit orchards.

Above me the body twists in the breeze. The animal has been hanged by the tail. His front legs, bound with telegraph wire, stretch down to below his head. As he revolves, he resembles one of the brass reindeers I assembled above our Christmas candles, except he isn't tinkling. A drop splashes my face.

"He's got something in his mouth," says Sucre.

I step back. The jaws have been forced open, something holding them apart in a frozen pant. A placard hangs down from the legs.

Twice I jump up, but the dog is too high. My attempts to pull him down disturb the flies at his eyes. I drive the car onto the curb and stand on the roof to cut the wire. The body drops to the ground, expelling a gasp of air. In the orange light I read the words "Deng Xiaoping."

I untie the placard and hand it to Sucre. Puzzled, he reads

aloud the message written below: "Your fascist leadership has betrayed our world revolution."

He frowns. "Who's President Ezequiel?"

But I am concentrating on the dog. From the mouth pokes a narrow truncheon of dynamite. My first thought is for the traffic below.

The sun would rise on dogs hanging from streetlamps in Belgrano, Las Flores and Lurigancho. Four more mutilated animals were found along the highway to the airport and another outside the Catholic University. People gathering beneath them experienced the same bafflement. No one had any idea who or what Ezequiel was. Nor his world revolution.

In the morning I spoke to the Chinese Embassy. Despite the references to Deng Xiaoping, no threats had been received. After a fortnight without more such incidents, I put the events of that evening from my mind.

Sylvina was relieved to be back in the capital. I had not seen her so happy since the early months of our marriage.

For about a year we rented the flat of her cousin Marco, who had moved with his wife to Miami. Eventually we found a modest basement apartment in Miraflores, three blocks north of Parque Colón. It wasn't as nice as Marco's flat, or the flat we had lived in six years previously, when I worked as a lawyer; and I couldn't easily afford the lease. But her mother's death had left Sylvina with a modest inheritance. How we would cope when this source exhausted itself, neither of us found the courage to contemplate. Meanwhile the inheritance paid for a cleaning lady and the subscription to the tennis club in San Isidro where Sylvina played four afternoons a week.

Our daughter Laura was growing up to look like my sister: large brown eyes, a strong body and masses of black hair which Sylvina insisted on braiding into a plait. Already Sylvina was talking about ballet lessons.

We had lived a year in the new apartment when I was pro-

moted to assistant head of the Diplomatic Protection Unit. Despite
that, Sylvina remained convinced that I was crazy to stay in the
force. Who could imagine becoming a policeman? They were all
either psychologically disturbed or they'd had run-ins with the
law. "And all of them are poor." But I worked regular hours, and
it was a quiet time in our marriage and in the capital.

One morning in November I am summoned to an office on the
third floor of a building in Vía Expreso.

I reported here for duty on my return to the capital, but have
had little occasion to come here since. It is a cheerless place, and
when the wind blows off the sea, as it does this morning, the
corridors smell of car fumes and maize cobs and urine. Because the
place was always known as one of the ugliest office buildings in the
city, money has been spent to brighten up the exterior with an
unnatural-looking green wash which makes it even more charm-
less. The color does not sit well with the barbed-wire emplace-
ments at the entrance or the concrete blocks which prevent people
from parking.

General Merino is a large-shouldered man with the trace of a
mustache and small shining eyes pouched into a gray face. He
wears a black turtleneck shirt, a half-sheepskin jacket with belt-
flaps, and looks at me from one side of his face, then the other, like
a chicken. There is no tic at the corner of his eyes, as there is to be
later. It is a benevolent look.

Merino is our most distinguished policeman. As a cadet in the
sixties, he helped crush Fuente's revolt, and he protects his service
with a similar ferocity. He has a reputation for hating the army
and is known to be honest, brave and overworked. His joy in life is
fishing. A rod is propped against the map on the wall behind his
desk.

"You speak Quechua, right?"

"Yes, sir."

"You know the north well?"

"Yes, sir."

There is a glass bowl with oranges on his desk.

"Want one?"

"No thank you, sir."

He takes an orange and peels it. "To corner a tomcat, Colonel Rejas—I call you Colonel, you understand, because I am promoting you—what do you do? You don't send two Alsatians up an alley. They'll play havoc with the garbage cans and the cat just leaps up the tree. No. You send in someone who knows the area, the other's way of thinking, what he smells like. You send in another tomcat."

The General, I will learn, is someone who reaches a decision quickly, is reasonably intelligent, and once he has delegated a problem, he has no intention of being bothered with it again. He gestures to a thick blue folder on his desk. "I want you to be our tomcat, Rejas."

He gives me until next morning to acquaint myself with the contents.

At home I slip open the adjustable metal fastener. The files catalogue incidents in the countryside since 17 May 1980, the day of the last general election. On that night, seven months before their appearance in the capital, dogs were hung from lampposts in four villages of Nerpio province. The symbol was, apparently, a Maoist one. "In China a dead dog is symbolic of a tyrant condemned to death by his people." Nor was it limited to the Andes. In the weeks ahead, dead dogs would hang under the streetlights of Cajamarca, Villoria and Lepe, culminating in the incident I have described on the bridge over the Rímac. The capital had no more such incidents after that first spate.

The animals that came next were alive.

In February, in Cabezas Rubias, a black dog ran through the market, frothing at the mouth. A fruit seller was chasing him away with a broom when the dog exploded. Three people suffered appalling wounds and a meat stall was blown all over the marketplace.

In Judío a donkey, galloping wildly, exploded into a thousand bloody pieces outside the police station. No one was hurt, but the blood seemed to have been etched into the stucco of the building.

In Salobral, during a meeting of the council, a hen was introduced into the Mayor's office and spattered the walls with feathered blood.

In none of these cases did anyone claim responsibility, but the dog and the donkey had evidently a placard around their necks proclaiming EZEQUIEL.

"A delinquent!!!" declared the Mayor of Salobral. "An Argentine," hinted the local bishop in a sermon recorded from the pulpit. "An American," avowed someone in a bus queue, this quoted by the correspondent of *El Comercio*.

There were also reports from the deep country areas.

From the police post in Tonda: eyewitness accounts of a public assassination, the victim accused of stealing bulls.

From Anghay: two prostitutes assassinated on a crowded street.

From Tieno: the assassination of the Mayor in a barber's shop.

Again, the name Ezequiel associated with these atrocities, sometimes scrawled onto the walls in the victim's blood, sometimes spelled out in rocks on a hillside: VIVA EL PRESIDENTE EZEQUIEL. VIVA LA REVOLUCIÓN.

This name repeated itself in valley after valley. Whoever this Ezequiel was, he was everywhere. At the same time, he was nowhere. He had published no manifesto. He never sought to explain the actions taken in his name. He scorned the press. He would apparently speak only to the poor.

This was why the government had ignored him.

You've spent time in my country. You must understand why Ezequiel could describe the capital as "the head of the monster." His "revolution" passed unnoticed there. His actions, if ever they reached the newspapers, were dismissed as an aberration, the work of "delinquents" and "thieves."

But you know what the capital is like. It believes itself to be the whole country. Everything beyond its limits is the great unknown. It only starts caring when the air conditioner is cut off or there's no electricity for the freezer. So long as he operated in the highlands, Ezequiel was no threat to our metropolis. And all this while his movement was stealthily encroaching underground. A gigantic scarab growing pincers and teeth. Ignored. Until the moment, one week before General Merino summoned me, when a boy nearly the same age as Laura walked into the foyer of a hotel in Coripe and blew apart.

That frightened people.

The photograph from the *Diario de Coripe* is dated 10 June. It must have been taken in a photo booth, because doubt is wandering onto the good-looking face. He holds his smile, uncertain, waiting for the flash.

In the article his profile is placed alongside a shot of the hotel's gutted lobby. Six bodies are arranged on stretchers. Paco, according to the manager, who survived the blast, was dressed in smart Sunday clothes with a brown leather satchel slung over his right shoulder. The manager remembered seeing his face, shielded by his arm, appear at the door. Local parliamentarians had convened in the foyer to discuss the building of a milk-powder factory. Catching sight of Paco's eyes bulging against the glass, the manager opened the door. The child had an urgent message for his father, the chairman. He must deliver it personally. "Over there," said the manager, indicating the chairman already rising to his feet, puzzled by the boy running toward him, holding up a satchel, and calling out "Daddy, Daddy!" The fact was, he had no son.

"Viva El Presidente Ezequiel!"

"This Ezequiel, sir, do we know anything about him?" I asked General Merino next day.

"Motherfuck all. Nothing beyond what you will find in that file." The General had trouble grasping anything in the abstract.

"We were a small unit, never more than six in the early days. Our brief was 'to investigate and combat the crimes perpetrated in the name of the delinquent Ezequiel.' But it is hard to establish an effective intelligence system from scratch. You need money—and we had little of that. One year we couldn't afford new boots. It takes also time."

"You had twelve years," Dyer pointed out.

"You sound like the General. And I tell you what I told him. Intelligence is no different from any other art. It's about not trying to push things. It's about waiting. Do you know how long it takes a sequoia seed to germinate? A decade. Of course, there's a time for impatience, when you must act quicker than you've ever acted before. Until then it's about collating and analyzing information.

Ezequiel, remember, had prepared his disappearing act since 1968. Once he disappeared, we would spend another twelve years tracking him down. But that's how long the Emergency lasted in Malaya.

"Success might have come sooner had we reacted earlier, with a clear policy and an image of the state as just, generous and firm. Unfortunately, the state wasn't that. It was directionless and its mongrel policies fueled Ezequiel's appeal to the country people and, of course, eventually also to people in the cities. By the time we decided to take note of him, it was too late. He had gathered momentum to such a degree that he could not be contained.

"I was glad to be entrusted with the case. My vocation, for which I had abandoned a prosperous position, had fallen short of my hopes for it. So I dedicated myself to the pursuit of Ezequiel.

"From the start, I was amazed by the fanaticism of his followers, by the degree of their subjection to his discipline. His cells proved impossible to penetrate. They relied on no outside group. They stole dynamite from the mines, their weapons from the police. We rarely made arrests, because their intelligence was better than ours. The few we captured refused to speak. When someone talks, it's to get off the hook, but not in the case of Ezequiel's people. It was evident they had been training since they were children. A good many of them *were* children. And when Ezequiel tapped a child on the shoulder, that child became a killer. To a ten-year-old boy or girl, it was a game. They competed. Put a satchel of dynamite or an AK-47 in the hands of a ten-year-old and annoy him—you don't want to be around.

"The finding of Ezequiel and his top echelon was my aim. My orders to my men didn't change. To defeat our enemy, we must be aware of his attractions. If we wanted to capture Ezequiel, whoever he was, we had to win over the same people. In no circumstances would we kill or torture a suspect. Frustrating though it was, we stood for the rule of law. Oppression must be seen to come from the other side. Intimidation wouldn't give us the answer. We might learn about the past, what had happened. But we forfeited a suspect's cooperation in the future.

"We were far more likely to achieve success by 'turning' a suspect. We should concentrate on scrutinizing those in the community who betrayed any sympathy for Ezequiel. Through details, however tiny, that's how we'd find him. The color of a wallpaper, the pattern of a dress, the contents of a garbage can.

"So we stacked up the evidence.

"We rifled garbage cans. We watched houses. We noted what suspects wore. Slowly, patiently we would build up a picture until we could present our suspect with a stark alternative: Prosecution or Reward. Any human being when faced with two doors, one saying LIFE, the other DEATH . . . well, you can predict which one they will choose.

"Which is what happened when I confronted the sacristan in Jaci."

He was awkwardly thin, his crinkled skin hanging on his face like something borrowed. I found him in the church, removing the candle stubs from a row of spikes. It was vital that he should not view me as yet another official from the coast conversing in a language he didn't understand. This was why the General had asked if I spoke Quechua.

We sat on the front bench.

"This is you?"

"Yes."

In the photograph, taken from the roof of the village school, he was receiving money from a masked figure. His benefactor's other hand clutched a captured police rifle.

"And this?"

The sacristan sat in a boat, two armed men in the prow.

"I can explain." The hospital would do nothing without money. He had taken it to pay for an operation. His mother was dying. Cancer of the lymph glands.

"A judge would give you twenty years. Maybe more."

"You don't understand."

"I do."

There were four more photographs, but he had seen from the start that I had the evidence to convict him. His face collapsed.

After he had agreed to help, I spoke to him with sympathy. I promised to have a word with the hospital. I tried to win him over.

I don't know if I succeeded. But he said he would have the information ready—names, dropping-off points, dates and places of future actions—when I returned.

I came back in plain clothes. The village lay in a bowl surrounded by steep, treeless hills, by a river with little water. It took three days to reach by bus and another morning in the back of a lorry. The driver was buying cheap potatoes. Passing as his mate, I helped load them into sacks.

I had arranged to meet the sacristan at midday. As I walked toward the church, I heard hooves galloping over loose timbers. In the street, there was a stirring. People gathered up their produce, speaking in quick, hushed voices. Doors slammed. The horses must have crossed the bridge because the clatter faded. Then they rounded the high wall of the school.

I could tell who the riders were. They were masked, about ten of them. Teenagers, led by a woman, her hair tucked beneath a baseball cap. Her short legs, bulging in their faded jeans, kicked the horse in the direction of the church where I was headed. The ground vibrated as she galloped past. She rode up to the church door, urging the horse up onto the stone step until its head and bristling shoulders filled the doorway. Then she got down. One of the masked riders took her reins. She hoisted up her belt, from which hung a machete in a leather scabbard, and walked into the vestry, where the sacristan awaited me with his information.

I fled uphill, up a narrow twisting street, to find a hiding place. The villagers had vanished behind their shutters, but I could feel their eyes. Eventually I took refuge behind an adobe wall—nothing but empty fields behind me—from where I looked down on the church. Minutes later, to the ringing of bells, five men were pushed into the square. The riders had known who to take, where to find them. The Mayor, two adulterers, the driver of the lorry which had brought me. And the sacristan. They were forced to their knees while the villagers watched. The bells fell silent and a young woman's voice burst from the loudspeaker tethered to the ankle of a stone figure above the church door. She spoke in fluent Quechua on behalf of Ezequiel. He had come to free them from their past. For Ezequiel the past was dead, as—shortly—these criminals would be. The five men symbolized a world in total disorder. The only way to change it drastically was not through reliance on natural political means but through the agency of someone divine. Ezequiel was this divinity. He was the Eternal Fire, the Red Sun, the Puka Inti, beyond human control. In his presence it was impossible to remain neutral. He was not just a law of nature but the fulfillment of our oldest prophecies.

"Weren't you promised clinics?"

Several heads nodded.

"Weren't you promised roads?"

"Yes."

"Weren't you promised telephones?"

"That's right!"

"Ezequiel will bring you telephones, clinics, roads. He will strip the flesh of the reactionaries who denigrate your customs, and throw the scraps of their offal into the flames." She held up a fist. Her voice rose to a strident pitch. "Under his banner the unbribable soul of the people will triumph over the genocidal forces of the law."

From the wall, after adjusting her shawl, an old woman hurled a stone at the men kneeling in the dust. I had stopped at her stall earlier to drink coca tea.

"This Ezequiel, you support him?"

"Yes."

"Why?"

"I am no longer a cabbage," she had said, not looking at me.

"Have you seen him ever?"

"Yes."

"What does he look like?"

She had pointed to a configuration of stones on the hillside.

Below, the campesinos were being as easily won over as a child with a sweet. Terrifying. He was using our myths for his purposes. But even had the villagers understood, they wouldn't have cared. Today in this square he offered what for five centuries the government had denied them.

A murmur fluttered through the crowd. In the sun, something metal flashed. There was a shout and one of the masked riders jabbed a rifle into the sacristan's back.

"Forward!"

The man's head rested, bowed and shaking, on his clasped hands. The force of the blow had knocked his cap to the ground.

"Go forward!"

Another blow on his shoulders. I heard him whimpering. He babbled about his sick mother, how she needed medicine. My fingers scratched the earth. He was about to be punished because of me. If I had been there, I would have been seized too. Who had betrayed him? Where was the information he had prepared for me?

He threw back his head. In a hoarse summons to the surrounding bowl he shouted, "Rejas!"

My name ricocheted from hill to hill.

"Forward, traitor!"

One knee tested the ground an inch ahead. Then the other. In minuscule shuffles he advanced toward the masked figure with the machete.

She tested the blade with her thumb.

"Rejas!" And madly his eyes followed the echoes, as if they would delve me into the open.

"Viva El Presidente Ezequiel!"

I tell you, I still wake up and it's his call I'm hearing. Rejas, Rejas, REJAS.

In this fashion Ezequiel persuaded the people to consider him divine. As a man of flesh and blood, he had ceased to exist. He had dismembered and scattered his body, and now thrived like a monstrous Host in the heart of anyone invoking his name. One day he was in Jaci, his name daubed in dripping letters on the church wall. On the same day he was six hundred miles east, robbing the Banco Wiese. If ever we approached him, the old coca lady had warned, he would transform himself into a canopy of feathers and lift into the sky. "He can never be caught."

But Ezequiel was no condor or circle of stones. He existed, all right. Who he was and what he looked like—small, large, one-legged, wall-eyed—we had not the least idea. But someone who condoned public beheading; well, we didn't think to look for a man of culture. We had marked him as a jungle-tested leader in the mold of Guevara or Castro, or those revolutionaries whom the General had fought in the sixties. Which is why it was such an extraordinary shock when we discovered Ezequiel's true background.

Six months after the execution at Jaci, Sucre led into the office a senior lecturer in philosophy from the Catholic University.

"He says he knows who Ezequiel is."

The philosopher—stooped, bloodshot eyes, white mustache—was frightened. A colleague had overheard his boast and mentioned it to another colleague, who at some point had told Sucre's cousin, a second-year student in the same faculty.

Contemptuously, Sucre piloted him to a chair. "He now denies it."

"Who were you talking about?"

"It doesn't matter. It was a quarrel, a long time ago."

He wore a maroon corduroy jacket buttoned up, which he undid to reveal a brown cardigan, also unbuttoned, covered with biscuit crumbs. His skin was drink-ruined, and he had the deflated cheeks of a boaster.

"Tell me about this quarrel."

It was nothing serious. Just an academic squabble.

"About Ezequiel?"

"No, with Ezequiel."

"You're telling me Ezequiel was an academic at your university?"

In the corner Sucre chewed air.

"He was a philosopher of no small distinction." Tetchily, he drew the wings of his cardigan over his shirt. "Only he didn't answer to Ezequiel. His name was Edgardo Rodríguez Vilas."

And slowly it came out.

It had happened in Villoria, in the mid-sixties. Our informant—let us call him Pascual—had been recruited to the newly opened University of Santa Eufemia. He had been happy in his position, until the appointment of this man Vilas to the same faculty.

Vilas was a Maoist, Pascual a Marxist. It was the time of the Sino-Soviet split. They'd argued.

"I was pro-Castro. Vilas thought Castro was a chorus girl."

One day Pascual complained to the Dean. Said he didn't approve of what Vilas was doing. A sinister, antihumanist influence. So fixed in his political ideal that all things became instrumental to it.

Somehow his complaint reached the ears of Vilas. In charge of personnel, he removed Pascual from the faculty board.

There was an added complication. One student over whom Vilas had exerted his influence was Pascual's girl. Vilas had gone off with her.

"You mean an affair?"

"To my knowledge, he did not actually have a physical relationship with her," he said coldly.

"Then why did she leave you?"

"I understand she found his absolutism attractive. Such people are always hungry for imperatives when those imperatives coincide with their own."

"Which were?"

"Like a lot of types unable to relate to others, he could excite in them a romantic possibility of violent revolution."

"Which you couldn't?"

He buttoned up his cardigan. "I tend to see the other side of the coin."

"And your colleague Vilas, he was capable of violence?"

"Possibly. He was always talking world revolution. But it was the sixties. Weren't you?"

"Where is he now?"

"Look, he's probably still in Villoria."

"Describe him."

"This was twenty years ago."

"Concentrate."

"Average height, glasses, black hair, thin."

"Do you have photos?" My attention had waned. At that time

a lot of radical professors, because of the expansion of the universities, woke up in positions they didn't have the intelligence to maintain. Suddenly they had power. They possessed the truth. So they used revolutionary ideology to shatter the system. Until it threatened their pension plans.

"He would never be photographed," Pascual was saying.

"Really? Why not?"

"Hated it. Which we found odd because he wasn't shy. If you ask me, it was vanity. He had this skin complaint."

My interest quickened. "Get the albums, Sucre."

There were six of them. "Take a look."

The philosopher turned the laminated pages. On one side we had stuck pictures of Ezequiel's victims; opposite, the faces of those so far interrogated.

"I didn't realize . . ."

"No one here does."

He leafed through the album. Page after page of mutilation.

"He was responsible for this?" He stared at the sacristan's corpse. He was frightened. He remembered something. Something was coming back to him.

He reached the end. "No, not there."

"Try an earlier one."

With relief he closed the second book. "Nothing."

"Another."

We were nearly done. His cardigan buttoned up, he wanted to go.

"Tell me. You're a man who understands history," I said. "If you want to start a revolution, why not issue a manifesto? Why not show the people who you are, what you're doing?"

He leaned back, grateful to explain. "That's perfectly understandable. Socrates wrote nothing down. Neither did Jesus. The problem with text is that it assumes its own reality. It cannot answer and it cannot explain."

"So if you wanted to be effective, you'd leave no trace?"

"That's right."

I opened another album, the earliest. "Last one."

Impatiently he turned the pages. Halfway into the album he dislodged a photograph. I retrieved the print from the floor and inserted it back under the plastic sheet. Pascual lifted the next page, and even though he had not been concentrating, I saw the hairline hesitation. His hand came up, scratched the side of his nose. Something forced him to hurry on, cover up the image which had made his eyes contract.

"Stop!" I pressed my hand down on the album, turned the page back.

"Is that him?"

The philosopher's cheeks sagged. His eyes flicked wildly over the face. I could only see it upside down. I wrenched the album from him. He had been trapped by a photograph of a man wearing a brown alpaca scarf, taken on a scalding morning near Sierra de Pruna. Taken by me.

A curious and not very comfortable feeling comes over me when I look at prints of my wedding or of Laura's christening: as soon as I see them, my memory of the occasion is subverted. In a vital way, what they celebrate has ceased to exist for me.

So it was with that photograph of Ezequiel. Each time I looked at it, I remembered less. The image, already distant, became encrusted with a further memory of my failure to remember anything more. The live face was, if you like, lost, bullied out by subsequent events.

At the office there was jubilation. At last we knew who he was and what he looked like. Professor Edgardo Vilas was the laborer Melquiades Artemio Durán, who was the Maoist revolutionary leader Ezequiel. The General hoped the sight of him might prompt additional memories, as if, by remembering one tiny detail extra, all would be solved.

"Think hard, tomcat. Think back. There must be something other than his Yankee cigarettes and the rash on his neck."

But there wasn't. Lifeless, unreal, boiled in time, he had become a nonface. He wasn't a man anymore. Not someone you could see in a café drinking tea and say, "Yes!" He had become an icon. When I looked into those narrow black eyes, all I saw was a stiff tail sticking out of a sack.

Pascual couldn't help. Two days later, when he was required to come back in and verify the photograph before General Merino, the faculty informed me that he had taken unexpected leave. He never did come back.

It does seem incredible in the age of the camera that someone can avoid having their picture taken for thirty-four years. From outer space it is possible to frame the scowl of a man perching on a beer crate in a country yard, yet for all this time what printed image did we have of Ezequiel? Apart from that black-and-white print, not one. Think of it: no high school portrait, no family picnic, no face gazing from among a group of friends. That this distinction should have been achieved by the holder of a prominent chair at Santa Eufemia University is remarkable.

With the same reverence for detail that characterized his dissertation on the Kantian theory of space, he had excised from the record all trace of his physical presence. When I inspected his dissertation, his appointment to the professorship, his library card, I found in each case the same rough, near transparent patch, lighter in color than the surrounding page, where a photograph had been torn out or removed with a knife.

It is not the first time an intense search has yielded nothing. At the Police Academy we were lectured on the American D. B. Cooper, who was the first person to hijack an aircraft. Our tutor credited Cooper with being the forerunner of modern terrorism. Decades later he may be still at large, walking cheerfully down some main street in Mississippi, popping his pink gum at the sky. For three hours, the length of the flight, he existed as D. B. Cooper, after which no one saw him again. He parachuted out of history, and the last image anyone had of him was the light on his silk chute drifting toward the pines.

Once he had climbed back into his pickup, that's how it was with Ezequiel.

———

I won't go into detail about the months and years which followed. The people who had met him, the rooms he had lived in, the shop where he had bought his mineral water—all these I traced until the moment of his disappearance. But I was trying to carve a statue out of shadows. I might have been excavating one of those burial mounds at Paracas. To the General, my exhibits appeared indistinguishable from the sand.

It proved impossible to conjure Ezequiel from such remnants. He was not a man to whom stories attached themselves. His character, assembled from hundreds of interviews, was a hollow, papier-mâché construction. The sentences canceled each other out. You heard only the echoes.

"He wouldn't hurt a fly." Classmate, San Agustín College, Galiteo.

"He said that violent revolution was the only way to seize power and transform the world." Classmate.

"He had no girlfriends." Classmate.

"Women pushed and shoved to be near him." Pupil, Santa Eufemia.

"His lectures were repetitive. He was not a particularly interesting phenomenon." Fellow teacher.

"He was handing down the Commandments." Pupil.

"He only bought mineral water." Shopkeeper, Lepe.

"I saw him smile once. It was in the street and he was drunk." Fellow university student, Lepe.

"He said that flowers made him sneeze." Secretary at Faculty of Philosophy, Santa Eufemia.

"Every day for lunch he ordered the same dish: a flavored yogurt." Cashier at university canteen, Lepe.

"He asked me to turn down my music." Neighbor, Santa Eufemia.

"In the middle of a conversation he would tell you Albanian olive oil was the best in the world." Visiting Peace Corps lecturer.

"He never took off his jacket. He always wore a scarf." Pupils, various.

Read cold on the page, these statements were inert or comical. One element united them. In each case, I heard the hush in the speaker's voice, the kind of hush people use when they should not be speaking.

Where was he?

Possibly he was not in the country at all. He could easily, without risk to himself, have directed his operations from some hotel in, say, Paris. But I didn't think so. My instinct told me he remained locked into this soil, driven into it with the force of an axe, identified with his revolution so as to be indivisible from it.

He really was a charismatic leader, you see. This was a man in command, who was not commanded. An unquivering spirit seemed to lie at the center of him, stilled into place by a terrible ambition. He didn't have to participate himself. I doubt he ever fired a gun. But by the act of being there, of showing his face, he could infuse a terrible energy into his followers.

And the throat slittings and the killings and the bombings and the robberies and the kangaroo trials and the dogs hung from lampposts—these ceased when he left an area. They followed him wherever he went, and when he was no longer there, they stopped. He was, if you like, one of those washerwomen in times of plague who contaminate everything they touch even as they wash it. Our own Typhoid Mary, except he believed he was making clean the lives of our people. He was scrubbing out the dirt and the corruption and the abuses which had oppressed us since the Spanish Conquest. He was leading us toward his fresh new dawn.

That's how he earned his nickname at university. Behind his back they called him Shampoo. Because he brainwashed people.

He wasn't abroad, but where was he? Believe me, it is difficult to disappear. Your ability to hide is restricted if you stand out in any sort of way. If you are bigger or more intelligent or if you come from somewhere else. Ezequiel would have stood out.

When people are after you and want to kill you, you have three choices:

You go to a place where there are no people.

You never leave your room. But it's not easy to hide an extra person; you knock over a chair and always there's someone downstairs who had thought, until then, that there was no one else up there.

You remain in the open, but you change yourself in every way possible. If you are an obsessive coffee drinker, you drink tea. If you wear glasses, you change to contact lenses. If you like to wear your hair one length, you wear it another. You put tacks in your shoes so your mother would not recognize your walk. You change your instincts. The Gestapo caught one of your agents in Paris because she looked to the right as she crossed the road. If you have to go into the street, you guard against anyone catching sight of your profile. Even on a rainy evening it's easy to recognize a person you know. You might not have seen them for twenty years, but no downpour will disguise the contours of a familiar cheek spotted through a car window.

In short, you change your habits, your instincts, your face.

But one thing you can't change is your illness.

You remember how I typed "eczema" on the basic description of Melquiades Artemio Durán? Well, Ezequiel suffered from psoriasis.

It's not a pretty disease. The new cells push up before the old cells are ready to leave and you erupt in nasty weeping yellow scabs. But what's odd about psoriasis when you consider Ezequiel is that you don't find it among the Indians. It's a Caucasian disease. A white man's disease.

It's also incurable. It might fluctuate and there may be periods when it's not present, but always it comes back. What you've got to watch out for is the stage when it becomes rampant, because that's when the sores become infected and the smallest movement is agony.

For a long time Ezequiel's bad skin was my most concrete lead. After any attack by his people on a village, I would interrogate the chemist. Sometimes they'd lie, sometimes there would be no records, but where records existed, these often revealed a sale of Kenacort E.

It suggested Ezequiel's illness might be worsening. If this was the case, I was confident he would be forced soon to abandon the high altitudes. You see, at a certain altitude his blood would coagulate. He wouldn't be able to go on breathing, and that's why he would want to make his way down to the coast.

I have no proof to back this up, but I suspect Ezequiel's ailment was connected with his decision to go underground. His behavior did suggest a certain vanity. All those spots—would you want to be seen in that condition? How else does one explain the quantum leap from Professor Edgardo Vilas, the mild-mannered philosopher, into President Ezequiel, the revolutionary?

I am not a Kantian philosopher. I find his work hardly intelligible. But I understand it enough to know that Ezequiel took an à la carte attitude to Kant's works, and made such a meal of his philosophy that its originator would not have recognized it.

Kant does have one image which holds some meaning for me: the bird which thought it could fly faster in a vacuum, without air to beat against. For me, that is where Ezequiel's reading and his texts and his philosophy had led him, to airless haunts where all gusts of life were extinguished. He'd started out with his ideology, but he was dealing with people for whom ideology meant nothing. Blood and bone and death were all that mattered to the people in my valley. It was idiotic to think they would care about Kant or Mao or Marx, and so he taught them in blood and bone and death, and he had become intoxicated.

My pursuit went on.

I got used to the overlarded soup of the canteen, the wary nods in corridors, the unanswering shelves of documents and photographs, the despair of an unfinished case.

I drove home.

I crouched before Laura as she sat in her playpen and shielded with both hands the flicker of my love for Sylvina. But my vocation had generated a deepening hostility. The unsolicited touch of our first meeting, that look across the table in the faculty library, such intimacies had fled into a darkness from which I could not retrieve them.

Day after day passed like this. Year by year. Twelve of them.

It came as a shock, therefore, when Ezequiel's death was announced. On 3 March 1992, Alberto Quesada, Minister of the Interior, gave a television interview in the course of which, questioned about the insurrection in the highlands, he adopted this line: Ezequiel, a criminal, a one-off, was certainly dead. If he wasn't dead, why didn't he show his face? He was the Eternal Flame. How could you conceal his splendid blaze?

Because, Quesada jeered, he had perished. He was like one of those tyrannical sultans whose death is not admitted, and whose pavilion is raised each night. He was like El Cid, and they had strapped his carcass to his horse. He had, in short, been blown out.

It was tempting to believe Quesada. But his bellicose message was as crude as the posters distributed by his ministry, showing my photograph of Ezequiel prancing on cartoon cloven feet and embellished with the tail of a devil. If such a pivotal figure were dead, there would be some sign that he was no longer on the scene. If the army had killed him in a shoot-out, they would have flaunted the body. They would have treated him like Che Guevara.

My own belief, which I had submitted in my latest report to General Merino, was that, on the contrary, Ezequiel had never posed a greater threat.

I expected to hear back from the General, but three weeks after Quesada's broadcast the police went on strike. None of us had been paid for two months. Outside the Ministry of the Interior a thousand policemen held up our symbol, a worn-out boot. The strike ended with Quesada giving his personal assurance that all salaries would be paid by the end of the week. Two days later the General summoned me. It was, the summons said, important.

I never could predict what the General regarded as important. I hoped he wanted to discuss my report. But he might want to talk about Quesada's pay settlement; or possibly he wished to know more about Hilda Cortado, a woman we had arrested the previous afternoon for distributing subversive leaflets. It was rare to catch someone red-handed like this.

In fact, it was about none of these things.

Preparing his tackle, he fiddled with a lure dangling with

hooks. "Forget it, tomcat. It's over." He rolled down his turtleneck and, with the lure, slit the air an inch from his neck. "Your pal Ezequiel, he's dead."

He sketched the details for me brusquely. Skirmish on a dirt road above Sierra de Pruna. Lorry refuses to stop. Army opens fire. Lorry, packed with dynamite from copper mine, explodes. Body found. Ezequiel.

Merino was annoyed. "We work on this for twelve years, then the army waltzes in. General Lache is going to be unspeakable."

"When did this happen, sir?"

"A month ago."

"A month ago! Why weren't we told before?"

"Lache wanted to be certain. He tells me Quesada's very happy."

It was true I had observed a lull in Ezequiel's activities. Normally during this period we might have expected forty, fifty incidents in the provinces. Since Quesada's broadcast my unit had reported seven.

Could Ezequiel be dead?

I expected the story to lead the news on Canal 7, but it was transmitted near the end, after an item on the national women's volleyball team. In the capital Ezequiel remained virtually unknown. The announcement of his bandit's end on a dust road a thousand miles away merited twenty seconds. There was film of a truck on its side and a plump corpse covered with an army blanket. An anonymous hand drew back the blanket, and the camera closed in on a man's head, lingering over charred features and a body which resembled a burned sofa.

Sucre looked to me for confirmation. "That's him. Isn't it, sir?"

"It could be."

You know how you look forward to something which you never believe will happen, and when it does, you are overcome with exhaustion? That was my feeling on seeing the blackened mess which was Ezequiel's face. With this fulfillment of my task, desire had faded. There was none of the anticipated elation. I felt stripped of my shadow.

Quesada, a small dapper figure in a white suit, was filmed clapping the shoulder of General Lache, who looked massively pleased with himself. Delighted, the Minister knocked on the camera lens. "As of this moment, Ezequiel no longer exists."

General Merino would have attributed it to professional resentment, but I had no wish to see the body.

5

"When did you next see Ezequiel?"

It was the second night and Emilio had removed their plates. Dyer, arriving early, had found Rejas already sitting at the corner table.

"See him? Five days after he was pronounced dead. But I didn't know it was Ezequiel."

"Who did you think it was?"

"How well do you know my capital?"

"Reasonably well."

"Then you know Surcos?"

Dyer did. A prosperous new suburb in the northern outskirts. Rejas leaned forward, raising his chin.

Picture this. It's about eight-thirty at night. I've parked my car and I'm looking up at the first-floor window of the building opposite. A yellow curtain—it is obviously a child's room—is drawn. There are cartoons of some sort decorating the fabric, but since the room is in darkness, I can't tell what they are. The sliding window is open at one corner, where a breeze sucks at the curtain, distorting the characters. I am trying to decide who they are—whether it's Mickey Mouse or maybe Dumbo the Elephant—when a light cuts on and a strange blue glow, full of underwatery movements, flickers over the ceiling. A figure moves across the light. I see someone pause behind the curtain and very slightly part it.

Although bracing myself for an uncomfortable interview, I do remember wondering who is in that upstairs room and whether the person framed by those eerie fluorescent shadows is Laura's teacher—or whether the apartment is even part of the dance studio.

It's Laura's teacher I'm waiting to see. There's been an embarrassing incident. Due to Quesada's delay in paying our salaries, my check for Laura's lessons has bounced. I hope the embarrassment is temporary. Deprived of Ezequiel's terror, I have tired of my profession overnight. It's as if Ezequiel's death has set me free.

But Ezequiel is not dead.

Surcos, if you have to live in the capital, is a pleasant enough suburb. It's about thirty minutes' drive from Miraflores and twenty from Laura's school in Belgrano. It smells of cooking oil, geraniums and, before it rains, fish.

Calle Diderot is a wide street, well tended, and you can imagine children running along the pavement or playing on the tidy beds of grass between each house. Populated by lawyers, doctors and teachers who have migrated from the coast, the street has a café, its own video store and an estate agency operating from a garage.

Jacaranda trees on each side of the street give speckled shade to eighty houses, painted brightly to remind owners of their fishing villages. The houses are modern, two-storyed, with barbed wire between the roof terraces. Their little front gardens are enclosed by walls or by iron fences, sometimes with a dog's muzzle poking through.

That's how it is now, and that's how it was then, on the night I'm talking about.

The ballet school was unremarkable, and was entered through a wall painted the same peppermint-green as the building it concealed. One by one the mothers pulled up outside to wait for their daughters. They parked bumper to bumper and sat in their cars, varnishing their nails. Now and then one of them would turn to shout "Get down!" at an uncontrollable poodle.

Many of these women had been Sylvina's friends since childhood, but they didn't marry policemen. They drove new cars, lived in properties facing the sea and could afford cooks. Sylvina saw them often. Iced coffee at the Café Haiti; tennis at San Isidro's Country Club; aerobics in the Hotel María Angola; and—the latest excitement—a literary dinner which required the wife whose turn it was to host the event to deliver a short talk on a modern novel, explaining why it interested her.

"Agustín!" Marina, sitting in her cherry-red BMW and tilting her face to the side mirror, had been applying her lipstick. She had returned from Miami with a slightly different profile, a little less nose, a little more chin. She left the car and crossed the road.

"I haven't seen enough of you!" Divorced from Marco, she had been two months back in the city.

We kissed. Miami had given her a taste for tight pants, long fingernails and streaked hair.

"I've been busy."

"How pleased you must be. I saw the news on television. I didn't realize until Sylvina told me he was the one." She touched my arm, partly secretive; partly not. We had asked Marina to keep quiet about my profession. When the girls at Laura's previous dance school found out I was a policeman, they had teased her. So had the ballet mistress.

Marina, squeezing my arm, said, "What will you do now?"

"I don't know. Maybe it's time to go back to the law."

"Sylvina will be thrilled!"

"I suppose so." That's what I'd promised my wife. Once Ezequiel was caught, I would look for a better-paid job.

"Is Sylvina all right?"

"She's at the vet."

"We're looking forward to her talk on Wednesday. You know we're meeting at your place?"

"She's very excited about it."

"I can't fault Marco. He's been extremely generous, sending us copies of the novel. Which I still have to read." The divorce, Marina wanted us to gather, had not been acrimonious.

"And Laura," she said. "Is she happy with her new teacher?"

"Oh yes. A great success."

"When I heard how miserable she was with Madame Offenbach . . ."

There was a commotion behind Marina. The ballet class filed out of the door in the green wall. Beautifully turned out, erect, with splay-footed steps they scattered toward the cars.

Marina, recognizing a pampered girl in pink tights and a smart blue leotard, said, "There's Samantha! Bye for now."

It was easy to tell my daughter apart. The other girls left talking to each other. She was by herself. Slightly heavier than the rest of them, and smaller, she was made taller by a head of hair which she pulled back in a way that gave a crushed look to her features. It was hair she could sit on, long and thick, the color of freshly made coffee. The other girls in her class had the blonder hair of their mothers; and the lighter skin.

Laura, seeing the gray Peugeot, walked toward me at a tilt. Conscious of her short neck, she held down her shoulders. Despite the warm night, she hid her body with leggings over her leotard. Sylvina was always after her to lose weight—"If you're not careful, you'll see your dinner in your behind"—and she would prepare a special fat-free chop which Laura devoured in a second.

Continually struck by the girl's resemblance to my sister, I asked on one occasion, "What's wrong with her? She looks all right to me."

Sylvina flicked the white hands which had once fascinated me. "Certainly she looks all right. Now."

My wife was the force behind the decision that Laura should take up ballet. This was what her friends did with their children. Through Laura, Sylvina could live out the dreams she had harbored for her younger self. She wanted Laura to be pretty, to walk nicely with ribbons in her hair, to be up there onstage as a Cinderella fairy. In other words, she wanted Laura to put on a tutu and forget where she came from.

The matter was never brought up; it lay unexploded between us. I had once overheard Sylvina speaking to Marina on the telephone. I wouldn't have listened had she not been talking in such an apologetic tone. "Samantha's so lucky with her looks. Laura's very dark, you see."

Quite why this should have cropped up then, I don't know. It had never been an issue before. When I met my wife—at university in the late sixties—it was a time of "indigenism," the country enjoying one of its spasmodic celebrations of self-discovery. For Sylvina it was an assertion of identity to be seen in fashionable company, white hand in brown, and I was not immune either. Now, twelve years on, she believed learning classical ballet might go some way to removing the jungle from Laura's face.

But you only had to look at Laura to understand she wasn't built for classical ballet. It agonized me to watch her struggling, bewildered, before the mirror we had installed in the hall. I could see the pain she inflicted on herself, trying to make her joints go in a way they were not meant to; doing things which did not come naturally to her body.

When I mentioned this to Sylvina, she said, "To be a good ballerina, you have to deform yourself."

I said nothing, but it made me angry. Laura had her own poise, her own beauty. She required nothing more.

However, this was not the matter I needed to discuss with her teacher.

I asked Laura to sit in the car.

My knock resounded in the street. Over the wall I heard a sliding door being opened, footsteps, the drawing of a bolt.

She was dressed in black: black round-necked leotard with long sleeves, a gauzy black ankle-length skirt over it, black ballet slippers.

"Yolanda? I'm Laura's father."

She pointed to her smiling mouth, which was full. She put a hand to her throat, as if this would make her swallow quicker.

"There. Sorry." She held up a slice of banana cake on a paper plate. "I've just made it. Want some?"

"No thanks."

"But Laura's left. Haven't you seen her?"

"She's in the car."

"Do you want to bring her in?"

"I'd rather not. It's about your letter."

"Oh. Yes," she said, as if she had forgotten. It's an embarrassing thing, to tell someone their check has bounced.

She unfastened the door chain. Beneath the streetlight her face gleamed pale, still wet from where she had toweled off her makeup. Wide brown eyes set on high cheekbones, a clear skin, fine dark hair. She looked frank, honest, conscientious—the kind of person you might tell everything to on first meeting.

"Please. Come through."

I followed her across the patio. We entered the studio through a glass door and she slid it shut after me.

The room smelled of cigarettes, sweat and the musky scent of rosin. A wooden barre, slung with pink tights and tracksuit tops, ran around two mirrored walls. Laid out on the shiny parquet floor were inflatable gray mats for breathing exercises and, against the near wall, a cassette player, a tin box scattered about with white powder, and a leather trunk. One door, half-open, covered in photographs of dancers, led into a kitchen; another, also ajar, into a shower room. The mirrors were steamed over.

She put on a tape, Tchaikovsky—quite loud, as if that were what I would expect—and raised her arms in an apologetic spread at the tatty state of her studio. "So. This is it."

Beneath the strip lighting, there was something original and unfeigned about her. Also a graveness, as if she had been marked by a bad love affair.

"Laura warned you? Once inside, you have to do everything I say."

Before I could answer, she raised one hand above her head and slid her fingers down an invisible rope to her neck. Speaking in a strict Germanic accent, she said, "The best position for a dancer is the one when you're hanged, because it's very well placed. The hips are over the feet. The shoulders are over the hips. The head is midway. *Ja,* it's a wonderful position." The imitation was good. She made me want to laugh.

"Madame Offenbach?"

"Not a success, I gather?"

"No."

I could see Yolanda wanted to say, "I hope Laura's happier here," but she held the words back, her lips skewed sideways, her front teeth showing at the corner of her mouth.

She scooped something from the floor. "They never pick up their plasters!"

She threw it into the rosin box "Coffee? Or would you like lemonade, if they've left any?" She watched me, biting a nail.

"Laura's waiting. I'd better not."

To Laura, not Sylvina, she had entrusted her simple note:

> Dear Señor Rejas,
> I regret to tell you the bank has refused to honor the money you owe me for Laura's ballet lessons during December and January.
>
> > Yolanda Celendín

I was nervous, which made her nervous. "Here's the money I owe. I'm sorry about the check."

With a smile all neat and laced, she said, "We hadn't met, but I thought it was better to tell you than Señora Rejas."

"My employers are two months in arrears with their salaries."

She accepted the money and, without counting it, folded it onto the plate beside the remains of her cake. "That's terrible. Already I've had to let three girls go because they couldn't afford it. I've regretted it ever since. They came every day from Las Flores. They were so excited, the parents. They watched their daughters in their beautiful dresses and they dreamed. I should never have let them go. They were three lovely dancers, I could tell as soon as I saw them."

"Can you tell, that quickly?"

She nodded. "Some girls, you only have to see them standing still to know they're dancers. Others might be good at barre work, but when you bring them into the center, they're terrible."

"And Laura?" I risked.

"Your girl, she's a spot of sunshine. That's a real child you have. Not a little adult in lipstick." And she imitated with exaggerated eyes someone I knew at once to be Marina.

At my laughter, she raised her hand. "No, I mustn't be so disparaging. They're probably your friends. It's just that in six months I have attracted the worst sort of ballet mother."

I was still smiling. Her mocking of Marina's values struck a chord. She was not the dupe of anyone's wealth. But she hadn't answered me.

"It's hard for a parent to ask this. Should we encourage Laura?"

Her face remained serious. "How much do you know about ballet?"

"Not much." Through Sylvina I had met a few dancers. They seemed to me dim, uneducated and self-absorbed.

"Laura has nice ideas," she said, "but she should take risks. I love people to take risks. Very often it works."

"She wants to join the Metropolitan."

"You've put her down for classical classes, which is fine," she said carefully. "You can't be an engineer without studying mathematics. If you've been classically trained, you can do things in modern dance no modern dancer can do. But she might find her natural aptitude is for the kind of contemporary dance I'm involved with. It can't hurt to try."

Politely, conscious of the time and of Laura waiting in the car, I said, "Do you still dance?" I knew nothing about her. We had found the school through Marina. Keen for Samantha to maintain the standards of Miami, she had recommended the teacher in Calle Diderot as a first-rate communicator. But I had no idea whether the teacher performed.

"I did and then I didn't and now I do again. As of this moment I'm meant to be preparing a ballet with a small group at the Teatro Americano, but it's getting desperate. I can't find a subject." She tucked her hands behind her back. "But you're not here to discuss my problems. Is there anything else about Laura?"

In fact, there was. I was worried my daughter was the one the pretty girls laughed at. I knew they called her Cucumber Body after a livid green all-over which Sylvina had bought in a sale. Once through the kitchen door I had heard Laura, in tears, telling Sylvina, "Samantha says my feet are claws around a branch and I look like a parrot in a storm."

But if Laura had been teased, she wouldn't want me to know. And no parent cares to inquire too closely into the particulars of their children's suffering. So I said, "I'm worried about her feet."

"Her feet?"

"Is it right for Laura's feet to bleed?"

"Can I ask you something? Laura wants to join the Metropolitan, but how serious is she—I mean, about wanting to be a dancer?"

I pictured my daughter night after night before the hallway mirror, beating her new shoes with Sylvina's toffee hammer to make them quieter, soaking her feet in salt water, spreading mustard on her blisters, inserting foam between the toes, raising one leg and then the other, her legs taut as triggers, her breasts shuddering as if she were going to be sick, her body crying out with fatigue.

"She is serious."

"Then she'll have to go through this hell. If you want to be a dancer, you can't have a normal life. You don't have boyfriends. You're not really a woman in most people's eyes. There's a sense in which you have to dance yourself to death. You're aiming for a perfection which your body isn't meant to give you. The pain is intense. Intense. You dance with pain. But the feet, you don't have to worry about them."

She hiked up her skirt, easing off her ballet shoes. In a graceful movement she lifted her leg until her bare foot rested in the air, perfectly still, not far from my face.

"See those corns? When they're well set in, she'll be able to dance on them. They'll be deformed, but her feet won't bleed anymore."

Yolanda's foot, it was more a sea creature's flipper. Ugly, discolored, with red calluses, the nails ridged into shapeless chips, the skin on the toes sharpened into a permanent crease. It reminded me of the turtle with a bitten shell I'd seen on the beach at Paracas.

I averted my eyes. "Does she have to starve too?"

"I don't understand." She lowered her leg.

I told her about the diet Sylvina insisted upon.

"Laura's not on a diet? You must take her off it. You'll never get a classical figure by dieting. She's growing. She needs energy. Oh, these Western ideas of beauty make me sick. Little girls' looks are just different. She's beautiful as she is."

I thought so.

"Of course she is! She should treasure what she has, make the most of it. That's what'll make her a dancer. Your daughter's much richer, much lovelier than all those Miami babes with chocolate-chip noses and frosted hair. Look at her. She has all of our country in her face."

I had never heard anyone talk like this. Those elements which Sylvina found distasteful in our daughter were mine as well. By supporting Laura, her teacher had given me, my origins, validity.

"At the Metropolitan I got into the most awful fights with the teachers. Be honest, look at us, I'd say. Most of us, we're brown-skinned and stocky. Classical ballet was invented by the Europeans, and is danced with different bodies in mind, different sensibilities. We have Andean bodies, Andean minds. How can we respond to what is going on around us if we're dressed like this and all the steps are spoken in French. We can't!"

"What did they say?"

"They'd laugh, except the Principal, who was English. Señora Vallejo was sympathetic, but she wasn't allowed to sack anyone. For the other teachers, the world didn't exist outside that European stage." She looked at me, amused. "In my last term I put on this dance. A scandal it caused with the parents. Much too dark, they found it. We don't understand your work, that dance you did with spiders. Spiders, I asked? Or was it homosexuals? Do you know what it was? The Condor Festival, one of our oldest ceremonies. And they thought this was sodomy!"

Until this moment I had thought of Yolanda as someone a little bit nervous who was talking a lot. I had said to myself, She's bound to be edgy, it's after-hours, maybe she's worried she's about to lose another pupil. I will give her the money I owe and after a polite interval I will leave. Now I wanted to stay.

"Haven't you forgotten about Laura?" she said.

Laura sat in the car, one foot over her knee, peeling off skin. When she saw me, she leaned across the seat and opened the door.

"Isn't she nice! I knew you'd like her. Was it about that letter?"

"A little bit."

"Was it a love letter?"

"About you."

"What have you been saying?"

"You should try modern dance, she thinks."

"I'd like that." She uncrossed her leg. "Today I danced a painting."

"How did you do that?"

"It's easy. She said, 'This is a painting. These are the dark colors. These are the light. Now express the colors for me.' I was the light. Then she divided us into two groups. 'Over here you're angry. Over here you're not interested. Dance it.' "

"Which were you?"

"I was angry, which was fun."

It was a world away from cloche-hatted Madame Offenbach. "You haven't told her what I do?"

"No, Daddy."

"If she asks, say I'm a lawyer."

"I need new shoes."

"Mummy will get you some."

She slipped on her ballet slippers. Their color was disfigured by a watermark and the toes were rusty with spots of dried blood.

"And unlike Madame Offenbach she can dance," Laura went on.

"Is she a good dancer?"

"When she left the Metropolitan, she was the best ballerina in the country. That's what Samantha told me. She danced a wonderful story for us today which she'd picked up in the mountains. She called it 'The Dance of the Weeping Terrace,' after a terrace people go to when they say goodbye. They hug and cry because they don't know their destination. That's why it's called a weeping terrace."

"Darling, I told you there was a terrace like that in our valley."

"Did you? No, you didn't. I wish you had."

Her teacher had made it more memorable.

"You promised to take me to La Posta," she said cunningly. Until now Ezequiel had been the reason we couldn't make the journey. According to intelligence reports, his men had been observed in the lower valley.

"You've no excuse now."

"I'll have a word with Mummy."

"Do you mean that?"

"Of course I do."

"And we can see the coffee bushes and Grandma's parrots and

Grandpa's library?" She had never met my parents. Like my sister, she would have run rings around them.

"That's right."

"You are coming home tonight, aren't you, Daddy?"

Often I didn't come back at night. I might be in the sierra, chasing some shadow connected with Ezequiel, or, if in town, I might be watching a suspect house. The extra money I earned from surveillance had—so far—covered Laura's tuition fees.

"Yes."

Beside me Laura loosened her damp hair. She gathered it up, fastening it with an agate hairclip I had given her. In contented silence we drove toward the supermarket in Miraflores.

"We must remember the cat food for your mother," I said.

The night was sticky and at the traffic lights on Parque Colón I shrugged off my jacket and laid it on the backseat.

"Aren't you hot in those leggings?" I asked Laura.

"Daddy, do you have a girlfriend?"

I was unable to reply for a second or two. "Darling! What makes you ask such a thing?"

"You never come home."

"I've been working, Laura."

"Samantha says her mother likes you."

Feeling angry, I was about to say "Well, I don't like Samantha's mother" when, without even a warning flicker, the lights in the street went out.

Laura looked outside. "What's happened?"

"Just a power cut."

The supermarket was a block away. An assistant shone his flashlight over the pet food shelves. He hoped it wouldn't last long. At nine there was a volleyball match.

There hadn't been a power cut since the military coup, but I was not concerned. At the plant in Las Flores they had been rumbling on for months about low pay. I was more put out by Laura's question.

We were about ten blocks from home when my jacket started to bleep. Sucre. I pulled over outside the Café Haiti. Lanterns had been placed on the tables. In the subdued light I saw men speaking into their mobile phones, checking to see all was well at home, in the office.

I listened to the confused details. The darkness sheeting the city had nothing to do with industrial action.

"Have you told the General?"

"He's on his boat."

"I'll meet you at the theater."

I gave Laura the handset. "Take this."

"What is it? What's wrong?"

She realized something terrible had happened. She fiddled joylessly with the machine. She was trying to imagine this terrible thing.

"It's Ezequiel." I said the words quickly, not hearing what I was saying.

"But Daddy, he's dead."

I accelerated along Vía Angola. Our street was not far now. I braked noisily outside the house, leaving a track of rubber.

"Listen, honey, I'm sorry. I'm not making sense. Explain to Mummy I can't stay."

I pulled the door shut behind her and drove flat out along Calle Junín. Sucre's message had resurrected the dread which Quesada only five days before had put to rest. It meant one thing: Ezequiel had not lain blackened and featureless beneath a coarse army blanket; instead, he had taken a tighter grip still on our destinies. It meant he was alive after all and had decided to rise from the earth. It meant he had descended finally to the capital. And the capital, "the head of the monster," was the perfect place in which to hide.

6

B y the time I reached the theater, the audience had bundled out into the street and were assembled on the sidewalk in a state of shock. My men had arrived and were attempting to detain them, but many had slipped away already. The crowd spread out under the plane trees and waited for taxis. Some, nervous as birds, stumbled between the tramrails. They followed the rails to the sea, not caring where they walked.

From a French playwright who had been sitting five rows from the stage I pieced together what had happened.

Lionel Grimaud, unaware of the power cut outside, had taken the blackout to be a part of the experimental drama he was watching, in full keeping with the poster which had beguiled him here.

The poster showed a young woman with white-chalked cheeks and eyes made up to look like a cat. She peered at her right hand, in which she held a minute version of herself fashioned into a glove puppet. From the tight ceramic mouth poured the words:

> Literature! Dance! Theater! Film! All this in a drama that is absolutely contemporary. Are you sick of injustice? Are you sick of feeling helpless? Are you sick of believing there's nothing you can do? Our actors will startle you out of your indifference. In *Blackout* you will see human existence taken to its extremes. You will see fanaticism. You will see darkness. You will see intolerance. You will see hope. AND YOU WILL SEE *Blackout* TONIGHT!

Twenty minutes into the play the theater lights went out. Already a negroid face, filmed behind an empty desk, had appeared on a large screen talking about alms. Then an angel had skipped onstage. Dressed in red rubber gloves, a gray suit and cardboard wings, he had hurled the contents of a bucket of water into the front row.

As an irritated section of audience mopped themselves dry, the voice of Frank Sinatra could be heard singing "This lovely day will lengthen into evening, / We'll say goodbye to all we ever knew . . ." The angel floated off, wiggling his red fingers, to be replaced onstage by four dancers, their backs to the audience.

Grimaud—who was emphatic on this point—said the dancers were girls. Each wore a black stocking over her head, with a thin black garter strap binding her face. They bent into a provocative stance, waggling their buttocks and slowly turning until they faced the audience on all fours, their tongues out. The only sound was of a fast breathing—"the sound of dogs panting"—and this, mixed with Sinatra's voice and, at the edge of the stage, the silhouette of the angel lip-synching his words, provoked a horrifying impression.

Sinatra was singing "I loved you once, in April . . ." when the moan of a recorded siren interrupted the words, followed by the rattle of gunfire.

It was then that the blackout occurred.

"We couldn't very well understand what was going on," admitted Grimaud. Onstage a disembodied light swung up and down. All eyes fixed on this erratic firefly, which plunged swiftly into the auditorium. There was the clatter of several people being tugged against their will onto the stage.

The audience shifted uneasily. Behind Grimaud an elderly woman hissed, "Claudio, you did not warn me that it was one of those audience participation plays. We should have sat farther back."

Then three shots, in quick succession.

The same woman said, for all to hear, "You promised it would be a musical."

Things were by now so confused that people didn't know if

this exchange was part of the play. The smell of cordite wasn't agreeable either, nor a warm sticky substance like scrambled eggs which had landed in several laps. After five more minutes of waiting in the dark, those in the front row who had earlier been sprayed began to hiss angry asides.

But even so, they sat there. And this was the strange thing: at least ten minutes passed before anyone had the nerve to stand up, and only because they saw, shining behind them down the aisle, another flashlight.

It swept along the rows, giving substance to the people sitting there. Soon it reached the stage, jerking upward to reveal a drawn curtain and three figures sitting on deck chairs about six feet from the back wall.

When you light something from below, you know how exaggerated it becomes? Imagine the sight of those bodies. The beam wavered across their legs and chests, magnifying huge shadows on the back wall.

They sat at an angle. Something had happened to their faces.

Quesada, his body bent backward, had a red caste mark on his forehead. The back of his head was no longer there, but you could see the eyes, nose and cheeks. His mouth had been gagged with theater programs screwed up into little balls.

Beside the Interior Minister sat his wife. You could tell it was a woman from the shadow cast on the ceiling by her curly, well-cropped hair. Her neck was twisted, with one shoulder thrust back to show her lapis necklace. They had shot her in the left eyeball, through her glasses, and her hair was sparkling with broken glass and what looked like phlegm, except it was her eye.

The bodyguard slumped forward next to her. The hollow-point bullet had entered the back of his head and his face was somewhere in the audience.

The silhouettes slipped back into the darkness as the manager rested his flashlight on the stage and climbed up. You saw its beam pointing at the woman's feet, where there was an awful lot of blood. The manager picked the flashlight up and staggered through the puddle toward the chairs, shining the beam directly into their faces, so now everyone could make out those terrible looks, the splatters on the stage set, like ink blots from a fountain pen which has been shaken violently, each splatter larger than the head, each self-contained, except for a thick vertical mark behind Quesada's chair where a chunk of his skull had struck the wall and slid down.

The light scanned the wife's sparkling hair, the pulpy red mask of the bodyguard and Quesada sitting there, a cardboard notice on his paunch, the lettering, sketched in his blood, reading DEATH TO ALL TRAITORS. VIVA EL PRESIDENTE EZEQUIEL!

The manager gave a choking sound. People in the audience gasped.

"Believe me," came a man's voice, "this is part of the play."

As soon as I read the sign around Quesada's neck, I knew that Ezequiel had come down from the mountains. He was among us in the city. Anywhere in the city.

But he was not just "anywhere."

I now realize that, earlier in the evening, he would have turned on the television. Careful to cut out the sound, he wouldn't have wished to attract the attention of the ballet students below. Laura's class had ended. The girls having taken their showers, he would have walked to the window to watch them leave. He would have pushed back the curtain with the back of his hand—and that's when, through the narrowest of gaps, he would have seen me.

Admittedly, in the dark neither of us could make out more than the outline of the other. But for a second or two we looked at each other. All that separated us was a yellow nursery curtain.

That curtain was permanently drawn. Ezequiel would stand behind it for minutes on end, absorbing the street. He liked to stand in the same position, his face against the glass of the window, which he would slide open a few inches. At the end, when I was observing him through my binoculars, I could see him inhaling the air, feeling it on his raised face like a dog pressing its nose to a car window. That's probably what gave him his cough, because a few days after Quesada's death Laura came home with a fever, and by the end of the week Sylvina had caught it too.

I can describe what he would have seen through that chink. By the time I ordered in my men, I knew everyone in that street, what they did, when they left home, what time they returned, their love affairs and peccadilloes. Afterward I wandered a lot around that room, standing where he used to stand, imagining him. Once, a movement drew my eyes to the house opposite. A young girl pushed a man, laughing, onto a bed. A leg was raised at right angles into the space where they had stood, then it disappeared. When the girl next passed the window, she was naked. Seconds later I heard the sound of a toilet flushing.

The toilet was fed from a water tank on the roof. It's a funny thing, but for six months almost the only word Ezequiel would have seen in the world outside the room was the manufacturer's name: Eternity.

If I close my eyes, I can follow the street to the hill at the end. Sometimes the outlines of the slope are clear and I can make out paths and the colors of a garbage dump. On other days it remains a blurred shape, the same color as the fluffy gray sky which our poets liken to a donkey's belly.

I hear the sounds of a middle-class street. A gate closing, a car door opening, a bird singing. The tree where the bird sits is a jacaranda. It's been growing purpler by the day, as if someone had dipped the branches in the afternoon sky. I don't know about you, but I hate the sound of birdsong in the evenings.

Opposite, below the lovers' room, Milagro, the maid, starts to beat an imitation Persian carpet against the fence. The noise causes an Alsatian to leap up, paws spread against the railings, barking. A while ago, while reversing into the street, Milagro's employer ran over one of this dog's puppies. That's why she paces up and down, thrusting her snout between the bars, her black eyes roving over anyone who passes.

Milagro shouts for the Alsatian to be quiet, but is ignored. She is habitually ignored. Every day she bustles after the boy who collects bottles. Too late she hears his shout. She scuffles in the wake of his bicycle cart, but never attracts his attention.

"Bottles!" shouts the boy. Casually he lifts both hands above his head, so that for a few dangerous yards no one is steering the cart. Then he grips the bars, leans into the corner and disappears.

Milagro lurches one or two paces and stands in the middle of the street, panting helplessly, holding to her breast a bag which clinks with empty Cristal beer bottles. "Señor . . . Señor . . ."

The barking frightens a face to a window of the house on the corner. Did Ezequiel know what went on in that room every afternoon? The face at the window belongs to Señora Zampini. At three o'clock, when Dr. Zampini is lecturing on geriatric oncology at the Catholic University, an orange Volkswagen Beetle draws up and out steps a tall man in a brownish suit with shiny dark patches on the elbows of the jacket. He stands up stiffly, pulling his shirt cuffs back down his sleeves. He's not as excited as he used to be. He comes without the verve or the flowers that attended his earlier visits. Has Señora Zampini noticed his listlessness? When the door opens, hers is the face in the shadow, grim with anticipation. He enters, kisses her hand. The door is bolted behind him.

What else do I hear? The conversation from the corner café over cups of scalding, cardboard-tasting coffee. Cars leaving for the beach, their drivers hooting as they pass the video store, the air sweet with the lotions they've rubbed on their arms and faces. The panting of two middle-aged joggers, women in turquoise tracksuits, their hairdos ravaged by sweat.

It is easy for me to picture myself as Ezequiel. How hungrily I watch the street. I yearn to be outside, moving. There are occasions when I want to yield to the violence I have unleashed, taste it for myself, experience the fear I have become immune to. I touch the window and cough. I feel the air against my hand. Despite my cough, I press my cheek to the draft. I belong downstairs, not in this locked room. I touch the door handle and dream of the world downstairs. At half past three every afternoon, Kant walked under his lime trees. For six months I haven't abandoned this space.

So there Ezequiel stands, waiting for Laura's class to leave, waiting to count the girls out so he may watch television or listen to his music.

There is a box crammed with loose cassettes—Beethoven, Schumann, Wagner and a Donizetti opera, *Lucia di Lammermoor*. There are also recordings of Frank Sinatra, but they haven't been played in a while. Ezequiel's taste in music has changed since he left the mountains. As the psoriasis devours him, eating its way between his buttocks, he no longer wants to hear a human voice.

Not that he spelled any of this out during our interrogation. I had to retrieve these bits and pieces from a tide of belligerent nonsense about fascist continuismo and the Inevitable New Dawn. The utopian garbage he spouted contained few clues about what actually went on in that room. Only the room told me anything.

It was not much bigger than my office. There was a double bed and at the center, with its back to the window, a high-backed armchair covered in red velvet, in which he spent much of his time reading.

His books were arranged in alphabetical order on a shelf above the cassette recorder. This was Ezequiel's third safe house in eighteen months and he had with him only essential texts, each one annotated in his close, backward-sloping handwriting. Had they let me study them, I might be able to tell you more about the way his mind worked. But they didn't.

On the arm of the chair, a tin Cinzano ashtray overflowed with Winston stubs. He loved American cigarettes. That, and his psoriasis, and his passion for Kant, and the fact that he liked drinking mineral water constituted pretty much the whole of the picture I had of the man until I met him face to face in that room. By that time there would be no yellow curtain between us, no merry cartoon elephants floating down on striped parachutes. Down to what, I don't know.

What else was up there? In such a space everything becomes an icon. Two pairs of shoes on the floor, making steps without him. On the white walls a small picture of Mao and a framed photograph of the Arc de Triomphe at night. He'd never been to Paris, but he admired Napoleon. These types do. A hotel trolley which he used as a desk, and also to eat from. The food, prepared in a back kitchen, was brought to him by Comrade Edith. She was the only person allowed to enter his sanctuary, kept locked at all times. Edith was the reason, I am sure, he had abandoned the mountains. His wife Augusta was the girl who had driven the red pickup (and was formerly the girlfriend of Pascual). She would have wanted him to remain in the countryside. Like him, she had envisaged the revolution achieving its triumph after his death, in much the way that cathedral architects were content not to see their work completed in their lifetimes.

But that was a young man's dream, the fantasy of a provincial idealist. Augusta's death and his disease had pinched him back into this life. He no longer had the patience of a snake. He had grown restive, and Edith found it easy to exploit this impatience. She urged him to enjoy the fruits of his revolution now, in his lifetime. All they required was one final, decisive action. But for this he must come down to the capital. His physical presence was needed to plan the operation. To monitor and inspire it. To be there when his people removed, once and for all time, the rotten, crumbling keystone of the state.

I don't know whether he and Edith slept together in that unmade bed. Rumors said he slept with all his female followers, who regarded him as holy. But I don't believe that.

A small bathroom led off the bedroom. Here he swallowed his capsules and applied his creams. Have you smelled petroleum jelly? Well, that's how the bathroom smelled. There were medicines everywhere, on the floor beside the perished rubber mat, on the shelf below the shower, ranged along the top of the cabinet above the basin.

What struck me was the lack of a mirror. I can only suppose that Ezequiel had become revolted by his image and no longer wished to be reminded of his obese, diseased, almost immobile self.

So here he stood, this sick body—the psoriasis worsening by the day—restless, in pain, and of course he was going to be aware of the beautiful girls below. Since he couldn't see them, they must have been the more beautiful in his imagination. You see, the dancers' bathroom was directly below his. He would have heard snatches of conversation as they soaped their exhausted bodies under the shower. Think of it. Here was a man in a locked room preaching liberty while downstairs, only a matter of feet away, they were free.

They were being trained to fly and he was caged. Doesn't that make you laugh?

He must have seen me get out of my car. I'm not sure what can have passed through his mind when he saw me crossing the street.

I guess while I talked with Yolanda downstairs he would have sat in his armchair and watched a silent television screen. Then, when the power cut came, he would have waited for news from the theater.

I left the Teatro de Paz at three in the morning and drove cautiously home. The only lights came from cars and a few candles twitching behind windows. The city was quiet too. All I could hear were the waves stampeding on a dirty gray beach. Not until I reached Vía Barranco did I learn why the silence was sinister.

My headlights picked out packs of children tearing along the sidewalks. They were sticking paper sheets onto doors and windows. I swerved at them and they ran off. Getting out of the car, I walked toward the face which stared at me from this door and the next, and from the doors of every house in Vía Barranco.

My photograph of Ezequiel, blown up by Quesada's ministry and used in the countryside, had been translated into thousands of head-sized posters. They were signed PRESIDENTE EZEQUIEL, while across the top of each, in the same handwriting, were the words BLOOD DOESN'T DROWN THE REVOLUTION BUT IRRIGATES IT! EZEQUIEL'S THOUSAND EYES AND THOUSAND EARS ARE ON YOU!

I had the sensation that the eyes in the poster mocked me personally. As a clue to what I look like now, this morning, they said, this face is worthless.

The dawn confirmed his prevalence. In San Isidro a general's widow woke in the half-dark and thought she had died because Ezequiel's face, which she mistook for that of her husband coming to greet her, had been pasted over both bedroom windows. His uninhabited eyes stared from the garbage cans, from movie posters, from beneath the glass tops of the tables left overnight outside the Café Haiti. He floated in the fountains of the Plaza San Martín. He was caught in the treetops of the Jardíne Botánico, as though dropped from the sky. He looked up from doormats in Belgrano, having been slipped, like a locksmith's circular or a Chinese restaurant menu, beneath the front doors.

Like the Passover Angel, he had spread his wings over the capital.

So long as it stirred the dust of unseen terraces far from the capital, no one believed much in Ezequiel's revolution. Now everybody was fervently interested. When there is a victim at once familiar and powerful, the anxiety of a nation is easily engaged. The identity of the murdered Minister underlined our gross incompetence. The man onstage, his mouth grotesquely stuffed with theater programs, had, among his other responsibilities, been head of the national police force. He was, politically speaking, our boss.

At eight-fifteen in the morning on the day after the Teatro de Paz killing, General Merino called me to his office. When he had learned the news of Ezequiel's death, already he had taken a holiday. He should have been on his boat. Instead, he stood by his desk and looked at me with misgiving, his lower lip pushed forward a little. He was slightly tipsy and smelled of the cigarette he had cadged off his secretary. Because of the power cut, the air-conditioning wasn't working and he had removed his jacket.

"I've been asked to stand by. Calderón wants to speak to me."

"Fuck," I said.

" 'Fuck' is right."

He grabbed an orange from the glass fruit bowl and started to dismantle it. A sticky hand indicated a poster on his desk, black letters screaming SICK OF INJUSTICE? SICK OF FEELING HELPLESS? SICK OF BELIEVING THERE'S NOTHING YOU CAN DO?

"Once," he said through a mouthful of pulp and juice, "I made the mistake of buying a ticket for one of these so-called plays. Believe me, there was nothing I longed to do more than climb onstage and grab the actor by the throat and say to him, 'This is no damn good.' "

He shook his head and sucked at a segment of orange.

"You know what Calderón is going to say, tomcat. How did we so completely underestimate Ezequiel?"

"We didn't, sir."

"What's that? Speak up, can't you?"

"A copy of my report was sent to the President's Office."

The warning had been there on the first page. In the third

paragraph, I referred to the mimeographed pamphlet discovered on the woman we had arrested in Las Flores. This pamphlet, entitled "Washing the Soul," constituted Ezequiel's sole declaration to date. "Our process of the people's war has led us to the apogee; consequently, we must prepare for the insurrection, which becomes, in synthesis, the seizure of the cities."

My message, underlined in yellow marker, was clear. On the presumption that the pamphlet was not a forgery, and regardless of the welcome lull in Ezequiel's activities, we ought to brace ourselves for an escalation of violence. "We cannot rule out that he will try a political assassination."

I doubt whether General Merino had read the report. He was unable to take Ezequiel seriously, regarding him, with mannered disdain, as a college professor who had dropped out. Revolutionaries who showed their faces—that's what he was used to. But Ezequiel was sneaky. He wasn't a manly Castroite like Fuente, who boldly and openly entered a bar and, in full view of his victims, shot dead fifty of them. The General, faced with my attempts to describe Ezequiel's revolutionary philosophy, would dismiss them with an air that suggested he had seen it all before, in far more virulent form.

"You think Ezequiel's people know about Mao and Kant and Marx, but they're just going back to the same buzzwords. They sit around the fire and pretend to warm their hands with European nostalgia. Really, they're itching to get out their knives. Especially the women. They adore to kill. It's an event. Then they make love for three days after. No, tomcat. This isn't a world revolution. It's a fuckathon."

His attitude exasperated me, but his hands were full elsewhere, his mind preoccupied with staff morale, pay, an epidemic of internal corruption. There was pressure on him from the government, the military, the drug enforcement agencies. The "world revolution" came low on his list. The capital was the General's priority, and to date Ezequiel had restricted his actions here to one or two attacks on the Central Highway, some tires burned and a demonstration on Labor Day. And dogs hanging from the streetlights, of course. He was irritating in the way a cigarette butt in the lavatory is irritating, still bobbing up after every flush. So the General had left me to deal with him. I wasn't on the take, so he could trust me. Because of my Indian blood I could be expected to shed light on the phenomenon. Better than some of his officers anyway. And most important to his way of thinking, I'd met Ezequiel, hadn't I?

Now the lavatory had blown up in his face.

He'd had a presentiment of this. Or so he would confess in one of the watchful nights ahead. One evening after work he'd be sitting in his favorite bar by the port, dreaming fish, and—snap!—the lights would go out. He would order another drink while they hunted for candles, and half an hour later a tapping at the window would divert him from his cinnamon-flavored brandy and Sucre would be making goldfish lips against the glass.

"What's that, Lieutenant? Stop that nonsense. Come inside."

"It's Quesada."

"What about him?"

"He's been shot."

And he'd feel this pain—actual pain—in his clouded head and all the bright days when he shouldn't have taken the boat out would slyly wink at him from his brandy glass.

The prospect of a meeting with Calderón filled him with apprehension. He began adjusting the position of his mobile telephone.

"It's in your report, I know. You've done a good job, tomcat. But remind me. How did this begin?"

"In Villoria. At the university."

"Villoria, eh?" He looked at the map on the wall behind his desk. An orange slice moved uncertainly over the Andes. "Now Villoria," he said, as if considering the matter for the first time. "Isn't that a strange place to start a world revolution?"

He turned to me. And the questions fell out of him until they lay between us in a pathetic heap. Why weren't we catching him? Where did he get his funds from? What did China have to do with our country? How many men did he have? Why communism? Wasn't communism dead? On and on, with me doing my utmost to answer, until he finally said, "What does he want, for Christ's sake?"

"Absolute power."

"Why?"

"He says the state doesn't care for the people."

"Amen to that," said the General.

He sucked at another orange quarter, then looked at me over the rind. "You know what worries me—"

The telephone on his desk began ringing, long pauses between each ring. He rolled his eyes despairingly and threw the peel into the bowl.

"Time to swallow the hemlock," he said.

He extended the mobile's aerial and climbed inelegantly to his feet, walking to the window. "Yes, Captain," said the General. "Speaking." Perhaps he decided he was being rude, or maybe he wanted me to share the burden, because he walked back to where I was sitting, drew up a chair and sat down next to me, facing his own empty chair across the desk, and held the mouthpiece between us so that I could hear too.

The voice was clipped and quick, too low for me to catch.

"I do understand," said the General reasonably. His cheek all but touched mine. I smelled the brandy.

"Do you think we haven't—"

The other voice broke in. The General listened, breathing heavily until it subsided.

"It is a sorrowful state of affairs. Twelve years . . ." He was echoing the words he'd just heard. "It's difficult to say, Captain. Perhaps you have no idea how diff—"

Another angry outburst. Again he listened, nodding. He reached for the fruit bowl, edged back. "Do you think that is necessary? I mean—" He looked at the space above the chair where he had been sitting.

"Of course. I understand, Captain. I will do what I can."

He slapped down the telephone and shook his head from side to side, testing the bridle of Calderón's order.

"I tell you. Tomcat, I feel just like . . . like . . ." The simile escaped him.

He walked around his desk and collapsed in his chair. "He's canceled all leave."

"I'll tell the men."

"If we don't find the assassins, he'll bring in the army."

"I have no names for you," I said.

"Then who do I tell him was responsible for putting a bullet through our boss's head?"

"They were dancers, sir. A man and four women."

"And why can't we catch them?"

"They're known as 'annihilation detachments.' Twenty years old, often younger. They probably came in from the countryside and disappeared there afterward."

"Who helps them?" No pause for breath.

"No one who helped them would have known who they were."

"Women? Jesus. What's happened to the women in this country? Have they gone nuts or something?"

"I don't know, sir."

"There must be thousands of poor bastards who don't know what's going on in their women's minds. The point is not that these women are terrorists, but that there are all these stupid husbands who don't know what the hell's going on."

I said nothing.

"These women, have we ever convicted any?"

"The evidence is never enough."

"We let them go?"

"Yes." He knew all this.

"Don't we have any suspects at the moment?"

"There's the woman we arrested with those pamphlets—"

He leaned forward, alert. "Who is where?"

"Downstairs. We have her in detention."

"Then we have nothing to worry about," said the General, springing from his chair.

The lift was not working. We walked downstairs, the General stumbling behind me in the dark. As we reached the basement, the lights flickered on.

Hilda Cortado sat on the corner of her bed, rubbing her eyes. We studied her sad face through the grille. She was muttering to herself, readjusting to the light. According to my notes, she was nineteen.

"She's a sexy drop," said the General, polishing another orange on his shirt. "Where's she from?"

"Lepe."

"Indian, is she?"

"Yes, sir."

"At police college we used to make the Indians eat dog shit," he said wistfully.

Hearing him, she turned to face us.

The arrest of Hilda Cortado a week before had, for me, first raised the possibility that Ezequiel might be preparing the fifth and penultimate stage of his New Democracy: the assault on the capital. Deceived by Quesada's broadcast, by a cindered corpse beneath a blanket, we had overnight lost interest in her. Now she incarnated all the General's earlier failures to take notice of Ezequiel.

"Okay, tomcat, I'll be the good cop," said the General genially, unlocking the door.

Once inside the cell, he took up position in the corner farthest from the bed, beaming.

I approached Cortado. "I have some questions."

The spit landed on my forehead. I left it there, not reacting, then stepped toward her. Her eyes flared and she braced her head, expecting to be hit. Holding her stare, I wiped the spit from my forehead and touched the wet fingertips to her lips. She pulled back, tightening her mouth.

I crouched before the bed, looking down at the floor. It hadn't been swept. She had scratched some words in the dirt: VIVA EL PRESIDENTE EZEQUIEL.

I took a breath and became the bad cop.

"Hilda Cortado," I began. My voice rose. "Listen up, bitch."

"Hey, calm down, buddy, calm down." From the corner the General made mournful eyes and shook his head. "She's young. She's got a right to her silence."

I turned from him to glare at her. "You had something to do with planning that business last night, didn't you? Didn't you?"

She sat very still, unblinking, her expression not altering. If I accused her of too much, she might confess to something. That was the idea, at least. But I'd interviewed her already. I knew she wouldn't confess to anything, even if I had found her with a dripping knife in each hand. Yet I wanted the General to see this for himself. I wanted him to understand that Ezequiel wasn't an invention, a rumor, an abstraction. I wanted him to know the frustration of dealing with people who never speak.

"Three murders," I said. "That's a life sentence. Three times over. The rest of your life in a cell like this. And you know who we're going to pin those murders on, Cortado? You." I held up a pamphlet, one of two hundred we'd found in her bread basket. I opened it. "Incitement to rebellion. Ten years for that. But after last night I think most judges would link you with Minister Quesada's death. Don't you?"

Her expression didn't change. Even if she didn't know anything about the Quesada operation, she wouldn't say. She had been trained for this.

"But that's not an option, is it?" I said. "Oh, no, Cortado. Because you know what we do with assassins like you, don't you?"

She'd know about the cattle prods, the buckets of water, the magnetos wired to genitals. Fuente had been sat on a box of dynamite and blown into the sky.

I produced a pamphlet and stroked it back and forth against her nose.

"Where did you get this, Hilda? Who gave them to you?"

"The wind blew it into my hand." She hissed the words. Her lips had no sooner opened than they clamped shut.

I rubbed out the letters on the floor. My fingers were still damp with her spit, and the dirt stuck to them. I began again, quieter. We had been preparing for this interview when General Lache's men blew up "Ezequiel" in his truck.

"Lepe, eh? I used to race around that square when I was your age. Jorge, the grocer, remember Jorge? I could beat him."

She wasn't looking at me, but listening. No one beat Jorge, the grocer.

I wiped my hand on my trousers and glanced up, catching her eye. She turned her face away.

"Benavides? Remember how he used to let down our tires?" She closed her eyes. I no longer saw her large pupils. I knew too much. The thought of that possibility beat at her defenses.

Kindly, I said, "And Domingo. You know my godson?"

On the bed the body tensed. Another hiss. "He never mentioned you." This time the lips remained open, glistening with spittle.

"Remember that ship in a beer bottle? On the shelf where he kept his music? Remember his guitar eyes, Hilda? Remember him going on about Mao and Marx, reading aloud from those books? Well, I gave him those books." I straightened. "We're fighting the same people, Hilda."

She stared at me, her body slumped, miserable, the slope of her shoulders like Sylvina's after an argument.

From the corner I heard the moist slap of the General's tongue. I was being too gentle. This, after all, was the role he had elected for himself.

I brushed the pamphlet against one cheek, then the other. "Ezequiel, where can I find him?"

But the General had heard enough. He stepped from the shadows. "Get out, tomcat," he ordered. "Let me stay with her a few minutes." He looked toward the bed, his eyes filled with consideration. "Hilda, can I have a word?" Even someone who knew the trick usually ended up telling the good cop something. But the General had never dealt with anyone like Hilda Cortado.

Full of concern, he went on smiling at her. "I'm sorry about my colleague here. He's a hothead," and he jerked a thumb in my direction. "He gets out of line sometimes." He put a hand on her cheek and tilted her head, like a man studying the label on an unfamiliar brandy. "Want a piece of orange, kid?"

The spit hurtled into his left eye.

If she was surprised by the ferocity of the General's assault, she didn't show it. Without blinking, she allowed herself to be slammed against the wall.

"Tell me where Ezequiel is, you bitch."

For the first time she smiled.

The blackout had sent the clocks haywire. I found Sylvina
stacking plastic bags of thawing food on the kitchen table.
The freezer door was open and ice dripped into a bucket.

"Thank heavens you're home. I've no idea how to reset anything."

I lifted the clock from the wall and turned back the numerals
to 19:20. Then I advanced the date from 24 to 25 February. I
could sense her eyes scanning the side of my face.

No one had told her about Quesada's death. She had been
asleep when I returned in the early hours, and I had driven away
before she awoke. But she had guessed. We had enjoyed our burst
of hope and we had been deceived.

The weekend before, to celebrate, Sylvina had borrowed a
beach house in Paracas belonging to one of her tennis partners. A
hired boat chugged us to the island, where Laura threw potato
chips at the sea lions. On the shiny brown sand she danced between the jellyfish. After dinner Sylvina and I made love.

"What will you do?" she asked.

"I'm not sure." In the dark I heard the dislocated bark of the
seals. For as long as I could remember, my thoughts had con-
densed on the harassing figure of Ezequiel.

"There were times when I suspected he might not be a he."

She deserved to be happier than my circumstances had allowed. I would make it up.

"Maybe it's the moment to leave," she whispered in my ear.

We had met in my second term at the Catholic University. I

was standing in the canteen after a lecture and she stood one place ahead. Round, elegant spectacles, a brooch at her neck, and white hands seamed with blue veins. I couldn't take my eyes off those hands, so different in color from my own. She waved them, exasperated, then noticed that I was looking at her. "Help me. What shall I have to eat?"

Sylvina took another bag from the freezer and put it on the table. "I hope there won't be a blackout for my party. What was going on last night anyway?"

"They've killed the Interior Minister."

"Quesada?" She stopped, still holding the plastic bag, its contents obscured by droplets of condensation.

"Yes."

"So he's not dead? After all that?"

I put the clock back on the wall. "Does that look right?"

"Christ, I was at school with Quesada's wife."

"She's dead too."

"What happened, Agustín? Tell me. You might as well tell me."

I described the events at the Teatro de Paz. It was the kind of play Sylvina might have enjoyed. Patricia, who had lent us the beach house, was on the theater's board and occasionally gave Sylvina tickets.

"Lucky she didn't this time." Her eyes had watered, but she tried to sound bright.

We talked about her literary evening. She worried the blackout might have ruined the casserole. "How long do you think it can keep?"

"Did you cook it with milk?"

"It's the one I make with smoked trout."

"If it has milk, are you supposed to freeze it in the first place?"

"I guess that means I shouldn't refreeze it."

"I'm sure it's all right."

"Or is it pushing things?"

"If it was me, I'd put everything back in the freezer."

"But I thought you said it couldn't be refrozen."

"Maybe I'm wrong."

"I also broke the pepper grinder. I can't get a new one anywhere . . ." She ran to snatch the bag from the cat, and immediately relented.

"She's eating!"

She seized a spoon, urging onto a saucer more of the half-frozen casserole.

"Look, Agustín. She's eating!"

She turned and looked at me. There was a spark of pleasure in her eyes and I wondered if she was seeing again what she had seen when I was a stranger?

I stroked the cat, as though I would benefit from the affection. I took Sylvina's hand, but she drew back. She pointed to the telephone on the trolley. "You haven't reset the answering machine."

I rewound the message tape and heard myself apologizing for not coming home: "I'm sorry. I'll explain later. You'll understand when I tell you . . ." The voice, high-pitched, aloof, uttering the decayed phrases of conciliation, didn't sound like my idea of myself. Though I stood only an arm's length from Sylvina, I seemed to be eavesdropping on some private grief.

She slithered the rest of the bag's contents into a blue container. "Laura said you had plans to take us to La Posta."

"She's keen to go."

"You can't. Not now."

"What shall I do? I did promise."

"You'll have to tell her it's out of the question."

"Where is Laura?"

She looked at the clock. "I'm collecting her in half an hour."

"She seems nice, her new ballet teacher."

"I'm not sure about this sudden interest of Laura's in modern dance."

"Can it hurt?"

"I haven't decided. I don't want anything to interfere with her chances at the Metropolitan."

"Isn't it her birthday soon?" I had been reminded as I fiddled with the clock.

"Next Thursday."

"How old is she?"

"Twelve, Agustín."

"What are we getting her?"

"Some ballet shoes, I thought. I'll also need some money from you to pay back Marco."

"Sylvina, why do we owe Marco anything?"

"He sent me the book I've got to talk about tomorrow."

Marco was her second cousin, a lawyer I disliked even more than I did Marina, his former wife. I felt bad when I complained about them to Sylvina, but the pair of them appealed to her worst instincts. They had gone to live in Miami soon after we married, and at their farewell dinner Marco had made me intensely angry. Standing by the fireplace in his creamy Nehru suit, he had told me that I ought to get my money out of the country: there was no future in a place where half the population were Indians who couldn't speak Spanish. I realized that he thought I was like him, and it enraged me. I had drunk rather a lot, and had begun to feel Sylvina was also looking down on me. I lost my temper. We were the ones who should be setting an example, I said. Instead, he was fleeing to Miami. I can't remember what else I said. Too much, probably. It makes me embarrassed to think how self-righteous I must have sounded. I remember the contemptuous look on his face. "So what are you going to do?" he said to me. "Become a fucking policeman, or what?"

I'd never thought about it before that minute, but that's exactly what I did. Laura was born in July. In August I was accepted by the Police Academy of San Luis, and things were never the same.

The knowledge that I owed money to Marco spurred me to tackle Sylvina about our financial circumstances. I was about to say something, but her mind was exercised by her literary evening, now only twenty-four hours away.

"You will be here to help, Agustín? You won't wriggle out of it."

I counted out the notes for Marco. "No, darling."

The prospect of having to talk for fifteen minutes about the novel Marco had sent had unnerved Sylvina for several days. At Paracas, lying on the beach, she had explained the plot aloud to clarify her thoughts. "It's about a cowboy who's also a photographer and he's always bringing light into these women's lives. Marco saw the guy who wrote it on a television show. Apparently he's really interesting, and he sings as well. Marco's sure the women down here would love him. I just hope Marina doesn't find out where I got the idea."

Over the weekend she had shown me passages from the book. I didn't care for it.

"I think this is trashy."

"Well, Marco doesn't. He thinks it's good."

She lodged the blue container in the fridge. "I don't care a damn what Ezequiel does, you've got to be here."

Poor Sylvina. Nothing went right for her, no matter how hard she tried. When he chose his next victim, Ezequiel couldn't have known that among the casualties would be my wife's literary dinner.

On that day I would complete my investigation at the Teatro de Paz.

None of the theater staff had seen the performance. *Blackout* had been a low-budget production and the players—students, it was thought—had insisted on operating the lights and curtains. They had left behind no trace save for a cassette, discovered under a chair, of Frank Sinatra's album *Point of No Return*.

"I . . . I was grateful for the business." Sixtyish, mustached, polite, the manager was the sort who likes to greet his audience as they leave. He sat on his hands wearing a formal satin jacket, which he refused to take off, apprehensive about his future. Nobody would want to be part of an audience where you risked being dragged onstage to have your head blown off.

He knew nothing of the cast. The one person he did remember was the director. He had been in his late thirties, of average height and build, with his hair concealed under a soft black cap somewhat like a beret—"but not a beret." He had spoken courteously in the accent of the capital, with a discernible whistle when pronouncing certain words—although which words exactly the manager couldn't remember. At first he described him as clean-shaven; later, he would not be confident even of that. The man had rented the theater for a fortnight, paying cash, with the option of extending the period should *Blackout* prove the success he sincerely believed it would be. Madame Offenbach's production of *The Nutcracker* was two months away. Rather than have his theater lie empty, the manager had accepted payment in the name of a student theatrical group from the Catholic University.

I don't need to tell you, no such group existed.

I never found out why Quesada let himself be lured that night to the Teatro de Paz. True, he had a liking for theater, but even so—*Blackout?* You see, Ezequiel couldn't have orchestrated his death without feeling confident he would be in the audience. Free tickets had been sent to five other government ministers and eight ambassadors; later, another of the envelopes was found unopened in a pile of correspondence addressed to the President. The publicity material, fortunately, attracted nobody but the Minister of the Interior. One can imagine the devastation had Ezequiel decided to stage, say, *My Fair Lady.*

I had the envelopes analyzed for fingerprints, but the technicians failed to come up with a match. I also submitted the handwriting on Ezequiel's poster to a graphologist. Her findings reached me late in the afternoon and told me nothing I didn't suspect. The low slope of the letters combined with thick, clublike finals indicated a cold character ruled by the head. It was the hand of a male; clannish, methodical, authoritarian and determined to succeed in spite of every obstacle. The lasso loops suggested a lover of music. From the short downstrokes she judged that the author suffered from an illness or physical weakness.

The analysis concluded: "This is a person who is successful in what he does, but who derives little pleasure from life."

Sylvina had a sweltering day for her dinner. At five-thirty I telephoned to say I was on my way.

"What happens if there's a blackout?" she said.

"There won't be."

"It's so hot."

"Borrow a fan, then."

"Who from?"

"The people upstairs, they'll lend you one."

"I can't. I complained to them this morning about blocking the garage."

"How's the casserole?"

Twice at breakfast she had opened the fridge, run her nose over the lid and sniffed.

"It should be all right. Although I did ring Marina to check. She says the amount of time is much longer than you're meant to keep something cooked with milk. I didn't tell her it was what we were having tonight."

"Have you worked out what you're going to say?"

"I've written two pages. That's enough, isn't it?"

I had suggested she practice her speech in front of the mirror, without looking at what she had written.

"You will be home, Agustín?"

"I'm leaving now."

Knowing the center would be congested, I headed through Rímac. There was more traffic than I expected, but that was all right. She didn't expect her guests until seven. I would arrive in time to insert the leaves into the dining room table, remove the two armchairs to the bedroom and act as a supporting presence. I would devote myself to making Sylvina happy, and afterward . . .

The mobile rang inside my jacket pocket. I pulled the car over onto the shoulder. The transmission was half drowned in static.

"What is it?"

"Sir, can you hear me?" Sucre.

"I'm here. Go ahead."

"It's Prado."

"Oh God." Admiral Prado, the Defense Minister, had been one of the other officials who had received free tickets for *Blackout*.

"Two girls. They've shot him."

I stopped the car. "Where?"

"La Molina, outside his house."

This morning I had been on the telephone to Prado's office. "No restaurants. No beaches. Not even a church."

"I don't believe Almirante Prado is a churchgoing man," said the secretary.

Yet even with the Defense Minister on his guard, Ezequiel had been able to strike.

A girl no older than Laura had killed the Admiral on this hot afternoon. There had been little to distinguish her from the thousands of schoolgirls who spilled into the streets after class. The Admiral and his driver, about to leave home for the Assembly, would have sat in the car, watching the bulletproof security gate slowly rising and the young legs juddering into view. The attention of both men would have been tantalized by the blue canvas shoes growing into the white ankle socks, the sunburned calves into bare knees, the thighs spreading into the neat hems of a brown and yellow summer dress just like my daughter's. Perhaps the driver kept his whistle to himself. Perhaps the Admiral whistled. His corpse would have the exhausted face of a womanizer.

She stood in view. They would have noticed her white headband. Two other girls joined her on the drive, blocking the path.

The driver hooted. Indifferently, they stood aside. The girl in the white headband rummaged in her satchel, tilting it toward the rear window, as if searching for a crayon.

The driver spotted the aimed satchels and delved inside his jacket.

The Admiral, his smiling face flattened to the glass, was shot twice in the neck. According to the Admiral's maid, who had run to the window at the first two shots, there was then a single explosion. In fact, three more bullets were fired.

Two rounds struck the driver. The car jerked forward and stalled in the road. The third hit the Admiral's assassin, who fell to the pavement, her jaw blown away.

Somehow the two unwounded schoolgirls managed to tug Prado and his driver from the car and lift their injured companion inside. The maid saw the dark blue Mercedes driving southward.

I turned my car around and headed for the house in La Molina. Five minutes later Sucre rang back. A teacher had contacted police headquarters.

"There's a car abandoned near her school in Lurigancho. It sounds like the Mercedes."

It was. I found it sideways in a ditch on the edge of the road to the airport, two wheels in the air. A tracery of blood covered the windshield, and more dampened the back and front seats. Flies buzzed between the sticky surfaces. In the heat the blood had begun to smell.

A hundred yards from the car a group of children volleyed an orange ball over a rope strung between lampposts. It was growing dark, but the ball remained bright, as if drawing to itself the fading light. I left my car beside the Mercedes and walked over.

The children—five girls, five boys—continued thumping their ball, not looking at me. I waited until the ball came near, then caught it.

"That car," I said to the girl who ran up. "Who drove it?"

She squinted at the Mercedes.

"Never seen it before, chief."

A boy with a peaked Coca-Cola cap sauntered over with the other boys. They looked from the car to me, hands on hips, panting.

I ignored them, and I asked the girl, "How long have you been playing here?" She drew an arm across her nose, sniffing.

I walked between the boys to a little girl at the back.

"You? How long have you been here?"

Her black hair was matted with sand where she had fallen.

"Ten minutes," she whispered. They had started late. It was too hot to play earlier.

"You saw nothing?"

She shook her head, concentrating on her toe as it scraped a meaningless doodle in the dust.

Kneeling before her, I'm thinking I ought not to be here. Sylvina expects me at home. Six-thirty. Her friends will be arriving soon.

"What's the score?"

At this, the girl smiled. "Three–one. To us."

"They would have come this way—the people from the car." I bounced the ball. The boy with the peaked cap made a grab for it, but I was too quick.

In houses around us the lights snapped on. A shadow moved, drawing my attention to a girl I hadn't noticed. She bent over, transfixed by a patch of ground at her feet. I walked along the shadow toward her.

"What have you seen, little one?" I squatted on my haunches beside her, but she didn't answer. She didn't have to, because as soon as I touched a fingertip to the dark spot on the sand, I realized it was blood.

I ran back to the car to radio Sucre for help.

"Here's another!"

I replaced the mike and saw in the distance the boys gathering in a huddle. They strode back across the pitch in a group, led by Coca-Cola Cap.

"Chief, what will you pay us for every drop of blood we find?"

"If we find what I'm looking for, I'll give you something."

"No."

My men wouldn't arrive for another ten minutes. There wasn't time to barter. "One peso."

Two boys nudged each other.

"Five," Coca-Cola Cap insisted.

"Two." I wouldn't be able to claim it on expenses.

He looked at me, weighing up my offer, old eyes in a young face.

"Three."

"Okay, three."

His lips came together in an awful smile. He half turned and, inserting into that smile a dirty forefinger and thumb, he whistled.

I watched his acolytes haring up the bank. The girls didn't follow. They remained on the pitch, picking up their jackets, reluctant to take part.

I heard a shout: "Here's one!" As before, the boys gathered around it. The drop of blood held them in, then released them.

"Here's one!"

"Here's one!"

They receded in the deepening dusk, drawing together, then separating again, a monstrous anemone expanding and contracting in the dark.

I tossed the ball to the girl with sand in her hair and set off after them, unfastening the holster on my belt.

The drops of blood led into a labyrinth of pale brick houses. Rusted angle-iron entrails poked from the roofs, and corrugated sheets leaned in bundles against the unpainted walls. I pictured the wretched group struggling this way. Had they known where to go? Was there a safe house in an emergency? Were they expected?

The boys had assembled outside a single-story house with low railings around it. They pointed to the steps, the concrete specked with blood. I drew my pistol. The boys stepped back a pace, all but for Coca-Cola Cap, who stood with his hands in his pockets, head at an angle, eyes missing nothing. I spoke again on the mobile. The nearest car was six kilometers away. I would have to act now, this minute.

I opened the gate and walked up the path. I felt no terror. That would come later, in the car driving home, in bed with Sylvina.

The door opened to my touch. I stepped into a narrow corridor. Ahead was a kitchen, to the right a glass door. Somebody flitted behind the glass. I pushed down the handle and kicked the door open, keeping back.

A body faced me on the floor, half propped against a black vinyl sofa and covered to the neck with a blanket. The head had been clumsily wrapped in a pink bath towel. All that could be seen of the face was a mouth, open at an angle, as if the skull underneath had twisted around and no longer fitted the skin. From the mouth came a wheezing sound.

Out of sight, a window rattled. I rushed into the room in time to see a flash of yellow hem disappearing over the sill. There was a loud report and the body at my feet jerked. I threw myself to the floor, in the same motion firing twice at the window. I counted to five. When I ran to look, there was no one there, and no one in the alley outside, and no noise.

I hurried back to the sofa. Under the bullet's impact the head had dropped to the floor and the blanket had slipped, revealing the brown and yellow uniform beneath. I peeled off the sodden towel. Still recognizable above the shattered jaw were the nose and eyes and hair of a young girl. Dead.

My mobile bleeped. Sucre, by the Mercedes, needing directions.

Outside, the volleyball team waited for me. When they heard the door open, they jumped off the railings. Their leader advanced up the path. He held out his arm, opening his fist. He was even younger than the dead girl inside, younger than Laura.

"Two hundred and forty-nine pesos."

That night, after the ambulance had removed the body to the police mortuary, we continued our search of the house. Sucre and I went through the front room while the forensic people completed work on the sofa. They had marked and tagged the towel and blanket and were tweezering the last fabric samples into a zippered plastic bag.

Around us, the havoc of a dismantled room.

"Hello." Sucre had unscrewed the back of a stereo loudspeaker. Wedged inside, a black leather Filofax.

I flicked through the pages. There were some words written in blue Biro, making no sense.

"I'll look at this tomorrow."

I drove home.

The kitchen clock said ten to midnight. Sylvina was washing up. Her guests had left half an hour earlier.

"They killed Prado," I said.

She didn't look up from the sink. "I know." Consuelo, the last guest to arrive, had heard the announcement on her car radio.

"How was your evening?"

"It went well, thank you."

Her shoulders betrayed her. Last night she had looked beautiful when trying on the dress.

"Sucre did call you?"

"Yes. Thanks." She was angry, but pretending she wasn't.

"I'm sorry I couldn't be here."

"I know. I understand." She might have lost her temper, but she understood.

She stacked another bowl.

"I've kept some food for you." She fetched the plate from the oven. Looking up, about to say something, she saw my shirt. "Agustín! You're covered in blood."

Fourteen years ago she had rushed toward me like this. It was my third week at the Police Academy. Then it hadn't been blood, but dog shit.

She made me take off the shirt, emptied the sink, filled it with hot water, dropped the shirt in it.

I sat down and began to eat.

"Probably it's disgusting," she said.

"She was only eleven or twelve."

"Who was?"

"The girl from the group who killed Prado."

"A street child?" She didn't mean to sound bitter.

"No."

You can tell a lot about a corpse. She'd come from a family like ours. Mixed blood; good dental care in the few teeth spared by the bullet; tidily dressed—the headband we later traced to a sports shop used by Sylvina; and little opal earrings concealed by the hair she must have washed only yesterday. This wasn't a deprived child or an orphaned child or an illegitimate child abandoned to the streets. This was a well-tended child from a good home, and with parents who loved her.

"This is the extent to which Ezequiel indoctrinates people."

I looked up. By the way Sylvina was pounding my shirt in the sink, I realized that I was behaving with no consideration for what my wife had been through. If you worry about something, you worry about it. She'd listened to me, but she had suffered her own miserable evening.

"Tell me about your dinner. Were you terrific?"

"Not here, Agustín. I'm tired."

In bed, naked together, she said, "Please don't. I can't. I don't want to."

I rolled back, lying beside her in the dark.

"Do you want to hear or don't you?"

"You know I do."

She spoke for half an hour, conducting her own postmortem. She talked at random, remembering what someone had said, providing another person's reaction. Until she drifted into sleep, one arm across her forehead, I was able to lose myself in another person's wretchedness.

I'd attended one of my wife's dinners a year before. The vogue then was charity, not books. Within six months they'd stopped raising money.

I conjured up her friends, braying women with their teeth in braces, tugging dogs into the hallway, plucking their blouses from their shoulders because of the heat. The images volleyed back and forth, and sometimes they were mine.

"But Sylvina, what a wonderful pied-à-terre."

She was too ashamed to invite these women home. I pictured them clinging to her in the gloom cast by the fluted Portuguese lamps, devouring with their degrading glances the tiny front room, the chairs in which they would sit before and after the meal, the lacquered dresser behind which Sylvina had tenderly arranged an incomplete set of green French coffee cups. From such inherited belongings she wove the mantles of her nostalgia.

I see Sylvina, elegant in her mother's dress and bracelets, hastening to close the kitchen door, calling over her shoulder, "I'll just do this as an anti-cat measure," before urging Patricia and Leonora to leave their dogs in Laura's room, where I hear Patricia whisper, "She looks like she's robbed the burial mound at Ur!" and I watch Leonora nod, indicating with a cruel uplift of her brow the tutu which Sylvina bought secondhand, and after they have shooed from the door their pets, a red setter and a dachshund, I follow them down the corridor, follow them past the mirror, observing their little flounce, follow them into the stifling room, where, bounding up to their hostess, they say in unison, "What a dear little flat you have," and Sylvina, blushing a little, starts to thank them when Marina interrupts, "Where's Agustín?" and Sylvina replies, "He's sorry, he has to work late," and Marina says, "Consuelo's just told us, isn't it terrible? I mean, tonight Prado, Quesada on Monday, and weren't we at school with his wife?"—this stimulating Leonora to admit through the braces on her teeth, "It's awful, I always found her so difficult," prompting from Patricia, "They tell me at the theater it was a woman who shot them," and Sylvina to react, "Oh, I think I can relate to that.

We have a repressed internal violence. Don't you think so?" which shocks Marina into saying, "But could you kill, Sylvina?" and Sylvina to answer, with her mind on me, on her smoked trout casserole, on the carnal adventures of a photographer cowboy, "I feel I could kill. I say that, but I don't know why," before leaping up, having spotted a tail under a chair, "Pussy! I thought I'd locked you away!"—this provoking Bettina to apologize, it must have been her, she'd mistaken the kitchen for the bathroom, but gosh it looks good, whatever it is, which reminds Marina to ask Bettina from the side of her mouth, "The bathroom, tell me, I've forgotten?" and Marina walks from the room trailing in her wake a silence which is filled by the sound of Consuelo's electric fan— she's brought it with her—and by Patricia, who says, "Remind me, did Marina leave Marco or did he leave her?" to which Sylvina, getting up, replies diplomatically, "Oh, I think it was mutual," as she prepares to offer each guest a monogrammed napkin and a plate arranged with slabs of veal pâté and thick sausages of cheese, which she encourages them to spread on squares of bread—"I'm sorry it's so soft, but I can't bear cheese that's been in a fridge"— and so on around the room, all accepting save Amalia, who declines with the words, "This man everyone's talking about, Eze-quiel, doesn't he sound fascinating?" to which Sylvina says, "Amalia, how do you keep your skin looking like that?" causing the other women in the room to concentrate, first on the portrait above the electric fire of Sylvina's great-uncle, for six months a Vice President during the Bermudez dictatorship, and then, more respectfully, on themselves caught in the hallway mirror, which, noting the direction of their glances, Sylvina explains she has erected for Laura, who now has a marvelous teacher, "All thanks to Marina," so releasing everyone to talk at once, even the taciturn Consuelo, the hostess of their last literary evening—a splendid affair on a lawn—who bursts out, "Don't tell me! That's wonderful," this encouraging Sylvina, on her way to collect the casserole, to add in a raised voice, "She's hoping for a scholarship at the Metropolitan," leaving her guests to nod to one another as if to say, "That dumpy little girl!" while they wait for her to wheel out the trolley—"No, it's quite all right, I can do this"—and out of politeness accept a small amount, "No, far too much, although it does look good. Really, I don't know how you do this on your own," as Sylvina resumes, "She'll be able to dance in New York, London, Paris," to which Leonora says, "Where our dogs come from," and Amalia jokes, "And some of our second husbands too!" and everyone laughs, before they coax the evening to its climax, the unavoidable moment when eight faces look up from their abandoned plates and forget the casserole and the heat and the absence of her antisocial husband and reassure Sylvina in a chorus warbling with anticipation, "Isn't this delicious? Isn't this fun?" and merge into a single creature, an oriental goddess with sixteen arms who pats her cat, her chair, her arm, and says, "Now, Sylvina, this book you've made us read . . ."

In less than a week Ezequiel had scrambled from the unmarked grave prepared for him by Quesada. From now on he would seek to burn his name on hillsides which could be seen from China to Peru. Every Cabinet Minister daily expected death.

We had no leads for Quesada's murder. At least the assassination of the Defense Minister provided two solid clues. They survived the night and were there when I awoke. There was the small body in the mortuary, which might be traceable. And there was the Filofax Sucre had discovered in the loudspeaker.

The diary pages were blank save for two entries, which read like assignations: "C.C. 9:30" (23 April) and "C.D. 6:00" (15 July). Maps of the capital and of Miami were inserted into the front, and a guide to phrases in English: "Please give me Thousand Island dressing"—that sort of thing.

The importance of Sucre's find was limited to two unlined pages clipped into the Filofax immediately after the diary. These had been filled in arbitrarily, with the randomness of notes jotted down at different times. One page consisted of a crude diagram in the shape of a church door, four mathematical calculations and a reference to page numbers 27 to 31 of the medical journal *The Lancet*. We would trace this eventually to an article, two years old, on a breakthrough in the treatment of erythremia. The sums might have been straightforward adding and subtracting—somebody bal-

ancing their checkbook or checking a grocery bill. Or they might
have meant something else.

Ten phrases were listed on the facing page. Some, obviously,
were book titles, but it wasn't clear if these were works someone
had read or books to be bought from a shop.

Life of Mohammed, W.I.
Rhetoric and dialectic in the speeches of Pausanias
Revolution among the children
Revolution No. 9
To know nothing of oneself is to live
There is always a philosophy for the lack of courage
Arquebus
Situationist Manifesto
One invariably comes to resemble one's enemies
Kant and samba

Most I couldn't decipher. For all I knew, "Arquebus" was a
racehorse—or was it some cold-blooded code word? The few
words or phrases I understood meant nothing. "Revolution No. 9"
is a song by the Beatles. "Pausanias" was a Greek traveler and a
tedious character in Plato's *Symposium*. I guessed "W.I." to be
Washington Irving—and this in fact I verified when Ezequiel, during my interrogation, began quoting a passage about how certain
desert tribes, if their dedication were great enough, could gallop
out of nowhere to conquer an empire.

As for the other phrases, well, only last week I was sitting here,
reading a book—Pessoa, it was—when that line about knowing
nothing of oneself leapt out at me. It made me think that if I live
long enough, perhaps I'll come to understand the rest of them.

Nothing on that list was as important as the three handwritten
addresses on the reverse of the page. All were in the capital. One
might be the house of the girl with the white headband.

They didn't let you smoke in the mortuary. The pathologist finished his cigarette in the corridor, then pushed open the door. He

slid her from the refrigerator and with both hands drew back the sheet. He repeated the process with the Admiral and the Admiral's driver until the three bodies lay side by side, as if members of the same family. The ammoniac smell reminded me of Sylvina's sink.

Two reddish mosquito bites pimpled the Admiral's chin. Otherwise his face, frozen into its tired expression, had the bluish white blush of ice. The skin wrinkles had stiffened and there were scabs of mucous about his nose. More disturbing than the fatal mess to his neck was the bloated angle of his penis. Resting against his stomach, it seemed cocked in the semiarousal which sudden death, pathologists tell us, can bequeath.

The eyelids had sprung open. The pathologist closed them.

When you get down to it, a dead body isn't something most of us can bear to talk about. We treat death by conventions. People are neatly removed by a single bullet. They drop to the ground in midstride. They die immediately.

Except that they don't die immediately. They keep moving. Breathing. Thinking. The Admiral died as instantaneously as it is possible for a man of sixty-five to die. Shot twice in the throat, he had suffocated to death. He had to have blood and he had to have oxygen, and both had been cut off by the girl's bullets. He was three minutes from the end when the first round caught him, but three minutes is three minutes. Struck by the bullets, he had passed into shock, yet his brain had continued working. For three minutes he would still have had his thoughts; confused and delirious, but thoughts nevertheless. He would have felt some pain, although not to the degree you might have imagined, since that part of his brain which enabled him to feel pain was dying.

Certainly he wouldn't have experienced the kind of torment his assassin suffered over the next two hours. She had had a much harder time. Until the moment she was fired at from the window, she could still breathe.

It is not usual even for policemen to come across dead children. I forced my eyes from the calm forehead to the ruined face. The jaw was a frayed tangle of blackened flesh. Part of her tongue fell free, tasting the air where her chin should have been. The face was the same color as mine, except at the back of the neck, where the blood shone purplish through the skin. The upper teeth, intact and healthily white, formed the top half of an expression. Whether of pain or something else I couldn't tell.

What had she been trying to do, this girl? Had this been a game? When the bullet removed her jaw, did she see everything in a different light? Or, even then, was it worth it?

For a few seconds she had been alive with me in that room in Lurigancho. Four feet away, that's how far apart we'd been, the same distance as now divided her from the Admiral—and I had heard her breathing. After I kicked open the door, her eyes blinked up at me, but because of the towel around her face it was impossible to read her expression. Did she know what was going on around her? What had that look meant? It had to mean something, from such a small creature in such extremity. Because the horrible thing about pain is that you're alone. No one can help you. I might have been able to help her, a little. But then the people she had thought her friends had fired a bullet into her chest.

The pathologist was speaking. "She had a nice little lunch beforehand. Lettuce, rice, meatballs, swallowed down with Inca-Kola, topped off with a Mars bar." He pulled back the sheet. "Before I tuck you away, little one, I'm going to put these up your nose." He talked to her as though she lived: to cope, I suppose. When I arrived, he had just sawed apart her chest.

It may sound silly, but in the days ahead I hoped someone would recognize her. To track down her parents, her grandparents, anyone who had known her, we circulated an artist's impression to schools. For any person in the world, there are hundreds of people who recognize their face. Think of those who would have come across this girl. She must have ridden on a bus wearing her brown and yellow uniform. From someone she must have bought her Mars bars and her Inca-Kola. To someone she must have shown off her little opal earrings.

We heard nothing. No one came forward. That, to me, was Ezequiel's most terrible legacy. The idea that someone could not only send this child to her death, but not claim her.

Later that morning General Merino returned from the Palace.

He had driven off at nine o'clock, flanked by two police motorcyclists. He sat upright in the middle of the backseat, clutching my report, rehearsing, not seeing the houses he once cherished, dreading the interview ahead.

The room was almost pitch-dark, he told me, just a light in a corner by a leather armchair. Calderón, in a black suit, finished writing something on a pad. He did not offer the General a seat. He stood up and sat, one leg dangling, on the edge of the desk. He wore black lace-up shoes, a tie of red and white horizontal stripes, round tortoiseshell glasses. His receding hairline was lavished neatly back, emphasizing the shape of its M.

"One of those faces you see in the business pages, tomcat, with a smile thinner than his shoelace."

Calderón had folded his arms. "Let us imagine that I am your superior."

"Yes, Captain."

"I would wish to know why this man, this delinquent . . . No. Let me put this another way. I want what you have on him. Everything. All records. Is that understood? Nothing kept back."

"No, Captain."

Merino had seen the goblin shark, and it was kinder.

Without energy the General walked to the window and looked out toward the sea. He spoke rapidly, his hands behind his back, getting rid of the words as fast as he could. "Calderón's ordered a curfew. From ten o'clock tonight. He's letting in the military. From now on it's a joint operation. We furnish the army with copies of our files, help any way we can. He has no choice. Prado was their man. Lache feels he's been made a fool of, especially after receiving Quesada's televised congratulations. His blood is up. It's bad, Agustín, bad, bad, bad."

Already he'd had General Lache on the line. "A heap of underperforming blubber, that's how he described us."

Behind his back, one hand twisted inside the other.

"Let us imagine Calderón's orders to Lache. 'If you catch anybody who looks mean or looks like they once had a mean thought about the way things are here, slap him in jail. Use any means. Screw due legal process. Plant drugs, torture them, keep them by force. If necessary, shoot them. You can't treat these people like rose petals.' "

He turned, looking at me. "You can see their point, tomcat. We've been in charge of this for twelve years and what do we have to show for it? A girl from Lepe whom we haven't yet charged because she won't speak." He brought one hand out from behind him, grimaced at his watch and made a calculation. "Well, forty-five minutes ago, four of General Lache's men went careering into the basement to sort out that particular problem. God knows where they've taken her, what they'll do." He turned his head from one epaulette to the other. "I'm sorry, Colonel."

I was leaving when he called me back. Something he had over-looked. Calderón, to finance the army's assistance in this joint operation, had trimmed our budget.

"It means no more overtime."

The cancellation of my overtime was a blow, I admit. The bank agreed to extend my overdraft for a short period. Regrettably, they could not increase the limit. Too many customers shared my pre-dicament—those who hadn't had the sense to transfer their money abroad.

The need to discuss money with Sylvina had become more pressing than ever. But I dreaded the thought of her protestations. I knew what I meant to say, and quailed. She, not I, was in the right. She had been good about money. She had spent her mother's inheritance on us. She took care to buy everything as cheaply as possible. Yet for twenty years she had been forced to endure the torture of her friends' sympathy.

It shames me to acknowledge this, but I found in Sylvina's demoralization a further excuse to prevaricate. Her nerves had grown frailer in the phoenix days following Ezequiel's reappear-ance. Two days after her literary dinner she had a noisy row with the couple in the flat above, newcomers from the coast, who parked outside our garage. About to leave for work, I had asked the husband to move his car. He obliged, but then his wife started shouting from the window. This was everyone's street. Just be-cause we'd been here longer, it didn't mean I had a right to tell people where to park. "We're proud in Judío, too!" She withdrew her head, then, as an afterthought, yelled, "Poof!" I drove off, but unfortunately Sylvina, coming outside to see what the matter was, heard the insult. She stood in the middle of the street and raised her fist. "My husband is not a poof! Park your bloody car somewhere else!"

Once more the woman stuck out her head. "Poof!"

This was too much for Sylvina. She marched back inside and reemerged clasping a long screwdriver. In full view of the street and ignoring the woman's anguished cries, she scraped and scratched at the offending hood. She stood back to reveal the words: THIS STREET SHOULD NOT BE LIVED IN BY PEOPLE LIKE US.

I agreed to meet the repair costs, but that, together with the blood money I had paid Coca-Cola Cap, meant I was almost at the limit of my overdraft.

The curfew lasted from ten o'clock at night until six in the morning. Any person stopped on the street between those hours without a permit risked arrest.

Hungry for information, people started to pay attention to earlier reports from the provinces. As the press caught up with nine-year-old atrocities, mothers throughout the city could be heard telling their children not to accept parcels from strangers, no matter what they offered.

Nothing retained its innocence. A group of schoolgirls on a sidewalk shimmered with menace. In the suburbs, schools broke up early.

The curfew, introduced to defuse tension, exacerbated the panic. Ezequiel's shadow had darkened us. Not a day would pass when we didn't feel the draft from his wings.

In the cathedral, minutes before a service due to be led by the Arch-Cardinal, a bomb constructed from mining gelignite was discovered under the altarcloth.

The president of a television channel sympathetic to the government was shot in the chest outside a flower shop.

Four civil servants died at a restaurant in Monterrico when a beer can, hurled through the window from a llama sling, landed hissing on their table.

Car bombs exploded outside the Carnation Milk Factory, at a

Miss Universe Pageant and outside the American Ambassador's residence.

Criminals fed on the chaos. In the richer districts, families prolonged their holidays, leaving their houses inadequately guarded. Sylvina's friend Patricia returned from Paracas to discover the contents of her living room missing, down to the brass light switches.

Soldiers patrolled the streets to meet the unseen threat. Tanks rolled into the square outside the Palace and took up positions from which they rarely moved. At night you saw the gun barrels aiming at the stars, the drivers watching the buildings through night glasses. Somewhere, inextinguishable in that darkness, murkier than any vapor, lay Ezequiel. But the army hadn't been trained to swat shadows. The soldiers couldn't grasp what they were fighting. Desperate for a severed head to brandish to the crowd, they could produce no one except Hilda Cortado, the nineteen-year-old pamphleteer. She was executed—God knows how—keeping her silence to the last.

Three weeks after the blackout at the Teatro de Paz, General Lache lost patience. In a crude parroting of Quesada's assassination, he exacted his reprisal on a group of drama students.

I have no doubt the Arguedas Players were innocent. I know that the man in the beret who booked the theater for *Blackout* had mentioned the Catholic University. A student theatrical group, remembered the manager. But, crucially, no name. My men had three times interrogated members of the Arguedas Players, the university's sole drama group, and absolved them of suspicion. Humiliated, dishonored, furious, General Lache reopened their case.

On the first Tuesday night in March, due to the director's car running out of petrol, the Arguedas Players started their audition for *Mother Courage* thirty-five minutes late.

The group which assembled in a lecture room of the agronomy faculty comprised ten men and six women aged between eighteen and thirty, the number increasing to seventeen with the arrival of the director, an untidy, square-faced man. Apologizing energetically, he unpacked from his wife's shopping basket five large bottles of Cristal beer and a pillar of paper cups.

At seven forty-five the caretaker looked in to tell them he was locking up at nine. He had the drama group marked down until eleven o'clock, in fact, but the booking had been made before the curfew order. With little to do, he asked if he might watch from the back. The director saw no objection. The caretaker would be the only survivor.

At seven fifty-five Vera, a nervous, striking-looking girl who hoped to play the lead, began reading from the text in a singsong voice. She spoke a few lines and stopped. She stubbed out her cigarette and, after a cough, began from the top, less mechanically this time.

She had read for perhaps a minute when there came a crash from the corridor. The door burst open and twenty men in black masks kicked their way through the chairs toward her.

Vera, unsure whether to continue, sought the director's cue. The script was slapped from her hand. An arm was clamped over her mouth, ripping her blouse at the collar. Someone forced a sweater over her head and, with her arms twisted behind her back, she was bundled outside.

On his hands and knees under the table, the director screamed for help until one of the masked men jerked him out backward by the ankles, smashing his nose on the floor.

Two minutes later a postgraduate student ran down from the library into an empty room. Scattered about the floor he found women's shoes, spectacles, pens, cigarettes and a script foamy with beer. At the back sat the caretaker, unhurt.

Not one of the Arguedas Players had been seen since.

General Lache laid the kidnapping at Ezequiel's door. Few believed him. The press interviewed distraught relatives and lovers—in one article mentioning by name the officer believed to have led the squad. It made no difference. That was the terrible thing. Among Sylvina's friends it was felt that the army wouldn't have acted without a reason. Therefore, those drama students must have been guilty.

"But, Sylvina, if we kidnap people without proof, we're no better than Ezequiel. Why choose us rather than him?"

She had come to equate me with the problem, not as part of the solution. "I don't care. It shows something's being done."

While the army retaliated—searching schools, arresting the innocents, filling prisons—I sat in a parked car and watched one or other of the three houses listed in the Filofax. About the addresses there could be no dispute. They were bricks and mortar. They existed.

Title checks couldn't tell me whether the houses belonged to friends or enemies. They were innocuous, well-kept buildings in the south and east of the city. They were lived in by a chiropodist, a professor of ethnology from the Catholic University and an American in the fish business, recently married to a pretty girl from Cajamarca.

Maybe these people were potential targets, people Ezequiel wanted to kill. Maybe they were his assassins. I had no idea. I just knew some violence was in store, some catastrophe, and I didn't want to risk questioning anyone in case we scared off Ezequiel. For this reason I had not relinquished the Filofax to the army. I felt I couldn't do anything for the time being except watch and wait for something to happen.

So that's what I did, day after day, night after night, collecting the trash bags, sitting in the car, looking for signs, watching.

The driver's seat became a sanctuary. I never used the same car twice in succession. I hung a dark blue suit against the window and leaned against it, pretending to sleep, or I read a newspaper as though I were waiting for someone. I knew the form of many racehorses. The Lova, On the Rocks, Last Dust, Petits Pois, Sweet Naggy, Without a Paddle, Zog, Nite Dancer.

I had a lot of time to think. It upset me, the way my unit had been treated. We might on paper share responsibility with the army for Ezequiel's case, but in reality we were not governed by compatible regulations. We had ceased to be the people's guardians. To my counterpart in the military, a burly colonel who reminded me of the cadet at the Police Academy who led the bullies, we were indistinguishable from the mob.

Calderón, by relying on the army, had marginalized us. Yet,

pushed out to the edge, I found Ezequiel coming into a perspective that disarmed me.

I remember, in one of the books I would find on his shelf, Ezequiel had underlined a saying of Mao: "People turn into their opposites." It is curious, but if you have been looking obsessively for someone—if, as I had, you had been stepped in Ezequiel day and night—after a while you do start to assume the characteristics of the person you are hunting.

Look at my hand. I can warn you I am about to touch this vase—and I do so. Or this book. But what if I told you of occasions when my hand didn't respond, when I mimed a bodily memory independent of my self—and instead of turning a page I watched with a grinding horror as this hand glided over my chest, to the base of my neck, searching for an itch which I couldn't feel but which my fingers desired, in spite of everything I might do to prevent them, to scratch?

I don't mean that I had moved any closer to finding Ezequiel. His character still seemed to me impenetrable—like the despair into which he cast us. But as I sat in that car, I had the sensation that I stalked nearer to the rim of some understanding.

Then, at the end of March, there was a swirl in the air—and I knew I'd disturbed him.

I had been watching the house of the American. He'd made his fortune in the States from pond-raised catfish. Ten months earlier he had come to this country to buy some Amazonian strains and to walk the Inca trail. At the travel agency in Cajamarca he met a very sexy, large-breasted girl, a model. They married, and in February flew down to the capital. A love story, he told his friends. He'd never left America before and within six weeks he was married! But it wasn't a love story. You see—and I'm not sure how well I have conveyed this to you—Ezequiel's assassins could be anyone. One day you might switch on the television and find the killer was your daughter. Another day, it might be your wife.

I spoke with him a few hours after he had found out, a fat man in a yellow golf shirt and tight-fitting Sansabelt slacks. He had a straw-colored beard and expensive glasses. Beneath his glasses his eyes were bloodshot.

He leaned over Sucre's desk, both hands flat on the desktop, talking uncontrollably. I was on my way to the basement when I heard him. Recognizing his clothes, I paused.

He had reached a point in his story which caused him to rub his eyes. He was telling Sucre how he'd been making dinner. He'd taken his carrot soup out of the microwave. In the act of settling down to watch the television news, he'd looked up and gone through hot flushes because there on screen, smiling, chic, looking out from the latest *Vogue,* was his wife. She was a model, see. That's how she paid her way. Then comes this news she's been captured. Oh no, he thought. They've got her, she's been caught in a car bomb, and they've got her. But it wasn't that. It was crazy, it was totally crazy. They were saying she was a terrorist. A killer.

He held Sucre by the shoulders, shaking him. "You've made a mistake, bud. She's not one of them. She's never voted in her goddamn life." He questioned whether she knew the President from her ass. "You've gotta let me see her, pal."

"Sucre," I intervened. "Let me."

Hearing my voice, he turned, his arms subsiding.

"You're American?"

"Yes."

"Where from?"

"We've got houses in Jupiter, Florida, and Lake Tahoe. I was born in Boston, Massachusetts."

"Didn't William James come from there?" My father had been an admirer.

"I have no fucking idea."

I took him to the video room. He sat meekly down while I poured him coffee, added lots of sugar and inserted a videotape.

He was close to tears. His wife was innocent, he kept repeating. He was one hundred percent certain. He believed all she told him. They had been married seven months, were so happy.

The screen brightened, filling with jerky images filmed by Sucre through the windshield of our car. A slim woman with long, stockinged legs was climbing into a black Suzuki Jeep. With both hands she hefted a Puma bag, sliding it onto the passenger seat.

"That's our car!" He was childish in his recognition. "She's going to her aerobics class."

I fast-forwarded the tape, chasing the Jeep through the afternoon traffic.

"She has this studio in San Isidro, Calle Castaños."

Out along the Malecón, past streets of substantial houses, their turrets rising over the walls, past Calle Castaños.

"She's picking up a friend. She does that sometimes. They take turns."

Out along the Pan-Americana, the dust bowl visible beneath the billboards advertising Hush Puppies and swimming pools.

"Some of them live as far out as La Molina."

Past rows of nondescript, squat brick houses with tin roofs.

"I don't know, maybe she's going to the Inca Market."

Past derelict, window-shattered warehouses from the days when we were a country.

"I guess she's meeting someone at the airport."

Past featureless districts, as yet unnamed, through untidy grids of adobe hovels, without electricity, without water.

Into more featureless districts, the hovels the same pigeon-gray as the dust, not adobe any longer but rush matting, a family to each roofless hovel, five hundred new families a day, jumping down off the trucks, dazed by the journey, run out of their valleys, no one to turn to, terrified.

By now we've slipped back so she doesn't see us. We've got her in the zoom. She bounces off the road, trailing a dust devil through a bank of rush-mat shacks, stopping outside a low white shed, one of the few concrete buildings in sight.

"Sometimes she does charity work." The words could hardly be heard. His face was shrinking. I could see the wide pores on his nose.

She looks around, hauls the bag off the seat and, without knocking, enters the building.

I fast-forwarded again. We'd waited a minute before going inside.

The tape wasn't well filmed, and once or twice crossing a slippery tiled floor, Sucre lost focus. But no one could mistake the look of the woman kneeling there as she jerked around to see us, nor the bag from which she had begun to unpack three submachine guns.

"Paulita," he said, a hand over his mouth, not believing it.

I had been on my way to the basement to interrogate her further. It was time I returned there. There was no point in telling the American, but this evening we would have to turn Paulita over to the military.

Already I'd spent six hours with his wife. So far she'd said only four words, repeated over and over again.

"*Viva El Presidente Ezequiel!*"

O n the next day my bank refused me credit.
Have you been in that situation? I notice you use a MasterCard to pay Emilio. But supposing tonight he came over and said, "Sorry, señor, can't take this"—think how you'd feel.

The cash dispenser was near my office. When it refused to return my card, I stood absorbing the flashing message, the cramps of impotence. Behind me concerned voices asked, "What's wrong? Is it out of cash?" Shamed, I walked down Calle Irigoyen. A couple, smartly dressed, entered a restaurant. What would the meal cost them? A hundred pesos? Across the road a man inserted his tip through a taxi's window. Inside a shop a woman decided on a dishwasher. Everywhere my eyes settled on people spending money. How could they afford it?

I counted my change. Three pesos. Enough for a pair of underpants.

Perhaps I could cash a check. Or request an advance on my salary. I saw myself reduced to telling Sucre I'd left my wallet behind, and might I borrow twenty pesos to tide me over?

At home I found Sylvina sitting on the end of our bed.

"What's wrong?" She had been weeping.

She looked away. "The shoemaker cut up my credit card."

On the bank's instructions, El Chino had before her eyes scissored in half the credit card with which she had tried to pay for Laura's birthday present, a pair of goatskin pointe shoes. "Thank God, I was able to put it on my Visa." But she had never been so humiliated. El Chino, an unpleasant man who kept a raucous crow

in his shop, was a gossip. When he went around the dance acade-
mies with his box of sample shoes, he would relish peddling the
story of Señora Rejas's MasterCard.

His shop became a place of horror. And not just his shop, but
the department store where she had hoped to buy Laura a leotard.
She had come home disgusted with herself.

"Why, why, why?" She wasn't extravagant. "Why, Agustín?"

I couldn't answer. Her friends bought dance shoes, but they
could afford them.

She held up a red-wrapped package. A present for Laura had
got her into this mess. Now everything was called into question.

"Maybe I shouldn't have bought these." She turned the package over, squeezing its contents. "Maybe they were too expensive." She started to unwrap the paper, then passionately hurled
the parcel away from her and collapsed back on the bed, her face
white and glittering with unhappiness.

"Sylvina, why—" I began.

"Why do you say 'why'?" She spoke to the ceiling. She
propped herself up on her elbows, her skirt drawn tight about her
thighs. Her legs were askew on the bed, heels caught in the
bedcover.

"We are—"

"Were. Were. Were," and she lay back again, a hand over her
face, sobbing.

I sat down beside her, picking up the package from the floor
where she had thrown it. I removed the red paper, laid the shoes
on the bed, then, tenderly, pulled my wife's hand away from her
eyes. One by one I separated the fingers, but they were not there
for me as they once had been.

She talked mechanically, as if making a list. There was the
telephone bill, her tennis club subscription, the groceries. How did
I expect her to buy food?—talking of which, there were no pears
today at the market.

"This is the time of year for pears. Why aren't there any,
Agustín?" She snatched back her hand. "How can I make you a
pudding without pears?"

"I don't know, darling." Whenever she wanted to forget something, she shopped.

"I still can't find a pepper grinder."

So it was on that bed that I confronted Sylvina with the true state of our finances. "I'm not accusing you of anything, but that's the way it is."

She sat up. Instead of reacting defensively, she said with great calmness, "What about Marco?"

"Marco?"

"I have discussed it."

"What do you mean?"

"He made the offer himself. He'd heard things were bad down here. We could rely on him, he said."

We had a terrible argument, after which she shut herself in the bedroom and telephoned Miami.

The following evening, without telling Sylvina, I drove to the ballet studio in Surcos. I made certain the mothers had driven away before ringing the doorbell. Yolanda had no telephone. If I wanted to catch her, it would have to be at the studio.

The street had fallen quiet. A bolt rattled and the door in the wall opened a few inches. I recognized her silhouette. Seeing who it was, she drew the chain.

"Señor Rejas?" Under dark eyebrows her look was intense. "But Laura's just left, with Samantha."

I knew this. I had watched them leave. Since I could no longer be certain of my movements, we had decided that Sylvina would alternate with Marina in collecting the two girls.

"It's about Laura I need to talk with you."

The door opened farther and a finger of light slanted down one side of her face. Her mouth was traced unevenly in dark lipstick, as though she expected someone. She wore a clean, faded pink shirt, which she must have changed into quickly, because it was misbuttoned.

"Do I disturb . . . ?"

"No, come in."

I don't know what questions passed through her head as she led the way through the sliding glass doors. Private teachers must expect the worst.

In the studio, as before, she put on a cassette.

"Dvořák, isn't it?" I asked.

"We were dancing to it just now."

She listened to the music, then turned down the volume. On her neck a tendon vibrated. "I can't offer you much. A coffee?"

Walking back from the kitchen into the studio, she dragged over two inflatable exercise mats. She blew them up until her face colored. When she inserted the stoppers, I saw that her fingernails were bitten to the quick.

"Sorry. These are all I've got to sit on. I don't encourage visitors. To begin with, I let the mothers watch, but I banned them after a week. They all sat in a row, which was rotten for the child who fell over. Mind you, some of their children I could push myself."

She laid out the mats. I sat cross-legged. She sat upright, her legs folded to one side, and drew a white handkerchief from her sleeve.

"I've got a bit of a cold."

I was about to tell her Laura had caught it, too, when she exclaimed, "I like your daughter so much! She's unsure of herself and anticipates the music and doesn't loosen her neck, but we were so right to try her on modern dance!"

Laura, with Sylvina's agreement, had exchanged a classical class for a modern one. Which was now immaterial, of course.

"I'm afraid I have to take her away."

A plaster had stuck to her mat. She peeled it off and looked at it intently. "What do you mean? Am I too strict?"

"No, she's very fond of you."

I explained my situation. I didn't want to withdraw Laura, but I could no longer afford the fees.

She kept staring down, and I thought she didn't believe me.

It wasn't merely a question of my salary being late. I'd been paying for Laura with my overtime earnings. Now all overtime had been canceled.

I was humiliated and she could hear it. She continued gazing at the plaster, then tossed it over her shoulder.

"That's all right. I'm happy to carry her until you can meet the fees."

Is this why I decided to talk to her before Sylvina? It must have been at the back of my mind, Yolanda's reluctance to disrupt her class.

Before I'd even thought about it, I said, "Next month. I might be able to pay then."

"Pay when you can. But don't tell anyone. Please. You can't imagine the misery my life would be if some parents found out."

I started to thank her, but she interrupted. "I've been teaching children in the mountains for free. Anyway, it's not kindness. I'm thinking of the others."

"Laura tells me you get your ideas from the sierra."

I knew that, before opening her school, she had studied traditional dance in the highlands. But I had mentioned the sierra only out of politeness.

"I've been studying the dance groups at Ausangate."

It is possible for a word to leap out and slap you after twenty years. "Ausangate," I repeated, and she must have thought I didn't understand, because she started to explain.

I wasn't listening. The word, last spoken by my mother, had exploded in my head. Now, on this dance floor, its mention extinguished the smells of rosin and sweat and cigarette ash and I was standing on a narrow path called the Knife Edge.

It was four in the morning. The moonlight blazed on the ice. We had been walking for three days and I was playing my flute to a sheer white cliff across a gully. We listened in awe as the glacier sent back my music, giving us the strength to climb to the summit.

I said, "I was once a pilgrim to the ice festival."

"You weren't!"

"Thirty years ago. I was Laura's age."

"You're the first person I've met in this city who's heard of it."

"I played the pipes in the *wayli* dance."

"No! Which pipes?"

A word formed on my lips—"*Pinkullo*"—and in uttering it I felt the sores in my mouth. The cold air cramped my chest. My neck ached and I heard the reedy notes of my flute and, from the pilgrims around me, voices imitating the animal whose costume we wore, whose bells tinkled round our necks, whose spirit we had been transformed into while the festival lasted.

"Then you know what I'm talking about!" Yolanda jumped up. She kicked off her slippers and raised one arm until I recognized the wrung neck of a dead bird. With her other hand she masked her face, kicking back a leg to mimic a creature scuffling out its urine. She danced a few steps, her body slim and decisive, then sat down again, eager to hear more.

"So you provided *kun*—what is it, the word for comfort and joy?"

I laughed. *"Kunswiku,"* and there was no way to halt the sequence of images: the short spears of frost on the stubble; the blast of orange heat from the candles in the sanctuary; Father Ramón, breathless, not used to this altitude, awaiting our return with Santiago beside him; while up ahead, leading us, scrambling onto the glacier with his axe, the distant figure of my friend Nemecio.

She touched my knee, forthright as a child. "Is it true every year someone dies? As a sacrifice?"

I was evasive. "There are accidents."

On the last night, we climbed to the summit and fought. There must have been a thousand people milling on the glacier, all from village groups like mine. At that height, in that strange light, something happened. Without anyone to guide us, we divided into two bee swarms. For an hour we ran at each other, throwing snowballs and yelling. The noise—rattled bells, shouts, drums—echoed off the ice as we rushed forward and retreated until someone slipped too near a crevasse. That year it was a pilgrim from Pachuca. We knew it as soon as he fell. We stood in the snow, not moving, and I'll never forget the relief—that it wasn't someone from our village whom the mountain had chosen.

She shook her head. "To think you played that flute. I can't believe this. So that explains what I've noticed in Laura. I wondered what it could be. She has her own way of moving, which you can't teach, just like the girls I've been living with in the sierra. She's also got that plumbline of balance these rootless Westerners don't have. She should be studying the *wayli,* like her father, not *The Nutcracker Suite!*"

Yolanda stared into space. I looked at her face. For whom had she inexpertly applied her lipstick? She lowered her gaze, unsettled again.

"You're sure I haven't disturbed you?" I said.

"No, it's nice talking. You don't meet many people outside the studio, and never anyone who's been to Ausangate. What were we talking about? I've forgotten."

"The Nutcracker Suite."

"Why does Madame Offenbach do it? Every year she still sends letters to Panama on Margot Fonteyn's birthday and every year she puts on *The Nutcracker.* Is that our response to the kidnapping of those drama students, to dress up in white tutus and behave like fairies or flowers?"

"And that is why you left the Metropolitan?"

She ran a hand down her leg at the memory, rubbing her ankle. She wore no stockings. On her ankle was a narrow scar, the same pale color as her skin, but shiny.

"No. I had a leg injury. Every time I tried to get my heel down to jump, it was agony. One day Señora Vallejo was watching to see if I'd recovered from my accident. There was an idea I might be the prima ballerina. Well, I put my leg in a developpé and I did this unheard of thing."

She stood up quickly, faced the mirror and unfolded one leg, the foot higher than her hip, then slowly lowered it.

"I thought: I'm giving up, I'm stopping. This is ridiculous. I put my leg down and I left the studio. Everybody knew what that meant. They knew it was final, as if I was in the army and had disobeyed an order. I ran into the dressing room, everyone's clothes hanging on pegs like ghosts. I heard the music outside, still carrying on. It was a Brahms adagio. At last, no more struggle, I thought. I want to go out into the world. So I went to the jungle for two years—I'd always longed to be a missionary. I dropped everyone in the ballet world and went to Iquitos, with the Teresiana nuns. For two years I couldn't bear to hear ballet music. I pretended I'd never been a dancer."

She had noticed in the mirror that her buttons were done up wrongly. She undid her shirt and rebuttoned it correctly.

"You gave up dancing, yet you started your own school."

"Because I can't help it," she said with feeling. She stood, arms crossed, chin up, on the tips of her toes.

"What do you mean?"

"I mean that everything that goes on inside me—joy, passion, rage, love—I want to show it with my body." She whirled around. "Don't tell me you didn't feel the same way at Ausangate."

"And this feeling, it came back gradually, or in a flash?"

"A flash." She pointed at a poster pinned to the kitchen door. "I was taken to see these Cuban dancers at the Teatro Americano—where soon I have to do my ballet. They reminded me of what I had forgotten."

"Which was?"

"Something Señora Vallejo always quoted. 'Movement never lies.' She never tired of reminding us that dance is a contemporary art form. It can incorporate our reactions to what's going on now, this minute. It can allow us to be ourselves, not parodies of some European ideal."

"Have you found an idea for your ballet?"

"It's unlucky to talk about work in progress."

That I could understand and respect. "Forgive me."

"Silence is part of the dance," she joked. Her face became serious again. "I'm going to dance a ballet in memory of the Arguedas Players."

"The drama group?"

She bit her lip and her nostrils flared a little. "Wasn't that terrible? Poor kids. I feel such hatred for anyone who could do that. What would you feel if one evening Laura was seized by a group of gangsters and that was the last you heard of her? No, that's a terrible thing to say." But she looked at me. "Do you think they're alive?"

"Who knows?" I'd wondered the same things myself.

"It's been three weeks. The parents have heard nothing. I've a pupil here—her cousin Vera was one of the students. Everyone knows it was the army behind it. They're dead, they must be."

"Probably."

"The other day I watched a program about their abduction. Then I had this idea."

"To dance the kidnap?"

"No, to dance *Antigone.*"

"*Antigone?*" I was out of my depth. "Isn't that a play."

"But, you see, that's it! That's the reaction I want. If I had told you I was going to dance something called, I don't know, *Hexagramma,* then all I'd hear from the ballet mothers is 'Why do you have to do pieces like this? Why do you have to show us all these dead bodies?' That's why I'm going to go back to Sophocles! Something everyone will think is taking place a long, long time ago, but which we're living now."

"Can I see this ballet?"

"You wouldn't like it."

"You said it was at the Teatro Americano."

Upstairs someone moved. She raised her head. "What's happened to our coffee?"

Yolanda went into the kitchen, flicked the switch on the kettle and waited for it to boil again.

She was pouring the water when the lights blacked out.

People think they know how they'll react in extreme circumstances. I *think* I know how I would react if this ceiling fell down. But I can't be sure. Nothing so far had indicated to me that Yolanda would behave as she now did.

In that first shock of darkness I heard her cry out. Something crashed to the floor.

"Are you all right? Have you hurt yourself?" There was no sound.

"My arm," came a thin voice. "I've scalded it . . ."

I fumbled my way across the dance floor into the kitchen. My hand sent a tin object clattering into the sink, an ashtray by the smell of it. Dampening a cloth, I felt my way to the fridge, probed inside until I found the metal tray, then pummeled out the ice cubes, packing them into the cloth.

"Where are you?"

"Here. Over here." Her voice rattled with panic.

I knotted the cloth around her arm, but it was impossible to tell how bad the burn was. She clung to me and I heard her taking in gulps of air.

"A flashlight, have you got one?"

I had to repeat the question.

"I don't think so."

"Or candles?"

"No, no. I don't know where they are. Can we get out of here?"

In the studio the mirrors, reflecting the night sky, smoldered with a reddish glow.

I slid open the door and guided her outside, across the patio, then out through the door in the wall. There was chaos in the street. Cars hooting. Names shouted. "Inez? Margarita? Juan?" Crazed parabolas of light and voices calling, "Watch out! Where are you? Over here!"

The blackout had blindfolded the city, save for the starry firmament above, like recollected dazzle, and one ember-red patch above the roofs.

"Miraflores," I said. "They must have electricity."

I helped her into the car and drove at a crawl toward the red tint in the sky. Tall buildings blocked our view of the hills. So we couldn't see what they were staring at in Las Flores and Monterrico and La Molina, a pattern of blazing oil drums that spelled out in acrid, flaming letters, brighter than any star, the single word EZEQUIEL.

"I'm sorry." Her voice was calmer. "These things always take me by surprise."

"We should look for a chemist."

She seemed distracted. But she wasn't concerned about her burn. "I never know when to expect them. And I wanted to play you some flute music."

By the time we drove into the light, she had recovered.

"You don't want anything for your arm?"

"No. Thank you."

"Let me buy you a drink then," I said.

"I'd like that very much."

The Café Haiti was packed. I checked the tables for Sylvina, who had been playing doubles with Consuelo. Would she be here? I wondered how I would explain myself. You must surely know that if you go somewhere with an attractive young woman, even if the occasion is an innocent one, and you don't tell your wife, you can't help feeling guilty. But there was no one I knew in the café.

The waitress, shy, with expressive eyes in a highland face, waited for our order.

"Whatever you're having," said Yolanda.

"Two beers."

"Here, let me pay."

"No."

"An hour ago, you were telling me you had no money," she teased. She was flirtatious, though there was nothing more behind it. I felt a rush of affection toward her.

From our corner table I took in the room. There was a lot of shoulder tapping and chairs leaning back as news of the blackout was broadcast and digested. It was strange to consider Miraflores as a beacon in a blinded city. For the first time the café struck me as beautiful.

I felt a sudden sharp pain in my hand. Yolanda was examining the fingers.

"You've hurt yourself." When thumping out the ice, I must have stripped the skin.

"How's your arm?" I asked.

She drew up her left sleeve. "I look idiotic wearing this dishcloth, but—truly—I hardly feel a thing."

Relief to be in the light again showed in her face. All her movements were revealed in the unreflected suddenness of her smile.

"I'm sorry about my panic attack. I don't like the dark."

"Is there a reason?"

"Do I need one?"

"I suppose not."

"I've never been able to sleep without a light on in the house. That's why I'm so relieved you were there tonight."

"I'm glad I could help," I said.

"Last time there was a blackout, I was rehearsing and I lost my balance. I couldn't see myself in the mirror and everything went to pieces and I fell flat on my ass."

"Is there no one you can call?"

"What can they hope to achieve, really?" clucked a voice from the table behind us. A woman in sunglasses, with flattened down, very golden hair, spoke to a woman with prominent, heavily mascaraed eyes.

"But haven't they got a point, these poor people?" said her companion.

Yolanda looked around as the blond lady removed her sunglasses. A reflection was admired in the lenses, some grease was polished off, and the glasses were restored to their perch on a large nose.

Through them, the blonde appraised Yolanda. There's nothing like the sight of an ugly woman taking in an attractive one. Wistfully, the blonde said, "Perhaps they'll kidnap Maimée."

Yolanda leaned forward toward me in a confiding way. She was about to speak when a woman's voice, obviously trying to be heard, announced, "You know, I've always been on the left, deep down."

Neither of us could help it. We burst into laughter.

Rejas glanced at Dyer. He seemed to have forgotten where he was. An all but empty restaurant. Not a ballerina sharing his table, but a man pretending to be a historian.

A foghorn prompted him to check his watch. Dyer saw the relief with which he said he must go. Somewhere in that night, in a house Dyer would never visit, Rejas had another woman to attend to.

"Emilio!"

Rejas, having called for his bill, began to stroke some bread crumbs into a line with the back of his hand. Unexpectedly, he reached across and removed the knife from Dyer's plate. He held it by the handle, over the table, between thumb and forefinger, blade pointing downward.

"How long do you think it takes a rat to drown?"

The question surprised Dyer. "Half an hour?" he guessed.

"It's a story I was told by Ezequiel," said Rejas. "He used it to explain to me the sheer will he managed to unleash in our people. But which could apply to any of us."

"How long?"

"He told me that if you drop a rat in a tank of water, the rat will swim about for fifteen minutes and after fifteen minutes he will drown." Rejas released the knife. It clattered on the table. His eyes blurred with despair.

"But if after fifteen minutes you pick the rat up by his tail and give him a good shake to start him breathing again and drop him back in the water . . ." He gazed at the dull blade. Once more he took the knife by the handle and dropped it. The noise bounced through the room. Dyer was aware of Emilio swiveling from the till.

"How long do you suppose he swims after that?"

"I don't know."

Rejas sat back, though his eyes never quitted the blade.

Dyer, too, stared at the knife. "Half an hour," he guessed.

"Two days."

"Two days?"

Rejas accepted his bill from Emilio and counted out the money. "I must go back to my sister."

The Colonel stood, but Dyer sat there, still imagining that creature swishing through the water.

"Her condition, is it serious?"

"She's in a coma. Well, in and out of it."

Dyer had failed to understand the seriousness of her illness. A case of food poisoning, he'd thought. Was that why Rejas had talked all this while, all these evenings—to take his mind off his sister?

"There's a good hope she'll recover, surely?"

"Hope? That's what it boils down to."

Rejas was not talking about his sister.

9

When Dyer entered the restaurant next evening, Rejas wasn't there.

Half an hour passed. Still no sign of his coming. At eight Dyer ordered Emilio's grilled fish, though reluctantly.

It had been very hot during the day. After writing down the policeman's story in a yellow spiral-bound notebook, he had slept late and again in the afternoon taken a long siesta. Now a little breeze came through the window.

He turned a page, listening for steps. Outside he heard the imperturbable throb from the fortress, and the peacocks in the bird market screaming from their cages. He tried to read, but could not concentrate. He looked at his watch. Eight-thirty. The policeman had never been this late. Had Rejas found out who he was, or had he, for whatever reason, suddenly thought better of telling his story to a stranger?

Dyer had not asked Rejas why he might want to talk in this way. It helped that he was Vivien's nephew, of course. Besides, people do tell their secrets to strangers, and it stood to reason they would feel for each other a certain sympathy. They were men of an age, both miles from home. And like Rejas, wasn't he about to be discarded, or used in the wrong way? But that he should have hit his target inadvertently . . .

And yet, Dyer thought, isn't it the desire of wanting to hit the target that makes you miss it? If you want things too badly, you end up with nothing at all. It's the act of not hankering after something that somehow, weirdly, brings it about. And wasn't he himself a kind of target? He was one of the few people in the world whose fascination Rejas could rely on. Many of his countrymen, perhaps even his own sister, might not have given a damn. But Dyer understood. Hadn't he been looking for Rejas in the first place and hadn't they both chosen this restaurant in which to read—both of them—the same book? Which was why, as Rejas had begun talking, Dyer had been able to quell any doubt about the policeman's motive. He had simply thought, This is the story I've been waiting for all my career.

It was past nine when he heard the *click, click, click* on the stone staircase and the strands of the bead curtain parted. Rejas sat down, apologizing. The specialist had been on the telephone to discuss his sister's tests. Over the plate which Emilio served him, he continued to brood on her illness, slowly enfolding Dyer in his misery.

Two months earlier a storm had kept her overnight on an island opposite Pará. At one of the stalls by the jetty she had eaten undercooked pork. Soon after, she became lethargic, complained of headaches, a pain behind the right eye. One day her husband found her speaking incoherently about snails. The symptoms—vomiting, nausea, disorientation—were consistent with cysticercosis. As the seizures became more frequent, he summoned Rejas. She was thirty-seven, and quite likely to die.

For the past three weeks the two men had taken turns by her bed. Rejas kept vigil during the day, his brother-in-law at night. Her level of consciousness fluctuated from hour to hour. One moment she was quiet, the next agitated and disoriented. After she swallowed her drugs, her limbs shook. Frequently she hallucinated.

Who was that making coffee?

Why did Agustín wear so much eau de cologne?

Didn't he like this beetle she'd found by the river?

"She thought I was our father. As a girl, she was always coming into his library with frogs and snails."

In the mornings Rejas sat in a wicker chair and read aloud

from their father's books. Propped on pillows, she listened, stuporous, sucking her thumb. In the afternoons as she slept, he brushed the flies from her mouth and the liquid trails from the corners of her eyes. At six, when her husband returned from work, Rejas could leave the room. He would be careful in his movements in case she heard the wicker creaking. In that confined space it had the effect of a shriek. Once, waking up, she insisted on coming with him. She knelt, rummaging through a drawer for a favorite dress of black velvet. "Wait, Agustín, wait till I find it. We'll have such a good time."

The doctor, observing the deterioration in his patient, advised a lumbar puncture. The hallucinations could indicate that the drugs were destroying the parasites. Or her condition was untreatable. The answer would show up in her spinal fluid. With the two men's approval, she was laid on her left side, curled up like a baby, while a long needle was inserted into her back. The sample had been sent for analysis to a lab in Rio. That was a week ago. They were still waiting for the results.

"You think you're grown up," said Rejas. "Then you see your sister ill—and she's a ten-year-old again. But there are some people—their youth never leaves them. It's the only time of life which interests them and they respond to everyone they meet as if they were still ten-year-olds. Yolanda was like that. In some ways she could be grown up beyond her years, in other ways oddly childish—as ballerinas can be who've not been around people much.

"Then there are those like me who don't think about their childhood. Which is a common experience in the sierra. When their parents die, people who've moved away don't come home anymore, not to small towns. I'd gone back to La Posta only once after I left—with Sylvina for a fortnight's holiday the summer I graduated. After the military had seized our farm, there was nothing to go back for. I didn't investigate Ezequiel's influence in the valley, because you never think things are going to be so bad in your own village. Then Yolanda mentioned Ausangate.

"That night I lay awake, remembering in detail the village, my friends, the skipping-rope rhymes, our coffee plantation. It was at this period I learned the fate of our priest."

He searched for something in his trouser pocket. "Tell me, did your aunt mention a Father Ramón, who might have worked with her on the children's project?"

"Ramón? I don't think so."

"I was one of his altar boys. There were three of us—me, Nemecio and Santiago, his favorite."

Dyer had been so relieved to see Rejas this evening that for a while he didn't mind what the policeman talked about. Now he was anxious for him to continue his story. "Last night you were talking about Yolanda."

Rejas, his hand now rummaging in another pocket, ignored him. "This old man. He wasn't just any priest, you understand. He was a priest I loved. It's a terrible story. But it was he who led me to Ezequiel."

He had found what he was looking for. "I want to show you this. It's important."

It was an airmail letter, the paper so thin that the blue writing pressed through like veins.

"My last contact was this letter from Portugal."

Rejas waited for Dyer to read it. The hand was large and neat. "You remember my hope of one day visiting Our Lady's shrine at Fátima? My prayers have been answered. I have been lucky enough to be appointed religious guide for a tour comprising eighteen pilgrims from our diocese." The priest, who Dyer gathered had never before left La Posta, was excited by the airport, by the food on the plane, by the way the time changed as he flew. "Five hours of Palm Sunday lost! Where did that day go? Was it a sin not to be in church, do you think?" In Portugal he had eaten well, if curiously—a dish with pork and clams . . . "On the way to the shrine we took a bus to Coimbra, where I saw the library. Gold everywhere. Your father would have loved it!" At Fátima the shrine to the Virgin surpassed his expectations. "I walked on my knees all the way with the same speed as if I had been on my feet. You have no idea how holy this place is. The Virgin's presence is palpable. I said a prayer for you and your sister. Also for the village. Things are not so good in the valleys at the moment, Agustín. I have had to send five children to an orphanage in the capital. You will understand why Our Lady's message of peace has never seemed more needed. I prayed through the night—and I did feel I was listened to."

I had not heard from Father Ramón since receiving that letter. Then, about a week after my meeting with Yolanda, Sucre handed me a newspaper cutting.

"La Posta? Isn't that your village, sir?"

"Why? What's wrong?"

"They've killed the priest."

The cutting, three weeks old, reported that Maoist forces had executed Father Ramón because he had been "participating in the counterinsurgency struggle designed by the government and armed forces."

I heard the details later. It was hideous.

They waited for him by the Weeping Terrace, which is now an airstrip. He walked there every Saturday, composing the sermon he would broadcast over our local radio station. They seized his hat, his stick and the small Bible he carried everywhere—a gift of my father's, with gilt-edged pages. He was forced to his knees on the grass, his hands tied behind his back. A woman knelt in front of him. She searched the Bible for the appropriate page.

"Read it out," she ordered.

The passage was from Job. He started reading. His voice was famous. He would have said the words as if he was touched with their emotional truth.

" 'His breath kindleth coals and flame goeth out of his mouth. In his neck remaineth strength and sorrow is turned to joy before us.' "

She tore the page out, screwed it into a ball, forced it between his lips. "Eat."

"What do you mean?"

"Eat!"

I picture his lips parting.

"Swallow."

I see him making the effort to swallow and the woman, a dreadful expression on her face, tearing the first page of Genesis, telling him, "In the beginning God created the heavens and the earth," making another ball, holding that to his mouth. I see him willing himself to transform this page into the Host. I remember there are six hundred and twenty-seven pages.

After he passed out, he was stabbed repeatedly. They scooped out the guts and filled his stomach with the rest of the Bible—which, according to a message left inside his hat, had been written as a propaganda tool.

Lastly, they attacked his face. Those who found his corpse couldn't tell if it belonged to a man. But when the face is mutilated like that, it means one thing: the killer is known to his victim.

Father Ramón had baptized her.

My father, a timid man with few close friends, believed that a part of the reason we love someone is because of the person we become when we're with them. When they're dead, we can never be that person again. It's that other person, my father would say, for whom we're grieving. When I read the bald fact of Father Ramón's death, I had no intention of journeying to La Posta. But I had to speak with others who had known him.

The three altar boys had drifted apart. The last I heard of Nemecio, he was teaching in Cajamarca. Santiago was in a seminary. I had no idea where they were at that time.

As you will see from that letter, Father Ramón mentions several of his fellow pilgrims. One of them was Santiago's mother.

Rejas waited for Dyer to find the reference. Although it puzzled the journalist—this concern for him to know every detail—he reread the passage.

> My feelings for Leticia Solano will always be informed by the utmost tenderness, but I will be relieved when we part. She would prefer it if her feelings toward me escalated to a level of greater intimacy, although this I attribute to her failing eyesight. We have known each other a long time—most of my life!—and she is so possessive of my company that once or twice it has led to friction with other members

of our group. Since leaving the valley—she lives somewhere in Belgrano: is that near you?—I hear she is more troubled than ever. I do not know if Santiago is at the root of her disquiet. I believe there has been a falling-out. Do you see your friend ever? We lost touch when he abandoned the ministry. It grieves me to think he didn't trust me enough to share his doubts. I would have told him what my Bishop told me when I contemplated the same action: maybe God doesn't exist, but people who believe in Him generally lead better lives.

I found two Solanos listed as living in the Belgrano district, one of them with the initial *L*. The telephone company said the line had been disconnected owing to nonpayment.

One evening I followed an orange cat between puddles up an alley, looking for Solano, L.'s house.

Clap, clap, went the echo of my knock on the shabby door. The cat darted under a gate. Beyond the wall a fig tree writhed unwatered. Presently a shutter rattled open. A bowl of white azaleas was shoved aside and, partly obscured by a line of drying clothes, an old woman's face appeared over the ledge.

"Yes?" She looked down between a pair of black stockings.

I stepped back. "It's Agustín. Agustín Rejas."

She weaved her head. "Who?"

"Santiago's friend. I've come about Father Ramón."

"What does he want?"

Her voice was bothered, her face lost in the flowers.

"Can I come in?"

She withdrew. On the sill the cat watched me. I thought, Why do people who go to pieces like cats so?

I heard a shuffle of feet and then metal squeaking. A gruff voice reminding itself, "Rejas, Rejas. The coffee farm."

We sat upstairs in a dingy kitchen, where she warned, "I've nothing to give you. No coffee." Her face and chest had flattened and she couldn't see very well. She relied on a neighbor's boy to bring provisions. He hadn't called today. She was thinking of Father Ramón, but too proud to ask.

"I wanted to get in touch with Santiago," I said.

Something fluttered across her face. "Santiago? Why Santiago?"

"We were at school together."

"In Pachuca?"

"No, before that. La Posta."

"Why didn't we meet?" She pretended she could see me. The eyes which had once caused havoc in the valley and beyond had a cloudy look. "Why didn't he bring you to the hotel ever?"

"He did. But you weren't there." She had abandoned hotel, husband and son for the alcoholic who pretended to be a wealthy cotton grower. Everyone but Santiago had known of the affair.

I said, "We both were servers at Mass."

I thought of walking with Santiago to the church. Horses grazing in the browned grass. A young goat shivering. Santiago wanting to be a priest. He looked very like his mother.

"I played the flute and he sang."

Santiago had the best voice in the village. I thought of Father Ramón, tone-deaf, encouraging Santiago to the eagle lectern; my friend's nervous face popping over those wings as though he were clinging to a condor.

"He gave up singing."

"Why?"

"Same reason he gave up the priesthood," she said bitterly. "He preferred to talk, didn't he?"

"What about?"

"Foreign names. All nonsense."

"What foreign names?"

"Why are you so interested? Why should I tell you?"

It's something I inherited from my father. If asked a direct question, I tell the truth. "I work for the ATP."

"The police?" She brushed the cat aside. Her cataractal eyes slunk back along the table toward me. "Paco told me they've found those actors you killed."

Bones had been discovered under the seats of a cinema which the university was restoring as a cultural center.

"That was nothing to do with us."

"The army, then. What difference does it make?"

"It hasn't been proved."

"Why are you all behaving like this?"

"I don't know."

"Why is it you want to see your schoolfriend?" The last word sarcastic.

"I want to talk to him about Father Ramón."

"That's what the others said."

"Who said?"

"Two men who came to see him."

"Who were they?"

"Friends from university. They needed Santiago, they said."

"When was this?"

"Two, three weeks." She lifted her head. "Why does everyone want to talk about Father Ramón?"

"What did they want to know?"

The cat had crept back. "His sermons—"

"They didn't like what he was saying?"

She folded her arms. "I told them to get out."

"Did you tell them where to find Santiago?"

"I have no idea where he is."

"Is that true?"

"Why should I tell you?"

"Then it's not true."

"He writes. He sends money."

"What do the letters say?"

"I don't know," she repeated, her eyes unable to make tears. "The boy who brings the food doesn't read."

"Don't you keep the letters?"

"Pass me that."

I unhooked the imitation leather bag from the back of a chair. She fumbled with the clasp and felt inside, bringing out an envelope.

The postmark was two months old, from La Posta.

She said, "Tell me, what does he write?"

I unfolded the letter. The page was blank, something to fold the money in so it couldn't be seen through the envelope.

"He says he loves you and everything is fine and he will write again soon."

The outline of a smile. "That's Santiago."

She moved her head to the wall. The thermometer was a Fá-tima Virgin. She bit her lip. "Tell me," she said more brightly. "How is Father Ramón?"

I requested a fortnight's absence. The General refused. The bowl on his desk was piled high with oranges, as if stocked against a great siege. "I tell you, tomcat, it's pandefuckingmonium out there." Calderón had given himself dictatorial powers. Everything went first to Lache. "If I know General Lache, the Arguedas Players, they're just the beginning. He's adopting the French solution— and the French haven't won a war since 1812. It's vital you stay here."

I held my ground. "And it's vital I go to La Posta, sir."

"Why?" He stood up and looked uncertainly at his map.

"Ezequiel has been trying to contact a friend of mine."

"So?"

"This friend may be involved."

It had burst upon me in Leticia's kitchen. All the time I had been searching for Ezequiel I had been looking in the wrong place.

10

On the morning I left for La Posta, Laura sidled into the bedroom. She was miserable. Children hold adults to their promises.

"Look." I watched her through the camera. "I'll take masses of photos for you."

Her face hardened.

"I'll bring you a flute—like the one I used to play. I promise."

She said nothing.

"The military have declared it an emergency zone, Laura."

To prove that she was the child I took her for, she locked herself in her room and sang aloud to the cat.

Sylvina drove me to the airport. An unusual peace had settled on her, and on the city we passed through. If you live with violence, you become acclimatized to it. After a car bomb, people will jog around the dead bodies. They will go to their tennis courts. One of Sylvina's cousins, to circumvent the curfew, had bought a second-hand ambulance to transport his friends to parties. There is a routine even to menace.

As we drove past the Inca Market, Sylvina said, "Agustín, I have a way we can make money."

She had been discussing our problems with Marco. She knew I'd be cross, which is why she waited until this moment to talk about it. The fact was, Marco had come up with a fail-safe plan for us to become millionaires. In the vague terms in which I grasped it, Marco's solution—upon which, shortly, all her hopes would fix—required Sylvina to sell certain beauty products to her friends and induce them to do likewise while taking a percentage.

"If you persuade people to work for you, you get ten percent of everything they sell, so if they sell fifty dollars, I receive five dollars, and if they in turn find two people to work for them, eventually I'll be at the top of the pyramid and it can't fail." A lavender Cadillac seemed to be involved at some point, because she brought up that again after the engine stalled at the security checkpoint.

"Marco's obsessed with it. Just in his own street two women have made millions."

We kissed through the car window. "You know what communications are like in the sierra," I said. "But I'll try to ring."

"Anyway, Marco's sending me a sample kit."

I flew in a military transport to Cajamarca, from where I caught a lift with a truck heading north. The driver was a round, thick-set man with an overhanging forehead and huge, offended eyes. We left for the mountains that night, splashing out through the mud, our headlights shedding a watery dazzle in the pelting rain.

The truck had been climbing for three hours when Ezequiel struck. We were approaching a high pass and the driver was telling me about his family, killed by the police. I sat, appalled, watching a bank of mist nudge into the sweep of our lights.

He said he knew the policeman who had killed them, knew his name and nickname, knew where he lived. Every night since his wife and daughters had been found in a sheep field, strangled with khaki webbing, he had driven back and forth past the policeman's house, fifty yards one way, then reverse and fifty yards the other way. Up, down. Up, down. Up, down. Until daylight. He lifted a plump hand from the wheel and pointed a finger at my temple.

"Pow!" he whispered.

"Watch out!" The headlight picked out a barricade of rocks in the mud.

He braked hard and the truck slithered toward the hillside, shuddering to a stop against a bank of earth. Soon another vehicle pulled up behind us, and another, until the lights of six cars illuminated the bend.

He slapped the flat of his hands against the steering wheel. "What the fucking hell is this about?"

It was ten o'clock. The mist was rolling in.

And then four figures solidified in the haze, stepping between the rocks, waving powerful flashlights, advancing through the rain.

The driver leaned from his window and yelled, "Let us pass."

"Shut your face." It was a young boy, speaking through a woollen mask. His gloved hands gripped what in that light appeared to be a gun, but might have been a stick. He wasn't nervous.

"Turn out your lights and wait in the cab." There was the flop of feet and he continued down the line of cars, flanked by his three companions.

The driver turned the truck's lights off and slumped back in his seat.

I said quietly, "If they order us out, we'll be shot." I carried no weapon, but concealed in my right shoe was a military pass and my police identity card. Should they discover these, there would be no mercy. Not for me, not for the driver either.

A shadow, then a tap on the window. A light beamed in my face. The door opened and a moment later my first gasp of the chill mountain air froze my lungs.

"Your money. Quickly." The light remained in our eyes while we groped for our wallets. A hand seized them, then the flashlight was flashed at my feet.

"That bag. Pass it here."

The bag was unzipped, a hand in a long, damp orange glove thrust inside. It emerged with my old Leica, one of the few nice things my father left me. On the film were pictures of Laura and Sylvina at Paracas: standing in the waves, offering potato chips to a sea lion, pointing at a turtle on the sand. I would later regret the theft of those happy images even more than I did now.

I could easily afford to contribute to the revolution, snarled the voice. This instrument was worth more than he earned in a year.

He jumped to the ground and ran off, leaving me to shut the door. Beside me the driver expelled his breath. There's something frightening about a twelve-year-old with a gun. Then, suddenly agitated, he twisted in his seat. "Hey," he whispered, "what's that?" The truck squealed on its chassis and we could hear the heavy boxes sliding in the back.

They were unloading his vegetables. With the hand that had been a pistol he covered his eyes and sobbed.

Five minutes later the boys came by again, not looking at us. They reached the rocks and switched off their flashlights; shadow-thin, sheathed in denim, they slipped down the bank and vanished.

It was something tremendous, this silence. We waited, waited, as the quietness dripped around us. Eventually the car behind switched on its sidelights, and after an interval a strained voice was heard calling, "Shall we risk it?"

Two men stooped over the rocks and began lifting them. The driver and I got out to help. We didn't exchange words. Then we climbed back in and everyone started their engines and we drove from that place.

Two days later I reached the valley where I was born. The road signs had been stolen, but I knew where I was.

I banged on the cab roof. As the pickup slowed, I jumped from the back.

The air smelled sharply of wet earth and the barky scent of catuaba shrubs. Gnats, bloated by rain, danced over puddles reflecting terraces of corn and cactus.

I paused at the top of the track. La Posta lay below, a village on the edge of a drop into a valley at the headwaters of the Amazon. I could see the white domed church, the ironwork bridge and the thread of road winding through the valleys beyond the town. It led to our farm, though the house was hidden by an escarpment.

You know how you feel when you see your name in print? I experienced the same shock of recognition. Nostalgia engulfed me and the landscape trembled a little and I walked down that track as if the rest of my life hadn't happened. The landscape hadn't changed—therefore, nothing else had either.

Just outside the village I heard a cry. A boy came around the corner, whipping a donkey with a strip of rubber. When he caught sight of my bag, he leapt off down the slope, not looking back. The donkey, ignoring me, lowered its peeled-back lips to the verge.

I was too excited to be offended. I walked on down into the main street. It was eleven in the morning, but I was shocked by what I didn't see.

I expected the sidewalks to swarm with women from the lower farms. Every morning they would sit cross-legged behind pyramids of coca leaf and manioc flour. At the same age as the boy with the donkey, I had loved to watch their hands sneak from under impossibly colored shawls, to ladle a cup of reddish chicha; turn over a chunk of sweet-smelling alpaca; or offer a roasted guinea pig with a mouth of charred teeth.

Today the muddied sidewalk was deserted save for three small figures hurrying away. I breathed in deeply. Even the air seemed tainted.

In the Plaza de Armas, steam gargled from an open drain and drifted over a scraggy hedgerow, smudging the knees of a statue. I remembered how, on Sundays, dissatisfied young women would loiter before our band, making eyes at the musicians. Parents would push their prams across the cobbles to meet other parents, and the benches would creak with watchful old men, tapping their feet to badly played tunes. This morning two girls knelt by the fountain in the square. They crouched at the spout, spraying water at each other from the dribble. José's daughters? They had the butcher's curly black hair. When they saw me, they ran off through the threadbare topiary into a house beyond.

On his plinth Brigadier Pumacacchua averted his concrete gaze.

I paused on the corner at the butcher's shop. Twice a week my mother would send me to buy the lambs' tongues for which my father had a weakness. The idea had entered her head that this was every man's favorite dish—Father Ramón included. She adored the priest and was always fussing over him, inviting him to dinner, serving him these tongues which, uncomplainingly, he ate, telling her they were wonderful.

Twenty-five years ago I'd been waiting my turn in the queue, a lamb's head resting on a blue chair beside me, when the door burst open and the printer we knew as "the Turk" bustled in holding a thermos flask of calligraphy fluid, warmed up, and a stack of blank invitation cards under his arm. "They've expropriated the coffee farm!" He didn't know I was in the shop, and at José's dismayed expression he turned, dropping the flask when he saw me. I watched the steaming ink spread under the chair, mingling with the lamb's blood until the floor was a vivid pattern of reds and blacks streaking one into the other.

"Oh no, oh no, oh no. I don't believe it," said the Turk, on all fours among his silvery thermos fragments.

I tried the door. It was padlocked on the inside. I pressed my face to the filthy glass. No meat slapped across the stone slab. The blue chair stood in the corner, its seat missing.

In the glass I saw my face. I looked disordered and alarming. Horrified, I found a comb and ran it through my hair. I was still combing as I turned into Calle Jirón and walked headlong into an old lady.

She was stooped beside a mound of potatoes. I was so startled I dropped the comb. The old woman—amazingly quick—darted to pick it up, then held it away from my reach, refusing to return it until I rewarded her. She extended her other hand toward me, pleading for money. Her face was terraced with age and she had an almost peaceful look.

Then her glance slid down to my bag and she screamed.

"*Pishtaco!*" She threw down the comb, gathered up the potatoes in her black shawl and hobbled away as fast as she could.

At No. 119, a white house with a red door, I paused. This was where my parents had lived after the military expropriated our farm. When my father died, my mother continued to share the house with his books. In her curt old age she saw in them the enfeebled crops and the money he should have spent on fertilizer and parrot killer.

I didn't want to see inside and walked on. The next street, parallel to the church, was Calle Bolsas. Outside Nemecio's house I put down my bag and knocked. Nothing. I pushed the door, but it didn't give and, pressing my ear to a window, I could hear no sounds.

At the bottom of the same street I tried another house, a metal plaque bolted to its door: F. LAZO, ORTHODONTIST.

A little girl opened the door. She had an Elastoplast on her arm and held a rag doll by the leg.

"Who is it?" asked a worried-sounding man from inside.

"I'm looking for Fernando Lazo," I called.

"But I know that voice . . ."

He came up behind the girl, holding her shoulders as if to support himself. It was frightening how little he had changed.

"Joaquín?"

"It's his son," I said.

Later, after the embraces and the disbelief, he led me to his office.

One always expects people to react more emotionally than they do when you haven't seen them for a long time. It wasn't me the dentist wanted to remember. During our conversation he called me by my father's name. What had happened to our library? It was a sad day when we left the farm. He had kept our dental records. Just in case.

"And you? You became a lawyer, right?"

"That's it."

"Didn't you have a sister?"

"She's married, lives in Brazil."

He contrived a smile. "So. How are your teeth?"

"No serious problems."

"That's good. Tell everyone how well I looked after you."

I sat on a stool beside his desk while he fidgeted with the cast of a jaw. It was odd once more to be in this room, more museum than dentist's office. Above the desk, thirty or forty burial urns were arranged on shelves reaching to the ceiling. As a younger man, Lazo had been an ardent collector of Chimu and Chachapoyan pottery. Once, he was treating my mother when his daughter, dusting the pots, felt one of them stir and, peering over the rim, discovered a knot of gray snakes. My mother had come home full of the question, wanting to discuss the puzzle of how they had got there in the first place. No one had any idea. Nor did they know how to get rid of them. Hot oil—the snakes might thrash and break the pot. Water—wouldn't they swim loose?

Fire—the pot itself might crack. Lazo decided to smother them. He sealed the pot with tinfoil, lowered it into a plastic bag and turned it upside down. It had stayed like that for days, a source of macabre and ceaseless fascination for his open-mouthed patients until, with a great song and dance, it was judged safe to remove the covering, and the pot, cautiously examined, revealed a withered tangle of what looked like strips from an exploded tire.

That morning I had disturbed Lazo while he was making a plate for the Mayor, who'd lost a front tooth.

"He has to have it today. Talk to me while I work." He inclined the white jaw to the light with the care of someone inspecting the innards of an ancient clock. He had seen to the teeth of three generations of my family.

"Says he slipped in the shower." He pulled toward him a jar of brown teeth. To tease us, he used to tell me and my sister that the teeth were really peanuts. He poured a selection onto a shoebox lid; suddenly I wanted to eat one.

"You've brought the rain, Joaquín," he said, bending over his work. "We haven't had rain for two years. Not rainy rain. Have you seen your coffee fields? There are cracks so wide you can't see the bottom." His voice quavered. He hadn't expected me. I brought back too much.

In the courtyard emaciated chickens, plucked-looking, poked their heads between the fenceposts.

"What's happened to the market?" I asked.

"Our friends destroyed the lower road."

He tweezered an appropriate tooth, a molar, from the box lid and clamped it in a small vise. "Anyway, there's no one left to feed. Just babies. You remember my daughter? You were friends. That's her little girl."

"Where is she now?"

"Graciela? In the capital. The young ones have all fled there, those that didn't join our friends, those that weren't put dead into a hole. We're a village of old men and women. With grandchildren to look after."

"When did you see her last?"

"A month ago. Just before Father Ramón died. I want to follow her, but I can't. They've confiscated our identity cards."

He unhooked his drill, directed it at the molar. When we were children, he used to fasten a piece of cotton wool on the drive cord. He hoped the white flash, zipping up and down the drill's pulleys, would distract us from the pain.

"We're sick of the army, we're sick of Ezequiel, we're sick of anyone we don't know. You're lucky you weren't lynched today." His voice was husky. The drill jabbed at the tooth like a weapon.

"Tell me about Father Ramón," I said.

He appeared not to have heard. I repeated the question.

He switched off the drill, sat back, watching the pulleys slow, the needle lock to a sudden halt.

"I can't do this and tell you." The Mayor's tooth could wait. Not every day did Joaquín's son sit here.

Two months before, the villagers had voted in a left-wing councillor. This was their angry response to officials who had ordered parents to pay an education fee. In the local elections, encouraged by the councillor, the village abstained. One morning the military came driving down the hill.

The councillor was not seen again.

But it didn't end there. The soldiers went from house to house, demanding to know who had supported him. It was then that Father Ramón stepped in. He insisted on an inquiry into the councillor's disappearance and would neither give up nor moderate his demands. He contacted the Diocesan Commission for Social Action in Villoria. To the Synod he sent letters and rolls of film chronicling the army's excesses. He accused the commanding officer to his face.

And then Ezequiel's men retaliated. They executed the Turk as an informer.

"Remember the Turk? He'd taken over the hotel after Leticia Solano left town. I don't know if he was an army informer, or if he wasn't. I don't know, Joaquín, really I don't. Friendships only last as long as we don't talk about these things. The fact is, they killed the Turk and they shot his wife as she tried to pull the hood off one of them."

Father Ramón had been enraged. In his broadcasts to the valleys he attacked Ezequiel, whose behavior was no different from the military's. He showed no respect for those he claimed to liberate. This killing was something intolerable.

"I had not seen Father Ramón so wound up since his visit to Portugal," said Lazo sadly.

One Saturday afternoon a month ago the priest walked down to the river, presumably composing his next tirade, and never came back.

"Nemecio found him. Identifiable only by his hat and his stick."

"Who killed him?"

Lazo stared at the shelves of primitive pots. His voice was tight, his eyes pinched and sore as though he hadn't allowed himself to cry.

"Who can say?"

Outside, the chickens pecked the ground. In the next room his little granddaughter sang to a doll.

"I thought Nemecio lived in Cajamarca."

"He came back to assist Father Ramón."

"Where is he now?"

Lazo shifted his gaze to the brown tooth.

"He was one of those in church."

"What do you mean?"

The dentist's eyes rippled in astonishment. "The massacre. I thought that's why you'd come . . ."

"What massacre? What are you talking about?"

He searched my face. "The military's reprisal for Father Ramón. But you heard about that, didn't you? Didn't you?"

Afterward, after he had stuttered it out, I had to tell him no one in my office knew. As soon as I heard his story, I saw that everything the General feared had overtaken us.

Falteringly, in a voice from which all emotion had been exhausted, Lazo described the military's revenge.

Ten days after Nemecio discovered the priest's body, the villagers watched two loose columns of men in black uniforms jogging toward the church. It was a Wednesday, about four-thirty in the afternoon, a time when Father Ramón would have conducted his Bible class.

Nemecio had taken charge of the class. Suddenly, from behind the altar, he heard a banging.

The men kicked down a door at the back of the church. They squeezed through a storeroom, knocking over boxes and paintings. The congregation were petrified. The soldiers fanned out along both aisles, leveling their guns at the twenty men and women, ordering them to kneel.

"Palomino Cordero?" they shouted. "Which one of you is Cordero?"

The man they wanted was the producer at the radio station. One of the soldiers gathered the identity cards, flicked through them, then handed the bundle to someone else, who repeated the process.

They didn't believe it. They had been misled. They searched the sanctuary, the pulpit; they tore off the cloth over the Communion table. But Cordero wasn't there. Their leader retreated to the altar to radio for instructions.

There was the rasp of static. A remote voice said, "Proceed as planned."

The soldiers grabbed Nemecio first. Then Lazo's son-in-law, the postman. They yanked all the men outside, leaving others to deal with the women.

"Sing!" they yelled. "All of you, sing!"

The women were terrified. What should they sing? One of them suggested a hymn. She led the way nervously. Her words were hesitant, her throat dry. From somewhere she found a voice.

"Louder!"

Guns cracked outside. One of the women screamed.

"Louder, louder," lashed the soldiers, from behind them now.

The voices rose in fear. *"Oh buen Jesús, yo creo firmemente que en el altar Tu sangre está presente . . ."*

They had begun the second verse when something bounced onto a wooden pew.

Lazo felt the explosion in his office. It was five o'clock. From Clemencia's shattered mouth he would hear what had happened. Nemecio's sister was one of two survivors. The other, a farmer's wife who lost both legs, died later.

Since then they had threatened Clemencia. If she opened her

mouth, they'd dig up her dead husband and make her eat him. Neither she nor Lazo believed this to be an empty threat. She swore she would say nothing. But while she was sitting in the dentist's chair—Lazo doing what he could with his inadequate supplies—her remaining teeth started to chatter.

When Lazo had finished, I said, "Weren't there bodies to prove this?"

"They used horses to carry them away," he said.

Horses were the only way of transporting the bodies to the airstrip. Ezequiel's men, after killing Father Ramón, had blown up the bridge. Near the hangar the soldiers had dug a mass grave, but three days later they'd come back with their shovels and dug it up again and thrown the bodies—wrapped in plastic trash bags—across the backs of the screaming animals.

"The smell wasn't any more pleasant to them, poor things, than it was to us," said Lazo.

The military must have feared an investigation, because four soldiers barged into his office and demanded that he hand over his dental records.

"Which I did immediately. But I have copies. I've foreseen something like this for years."

Anxious to know the fate of his son-in-law, Lazo one evening made his way to the airstrip. He'd smelled the decay lingering above the disturbed earth. Dug for a while; found nothing except the end of a candle, a strip of white cloth and a bunch of keys.

Saliva shone on his yellowed false teeth. He looked up at the ceiling. "When they buried them, not all the victims were dead."

Words formed, but I couldn't speak.

"Ask me. Go ahead and ask me. How do I know? One night a soldier got drunk. He began shooting in the air, yelling that he missed his mother. Knocking on doors. He demanded to see my documents. I invited him in, calmed him down. Then he put aside his gun and began crying. He was from the coast, hundreds of miles away from home; he'd been made to do these terrible things—and he described what they had done.

"I haven't told my daughter. She thinks her husband's just missing. But they buried him alive. They dug that hole and threw him in it and shoveled earth over him. Alive, alive."

Lazo fiddled with a gas cylinder by his feet. He flicked a cigarette lighter, holding the flame to the tip of a blowtorch. The gas blew it out, but lit at the second attempt, burning with a blue-orange flame. I watched him melt the amalgam and fix the tooth in the plate.

"There. That'll have to do." He turned off the gas and the flame died. It wasn't perfect, but the cylinder was running low and months might pass before he could get another. The Mayor was a sonofabitch anyway.

He swiveled in his chair. "I tell you, Joaquín, we've been afraid so long, we're not afraid. We're mad. Our blood has boiled over. It's bubbled into our eyes, our brains, and we're crazy. We'll strike at anything. I tell you this for your own safety."

Next door the girl began another song, a skipping-rope rhyme I used to chant with Nemecio.

"Este niño mío, no quiere dormir . . ."

Embarrassed, I said, "Señor Lazo, can I ask a favor?"

"Be careful, Joaquín, what you ask."

I told Lazo about the theft of my wallet at the high pass. "Could you lend me some money?"

He reached stiffly above him and tugged a pot from one of the shelves. He rooted inside, plucking out a bundle of notes.

"Take this. No, take it all. There's nothing to spend money on here. But pay it back to Graciela, would you?" On the back of an invoice he wrote down her address in the capital.

"Shall I take a letter from you?"

"What would I say?"

"You must have something you want to tell her."

"What? That she has no husband? No friends? Is that what you want me to write?"

"Then I'll tell her you're well and so is her daughter."

He closed his eyes and opened them. "No. In return for this money, you please tell her the truth. What happened."

"Very well."

I stooped, folded the address and the money into an inside pocket of the sports bag. I was about to close it when he said, "This is for you."

Lazo, hands trembling, held the portrait vase above my head.

A beautiful one, reddish-colored, with the traces of black brush-marked crosses and a face. He could have sold it in the capital for the equivalent of his annual income.

I got to my feet. "But that's—"

"Please, Joaquín. I'm too old to be argued with. I want you to have it." He was breathing fast, as if he had run up the road to bring it to me.

I turned the jug under the light. Off the shelf this was not a dull ornament in need of a good dusting. It struck me then—there, in Lazo's office—that within its simple shape, its rough patina, the nameless red of its pigmentation, the strong face, the sensual quality of its jaw and lips, there existed the gamut of beauty and terror.

He had dated it to the Chimu dynasty, he said. He'd bought it off a grave robber from the coast, near Moche. Probably it was the portrait vase of a king or shaman and had been buried with his shrouds.

I stammered my thanks, knowing what this gift meant to him.

"Your father, Joaquín. I loved him."

"Then I accept it in my father's memory." I wrapped the pot in a shirt and zipped up the bag.

He opened the door for me. "I keep the records in the other pots. In case we find the teeth."

We shook hands. There was a furtive quality to his touch, and I knew there was something he held back. Despite everything he had told me, about Father Ramón, about the army's reprisal, there was more to tell.

"*Porque el cuco malo está por venir . . .*" The song's words drifted from the dark hallway.

"Santiago Solano—was he killed too?"

"Santiago?" His fingers fretted at his temple. For a moment he was trying to recall whether that ditch had taken Santiago too. Then his face cleared. "No. I don't think so. I think he was out of town that day."

"Where would I find him?"

"He teaches at San Marcos."

I had to walk past the church to reach the school.

At my approach the pigeons on the dome exploded into the air, leaving the brickwork bald and white. Sandbags packed the entrance to the height of my chest. A chalked sign declared that the building was undergoing essential redecoration.

I felt the urge to pray. Between the sandbags a passage led to the wooden door. I assumed it would be locked, but the hinges were wrecked and it opened.

From my childhood I remembered aisles watched over by gold-haired saints, and a caoba wood floor dappled with green and blue window light, as if seen through deep water. My father, who calculated the windows to be three hundred years old, had traced their origin to a glassmaker from Salamanca. The grenade had blown them out.

I walked into the nave, one step at a time, over creaking floorboards. I had been baptized in this church. My parents had married here. Beneath the pulpit I learned to play the flute. Yet I didn't recognize the place. No plank pews. No saints. No Communion table. The nave glowed with a hygienic, Protestant light from the empty casements.

A plywood board, an inch thick, rocked beneath my feet where the grenade had landed. A stain darkened the floor all the way back to the entrance.

Whose body had they dragged outside? Nervy Jesús, who smiled with relief at her friends every time she sat down after reading the Gospel? Or Aguilina, who wore a hairnet, which gave to her head the appearance of something imperfectly, patchily dyed? Or Prudencia—a gossip with balcony-hardened elbows—always patting her wet hair and saying "La Posta is such a dirty place"? Or María, who had never been the same since the Turk's tin sign for paraffin had fallen on her head in a gale?

Perhaps this bloodstain wasn't a woman's. Perhaps one of the men had crawled back into the church. Lazo's son-in-law, the postman, who often delivered letters to the wrong houses, a nice man with a pencil-sharp chin whose name I couldn't remember but didn't have the courage, just now, to ask for. Or Nemecio.

The afternoon sun simmered on the pillars. Blotches of cement spoke of an attempt to conceal the damage. Limbs, eyes, blood, glass, screams. Standing on this spot, I hated myself. I had left this valley to work for the law—and this was how the law had repaid my people.

The soldiers had thrown the headless saints into the storage room. Chips of gold plaster scattered all over the floor. There were ripped hassocks and cigarette ends and something metallic. When I held it to the window, I saw that it was a spent cartridge case, regular army issue.

The mahogany lectern toppled at an angle against a twisted metal chair. I pulled the eagle upright. The blast had removed one wing. I wanted to feel an emotion, be moved, but my only desire was to get outside. I had reached the storage room door when my eye was drawn to the wrecked diptych behind it. Through the mangled fronds of canvas I saw Father Ramón's cassette recorder. There was a tape still inside.

On this machine, every Saturday, the priest would record his twenty-minute talk. He would give the tape to one of the altar boys—Santiago usually—who would then run with it to the radio station. His sermons were immensely popular, their influence extending into the neighboring valleys. On a tape like this our priest would have recorded his attacks on Ezequiel.

I pressed the start key. The spools revolved. In a voice from which he couldn't keep his delight, I heard Father Ramón telling a story about Leonardo's *Last Supper*:

". . . try as he might—and how hard he tried!—he couldn't find the model for Judas! He had painted all the disciples. There was this one blank. Years passed while he searched for a model with the appropriate expression. But no. There the fresco stood. Incomplete. And I have to tell you that Leonardo had given up on it. Until—incredibly—one day in the market he found the face he had been seeking all this time. Judas to the life! He showered money on the man, flattered him, dragged him back to his studio and set to work. Can't you imagine the energy with which he picked up his brushes? Then he looks up and what do you think he sees? His model, head buried in his hands, is weeping uncontrollably. What's up, asks Leonardo? What's wrong, man?

"At first the other shakes his head, like we all do when we

don't want to confess something. Finally, he blurts out the reason for his distress. Many years ago he had sat in the same chair. He had sat like this, exactly as he was required to sit now. But then he had been posing as Christ . . ."

I stopped the tape. I didn't know the moral of the story, didn't care. I was conscious of my own tears tickling my cheeks. Blindly I tried to get out of that room. I knocked an object to the floor, and I might have left it there, whatever it was, under the lectern where it had fallen. But something made me retrieve it.

An ashtray from Fátima. In the center was a reproduction of the apparition of Our Lady. Three children, watching in rapt attention, prayed to the Virgin, who was balanced on a cloud above some sheep. She held, flaming in her hands, a human heart, in shape and color resembling a red pepper. Circles of dark brown tar obscured the Virgin's face and part of a message reading GOD'S FIERY SIGNATURE.

I packed the ashtray in my bag and went to look for Santiago.

He was teaching a class of bored children. He lifted his arm and scratched a sum on the board, savored its meaning and chalked another sum, not glancing around.

After the class he came up to me and we stood there and looked at each other. His face, always so much his own, seemed composed of other people's features. He hadn't shaved and his beard escaped from his chin in wisps, while his fairer hair sprang straight from the scalp as if something had shocked it. When young, his eyes had had the expression of a child in a playground. Now, thin as a lamppost, he had the stone-gray eyes of a plundered soul. Perhaps that's what he thought about me.

"Hello, Santiago."

"What brings you back?" He was not surprised to see me.

"It doesn't feel the same place."

"Blame your people for that."

"They're not my people."

"Military, police, what difference?"

"I've just seen the church. It's monstrous."

We walked out of the gates into the street.

"But any organization is like this," I said. "People can go mad within it."

He shot me a look. "Why have you come back? What do you want?"

"To see you," I said.

He strode a pace ahead, keen to get home.

I said, "I talked to your mother."

"We haven't been in touch."

"She hadn't heard about Father Ramón. I had to tell her."

He unlocked a door. The spirit of the sixties lingered like a joss stick in the room. A poster of a Brecht play. The sleeve of a Beatles record. Books stacked against the wall: Marx, Kant, Bakunin, Camus. I had parroted their ideas during Fuente's revolt. Once, in an "underground" café in Pachuca, I had listened to Santiago quote Lukács in defense of murder, a hint of madness in his eyes. My revolutionary ardor dimmed when the left-wing military took power. I ought to have approved of their seizure of the coffee farm. My correct reaction should have been: if our hacienda, seized in the people's name, would better serve the masses, so be it. But that's not what I felt.

"Weren't you going to be a priest?" I put down my bag and sat. The sofa, covered in pillows, lacked an arm.

"I changed my mind at university." Santiago, holding a tray, came out of the kitchen. He poured a mug of strong tea.

"You're not drinking?"

He patted himself. "Stomach upset."

He drew the curtain and sat down, crossing and recrossing his legs.

"What with the drought and the bridge being closed, we haven't eaten well."

Do you have friends you half apologize for, but whom you would hope to defend if they were criticized? At school Santiago had possessed a guileless quality which moved me to protect him. What had kept our relationship from developing into the sort of friendship I enjoyed with Nemecio was his stubbornness. No sooner did he find a phrase that pleased him than he would repeat it like a rosary. The same with his ideas. If anyone interrupted him, his lower lip would tremble. He had the inflexibility of an actor who has grown too much into his part. An unscripted line he saw as a terrible threat.

I think this explains what happened after his mother left the valley for a stranger, a man much younger than herself. I was already at the Police Academy when she discovered her lover's cotton fields were no more extensive than the bar in Cayara where he was employed to collect empties and wipe the tables. My sister wrote to say Santiago had been badly affected by his mother's defection. It must have been at about this time that he shifted the focus of his reverence.

"What did you study?" I asked.

"Religion, for a term. Then philosophy."

"The opium of the people, eh?"

"If you like."

"Because you were very religious, and all of a sudden you changed your mind."

"It seemed irrelevant to what was happening around us."

"Do you think Father Ramón was irrelevant? You used to admire him, all the good things he did. What seems irrelevant to you is the fact he's been killed."

"At least Ezequiel has drawn the attention of the government—who would rather forget us. We ask for clinics and what do they give us? Grenades. No, Agustín, the revolution must put up with its own violence or be fucked."

"Then you accept Father Ramón's death?"

His mouth folded up. "That—it's not something I can explain. It—"

"Don't you feel disgusted?"

His eyes blinked, gray, nervous, strained.

"Well, no. Not really. But yes."

"If there's a word to justify such an action, then tell it to me, Santiago."

He stared at the back of his hands, licking his lip.

I said, "Then you understand how I feel when I'm confronted by the sight of that church as evidence of what I'm doing, or what my side is doing. But I tell you this. I'm leaving here tomorrow and my first action will be to file a report. I want to see the people who did this in prison as much as you do. You, on the other hand, have to play your part. What happened to our priest is no less reprehensible. You didn't kill him any more than I threw that grenade, but if this sort of thing is to stop, we must help each other."

"There are bound to be accidents," said Santiago. " 'To act immorally is the highest sacrifice the revolution demands.' Remember? Besides, Ramón had been speaking out against Ezequiel. He was judged an enemy of the people." The rhythm of his speech was too fast, too stuttering.

"Rhetoric is rhetoric, Santiago. Could you have stood there and spouted that stuff as they forced him to eat his Bible? Any more than I could have stood and watched that soldier toss his grenade into the church? I would have done all in my power to stop him."

"Kant says—"

"What does Kant have to do with anybody in this valley? Didn't they teach you Plato, for God's sake? Philosophy is impossible among the common people."

"The communists ban Plato."

"So do the fascists," I said.

"Kant is relevant. If we live according to his precepts, we will achieve perpetual peace."

"And old priests will be found slaughtered on riverbanks till the end of time."

"Through Kant and Mao," he persisted, "Ezequiel has constructed a cosmology that can be understood by the masses."

"Reality is stronger than any cosmology. Ezequiel's ideology has no basis in fact. Look around you, man. Communism is dead, even in Albania. If Ezequiel is the rational person he claims to be, he would have come to accept the changes in the world. He's like a chicken tottering about after its head has been cut off."

"I promise you, his revolution—"

Santiago was scrambling now. He retreated into the bleak, unsubtle territory of revolutionary socialism, the Kantian dialectic as promoted through the books strewn on his floor. Capitalist society reduced our people to objects. Those old women outside were of no more importance to the state than their pathetic shawlfuls of potatoes. Clinging to the wreckage of familiar jargon, he addressed his words not to me but to the world. But it was the shadow of a speech composed by another.

I listened, and I understood what had happened. At university, while I studied law, Santiago had transferred into the political sphere this moral stubbornness of his, this obstinacy that brooked no opposition. He had wanted to be a priest, but he had come up against an absolutism more attractive than Father Ramón's bustling humanity.

Such people are always hungry for imperatives when those imperatives coincide with their own. And who was it who supplied what Santiago sought? Ezequiel, that poisonous red mushroom created by Kant. My fellow altar boy would, of course, have perceived in Ezequiel's Kant a disembodied Christianity. Treat all mankind as your equal, everybody as a person, nobody as a thing. Look to yourself as the source of order. How alluring it must have seemed. But it was not what Ezequiel had meant at all.

I had heard enough. I interrupted the speech. "It's cowardly to set philosophy above life when such atrocious things have happened, are still happening. Cowardly and evil. Tell me, why is it that people who espouse Kant's liberation doctrine always end up putting other people in chains? I could use Kant to justify bourgeois morality, yet you use his categorical imperative to justify Father Ramón's murder. Why, Santiago? Why?"

"So I'm nuts, completely nuts. What do you want me to say?"

"I want to know who killed him."

"Forget it."

"Under the Emergency Code, I could arrest you for everything you've said. These books alone—"

"Look, don't make threats about arresting me—I just need to yell 'police' and everyone in town will come running."

"Fine. I'll go away. I'll build the evidence against you. I'll watch you night and day. And then I'll come back. Do I have to spell it out?"

He looked down at my feet. "Why do all policemen wear white socks?"

"Who supplies the food? Who are Ezequiel's contacts in the village?"

He threw himself back. "I don't know. I don't know."

"But you know about Father Ramón. I'm certain you do."

His lower lip trembled and he clutched his knees. When he raised his head, his eyes were not looking at me but at the side of my face. "You don't understand. I've signed a blood pact with these people."

"You're a lot better off dealing with me, buddy. You know Ezequiel's ways. If he discovers we're friends, he is likely to make the same moral sacrifice of you that he made of Father Ramón. And you've seen how the military behave. It's a miracle they didn't get you last time. You're fucked, Santiago."

I gave it time to sink home. Then I said reasonably, "It could be lucrative, you know. How much do you earn teaching algebra? I can offer you more. A reward. Start-up capital. Settle you in a new country, new identity, leave all this despair behind. Miami. White beaches. The good life."

"Go on, Agustín, squeeze my balls some more."

"Don't you see? Ezequiel's made an idiot of you. Is that what you wanted when you were an altar boy? To see your priest, the person in the world you most wanted to emulate, choke on his Bible, see him gutted like a fish, see his face sliced off?"

No reply. He was not listening. In a faraway tone he addressed the sofa beside me, breathing uneasily. "They came here after they'd done it. They wanted bed and food."

"How many?"

"Three."

"Male, female?"

"Two men, and a woman who was in charge."

"How old? Where was she from? Was she educated?"

"It was Edith."

"Edith? From Pachuca?" A girl with cold, mint eyes and makeup who wouldn't dance with us.

"Ramón had to be punished by someone he knew," he said doggedly.

"Where is Edith now?"

"No idea. They operate away from home. Like your army friends."

"But she used to live in the next valley."

"Not for twenty years."

"How did she behave? What did she say?"

"She said be patient, the revolution was in our grasp."

"And the men with her?"

"Kept pretty quiet. Said almost nothing."

"You knew them?"

"No. They were from the capital."

Had Edith slept on this sofa afterward?

"Did they want you to lead them to Father Ramón? Is that what they wanted?"

"They were angry about his sermons. His attacks on Ezequiel."

"He had also spoken out against the army."

"Anyway, I wasn't here."

"But you were here when they came back."

"That's right."

"Where were you, Santiago?"

Dismally, he said, "A woman. She's married. I see her in the afternoons. You can have her name, if you like."

I didn't want to hear more. "How do you feel? You waited all these years for the call, and this is what the revolution demanded—and you weren't even here. Nor when they killed Nemecio and the others."

"No, I wasn't. And by God, Agustín . . ."

"How did you know who these people were? How did you know they weren't spies?"

Santiago got up and went into his bedroom. A cupboard creaked. He came out again, unfolding a piece of paper.

"Here. This is all I can offer you. This is all I know. This is all I have."

A photocopy of a computer printout. Four names, each listed for a village in the area. At the bottom, on its own, a telephone number prefixed by the code for the capital.

"You're 'Comrade Arturo'?"

"That's what they called me at university. I had no choice. Don't ask who the others are. I've no idea."

"What about this number with no name?"

"She said to use it in an emergency."

I copied down the information.

"Do you still play the flute?" he said in a not very interested way.

"No."

"I'll never forget the sound you made as we came down the glacier."

"And you, Santiago, do you still sing?"

Before he could answer, voices sounded in the street. He jumped up, parting the curtain. "I told them to play in the yard!"

Someone pounded on the door. Santiago said, "Excuse me." He puckered his lips in a schoolmasterly way and charged out into the street.

I heard animated snatches of conversation. Then he came back in. He shut the door, leaning against it. "The class is waiting. I have to go back."

I picked up my bag. For the first time Santiago seemed to notice it. "Wait. Where are you staying?"

"Your old hotel, if it's still open."

"When did you arrive?"

"This morning."

"You had no problems?"

"What kind of problems?"

"I don't know. From the people."

"An old woman screamed at me. A donkey boy ran off when he saw me."

He blocked my way, staring at me hard. I had seen the same look in Lazo's eyes. He looked down at my bag again. "They've had enough, Agustín."

"What do you mean?"

"They're suspicious of everybody. A man carrying a bag like yours, he was killed last week."

"A man? From the village?"

"Nobody you'd know. A commercial traveler from Pachuca."

"What was he carrying?"

"Just samples."

"Samples of what?"

"Brushes, scissors, combs, the usual stuff. He was going from door to door trying to interest people. But the whisper went around. He was a *pishtaco*. He'd come to abduct our children, cut them up, boil their limbs for grease."

Do you know the *pishtaco* myth? My mother, who worshipped mountain spirits, tried to make us believe in this creature. She warned us not to go out at night or we would find, waiting for us, a stranger in a long white cloak. He had been sent by the authorities to rob us of our body grease. He would carry us to his lair, string us upside down and collect our dripping fat in a tub. She said the *pishtaco*'s favorite delicacy was the meat of young children, which he sold to restaurants in the city. My sister and I assumed she used this bogeyman to stop us roaming too far from the farm.

I said to Santiago, "They can't believe this. Not seriously?"

"They don't know what to believe. They say those who have disappeared are demanding some explanation. They say policemen in disguise have been sent to extract our grease. They say that with this grease the government can buy weapons to fight Ezequiel."

"Who believes this?"

"Who doesn't? I'm telling you, don't go out at night, Agustín. Because that's when they seized this man. He'd been trying to sell to the barber and they descended on him. A crowd, fifty at least, old men and women, terrified for their grandchildren. The noise, I can't describe it. They were beating pan lids, screaming and chanting. One of my pupils saw it from her bedroom. They knelt on him. They searched his pockets. Nothing. Then his bag. Inside they found scissors, nail clippers, penknives, needles. That proved it. So they lynched him. It was like a *ch'illa*."

You see, this was another thing about a *pishtaco*. You couldn't shoot him. My mother said the only way to kill a *pishtaco* was to gang up and use his own methods on him. A *ch'illa* was how the farmers sacrificed their llamas.

"They tore out his eyeballs, but they didn't stop there. They ripped off his balls and then they plucked out his heart. He was still alive. I heard the screams from this room."

The army buried him near the bridge. No one knew his name, nor what he had looked like. The people had dragged him through the streets until his bones showed through the scraped flesh.

"I hear the pan lids every night."

"Is that what you were discussing outside?"

"One of the kids spotted someone on the upper road. It's exciting for them. In daylight it's easy to dismiss as a joke. But it's not. If you go to the hotel, take my advice. Stay inside." He nodded at the sofa. "I'd offer you a bed here . . ." He couldn't hide his thoughts.

"It's all right, Santiago." I had exacted enough.

He jerked up his thumb, relieved. "So long, then, Agustín. If you catch Ezequiel, give me a call."

"Look, I'm serious, what I said about money. About a reward."

Emphatically, he shook his head. And that's how we left each other, making vague promises which neither of us thought we would keep.

I decided to sleep the night at our farm.

The bridge had reopened days before, repaired by army engineers from a base in Pachuca. Below me the gully squeezed out a torrent of icy water.

The rain had come too late to work its miracle on the valley. The drought had filched the colors from the mountains, and the familiar contours were streaked with the dark brown shades of a buzzard's wing. The sight of the pinched terraces, slipping away into ridges of cracked earth, ploughed up buried voices. I heard my mother saying, "If you don't play your flute, the rains won't come and the coffee won't grow."

I followed a line of hoofprints. They stamped ahead of me over the clay, disappearing off the road down a steep track. Down that track the frightened animals would have stumbled to the airstrip. I stepped onto the verge and looked from the river—glinting, a little swollen, through a bluish haze—to the flat field below. Unable to contemplate the passage of the horses and their load, I grasped at another image.

I thought of the day I left home.

My mother is driving our truck along this road so I can catch the bus. I'm eighteen, going to the capital to study law. I sit between my mother and my father, who has my sister on his lap.

Since it's my last day, everyone is making an effort. But it isn't a happy occasion. A week ago an army jeep delivered an envelope to my father. We haven't been told what it contained, but after overhearing the Turk in the butcher's shop, I know.

I am about to speak when my sister points. "Look!" Covering the field, a flock of green parrots.

You must have seen them. You can tell you're up north when you hear those birds. They're hard to make out on the ground. You see a green bush, and then the whole thing lifts and the way the light falls on their feathers as they tilt makes it seem the birds have changed color in midair. What has been green is violent red, and you are looking at another creature.

I expect my mother to stop the truck and shoo the parrots from the bushes. She detests these creatures. They eat the crops and she is forever asking my father to buy some poison. Whenever she hears a wingbeat, she dashes into the field and raps a kettle, shouting "hey-hey-HEY!" until they rise, shrieking, against the mountain.

But, as she sits beside me, her lips are closed.

We reach the road. My father slides out of the truck to open the wire gate. He waves my mother on, closes the gate and climbs back in. Normally this is my job. Today it's his treat to me.

I look back at our farm. It is an honest house and the view over the split-wood fence is identical in every direction. Bleached grass on the terraces. The shadows of large birds. Rain-streaked rocks. In winter, shoals of puffy clouds neatly arranged to the horizon. In summer, nothing but the sky. When it grew really hot, you'd get fireballs. On that sort of day the eucalyptus trees would explode.

Ezequiel grew up two hundred miles to the north, his house not unlike ours. He shared our river too. The Marañón springs from a limestone basin above the village. It becomes the Amazon a thousand miles away, but is already a substantial flow by the time it passes our fields. From the truck I can see the rapids.

"You'll miss the river," murmurs my father.

Last week when the moon was up, Santiago, Nemecio and I

tied hunks of meat to a string and threw the bait in the water. When the string went taut, we scooped the net under what clutched the meat and boiled up a paraffin can.

"You won't eat crayfish like this in law school," said Santiago.

My father, leaning against the window, observes his fields. The farm has been in his family since 12 August 1580, which he has read was a Wednesday. By the time he inherited from his uncle, it had dwindled to an estate of a hundred acres. But still large enough for the military to expropriate.

"Ouch," he says, adjusting his position. "You've become too heavy." This is an excuse. He wants to shift my sister off his lap so he can see the black roof now coming into view between the trees. His library.

I've never met a man so interested in books. Any hope of establishing a conversation with him is predicated on your being interested in what he is reading. Otherwise, as my mother says, it's a long cold night.

She jokes he is more concerned about his books than his family. The reason he pays attention to my sister is because, from when she was a small child, she liked to show him animals she'd captured by the river. She would ostentatiously play with them at his feet—toads, beetles, lizards, snails she'd scraped from the cactus. But he is not often seduced from his text, unless he treads on something on his way to the shelves. Scraping a snail from his shoe, he would exclaim, "The boys throw stones at the frogs in sport, but the frogs do not die in sport, they die in earnest."

At four o'clock every afternoon my mother joins him in his library, nudging open the door, with a glass of red syrup for his chest. Together they raise Pachuca, the nearest big town, on the transmitter and take orders for coffee beans—fewer and fewer orders since the creation of the government cooperative. Then, until it is time for dinner, she abandons my father to his books.

And last week a man he has never met, made important by a soldier's uniform, has written to say: all this, it's over; it's no longer yours, it's mine.

He jerks his head. "Martha . . ."

"Yes, dear?"

We wait for him to speak. But it's my last day. "Oh . . . nothing," and he investigates his foot.

My mother is an Ashaninka, pure. She has been his housekeeper since he was twenty and is sharp and sweet. She has high moral standards and shoulders lopsided from picking his coffee. If I look at my face, I see my father's Spanish nose. From my mother I inherited my coloring.

"I've packed your flute," she says.

"Oh, good. Thank you." I had wrapped the *pinkullo* in a sweater and hidden it in the back of my drawer so she wouldn't find it.

"They'll keep you busy at university, but try to practice."

"I will."

Her eyes, which nest in the fine lines of her round face, smile trustingly. She wipes the condensation from the windshield and drives off the road, down the track, toward the Weeping Terrace.

Before I catch the bus, family and friends are to assemble on this field where by tradition the villagers meet to say goodbye. It's a rare event for any of us to leave the valley and we will hug and cry and sing special, very sad songs. I've witnessed these farewells, and hated them. My mother has forced me to learn the flute so I can participate in ceremonies like this one, but I don't believe in her music any more than I believe in my father's books. They haven't saved the farm. These rituals embarrass me.

Political, ignorant, mad to get away, I am a young eighteen.

We are early. We wait on a bank of sharp sedge grass while my mother extracts the *pinkullo*. She plays some notes and hands me the flute.

"Dirty girl," says my father, picking grass from my sister's back. But the set of his shoulders says, What are we going to do, Martha?

"Papa . . ." I wish he'd speak to me. He wanted me to inherit the farm.

"Look, there's Father Ramón!" My mother points at the priest, who is stumbling toward us down the hill.

"You'll trip over your surplice," she calls.

"Agustín! Agustín! Thank heavens, I've caught you . . ." He

slows to a walk as he nears us, then stops and slaps his belly, catching his breath.

He has been at the radio station, he gasps. Delivering his sermon early so he could join us. He grips my shoulder while addressing my mother.

"Before I forget, thank you for the most delicious dinner last night. The tongues were excellent. Nemecio and I agreed . . ." and the rest of his sentence is consumed in a fit of coughing.

"Shouldn't smoke, Father," flirts my sister. She is the one who gets around everybody.

"Now, now," and he coughs louder.

I ask, "Where is Nemecio?" But I can see him with Santiago, waving from the road above. He spreads his arms into wings and zigzags down the bank. It's the last time I will see him.

"Agustín, I want to give you this." Father Ramón hitches up his surplice, revealing dirty tennis shoes. He plucks a hand from the folds. "No." I take a step back. "I can't. Not possibly."

Coiled in his palm, his silver chain with its pendant. Our Lady of Fátima.

"Trust her, and you'll get through your law exams." He advances, spreading the chain into a circle. "Always remember, God's mercy is more powerful than God's justice." He drops it over my head.

Look. I still wear it.

I got to our farm in the late afternoon.

It stood at the end of a subdued avenue of eucalyptus. The view of the house held no surprises, but I was not prepared for the emotion it aroused. I hastened toward the buildings as if the river would drag them away before I reached them.

The trees opened into the yard where we would heap the dispulped berries. I stood by the concrete water tank. Faintly on the air came something I hadn't smelled for twenty years: the scent of the rotting honey which coated the beans.

The buildings were deserted. All I heard was my breathing. Lack of sound in these valleys meant lack of life, another reason my mother made me learn the *pinkullo*. Music and dance for her were practical necessities, the melodies she urged me to collect as vital in their way as my father's crops. Silence spoke only of blight.

Now, up close, I saw the devastated fields around the house. The earth had separated into fissures wider than my outstretched arms. Shrubs poked into the air, unprotected against the sun, strangled by vines. My father had not been a successful farmer, yet those who replaced him had understood his crops less.

I walked through the rooms, not taking much in. Broken glass on the kitchen floor. In my bedroom, a cardboard box spilling over with magazines. A drawer chinking with dead light bulbs. The farm had been seized in the people's name, and the people had not known what to do with it.

I crossed the yard to the old depot. Beside the door, on its side, crouched the rusted carcass of the English-built generator. My father boasted that it had pumped in the same peevish rhythm since 1912. It had powered the dryer for the berries and the transmitter in his library and the lamp by which he read.

The door had been torn away. The floor was a mess of empty sacks and gasoline drums. Termites had crumbled the pillars, and the roof in listing had shed most of its panels to the floor. I approached a heap lying at the end of a beam of sunlight: the blackened remains of a gut-shot dog, the floor showing through its eye sockets. I heard my father's voice: "Wherever you see the military, you see stray dogs."

Something smelled; the dog, I thought—but it was me. I had worn the same clothes for three days.

I washed everything in the river, including myself. On the opposite bank a thin mare was eating a mouthful of yellow grass. Like a ballerina, she rubbed her head against an outstretched leg. When I fell backward, naked, into the water, she cantered off, kicking against the flies.

The sun was hidden by the mountains, but the air was warm and when I got out of the river my skin dried quickly.

I was hungry. Tucked under the bank, in a pool where we often trapped trout, I noticed two dark shadows and a lazy bubble trail. I went back to the house, mended a net I found hanging in the library, and in a short time landed two small fish.

I gathered firewood, built a fire in the yard and cooked the trout. But I could barely keep awake to eat. I had spent the previous night rolling and bumping in the back of the pickup from Pachuca. The night before, I had sat unsleeping in the truck. I changed into a fresh shirt, rested my head against my bag and fell asleep beside the fire.

A penetrating cry dissolved into stillness. The cry rose again. It became part of my dream, a dream in which I saw the eye whites of terrified animals, hooves kicking against a stenchy load, teeth tearing at their own necks. I heard the whinnies of those creatures as they picked their way, or were dragged or beaten, across the stream. And, again, the cry.

I scrambled to my feet. The road above jittered with orange lights. Tall shadows flared on the cliff. The sides of the gorge magnified the clamor. I heard animals howling, men shouting, a clashing of steel like the sound of my mother beating her kettle.

The flames jerked down the bank. A line of upright shapes stumbled into the avenue. Dogs barked. Back and forth, torchlight flashed on the eucalyptus, shooting up the trunks to a great height. Then the lights were snatched away to kindle another patch of darkness.

The shouts were distinct now, male and female, but mostly female, older rather than younger; after so many years of frugality and silence, a hysterical release of pent-up rage, despair and grief.

"Pishtaco! Pishtaco!"

I leapt back from the fire, ran across the yard, took refuge inside the library. The blood seethed through my head. Who were these people? Whom were they chasing? Did I know the person? Half-asleep, exhausted, I asked myself these questions. I believed they had pursued their quarry all this way from the village. They had frightened him into the fields and now were flushing him out with their pan lids and burning brands.

I peered down the avenue, expecting to see a figure flitting like an exhausted bat between the trees. Nobody. Nothing moved toward me, save for those flames.

Now I could make out the forerunners. As well as their torches, they held sticks. The dogs tossed their heads, teeth flashing in the lights.

Then from that swarm of shadows I heard a woman's scream.

It was a sound from which all the flesh had been removed and only the raw bone showed. A voice ecstatic with hatred.

"Pishtaco! There he is!"

I ran to the river, wading into the fast-running water, the bag with Lazo's jug in it poised over my head. In midstream I slipped on a stone, but the current buoyed me up and I allowed it to bob me along. A short distance away the river broke into rapids. I floated on—not far—to the next bend and found my feet, splashing to the bank. As soon as I reached the level of the field, I doubled back through the shrubs until I knelt about fifty yards from the crowd. Slowly I raised my head.

They hadn't followed me. They trained their attention on my fire. To a frightened people looking for what they needed to find, these flames in a deserted farm signaled one thing. *Pishtaco.*

An old woman—perhaps the one who had screamed—danced toward the fire. She stamped her feet, sending up scuffs of earth, twisting her body in an untidy sway. Once, livid with my father over something, my mother had shuffled the same steps.

Spread out around the flames were other shriveled figures. Chanting together, they urged her on. Light played over their quivering throats, their downturned mouths, their brainwashed faces. They looked like creatures made of earth. *"Pishtaco, pishtaco, pishtaco,"* they sang tonelessly.

The woman was dancing away the alien, the flesh-eater.

She finished. A man's voice said, "He's not here. Where is he?"

The faces disappeared. Dogs were called and the lights doddered through the house. Sparks drifted up through the library roof. A fierce beam of torchlight investigated the rafters.

"Over there! Something moved!" But it was another's shadow.

From the river, in a voice I thought I knew, an old man shouted, "He's in the water!" My shirt and trousers—which I had spread on the rocks to dry—were brought for inspection, then cast into the fire. The thrower knelt down, puffing at the embers. The flames illuminated a face that could have been Lazo's—but from that distance, in that glow, I was not certain of anything.

If it was Lazo and he caught me, would I be able to reassure him, make him call them off? Or would he tear out my eyes?

An old woman, her back framed by the fire, suddenly turned

and scrutinized the darkness that engulfed me. She held up a lantern, and its light slanted across a ravined cheek. I heard her say to two other women, "Come on, let's check this field." One of them whistled. A dog lifted its nose from the fish bones. Swiftly—very swiftly, given their age—the three of them struck out in my direction.

I scrambled through the undergrowth. Brambles tore at my face. I wasn't sobbing yet, but I felt a stab of terror. I crawled on hands and knees, feeling a way between the roots and over ditches. After twenty yards or so the ground suddenly gave way and I fell through black air. My arm flailed, striking a bush—which I grabbed. Rigid with dread, I hauled myself back to the surface and lay on the lip of the crevice, hugging the bag to my chest, panting and trembling. Branches snapped. A dog barked. Daggers of light converged toward me. I had no time left.

How wide the crevice was, I couldn't tell. I kicked out and touched earth a yard away. But how deep? *There are cracks so wide you can't see the bottom.* To measure the depth, I gripped the bush and lowered myself, feeling for the bottom with one foot. The sides started to narrow almost immediately. I let myself down a little farther. The crevice seemed to shrink to the width of a man's waist. But I could not feel the bottom. The ground reverberated with trampling feet. What if Lazo was right? What if this plunged into the heart of the earth? I twisted my head. The tips of branches glinted twenty yards away. I could hear a hungry snuffling. A bush shuddered.

I released my grip and slithered down until I was wedged. Above me was the vast indifference of the night. Then sparks drifted among the stars. They had set fire to the house.

At that moment I wanted to kill Ezequiel. Had he been sandwiched in the earth and I had appeared on the lip, I would have stamped him into that bitter-smelling oblivion.

11

Next evening, waiting for Rejas, Dyer had opened a second packet of breadsticks. Without a word, Emilio lifted the book and flicked the crumbs into his cupped hand. Then, in his grubby, overlarge jacket, his bow tie at an angle, he walked ponderously onto the balcony and flung out his hand, scattering the crumbs.

Nine o'clock. A samba racketed from the fortress. Through the window drifted dog barks, engines panting and the leathery smell of night.

"Where is he?"

Coming back inside, the waiter shrugged.

"Do you know where his sister lives?"

Emilio flicked a napkin over the seat of the empty chair, avoiding Dyer's eye.

"Do you know her name?"

No reaction. Across the river, darkly spread against the last traces of a dramatic sunset, the jungle lifted ragged wings. Dyer could see, between the acanthus scrolls of the balustrade, the water rolling by and foam curling from a prow. A garbage boat. Sluggish, unimpressible, varnished by a low moon, the river had Emilio's face.

Dyer ordered a beer. At nine-thirty he heard someone on the stairs. The curtain rustled and two faces poked, one above the other, through the beads. The taller, European-looking, wore a ponytail and chewed a mango noisily. At first Dyer thought they were musicians, wondering whether to play. Then he saw a pair of flippers dangling from the taller man's neck, and, attached to his belt, some goggles. Two divers, more likely, looking for a buddy or a good time. "Come on, Mr. Silkleigh, there's nothing for us here," decided the lower head, impatient. "Righto, old thing." The discussion over, they withdrew. Dyer heard their footsteps descending and a catcall from the square.

Ten o'clock.

Last night Rejas had left Dyer down a dark hole, expecting to have his eyes torn out. Surely he couldn't have intended to leave him hanging at such a point? Dyer had listened to people's stories all his life. Why was he so engrossed by this one? However dimly, he must have suspected where Rejas was leading. The policeman's narrative beckoned, and not just because he had fought against a darkness unlike any Dyer had known.

"Another beer."

That darkness, that darkness—suddenly it flickered through him like a nausea. Jaime, wasn't that his name, the journalist from Villoria who'd had his tongue cut out? No, Juan, that's who it was. Or maybe it was Julio. Dyer had met him only once, for a beer, at the Versailles Bar in Plaza San Martín. Gray jersey, shiny black bomber jacket, fattish. Dyer must have seen the tongue when Julio licked his fingers to turn the pages of the thesis he had brought with him. He'd written this about Ezequiel, his years at Santa Eufemia University. It was one of three copies; the military had one, Ezequiel the other. The two professors assigned to supervise had both resigned out of fear. Ezequiel's comrades had rung him. A strange voice said, "Burn your copy. Show it to no one." If you're afraid of dying, you'll die many times. But if you've spent four years writing six hundred pages, what you want most in the world is readers. That's when Julio licked his fingers. The world needed to know this, how it started. He had been vehement on this point, fervent, but Dyer couldn't tell him that the world didn't care a fig, could not say that to a colleague, so he asked him, "Jaime, listen, who've you shown this to?" And Jaime had listed them, this American journalist—who Dyer knew was CIA—also a French journalist and one from Reuters, and now he was showing it to Dyer.

Wasn't he in danger? Oh, no. No, no. No. Besides, who would find out? Jaime didn't believe in Ezequiel's thousand eyes, Ezequiel's thousand ears. Propaganda.

Journalists can get like that with a story, when it becomes more important than their lives.

But someone found out. Must have. Jaime had been so pleased too. Kept saying "scoop." Wanted to know if that's what they called it in English. "Scoop?" In fact, that was the last word Dyer heard him say as they were leaving the bar, Jaime hopping from one leg to another, terrifically pleased with himself. A group of Ezequiel's followers imprisoned in Lurigancho had agreed to speak to him. In jail. "A scoop."

It was too. None of the press corps had been able to interview Ezequiel's people. This was Ezequiel's policy. He didn't like journalists. Journalists took sides, he said. So far he had killed forty-two.

Well, the prisoners granted Jaime his interview. The guards unlocked the door into the compound, let him through, turned the lock after him. An hour later a hand scratched at the grille. They had cut out his tongue.

Perhaps it was Jorge. The name didn't matter. The point was the tongue, and once Dyer thought of that gargling hole, he couldn't stop himself. The awful daring of a moment's surrender, wasn't that what Eliot had said? Or Pound?

Unasked, Emilio brought him another beer.

He was drinking to forget what he couldn't remember. Now that he thought about it, had Jorge's tongue in fact been cut out? Dyer hadn't seen it. Had anyone seen the tongue or the absence of tongue? What was to say that it didn't happen? That the whole story had been made up, its horror improved with the telling? Hadn't Dyer been culpable of treating Ezequiel like this? Hadn't he boasted he knew all about Ezequiel—yet if he was honest, if the man were sitting right opposite him now, in the seat he'd reserved for Rejas, who wasn't coming by the look of things, did Dyer know anything about the man? Really know? Some people devoted whole lives to this subject. Forty-two of his peers had given their lives to it. Dyer had been lucky so far, but there was no reason why his luck should continue. If he hadn't had connections, and Vivien Vallejo for an aunt, nobody would have had anything to do with him.

And Brazil? What did he know about Brazil? Come to that, what did he know about South America? He knew Spanish and Portuguese and a smattering of Guarani, but not so well that any-one would take him for a native speaker. In his articles he was able to present the continent as a novelty in England, but what right did he have to act as an intermediary?

His heyday had been the war in the Falklands and its after-math. His dispatches towered above the others, not just because he spoke Spanish but because, by virtue of his upbringing in Latin America and his marriage to a Brazilian girl, he already had unri-valed contacts in the region. He won two consecutive press awards—one, for his interview with Lieutenant Colonel Rose, minutes after Rose had brokered the peace in Port Stanley; the second, for his investigation into the treatment of Amazon Indians. Excited by Latin America for the first time since Perón nationalized the railways, his newspaper had opened a bureau in Rio.

But interest had quickly flagged. Either he could keep up a steady flow of revelations about the destruction of the rain forest or Nazi-hunting in Paraguay, or the public did not want to know. *Our C2 readers aren't switched on to your neck of the woods.*

And now his aunt had disappeared and it was eleven o'clock in Pará and Rejas hadn't turned up and he felt like a shit because he hadn't told him who he was. Rejas had thought he was talking to a receptive stranger, but had grown suspicious. He must have used his contacts in the police force and found out about him and that was why he wasn't coming tonight and why Dyer would never see him again and would spend the rest of his life thrashing through the water without having heard the end of the story.

When he got to his room in the Hotel Seteais, he threw up. It had been a mistake not to order dinner.

In the morning Pará celebrated Corpus Christi. The young priest stood beneath an awning in the bed of a lorry, which took him at walking pace across the square, stopping at the steps of a church with three clockfaces. Attached to the fringed awning, two coffin-sized loudspeakers distorted the Eucharist. The congregation, dressed up, fanned their throats with hymn sheets until invited to sing. Their words emphasized the connection between Pará and the Old World: "O Jesus, you were born in Bethlehem, our brother city." Firecrackers burst noisily between the hymns.

Shaken from his bed by the din, Dyer got up—still in his clothes from the night before—and walked to the square.

His mood was penitential, but he lacked the energy to insinuate himself into the crush. His mouth was dry and he had an undergraduate's hangover. What he wanted most was coffee and a large glass of orange juice. He looked toward the restaurant, peering over the hymn sheet someone had given him, to see if Emilio had opened his shutters, when he saw Rejas standing in the recess behind the balcony.

Dyer, climbing the steep stairs, was worried in case Rejas might want to avoid him, but the policeman regretted his absence the night before: he had not been able to leave his sister. She had been unwell all afternoon. When she opened her eyes, her left pupil was turned outward and didn't respond to light.

"No news yet from the lab?"

"No."

They watched Emilio put down the coffee and orange juice. Rejas waited until the waiter was gone, then said, "You've been suborning my friend."

"I did ask him where your sister lived," admitted Dyer, embarrassed. "But he wouldn't tell me."

"No, he wouldn't. He comes from my valley. His family used to work in the hotel when it was owned by Santiago's mother. His wife looks after my sister. They were driven out by Ezequiel's people. My sister was happy to take them in."

"He's very protective . . ."

Rejas, changing the subject again, said, "What did you do yesterday? Did you find some Indians?"

"There's something I need to tell you," said Dyer.

"What is that?"

"I told you I was a writer. That's not the whole story. I'm a journalist."

Rejas gave him a quick, hard look. "I know who you are. I know your name, and your date of birth, and the name of the paper you write for."

"How did you know all this?"

"I knew it as soon as you told me that Señora Vallejo was your aunt. I've read your work." Rejas mentioned an article which had been translated in *La República,* one of the first studies of Ezequiel's movement to have been published in the West.

"Well, yes—yes, actually, I did write that."

Rejas said, though not disagreeably, "It was rather shallow, I thought. There were some inaccuracies too. And another article which upset a great many people in my country."

"I hadn't known until quite recently that it caused this offense."

"It doesn't matter." His smile was more a shrug than a reprimand.

"They were rather shallow," agreed Dyer. "What I write is bound to appear shallow to a participant. Journalists can't tell the whole story." He stopped. "But if you knew I was a journalist all along, why tell me your story? You must be aware of the risks."

Rejas, face between his hands, evaluated Dyer. "Do you write everything you are told?"

"If I judge it has political interest for my readers, yes."

Rejas considered this. "When you came here, what actually were you researching?"

To be able to tell the truth was suddenly more welcome to Dyer than fresh air. He explained the background to his journey to find Vivien, his failure to get an interview with Calderón.

"It seems I may have blotted my copybook."

Rejas shook his head. "Frankly, you ought to have known he wouldn't speak to you. He's practically ungetatable. That is the source of his power, as it was for Ezequiel. Why should he see you? He won't even see me."

"Calderón has reason to be frightened of you. It's hardly any wonder."

"No, it's not that. He just doesn't see people. That's not the way he works."

"But why would you want to reach him, Colonel? Except to tell him of your intentions."

For three nights, Dyer had kept his ferreting brain in check, hoarded the questions he wanted to ask. Now they tumbled out. "Ledesma of the PLP is vying with Temuco of the CPV for your hand in political marriage. Yet here you are, miles from home. All right, your sister's ill. But surely you have a plan? You must know that if the elections were held tomorrow, you'd have a chance of winning. You're an ideal figurehead for the People's Party. You would have an immense following. A great many people outside your own country, too, are aware of you, what you've done. The Brazilian press, if they had any idea you were here, would be marching up those steps in battalion strength."

He watched Rejas, waiting for a reaction. But he was trapped by the other man's unblinking gaze into rushing on. "So what would stop you running? What is stopping you running? Is Calderón frightened of your popularity?"

Rejas, a little impatient, said, "Who can say what Calderón thinks? I've left the stage, haven't I? I've gone away—which is what he wanted. I can't help it if the stage keeps coming back to me."

"I don't want to appear impertinent, but I have to ask. Will you run?"

"Maybe not. Maybe I will. Today is too soon to say. Neither yes nor no is yet the right answer."

"What do you need, then, what are you waiting for, to make up your mind?"

Rejas threw back his head, exasperated. "Let's just say that I need, in some way I haven't been able to arrive at, to reach an understanding."

"Are you talking about a deal? I can perfectly see, Colonel, what you could offer Calderón. But what could he propose to you?"

Rejas looked at Dyer a very long time, as if weighing whether to continue with the discussion.

Finally he said, "Let's get to the end of the story."

12

I returned to the capital by bus. The journey took three days. What sustained me was the piece of paper with Edith's emergency number on it. I had no idea of her position in Ezequiel's hierarchy, but she was obviously high up. If I could locate the address, I believed it would connect me to Ezequiel. I knew that number by heart.

We reached the outskirts at dusk. There was a blackout. Blue fireworks spattered the sky, a signal of some kind. I was certain a message lay encoded in those bursts of color, but could not guess what it might be.

The bus inched through the crowd. Fanned out beside the window, panicked men and women, heads down, walked rapidly from something. Families fleeing with their children, heading they didn't know where. A face twisted up at me, mouth open.

I had been gone nine days. Terror had sunk its fangs into the city.

We drove through the blacked-out suburbs. Pyramids of truck tires blazed on a hillside. The night smelled of burned rubber. Inside the bus we started coughing.

At eight-fifteen we were spat out into the chaos of the terminal. I pushed my bag through the crowd. The streets dinned with people bashing their car doors, hooting. In the middle of the road, as if answering to some weird impulse, a barefoot figure in striped pajamas and brandishing a straw hat directed the traffic.

"That's it, straight on. You'll get there."

Figures weaved between the car bumpers selling objects they

had looted. Beneath a set of dead traffic lights, a boy held up a canvas, ornately framed, of a peaceful European river scene. An accomplice, in jeans and a woolen hat, lowered his head beside a driver's window, offering a silver goblet to an alarmed woman.

I crossed the road, searching for a bus to take me to Miraflores. Another firework exploded. A few feet away an antlered head reared glassy-eyed over the car hoods. Its throat lifted skyward, and then with a desultory toss, the head tilted and disappeared. Gripping the horns, a disheveled man in flapped-open coveralls said, "Twenty pesos, señor?"

There was no blackout in Miraflores. The bus might have rattled out of the darkness into another planet. Couples sat on benches, holding hands. In a café, brilliantly lit, a girl raised a glass of iced coffee to her lips and, laughing, wiped a cream spot off her nose. By the flowerbeds a man slapped his green mackintosh and called to his dog.

I stepped off at Parque Colón and hurried toward our flat.

I had not spoken to Sylvina since she'd driven me to the airport nine days before. I hoped she had not started to worry. Whenever my work took me outside the capital, I made certain to telephone. I would write down a list of things I wanted to say and never get around to saying them. But always I called.

This evening I desperately wanted to talk to someone.

Laura, her face lifted to the ceiling, sat at the end of the table while Sylvina applied a gray paste to her cheeks. A pink vinyl case gaped open, and scattered about it were a number of small gold pots with their tops off.

Sylvina stood back. Her mouth shone unnaturally bright and her eyes had the undaunted stare of the convert.

I looked at Laura. "What is going on?"

"Laura's been filling in for one of my clients, haven't you, darling? No, give it time to set."

"Clients?"

She kissed me, but not so as to disturb whatever she had smeared on her lips. "I've got six, Agustín. Six in three days! Patricia, Marina—I won't go on. They're coming tomorrow. Consuelo said she'd pop in, but wouldn't buy anything. Otherwise they've sworn to place an order, even if it's only an eyebrow pencil. People are wonderful."

Sylvina's scheme. Our salvation. I'd forgotten. From a leaflet on the table, a frosted blonde, teeth framed between bright lips, smiled at me. STRATEGY. A REVOLUTIONARY SKIN CARE FOR THE MATURE WOMAN.

"I know you don't like him, but Marco's office expressed these samples last week." She'd spent the last two days with Laura, learning the spiel, how to apply the cosmetics. "It's so exciting, Agustín."

My tired eyes took in the gold pots. Lip gloss. Throat creams. Concealers. Moisturizers. Foundations.

"We're going to make money, darling. Thousands of dollars in weeks. It's the Sally Fay promise. They're keen to get into our market. There's no one doing this here."

Laura lifted her head, trying to say something.

"No, don't speak yet. She's been very good, listening to my pitch. There's this pack of promotional material I'm expected to memorize."

"Sylvina—"

"They want me to put over the idea that Sally Fay works best when the products are used together."

"Sweetheart—"

"I've asked everyone to come over tomorrow without their makeup—so I can confirm their skin types."

She had stopped paying any attention to me. Here on this shrinking island of Miraflores she had found in that vinyl briefcase her answer to the horror.

She inspected Laura's closed lids. "Yes, it's ready to come off. How was your trip?"

I pulled out a chair. I wanted to tell her, but my words dissolved in the air between us.

"I'll tell you later." I sat down. "What's been going on here? You know there's a blackout in the suburbs?"

"To tell the truth, Sally Fay's been devouring my time. But you remind me: I must get more candles."

I turned to Laura. She was rubbing off what looked like dirt. "How are your new classes?"

Sylvina said on her behalf, "Going well, aren't they? I do like her teacher. Deliciously pretty and so dedicated with it. Nothing too much trouble. But it's all dance, dance, dance. I told her—not too sternly, I hope—'I want to see you with a boyfriend. This city is no place for a single girl.' By the way, Agustín, remember that pepper grinder? I can't find a new one anywhere. There. Show your father."

"How do I look?" said Laura.

"All right." The paste had turned her skin blotchy, as if she had stood too long in the shower. It made her resemble Marina's daughter.

She spat something out. "It tastes like seaweed."

I made myself a sandwich in the kitchen. I hadn't eaten since breakfast. The radio, which Sylvina sometimes left on for the cat, was playing classical music above the fridge. I made an unconvincing animal noise and the cat bolted.

A moment later Laura entered, holding it in her arms.

I looked at her and my heart turned out. "You wouldn't have enjoyed it."

She stamped her foot. "How do you know?"

"You couldn't have seen the Weeping Terrace. It's become an airstrip."

"Did you bring me a flute?" She saw I'd forgotten. "Oh, Daddy . . ." The cat leapt from her arms as she ran out.

I finished eating the sandwich and made a pot of tea. Outside I heard Sylvina speaking.

"What?" I put my head around the door.

She had taken up position in front of the mirror and was speaking to herself.

"All those companies you can't pronounce. It's so easy to understand and say Sally Fay. We're not trying to hide behind some exotic French name. Sally Fay takes you into the next millennium of skin care without you having to leave the comfort of your own living room . . . Laura? What comes next?"

". . . and because we don't have overheads . . ."

I took a shower. She was still speaking to herself when I came out of the bathroom, smiling in a way I'd not seen before.

She offered the mirror a tube.

"Now this is a really good defense against skin fatigue."

As soon as I awoke, I telephoned Sucre.

"Any luck with the chiropodist?"

"Nothing."

"Dr. Ephraim?"

"Ditto. No one suspicious."

"And the trash?"

"Nothing out of the ordinary, sir."

I read him the number Santiago had given me. "I want to know the address. A month ago it was hot."

"It could take a day."

"Take a day."

"Where can I reach you?"

"I'll ring in. I've got to repay a loan."

Lazo's daughter worked in a cavernous, ill-lit bakery opposite a tin-roofed church.

The manager agreed to spare her for five minutes. I didn't tell him who I was. Family business, I said. I'd come directly from the bank.

"Agustín."

She met me at the door, sleepy-faced. She had her father's eyes and her daughter's tight mouth. We kissed. Her cheeks smelled of flour.

"How did you find me?"

"No other bakeries on the hill."

"Your voice, it's deeper . . . but the same."

"You haven't changed either."

We were being polite. If you know someone as a child, you'll recognize them as an adult. For a few seconds she was the Graciela who loved detective stories and pizza with grated cheese. And I was the Agustín who played in a band.

"You're crazy, Agustín. Look at me. I'm exactly the same as I was twenty something years ago? Is that what you're telling me?"

Coquettishly, she fanned out her dress, releasing a floury puff, and pushed out a cumbersome hip.

The day was hot, but I could feel the hotter blast of the ovens. From inside, a man shouted.

"I'm coming," she called—then with sudden anger over her shoulder, "Jerk." She rubbed an eye. "Tell me, how is Papi?"

"He sends you his love. And some money."

"Didn't he write?" She leafed through the notes. "Nothing for me, no word?"

"He couldn't talk for long. He was mending the Mayor's teeth."

"Agustín, they—the military, I mean—found a piece of red cloth in my bedroom. It meant nothing. Tomasio used to wave it at the bulls. They said he was one of Ezequiel's men. I had to leave . . ." She looked down the hill, over the ghetto of dust-colored houses. This was not what she'd anticipated when she stepped onto the bus in La Posta. The night before, the second in succession, the army had choked the streets of the capital, had beaten down doors, had thrust people into vans.

"But you say Papi's well, and Francesca, did you see her, how does she look, Agustín? Has she lost that sore on her arm? It wouldn't go away."

"Your daughter's well."

"I want her here with me, but I'm waiting to hear from Tomasio. Did you see Tomasio? He said he'd write—but I haven't heard."

"I didn't see him."

"It would be just like Tomasio to send his letter to the wrong address."

In return for this money, you please tell her the truth. What happened.

I could not look her in the face, embedded my stare instead in her dress. Then, gently, I asked if we could find somewhere quiet to sit down.

An hour later, exhausted and on the verge of retching, I drove over the Rímac bridge.

I could taste the Styrofoam cup which Graciela had filled with lukewarm coffee. Not thinking, I drove to Miraflores. Whenever Sylvina needed to forget an unpleasantness, she shopped.

I walked into an arcade, looking for presents for my wife, for Laura. But in each window the glass reflected back a dress scrunched at the knees, and two flour-covered hands clawing at printed yellow flowers, mashing them.

I turned away. What was I doing in a shopping arcade? I couldn't afford presents anyway. I moved toward the daylight—and it was at that moment I recognized the silhouette of Laura's ballet teacher.

She wore, despite the heat, a pale pink sweater—V-necked, far too large for her, made of some fluffy angora stuff like kitten fur—over a black leotard and leggings. She stared at an enameled urn in the window.

"Yolanda!"

She had a Walkman on. Her head swayed from side to side and her knees brushed against her shopping bag in abbreviated movements, shorthand for a dance.

"Yolanda!"

She had her hair pulled up with a dark green band and was wearing black Doc Martens—like combat boots, only with something very childish about them. Laura has a pair. They made her legs look thin.

Yolanda moved off, clasping a plastic bag to her chest. Not looking around, she walked out of the arcade, her stride long and loping.

Running into the street, I touched her shoulder.

She spun.

"Yolanda! It's me."

The muscles of her neck relaxed.

"I didn't see you," she called. She plucked off the headphones, slipping them over my ears. Her face, excited, awaited my reaction.

Have you had this feeling? You are sitting in a car, radio on, and across the street someone tunes in to the same frequency—but much louder. For a second you are physically somewhere else. That's how I felt. I was looking at Yolanda, but at the sound of those pipes a different air filled my chest and I knelt on the moon-blue rim of a glacier. I was planting candles in the ice while, beside me, Nemecio axed out a block to carry on his shoulders. The ice, melted into holy water, we would use as medicine.

"For my *Antigone.*"

"What do you mean?"

She stopped the tape. "That's the music I'm going to dance. I'd been stuck on something totally inappropriate—Penderecki. Then we—you and me, I mean—started talking about Ausangate and I had the idea."

I returned the headphones. "So your ballet, I haven't missed it?"

"It's this Sunday. Since I last saw you, I've been rehearsing, rehearsing, rehearsing. Suddenly I felt I had to get out or I'd go mad." She dropped the Walkman into her bag.

"It's wonderful to see you." My voice sounded far off to me, as if on the mountain.

"You're thinner," she said.

"I've been away." I hadn't combed my hair and my fingernails were filthy and she looked so alive with the sun on her face.

"I've missed our conversations. I've thought a lot about the other night. But what are you doing here?"

I shuffled my feet. I hadn't polished my shoes. My hands felt large, my palms sticky. "I was looking for a pepper grinder. And a flute."

"A flute? Don't you have one?"

"Let's see, what have you bought?"

She opened her bag. "A jersey for my brother."

"Let's see."

She held a yellow alpaca cardigan against my chest. I sucked in my stomach, conscious of the white-flour fingermarks on my shirt. Afterward, I'd held Graciela for ten minutes.

"He must be big, your brother."

"He is large."

I peered inside again. "And underpants!"

She folded the jersey back into the bag. I noticed how her nostrils flared a little whenever she wanted to change the subject. She said, "I've spent my money, but the real reason I came out was to buy a jug."

For a second time that day, I reached for my wallet. "I've just been to the bank. I owe you six weeks' tuition at least."

"Are you certain?"

Having paid Graciela what I had borrowed from her father, I had intended the rest of the money for Sylvina. Marco's dollar guarantee had not solved the problem of our finances, but because of it the bank had agreed to extend my overdraft.

"Take it while I have it." I waited while she tucked the money inside the jersey in her bag. "Where are you going now?"

"The theater where I'm dancing on Sunday. I must check the stage. Do you want to see?"

I needed to ring Sucre, but it could wait. "Is it far?"

"Five blocks. Come on." She touched my arm.

I must tell you about this in the right order. Before today I had met Yolanda twice. I had liked her, but it would be stupid to pretend that the thought of Laura's teacher sent me into a state of excitement. When, in the truck from Cajamarca, I had tried to recall her face, it had eluded me. She had contracted into a ballet dancer with a good figure and shoulder-length black hair.

As we walked up Calle Argentina, I found myself drawn to her again. You know how some people affect the air around them? You enter a room, a party, and immediately the crowd divides into those—the majority—who suck energy from you, and one or two who with their every look and gesture restore it. Yolanda was like that. She had—well, she had life.

She took my arm. "I thought you were afraid of me." Her cry was full of affection.

"Why?" I cut my eyes away to a stumpy man who was staring at Yolanda's chest: the low V of the fuzzy pink sweater, the scoop of leotard beneath it. He walked by, swinging his arms higher.

"You never come to the studio," she said.

"I've been away."

"You've been in the mountains. Laura was upset not to go with you. I want to hear everything."

I looked back at her face. The light falling through a tree played over her collarbones, her cheeks, the dark notes in her hair. Her eyes were big and slanted, but in a beautiful way. I felt an urge to tell her everything.

"The new classes—are they a success?"

She stopped. "That girl of yours, now there's someone who can really do it. She's talented and it sings out, and then doesn't she know it. She knows. I told you I was right. If you'd watched her last week . . ."

I couldn't listen very well. All I could see was the distinctive slant to her eyebrows and the lipstick which didn't suit her, and then suddenly I could think only about the woman I'd left in the bakery.

"I'd recorded this group of women from Chimbivilca. Their song—well, it describes how they ride like horses through the snow, celebrating the gold they have been given. A new age, if you like. Laura took to the floor and danced as if she had known the steps all her life! The other girls are starting to be jealous."

"Thank you for encouraging her."

"Hasn't she said anything?"

"I haven't caught up." I tried to describe what I'd found on my return home, but my head buzzed as I spoke.

"That is hysterical."

"That people should be worrying about oily skin . . ."

"Actually, your wife came to the studio a few days ago."

"Sylvina?"

Very funnily—as I said, she had a gift for mimicry—though not unkindly, she imitated Sylvina's voice. " 'I hope you're not teaching my daughter anything too absolutely contemporary.' "

She walked on in her loping gait, her feet in their heavy boots rising unconsciously on tiptoe at each step. Without warning, her face grew solemn.

"You know, the only moment I was possessed by dance, really possessed, was at Laura's age, before I knew too much. It's what most of us lose as adults. The older you get, the more you edit out the daydream. Discipline takes away that feeling. You become so controlled."

She withdrew her arm from mine and swapped her bag into that hand. She fell silent, thinking something over.

The Teatro Americano, a cream-painted colonial building, lay behind spiked railings in a rectangular garden planted with lavender and cassias. It was currently being used as the venue for an exhibition by a Chilean artist. A placard on the railings announced A HISTORY OF THE HUMAN FACE.

The attendant, slim with a scanty mop of gray hair, was about to tear us tickets when she saw Yolanda. She chucked back her head and called a name through an open door. A short young man with a close-cropped beard and cautious eyes strode out. "What is it?" At the sight of Yolanda he threw up his arms. He hugged her, speaking into her ear in a jaunty, whistling voice. "I have the lights, the loudspeakers, two hundred chairs. I've rung Miguel. He promises to write a review."

Over her shoulder, he peered at me from between heavy, red-veined lids.

"Lorenzo, this is my friend Agustín. I wanted to show him the stage."

He pulled back. "Sure, carry on. How's everything going?"

"I'm not there—yet."

"You need help?"

"That's sweet of you. I'll manage."

He looked at me, then in a low voice said to her, "I'd love to see a dress rehearsal. The others would too."

"There really isn't that much time."

He thought about this for a moment. "Listen, I've someone on the line. We'll be in touch." He squeezed my shoulder. "Good to meet you, Agustín."

We passed into a lofty room hung with silk sheets. She whispered, "Lorenzo, when he isn't running this theater, is a depressed choreographer." She glanced back. "We used to work together. You can't believe his jealousy. Worried continually I'd run off with his steps."

The room, arranged with uncomfortable-looking cane chairs, was lit naturally from a glass roof which revealed the gray-wool sky and the top of a palm tree. Stage lights cast elaborate shadows across a stained wooden floor.

Yolanda waited for two students to leave the room, then slipped off her shoes, handing me the shopping bag.

"I need to measure this." She walked to one wall. Abruptly, she pirouetted once, twice, three times, then leapt five paces across the floor. "Zsa, zsa, zsa, zsa, chu!"

Burned in my mind is the flash of her feet, naked and white, through the bright air.

A yard from the opposite wall she stopped. "That's fine. I was worried about the width."

Another couple wandered into the room. She retrieved her shoes. "Isn't this a nice place?" She spread her arms and her voice rang beneath the glass. "In my first year at the Metropolitan I danced Stravinsky's *Symphony of Psalms* here. Hey, look at these faces."

My attention fixed on Yolanda, I had failed to notice the faces staring at us from the silk sheets. Up close, they defined themselves. They had been lifted from newspapers in Chile dating back thirty years, blown up to life size and printed on the silk.

The faces of pickpockets.

The faces of murderers.

The faces of terrorists and freedom fighters.

The faces of their victims.

The faces of their pursuers.

The faces of their judges.

The faces of patients from a schizophrenic ward.

The faces of extinct aborigines.

"Many of these people had one thing in common: they were not included in the society that was photographing them—either for the purpose of anthropological observation or as objects of police control. Are you a good judge of character?" she asked.

"I think so."

"Everybody thinks they are. Let's see."

We played a game. She darted to a sheet, covering a caption with her bag. "Now, answer me. What kind of person is this?"

"Thief?"

She raised the bag. "Murder victim." She ran to another face. "What about . . . her?"

"Policewoman?"

"Policewoman it is. Him?"

"Judge?"

"No. Murderer. Her?"

"Freedom fighter?"

"Schizophrenic. Him?"

"Extinct Indian?"

"Right. Two out of five. Which means that half the people you meet, you get wrong."

Across the room the couple, who had been watching us, began to copy our game. They likewise had been confident of their ability to distinguish a murderer from a freedom fighter, a general who had been blown up in his bed from a Yaghan who had died of a common cold. But this was the artist's challenge. He was saying: put them side by side and the schizophrenic assumes the personality of the judge.

"In other words," said Yolanda, "we know nothing about anybody."

Not every face had been alive when photographed. I had been about to test Yolanda's skill when she halted before the mummified features of a body in a dress.

"Yaghan?" I asked.

"Look."

The caption read, "One of General Pinochet's disappeared. Eva Vásquez, student, for seventeen years buried in a mine shaft."

Yolanda said, "It's the same story, over and over again." She added, fiercely, "Bastards."

I looked at the torn drum of skin, the wretched angle of the head, and thought of Nemecio, his mouth filling, drowning in earth. Thought, too, of a widow five miles away, scrunching her dress at the knees. My years as a policeman, what had they achieved? What if I had followed Santiago's path? A sense of my emaciated duty all at once made ridiculous the distinction between Ezequiel and Calderón. You might have asked me to choose between Emilio's grilled fish and his grilled pork.

Yolanda said, "I don't know what you are like, Agustín, but I can't look at a face like this and say nothing. What happened to her is happening to us, now."

She told me that while I'd been away the university had held a service for the Arguedas Players. She had joined the parents lighting candles for their missing children. The remains found under the cinema floor included a scrap of green blouse and two keys on a keyring, one of which fitted Vera's locker. But no body, or at least not enough of one to be identifiable.

Yolanda, looking at the desiccated face on the silk, spoke as if to herself. "You have to have a body to be able to grieve. It's something you can't understand unless you've seen a loved one die. You have to see the corpse to be certain they're dead, so they can begin living in your memory. Without a body, you can't be rid of the horror." She broke off, covering her eyes. "Stop it, Yolanda, stop it, stop it." She composed herself, not without effort. Giving a quick look around, she said, "Come on, let's leave."

Outside, people pushed their baby carriages or stretched out on the grass, reading. Through the railings I saw a yellow handcart and bought two lemon water ices on sticks. We sat on the grass, but a darkness had brushed Yolanda and she had retreated into herself.

"What would you do," I asked, "if you were Eva Vásquez and your boyfriend asked you to fight that war?"

"I don't know." She nibbled at her ice. Her eyes were red. "I don't have a boyfriend."

"I'm thinking of Laura. If I were her age, I'd be tempted to fight."

"She's a dancer."

"Does it frighten you, that I talk like this?"

"No, I'm thinking. What I would do." But she had retreated from me as well. She finished her ice and buried the stick in the grass. "I give up. I need a cigarette."

Ten yards away a young man lay on his stomach, reading a newspaper. Yolanda went over and talked to him. She came back, drawing on a cigarette.

"I didn't know you smoked," I said.

"I don't. I feel like one."

Forcefully, she blew out the smoke. "What about you?"

"I don't smoke."

"I mean what would you do?"

Something about the jut of her chin, her glowing eyes, must have reached me, stung me even. I said, "There was a moment when I sacrificed everything."

"When was that?"

"I was younger than you."

"What happened?" She had been distracted. Now she was focused.

"I had a good job with a law firm. I was just married. I was going to be rich, maybe become a judge. One day my conscience spoke to me. When I heard it, the barriers went down. My wife, career, friends. Nothing mattered when I heard this voice. Next day I left my job."

Her hand slapped the ground. "That's what she felt!"

"Who?"

"Sorry, I see everything through Antigone. She didn't want the dogs to eat her brother's corpse. She was saying, life and death, those obligations are more important than a state's decree—and that's how I feel. I value Eva Vásquez's life—or Laura's, or yours—much more than the laws of this country."

"So our political situation can never change?"

"I'm not interested in politics. The only command you have to listen to is the one inside you—which you listened to."

She flattened a hand against her chest. "I'm interested in doing the things you know in your heart are right. Burying your brother is one of them." She spoke like a child, seeing what a child saw, then became serious again. "That's what stirred me up about the Arguedas Players. They were people's brothers and sisters." She was crying.

"Lovers and sons and daughters too."

She shook her head, coughing, stubbed out the cigarette. "Not so important. You can find another lover, give birth to another child."

"You mean, you'd sacrifice your child?"

She stroked the grass. She spoke as if she were onstage. "It doesn't take much to break a man-made law. A little dust, that's all. So what can we do, Agustín? We can follow orders and do nothing. But aren't there other demands? You've been back to your people. Don't they need our help?"

I didn't move. She stared at me, her face swollen. The path her tears had taken shone down her cheeks. In a hurt voice, she said, "Agustín, do you have a reason for not telling me about your journey?"

I had been concerned to protect Yolanda from knowing the things which churned me inside. My eyes fastened on her ankle and the scar an inch or so above her boot where the leggings had pushed up.

"I'm not who you think I am. I've deceived you." I nodded at the Teatro Americano. "I'm like one of the photographs in there. Laura may have told you I was a lawyer, but I'm not."

I couldn't reveal to her the work I did, but told her that it involved lies, violence, death. I had been engaged in it when I returned to La Posta. I kept back the details of Father Ramón's murder, but not the church massacre, nor the communal grave at the airstrip, nor the people beating their pan lids along the eucalyptus avenue.

"They never found me, nor did their dogs. I can only think it's because I had changed my clothes."

I told her how I had lain tucked under a lip in the crevice throughout that cold night, my clothes damp with urine, insects crawling over my face, under my shirt. At sunrise I climbed out of the hole, my arms and legs aching. I was filthy.

After washing in the river, I walked back to the village. During the night I had made a decision. Because of it I had to move with extreme care so that neither the Mayor nor the army would discover my presence.

I wasn't going to leave La Posta until I had gathered depositions.

"People were too scared to talk to begin with. But when word got out it was Agustín from the farm, they filled Lazo's office. I didn't like to think how many of those faces had chased me the night before."

I spoke still to her ankle. I was conscious of my hand jerking in the air and the lemon ice melting, running down between my fingers.

"For many, this was the first time anyone had paid attention to them since they'd been at school. They reverted to the elementary habit of raising their hands to speak. One old lady, no longer able to walk, told how three soldiers had escorted her to the far end of a field and raped her, beginning with the officer."

Yolanda took the stick from my hand and poked it into the earth.

"Another woman lost her son when soldiers found the toy gun he carried for the Independence Day Parade."

She rested her hand on my hand, the lemon ice sticking her skin to mine.

"There was a woman holding a baby, born as a result of a rape she'd suffered on a previous invasion by the military. She'd been asked for her identity card. The soldier had ripped it up, put the pieces in his mouth, eaten them. He had repeated his demand. 'Where's your identity card?' "

Yolanda raised my sticky hand to her lips. She spread out the fingers. One by one she inserted each finger into her mouth and licked it clean.

The air went still and in that instant something altered between us. It was as unsuspected as a conversion, and as explosive.

Absentmindedly I rubbed a damp finger over her eyebrows, down her cheeks. She pressed her head to my knee. Her face had a cracked look. Neither of us said another word, but when we got to our feet, she was no longer Laura's teacher.

Much later I contacted Sucre.

"Still no luck with that number," he said.

"It must be on the computer."

"The exchange is down, sir. Truck bomb."

"If you hear anything, call."

I had collected the car from where I'd parked it behind the shopping arcade and driven home. The lights blazed in our street. On the night of my wife's presentation, Ezequiel had decided to be charitable.

I could hear Sylvina talking. I closed the door softly behind me. Reflected in Laura's mirror, six ghostly visitants sat chin-up in a line, towels bibbed under their necks.

Sylvina was saying, "You risk tragedy if you mix different products from different cosmetic companies."

"I've just spent a lot on a new Estée Lauder." Marina's voice.

"Well, you could try Sally Fay's under-eye cream and see how you like that."

"We're not supposed to mix, you said."

"I was thinking of having a facelift," another said, doubtfully. "Like Marina's."

"Then I suggest before you undergo the knife, Consuelo, you try this alpha-hydroxide cream. It works something like an actual facelift—it's the most revolutionary product we've created."

"It does exactly what?"

"It will protect you against environmental damage. It will combat free radicals. It's even got Vitamin E. Here, put a little under your eyes. No, let me help you. Maybe on your chin, I see a little blemish there."

She took up position behind the next chair.

"María, you have reddish undertones to your skin, so we're going to use this color to even them out. Yes, it does seem a little green, but don't be scared . . . Oh, Agustín—"

"Don't get up, don't get up." Six hands gesticulated from beneath their towels. "How's it going?"

From the chairs an uncertain chorus. "How do we look? Horrible?"

Necks extended, they peered at Sylvina's husband. My unpredictable hours, my weekend shifts, my unexplained absences in the countryside, ensured that many of them could barely remember what I looked like.

I gave an enriching smile of encouragement. "You're going to be angels."

Patricia said tartly, "If there's a blackout, we'll need to be."

I mumbled my excuses and went into the kitchen. Since leaving Yolanda I'd felt hungry. I toyed with the sandwiches Sylvina had made for her guests.

My appearance, far from discomposing the women, had relaxed a tension. I heard them swapping blackout stories.

Patricia had come home ten days before to find her angelfish belly-up. The filter had gone off and it had died of heat and suffocation.

Margarita, a cheerless woman who complained about bleeding gums, had come home to find the freezer thawed and already squirming with maggots. "They'd hatched in the beef—so there was not only this bad smell, but the meat was alive!"

Tanya's husband had not come home at all, having started an affair with a total stranger with whom he had been stuck for three hours in an elevator.

Sylvina spread her lotions.

"Now this is a really good defense against skin fatigue."

Patricia said, "This old man, he was directing the traffic in his pajamas."

"It goes on like silk, see, and it doesn't have to be reapplied."

"There are characters who like to direct the traffic," said Marina. "In Miami the nuthouses were full of them."

"It'll give you a more youthful appearance."

"Daddy!" Laura's head appeared at the door. "Those aren't for you."

I sprang up. I wanted to make peace with her.

"Someone's on the phone," she said, writhing away from my kiss.

Sucre had an address.

"Eleven twenty-eight. That one!"

He'd collected me in the Renault. Behind us Sergeant Gómez and three others sat in a van we'd borrowed from Homicide.

"Tell them to overtake and park the other side."

Sucre spoke into his handset. The van crept past. Its headlights uprooted a tree outside the house, kaleidoscoping its shadow branches against the blue stucco.

Santiago's last resort in an emergency was a flat-roofed, single-story building five minutes' walk from the sea. Paint curled from the wall in page-sized sheets. The shutters, unvarnished and lopsided, were closed. No one had cared for 1128 Calle Tucumán in a long time.

"Not much squeal on the place," said Sucre. "Lease ran out in February. Until then rented to a Miguel Angel Torre. Says he's a poet on his lease form."

"Where's Torre now?"

"We're looking for him. But someone's paying the bills. Electricity and telephone haven't been disconnected."

The van drew into the curb fifty yards beyond the house. Opposite, boys threw stones at a beer bottle on a low wall. One boy, spotting our car, detached himself and loafed toward us. He stopped some way away, trying to look uninterested. The radio in the car came alive.

"What's that up there?"

"A cage, it looks like."

I took the binoculars. A wire coop on the roof fluttered with birds.

"Stake it out for a day or two, sir?"

"No." Santiago might have alerted them. I lowered my gaze. Sprayed on the door in gray paint was the name of a novelist who had stood for President.

"Ask Gómez what he sees."

Sucre spoke into the radio. In the van someone, not Gómez, was saying, ". . . she promised she'd clean my straw if I let her go."

"Gómez, what do you reckon?"

Gómez came on. "Light in the yard at the back, sir. Otherwise no movement."

To me, Sucre said, "Go in now?"

"Tell Gómez to drive around the other side and keep watch. There might be a garden they can escape from."

I heard a snarl in the air. A helicopter tilted northward into a sky scratched with red fireworks.

"Red, what's that mean?"

"No one's worked out the colors, sir. Yesterday they were shooting blue. The day before, green."

All kinds of confusion had been going on when Sucre left the headquarters. Roads piled high with burning tires. Windows smashed. Stores looted.

"The General reckons some enormous piece of shit is floating down the pipeline." He took the binoculars and raised them to his eyes.

We watched the street, waiting for Gómez to radio back. The boy knelt in the road twenty yards away and retied the laces on his gym shoes.

"The General, you won't recognize him, sir. Calderón and Lache, they treat him like he's garbage. Cut him out of everything."

He unwrapped something from a sheet of newspaper. "Pear, sir?" They'd come from his farm.

A shutter opened in the house next to us. Through the window I saw a girl in a rugby shirt. One arm raised, she leapt to touch a slowly revolving fan. She reminded me of Yolanda. Everything did. A laugh floated out and a fat man in a vest appeared at the window. He leaned on the sill, glass in hand. Give his red nose a twist, I thought, and it would come off. After a while he stopped laughing and turned back to the room.

I ate my pear, concentrating on the girl, wondering why she wanted to touch the fan like that, when my vision was blocked by a hideous face. Sucked to the car window, the lips of its distorted mouth moved down the glass.

"Beat it!" Sucre, throwing the newspaper over his pistol, reached across me and slapped the glass.

"Can't I stand here?" The boy's voice, faint through the glass, sarcastic.

"No."

"Why not?"

"Just beat it."

His gaze roamed over our laps. Then he pushed himself upright. He sauntered back to the others, on the way stopping to pick up a stone. I heard the tinkle of shattered glass, followed by a shout. Then a quietness settled over the street. A quietness which terrified.

Gómez radioed that he was in position. A firework exploded, hidden by the roofs. Sucre, fidgeting with his pistol under the newspaper, said, "Ezequiel, if he's inside, I'm going to stop his clock for him."

If, behind those shutters, we did find Ezequiel, how tempting to believe it would cease overnight—the shooting, the murders, the knives at our throats—and the days would be unsoured and Sylvina could take Laura to the beach and buy her a balloon or polish her toenails in the sun. But Edith would not have handed out Ezequiel's number to a bit player like Santiago.

"What's that?" I said.

"Sounds like a dog at a trash can."

"Let's go."

Filling the house was the smell of a burned filter from a cigarette crushed into a mug. The television set was warm and the door to the yard was open. A lamp on the porch swayed in the breeze from the beach.

Sucre barged back in from the yard, followed by Gómez.

"They were tipped off, sir. We should have gone in immediately." He smashed his foot into the door.

I ordered Gómez to round up the boys in the street, then went through the house. Alerted by Ezequiel's thousand eyes, whoever had been here had left in a panic. Clothes jettisoned over a narrow iron bed; on the kitchen table a tin of peaches, half-empty beside an architecture magazine; in the front room, stacked on top of the television set—three videotapes.

A stepladder led through a hatch onto the flat roof, from where I watched Gómez running down the empty street. I waited, looking at the fences and rooftops. In the cool, dry night no shadows moved.

My presence had disturbed the birds in the cage. Agitated by the fireworks, they clawed against the wire, opening and closing their cramped feathers. I had assumed they were doves or pigeons, but now I saw that they were parrots. Raging, impervious to the screeching and scratching and clatter of wings, I heaved the cage to the edge of the roof and I pushed.

When I went downstairs, the ruined green wings flapped blood over the porch, and dying birds sang their pain through smashed beaks.

The Café Haiti, where I waited at twelve the following morning, was emptier than usual. I sat at a table in the corner and ordered coffee.

The waitress retrieved the menu. "I remember you."

The prospect of leaving Yolanda without having made a firm date for another meeting had been intolerable. I hadn't known how best to broach the subject. Then, talking about *Antigone,* she had said she was coming into town to collect her costume.

"Could we meet afterward—at the Haiti?"

I had had to extract myself from Calle Tucumán. We were going meticulously over the house. So far all we'd found were a black horsehair wig, a combat jacket on a door hook and a cardboard box containing more of the pamphlets Hilda Cortado had distributed. There remained the three videotapes in my briefcase. I'd watch them at the station, I told Sucre. Then, for the first time in my career, I played truant.

At twelve-fifteen Yolanda pushed open the glass door. She wore a sea-blue dress—sleeveless, loose, above the knee—and, over her shoulder, a bag of raw silk patterned with white llamas. She stood on tiptoe and looked about the café twice before she saw my upraised hand.

She walked over, head down, and we embraced clumsily. She had washed her hair and I could smell the new cloth of her dress and I knew she wore it for me.

"You look lovely."

"Don't let me forget this." She tucked her bag under the table.

"May I see?"

"It's unlucky. Not until I come onstage." She didn't want to begin on a wrong note and wasn't ready to catch my eye.

She said to the waitress, "You know what I feel like more than anything in the world? A *suspiros de Lima.*"

"We don't have them."

"Oh, dear. A *masita,* then?"

"Only *pan de árabe* or *pan de Viena.*"

"*Pan de árabe* then." She looked around. "Isn't this where we sat before?" Her eyes rested on me. "See? Already we have a history."

I don't wish to say too much about that afternoon. What I mean is . . . is that I can't be precise. What happened between us is not a complete picture in my mind, any more than is she. How long had we known each other? If I count up the hours, I don't suppose much longer than the time I've spent talking to you.

Put it this way. For many years I had looked neither right nor left, but stared ahead, my thoughts settled on one object: the capture of Ezequiel. Now, out of the blue, this young woman had taken me by the arm and offered something which I ought to have resisted.

There was still light in the sky when we left the Haiti. We spent the end of the afternoon walking. Toward the sea and along the Malecón. I had no sense of being curbed, only of endless space. When I looked at her, the ghosts of my happiest childhood moments nudged me.

"That sea," I remember telling her. "It takes you nowhere, but I love it."

And later: "I've been walking down this street for twenty years and never noticed that funny gray turret."

In some square—I was never to find it again—we sat on a bench.

"What are you looking at?" I asked.

"Your wrist. I was looking at it yesterday, on the grass."

"My wrist?"

"I always look at a man's wrist. Or the side of his neck, or his ankle. The vulnerable parts."

I inspected my wrist. It had never struck me as vulnerable.

"What does it tell you?"

"All intelligent people can fake modesty, Agustín, but you *are* modest."

Her hand suddenly flew at my face and I ducked away.

"What are you doing?"

"I'm not going to hit you." From the corner of my mouth, she neatly flicked away a large crumb of *pan de árabe*.

Was it on this bench that she released the few details of her life, or do I introduce these from another conversation? It wasn't much. Conservative upbringing. Only daughter of a construction engineer, to whom she had been close. Her mother, a pious teacher, made her attend the Fátima church in Belgrano four times a week. From an early age she longed to escape. The opportunity presented itself when she was fifteen. The nuns from the Sophianum school took her on a trip to the shantytowns. The Mother Superior led her to understand that she would regard it as something dreadful, worse than a lie, if Yolanda ignored the conditions in which these people lived. She decided to become a missionary in the jungle. Her father put his foot down. He wouldn't allow it.

"So I became a dancer."

Whenever she talked about her calling, a splinter of ruthlessness would enter her voice. "You may think I'm a nice person. But ask Laura. In my studio I'm different. Once you come inside, you're there to be disciplined, to get rid of your ego."

Another time she said, "You don't know how dance is. You can't talk about it—but it is a calling. You feel different. You feel special. You have to be very much yourself, but that's so you can be someone else."

"How do you mean?"

"Look, I have chubby cheeks. Too much flab here—and here. Nevertheless, people always say, 'You're so beautiful, Yolanda. What a marvelous body.' But to me a marvelous body is not interesting unless it can represent something. Because what are you? You are many people. I can't become real to myself unless I can also become, say, Antigone."

I had not met anyone like Yolanda. Yet if I describe her qualities, they sound slight. As I say, she was astonishingly alive—she really did excite the air around her. She was attractive, but didn't assume she could do everything. She was an idealist; at the same time, she could behave like someone who had lost her beliefs. She was tender. She was interested. Above all, she had this alertness. In repose, she always seemed ready to whirl about. Sometimes you had the impression she waited for a signal which none but she might register—and that it had sounded as you spoke to her. Then she would break off and her face would set in an attitude of the most intense expectation. She would look into space and with a jerk of attention focus back on you. She might listen deferentially to what you were saying—but a few minutes later something would distract her and she'd cry, "Isn't that man ridiculous? No, come to think of it, I'd like hair like that."

Prompted by the bag at her feet, which contained the dress she wouldn't show me, I asked about her performance. Who had choreographed the ballet, who was to be Creon, what props would she use?

She rolled her eyes. "Oh, it's a mess. There were going to be four of us, including Lorenzo. Remember, you met him at the theater? We'd been looking to dance a drama. Then I saw this piece on television about the Arguedas Players, and that's when I had the idea. What about *Antigone*? So we read Sophocles. Then Anouilh. Then Brecht. Then fought a lot. When the group broke up, two of them wanting to direct, all of them wanting to dance *Antigone*, I said, 'Forget it. I'll dance on my own.' "

We walked around the square. Prim houses. A woman behind a grille who looked up from her book. "Did you see that lady smiling to herself?" A couple not talking in a car. "What is she doing with him?" "What is anyone doing with anyone?" Laughter.

On the edge of the square a large dog, black with a spine of orange fur, hurled himself from the leaves and nudged his head between us, panting.

I pushed him away, afraid he might attack Yolanda. He bounded to her side and licked her hand.

"Down, boy, down." She stroked his shining face, then took my arm.

"Tomorrow I will be twenty-nine."

"How will you celebrate?"

"Rehearse. Then classes. Then more rehearsing."

"On your birthday? What about your family?"

She looked abstracted. She might have been working out a complicated dance step.

I thought of the yellow cardigan she had spread against me. "Isn't your brother going to take you out?"

"But, Agustín!" she cried. "My dance is one week away. I haven't finished the choreography. I'm having nightmares."

"Nightmares? About what?"

She pressed the fingers of one hand to her chin, contemplating the dog, which had run on ahead. "Very well. I dream I am late for the performance. I hear a flute in the background—maybe it's your rain pipe!—and I can't get to the stage, I can't run. Something, someone holds me back. At the last moment I break loose and it's dark onstage and there isn't enough light to see."

"But you shouldn't spend your birthday alone . . ."

"It's not a problem."

"My wife is worried you have no friends."

She burst into laughter. "Your wife is right. Yesterday, before I bumped into you, I felt so useless. I wanted to pack it in. Then I said no, better not, too much work to do."

"That's why you have no boyfriends?"

"Oh, I've catted around," she said unexpectedly. "And I was engaged, to a poet, a frivolous poet who only liked cars and clothes."

"You didn't love him?" I said, without reflecting.

"I loved him. But work got in the way."

Childishly, she withdrew her arm and dashed up the path to kick a can. She kicked it again and the dog chased after, pushing the can away from her with his nose. Then he trotted off, the can in his mouth. Yolanda looked back at me, raising her arms in a shrug. I felt another stab of intimacy, and I knew a strength in me had lapsed.

I drove Yolanda home and around seven o'clock returned to police headquarters. In the viewing room on the fourth floor, I gave the videocassettes from the house in Calle Tucumán to Sergeant Clorindo and went to fetch a cup of water.

"Okay, Clorindo. I'm ready."

I settled down without much expectation. I held the cup to my lips, about to drink, when on screen there appeared the face of Quesada, our late Minister of the Interior, making a televised speech to the Assembly. I finished the cup and sat back. Already this promised to be a waste of time. Probably the other cassettes were movies. I was so used to disappointment.

It would last less than a second. It was no more, really, than a trivial act of clumsiness. But our smallest gesture is never so small as we think. You hand over a camcorder, you rub a crumb from someone's mouth. The consequences are incalculable.

The first tape was a compilation of news reports. Quesada's triumphant speech. Quesada, wife and bodyguard onstage at the Teatro de Paz. Prado's body on the roadside. All items recorded from Canal 7, fifteen of them.

The second tape featured exteriors filmed through the back of a fast-moving car. The Presidential Palace; a barracks in the south of the capital; two houses I didn't recognize. The sites, I presumed, of intended targets.

I did not immediately gauge the significance of the last tape. It consisted of a single grainy recording, rather blue in color, as though it had been copied from another copy. Filmed in a nondescript room, a group of darkly dressed men and women danced in a ritual celebration.

"Turn up the sound."

Clorindo adjusted the volume to a high-frequency, insect hum. "There isn't any," he said.

The floor was strewn with flowers. The celebrants surged back and forth, arm in arm, stamping on the blossoms. At the same time, their faces concentrated on the dancer who held the camcorder, about whose expertise, despite the uncomplicated eagerness of their smiles, several eyes implied reservation. From the angle of the pictures, it was obvious that the dancer/operator, who moved in a sort of inebriated sway, didn't know how to work the machine. A short-haired woman, rather flat-faced and with a mannish mouth, could be seen shouting directions. Then a hand must have found the volume control.

There came the sudden loud sound of stamping feet and reflected voices and Frank Sinatra singing "Summer Wind." I could hear the cameraman's heavy breathing, like the wow-wow resonance of a seashell removed from the ear.

The flat-faced woman pleaded, "Give it here, give it here."

As she took the camera, I glimpsed the person behind it—a large man in a pale jersey, filmed from the side. When he realized the tape was running, he flinched, held up a hand, spread the fingers over the lens. The tape ended there.

"Go back to the beginning," I told Clorindo.

Could that blank-looking face be Edith's? I remembered a woman with thick makeup and longer hair.

"Let's see the color of her eyes."

Clorindo froze the tape. He connected the image enhancer and blew up the pixels. An icon appeared in the corner, which, with the computer's mouse, he dragged down to her eyes. He clicked twice. The image needed sharper definition.

"Try a different algorithm."

He typed in the coordinates. Once again he grabbed a frame and digitized it. Her eyes became the screen. They were the same color blue as the print. But I knew them to be green. I was looking at Father Ramón's killer.

"Go forward." I wanted to see the dancer at the end, the operator.

Edith, animate again, took hold of the camera. It jerked to the floor, recording several pairs of trouser legs. Then it arced up, over the walls, filming the man's shoulders.

"Wait. Focus on that area."

The icon was clicked. The hand juddered frame by frame toward the lens. I could see between the fingers a fuzz of beard, the black frame of a pair of spectacles, two narrow eyes.

Ezequiel.

We reran the tape. It's amazing what you miss when you're looking for something else. I was concentrating so much on Edith and the bearded dancer that I did not notice the road sign until I'd played the tape a dozen times.

The three letters had been recorded during the fumble when Edith took the camera. At first I had assumed they belonged to a picture on the wall. It was Clorindo who said, "That's not a picture, sir. It's a window." The window overlooked a tree. Outside, it was night.

"Can't you make it clearer? Try a vector map."

The computer enhanced the definition. From the letters and the way they were formed, it was a street sign. The window frame cut off the left-hand end of the word, and branches hid the last letter, but clearly visible was ERO.

I ran downstairs. Ordered a computer search, a list of all streets containing this sequence of letters. Nothing said this was a street in the capital, but I wasn't going to widen the search. Not yet.

How long would it take? "An hour, two hours?"

My secretary said, "Maybe an hour."

I rang Sucre. He was still picking through the house in Calle Tucumán. The General, eager for such propaganda as he could make out of our raid, had been on his back.

"He's keen to speak with you, sir. He wants to inform the media."

I didn't want to talk to the General. I told my secretary I'd be back in an hour and returned to the viewing room. I had intended to spend this evening plotting my report on the army massacre in La Posta. But suddenly nothing was so important to me as this tape. I had Clorindo play it again and again, trying different filters. For the first time since I had questioned him in Sierra de Pruna, I had a tangible sense of Ezequiel's presence. Over successive generations the image had become degraded. His features were blurred and imprecise, as if seen in the light of an eclipse, but I had no doubt in my mind: those fingers clawing at the lens and the eyes they half concealed were his eyes. His fingers. Ezequiel the cameraman. Ezequiel the dancer.

At ten-thirty I received the printout. There were two addresses. I knew them both. Calle Perón I remembered from my days spent guarding diplomats. A smart cul-de-sac with several banks and embassies.

I was familiar, too, with the second address, a quiet, tree-lined street in the suburb of Surcos consisting of a hundred or so houses. And my daughter's ballet studio.

13

From the very first I deployed two teams to watch Calle Diderot and Calle Perón, five in each team, men and women, disguised as sanitation men, municipal gardeners, loving couples. They were to report on everyone's movements, what time they left home, returned; whom they let through their doors. In the evenings the refuse from both streets was to be collected in a special sanitation department truck and sifted.

"Get a list of chemists in both neighborhoods," I told Sucre. "Who's buying what ointments, how regularly. Anything to do with psoriasis, I need the details. Same with tobacconists. I want to know of anyone who always buys American cigarettes: Winston, Marlboro, Camel, L&M. And a list of householders. Occupations, how long they've been there, where they've come from. Everyone is suspect. Even the Argentine Ambassador."

Except Yolanda, of course. I had to warn her.

Yolanda, when she spoke of it, had tried to play down her birthday, but she couldn't hide from me the child in her who wanted to celebrate. The occasion became my pretext.

At nine o'clock, half an hour after the modern dance class ended, I walked down Calle Diderot and pressed her bell. I carried a package, not well wrapped, and a flat box containing a banana cake.

The cake wasn't the cake I had wanted to buy. I'd seen a

beautiful *suspiros de Lima,* positioned cleverly in the window so as to convince me that I could afford it. When the girl inspected the pedestal, she discovered it had a much higher price. What I could afford was something pitiful. Anxiety assailed me as soon as I had left the shop. The cake wasn't enough. What else could I give her?

The present I chose in the end was meant only as a friendly gesture. Now I wondered if the act of bringing both a cake and a present could be taken for a sign of something else—something more emotional. Was I fooling myself? What was she going to think?

The studio lay in darkness. Upstairs, screened by the yellow curtains, someone watched television. I rapped on the door. Part of me hoped she had slipped out. I was falling for her and not wanting to. Yet my job had taken me to where she was.

I knocked again, then gave up. I had walked two or three steps when I heard the door open.

"Agustín?"

She leaned in the doorway, one leg lifted so that the foot pressed against the frame, her hands on her cheeks.

"Happy birthday," I said.

She brought her brows together and looked at me for some time. She had hurriedly thrown on a thin black dress and her hair was sticking in wet strands to her cheeks.

"Why didn't you knock properly?" she said at last.

"I thought I did."

"I shouldn't let you in." She withdrew a hand and tugged at the straps of her dress. Her shoulders were red from the shower.

"But you can't dance all day. To be cooped up, these four walls—"

"What's that you've got?"

She looked at the parcel, her eyes curious. She wasn't sure what to do.

"And a banana cake." I held up the box. "We could eat a slice. Then I'll go."

She stood aside to let me come in, then shut the door and walked ahead, barefoot, through the sliding doors into the studio.

"I was washing my hair." She pushed a cassette into the

player—the Pretenders singing "Stop Your Sobbing"—and turned up the volume. She was pleased to see me, but she didn't want me there.

I gave her the parcel and we sat down cross-legged on the floor and I felt like a teenager again, sitting in a chairless room with music playing loudly and a pretty girl and from somewhere the smell of lilies.

"It was nice of you to remember." She pulled the string loose. Raising Lazo's red pot to the light, she gave a little gasp of pleasure. Turning it over in her hands, she let her fingers caress the rim.

"It's a portrait vase."

"You're giving me this?"

"Didn't you need a jug for *Antigone*?"

"Could I put in flowers?"

"It's very old. And porous, probably. The water might leak."

With a fluent motion she lifted her hands and waved the pot from side to side above her head. When she moved her arm, I could see soapsuds in her ear. She flung the jug into the air.

"Careful!"

She caught it, swung it gracefully to her breast.

"See, now it's a baby." She was overcome. "It's beautiful. Thank you." On all fours she crawled over to where I sat and kissed me on the cheek. A soapy smell mingled with the sharp scent of her skin.

"Now I have something for you." She scrambled to her feet and skipped from the room.

I was taking off my jacket when she ran back holding a long wooden flute.

"I bought it at Ausangate. It's a *pinkullo*. Play something." She turned off the music and lay down on her side, her legs tucked in, watching me.

I pressed the mouthpiece to my lips. Pushing out my chin to raise the pitch, I played the opening notes of a rain melody. Followed by Yolanda's eyes, my fingers opened and closed the six holes as I blew, producing a muffled, flattened sound. It wasn't a *pinkullo*, it was something else, and I had no idea how to play it.

"It's for you," she said, face shining.

"No, Yolanda. This is too special. Please. You keep it."

She rubbed a hand up and down one leg as if she were cold. The soles of her feet were black from the patio.

"But didn't you want a flute? Weren't you looking for one?"

I didn't want to distract her by bringing Laura into the conversation. "I suppose so." It sounded graceless.

She sat up, put her hands on her thighs and rose lithely to her feet. "I'm not accepting this jug until you accept my flute." But before I could reply, she added, "Now let's try your cake."

I followed her into the kitchen. A hotplate beside the sink was stacked with half a dozen unwashed mugs and an ashtray piled with cigarette ends. A green oilcloth covered the table on which was a fountain of lilies in a cream-cracker tin. There were two chairs and a fridge. A door in the far wall led—presumably—into her bedroom. The ceiling beams were decorated with photographs of dancers.

Impatiently, Yolanda pulled open the cake box. She cut two slices onto a plate.

"Here, have some," and she fed me one piece, putting it into my mouth, making a mess. She ate hers quickly, with a child's appetite.

"It's good."

"Isn't it." But I thought of the cake in the window.

Before I'd finished eating, she jumped up, mouth full, and ran to the kitchen cupboard, bringing out a bottle of red wine. I opened it and filled two glasses.

"To your birthday."

Suddenly she hesitated. "We shouldn't be doing this, Agustín. Our birthdays are not important." Her voice was chastened, different.

"Nonsense. How old did you say you were?"

Soon the bottle was empty, the last of the wine in our glasses. An impish smile spread over her face. "Shall I tell you something? Shall I tell you a big secret?"

She crossed her legs. I looked at the scar on her ankle, like an anchovy. My heart stopped and I thought, She's going to tell me she's fallen in love.

"Oh God, another plaster!" She peeled something from her heel and rubbed it between her fingers until it was tight enough a ball to be dropped into the ashtray.

"What's the secret?"

"No, no." She had changed her mind. "I won't. I can't."

"You're probably right." I put down my glass. My hand had begun to shake. "How is the ballet going?"

"I'll show you."

She got ready in the bathroom. To busy myself, I removed the plates to the sink. My eyes strayed to the door at the end of the kitchen. On it were pinned a list of pupils' names, with ticks against each one; a poster of the National Ballet of Cuba; and photographs of ballerinas: Patricia Cano, Carolina Vigil, Vivien Vallejo at the Colón in 1951. I was looking for Laura's name on the list when a hand covered my mouth and Yolanda said, "Come."

We took our glasses into the studio. She wore a loose Andean dress, sand-colored with braided edges, reaching nearly to her feet. She sat me down on the leather trunk and picked up the rosin box, tapping out a small heap of powder until its musty odor vied with the scent of lilies. From a hook on the wall, she lifted a pair of platform clogs and a white mask. She set them beside the rosin and put another cassette on the machine. As the tape hissed, she took up her position, her elbow rubbing a hole in the steamed-up mirror.

She rose on tiptoe, checking herself. One hand gripped the barre, the other performing small involuntary gliding movements as though a live creature lay beneath her skin. A foot caressed the air. Her doom-eager face was beautiful, as implacably set as Lazo's jug. She was ready.

The notes of a pipe—similar in tone to the one she had given me—zigzagged through the room. Her body stiffened. She picked the jug up and tracked in hesitant steps to the opposite mirror. Back she flitted to the rosin heap, her feet squealing on the parquet. With a bump she put down the jug, tied the mask over her face and bent double, gathering her dress up between her legs, like a pair of trousers. The music quickened. A charango strummed and she became her helmeted brother, riding across the plain, fleeing the battle. She was breathless, but she had clearly been a marvelous dancer.

A brash clap of cymbals broke her advance. She halted. No longer her brother, she slipped onto the high clogs and kicked away the mask, which skimmed with a crack into the wall. Now she danced her uncle, Creon, stamping about the floor, one hand lanced toward the jug, forbidding Thebes to bury a disgraced brother.

There was a final crash of the cymbals. Upstairs, a chair shifted. Then, unaccompanied, a *pinkullo* began to play its pithy notes. I recognized the instrument, and the music snatched at me. Yolanda freed her dress and lay down on her stomach, her arms stretched forward in the air, begging. She was Antigone, entreating her uncle—but her fingers also reached out to me. I caught her eye. Did it mean anything, the way she looked at me? I held her gaze and felt a blast of desire.

Slowly, elegantly, she stood up, preparing herself for the movement she had practiced at the Teatro Americano. She pirouetted, once, twice, three times. And leapt. Then the lights went out. The music stopped, and a thump resonated in the darkness.

"Yolanda!"

She lay against the sliding doors. I tried to lift her, but she pushed herself up and away from me. "This time I was prepared."

She stumbled to the leather-covered chest. Inside, there were candles. She lit two, sticking them upright in their own melted wax. We sat, close together, on the floor. In the candlelight her skin had a lustrous shine. Sweat polished her shoulders and rolled in bright beads down her throat, between her breasts. Her nipples pressed dark and hard through the sandy-yellow dress. The last blackout had panicked her. This time she was aroused.

I had to remember the reason why I had come to the studio—to warn her. I put an arm on her damp shoulder. I forget what I said, but I spoke vaguely, in hints. It was not possible for me to confide to her the nature of my business in Calle Diderot, nor could I reveal that I would not be far away in the days to come. But I had to alert her to the danger.

I was telling her of the need for vigilance when she interrupted. "But I am careful," she said. "Everybody has to be careful these days. You too."

I took her hand, feeling the rough-bitten edges of her fingernails. How could I say what I had to say? That they wouldn't care if she was a dancer. That they wouldn't care about her girls. That, to them, we were expendable. All of us.

As if to tell me not to worry, she tapped my wrist, then lightly kissed my cheek. She wanted to get up. "We can look after ourselves."

"I know. But I was worried for—"

"Stop it. You're scaring me," she said, and the moment had passed. She stood straight. "Anyway, I haven't finished."

"You want to go on? In this light?"

Above me, her face had been sculpted by the candlelight into something older, stronger, fiercer. "I can see perfectly well."

"But what about music?"

She picked something up from the floor. "Here."

That night in Yolanda's studio I mustered the notes of a forgotten tune. I didn't really know how to play it, the flute she'd given me. It was hard to produce a good clear tone. But as my breath warmed the wood, the color of the sound changed. The flute vibrated to the same pitch as my body, as though it were another limb, another flow of blood. And Yolanda, dancing her forbidden steps, became the music of this flute made flesh.

She cradled the pot to her breast, then moved on scissor legs toward the rosin, scooping handfuls into the pot. Her body was something unimaginably alive. She wept with her limbs, yet at the same time they blazed. She truly was making something unseen visible, so that I never doubted her identity as the sister about to cover a mangled corpse with dust.

She pirouetted and jumped. In that leap her body was in complicity with the air. Her legs dismissed the ground, her shoulders expressed their wings, and the image of her flight was painted there.

"Play. Play." She spoke to my reflection. The steam had cleared from the mirrors and in them I could see her body from every angle. With trembling arms, she raised the jug above her head—and I am certain that, with this frozen gesture, as if offering a libation, she intended the ballet to end.

"Don't stop, Agustín." A whisper.

She was then to do something I will never forget. It was the last thing I expected, and I doubt whether the idea had entered her head until that moment. She stared up at the base of Lazo's jug, and I wondered if she had seen something there. With a tidy flick of her wrist, she overturned it. A torrent of white dust poured down her hair, over her dress, puffing out over the candles, where it burned, sparkling, in the flames.

Rejas fell silent.

"Go on," said Dyer.

"Half an hour later I left the studio, having promised not to see her until Sunday."

Dyer was not certain he had understood correctly. "You mean, you wouldn't meet again until after her performance?"

Rejas blushed. "That's right."

"Why?"

His fingers tugged at the chain around his neck. "She was an artist. She was consumed by discipline. She needed her privacy— her loneliness, even."

Dyer's eyes hadn't moved from his face. There was more to be said, but he saw that the other didn't want to say it. At that moment Emilio appeared with two dishes of pork and pineapple. Dyer supposed that Rejas would have no appetite, but he ate hungrily.

When Rejas resumed his story, Dyer hoped he would pick up the thread in the ballet school. But the meal had restored in him some sort of equilibrium. He wanted to talk about Ezequiel.

Ezequiel signed his name when he handed the video camera to Edith. I knew as soon as I discovered the street he had filmed that I would find him. You might have thought this would be easy: I just had to look for a house near or opposite a street sign. But on either side of each street, vertical posts stood every hundred yards beneath the jacaranda.

There are ninety-six houses in Calle Diderot. In Calle Perón, fifty-four. I took charge of the Diderot operation. I'll spare you the details. Watching a street, vital as it is, is tedious work. Compare it to the act of blowing up an air cushion: although nothing appears to be going on, no breath is wasted. It is only with the last few breaths that the cushion takes shape. Yet you have to keep blowing.

Some people get a headache just waiting for something to unfold. Hour upon profitless hour. Contemplation immobilizes them. They end up like my father, drugged by doing nothing. They become disciples of sitting down and facing a blank wall whenever they feel a storm of rage or passion. Because it is not enough to be patient. You have to know how to be impatient, when to act quickly. The trick is to recognize the moment.

The Calle Diderot team worked eight-hour shifts. It was a crude operation by Western standards. But anything more sophisticated at this stage might have aroused curiosity. Sucre was the sanitation man. Gómez, alternating with Clorindo, did wonders in the blue and yellow outfit of the municipal gardener. A couple transferred from Narcotics spent hours in the café and nestling in the front seat of their worn-out Volkswagen. The operation was kept secret even from the General, whom I had not told what we had found on the videocassette.

I used a different car for each shift. Sometimes I parked in a narrow cul-de-sac, sometimes on the corner of Calle Leme. People aren't that observant. They don't stare at particular cars in the street—and I wasn't driving a lavender Cadillac. I listened to the radio. I read the newspaper. I broke up the day by using the lavatory in a bar on Calle Pizarro where they sold sandwiches. I sat for eight-hour stretches, watching passersby.

At night, since it was too risky to rent a room from anyone in the street, I exchanged the car for a van. I used a blue engineer's van, no windows at the back and with a black stripe along both sides. From the outside it looked like a band of paint. In fact, it was darkened Perspex, and I could see through it.

I sat on a folding chair in the back. I had night glasses and a bottle to pee in. One of my men, usually Sucre, would park the van, get out, lock it and walk away. At the end of the shift he would come back, repeating the process in reverse.

I soon became familiar with the faces of the street, what preoccupied them, whom they liked or didn't like. No one seemed ill at ease or fearful. This was a prosperous neighborhood, far removed from the tension of the outskirts. A bird sang in the jacaranda. A dog lay asleep on a porch. The very tranquillity of the scene was reason enough to be on guard.

I compiled notes. On that first afternoon, for instance, at about two-fifteen an elderly man, tall with patched sleeves, entered No. 339. After forty-five minutes he drove quickly away in an orange Volkswagen Beetle.

An hour later the maid from No. 345 visited the Vargas Video Store. She came out holding two cassettes, talking to herself. The storekeeper charged extra if you didn't rewind the videos.

At four o'clock a female jogger, late forties, in a turquoise tracksuit, left No. 357. She returned after thirty-five minutes, walking.

Ten minutes later a young woman, tidily dressed, arrived at No. 365, the estate agency run from a garage. I could see the car behind her desk. She left at five-thirty carrying a handful of envelopes.

Which of these people was hiding Ezequiel? You see, I was certain he had settled here or in Calle Perón. He had remained as silent and derisive as a god right up until the moment I saw him on the videocassette. A few frames of film had made him fallible, human at last. The sound of him may have been no louder than the distant thrumming of an insect, but in those warm nights I felt his presence.

I am able to picture him in that room. He's lighting another cigarette. He is listening to the music we would find in the cassette player: Beethoven's Ninth. Perhaps it is the last movement playing as he leans in his customary position by the window, having watched the sixteen girls go into their class.

It strikes him as a warm evening, but he often misjudges the temperature, so that Edith, wearing a thick sweater, will come into the room and find him with nothing on but a vest.

I see Edith nudging open the door with a tray. She rests it on the trolley while he lingers at the window, watching two lovers go by. He hears a bird. He scratches his neck. For twelve years he has been cooped up in airless rooms like this one.

Edith confirms the meeting on Monday. At eight that morning the Central Committee will present details for his approval. Nothing can go wrong. In less than a week the final act of the Fifth Grand Plan will be played out.

He listens, eating. He planned it himself, twenty years ago. The strategy has remained unblemished in his head. He nods and forks toward his tongue another mouthful of ceviche.

The night crackles. Edith parts the curtain a fraction. Yellow fireworks confirm the operation tomorrow, against Cleopatra's Hotel. She comes back into the room and sits on the edge of the bed, plucking hairs from her black trousers.

At seven o'clock she turns on the television, keeping the volume low. The police announce an important breakthrough in the hunt for Ezequiel. A police general, interviewed outside a blue house, holds up a wig and says, "Have no doubt. We are closing in."

Ezequiel watches for a minute, then picks up his book. There are marks on the page where wax from a candle splashed during the last blackout. It upsets him because it is a good edition.

Edith says, "Is there anything else you want? Cigarettes? Water?"

"I need more Kenacort." He doesn't need to speak loudly to be heard. His voice is a solid thing, the words creating in the room another presence. This second figure stands at his shoulder, like a maquette of damp gray clay, arms crossed, featureless—but watchful.

"Is it bad?"

He nods. The rash has started to creep inside the membrane of his penis. When he pissed this morning, he wanted to scream.

He brushes her hand from his knee. Reluctant to pull herself away, she watches him drink his water. She decides to make the bed. The Dithranol has marked the sheets with purple-brown stains. She strips them off and is about to leave the room, pregnant with dirty bedclothes, when she hesitates, returns to his side.

His mouth is full of water, his tongue and lips dry from the Acitretin tablets. He swallows. "What is it?"

"It might be nothing."

He listens as she explains what is troubling her.

"Should I have him followed?"

"No. I've seen him. It's nothing. He's infatuated, that's all. Another Gabriel."

"Are you sure?"

Although the words are quietly spoken, his black eyes are charged. "You can't check everybody." He drains his glass and pushes away the tray.

"You're finished?"

"Yes."

"Do you want to watch some more?"

"No."

She switches off the television and leaves the room. She will not come back tonight.

From below he hears the squeak of shoes, a sound as of something sharply wrenched. He looks down to the rug. Downstairs they are beginning their exercises. For the next hour and a half the floor will become a sounding board for the thud, thud, thud of feet and the "one two three, one two three, one two three" of the teacher calling out the rhythm, and for the music, interrupted again and again, of his favorite composers.

These interruptions are a torture to him. At the same time, he demands in his followers the same obedience as the ballet teacher seeks from her pupils. He makes tolerable these evenings by recasting the girls beneath him into the image of his invisible army.

Tonight it is a classical class. The girls begin at the edge of the room and, in a quickening tempo, proceed to the middle. At the end of the lesson they will have exercised every part of their bodies—except the vocal cords. On the dance floor, only the teacher speaks. They listen to her, not talking, because she can make them perfect.

"Okay, we'll start with the same plié as yesterday. Let's remember what we discussed, about keeping the strength in the middle and freeing the arms."

He slips a finger under the page as he reaches the bottom. He is rereading Kant. He turns the page.

"Listen to what I'm going to play, and push from the front foot. Good, Christina. Practice that."

They're dancing "The Song of the Moon" from *Rusalka*. Hands wave in the mirror. Bodies sway like branches in a wind. The hands and bodies flow to the Dvořák composition he most loves. He stretches a leg.

"Down and up, down and up. Hips back. Listen to the music. You're not listening to the music, Gabriela." It stops in midbeat. "I'm sorry, girls."

Shoes brush across the parquet. The teacher, he imagines, will be adjusting a head, plucking up one shoulder, placing a finger in the small of the girl's back.

"Now, your arms are condor feathers."

The music strikes up, accompanied by a handclap in time to the beat.

From the trolley he picks up a fountain pen. He unscrews the cap and with an effort writes in the margin: "Can we then infer from the natural world that man ought to be free? Is that bird I hear free?"

He reads another paragraph, but the words are evasive. They, like the music, fail to move him. He coughs, catching a movement on the blank screen before him. From the television his reflection is beamed back at him. Sitting behind the trolley, he is made shockingly aware of the contrast between this body and the hands which tremble at full stretch below him, taking aim at the ceiling.

"The eyes must go up," says the voice downstairs. "Open them, open them, look at the ceiling."

Ezequiel turns a few pages and lays the book, pages down, on the arm of his chair. He pushes himself up and walks to the door. He unclenches his hand, lets it hover over the stainless-steel handle. But he does not make contact. In the end the hand drops back to his side.

"You must be careful of that foot, especially Adriana."

Grimacing, he unwraps his scarf, throws it onto the bed. The meal has made him sweat. He feels the jowls dragging on his face and the weight of his belly. What can he expect if he eats and doesn't exercise? Sliding a hand under his vest, he begins to scratch.

The move to the city has not arrested the spread of the disease. His hairless chest is patched with white fleck marks where the skin is peeling. These sores, the shape and size of tears, also speckle his arms and the insides of his legs, while a thick red rash torments the back of his neck. An unkempt graying beard conceals the eruptions on his plump face. His scalp shows pinkly through a thin scrub of curls. If he scratches it, the fingers come away stuck with the hairs.

To handle a book, even, is an agony. There are brown pustules on the palms of his hands, on the soles of his feet, on the skin of his armpits and inside his ears and belly button. Since he left the jungle six months ago, his nails have grown crumbly. On his right hand, three have lifted from the nailbed. He bathes them every morning in a bowl of warm oil, but the delicate flesh around and under them is weepy. Against the pain, a doctor has advised, "Find an image you like. Imagine yourself on a beach, or your skin being soothed by the sun."

The only thing that can help is to be in the sun.

He tries light therapy. In the evenings he sits under the sun-lamp and reads, but it is never wise to read for long. He has articles brought to him on the current state of research into his condition. He experiments with the latest medicines. He prays for a miraculous breakthrough, but his head tells him there is no cure. A doctor has told him, "It's your Spanish blood coming through." But he still hopes.

Downstairs the tempo quickens. The girls have changed into pointe shoes and are leaping through the air. He hears the yelp of the shoes, the thump of feet as the dancers land, the occasional, less exact, sound of someone falling over, the teacher's handclaps passing like gunshots through the floor.

"Laura, do you want to have a go?"

Ezequiel closes his eyes.

He is awakened by the young dancers applauding their teacher.

A mosquito feeds on the back of his hand. He watches the blood fill its belly. He lifts his hand and the insect is gone.

A minute later he limps into the bathroom and claws a flattened tube from the basin. He squeezes a length of greenish jelly onto his fingers and rubs it into his neck and behind his ears and on his chin until the beard glistens. Lifting his vest, he smears the foul-smelling stuff over his stomach. Then he unbuckles his trousers and does the same on the inside of each leg. Having shielded the exposed skin, he spreads the Dithranol—very carefully, since it burns. Finally, he swallows the last two pills from a brown box. He has been taking these pills since June. They make him liverish, but on parts of his body he has noticed the rash has stopped spreading. He drops the empty carton into a bucket under the sink.

Beneath his feet, below him, he hears the girls turning on the showers. The sounds are distinct. He hears their giggles, the water hosing their bodies, their complaints about the lesson.

"I told her from the start my neck's out from last night."

"Doesn't she understand we're exhausted?"

"My physio told me I shouldn't be pushing it, and there she was—pushing it."

"Shit, my feet are bleeding again."

Sometimes the girls talk about sex while they soap themselves, or as they whip their long hair from side to side under the hot-air vent. But tonight in the shower they talk about Laura.

This dance they're talking about, she had performed it while he slept.

"You used to dance like a lollipop," says a grudging voice. "What happened to you?"

They ask questions, trying to sound nonchalant.

"Was it as amazing as it looked?"

"Go on, Laura. What was it like?"

The girl called Laura speaks. She sounds embarrassed. She dreamed she was standing in the air.

Twelve hours after I last saw Yolanda, in the early hours of Friday morning, a car bomb exploded on a traffic circle in the main street of Miraflores, killing twenty-seven people and gouging a truck-sized hole in the road outside the Café Haiti. The debris maimed scores of others, among them the cheerful waitress from Judío, whose nose was sliced off. There was no doubting the intended target: Cleopatra's Hotel, where the Foreign Minister was to have entertained ambassadors from countries of the European Community at breakfast. But an accident spared the hotel. At the traffic circle the getaway car crashed into one loaded with a mixture of fertilizer, diesel oil and dynamite. Their bumpers became entangled. When the café's security guard walked over to help, the drivers ran off across the park. The collision must have damaged the detonating mechanism, because ten seconds later the front car blew up, the force of the seventeen-hundred-pound bomb catapulting it into the Café Haiti, which caught fire.

I heard the thunderclap from ten miles away, having just arrived in Calle Diderot. It was seven in the morning and the street was rubbing its eyes. Opposite, a schoolgirl leaned against a wall talking to a friend, their legs the color of cooking oil in the sun. The bottle boy cried out and they glanced up, which encouraged him to bicycle past waving both hands in the air. Red-faced, talking both at once, they turned back to each other, ignoring him.

"Bottles! Bottles!"

The earth jolted between his cries, but the girls did not look up.

There were few details to be had over the radio link with headquarters. I tried to contact Sylvina on the mobile phone. As I left, she had murmured about some shopping she needed to do. I rang home, but the line was engaged. I waited five minutes and tried again. Still busy. An hour later she answered.

"Yes?"

"It's Agustín." I was so relieved to hear her voice.

"What's wrong? Are you all right?"

"What about you? What about the bomb?"

"Bomb? I thought it was the gas mains."

"You're not hurt, then?"

"No. I was washing my hair. I was going to complain. The oven's not working."

"You know I love you."

There was a pause. "Agustín, you can't just ring up and say

you love me as if that will make up for not saying it when we're together. It won't."

"Darling, I was worried."

"I was expecting another call."

My news had disturbed Sylvina. She wanted to know from me how I thought the bomb would affect her presentation on Sunday night. She'd had acceptances from ten prospective clients, including Leonora—which was a coup (although Leonora's dachshund had become pregnant by Patricia's Irish setter, and Leonora was worried the puppies, expected to be premature, might have to be born by cesarean). Sylvina didn't know how she was going to seat everyone. She needed extra chairs, but she refused point-blank to ask the people upstairs before I had even suggested it.

"Do you think the bomb will affect international flights?"

"Why should it?"

"That's another thing. I have to go to the airport."

"What on earth for?"

"I'm expecting more samples this afternoon."

"Can't they wait?"

"No. Patricia placed her order on the strictest condition she had the lipstick in time for the American Chargé's party tomorrow. I've been invited too, which is very sweet, since I've met Señora Tennyson only once. It's her fortieth birthday, which means a present, I suppose . . . Perhaps a nourishing night cream . . ."

Dr. Zampini drove by, raking a hand through his long gray hair. The bus drew up and the two girls climbed aboard.

Sylvina said, after another pause, "Agustín, would you do me a favor? I've spoken to Marina. She's free to collect the girls later tonight, but she doesn't think she can take them to their lesson. Would you do that? I don't often ask and it would help matters."

"Shouldn't we pull Laura out of the ballet—for the moment?"

"When everything's going so well for her? Agustín, I simply don't read you sometimes."

Gómez relieved me at three o'clock. I drove back to headquarters.

In the corridor a long-faced Sergeant Ciras gave me an update.

When the car crashed through the Haiti's window, twenty people were in the café. The dead included a director of the Banco Wiese and a junior Foreign Office minister, blown up with his undelivered speech in his briefcase. And there were yet more injuries when tenants of the high-rise blocks recklessly tapped out the shards from their smashed windows onto the pavements below.

I walked upstairs, thinking of an obliterated corner table.

When the General heard I was in the building, he sent for me. "What's going on?" he said woozily, as if he had fainted. He grabbed my arm and shut the door. "Calderón has been shitting on my shadow all morning." He sat down heavily. The fruit bowl was all but empty. The crisis had stripped away his eccentricities, of which the final remnant was one shriveled orange. The General started to peel it.

"Latest orders: whoever captures Ezequiel, we turn him over to Calderón and keep it secret." He put the first segment of orange into his mouth.

"What does that mean for Ezequiel, sir?"

"It means they'll shoot him."

He pulled a face and spat out a pip. "The army's become the government—the government's so desperate they're trying to buy their way out. The reward for Ezequiel's capture is now ten million dollars. I've heard they are debating bringing in the Americans."

He leaned forward, rubbing his cheeks. "I tell you, tomcat, this is a cluster-fuck."

His face had a bedraggled, unimportant look. "Tell me, anything in Perón and Diderot?"

"So far nothing."

"Gut feeling?"

"Gut feeling is we're close, but we mustn't hurry—"

"Yes, yes, I know about your inflatable bed theory." He played with the orange peel, plucking out strands of pith, which he dropped into the bowl. In a voice so quiet that he might have been speaking to himself, but didn't mind if I overheard, he said, "Fact is, tomcat, in one sense Brother Ezequiel's won already. The Americans, who believe everything they read in *Der Spiegel*, reckon he's taken control of the country."

He lifted his head. "It was a pity he had to bring in all this Mao and Kant, you know. It was perfectly understandable without that claptrap."

I sought out Sucre in the basement. He stood behind a table, face mask pushed up over his hair, tagging a card to a trash bag. He had opened the door to allow in air from the courtyard, but the place stank. Bunches of flies rose from the concrete floor as I approached.

"What's exciting today?"

Behind Sucre, dressed in coveralls and wearing blue rubber gloves, other men raked through a little hill of filth.

"Nothing to give you gooseflesh."

He studied a chart, wrinkling his nose. "Best of the day? Calle Perón. Item One: three copies of *Marxism Today* from No. 29. Item Two: traces of cocaine in envelope addressed to cultural attaché in No. 34. Item Three: serrated bone-handled knife from No. 63, probably thrown away by accident, since the bag also contained duck à l'orange."

"Any medicines?"

"Aspirin, Nivea, French talcum powder, mouthwash, yards of dental floss, used Trojans. What you'd expect from diplomats."

"Calle Diderot?"

"We're collecting tonight. You told us not to be too clockwork. Make the customers uneasy."

"Clorindo report anything?"

"He frightened off a man climbing into 456. Probably just a thief. Otherwise he's whitewashed most of the trees."

"Gómez?"

"Problem with the maid at No. 345, who said her employer liked to plant the geraniums himself. Yesterday he put in all the annuals I gave him." He set down the paper and tried to wipe off a grease stain he'd made with his thumb. "Soon everyone will want to move in."

At six o'clock I drove one of our surveillance vehicles to Laura's ballet school. About the dangers posed to my daughter, I suffered a father's anguish. Should I tell Sylvina, who, in a sort of ecstasy, spent each day ordering lipsticks? Should Laura from now on ride to and from her class with Marina? I didn't want her associated with me. Ought I to remove her from the school? Would you have wanted *your* child to go to dance lessons in that street?

"Laura!"

She didn't recognize the car. I repeated her name, but she turned away.

I opened my door and shouted. "Laura! Samantha!" They turned, walked over.

"Where's Mummy?" said Laura, climbing into the backseat.

"She's gone to the airport."

"Is she leaving?"

"She's collecting something. It's for her presentation on Sunday. Marina will take you both home later."

In the mirror her face was serious. "Daddy, do you think we'll ever be rich?"

"No."

"Yes, we will be. Mummy says we're going to be rich and she's going to buy a house in Paracas and drive us there every weekend in a big purple car."

"Let's not argue in front of Samantha."

At this Marina's daughter, small-eyed, ruddy-faced, looked superior. The month before, she had stabbed Laura with a pencil.

Laura looked out of the window. "This isn't the way."

I was driving along the coast road. The streets around the Haiti would be blocked off. "There's been a bomb."

"Samantha knows one of the people who was hurt."

I looked up. "Is that so?" In the back Samantha tried to feign sadness but looked proud.

"It's not my friend, Laura, it's Mummy's."

"You said it was your friend."

"I did not."

"How's your flute?" I asked Laura.

The night before, I had come home from the ballet studio. After taking a shower, I found her in the kitchen. She threw her arms about me.

"Daddy, thank you! I was so horrid. I thought you'd forgotten. Mummy said you must have been keeping it as a surprise."

"What are you talking about?"

"I shouldn't have opened your briefcase, but I was looking for your newspaper . . ." She slipped her head from beneath my hand. Her fingers, their span not yet great enough to cover the holes, clutched Yolanda's gift to me.

Behind me in the car, Laura's voice: "The flute's all right."

"Is that all?"

"That's what you say whenever we ask you something. I can't wait to show it to Yolanda."

"I don't want you to take it to the studio," I said hastily. "It's too precious."

"But Daddy—"

"What have you both been dancing this week? Samantha?"

"Yesterday we danced *The Nutcracker*. The day before we tried a dance from the sierra."

"What dance?"

Laura, reminded of her aborted trip, said, "You won't have heard of it."

"Try me."

"I know what it's called," said Samantha, perking up.

"Don't tell him."

" 'Taqui Onqoy'," pronounced Samantha, accurately.

"The dance of illness?" It was a messianic dance.

"Samantha has an audition at the Metropolitan," said Laura.

Samantha, looking out of the window, said in a lethargic, grown-up voice, "But I don't really know if I want to go there. Daddy says I might be better off in Florida."

"What about Yolanda," I said, "are you pleased with her, both of you?"

Laura came forward, hugging the headrest on my seat, her breath on my neck.

"We think she's got a boyfriend," she said slyly.

Both girls giggled. I flushed. Were they talking about me?

I adopted Samantha's bored tone. "Who is he, do you know?"

"Christina saw a birthday cake in the fridge," said Laura. She had removed her hairclip and now shook loose her hair. "And the two wine glasses, Samantha—remember?"

"Someone's given her an old pot," Samantha added. "She was furious when I put out my cigarette in it."

"Samantha! Sssh!"

I was too interested in Yolanda to take up the matter of a forbidden cigarette.

"Must it be a boyfriend?"

"Oh yes," said Laura. "She's changed, don't you think, Samantha? She's started worrying what she looks like. She never did before."

I felt an unpleasant tingle at the back of my neck. Perhaps Yolanda did have a boyfriend.

"Daddy," whispered Laura, "you shouldn't scratch like that. Your neck's covered in spots."

"You've missed the studio," noted Samantha.

"I'll drop you both here."

I parked on the corner and they climbed out. I tilted my side mirror, watching them walk back a block until they stood outside the door in the green wall. Samantha pressed the bell. Laura fiddled with the zipper on her Adidas bag. Aware that I was watching, she refused to look back. She tugged up one leg, then the other, exercising. She was the only reason my marriage survived.

The door opened. I saw Laura's face light up.

I drove past Gómez, who followed me at a distance to a car park behind the Banco Wiese in Calle Salta. I then climbed into Gómez's van and he drove me to Calle Diderot, parking in the narrow cul-de-sac opposite the studio. After he got out, locked up and walked away, I took up position in the back. Through the Perspex I could see the studio's strip lights. Laura had left her hairclip in the car and I held onto it, thinking of her inside with Yolanda.

You have to realize, watching—it's also about desire. I was deeply shaken when I sat down in that van. *We think she's got a boyfriend.* Laura's words were a punch to my heart. She was Yolanda's pupil and I was her father and Yolanda had *Antigone* to think about. It was none of my business—but suppose there *was* someone else in Yolanda's life? She'd mentioned a fiancé, had said,

Oh, I've catted around. Then there was the matter of her visit to the sierra. Had she made the journey to the ice festival alone? Or had she been with a lover when she was researching the dance groups? People tend not to mention former companions when talking to a third person they are fond of—and I didn't doubt Yolanda liked me. But how much? And was her brother really her brother? Or was I being jealous of myself?

How many times did I tell myself none of this should concern me? But after what both Laura and Samantha had said, my hopes and suspicions ran wild. One minute I was elated. The next, I felt the cold feet of jealousy climbing into bed beside me. With everything else that was going on, it was hard to reconcile myself to the fact I was in love.

There's no point trying to understand why people fall in love. My contact with Yolanda had been so snatched, yet the impact had been intense. I was forty-three years old, but I had lived only for a few days. Once you wake up like that, you don't drop back into sleep. Not easily. Since Monday, when I had bumped into Yolanda in the Bullrich Arcade, I had hardly slept. My heart had become a vast and uncomfortable thing. It reared out of my chest, throwing back my head so I could breathe only with difficulty. As I pressed my forehead to the dark Perspex strip, I could no longer hide from myself the reason for these feelings, this behavior.

In the few hours that remained until I saw her again, this is what I argued: I was in the saddle of a passion which could lead nowhere. I sifted Yolanda's character for faults, fumbled with them to that narrow bar of light. She was immature, unpredictable. She had chubby cheeks, an unquenchable appetite for cakes, ugly feet. I pictured her in revolting positions. I summoned her feet and stamped their deformed features on her face, over her eyes. There! Could I find her attractive now? I did. I did! I was in pain. I was miserable. I was ashamed. I was thrilled. The smallest detail rang with her name, from the outline of the jacaranda to the pattern of specks on the Perspex.

———

You remember I told you how she flipped the jug in the air? Well, what happened . . . happened shortly afterward. She remained in that position, eyes closed, arms raised, holding her breath. I can only say that, to me, the air about her was charged with the naked thrill of what she had done. She looked as if some extraordinary truth had dawned on her. I mean, think of it. She had with that simple gesture buried her brother, the state, herself.

Then she lowered her arms and this expression vanished and her breath returned in chokes. Her throat and shoulders were sweating. Tiny crystals of rosin sparkled in her eyes, on her breasts. The dress had opened at the front. Her dark ruby nipples showed through the thin cloth, catching at the material. She was devastated, but also intoxicated.

We fell against each other. I felt her hair rubbing my cheek and her breath, flavored with wine and banana cake, scorching my neck. Her closeness was unbearable. I longed to move my hands down her sweating back, to take off her dress. Her breasts pressed hard against my chest and I smelled her coppery skin. In that moment I wanted her more than anything I had ever seen or known or done.

I touched her and became something else. All the vital experiences of my life had predicted this moment. Touching her, I repossessed them and relived them, felt their reverberations. I was a candle burning in the snow. I was my father carrying my mother in his arms. I was grief and joy.

Slowly, she tilted back her head. She held my face between her hands and she kissed me.

Then she pushed away. "Oh, my darling, what are we going to do?" She blinked, putting out a hand to the barre. Rosin had fallen into her eyes. She rubbed them with the back of her hand.

"It's not allowed, you know that. What are we going to do? I—"

She couldn't escape my face in the mirror. Nor the effect on me of her words. "And believe me, I want to, I want to . . ."

Now she folded her arms, bowed in pain. "Agustín, you must go. It's impossible. It's nearly the curfew."

My voice came out thick, desperate. Our kiss, which had made her all of a sudden vulnerable and tense—like someone without a skin, really—had brushed me with fire.

"Tomorrow, can I see you tomorrow?"

She unfolded her arms, clasped and unclasped her hands. "It disturbs me very much to have you here."

"Disturbs you?"

"This is a really important decision. For us both. It is not one I can make now. Not now. The dance is an impediment, Agustín. I've been working too hard. I'm not clearheaded."

She glanced crookedly up at me in the mirror. It was easier to fend me off there. In a ravaged voice, she said, "It's not something to be entered into lightly. After the dance—after that, let's talk about it. Let's be sure."

The ballet class ended at eight-thirty. Through the Perspex I watched the girls being collected. Marina drove off in her red BMW, Laura and Samantha squabbling in the back. I trained my binoculars on the door, but I did not see Yolanda.

A mosquito wailed in the air near my face, then fell silent. I slapped my cheek.

Some time later, there was the noise of a key in the lock. The door opened and Sucre climbed in. The chassis rocked as he clambered to the back. I unfolded a chair for him. He had inspected the garbage bags from Calle Perón. Nothing of substance. He took a paper bag from his jacket pocket. "Sandwich, sir?"

He reeked of the basement. I had to ask him what the sandwich filling was.

The streetlight threw a band of orange across our faces. Sucre touched his cheek to indicate the spot. "You've been bitten, sir."

I wiped my face and looked at my finger. There was blood on the tip.

"I've a can of spray in my truck."

"It doesn't matter. I'm leaving soon. Tell Gómez to be here at ten."

Sucre would start collecting the trash once the curfew started. Piled outside each house, the black sacks had materialized throughout the day. As ten o'clock approached, they stopped appearing. The curfew wasn't for another twenty minutes, but its shroud prepared to wrap the city. Everything fell still and you heard sounds you never normally heard. The fragile hum of a drunk. The receding gargle of a motorbike.

The clink of a garbage bag against a doorframe.

I heard the noise, glanced across the street. What I saw made me sit bolt upright in my chair. All day I had longed for this sight. It jarred me to see her.

Yolanda, in black leotard, black tights and bright red head-band, squeezed sideways through the door in the wall and onto the sidewalk. She held one trash bag against her chest and dragged another behind her. She swung them onto the heap at the base of the lamppost and wiped her hands. I expected her to return inside, but she paused under the light.

I focused the binoculars. That I was snooping shamed me. What would she think if she knew that, fifty yards away, I sat spying on her?

With her feet turned out, she walked two or three paces toward me. Her shadow lengthened out and revolved against the wall. Rising on her toes, she gazed down the street.

My head swirled: She's expecting somebody.

"That's got a nice little walk on it," observed Sucre. "Your girl's teacher, isn't it?"

"Yes."

"Single, is she, sir?"

"That's right."

"You know, a single girl like that—it's kind of tragic."

Balanced on the tips of her ballet slippers, again she looked down the street.

"Although," said Sucre, "that's a lot of garbage for a girl on her own."

She turned and loped, head down, toward the studio. I adjusted the focus, following her inside. I expected her to shut the door and draw the chain. Instead, she stood on one leg, eased off a slipper and wedged it between the door and frame.

Sucre scratched at the plaque on his teeth, sucking. "Hello. She's waiting for someone."

We think she's got a boyfriend.

Before leaving the van, I put my pistol in the glove compartment. "Time to start collecting the trash."

She saw me the instant I entered. All those mirrors—you're aware of who's walked into the studio without having to look behind you.

"It's you." She stood with her back to me, not turning, one arm up, one leg raised in an arabesque.

"You're still rehearsing?" I looked at Lazo's jug and the tapes, which she hadn't moved—which she had played for me. I looked at the two glasses on the floor where we had left them, the wine evaporated to a powdery red blush.

"I didn't expect you."

I put into my voice all the passion I felt. "I wanted to see you."

She lowered her leg to the floor.

"I love you."

In an empty dance studio—or anywhere else, I suppose—a whispered love is a deafening thing. I had not known I was going to say the words. But in the van, when I visualized our scenes together, I had been drawn back to everything that was truest about myself.

She bowed her head as if someone were saying grace. "Please don't."

"But this last week—"

She whirled toward me. "And I meant everything I said."

Then she crumpled to the floor.

It's funny, the memories you keep of people. The moments which fix them in your mind aren't always the most obvious. My last image of Father Ramón is the vision of him in dirty tennis shoes spreading a silver chain above my head. I remember my mother shooing parrots and my father in too large a suit at my wedding and my wife leaning against the kitchen window, tapping at the glass. She was tapping like that to make a bird on the lawn fly away, to save it. But, startled by the noise of her fingers, the cat pounced. "And Agustín wanted to put you down," she said afterward, stroking it.

This is almost the last memory I retain of Yolanda. It's a sight that stops my heart. She is seated cross-legged on the parquet. Her long hands are thrust over her face, her hair falls through her fingers, and the red headband is about to slip off. Lazo's jug is beside her and she sobs into her lap.

Curiously, I don't hear the sound of a woman weeping, but of a river breaking over the rocks and the wind dragging its feet through the grass and the slap of a tattered wind sock. I have this sensation I have led Yolanda along the bank and up a steep narrow path to the airstrip. I see the ice sheeting the mountains and the ancient field beaten from the valley floor and the moist square of earth where the grass has not grown back.

I said something and left.

You don't wake up, look at a blue sky and think to yourself, What a perfect day to capture Ezequiel.

It was another morning which began uneventfully. By ten o'clock the sky was overcast. The branches shifted a little, and from the window of the car—a Ford Falcon, I think—I watched a duck fly east. The air smelled of fish.

Everyone in the street agreed. Today, or tomorrow, it would rain.

At ten-thirty my mobile bleeped. It was the General. Last night a woman had been arrested near the city's main water plant. She had been carrying a bottle of urine

"The lab says it's contaminated with the typhus bacillus."

He was calling because he had no one else to tell. He saw no end to the giddying violence. He didn't ask if I had anything to report.

At eleven I called Sucre. He'd managed three hours' sleep and sounded exhausted. I waited for him to find his notes. Somewhere he had a list of those who'd broken the curfew in Calle Diderot.

Dr. Zampini, presumably on a hospital call. "But we're checking."

The owner of the video store. He'd come back at midnight, drunk.

Two women and a man going into No. 459.

I was slow to register. "But that's the ballet studio . . ."

"They turned up about fifteen minutes after you left with Gómez."

"In a car?"

"On foot."

"Description?"

"The man had a beard."

Lorenzo. The depressed choreographer. Of course! Why hadn't I thought of him before? *I'd love to see a dress rehearsal. The others would too.* He'd be bringing the members of Yolanda's dance group, the ones who had first wanted to be in *Antigone*. They would have taken a bus from the center. Perhaps the bus had been late, or they'd missed an earlier one. That's why Yolanda had wedged open the door with her ballet slipper. She didn't want them stranded outside in the curfew.

My jealousy eased. I felt happy.

"When did they leave?"

"They were there when I took away the trash. That was about midnight."

"What about the trash?"

"Seventy-six bags we've done."

"That leaves how many?"

"About the same number."

"When do you reckon to finish?"

"Five, six o'clock."

At three o'clock, after Gómez relieved me, I drove to headquarters. I intended to return later to Calle Diderot, spending the night in the van. For the rest of the day I would busy myself with my report on the military's atrocities in La Posta. I wanted to block out Yolanda.

> According to the deposition of María Valdes, 67, the officers who dragged her into the field were addressed by the nicknames Pulpo and Capitán . . .

But I didn't see an old woman in a dentist's office, raising her hand to speak. I saw an anchovy scar, an ocher dress snagged on a breast, a flash of calf through a torn leotard, a row of white teeth pressed into a bottom lip.

At five I telephoned Sylvina. She was excited. Fifteen people had subscribed for Sunday's presentation! Because of tonight's party given by the American Chargé d'Affaires, she wouldn't be back till late. Patricia promised that several ambassadors would be there and, with luck, some generals and their wives. I sensed her hands winnowing the air at the prospect of new clients. "I tell you, Agustín, we're going to be rich."

So, anticipating this, she planned to rearrange the apartment and change the color of her hair.

"And I've bought you a polo shirt." She described it, navy blue, sleeveless, from a store in the Bullrich Arcade. "Marina said it's time I spoiled you."

I drank a Coke. Midway through my report I broke off to write to Lazo, to say that I had repaid his daughter and discharged my promise. Then I asked him for copies of his dental records—in case, as was my hope, we found Tomasio's body.

At six fifty-five the telephone on my desk rang. It was Sucre, his voice hoarse. "Sir, I think you should come."

Sucre had isolated three tubes on the table. Also, two pillboxes and ten crushed cigarette packets. The stench in the basement dispersed the moment I saw them.

The tubes had been rolled up to the mouth. I flattened one out. Dithranol. The brown pillboxes had contained methotrexate and cyclosporin A. The cigarettes were Winston.

"Which house?" Even before Sucre answered, a numbness invaded me.

He smoothed out the neck of the trash bag, inspecting the label he had taped there.

It was seven-ten. I didn't have time to stop and think. My first impulse was to warn Yolanda, but the class had begun on time. Gómez, sitting in a green Renault, confirmed fourteen girls inside, plus Laura. If I warned their teacher, it would create panic among her pupils and alert Ezequiel in the flat above.

I told Sucre, "Find out how long the place has been rented, who the landlord is, whether there's a ground plan. Get everyone from Calle Perón to the Banco Wiese car park in Calle Salta."

I telephoned Marina. Today was Tuesday. Her turn to collect the girls. No one answered. I tried Sylvina. She had said she was going to the hairdresser. No answer.

Twenty minutes later I addressed the unit over the radio. There was no time to speak to each officer individually, so I told them to listen carefully. I had, I said, been inside No. 459.

The house was divided into two. Downstairs was the ballet school. Our suspect might be in the first-floor apartment. There was no access from the studio and the ballet mistress didn't know who lived upstairs. Probably our suspect relied on a staircase at the side or back of the building, but I hadn't seen it.

Once they were over the wall, they were not to open fire unless they were fired on first. Anyone found inside must be captured alive.

"There's a dance class in there. I want to wait until the class is out."

Before leaving, I again telephoned Marina and Sylvina, but there was still no answer.

At seven forty-five I drove to Calle Diderot. Apart from my team I had told no one.

Not a day goes by when I don't return to that scene.

Dusk is falling. I park in the cul-de-sac. There's a bright light shining in the upstairs apartment and I train my glasses on the yellow curtain. Behind the cartoon elephants a shadow blurs back and forth as if addressing an audience. The shape disappears and the only movement is the curtain being sucked in and out by the draft.

Gómez, in his gardener's overalls, halts his wheelbarrow beside the car. The directional mike is hidden in the rake. For thirty minutes he has pointed its laser at the first-floor window, picking up vibrations from the glass.

"Meeting broke up a few minutes ago. He's now watching television."

"Who else is up there?"

"Four others. They're resting in a room at the back."

"And the dance class?"

"Just now a lot of clapping, but no one's come out yet."

He trundles his wheelbarrow away. Sucre gets in beside me.

Neither of us says anything. Such a long time I've waited for this moment, but I don't feel tired. I'm concerned for Laura and Yolanda. I must get them out.

The clapping means the lesson has finished. I fiddle with Laura's hairclip, trying to imagine my daughter waiting her turn in the shower. The older girls will have lit cigarettes. They will be lying exhausted on the floor, their feet against the wall, higher than their heads. They will be looking at the ceiling. At Ezequiel.

Will he have guns, explosives? Will there be a secret escape route? Will he let himself be taken alive? Or will he want his world to die with him?

There's nothing to do but wait.

I feel the relieving breeze from the sea and hear the bottle boy yell out from the next street. The maid from the house opposite the studio is beating a carpet against the railings. Elsewhere, people are putting on their makeup, going to a birthday party, meeting for the first time, falling in love.

Against the fatigued sky the branches of the jacaranda are blots of ink. A bird flies down to a lawn which is being watered by a sprinkler. On the porch, darkened by the spray, a dog wakes up and shakes itself. The bird returns to the tree, a branch sinking slightly under its weight. The light is fading fast.

In the café beside the studio a tubby fellow with curly fair hair caresses a young woman's ear. They kiss. Their job has been to monitor my side of the street; also to protect me. They have been there since three this afternoon. Behind them, Clorindo, in a gray pigskin jacket, buys some cigarettes and gets into an argument about change.

At eight there's a honk. Dr. Zampini parks in front of his house. The door opens and a wedge of orange light reaches down the path, pulling him toward his wife. She stands on the threshold, her hair freshly sculptured, her arms raised in welcome.

"Here they come!" whispers Sucre.

The door in the green wall opens, and out of it troop the girls. I count them, holding my breath until I see, second to last, Laura. Yolanda follows, in a long T-shirt and the black gauze skirt she was wearing when I first met her. She stands on the pavement giving the ballet mothers her pleasant "hello" wave. When she lifts an arm, rubbing it against her headband, I can see that her neck is shiny. Sucre can't keep his eyes off her.

Laura leans against the whitewashed trunk of the jacaranda, watching the other girls leave. Marina is late. Suddenly I realize that no one's collecting my daughter. She is alone, without even Samantha to talk to. Later I learn that Marina, on Marco's say-so, has removed Samantha from the class in reaction to news of the Miraflores bomb.

One by one the ballet mothers leave. Eventually only Laura remains.

"Oh God," says Sucre, "she's going back inside!"

Yolanda is saying, "Why don't you wait in the studio?"

Laura gathers up her Adidas bag and heads for the door. I'm reaching for the handle when there's the sound of a car horn and Sylvina jerks our gray Peugeot to a halt outside the door in the wall.

My wife is dressed for her party. I can tell, thank God, she's in a hurry. She throws open the passenger door and shouts across the seat. Yolanda, hands pressed between her knees, stoops to the car window.

I hear Sylvina's words, "Good luck tomorrow."

"Come on, come on," I'm saying.

Sylvina checks herself in the driver's mirror. A quick hand through her hair, set in a new style. More lipstick, she decides. Leisurely, she applies it. Yolanda, embarrassed, seems to think she ought to wait. She sinks to her haunches and says something to Laura, touching her shoulder through the window.

"Get on with it."

At last the car starts. They wave goodbye. Sylvina drives past, running her tongue over teeth and lips.

A desire rises unsteadily within me, like a rage. I want to leap out, scream, run as fast as I can down the street to prevent Yolanda from stepping back inside that door. Unaware of my thoughts, unaware of the eyes upon her, she removes her headband. With it she dabs her temples, her cheeks, then stretches it back over her hair. With a toss of the head, she disappears through the door.

The street is empty, frozen.

"Look, sir. Upstairs!"

Upstairs the curtain parts; against the yellow folds the outline of fingertips, a cheek.

"That's him, isn't it?"

At first I move the focusing wheel the wrong way, so that he dissolves into the curtain. Then I have him.

The head swivels as if in pain. Through thick spectacles two black, bright eyes sweep the street. About the throat, loosely knotted, there's a scarf. A hand appears and begins absentmindedly to scratch at the back of the neck.

The car radio crackles. "Men in position." Sucre, his voice edged with terror, fears a blackout.

But I wish to prolong the moment. I know my life is about to change. In a room behind the green wall Yolanda will be undressing. She'll be turning on the shower. I can see her soaping her legs, her breasts. I see her squeezing the washcloth, wetting it, reaching over her shoulders to scrub her back. She screws shut her eyes and lifts her face to the jet. Cymbals and pipe music sound in her head. Everything is ready for her dance tomorrow. I hear her humming through the falling water.

The lights snap on in the street. I look down Calle Diderot one last time. The bottle boy bicycling round the corner. The maid whacking her cane against the carpet. Just now, after the spear shot of recognition when I saw the face at the window, a wave of calm rolled through my head. The hush ebbs and I hear the slow handclap of I don't know how many thousand dead.

Sucre again. "We're ready to go."

I put down the hairclip. I pick up the handset.

15

There really is very little more to say.
    I gave the order, after which seven of my men climbed over the wall. Finding no outside steps, they smashed into the studio through the sliding panels, and in the kitchen knocked down a door leading up a short staircase to the first-floor apartment. Ezequiel was sitting under a sunlamp with the *Critique of Pure Reason* still in his hands. The television was on. He was watching the boxing.

Sucre radioed me. "It's him."

The rain had started. I came in from the car and ran across the patio. Yolanda was struggling on the parquet with two of my men. There was glass everywhere. Oblivious to her screams, a third man was pointing a pump-gun at the ceiling.

Yolanda, aware of another presence, looked up. Shock blackened her eyes and left her cheeks purple and gray, the shade of an artichoke leaf.

Her eyes grabbed me. "Agustín! Help me. These bastards—"

"Let her go."

Gómez tried to say something.

"Shut up," I said.

He released Yolanda and she ran to me, throwing her arms around my neck, sobbing with relief.

I stroked her head. "Thank God you're safe. You don't know who we've got upstairs."

Behind my head, her arms stiffened. Extremely slowly, she disengaged herself.

"What's going on?" she said in a confused voice, her jaw at an angle.

I held both her hands. The veins in them stood out as she strained to pull away. "Don't be frightened. These are my men."

She glared at me. Some savagery transformed her eyes and there shot into them an expression I had seen on Laura's face. She stared into a middle distance that didn't exist, in which I did not exist.

She tore free one hand, punched the air and screamed, "Don't you dare harm him! You'll pay with your life if you harm him!"

"Yolanda—" As she whirled away from me, I felt the bite of truth.

"Viva El Presidente Ezequiel!"

Gómez seized one of her arms, Ciras the other, as she tumbled toward the floor.

Somehow I stepped past her, through the kitchen, up the steep, uncarpeted staircase, toward the dull nickel of my triumph.

He sat in his velvet-covered chair, a sick man wearing the yellow alpaca jersey which she had bought him. Sucre and Clorindo kept their guns on him.

He looked from Sucre to me and back to Sucre, who said, "Stand up before the Colonel."

Obviously in agony, Ezequiel slowly rose to his feet, watching me intently. Neither of us knew what to do. He offered his hand, and when I shook it, conscious of a rough-textured, vegetable skin, he flinched.

Sucre, encouraged by this contact, searched for a weapon. With care, as if he might not be dealing with someone of flesh and blood, he patted his hands down our prisoner's legs.

Ezequiel, still holding my hand, was calm. With his free hand he tapped his forehead. "You'll never kill this." He spoke with an insane clarity. His eyes were dark and unblinking, the black dots in their centers like shirt buttons. He was, I think, fully expecting to be shot. I had not even drawn my gun.

From a room at the back I heard women screaming. Edith and someone else, shrieking for me not to touch him. Downstairs, Yolanda's screams renewed themselves. Gómez must then have gagged her.

Since I wasn't in uniform, I introduced myself, addressing Ezequiel as "Professor." For the second time in our lives I asked for his documents. Gingerly, he emptied his pockets. He produced a spotted handkerchief, crinkly with dried phlegm. "I have none."

He did not appear distressed. I reasoned that someone who has caused so much havoc, so many killings, is not going to be worried by final capture.

"How many others?" I asked Sucre.

"Three next door—two females, one male—plus Edith Pusanga. Sánchez and Cecilia are covering them."

"And downstairs?"

"Only the dance teacher."

I turned to Ezequiel. Haunted by a ballerina with unseeing eyes, I couldn't distinguish the details of his face. "Is Yolanda with you?"

The beard opened and the answer slid out through a smile, stabbing me with the cold blade of understanding.

"Everyone's with us, Colonel. It doesn't matter if you shoot us. We're in history."

I told him that he must accompany me below. He wanted to take with him a Mao Tse-tung badge from a drawer by his bed. The Chinese leader had presented it to him personally.

I glanced at Sucre, but he was broken with emotion. I found the badge. After Ezequiel had closed his fist around it, I nodded to Clorindo to put on handcuffs. He seized Ezequiel's wrists and I thought, This is my victory. A sick man with nothing to say who wants to keep his memento from Mao.

Out of the room, he changed. He had been waiting for the coup de grâce. Once it dawned on him that he was caught, his personality abruptly weakened. He had no plan beyond this—not a Sixth or Seventh or a Twenty-fifth Grand Plan. Upstairs he could be Kant's dove, soaring in his own vacuum. Downstairs, when I took him into the street and the rain fell on his skin, he felt the beak of fear.

We used the back elevator to reach my office. I locked the door. Four men stood guard in the corridor outside. No one else was to be allowed entry. In accordance with the orders issued to me, and with enormous reluctance, I telephoned the office of Captain Calderón.

A clipped female voice told me he was attending a cocktail party at the house of the American Chargé d'Affaires. If my business was urgent, she was empowered to provide a contact number.

"It's urgent."

I started to dial. I was aware of Ezequiel in the chair and Sucre behind him and Gómez holding a gun. But my thoughts were not coherent.

I heard the ringing tone. I looked at Ezequiel, bright diamonds of rain on his yellow cardigan and in his hair. He must have felt an itch because he raised his hands and with the back of his fingers tried to scratch his temple. The handcuffs restricted his movements and he knocked off his spectacles. The sight of his naked face, suddenly revealed, brought a flash of recognition. I remembered the packed earth yard in Sierra de Pruna, the upturned beer crate, the cramped front room in the police post.

"Sucre, see to his glasses."

Ezequiel fumbled blindly on his lap, but his ruined fingernails caught in a fold of his trousers.

In the receiver at my ear a voice boomed in English, "Denver Tennyson, can I help?"

"Captain Calderón, is he there, please?"

"Who wants him?"

On the other side of the desk, Ezequiel grimaced. Suddenly I saw what the matter was. Gómez, in applying the handcuffs, had prised loose one of the fingernails. Ezequiel, when he dislodged his spectacles, had not been trying to scratch, but to press the nail back over the exposed flesh.

"I've made a mistake. I'm sorry to have troubled you." I replaced the receiver.

By that grimace, Ezequiel placed himself with the living. If, as were my orders, I handed him over to Calderón, he would be tortured and killed. I would be delivering him to the fate he expected, and against which he had prepared himself. He knew that in death he would become something else, a memory to spur his people on. To save his life was my greatest revenge.

I dialed Canal 7. "Cecilia, I have something for you. Yes. It's important."

At nine in the morning, having interrogated Ezequiel through the night, I presented him to the press. I learned more from our conversation than I am able to tell you, but nothing to make me alter my plan. Once word was out that we had him—alive and unharmed—the government could not shoot him. Your profession saved Ezequiel.

There was another consideration. I wanted to demonstrate that the institution I had served for twenty years was strong enough to ensure a fair trial. It was naive of me and it didn't happen. Yet he wasn't executed. Calderón drew up a Decree Law—even selected members of a naval firing squad—but the President feared the outrage abroad.

Calderón, if he couldn't execute Ezequiel, decided to humiliate him. He hit on the idea of exhibiting the captive in a cage. He dressed him up in a black and white uniform, like a cartoon figure, and locked him inside a large metal coop, a kind of box with bars, covered with tarpaulins. At what was judged to be the most propitious moment, Calderón had the covers removed. But it belittled us rather than Ezequiel. Like staring at a monkey in a zoo. As if we were superior. But you were there, with all the rest of those journalists. You saw how they treated him. That was in the piece you wrote.

"And Yolanda?" Dyer asked after a long interval.

Nothing in all his years as a journalist had hardened him to the despair in Rejas's answer.

"I was still interrogating Ezequiel when the message came through. Yolanda, Edith, Lorenzo and the two women from the Central Committee had been transferred from Calle Diderot to cells downstairs. Yolanda, I ordered, was to be put in a cell by herself. She had been hysterical, but the nurse had given her a shot. She was now asleep.

"I rang downstairs. 'I'll look in on her later,' I told the nurse. 'Please give her an extra blanket.' There was an astonished silence, so I said, 'She's my daughter's ballet teacher. She doesn't understand what's going on.'

" 'She doesn't, does she?' I asked Ezequiel.

"His hand opened and closed over Mao's badge, as it had throughout our conversation. Behind his glasses his eyes were tired. 'Comrade Miriam is not only a fine dancer, Colonel.'

"Even at this stage I hoped there had been some mistake. It didn't seem possible. Yolanda was naive politically, but if I could talk to her for an hour, we would find some way out of this. I didn't want to believe there wasn't a way.

"Minutes before the press conference, I tried to see her. I needed a special pass to enter the basement. My own orders. Sucre fetched the permit.

"The nurse looked at me angrily. 'Over there.'

"On a bench in a small cell, her face to the wall, Yolanda lay sleeping.

" 'When will she come round?' A blanket covered all but the top of her head.

" 'An hour or so. I gave her another shot at six.'

" 'She didn't understand what was going on,' I repeated.

"Behind me a drained voice said, 'You're wrong, boss.'

"Sucre nodded through the bars. His face had the look of someone who has steeled himself to say the unsayable."

Calderón gave me no chance to interrogate Yolanda. Twenty minutes after the press conference a convoy of trucks blocked off the entrance to the headquarters. Soldiers leapt out, followed by my furious military counterpart.

In my office he threw an official order down on my desk. It removed from my charge Ezequiel, the four members of the Central Committee—and Comrade Miriam, as Yolanda would from now on refer to herself.

I last saw her stumbling between soldiers, her head covered in a black hood.

Next evening Dyer crossed the square for the last time and climbed the stairway to the Cantina da Lua. The following morning he would take a plane out.

Rejas had ordered the wine. He began to fill two glasses as Dyer sat down.

Good news. The specialist had telephoned about his sister's tests. The antibiotic was working. Her cysticercosis, which they feared might have been a fatal strain, was curable.

Alert, no longer disoriented, his sister had no memory of her recent confusion. For the first time in a fortnight, she had asked Rejas to read to her. She wanted her mind to be taken out of that stuffy bedroom.

Rejas smiled. "I read a few pages of *Rebellion in the Backlands.*"

He poured another glass of wine, but he drank without tasting it. He had ordered the bottle to celebrate his sister's recovery. He was not drinking to celebrate.

He was coming to the end and he wanted Dyer to listen.

I have blanked out a lot since the night of Ezequiel's capture. Calderón forbade me to say a word, with very clear threats of unpleasant consequences if I chose to disobey him a second time. In the months ahead he would have me watched. But my wound was private. I hardly remembered how to breathe, or walk, or perform the simplest gestures. The press would declare repeatedly how, by my action, I had cured the country of "Ezequiel's pestilence." I had achieved all I had set out to achieve, but in achieving it I had lost what I most wanted. The truth was that I had sundered myself from all that was precious to me.

There followed the darkest days of my life. Why had fate determined that Ezequiel and I should be linked in this way? Nor could I get used to the coincidence that Ezequiel's safe house was the school where Laura learned her ballet. Every time I dropped my daughter off, I had been, without knowing it, delivering her to his lair.

I wanted to hate the person who had taken her hand, led her inside, but I didn't. I kept seeing Yolanda on the parquet, two men pinning her to the ground, her eyes loaded with hatred and madness combing her hair. I was stormed by her image and my heart could not bear it.

We know so little about people. But about the people we love, we know even less. I was so blind with love for her I hadn't been able to see. I had been like that American watching the video who could not believe it was his wife. *There must be thousands of poor bastards who don't know what's going on in their women's minds.* I had just kept making excuses and making excuses.

Shall I tell you something? Shall I let you into a secret about Yolanda?—and this is such a sad thing. I believe that until the last moment, when it could not have been clearer who I was, Yolanda had found a way of convincing herself. If true, it's pitiable—but how else do I explain our intimacy? On that day when we sat on the grass and I told her about the army massacre, she must have told herself I was on her side. I was one of them. Of course, she had no means of proving it. She couldn't run upstairs to Ezequiel and say, "I've just met this man . . ." That would have been a breach of his discipline. So she demonstrated her loyalty by not informing him. When she said to me, "Silence is part of the dance," she was speaking the truth.

At her level you weren't permitted contact with more than two comrades. And you'd address each other as Comrade this or Comrade that, so that you'd never discover who they were. After your mission you'd go back to being the person you had been before. It ensured you revealed nothing if you were tortured. That's why Ezequiel was effective.

But, isn't it funny? Isn't it the most appalling thing? There I was, pouring out my heart to Yolanda, all the time exhibiting the same tensions and worries she was suffering. It's possible some of the cryptic phrases I used to protect my work chimed with phrases she had been taught—and it would have been in her nature to think if she didn't recognize the code, the fault lay with her, not me.

Then there was this other problem. You see, in Ezequiel's world, love was forbidden. Sex was okay, but he demanded that his followers live a loveless life, dedicated to him. But for whatever reason, whether it had to do with her father or the sad figure who'd been her fiancé, poor Yolanda, who in every other way proved so perfect a disciple, wasn't quite capable of filling that emotional hollow with Ezequiel's philosophy. There was a gap which the revolution couldn't satisfy.

All her training, the nuns, the months in the jungle camp, ought to have drummed into her the unsuitability of a man like me. But in my comforting her during the blackout, something happened which she couldn't have predicted.

A week, ten days maybe, passed before I decided to speak to the one person who might reduce my madness: her old fiancé, the poet.

He was a thin, angular-faced man with trout-colored eyes and Yolanda's habit of staring into space. We walked through Parque Colón and sat on a bench, while, opposite us, a blue-and-yellow-uniformed gardener patted geraniums into the black earth.

The poet was reluctant to talk. He was still in love with her and so was I. We were rivals and I felt shameful, but I needed to see what he and I had in common, and if he bore any stamp of her.

I gave him little choice. Either he talked to me informally, here in the open air, or I would detain him for questioning. It was imperative we speak. There were matters I needed to clear up regarding Yolanda's trial.

It was a mild day, too cold to sit out really, and he was nervous. He spoke himself.

"I couldn't believe it. When I saw her photograph, screaming, I said, 'No, it can't be Yolanda.' And then it was Yolanda." He picked up a book wrapped with a battered-looking dust jacket. I supposed he had brought it along to prove his innocence. "It was as if I'd opened this book and it had exploded."

I asked to see the book. It was *When the Dead Speak* by Miguel Angel Torre. "No one pays attention to poetry," said its epigraph.

"Not a good time time for lyrics," he said.

I noticed a poem dedicated to Yolanda.

> . . . *world invisible,*
> *the skillful poison of*
> *your changeless pose* . . .

Envy overwhelmed me. This young man with the red mole on his forehead had felt the same as I did, but his desire had lived to enjoy its full flesh.

His shadow fell on the page. "She danced that one."

He started talking about her. Their first meeting, a friend's birthday party at the Catholic University. Her taste in music (she liked The Doors, Pink Floyd, King Crimson). Her passion for cakes. (A day later I found myself queuing at her favorite bakery in San Isidro.) A born seductress. Never said a bad word about anyone. Didn't have enemies. If she wanted to go from A to B, she went. Whatever the cost.

A force to be reckoned with.

Soon they were living in the blue house in Calle Tucumán. He installed a caoba wood barre in their bedroom so she could dance. That was a good time. They went to the beach, cooked, made love. Then, while she was convalescing from a leg injury, she was invited to Cuba, to a conference on the arts.

She was to be away for a fortnight. When she stayed a month, he became worried. Maybe she had met someone else. He was always jealous if, onstage, she danced with another man. But, no— there was no man. She had found the society in which she could believe. Four months after returning from Cuba, she resigned from the Metropolitan.

Classical ballet was too rigid. It was ballet for the bourgeois. From now on she would devote her energies to modern dance. Modern dance represented a liberation of the spirit from its state of repression.

"Her talk, it was all about dance. That's what I believed. But she was acting the whole time. She was seeing with other eyes."

"Did you never suspect?"

A hand squeezed his face. He was afraid. He had believed in many of the things she did. He also believed that to admit this to me would be to condemn himself. He feared, perhaps, that I would discover his status as an underground poet. But from my university days I had been familiar with the bars he frequented. Like him, I knew how to weave tough dreams from cigarette smoke. The Kloaka, the Dalmacia, the Café Quilca—these were the haunts of people who talk revolution, talk and do nothing about it. We were more alike than he knew, he and I. Yolanda would have branded us cowards.

"I thought what she felt was religious, not political," he said carefully. "There was a group of nuns she liked. Twice a week she would borrow my car and drive them to the shantytowns. She'd bake the children cakes, teach them to dance. At least, that's what I supposed she was doing. But she was very reserved, never talked of anything that was purely personal to her.

"Our relationship began to come unstuck when she wanted me to join in. 'How can you represent the masses if you don't live with them?' I had said. Besides, I was a poet, not a revolutionary.

" 'Then let's live with them,' she said.

"Early on, I might have done. But our affair was not as passionate as it had been. There were frictions. A writer has to live in his own world at one moment and relate to his public at another. A dancer needs to be the center of attention at all times. For Yolanda I had become something day-to-day, while every day she burned with a desire to impress a new audience.

"She attended a studio of modern dance in Calle Mitre, mixing with people I didn't approve of. She started coming home late, talking about Truth and Justice. She spoke of the Greeks, of Plato and Sophocles. She had read nothing—then Sophocles!

"Of course, you don't know her, so you can't imagine this. But Yolanda, reading Sophocles . . .

"One day she received a call from the youngest of the nuns. The army had stormed the prison in Lurigancho and killed two hundred of Ezequiel's men. I overheard the nun asking Yolanda to distribute leaflets about those who'd been murdered.

"I protested: 'Yolanda, those are Ezequiel's people.' And I forbade her. That night she came home late, driving my car.

"She didn't deny what she had done. She had brought back a potted plant for me. I threw it at the kitchen window. She swept up the glass, the earth, the terra-cotta shards. Later, when I apologized for breaking the window, she said, 'It isn't a window you have broken.'

"We didn't speak for a week. Then I found a pamphlet advertising a discussion at the Catholic University about the prison massacre. 'I want to go,' I said.

"The evening was dominated by this bearded chap—Lorenzo. He kept waving his arms about, shouting for everyone to rise up, assassinate the President. Afterward he joined us and he was very friendly with her.

" 'Yolanda,' I said, 'I don't want that man in our house.'

"Three days later I came home and he was sitting in our kitchen. I threw him out. It was the second time I had lost my temper. You couldn't lose your temper with Yolanda. She went with Lorenzo to the door and watched him leave. She didn't scream or say anything. But that night in bed she said she had begun to question our relationship.

"She became cold and distant. I worried for her health; among other things, she hadn't menstruated for twelve months. And ate nothing, only cakes. She'd become so thin she would put stockings in her bra to make herself look bigger there. But her belief was rocklike. I think she had already made her decision.

"Two days go by. Then at breakfast she says she's going on a retreat in the jungle with some Canadian nuns.

"I sat down and said, 'Yolanda, you're not going to a retreat. Are you?'

"She didn't lie. She didn't know how to lie.

" 'You're going to your political friends.'

" 'Yes.'

" 'Then we can't live together in this house anymore.'

"She packed and left. A week after that, when she hadn't come home, I abandoned the house.

"I saw her again about six months later. She was sweet, and talked for two hours about the jungle, what she had seen and done there. At the end of the conversation she asked for money. She had moved back into Calle Tucumán. She needed to pay the bills. I refused, said I knew what she wanted the money for. Now, for the first time, she lost her temper. She shouted at me, and then she turned on her heel and was gone.

"I saw her again once, walking along Calle Sol. I didn't recognize her at first. She had put on weight. I thought she looked terribly attractive. As she came toward me, I called her name. She walked past."

A man plonked himself down on the bench next to us and opened a newspaper.

We got to our feet. Behind us another gardener had been lifting turf. He didn't have gardener's hands.

We walked under the African tulip trees to the gate at the edge of the park.

"Is it possible she will recant?" I asked.

He shook his head. "No, this will have made her even stronger, even more determined. She'll never relent. Ballet gave her this discipline."

"What about her brother, was he involved too?"

"Brother?" he said. "She had no brother."

We stopped at the gate. I shook his hand, thanked him for his time. I knew he would have been distressed by our conversation. A barman at the Café Quilca had told me that he thought the poet had attempted suicide after Yolanda left. Now he was reluctant to let me go. There was a question which plagued him.

"Tell me, what was her relationship with Ezequiel? They say in the papers he slept with all his followers. She didn't sleep with him, did she?"

The same thought tormented me. We stood there, two rivals seeking from each other assurance it was impossible to give.

"There's no way of knowing one way or the other."

He nodded seriously to himself, zipped up his jacket, and I watched him sidle off, his head on one side, book under his arm, the other hand trailing along the railings.

Still, there are answers I can't find. What position did Yolanda hold? How did she relate to the Central Committee? To Edith? I would have bet on Edith being jealous of her. Yolanda was privileged, middle-class, not a jungle-tested killer. Or was she? Had she planted car bombs and cut throats? When I asked the poet, he remembered a Sunday lunch they'd had once and her squeamishness over a chicken. She couldn't sever its head and the creature had scampered around making the most awful mess until he had to finish the job for her.

I ask all these questions, but always I go back to her relationship with Ezequiel. What went on between them?

Yolanda's trial was a charade. The few details I have were passed on to me by the governor of the prison at which she is held.

She was flown to Villoria, and from there transported in a truck to a military base on the lake. The trial was staged so quickly that it would have been impossible to prepare a proper defense. She never saw her judges. They sat behind reflecting glass, and she spoke to them as she might have spoken to the mirrored walls in her studio.

The voices accused her of fifty-four charges. Her lawyer's plea that she was solely the errand girl for No. 459 Calle Diderot was dismissed out of hand. She belonged to the Section of Operative Support. She found safe houses, made connections, linked one cell with another. Her calling, her privileged position allowed her to move freely in society without arousing suspicion. The most damning evidence was a mention in her notebook of the name of the café outside which the Miraflores bomb had exploded.

She was sentenced to imprisonment for the rest of her natural life at the women's penitentiary in Villoria. The senior judge acknowledged the severity of the sentence. It attested, he said, to the state's determination to prevent "the superficial attractions of the accused from serving as a beacon to others." In passing sentence, he had acceded to the prosecutor's demand for a symbolic punishment.

She would be condemned to a cell without light.

I've never been to the compound in Villoria. And I suspect it's worse than I've been told. But I do have this certainty: if her cell is anything like Ezequiel's, it's unendurable.

Picture a tiny, windowless room thirty feet underground. If you open your arms, your fingers scrape unpainted concrete. If you raise your hands, you touch the ceiling. If you walk three paces, you smash your face.

Along one wall is a narrow bed with a mattress and a blanket. The air battles its way into the room through a vent in the ceiling. Apart from the bed, there is nothing other than a towel, a plastic water jug and a plastic basin which can be used as a toilet. At least that is what you see with the lights on. What it's like without light, I cannot even begin to imagine.

Do you realize the horror of this? A woman used to movement, who is afraid of the dark, who is used to a lighted stage, now living in absolute darkness, no one to acknowledge her except the guard who collects the tray. There are no mirrors. She can't know what she looks like. Perhaps her eyes will milk up, like one of those deepwater, dark-dwelling fishes they net from the lake at that altitude.

She can't see what she's eating, what she's drinking, where she's defecating. She can have no idea whether it's night or day. How does she know when to sleep, when to wake? Dreams must be her only light, but what can she dream of, and how does she feel when she wakes from a dream and there's darkness and she knows she'll be waking to this room for the rest of her life, that until the grave this is what will greet her?

Of course, one hopes that it won't be for the rest of her life, that there'll be a remission, an act of clemency. I think of Father Ramón's last message to me: "God's mercy is greater than God's justice." But in a way it's worse, not knowing. If she knew she was going to live like this for the rest of her life, she could simply give up. Or else she could take heart if she knew she would have to endure it only for a certain number of years. But to face so uncertain . . .

Rejas stopped. He started again, pausing between each sentence, measuring each word as if he had few left.

During the whole first year she was permitted one visit from a Red Cross official. Now her family are allowed a visit every fortnight. But she refuses to see them. She hasn't seen anyone for fifteen months.

It would be inconceivable, even in that lightless space, if she didn't attempt some form of movement. But if you're not born at that altitude, you risk *soroche*. You've been to Villoria—you can't jog fifty yards without feeling mountain sickness. So I expect she stretches to keep warm, gripping the bed for support. The nights are often well below freezing.

She still has touch, I suppose. But that's all she has. Her last anchor to this world is the feel of her bare feet on the concrete floor, her nose against the wall, the tips of her fingers on the ceiling.

I did manage to deliver some blankets to the prison governor, asking him to pass them on. The blankets were returned with a personal message: "Tell him I'm dead and I live only for the Revolution."

I know what people say. They say that what she fought for has enveloped her, that where she lies now is an appropriate punishment. Didn't Ezequiel for so long make this country a place of comparable darkness? Shouldn't she be held up as an example so no one will be tempted to follow this path?

But it is not what I feel. I think of her in prison like a candle burning down, her muscles degenerating. Soon she's going to be too old to dance. Such a waste. As if someone said you could never read again.

You will say that I feel this because I'm in love with her. But if you were to meet her, you would see the ballerina before you saw the terrorist. We're none of us, are we, just one thing? I am a policeman, but also a father, a husband for the time being, a nurse-maid to a sister who I pray will survive her illness. You are a journalist, a writer and I don't know what else besides. To look at a person from a single angle is to deform them. Even if Yolanda is guilty of protecting Ezequiel, she is also afraid of the dark. And I cannot forget that I put her there. In prison. To be in the dark forever.

Rejas had finished.

On the jetty the night-cart people loaded trash onto container boats. Black and yellow birds darted into the searchlights, and out in the river something splashed.

Astrud was buried in a cemetery overlooking Botafogo Bay. Hugo had picked out the black wood coffin, lined with bright blue satin. She was buried in her nightgown, the wrinkled neck of the dead baby girl in her shawl visible between her folded arms.

Dyer looked back into the room. "Why did you tell me all this?"

17

Her luggage had been left at the foot of the staircase. Dyer walked past it, chasing her laughter down a paneled corridor until he reached the conservatory.

Vivien sat holding Hugo's hand at the breakfast table, her other hand carving gestures in the morning light. She wore black velvet trousers, green ballet slippers, a white organdy shirt with an open collar and a sailor's bow loose at the neck. Ruby links—not Hugo's, he surmised—in her French cuffs.

"They should have been far, far quicker in the first act and they rushed the music in the second." Then: "Johnny!"

She jumped to her feet and stood on tiptoe to kiss him. "I'm telling Hugo about our performance in Pará. Although you, my dear, won't be interested in the least."

Hugo smiled his diplomat's smile at Dyer.

"There's coffee on the sideboard," she said. "You'll have to be nice and wait patiently until I finish my story."

Hugo, having heard about the ballet—a modern piece, specially commissioned—was fascinated to know what the Amazon looked like. "Can you see the other side?"

She touched him tenderly where his paunch pushed at his silk shirt. "It's too ridiculous. Two weeks I was stuck inside that opera house—and I only saw it for the first time last night. My dear, it's like any other river."

Dyer said nothing. He poured himself coffee and listened while Vivien described a party thrown by the Governor—"the girls nicknamed him Porpoise Eyes"—and the varieties of fish she had eaten.

At last Vivien clapped her hands. "Enough about me." She looked at Dyer, hard. "Johnny, darling, I want to hear what you've been up to."

Not until lunchtime was Dyer able to tell her.

She had booked a restaurant on the Malecón. "Just the two of us. Hugo, miserably, has another engagement. He says you were awfully sweet with him."

"I only took him to the Costa Verde."

"He couldn't stop talking about it. How did you find him?"

"In good form, I thought."

"He minded losing his eyebrows. Otherwise he is quite chirpy."

They ordered lunch. Vivien talked in her enthusiastic fashion about the orphanage, the children and a separate dormitory she had built for the girls. "Before my eyes they'd grown into adolescents. I'd find the boys the whole time under their blankets."

The details—cupboards, washbasins, new cooking pots— seemed fresh on her mind.

"Is that where you spent last week, Vivien?"

"My dear, why do you ask?"

"I went to Pará."

She held him with her pale blue gaze. "It's funny, I didn't somehow picture you with the Ashaninkas."

"I couldn't find you."

"Pará is a big place."

"Not as big as you would think."

She laughed, fiddling with a cufflink.

"When I found out there wasn't a ballet," he said, "I thought you might have gone there for other reasons."

"Darling, would I have done that if I suspected you were going to follow me?"

"Did you know I would?"

"Let's say I had an inkling. But how else was I to lose you? I had one or two things to do which I can do better on my own. I'm sorry I couldn't help with Tristan. But please understand why not. Your instinct always to find people in power morally dubious is perfectly commendable, but it doesn't go down so smoothly with those of my friends who happen to be political—not every time."

"You can help me now," said Dyer.

"Johnny, I can see it in your eyes. You're teeming with wicked ideas about what your aunt is up to. But it's not what you think. Without Tristan's patronage the orphanage would collapse. And I'm not going to jeopardize those children's future for the sake of getting you a newspaper interview. *Punto final.*"

"I've got something important to tell Calderón," said Dyer.

"Sweetheart, you're being childish. He's not going to see you. Not only is he not going to see you, he's not even going to let you past the gate."

"I don't want to see him."

"Good."

Dyer smiled. "You used a phrase once. 'My life has been a series of meetings and failings to meet.'"

"How very poetic."

"You were talking of your elopement with Hugo."

"That was forty years ago, my dear."

"I didn't manage to meet Calderón. But because of you, I bumped into someone more interesting."

Her eyes challenged him. "More interesting than Tristan?"

"Agustín Rejas."

Vivien put down her menu. "It's not true! You saw Rejas? Where?"

"In Pará. While waiting for you."

"My dear, no one's met Rejas. Do you realize how incredible that is? The press here are shrieking about how he's been out of the country, talking to the Americans. Now you tell me that he's been talking to you. What sort of creature is he? I've met his wife. She tried to sell me lip gloss. I want to hear everything."

Dyer's summary lasted through most of lunch. Vivien listened without interrupting. At the end she ordered another bottle of wine.

"Yes, yes, pour it out," she told the waitress in atrocious Spanish. "Why do you wait for me to taste it? If it was disgusting, I'd send it back. You didn't wait to see how we liked our fish, did you?"

She toyed with the glass. After a while she said in a sober voice, "So Rejas did fall for Yolanda. I'd heard as much. It's not surprising. She was lovely."

"Why did you never mention her?"

"I expect I forgot. So much was going on. I had rehearsals. Hugo had his stroke. All of us—the whole country—were picking up our lives after Ezequiel. You forget, the vast majority of people, like me, aren't interested in politics. I'm for a well-organized life. I don't like people dashing about with guns. I was simply relieved the lights worked again. It's only you, my dear, who goes on being fascinated by the bad news."

"That's not true."

"I never could share your obsession with Ezequiel. It is the one thing I won't forgive, the way he used that girl. A dance studio was the most brilliant cover. Who would have imagined that above those proper young ladies there would be this choreographer of violence?"

"Then—she was lovely? Yolanda, I mean."

"You're upset. I can tell."

"Everything Rejas said . . ."

"My dear, you're as bad as he is. This intense attraction, hardly consummated by a touch . . . He sounds as if he didn't know her—which is always for the best. Never get too close to the dance stage, Johnny."

"It isn't exactly my line, as you know, but she sounded so attractive, so—beguiling."

"She was, and she wasn't. I liked her, but then I didn't, or at least not so much."

"Tell me about her."

"Yolanda? I met her through Dmitri. Remember Dmitri?"

"The White Russian? Tall, bald?"

"That's him. He was a bit démodé, but great fun. Anyway, he was running the Ballet Miraflores then and he insisted I see this girl. She was fourteen, which is getting on a bit, but since it was Dmitri, of course I saw her. She came for an audition. Everyone performed a little dance and she did jazz, with a bit of mime and a

Paganini piece thrown in. She was glorious to look at and I was in tears at the end—Dmitri knew how to get to me, all right. She wasn't wishy-washy and she moved very well. Her mother, a small gray-haired Miraflorina, sat in the front and watched. Well, I accepted her and she was with us—let's see—nine or ten years. At one point I thought she might be prima ballerina material. But I must have decided she was too easily influenced. Then she had this problem with her leg."

Vivien took up her glass and sipped at it, then set it down on the table.

"She told everyone it was a dance injury. I wasn't so gullible. You don't get scars like that, my dear, not from dancing. Very suspicious, it was.

"One day she was helping at the orphanage and out it came. She'd been on a protest march at the Catholic University and had been tear-gassed. In the panic, the crowd trampled on her."

"Wasn't it a bit dangerous, to confess that to you?"

"Not at all. She knew I'd be sympathetic. She'd spent a good many Saturdays at the orphanage, cooking, washing clothes, teaching the children to do pliés. Initially, I'd been reluctant to involve her. Most do-gooders are a menace. Yolanda, I have to say, was different. A tremendous way with the children, she had. But after a few months she stopped coming.

"I have to say it was the same with her dancing. She started to find classical ballet too constricting. I thought she might like something more modern, more aggressive, even—Martha Graham, say—but no, she preferred folklore. Then she went to Cuba and that impressed her terribly. Came back with all sorts of ideas. Instead of getting down to rehearsing, we had to have these moral discussions, my dear. Fond as I was of her, I did start to find her a teeny bit wearisome. It was like talking to a glove puppet.

"But far worse than her debates, she used to skip rehearsals. That is no good, not if you're serious. She would disappear for a month at a time, and no one ever knew where.

"Then, one day, in the middle of a class, she gave it all up—poosh!—just like that. I understood, my dear. Or thought I did. I didn't know with her if it was love, or what. But politics—no, I never imagined politics. She was too naive.

"Who knows what was going on in her mind? She'd done nothing for other people, or so she felt. And then she must have met someone who talked about the creativity of the Indians, and how the only way to help them recapture their identity was to offer them salvation through revolution. A very romantic view of Indian society, my dear. It could have happened to a lot of women like that—educated, pretty, good family, religious. You start with a humanitarian idea, and before you know it, you're cutting throats.

"She soon dropped out of sight. Then two years ago I heard she had started her own school. I went to see her once or twice, for encouragement's sake; also to let her know I'd leave the door open if things didn't work out. I recommended her to a few parents. As far as I could make out, she seemed content. But I had other things to worry about. To me, she was a very good dancer who had stopped coming to rehearsals."

"Rejas is convinced she must have been exceptional."

"Some of my teachers have gone round making extravagant boasts on her behalf. But when someone becomes notorious, people do tend to say, 'Oh, my brilliant pupil.' Do you still paint your watercolors? If you had gone berserk with a machine gun, no doubt one or two people would have said, 'What a tragedy—he was such a good artist.' "

Dyer couldn't help smiling. "So atrocity is the province of the bad watercolorist?"

"My dear, I adore your paintings. We still have one in the spare room. No. What I'm wondering is, if she had been that good a dancer, would she have given it up?"

"You did."

"I had no illusions. The world was going to go on without me. I didn't think I would be able to go on without Hugo. That's all."

Vivien looked at him, a suspicion of sharpness in her eyes. "This doesn't make her fate any less unspeakable, but hasn't she become what she struggled to be on the dance floor? Isn't she entombed in her cave, like Antigone? All I'm begging you is, don't fold her into your life, please. I'm serious, Johnny. She is lovely, Yolanda, and it's easy to see what Rejas, poor man, must have felt. Imagine this attractive young woman walking toward him through the rubble of his life. Who could resist? That body! Those looks!

That sweetness! My dear, it must have been as though she had sat on his lap stark naked.

"But if I was stern, I could paint a different picture. I could say Yolanda had only her looks. I could pretend she wasn't blessed with the meat and gristle of character, and that when she grows old, this will reveal itself in her face. We old people aren't unfaithful to our characters. Your aunt here—what you see is the real thing. You can keep something suppressed a long while; then, at a certain age, your true self bounces out. Maybe in twenty years those big brown eyes will narrow, showing how thin the broth has been. Maybe her skin will grow dullish, her black hair lose its luster, her slender fingers flatten into hands like those of our dear waitress. Maybe the dungeon will snuff out her essential sweetness and she won't be lovely anymore."

"And I wouldn't believe you."

"The thing is, you'd be right," she said crossly. "But it's my duty to stop you forming sentimental attachments to people you haven't met—if only for your poor mother's sake."

She called the waitress for a plate to cover the fish against the flies. "No, don't take it away. I know we've had our pudding—but we might want to go back."

"What about her relationship with Ezequiel?"

"What does Rejas think?"

"He doesn't believe there was anything between them. Doesn't want to, perhaps."

"Men are so silly. Listen, have you any idea what Yolanda was like at the Metropolitan? She was wild, my dear. Wild. Blasts of vitality. No one was immune to her attraction—why should Ezequiel have been different? All those months in that compression chamber . . . Maybe they did, maybe they didn't. Does it matter anyway? No, don't give me that flinty look—Ezequiel I regard in the same light as the Devil, but he might have been amusing company with it. Perhaps he was considerate and careful with her. Women, who will tell themselves any number of consoling lies, forgive almost anything of a man who goes out of his way to be tender and make them laugh. A little bit of trouble goes a long way, my dear. I'm not saying that's what happened. But who knows what goes on between two human beings? And what did

Rejas himself say? That we know next to nothing about the people we love."

She sighed. "That goes for you too, Johnny. Sometimes I think of you as just another one of my orphans. I'm always saying to them when they leave, 'Get on with it, for Christ's sake. Up, up, up, on your own two feet.' And I wish you would do the same. When Hugo told me he'd been trying to fix you up with Mona, I said, 'That willowy girl is no good for Johnny. He needs someone much rounder.' "

Vivien drank her wine and looked serious again. "A ballet dancer would never do for you, my dear. Now. This message you have for Calderón—is it about the election?"

"It is and it isn't."

"Is Rejas going to stand?"

"What does Tristan think?"

"Don't play with me, Johnny."

"I think it's more a question of 'I won't stand if . . .' "

"What's the if?" Her eyes narrowed. Dyer had her complete attention. But he knew she was addressing someone else.

He saw this person clearly now, from their first meeting in the Cantina da Lua. Rejas, recognizing him from the start, had taken a gamble on the kind of person Dyer was—had gambled his all. By speaking freely, the policeman had broken the habit of a career. His anguish was unreachable, but Dyer, without being aware of it, had offered, through his kinship with Vivien, one feeble ray of hope. In order to win the journalist's trust, Rejas had told him everything, in the most careful detail, omitting nothing. At the same time, he must have hoped that when Dyer understood the reason, he would decide not to publish it.

Once he had relayed the message to Vivien, Dyer knew that he would put this story away. He would not forget it, but it was too personal, too unhistorical, too unpolitical to use as journalism. The only thing he could make of it would mean his having to leave the real elements out.

But it would not be wasted. Rejas had confessed to him for a reason—because Dyer was still capable of doing things that he could no longer do himself.

With Rejas's story, Dyer had the power to give Yolanda back the light.

"I'm bringing you a message for you to give to Calderón. Rejas wants to be certain that Yolanda—as quite distinct from Ezequiel—will be decently treated in prison, and that Calderón will use his influence with the President to release her in two or three years' time. If Rejas has this assurance, he will not contest the elections."

"You believe him?"

"Yes, I do. One, he is a just man. Two, Yolanda has no blood on her hands. That's why Ezequiel chose her. Three—he loves her, damn it."

"Didn't you see her on television? She was screaming blue murder for the revolution."

"Yes, but she's young. Rejas is convinced that she has never handled a weapon in her life. You knew her, Vivien. Was she a revolutionary? He's appealing to you."

"Did he mention that he'd given the orphanage the money from his reward?"

"No, he didn't. But I knew anyway."

"So his gift really was an *acte gratuit,*" she said reflectively.

"You can't think he gave you that money to get at Calderón. He announced his decision on the steps of the police building—the day after he caught Ezequiel."

Vivien nodded. "You should tell your friend he's done a wonderful job, but he's not presidential material."

Dyer looked down at the table, pushing a fork so that its tines left faint parallel tracks in the cloth. He looked up at his aunt again. It was vital he persuade her.

"He's a good man, Vivien. I trust him."

She sat back, returning his gaze. "If, as you seem so certain, Rejas doesn't go into politics—well, anything might happen. Then there is hope. That hair-raising story Rejas told you about the rat . . . He's right, you know. But if he decides to stand against the government, or even to speak out in any way, the risk is obvious: she'll continue to rot in jail."

"So that's the message back?"

Her eyes twinkled at Dyer's concern. "He knew what he was doing, didn't he? Quite apart from the fact that you are my nephew. It's a terrible burden, a story you're not allowed to tell which the world has got wrong. And what better way of keeping it quiet than to give it to a journalist who understands more or less what you're talking about, but whose readers at home will never be interested in South America? You know what they would have said, don't you? At the paper, I mean—'Nice story, my dear, but can't you set it in Provence?' Telling it to you, he was telling it to the ground. So don't worry about Rejas, Johnny. He chose you."

They walked home along the Malecón. The trees were in their last days of flower, and in a small open park on the clifftop, the blossoms were strewn across the dry grass.

"I have another favor to ask," said Dyer. "I promised Rejas I would speak to you about his daughter. Laura. Who was Yolanda's pupil."

"How old is she now?"

"Fourteen."

"Too old."

"Her dream is to join the Metropolitan."

"I'm sure. Or is it her father's dream? It doesn't matter, in any case. This is not a sentimental profession."

"You accepted Yolanda at that age."

"Yolanda had talent."

"I believe Laura's good. Really."

"Or Rejas does?" Vivien, who had been about to shake her head, looked amused. "And if Laura does succeed in becoming a dancer—a good one—then a part of Yolanda will live on? Is that what you're both thinking? All these people you haven't met, Johnny . . . All right, I'll give her an audition. Now, watch out for that step. You're walking too fast. I want to catch my breath."

They looked down at a gray sea dissolving into a grayer horizon. A freighter moved out of the docks. Through the cranes, as though hanging from them, Dyer could make out the shape of an island. Under its cliffs, white-stuccoed with guano, spread the squat roof of Ezequiel's prison.

He thought of Ezequiel's captor, still in another country. He could not forget the policeman's grief-colored face as they had shaken hands twenty-four hours before. Here was a man who had fought against not one system but two. What he represented was better than either. Yet his cure had been his destruction; and what he had called his "madness," his salvation.

Halfway across the square, Dyer had heard the clatter of the shutter against the wall and stopped to look back at the Cantina da Lua. Rejas was on the balcony, gripping the iron balustrade, and for a moment the other had thought he might have left his chair to wave. He raised his hand in salute, but Rejas was staring into the river. At first Dyer couldn't work it out. Then he realized. A strong breeze played over the current, blowing upstream, so that the river seemed to be flowing the other way, inland to its source. His eyes adrift on that water, Rejas had looked so lonely and little, a man with part of his soul broken.

"Thinking of Rejas?" said Vivien.

"Yes."

"It's like the end of a book. He'll live on. We're very resilient, human beings. Maybe he'll find someone else. I've survived ten revolutions and as many heartbreaks. What they say here is true. Love is eternal for as long as it lasts."

"Vivien—"

"I'm sure Tristan will find out what you've told me," she said abruptly. "But I do need you to get that slipper copied—I am serious."

They turned into Vivien's street, purple with jacaranda and lined, between the trees, with old-fashioned lamps from the time of the rubber boom. It was early afternoon, but jets of gas flickered behind the glass shades.

In Pará, Rejas would be sitting down to dinner.

———

Dyer sent his fax from Vivien's office.

> It wasn't the story I thought it was. This gives me all the
> more occasion for writing to say that I can't accept your
> offer to send me to the Middle East. This is where my life
> is, with or without the paper. I don't suppose Jeremy is still
> in Personnel, but could you put me in touch with someone
> to arrange severance terms?

Meanwhile he had a book to finish. He threw himself into the
project as soon as he had finished closing down the office in Joaquim Nabuco. He would rise at six and write until lunchtime. In
the afternoons he took to walking the length of Ipanema beach, to
the point where the Dois Irmãos slipped into the sea. As he walked
toward those mountains, he would often think of better ways to
express what he had written; on the way back he planned the
chapters ahead.

He began to enjoy the work. The book would have a limited
market, but it was a subject he felt uniquely qualified to write
about. As the weeks passed, he forgot about Vivien's promise to
audition Laura. It was the sort of thing his aunt would not think to
mention, and besides, she was hopeless at keeping in touch. He
had rather expected it to turn out badly; such vague attempts to
help usually do.

He had reached chapter seventeen when the letter came
through the box. The envelope had been sent to Dyer, care of
Señora Vallejo. Vivien had forwarded it and on the back she had
written, "Shoes perfect. Color, too. Thanks. V"

Inside, there was a postcard.

The legend was "Pilgrims ascend Mount Ausangate on the final night of the Corpus Christi ice festival." The color photograph
showed a zigzag of lights against a dark blue slope and, dotted on
the snowy summit, a line of curiously robed figures.

It was from Rejas.

His sister had died. Emilio would be staying on and doubtless
would be pleased to see Dyer if he chanced to visit Pará.

His wife had gone to live in Miami.

Ezequiel had signed a declaration stating that he agreed with the policies of the government.

Dyer would shortly read that Rejas had been made Minister of Native Affairs.

Whenever Dyer came to the capital, Rejas hoped he would make the time to dine with him again.

And, "Laura has been accepted by the Metropolitan. Thank you." And his initials.

That was all.

Nicholas Shakespeare grew up in the Far East and South America. He is the author of the novel *The Vision of Elena Silves,* which won the Somerset Maugham Award, and he was chosen by *Granta* as one of the Best of the Young British Novelists in 1993. He currently lives in London, where he is at work on a biography of Bruce Chatwin.

PUREBRED DEAD

A Selection of Titles by Kathleen Delaney

The Ellen McKenzie Series

DYING FOR A CHANGE
GIVE FIRST PLACE TO MURDER
MURDER FOR DESSERT
MURDER HALF-BAKED
MURDER BY SYLLABUB

The Mary McGill and Millie Series

PUREBRED DEAD *

* *available from Severn House*

PUREBRED DEAD

Kathleen Delaney

This first world edition published 2015
in Great Britain and the USA by
SEVERN HOUSE PUBLISHERS LTD of
19 Cedar Road, Sutton, Surrey, England, SM2 5DA.
Trade paperback edition first published 2015
in Great Britain and the USA by
SEVERN HOUSE PUBLISHERS LTD.

British Library Cataloguing in Publication Data

Delaney, Kathleen author.
  Purebred dead.
  1. Murder–Investigation–California–Fiction.
  2. Christmas pageants–Fiction. 3. Detective
  and mystery stories.
  I. Title
  813.6-dc23

ISBN-13: 978-0-7278-8501-2 (cased)
ISBN-13: 978-1-84751-603-9 (trade paper)
ISBN-13: 978-1-78010-654-0 (e-book)

All Severn House titles are printed on acid-free paper.

Severn House Publishers support the Forest Stewardship Council™ [FSC™],
the leading international forest certification organisation. All our titles that
are printed on FSC certified paper carry the FSC logo.

Typeset by Palimpsest Book Production Ltd.,
Falkirk, Stirlingshire, Scotland.
Printed and bound in Great Britain by
TJ International, Padstow, Cornwall.

ONE

Mary McGill stood on top of the library steps, trying to hear the person shouting at the other end of her cell phone. She could only make out every other word. It sounded as if they said the cow had run away. She should have learned to text.

'Where did the cow go?' She listened for a minute as the growing crowd made their way through the park toward the Victorian Christmas Extravaganza on Maple Street, one block over, wondering, not for the first time, why she'd agreed to once more chair the organizing committee for this event. 'Why we ever let the Maids a-Milking bring a real cow, I'll never know. Can you catch it? It what? Oh, oh. Keep me posted.'

She hung up, hoping Bobby Connors was right and he could keep the cow out of Mrs Wittiker's mums. She was pretty proud of those mums. Oh, well. It was a bit late for them anyway.

It was getting dark fast. Clouds were coming in. The forecast was for rain, but not until later tonight. Mary sent up a silent prayer it would hold off until at least midnight. It would take that long to get everyone out of their costumes, make sure all the animals were accounted for and back in their barnyards or kennels and any stray children found and returned to their parents. No matter how hard you tried, children strayed.

Her cell phone rang again. 'Mary here. Everything's fine. No, no sign of the cow. You tell Bobby to get on it. We can't have a cow running— Oh. Good. Where's the *posada*? The donkey did what? Is Luanne all right? Take care of her. She's about as far along as Mary was when they got to Bethlehem and I have no intention of closing this event tonight birthing a real baby.' She listened a moment. 'All right. I should hear the singing any time now.'

The library Mary stood outside of was in the middle of Santa Louisa's town park, almost directly across from St Theresa of the Little Flower Church, where the *posada* was supposed to end. Mary and Joseph would finally be welcomed someplace after all the inns set up along the procession route had rejected them. Mary would lay baby Jesus in the manger, the children's choir would sing a hymn, the people who had followed the procession would join in and a party would immediately commence. Libations were supposed to consist of lemonade and hot chocolate. Mary fervently hoped that was all that was served.

Many California towns had recently included *posadas* in their Christmas celebrations, but this was Santa Louisa's first attempt. St Theresa's had decided to hold the *posada* as their contribution to the annual Victorian Christmas Extravaganza and the plan, or at least the hope, was that after the singing and the breaking of the *piñata*, all the pilgrims would leave Main Street and move over to Maple Street and enjoy the extravaganza. Every house on Maple Street was lit to the hilt with Christmas lights, and almost every house offered some kind of tableau. This year it had almost gotten out of hand. The Maids a-Milking were really going to try to milk that cow while the lords were leaping all around them. How they could do that every fifteen minutes while people walked up and down the street, gaping at the exhibits, she didn't know, and was afraid they didn't either.

They weren't the only ones taking the 'extravaganza' seriously. Mimes, Morris dancers, a barbershop quartet, a storyteller, a group wearing Dickinson-era costumes while singing Christmas carols, even Ebenezer Scrooge, were all making an appearance. Evan Wilson played Scrooge every year. He came out on his balcony, dressed in a bathrobe and stocking cap, shaking his fist at the children, telling them to 'get off my property.' Then he'd throw down gold-wrapped chocolates. The children loved it. Mary didn't know how he did it. Evan was usually such a mild-mannered man.

The *posada* would come down Maple Street, turn the corner on 11th, a block before the extravaganza started, continue up Main Street and stop on the church lawn, where the manger scene was set up, just to the right of the church steps. Joseph, portrayed by Stan Moss, led the procession, walking alongside Luanne Mendosa who portrayed Mary. She was perched worryingly on the Bates' donkey, an animal that wasn't mild in the least. Shepherds walked behind, followed by the Three Kings, who had thankfully not been able to come up with any camels. They were mounted instead on Irma Long's three most elderly and unflappable mares. The townspeople came next, singing traditional Mexican songs, and in this case, traditional English Christmas hymns as well, pausing only to howl in disappointment each time they were refused entry by one of the inns along the route. They should make it to St Theresa's manger scene in – Mary checked her watch – about fifteen minutes. The crowd was already moving her way.

So many people. She thought back to the first extravaganza, over twenty years ago. She'd managed that one, too, but the crowd had been considerably smaller. Only a few houses were lit that year, the entertainment limited to a living manger scene, a barbershop quartet on the Martins' lawn and the high-school choir. Where they had set up she couldn't remember. What she did remember was her middle-school home economics class making Christmas cookies. How Samuel had laughed when he'd seen the few she'd brought home. Their nieces and nephews hadn't minded how uneven they were or how sloppy the frosting. They'd gleefully added them to the Christmas breakfast Mary and Sam hosted every year. Sam had been gone some seven years now, but she still missed him dreadfully. Her days teaching home economics were also gone but not missed nearly as much. However, she still presided over the extravaganza, which now attracted visitors from all over the state. She sighed and shifted her weight. Why she'd allowed herself to be talked into coordinating this mob scene 'just one more year,' she had no idea. Yes, she did. It was either that or prance around in a reindeer costume. The choice had been clear. She surveyed the crowd and checked her cell phone again. All quiet.

'Mrs McGill?'

Mary looked down at Dalia Mendosa. The child had climbed the steps without her noticing.

'Dalia. What are you doing here? Aren't you supposed to be over at the church waiting for the *posada* to arrive?'

Dalia nodded. 'I was. We have the doll and everything, but he won't get up and I don't know what to do. Ronaldo's there. He's holding the doll.'

Mary surveyed the ten-year-old and shook her head slightly. 'What are you talking about?'

'It's Doctor Mathews. He's lying in the manger, asleep, I think. He won't get up.'

The child's eyes were large and a little frightened.

'Old Doctor Mathews? The vet? Are you sure?'

Dalia nodded, her large green eyes wide with apprehension. 'We called his name, but he won't get up.'

Oh, Lord. Cliff Mathews. He'd been so good too. Why did he have to pick this night, of all nights, to fall off the wagon? Why did he have to pass out in the manger? She clicked on her cell phone. 'Tony? I think we have a problem. Can you meet me at the manger? No. St Theresa's. Now. Cliff's been drinking again and it looks like he's passed out in it. The *posada* will be here in just a few minutes. I can't get him out of there by myself.' She listened for a moment. 'Thanks.' She hung up and took Dalia's hand. 'Let's go.'

They crossed the street with some difficulty. People were everywhere. Strollers decorated with battery pack Christmas lights were pushed by parents who weren't looking where they were going; dogs on leashes, even though outlawed, wound themselves between people's legs, doing their best to trip someone. The traffic lights were off tonight and the sea of people that flowed in all directions, laughing, talking, kept Mary and Dalia from making much progress. Finally, they stood in front of the church. The lawn was clear of spectators. There was, so far, nothing to see, but as soon as the *posada* got closer . . . Was that singing coming their way?

'Where is he?'

Dalia pointed to a rough-built lean-to, open to the street. Inside, where the manger was set up and the animals were housed, was in shadow. Spotlights were ready, sitting at both the inside and outside corners, for the arrival of Mary. The place would radiate light, the North Star would shine from the oak tree and angels would appear. But for now, everything was in shadow. Mary could just make out the outline of what looked like a goat. It bleated as she came up. A couple of other animals hung their heads over small pens, staring at the figure overflowing from the manger in the middle of the display, waiting for Mary and Joseph to appear.

'Cliff Mathews, you promised.' Mary let go of Dalia's hand

and marched up to the manger. 'Get up right this minute. How you could—'

She stopped abruptly. Cliff wasn't going to get up, now or ever again. He lay in the middle of the manger, eyes staring up at nothing, the shadows failing to hide the front of his gray hoodie, stained bright red.

TWO

'So, there you are.'

The voice made Mary jump. She wheeled around. Father D'Angelo bore down on them.

'I told you two to stay where I could see you. I was scared to death. Why did you— Oh. Hello, Mrs McGill.'

'Good evening, Father.' Mary glanced down at Dalia. Why had she been out here, with the animals, unsupervised? It didn't matter. There were other things more pressing, like a whole procession of people following Mary and Joseph on their quest to find a place for Mary to have her baby. It couldn't be here. There was no longer any room in this inn, either. 'We have a problem. Can you call St Mark's right now and tell them we are rerouting the *posada* over to their crèche? They're right around the corner. Theirs is a big one, so please, do it now.'

The priest looked for a second as if he didn't understand, then, as her words sunk in, he began to shake his head. 'No.' He shook it emphatically as he thought about it. 'Why? We've planned this for months. It's our first. Why would we . . .'

Dalia moved closer to Mary and reached for her hand as she watched Father D'Angelo. It gave him his first view of the manger. His head stopped shaking and he drew in his breath with a hiss. 'What's that? There's someone in the manger.' He took a step closer. 'He has to get out. We can't—'

Mary's hand closed on Dalia's. She pulled her close and stepped in front of Father D'Angelo, blocking his assault on poor, dead Cliff. She thrust Dalia at him, making sure the child had her back to the gruesome scene. 'Please, Father. Take the children inside and make that call. Tony's on his way, and I'm going to call Dan right now. Or Hazel.' She looked around. Where was Ronaldo? He needed to go . . . There. Standing beside the sheep pen. One sheep had her head over the railing, watching them with what seemed to be great anxiety.

'Dan? Dan Dunham? Hazel? She's the dispatcher for nine-one-one. What are you saying?' Father D'Angelo quit trying to move around Dalia and stared at Mary.

She gestured toward the children and once more gently pushed Dalia toward the priest. The children needed to get out of there before the police arrived; before they realized what they'd found wasn't a living, breathing drunk but a very dead man. 'Ronaldo's got the baby Jesus doll. They can put it in St Mark's manger.'

The eight-year-old boy watched them with the same anxious expression as the sheep. Eyes wide, seemingly trying to decide if he should be scared, he clutched something tightly to his chest; something smaller than the doll, something that squirmed. Mary squinted to see better, but the lighting was dim. What . . . No time. She'd find out later. She turned back toward the priest. 'Maybe you, or one of the ladies, can take them over to St Mark's. Only, as soon as their mother gets off that retched donkey we're going to need you back here.'

Father D'Angelo took another look at the body in the manger, crossed himself, walked the few steps over to Ronaldo and reached for his hand. The boy backed up a step and clutched his bundle tighter.

'It's all right. You can take the doll with you. We're just going to St Mark's. We'll meet your mother there.'

Ronaldo stared at the priest but he didn't move and didn't speak.

Father D'Angelo glanced over at Mary, a helpless look in his eyes. He'd always seemed so calm, so collected when they'd worked together on events like the Cancer Run or the Special Olympics, but he wasn't collected now. However, Mary suspected he'd never found a dead body before.

She sighed. It was equally obvious he'd never taught school. 'Ronaldo, please go with Father right now. Dalia's going also. The *posada*'s not coming here, and you have to hurry to catch them.'

She was interrupted by a whimpering noise. The bundle Ronaldo held so tightly squirmed harder.

'What's that?' Father D'Angelo bent down.

Ronaldo backed up farther, pushing against the sheep pen.

'That's not the doll.' Mary also took a step closer to the cowering child.

'It's a puppy.' Dalia sounded torn between pride and fright. 'We saved it.'

Mary and Father D'Angelo turned toward her as one. 'You what?'

'Saved it. We came out to make sure the doll was here, ready for when Mom rode up on the donkey, and heard the puppy crying. That's when we saw Doctor Mathews. I called to him, but he wouldn't get up. Ronaldo picked up the puppy and I went to get Mrs McGill.' She paused, as if she hadn't yet told the most important part.

Mary held her breath. Surely they hadn't seen . . .

'It's black and white.' Dalia looked at her brother, as if for corroboration.

Mary let her breath out in a sigh of relief.

Ronaldo nodded and shifted the wiggling puppy.

'We can't . . .' the priest stammered.

'You have to.' Mary put as much determination in her voice as she'd ever used in her seventh-grade home economics classes. 'Take the children and the puppy. We'll sort it all out later.' She reached into her pocket and pulled out her cell phone. 'I'm going to call Hazel now. We'll get the procession rerouted, but the people at St Mark's need to know they're about to get several hundred people they hadn't counted on.'

Father D'Angelo took another quick look at the body in the manger, took each child by a shoulder and herded them back toward the vestibule of the church. 'I'll go right now,' he tossed over his shoulder.

Mary sighed and turned back toward the body as she clicked open her cell phone. Cliff. Poor old Cliff. What could possibly have happened?

'Hey.'

She almost dropped her cell. 'Tony! You scared me half to death.'

The tall, dark-haired man grinned. 'Sorry about that. Where's Cliff?'

Mary took a deep breath and let it out slowly as she'd learned in her Silver Sneakers exercise class, hoping it would keep her hand from shaking. 'In the manger.'

'In the— He would pick tonight.' Tony turned slightly to stare at the crumpled body. 'He's really out cold. Do we need an ambulance?'

'We need the coroner. He'd dead.'

She ignored the shocked look on Tony's face and spoke into her cell phone. 'Hazel? Mary. We have a problem. I'm at St Theresa's and Cliff Mathews is dead. In the manger. Send Dan and the troops and can you call Sister Margaret Anne? She's walking with the *posada*, but she's got her cell. Her number should be on your sheet. Good. They have to go to St Mark's. Don't let them come here. Father D'Angelo is going over there right now.' She paused. 'No. I don't know what happened, but the last thing we need is a few hundred people milling around while Dan and his people try to find out. Thanks, Hazel.'

Tony hadn't taken his eyes off the body. 'Where are my kids? They were supposed to wait in the church, with the choir, until the procession arrived. Are they still here? Inside?'

'They're with Father D'Angelo.' Mary paused.

Tony continued to stare down at the body as if transfixed. He'd made no move to touch anything but seemed to be taking in all of the details.

Mary had seen all the details she wanted or needed. 'I asked Father to take them with him to St Mark's and stay there until Luanne gets off the donkey.'

Tony managed to tear his eyes away from the awful tableau. 'She's the most stubborn woman – she's due any minute. Why she insisted on riding a donkey half a mile up the street is beyond me.' He looked back at the body. 'Did you find him?'

Mary hesitated. Tony wasn't going to like this. 'No. Actually' – she took a deep breath again – 'Dalia came and got me. She and Ronaldo found him. They thought he was asleep.'

Tony's face got red and he seemed to sputter. 'My kids saw that? That old man lying there – blood all over his . . . Why weren't they in the church, with the choir kids?'

'I don't know. I don't know anything right now. The children are all right. I don't think they realize what happened, and Father got them out of here so quickly they can't have seen much. Right now let's concentrate on keeping anyone else from seeing this.'

It took a minute but Tony finally nodded. 'Can you wait here? I'll head down the street and make sure the procession goes the other way. Dan should be here any minute.'

'Please go. I'll be fine here.'

'My kids – you're sure they're—'

'Father had them in tow. They should all be at St Mark's by now.'

Tony took another look at the manger and shook his head wonderingly. 'Why would anyone want to hurt poor old Cliff?' He turned and almost ran out of the lean-to.

Mary kept her back to the contents of the manger. She felt a little shaky and another look at Cliff's dead body wasn't going to help her feel better. Why would anyone hurt Cliff, indeed? He was a wonderful vet in his day; everyone in town said so. Everyone loved him. At least they had before he'd started drinking and had all that trouble. She sighed heavily. But he'd never been a mean drunk. Just a sad one.

A tear started to form. She blinked rapidly. She couldn't cry now, no matter how much she felt like it. They had a lot of the evening left and at least a thousand people wandering around the six blocks of lighted houses, most with tableaus on their front lawns, through the downtown displays and in and out of the restaurants. Crime scenes weren't in keeping with Christmas pageants. There was no way to keep this one a secret but maybe she could . . . She dialed again. 'Wilma. Have you got the choir in there? I need them. Now. Can you get them out here? They need to march down the street, singing, and meet the *posada*. Then they can lead it back to St Mark's.' She moved the cell phone a little away from her ear. 'You heard right. The *posada*'s going to St Mark's, and I need a distraction to keep people away from here. Those kids can be my Pied Piper.' She listened. 'We've had an emergency, that's why. I'll tell you about it later. Right now, I need those kids out on the street. Get their candles lit and get them out here. Hurry.'

Almost immediately, the church doors opened and children,

dressed in long red robes topped with white Buster Brown collars, gilded halos bobbing precariously above their heads, spilled out onto the church steps, laughing and talking. As one, they looked at the manger scene, chattering. Wilma Goodman, her graying bun starting to unravel a little, clapped for attention.

'We'll start our first song, children, and walk down the steps while you sing. Turn on your flashlight candles now and hold them just the way I showed you. Then I want you to follow me down the street, four by four. Just as we practiced. Now. On my count of three.'

The children formed themselves into rows of four, most quit their giggling and, on Wilma's count, started to sing.

A shiver ran through Mary as she recognized the hymn. 'Away in a Manger.'

How appropriate.

THREE

'Tony, I'm going to have to talk to them.' Dan Dunham, Santa Louisa's chief of police and Mary's nephew by marriage, faced Tony Mendosa and sighed.

Tony was out of breath from his sprint to St Mark's and back, but he had enough left to flatly refuse to allow Dan to talk to Dalia and Ronaldo. 'They're little. They don't know anything and all you'll do is scare them to death.'

'Tony.' Mary didn't think she'd ever heard Dan's voice more patient. 'We have to know why the kids left the choir room and what time they came out to the manger scene. Was anyone there . . . Was Cliff already . . . Did they touch him? We have to know what they saw. You and Luanne can be there the whole time.' He turned to Mary. 'Will you come? The kids love you.'

Mary didn't know what to say. The Mendosa family lived only two houses down from her, and the Mendosa children visited her kitchen often. They seemed to have a sixth sense when it came to cookie baking day, but she was still needed out on the street. The *posada* hadn't turned the corner yet. Many of the other displays were just getting started and she still didn't know where that blasted cow had gone.

'I can't. You can't have the kids yet, either.' She looked around. A crowd had started to gather to watch the *posada* appear, only now they stared at the police stringing yellow crime-scene tape that cordoned off the church lawn around the manger and started murmuring among themselves. The word would go out any minute that something not scripted was happening at St Theresa's, and Maple Street would be deserted. Every person able to squeeze anywhere close would be over here, wanting to know what happened. Not a good idea. 'We need to finish the *posada* and all the other events, find that damn cow and get this crowd out of here without completely overwhelming your crime scene. The kids are waiting for Luanne. Tony needs to go back there. I need to be back on the library steps and try to make sure nothing else goes wrong. The way things have gone so far, that doesn't seem likely. When this is over, Luanne, Tony and the kids can all come to my house. We'll wait for you. Bring Ellen. I'll make coffee.'

'You better have more than coffee.' Dan's face was grim but he nodded. The kids could wait. 'Tony, don't let them out of your sight. I have no idea what they saw, but if they caught even a glimpse of whoever did this . . . Don't leave them alone for a moment.'

Tony visibly paled.

Mary's heart pounded. If those children saw the killer . . . No. They couldn't have. They saw Cliff in the manger, though, and they saw the puppy. Where had it come from, anyway? Thoughts of the puppy vanished as a new noise intruded. What was that? Mary listened. The *posada*? The singing was close, too close. This wasn't the *posada*; it was another noise – laughter. A lot of laughter.

Mary glanced at Dan. It seemed he'd also heard it. They walked toward the front of the lean-to. A Jersey cow leisurely trotted down the street, swinging her head, making the broken lead rope hanging from her halter sway. She looked with seeming curiosity at the crowd gathered around the yellow police tape, loudly wondering what had happened in the manger scene. Almost as one, they turned their attention to the cow.

'You'd think they've never seen a cow before.'

'Some of them probably haven't, and I'll bet no one has seen one leading a *posada*.' For that was exactly what was happening. The cow ambled down the center of the street, turning right on cue toward St Mark's. Rounding the corner, right behind her, came the St Theresa's Children's Choir, halos swaying, flashlights making their faces glow like angels in an antique Bible, belting out 'We Three Kings' with gusto. Mary, perched precariously on her donkey, Joseph right beside her, came next, followed by four shepherds trying to keep a band of six sheep together with the help of Ben McCullough's black-and-white Border collie. The Three Wise Men, mounted on Irma's Arabian mares, were close behind, followed by a crowd of what Mary supposed were pilgrims, most of them in medieval costumes, singing 'O Little Town of Bethlehem' at the top of their lungs. They paused as they got to St Theresa's, puzzled when the cow, Joseph, Mary, the donkey and the angels headed toward St Mark's. Most looked over toward Mary, who waved them on. It wasn't until Sister Margaret Anne appeared, arm raised in a forward motion, that they obediently fell back into rows and, with only furtive glances at the police occupying the lean-to, disappeared around the corner.

FOUR

Mary sat in her overstuffed reading chair, shoes off, slippers on, surveying the people in her living room. She'd begun to think she'd never get away. Did the straw go on the fire truck, which was in charge of tearing down the inns along the *posada* route, could the maids leave the cow overnight in the Blake's garage . . . that one was easy. No. But finally all the questions stopped, the streets were empty and she was home. Luanne sat on her sofa, a child on each side, the puppy on what was left of her lap. It was asleep. The children weren't, but their yawns and half-closed eyes gave signs sleep wasn't far away. Her niece, Ellen McKenzie Dunham, was in the kitchen getting coffee, hot cocoa and the chocolate-mint cookies Mary had made that morning. Ellen. Her only blood relative left in this small town. There had been only one streetlight when Mary was growing up, and only one grade school. Today there were three grade schools, a much expanded middle school and more street lights than she thought necessary. The growth was largely due to the vineyard and wineries that had sprung up all over the county. They brought in large groups of tourists but the town remained small enough so she still knew almost everyone who lived here. Growth had been good for Ellen, a talented and hardworking real estate agent. It hadn't been as kind to Dan. A growth in population usually meant an increase in crime, and the grey that sprinkled Dan's light brown hair and mustache testified to the truth of that. He should be here any time now. He'd better hurry up if he wanted to talk to the children.

Tony paced.

'Tony, for heaven's sake, sit down. Or, better yet, go help Ellen with the drinks. Dan will be here soon. The kids can tell him what little they know and then you can all go home.'

Luanne moved one of Mary's pillows into the small of her back and leaned against it. The children moved closer to her. The puppy slept on.

'He'd better hurry. The kids aren't going to last much longer.'

Both children looked at him with half-closed eyes, as if determined to prove him right. Ronaldo's head slumped against his mother's arm.

The front door opened and Dan entered. He looked as tired as the children. The sight of Ellen coming out of the kitchen, carrying a tray filled with white porcelain mugs and the cookie plate, visibly brightened him. She smiled at him, walked across the room and set the tray down on the coffee table in front of the children. 'I put marshmallows in your cups. Is that OK?'

The two children sat up straight, their now wide-awake eyes darting from their mother to the cups and cookies. Ellen picked up a mug and walked over to Dan. 'Here. You look like you need coffee. Let the kids get a sip or two of their cocoa down before you start grilling them.'

'I don't grill children.'

'Oh, yeah?'

'Yeah.' Dan smiled, gave her a quick kiss on the cheek and took his mug.

Mary watched with satisfaction. It was a good marriage. They'd both had problems with their first marriages, but this one was working well. She glanced at Tony, who scowled at Luanne. Worry about her and the child she carried showed on his face. He adored the other two and was the only father they remembered, and they seemed to love him back. However, he had a hot temper and a tendency to think his way was the only way. She hoped this marriage worked out as well as Ellen and Dan's, but she sometimes had her doubts.

Dan set his mug on the tray and squatted down in front of the coffee table. 'Nice puppy. Where'd you find him?'

The children looked at each other then up at their mother.

'Tell him.' She squeezed Dalia a little closer and dropped a kiss on the top of Ronaldo's head.

'By the sheep.' Dalia squirmed until she sat up straighter, while holding her mug tight against her front.

Mary held her breath, but the child didn't spill a drop.

'He was crying.'

Dan shifted his weight slightly. 'Is that why you left the choir room? Did you hear him?'

Ronaldo shook his head. 'No. You couldn't hear him until you got out there, where the manger was.'

'Then why did you go?'

Mary watched Dan carefully. She'd never seen him work with children before and was surprised at how neutral he kept his voice and how quiet he kept his body. Nothing there to frighten two small people who'd already been frightened enough. Dalia, in particular, seemed to be coming around.

'We wanted to make sure the doll would fit in the manger. Ronaldo couldn't remember if anyone had tried it.' She paused and glanced over at her brother. 'I couldn't either.'

Dan nodded. He reached for a cookie, picked up three of them and held out two. 'You guys get a cookie yet?'

Dalia hesitated but Ronaldo reached out. He took one before he looked up at his mother. She sighed and nodded. Dalia transferred her now almost-empty mug to the coffee table and took the other one.

'So, what happened when you got out by the manger?'

'We saw someone in it.' Dalia talked around a mouth full of

cookie, swallowed quickly, picked her mug back up and washed the crumbs down with the last of the cocoa. She gave no sign of wanting to say more.

Dan's jaw tightened. 'What did you do then?' He turned to Ronaldo who, up to now, had said nothing. It didn't look as if he was going to begin now, either. Dan turned back to Dalia. 'Did you walk over to the manger?'

She shook her head. 'At first, we stood there. We didn't know what to do. He wasn't supposed to sleep there.'

'Could you see who it was?'

Dalia shook her head again. 'Not right then. That part came after we heard the puppy and the other man ran out.'

Mary forgot to breathe. They'd seen the murderer. Tony stopped pacing and stared down at the children. Luanne gathered both of them tighter. She bit her lip, hard, and stared at Dan. He rocked back on his heels a little and waved his hand toward Tony, who looked as if he was about to speak.

'OK. You watched a man leave, is that right?'

The children nodded in unison.

'Then you went over to the manger?'

They shook their heads together. 'We heard the puppy.'

'He was crying real loud.' Ronaldo seemed to come alive in his concern for the dog. He turned toward his mother and laid a hand on the puppy's head. It looked up, as if to see who was there, seemed reassured and dropped his head back on Luanne's lap and closed his eyes once more. 'We started looking all around. We found him, too. He was in with the sheep.'

'Did you climb over that fence into the pen?' There was not only disapproval in Luanne's voice, but a tinge of horror.

'Didn't have to.' Ronaldo looked at his mother with wide-open eyes. 'He was right by the gate. We just opened it a little, grabbed him and backed out.' He paused and gave them all a proud smile. 'I put him under my sweatshirt and he liked it. I know, because he got real quiet.'

So did everyone.

Finally, Mary spoke. 'Then what happened?'

'We went over to the manger.' Dalia leaned over and started to rub the puppy's ears. There was a tremor in her voice, and Mary was certain tears pooled in her eyes. The child had seen more than she thought. Should they be putting her through this?

Mary could see just the side of Dan's face, but it was enough. He looked as agonized as she felt. So did Luanne. Tony looked as if he was going to stop this. But they couldn't stop. Not now. The children had seen something – a man, quite possibly the murderer. The next question had to be asked.

'Dalia, honey, I know this is hard, but I'm counting on you. You walked over to the manger and then what?'

'We saw Doctor Mathews lying there, all crumpled up. He had blood on his sweatshirt.'

Mary's stomach lurched. Luanne's hand shook as she put her coffee mug back on the tray. A strangulated sound came from behind her. Tony. He'd walked around behind her sofa and stretched out his arms along the top, as if trying to envelop all three of them.

'Can you go on?' Dan no longer looked neutral. The lines around his mouth had tightened and his eyes had narrowed. He looked like a man fighting profound anger and losing.

'We didn't know what to do. That's when I told Ronaldo to hide back by the sheep and I'd go find you.' She lifted her head and looked into Mary's eyes. 'I knew you'd know what to do.'

Dan glanced at her and the lines around his mouth briefly softened into a sliver of a smile before he turned back to the children. 'Why didn't you go into the church and find Father D'Angelo?'

'We were scared.' Ronaldo looked as if he still was.

'With good reason.' Dan nodded. 'But the church was closer than Mrs McGill and the library. Why didn't you go in there?'

The children looked at each other. Ronaldo closed his mouth with an expression that clearly said he wasn't saying another word. Dalia's voice wasn't much louder than a whisper. 'Because we were scared to. The man who ran out?'

Dan nodded, encouraging her to go on. 'Did you recognize him?'

Dalia nodded then stopped.

'For heaven's sake, Dal, tell us.' Tony apparently couldn't hold it in any longer, but it didn't help.

The frightened look in Dalia's eyes intensified.

Luanne sent Tony a warning look and crunched Dalia closer to her side. 'It's OK, baby. We know how hard this is, but we have to know. Who did you think the man was?'

Dalia took a deep breath and, as she let it out, the name came with it. 'We think it was Father D'Angelo.'

FIVE

Mary's living room had never felt so still. It was as if time somehow stopped, leaving them all frozen in place.

It was Dan who finally broke the spell, only his voice didn't sound quite right. Cracked, somehow. 'Why did you think it was Father D'Angelo? Did you get a good look at him?'

Dalia and Ronaldo glanced at each other across their mother, who had them each squashed tightly into her sides.

'He had on a hood.' Dalia made the simple statement with confidence and Ronaldo nodded his agreement.

Dan waited a moment and took in a long breath and let it out before speaking again. 'A hood. Is that the only reason you thought it was Father D'Angelo?'

Dalia nodded. 'He doesn't usually wear it up 'cause it makes him look like something out of a scary movie. That's what he says.'

Father D'Angelo was a Franciscan priest. He wore the centuries-old long brown robe tied at the waist with a heavy rope and sandals. Mary couldn't remember ever seeing his hood – they called it a cowl, didn't they? – up either. She didn't attend St Theresa's so only knew Father D'Angelo from the events she helped put on for the church. He'd always seemed like such a nice man, never angry, so good with the children. A bit frazzled from time to time, especially when they were setting up for the church bazaar, but that certainly wasn't abnormal. Or frightening. He couldn't have . . . could he?

'Father D'Angelo never murdered anyone.' Tony's faced was flushed with anger, his hands rolled up into fists. 'He wouldn't harm a fly. You kids don't know what you're talking about.'

Luanne pulled the children tighter, if that were possible. Dalia gasped; Ronaldo gave a little groan; even the puppy yelped.

'For heaven's sake, Tony. They only said what they saw. There's no need to yell at them.'

'I wasn't yelling.' Tony glared at them then walked away from behind the sofa to stand behind Dan. 'Only, they're wrong. I don't know who they saw, but it wasn't the good Father.'

Dan sat back a little on his heels before pushing himself to his feet. He never took his eyes off the children, who had theirs firmly fixed on Tony. They both looked scared.

Dan sighed. 'Tony, let the kids tell us what they think they saw. Scaring them to death won't get us anywhere.'

Tony stiffened; the veins in his neck stood out.

He's going to explode.

But he didn't. His hands unclenched, he filled his lungs with air and let it out slowly, his shoulders dropped and he nodded. 'Sorry. It's just that— Go on. Tell Dan what you saw. I'm not going to say another thing.'

Luanne smiled at him and relaxed as well. The kids didn't, much.

Dan studied them a moment then smiled. He got no smiles back. 'OK. Tell me again about the puppy. Do you know why it was there? Was' – he glanced up at Tony – 'the person you saw looking for it?'

The children looked at each other. Dalia shrugged. Ronaldo stayed mute. Dan sighed.

'All right. I think that's all for tonight. Luanne, could you bring the kids—'

'Not the police station.' Ellen hadn't said anything until now, but there was no maneuvering room in her voice. 'Aunt Mary won't mind if Luanne brings them back here, or you could go to their house.'

'Why don't you do that?' Luanne looked at Tony, silently asking if he agreed, or perhaps telling him that was what was going to happen.

Mary wasn't sure.

'They're exhausted, and they'll feel more comfortable at home. Right after lunch tomorrow?'

Dan nodded and picked up his coffee cup. 'I'll be there. Right now, I've got to get back.' He drained his cup and handed it to Ellen, along with a quick kiss on the cheek. 'Don't wait up.' He turned back toward Luanne but made sure he included Tony. 'Please don't question the kids. Don't talk about it with them at all, unless they get upset and need to talk. The more you question them, the more they'll forget what they really saw.' He turned back toward the children, as if reluctant to leave them, but Ronaldo's head had dropped to his chest and his eyes closed, the cocoa mug dangling from one hand. Dan shook his head and turned to go.

He got to the door just as it opened.

'Hi. We thought we'd find you here. What happened out there tonight?'

Karl and Pat Bennington walked into the room, shedding coats as they came. Pat enveloped Mary in a huge hug, wiggled her fingers at Ellen and zeroed in on Dan. 'You're not leaving, are you? We want to know what happened to Cliff. Is it true he was murdered?'

Dan looked at Pat, then at Ellen. The Benningtons were their best friends, and Pat, as well as Ellen, didn't believe for one moment the police had any reason to keep anything from them. The press, of course, and other townspeople, maybe, but they were family, or as good as, so, of course, he should confide in them. 'Oh, a puppy.' Pat walked over to the sofa and bent down to touch the puppy on its head. 'Isn't he – she? – cute. Where did you get him?' She touched Ronaldo on the top of his head as well, but he didn't look up. Dalia looked at her through half-closed eyes but said nothing. Pat grinned at Luanne. 'So you're going to have two little things to housebreak.'

Luanne laughed, but it didn't last long. 'We're not keeping it.'

That woke the children.

'We saved her. We can't let her go now.' Dalia's eyes started to pool and she reached out for the puppy.

'I got him out of the sheep pen. He would have gotten trampled if I hadn't. He needs me.' Ronaldo's eyes had snapped open. He glared at his mother, his face set in stone. He also tried to grab the puppy.

It yelped.

Karl had followed Pat to the sofa. He reached out for the puppy and, without a word, the children let him have it. He spoke softly, stroked its long, black, curly ears while he held it in his other hand then turned it over. 'Sorry, Dalia, she is a he. Where did you say you got him?'

'The girls will tell you all about it. I've got to get back.' Dan looked at his phone, texted something, struggled into his jacket and reached once again for the door. He paused, his hand on the knob. 'I can understand you not wanting to keep the puppy, Luanne, but someone needs to. I want it close, at least for the time being. I suppose it's possible it strayed into the manger scene by itself, but I think it's a whole lot more likely it was brought there. I'd sort of like to know by who, and why.' He looked at the kids for a minute then smiled. 'So, keep him safe at least for tonight. OK? I'll see you guys tomorrow.' The door closed with a firm click behind him.

The children looked at their mother with hope written clearly on their faces. She shifted the pillow behind her back and sighed. 'He's too young to be housebroken. I really can't . . .'

'Your mom's not doing anything else today, or tomorrow, either. She's done way too much. That damn donkey jolting her all over – we're not keeping the dog.'

Both faces started to crumble.

'Why don't I take him home tonight and then tomorrow, we'll see,' Karl said.

All eyes turned toward Karl, even Pat's.

'You'd do that?' Tony looked torn between relief and skepticism.

'I'm a vet, remember? I have a clinic and am well equipped to house a puppy. We'll give him a nice, comfortable bed and lots of dinner. He'll be fine. Then, tomorrow, after you talk to Dan, we'll see.' He looked at the puppy, turned him over again, pushed his ears back and ran a soft finger over his nose and down the back of his head. He picked up each front paw and examined it before letting the puppy withdraw it. 'I'll need to look him over, anyway, to make sure he's healthy – all that.'

He'd already done a pretty good job of looking him over. Why? Professional compulsion? Or something else? Karl had a strange look in his eye.

'Luanne, I think you need to take these children straight home to bed.' Mary looked at her a little more closely than at Tony.

'You all look as if you could use a little time in bed. Go on, scoot. All of you. We'll see you tomorrow.'

The yawn Luanne gave was testimony Mary was right. She smiled, reached out for Tony's hand and got to her feet. 'Come on, kids. Let's go home. We'll visit the puppy tomorrow.'

'Promise?' Ronaldo scrambled to his feet as well and grabbed his mother's other hand.

She nodded.

Dalia sat for a moment, evidently thinking it over. Finally, she pushed herself up but bypassed her mother and walked over to Karl. She placed her hand on the puppy's little head then bent down and gave him a kiss. His tongue went out in search of her and landed on her nose. She laughed. Tony didn't.

'His name is Sampson,' she told Karl.

'How do you know?' Ronaldo let go of his mother to stand beside Dalia. He gave the puppy one last pet as well.

'Because I just named him.'

Mary almost laughed at the finality of that statement. However, now wasn't the time for a discussion on the merits of a name for a puppy they probably weren't going to keep, and Ronaldo's mouth was open with what Mary was sure was a protest.

'Where are your coats?' That ought to serve to get them moving.

'Mary, can you come over tomorrow when Dan comes? Before would be even better. I have some questions . . .' Luanne gave a quick glance at the children.

Mary nodded. 'We do have a few things to talk about. I'll see you all then. Tony?'

'Probably not. We're starting to prune the vineyards, and I have to be there to supervise the crew. I'll try to make it home for lunch, but I don't know yet.'

Mary nodded and held the door as they all walked out into a night that had started to spit rain.

'Hurry, it's starting.' Tony, clutching Luanne by one arm, shooed the kids ahead of them. He glanced back, gave a small wave and resumed guiding Luanne down the sidewalk.

Mary watched until they turned onto their front walk before she closed the door and turned to face the room.

Ellen made the rounds with the coffeepot. She poured the last drop into Karl's cup. 'I'm going to make another pot. I'm pretty sure we're going to need it. Don't say one word, any of you, until I get back.'

Mary walked across the room, sank into her chair and picked up the oversized NPR cup she always used.

'What on earth happened tonight?' Pat leaned forward slightly from the seat she'd taken on the sofa. 'I've never heard so many rumors in my life. Is Cliff really dead? Murdered?'

'How did that cow get into the act?' Leave it to Karl to zero in on an animal.

Mary almost laughed, but it wasn't really very funny. 'The Maids a-Milking brought the cow. They were going to try to milk it during their performance. Evidently, the cow took one look at all the people acting out the song and decided she wanted no part of it. How she came to lead the *posada*, I have no idea. Did anyone ever catch her?'

'Bobby Connors did. Tell us about Cliff.'

Ellen walked back into the room, crossed it and settled herself in the rocking chair beside the TV. She picked up the full mug of coffee she'd put down beside it. 'Coffee's perking. Yes. Tell us about Cliff. Was he really murdered? Did the Mendosa kids really see the murderer?'

A shudder ran through Mary. They'd seen something – or someone – and whatever, or whoever it was, it wasn't good.

'Yes. Cliff was murdered. I don't know how, but there was blood all over the front of his sweatshirt. The coppery smell filled the air.' She stopped, reliving the horrible scene. She fervently hoped the children hadn't seen as much as she had.

'Blood on the front of his sweatshirt?'

Mary nodded. 'A lot of it.'

Karl absently stroked the puppy as he watched her. 'That means he probably wasn't shot. If he was, he'd have fallen backward into the manger and all of the blood would have been around the exit wound. Maybe someone stabbed him with something and pulled it back out.'

The rest of them just looked at him.

'That was more information than we needed,' said Pat, finally.

'Why would anyone kill poor old Cliff? He wouldn't harm a

fly, and now that he'd quit drinking . . .' Ellen paused to wipe the corner of her eye. 'I remember when I was a kid and my cat got hit by a car. Cliff was wonderful, let me hold Fluffy's paw while he set her back leg, kept talking to me the whole time, telling me she'd be fine. She was, too.'

'Fluffy?' Pat's eyebrow rose.

'Fluffy. I was about Dalia's age.'

'She came up with Sampson.'

'Yes. I wonder where she got that.'

'Bible story.' Mary's tone left no doubt that was as far as they were going with that conversation. 'What I want to know is what Cliff was doing in the empty manger scene. He didn't go to St Theresa's, so he wasn't there to help.'

'Cliff didn't go to any church in town, at least, not on a regular basis.' Karl set the puppy down but immediately picked it back up. 'Mary, do you have any newspaper? I think we're going to need some, and soon.'

Papers were found and the puppy obliged, but the conversation didn't resume.

Ellen looked at her watch and said she'd better go. Unless she would rather have someone with her tonight?

Whatever for? Mary hadn't seen Cliff killed, or the murderer. It was the children she worried about.

Ellen smiled at her aunt as if that was the answer she expected, and pushed herself to her feet, empty mug in hand. So did the Benningtons.

'It's after eleven,' Pat said. 'We need to drop the puppy off at the clinic – unless we're taking him home?'

Karl smiled.

Pat sighed. She hugged Ellen and kissed Mary on the cheek. 'You did your usual wonderful job. Don't know how you do it, but nothing in this town would ever go right without your help. Ellen, you'd better call me.'

Ellen nodded and reached for their mugs. 'I'll just drop these off in the kitchen.'

'You'll do no such thing. I'll take care of them. You get your-selves home. You must be done in, all of you.'

'You're not?' Ellen looked at her aunt with a small smile. 'It won't kill me to stick these in the dishwasher.'

'It won't kill me, either. Get.'

Ellen obediently set the mugs down on the coffee table.

'Don't forget to lock this,' was Ellen's last remark as they went out the front door, running toward cars as they tried to avoid the rapidly increasing rain.

Mary closed the door, locked it, slipped the chain into its holder and leaned her back against it. The stillness suddenly seemed ominous. Why, she couldn't imagine. Unless, of course, the horror of the last several hours was just setting in. Poor Cliff. Why now? He'd been so good for . . . how long? At least two years. He had to be in his late sixties, early seventies. Certainly not a threat to anyone. Any fallout from the mistakes he'd made when he was practicing were long . . . well, maybe not forgotten but certainly tempered by time. Who could possibly have wanted to kill him, and in that bizarre way? Who'd brought the puppy into the manger? Mary agreed with Dan. The puppy hadn't wandered in. It had been brought. By who? Why? She sighed and pushed away from the door. Answers to those questions weren't going to come tonight. She picked up the coffee mugs and headed for the kitchen.

SIX

T he phone rang. Again. Mary paused in the act of slipping another tray of pumpkin/cranberry muffins in the oven and glared at it. Who was it this time? She'd already answered it six times and it was only nine in the morning. Why did all these people think she knew what had happened to poor old Cliff? She shut the oven door and looked at caller ID. Bonnie Blankenship. She needed to talk to her.

'Hello?'

'Mary, it's Bonnie.'

'Bonnie, yes. You're on my list to call. Did you manage to get the dog food?'

'Six cases.' She sounded pleased with herself. 'And, Mary, I talked to Evan at Furry Friends pet shop into donating some dog

collars and leashes. He's going to throw in some food dishes
too.'

'Great. There are so many families out there that have pets
they can't really afford to feed. Adding pet food and supplies to
our Christmas Can Tree Food Drive was brilliant. When can you
deliver what you collected?'

'That's one of the reasons I'm calling. I can't. Todd took our
truck to the hardware store this morning, my van won't start and
all I have is the MG. Can you possibly come out and get this
stuff? I think we can get it all in your trunk.'

Mary blanched. She had to get these muffins over to the Holiday
Bake Sale at the St Stephen's Lutheran Church, be back in time
to meet Dan at the Mendosas and be at city hall to open the
Christmas Can Tree Food Drive by two. They were going to lay
the first layer for the Christmas Can Tree. All the local press
would be there. As chairperson, she was going to put down the
first can. She also needed to make sure the city crew cleaned up
Maple Street as promised. The extravaganza was fun; the mess
it left the next morning wasn't. The homeowners cleaned up their
yards. The city did the street, but not without some persuasion.
She didn't really have time but they needed that pet food. She'd
promised the Humane Society that this year pets would be
included in the yearly food drive, and she'd been the one who'd
pressured Bonnie, as president of the Santa Louisa Pure Breed
Dog Club, to help out. If she didn't have that pet food today,
their contribution wouldn't be in the paper or on the local TV
nightly news, which was part of the deal she'd cut. If she hurried,
she'd have just enough time for a shower before these muffins
had to come out of the oven. She set the timer, told Bonnie she'd
be there in an hour and sighed. She was getting too old for all
this.

There were three new messages on the machine when she got
out of the shower. She didn't bother to listen to them until she
had the muffins cooling on the rack. Her box was already almost
full; these could go in just before she left. The Lutherans were
raising money for the Shelter for Abused Women and their children so they'd have something special for Christmas, a cause
close to Mary's heart. The thought of what those women went
through – but then, most of the causes she helped raise money

for were close to her heart. She'd felt guilty when she had to turn down the chairmanship for their fundraiser, but between the Victorian Christmas Extravaganza and the Christmas Can Tree, she couldn't do it. But she could still help by donating some baked goods, and pumpkin muffins always sold well. Hoping three dozen would be enough, she turned her attention to those messages. One was from the Santa Louisa *Post*, wanting an update on how she thought the Victorian Christmas Extravaganza went. Another was from the city maintenance department. They were on the job, but Dan's people wouldn't let them near St Theresa's, and it wasn't their fault if that part of the street didn't get cleaned. The third was from Evan. Could she stop by and pick up the leashes and things he was going to donate? He couldn't leave the store. No one asked what she knew about Cliff, thank God. Not that he'd been out of her thoughts. She couldn't seem to shake the picture of him, lying there, the blood . . . Why? That was the question that kept going round and round in her head.

If this had been a few years ago, she would have wondered if it had been someone who suffered from one of his 'mistakes.' Was it three years since he'd lost his license? No, closer to five. That was a long time to hold a grudge over what happened to your cat or dog, no matter how beloved they were. Although spaying Alma Maxwell's Champion cocker spaniel bitch, who was in the vet's for a pregnancy exam, was pretty close to unforgivable. Cliff had got her mixed up with another cocker spaniel because he'd been drinking. There had been several others, she couldn't remember them all, but that had been the mistake that had cost him his license. Father D'Angelo had also testified against Cliff at the veterinary board hearing. What was it Cliff had done? Whatever it was, Father D'Angelo's cat had died, and he'd been distraught. How distraught? Father D'Angelo was hardly the murdering type, even though the children had thought the man in the manger scene was him. He'd really liked that cat; he'd told her once it was his best friend. Mary shook her head as if to clear all those memories. That was five years ago. Cliff no longer practiced as a vet; he'd paid for his sins and stayed sober for, well, at least two years now.

If any of those people wanted to kill him, and she wouldn't have been surprised if, at the moment it happened, the thought had crossed more than one mind, they would have done it then. No one would carry a grudge that long, surely? So, what had he done to get himself killed now? She sighed. Dan was going to have his hands full with this one. She put the last few muffins in the box, closed the lid, reached for her car keys and purse and headed out the back door.

SEVEN

Mary slowed the car, conscious of those behind her, impatiently wanting to pick up speed on Hwy 46, that were forced to slow. Her directions said turn left at the Golden Hills Winery. There it was, and there was a left-hand turn lane. She thankfully took it. The winery was large and impressive, and she slowed to admire it, but not for long. She'd been meaning to come out here for some time. Naomi Bliss and her husband, Bill, owned it. She and Naomi were on a committee together at St Mark's, but somehow she'd never made the time to take the tour. It wasn't going to happen today, either. She was already behind schedule.

The women at the Lutheran church fundraiser wanted information along with their muffins. Most of them knew – had known – Cliff and were visibly upset. How could anyone . . . Was he really . . . Was Mary sure he hadn't had a heart attack? He hadn't been well for some time – surely he hadn't . . . Did Mary think . . . Was she really the one who found the body? Only one person mentioned the children. She glossed over the question about them quickly. The rest of the questions she tried to answer as best she could, but she didn't have any real answers. She'd broken away as soon as possible. She wanted to get the pet food Bonnie collected so she could sit in on the interview – she refused to think of it as questioning – Dan was going to conduct with the children. Dan would never bully them, but he needed to find out what they saw. Sometimes the police – well, zeal could take over good sense. She wasn't at all sure those kids knew what they'd seen, and too much questioning was only going to muddy the waters. They were sure about one thing: the puppy. Where he came from, she had no idea, but somehow he was important. So was finding the right street. This area was new, built up over the last year, and she had no idea where she was. She didn't know anyone who lived out here. It was a new experience for her and one she found unsettling.

'Blast.' Mary glanced at her watch. She was running late. She hated being late. Her mother always said— There it was. Mary Beth Lane. Bonnie had said her place was a yellow Spanish-style stucco house set close to the street at the end of the cul-de-sac. A dry fountain and a flower bed that needed weeding sat between the street and the circular drive. A high board fence defined the boundaries of Bonnie's pie-shaped lot, broken only by a wide gate along one side. It opened to reveal Bonnie, waving at Mary.

'What? I can't hear you.' Mary rolled down her window and leaned out a little.

'I said, come in here. It'll be easier to load up the dog food.'

Mary eased the car through the gate. Bonnie trotted ahead, gesturing for her to stop in front of a long, shed-type building. High-pitched barks serenaded Mary as she climbed out of the car.

'These are my kennels.' Bonnie gestured at the long, one-story red board building. There was a white door in the middle, with several windows on each side, trimmed in white boards. The barks came from wire-fenced runs barely visible along the back.

'The food's in here.' Bonnie opened the white door and entered. Mary assumed she was to follow but paused to look around. Bonnie's property backed up to a vineyard, the vines just visible as they rose up the hill. Golden Hills? Probably. There was an old two-story barn inside Bonnie's back fence line. The long metal pole once used to hoist hay bales into the loft was still there. So was an old rooster weather vane perched on top of the barn roof. The dirt driveway she'd entered on ran down the side of the property, past the kennel building, turned in front of the barn and continued down the far side of the property, toward the street, and ended in a parking area of some sort right behind the house. The driveway in front of the kennels was evidently a small spur. Did Bonnie keep dogs in that old barn as well? It would be a good choice. She doubted grapevines cared if dogs barked.

She entered the doorway and was in the middle of a wide aisle that ran the length of the building, chain-link fencing on the side facing her, closed doors into rooms that faced the drive on the other. The fencing on the kennels side was interspersed with gates leading into individual pens separated by smooth board fencing that ended a little more than halfway to the ceiling. Sliding doors open along the back revealed the long-fenced runs visible when she parked. What appeared to be a large exercise yard in the middle separating the runs contained a low automatic water bowl, an assortment of well-chewed toys and four puppies running circles, yelping as they ran. There were two black-and-white ones, one black and one a soft golden brown. The golden-brown pup was delicate looking, with an exaggerated indentation between the nose and forehead and large liquid-brown eyes. It looked at Mary, walked over to the fence, sat and cocked its head to one side. Her heart lurched. *Quit it. The last thing I need is a puppy.*

A single black dog stood by the kennels next to the exercise yard. He stared at Mary without moving, his ears long and silky, feathers on his legs and sides without a tangle.

'Oh. He's beautiful.' Mary didn't know much about dogs, but there was no mistaking this one was special, and knew it.

'That's Champion Seaside Manor Over the Moon. Better known as Bart.' The dog's stub of a tail wagged slightly and his head came up. 'He's used to being admired.' Bonnie's tone changed as she smiled at the dog. 'Aren't you, big boy?' The stub wagged harder. Bonnie's smile faded. 'He's bored. He likes to show. He also likes to breed. He's not scheduled to do either, which is a shame. A couple of bookings or a little prize money would help right now.' She ran an arm over her brow, leaving a faint streak, then looked down at herself. 'I've been cleaning pens.'

That explained it. Bonnie wore jeans that needed a trip to the washer, a sweatshirt that had been there many times and running shoes. Her usually immaculate red hair didn't look as if it had been combed yet this morning. It was the first time Mary had seen Bonnie without a full face of makeup. She had to be some-where in her fifties, and today it showed.

Bonnie flushed a little under Mary's scrutiny and opened a door across the aisle from the majestic black cocker. 'The food's in here. If you'll go pop your trunk, I'll carry it out. I'm sure there will be someone at the can tree who'll unload them for you.'

Mary glanced into the room, which seemed to be a feed and grooming room. There was a bathtub at one end and a table in the middle with a clipper that looked large enough to shear a sheep hanging from a hook above it. The side of the room closest to the door held brown sacks clearly marked 'Stillman's Special Mix Dog Food.' The shelves above them were stacked with clean metal bowls along with pails and measuring scoops. Six cases of canned dog food were piled up close to the door.

'Are you giving us all your dog food?' Surely Bonnie wouldn't do that, but she didn't see any more around.

'I don't feed canned. The dry food in those sacks is specially formulated. We start the puppies out with the little pieces, then they graduate to the adult food, and that's what they get the rest of their lives. Most people buy the kind you get in the grocery store, and that's fine, but these are show dogs.'

That seemed to say it all. Mary nodded, walked out to her car and popped the trunk. Bonnie staggered out of the kennel building with two of the cartons in her arms. She grunted as she thrust them in the trunk and let them drop with a clunk. Mary winced but decided the floor of her trunk was designed to bear heavier burdens than a few cartons of dog food. Bonnie was back almost immediately with two more. This time she seemed a little out of breath.

'Let me get one,' Mary said.

Bonnie barely glanced at Mary. 'I'm fine. I'm used to this.' She disappeared and returned with the last two. This time she leaned against the car, pulled a handkerchief out of her jeans pocket and wiped her hands meticulously.

What should she say? 'You have a wonderful place here.' That seemed safe.

Bonnie smiled for the first time since Mary arrived. 'Thanks. We've only been here a little over a year, but it's working out great.'

'Do you have dogs in the barn as well?'

Bonnie shook her head. 'Too far away from the house. Todd uses it to store inventory for the hardware store.'

'Oh.' Mary couldn't think what else to say. She needed to go, but Bonnie still leaned against her car. Mary tried not to fidget. Finally, Bonnie stood upright. Mary tried not to show her relief as she held out her hand, ready to thank her once more.

However, Bonnie wasn't ready to let her go. 'I'd like to ask you—'

Mary knew what was coming; the only surprise was she hadn't asked before.

'I've heard that Cliff – that you found him . . . Mary, was he really murdered?'

Mary studied Bonnie's face. The red-rimmed eyes. The tired lines around her mouth. Grief? Cliff was Bonnie's vet when she first started to breed cocker spaniels. She was now one of the most successful breeders in Central California and showed her dogs all over the country. She'd even taken one to Westminster. She was a local judge and evidently in much demand. Losing Cliff, whom she'd known much better than Mary, must have been a terrible shock.

Mary hesitated. What should she say? She didn't know much, and what she did know was bound to be on tonight's news and was probably already in the local paper. 'There was blood all over his front, and I don't think it came from natural causes.'

'Who would want to kill poor old Cliff? He suffered enough from all the . . . mistakes he made. I know he was trying to make up for some of it. How, I don't know, but he was always there for me, even after he lost his license. He came out when one of my bitches whelped to make sure she was all right and check out the puppies, even though he knew I'd take them all in to Karl. He loved purebred dogs in particular and felt awful about the . . . what he did.' She looked past Mary as if her eyes registered a scene only she could see. Then her eyes shifted back and she was her usual brisk self. 'Was there really a puppy in the manger scene? Do you know how it got there?'

Startled, Mary didn't answer for a moment.

Bonnie's eyebrows narrowed.

'Yes.' This came out slowly. How did news of the puppy get out so fast? As far as she knew, only Dan and the group at her house last night knew about it. No. That wasn't right. Father D'Angelo knew. Ronaldo had the dog with him when the *posada*

stopped for the last time. Someone else must have seen it. She
sighed. Probably lots of someones. 'There was a puppy. Where it
came from, I don't know.' That was absolutely true. What she
suspected was another matter.

'What kind of puppy?'

'Kind? A black-and-white one. Cute.'

'No.' Impatience showed on Bonnie's face. 'What breed? Or
was it just a puppy?'

'Oh.' Evidently 'cute puppy' wasn't enough of a description
for someone who knew about dogs. 'Karl says it's a cocker
spaniel.'

Bonnie had let her hand rest on the side of Mary's car. She
now jerked it away as if it was burnt. 'A cocker! No. That can't
be right.' Her horrified expression softened a little, replaced with
puzzlement. 'Karl thinks it's a cocker puppy? Did Cliff bring
it?' That last statement was almost an accusation.

'I have no idea. I don't think anyone does.'

'Is Karl sure it's a cocker?'

Mary fished her car keys out of her purse and edged past
Bonnie toward the driver's door. 'Bonnie, it's a puppy and it was
in the sheep pen. How it got there and what kind of dog it is, I
really don't know.' She managed to get the door opened and
started to slide in.

'Where's the puppy now?'

Leave it to a dog lover to put the puppy before everything
else. 'Karl and Pat took it. I guess they'll keep it until its owner
shows up.'

Bonnie didn't say anything. Finally, she nodded. 'I'd better
hit the shower if I'm going to make the can tree thing. Don't
worry about the gate. I'll close it.' She turned and walked away.

Mary shook her head as she started the car. Bonnie was often
abrupt, usually because she was absorbed in what she was doing.
She was president of the Santa Louisa Pure Breed Dog Club,
head of the committee responsible for the all-breed dog show
they put on every year, wrote a column for the paper about dog
care and breeding, did volunteer work with the Humane Society
and was largely responsible for the no-kill shelter the town
recently instituted, as well as taking care of her own breeding
business. Her husband, Todd, ran the only independent hardware

store left in town and put in long hours. Bonnie was left pretty much on her own. Her almost rudeness just now was probably due to overwork, grief and concern about Cliff. This wasn't going to be easy on anyone in town.

Mary pulled out onto the street, heading for town and the Mendosas' house. Her hands tightened on the steering wheel. There was something about that meeting with Bonnie that was very uncomfortable. The interview with the children wasn't going to be easy, either. This was turning out to be a very difficult morning, indeed.

EIGHT

D an looked up as Mary came in the door with obvious relief. His smile seemed strained. The children sat at the kitchen table, the remains of their breakfast in front of them. Luanne sat on a straight chair squeezed between them.

'I thought you'd got lost.' Dan faced them, an untouched cup of coffee cooling at his elbow.

She shook her head. 'I was out at Bonnie Blankenship's collecting dog food for the Christmas Can Tree Food Drive. Before that, I baked some muffins for the Lutheran Christmas craft show today, their fundraiser for the women's shelter. Want to try one?' She put the small box of muffins she'd kept back on the table and opened it.

The tantalizing aroma of pumpkin escaped, surrounding the table. The children smiled.

'Oh, can we?' Dalia crooned.

'May we,' corrected their mother. 'Yes. But only one each.'

Small hands reached out and worried faces dissolved into smiles.

'You make the best muffins.' How Ronaldo made that under-standable with a mouth full of muffin, Mary had no idea.

She handed him a napkin. 'How are you two this morning?'

Ronaldo was busy picking cranberries out of his muffin and didn't answer.

'We're fine. Chief Dunham said we didn't have to go to school this morning and Mom let us call Doctor Bennington. He says Sampson is fine too. We can come and visit him, if we want.' The bite Dalia took of her muffin was small. She put it down and stared at her mother expectantly. 'We can, can't we, Mom?'

'We'll see. Coffee, Mary?'

'You sit where you are. I'll get it.' She set her handbag down, slipped out of her jacket and headed for the cupboard where the mugs were kept. The first time she'd been in this kitchen was when Luanne's mother died of breast cancer. Even though Luanne went to St Theresa's, it was Mary who'd made sure everyone was fed, that family coming in from out of town was met at the airport and a list was kept of those who sent flowers or condolences. She'd been here, helping, when Luanne brought Dalia home from the hospital and when Ronaldo was born. She'd also been here when Cruz, the children's father, died in that terrible accident on Hwy 46. She'd organized food donations to take Luanne and her family through that terrible time and had made sure, along with some of her other friends, that errands were run, floors washed and laundry done until Luanne was able to function again. This kitchen held no mysteries for Mary.

She brought the coffeepot back to the table and waved it over Dan's still-full mug, He shook his head. Luanne did as well. *Watching her caffeine intake, probably.* Mary wasn't.

She poured her mug full and returned the pot to the machine. 'Are you two helping Dan?'

Ronaldo smiled. 'Yep. We told him everything.'

Dan looked at him with an impassive face. 'They're both trying really hard.'

Mary wanted more than that. What had they said? More importantly, what had they seen? Had a good night's sleep, which she fervently hoped they'd had but somehow doubted, helped their memory, or had facts slipped in that were somehow tinged with fiction? 'Can you tell me too? Remember, I came over late.'

Dan glanced over at her. Was that relief in his eyes? 'Now, that's a good idea. Why don't you tell Mrs McGill what happened?'

Ronaldo looked dubious, but Dalia seemed more than willing. She put down her muffin and turned toward Mary. 'Like we told you last night. Ronaldo was worried the doll would be too big to fit in the manger. It is kinda a big doll. Besides, we both wanted to see Mom ride in on the donkey. I've never been on a donkey.' She looked thoughtful, glanced at her mother and tore off a bite of muffin, which she put in her mouth. She swallowed. 'Ronaldo picked up the doll and we went outside to the manger. It was pretty dark in there.'

'It was scary.' Ronaldo looked up quickly and just as quickly dropped his eyes.

Dalia nodded. 'You could hardly see the animals. At first, I thought the man was a cow. He stood right beside the cow. She was in a pen by the sheep.' Dalia paused.

Mary nodded.

'Then we walked over toward the manger and I saw something was in it.'

'What did you do?' Mary held her breath, waiting for the answer.

'Nothing. We just sort of stood there. Then the man moved toward us and I saw he wasn't a cow.'

The corners of Dan's mouth twitched.

Not Mary's. There was nothing amusing in this story. 'Did the man say anything?'

Ronaldo shook his head.

'Yes, he did,' Dalia corrected her brother.

'Did not.'

'Did so.'

'What did he say?' Mary inserted that forcefully. She hadn't taught middle school all those years for nothing.

Dalia's face got red. 'I can't tell you.'

'Why?' Dan's face showed confusion for the first time.

Dalia looked at her mother and bit her lip. ''Cause it's a word I'm not allowed to say.'

Luanne glanced over at Dan then at Mary. She reached over and patted Dalia on the arm. 'You can say it just this once. Chief Dunham needs to know, but this is the only time. What did he say?'

The word came out in a whisper. 'Shit.'

'Shit?'

Dalia looked at Dan disapprovingly but nodded.

'Then what happened?'

'He brushed past us and ran out. That's when we heard the puppy and started to look for it.'

Brushed past them. He was that close. A shudder ran through Mary. 'Did you see his face?'

Dalia shook her head.

Ronaldo looked up from his pile of cranberries. 'His hood was pulled way down.'

'I felt his skirt. It was sort of swirling around his legs, he was going so fast.'

'His skirt?' Luanne's expression changed from confusion to awareness to something like despair. 'The man had on a skirt?'

Dalia nodded. 'A robe. Like a bathrobe with a hood. Or like that robe Father D'Angelo wears. He ran out so fast he didn't even know his stick hit me on the leg.'

'Stick?' Luanne tensed. This was the first anything had been said about a stick.

'What kind of a stick?' It came out before Mary knew she'd spoken. She tried to signal her apology to Dan, but he was too absorbed in the little bombshell the children dropped to notice. 'How long was it? Did you get a good look at it?'

The children looked at each other across their mother. Dalia shrugged.

Ronaldo shook his head. 'It was pretty dark in there.'

Dan sighed but looked thoughtful. 'I think we just expanded the range of our crime scene.' His fingers started across the keyboard of his phone so fast Mary thought flames would surely fly up any minute.

'Is that when you, ah, saw who was in the manger?' Mary was thinking as fast as Dan typed, trying to picture what happened.

'No. We heard the puppy and started to look for it.'

'*I* heard the puppy. You said I was hearing things. I found it too.' There was no room for argument in Ronaldo's tone. He didn't exactly glare at his sister, but the stare he gave her was just one notch short of one.

'I opened the gate so you could get him.' Sweetness dripped from Dalia's voice. She might not have actually saved the puppy, but her contribution was not to be overlooked. She smiled at Ronaldo, who sat back in his chair and sighed.

Luanne looked at both of them and also sighed.

Dan looked confused.

Mary almost laughed. 'Then what happened?'

This time Dalia got in first. 'I let Ronaldo hold Sampson and went over to the manger to see what was in it.' She paused. Her face grew white. So did her knuckles as she squashed the remains of her muffin. She didn't seem to notice. Her voice was soft and there was a little tremor in it as she went on. 'That's when I saw it was old Doctor Mathews. There was blood on him.' Her eyes locked onto Mary's and the fright in them was heart-wrenching. 'I called to him, but he didn't move. I thought maybe I should shake him, but I didn't want to. I told Ronaldo I thought Doctor Mathews was sick or hurt and asked what we should do.'

'I said we needed to get help.'

Mary thought he probably had said it in that same matter-of-fact tone. 'You didn't go back into the church, though.'

Ronaldo looked wary, as if somehow that decision got them in trouble.

Dalia shook her head. She didn't look any happier, but she seemed ready to defend their decision. 'We aren't really in the choir and we don't know the lady leading it. And—' She looked over at her brother. There seemed to be some silent communication between them before she went on: 'The man who ran out – he didn't go back to the church that we could see, but you can get into it from the side door. If it was Father D'Angelo . . . We talked about it and Ronaldo said he'd hide by the sheep and I should go get Mrs McGill. We knew she was on the library steps, ordering everybody around.'

Mary gave a little gasp at that one but swallowed it quickly to glare at Dan. His smile was just a bit too broad.

'You did the right thing. Tell us more about the man. He had on a robe like the Father wears and he carried a stick. Was there anything else that made you think he was Father D'Angelo?'

Together, the children shook their heads.

'Just the long robe with a hood,' Dalia stated.

'Excellent point.' Dan reached for his coffee and took a huge swallow. He held onto it, looking down into the mug as if the coffee were tea leaves that would tell him what to do next. The thought that Father D'Angelo might be a murderer clearly didn't make him happy.

'A good point for any day of the year but yesterday.'

Dan looked up from his coffee to stare at Mary. 'What do you mean?'

'Half the town was dressed in robes. The shepherds in the *posada*, also the Three Kings. A bunch of the *posada* followers got into the mood and dressed in medieval robes. The adult choir from St Mark's United Methodist was dressed in robes. There were three other living crib scenes along Maple Ave. They all had people who were shepherds, kings and heaven only knows what else. There was some kind of display or pageant on the lawn of most of the houses on our six-block tour. Even Evan had on a hooded bathrobe while he played Scrooge. Anybody in town could have been dressed like that and no one would have paid them any attention.'

Luanne, with no little difficulty, pushed back her chair and struggled to her feet. She swept up the pile of cranberries and crumbs in front of Ronaldo, handed Dalia a napkin and headed for the kitchen sink. 'Mary's right. It could have been anyone. People came and went during the procession. People watching us wore costumes, and everyone milled around so much . . . The only person it couldn't have been is Santa Claus. Dan, if you're finished, I have a doctor's appointment and need to get going. I don't think they have anything more to tell you.'

Dan pushed his chair back. 'We're done. Kids, you did a good job. Thank you.' He picked his coffee mug up. Luanne reached to take it from him, but he set it down and grabbed her hand instead. 'I'm going to tell your mom something and I want you to listen. For the next couple of days, you're to stay with a grownup. No park, no playground. Mom will drive you to school and pick you up. You need to play here, in your yard. In your backyard. Do you hear me?'

Two faces stared at him, their mouths slightly open, but no sound came out.

Finally, Dalia nodded. 'Because of that man? Because he's bad? Do you think he might try to hurt us?'

Luanne gasped.

Mary didn't. She expected something like this. They'd seen

him. Whoever he was, he couldn't be sure the children hadn't recognized him, or had seen something that could lead police to him. Whether he'd hurt them or not, she had no idea, but Dan was going to make sure they were protected. However, he could have gone about it a little more tactfully.

Mary looked Ronaldo and Dalia in the eyes, one at a time. 'No one's going to hurt you, or even try. Chief Dunham wants you to be careful for a couple of days until we know what really happened.'

The worry seemed to fade from Ronaldo's eyes. But not from Dalia's.

'Old Doctor Mathews. He was dead, wasn't he? He had blood on his front. That man we saw who ran away, he killed him, didn't he? Is he going to kill us too?' Dalia's voice rose and gradually faded.

Ronaldo's eyes got round. He looked at his sister first, then at Dan, then his mother. All it was going to take was one more scary statement and he'd burst into tears.

Luanne, blinking back tears, walked over and put her arms around him then reached out and gathered up Dalia. 'No one's going to hurt either of you. They'd have to get through me first, and that wouldn't be easy.' She looked at Dan. 'They'll have to stay in the waiting room when I go to the doctor. They can't come in with me. Is that all right?'

It might have been all right with Dan, but it wasn't with the children.

Ronaldo's eyes clouded over. Tears threatened but the set to his mouth was stubborn. 'No. I'm going in with you.'

Dalia didn't say anything, but she started to bite her lip. Tears appeared at the corners of her eyes. One more minute and the whole room would be awash.

'There's no need for them to go with you. Why, they'd be bored to death. I'm going to the Christmas Can Tree Food Drive opening ceremony and they can come with me. After that, I want to go see Karl. I need a donation from him. You kids can play with the puppy while I talk Karl into giving it to me.'

Fear evaporated. Smiles appeared. 'Can we, Mom?' Ronaldo looked at his mother, pleadingly.

Dalia was more practical. 'What's a can tree?'

'We're collecting canned food for the food bank. That's where poor people – homeless people – go to get something to eat. So, people who want to donate bring their cans to city hall and we're going to build a big tree out of them then give all the food away before Christmas.'

The children looked dubious but willing. It obviously beat waiting in the doctor's office and there was the puppy to visit.

'Good idea.' Dan smiled at Mary with visible relief. 'Can't think of a better place for them to be, or a better person for them to be with. That all right with you, Luanne?'

Luanne didn't look as if it was, but she'd been outmaneuvered and she appeared to know it. The kids would be happy and safe. 'Are you sure?'

'Positive. All right, we have to leave in' – Mary looked at her watch – 'five minutes. Go get washed up and comb your hair. Both of you. You aren't going anywhere looking like ragamuffins. Put on sweaters. It's getting cold outside. Scat.'

They did, their mother right behind them, issuing instructions.

Dan grinned at Mary but immediately turned serious. 'Don't let those kids out of your sight. Not for one minute. Someone drove something sharp and nasty into Cliff's chest. We haven't found it, so we don't know what it was, but it was long and pointed. It went in . . .' He shook his head. 'I think whoever it was hadn't left because he was looking for the puppy. Dalia said he was over by the sheep pen. He wasn't expecting those kids to show up. They must have startled him big time because he left fast after that. If he thinks they recognized him, well, I don't want to scare them, but I don't mind scaring you. Don't let go of them for a second.' He paused. 'You're going to see Karl?'

Mary nodded. She wasn't capable of speech right then. The picture Dan had painted of Cliff was more graphic than she'd needed to hear. She swallowed, hard.

'Ask him about the puppy.'

'Ask him what about the puppy?'

'I don't know. Only, I think it was brought there, and I'll bet Cliff brought it. Why, I have no idea. Why was he there? I've got a lot of questions and not even one answer. Just . . . ask Karl.'

He gave her hand a quick squeeze and left. Mary was out of

breath and strangely weak in the knees. This wasn't good. Not good at all, and somehow she was certain it was going to get a lot worse before it got better. She turned, gathered up the remaining dishes on the table and headed for the sink.

NINE

M ary slipped into a parking space in front of Furry Friends pet shop right behind a van that pulled out loaded with kids. What a stroke of luck. She had fifteen minutes to get in there, get the donations Evan agreed to make and get to the opening of the Christmas Can Tree Food Drive. There were so many people in town she was afraid she wouldn't be able to find another spot. She glanced in the backseat. Could she chance leaving . . . of course she couldn't. Anyway, the decision had already been made. Seat belts were off and the rear door opened.

'We don't have time to look at the pets.' She used her sternest middle-schoolteacher voice. 'I have to be at the Christmas Can Tree Food Drive in ten minutes.'

Dalia stood on the sidewalk and looked across the street. 'It's right there, in front of city hall. Why don't we just walk across the park?'

Why, indeed? 'We have to unload all that dog food, which means finding another place to park and someone to help, so don't get involved.'

Ronaldo opened the shop door and waited as she and Dalia walked through. *Unusual for an eight-year-old.* Someone had taught that boy well. That kind of politeness usually came later, when they, and the girls they were interested in, were more grown-up. She smiled and thanked him.

'Look!'

There was a low pen just inside the front door filled with newspapers and puppies. Black and white curly haired puppies. The children couldn't have been drawn more effectively with magnets.

'This one looks just like Sampson.' Dalia leaned a hand over the low side of the pen. A puppy immediately came over to investigate and started licking her fingers. She giggled.

'Mary McGill. I'll bet you're here for the donations, aren't you?'

Mary swung around.

Evan grinned.

She smiled back and nodded, thinking how unlike Scrooge he looked this morning. No nightcap covered his thinning blond hair, no bulky bathrobe gave substance to his skinny frame, and Scrooge wouldn't have been caught dead in the long-sleeved mauve polo shirt Evan wore, or the sandals he'd buckled over white socks.

'We're in a hurry, Evan. Sorry, but today's been a blur. I'll make sure the paper knows these are from your shop, though.'

'Not a problem. I've got everything right here.' He picked up a large shopping bag with rope handles and handed it to her. Mary almost dropped it. 'My goodness, you've given us a lot.'

Evan's face reddened. 'Had some food dishes that didn't sell very well. Thought some of those kids would get a kick out of having a special dish for their pet. They need collars and stuff too. You know, I've seen dogs running around with kids, no collar, no leash. That's no way to keep them out of the street. Maybe this stuff will help.'

'Is that why you've put in squeaky toys and a couple of balls?' Mary had the top of the bag open and pulled out a green elf. It squeaked as she squeezed. Evan reddened more. 'Well . . .' His voice got more muffled as his face got redder.

'Thanks, Evan. All this will be greatly appreciated, I know.' She patted him on the arm as she turned to go. 'Come on, kids. We have to go.'

'Come look. This puppy is just like Sampson.' Dalia held the puppy high for Mary to see.

'Who's Sampson?' Evan walked over by Dalia, gently took the puppy out of her hands and put it back in the pen.

'Ah . . .' Dalia backed up a little; a worried look took the place of the smile. 'Just a puppy.'

'We found it,' Ronaldo said.

Mary cringed. This was exactly what Dan didn't want to

happen. She took Ronaldo by the hand, motioned to Dalia with the shopping bag dangling from her wrist and headed for the door. 'Will we see you at the can tree opening ceremony?'

Evan was right behind them. 'No. I can't leave the store. Where'd you find a puppy?'

Dalia looked at Mary, fright in her eyes. Mary shook her head just a little and kept on toward the door.

'Aren't these the Mendosa kids? I see them playing outside sometimes. They're just down the block from me. Someone said they found poor old Cliff. Is that right?'

'They live right down the block from me also, Evan. They're staying with me this afternoon. Their mother is at the doctor. I've got to get over there and find a place to park. My trunk is full of dog food. Thanks again.' She pushed the door open and the children scampered out. She followed them, letting the door swing shut.

'Wait.' It was Evan, half in and half out of the doorway. 'Wait a minute. How many cartons do you have?'

'What?' Mary turned back.

Evan held the door open, gesturing at her. 'Dog food. How many cartons? I can get eight on my hand truck. I'll take them over for you. I can lock the store for a few minutes and that way you won't have to move the car.'

Mary looked across the park to the library. The can tree was to be built in the area between the library building and the city offices. TV trucks were already there. People carrying cartons of cans poured through the glass double doors. All the real estate offices in town had challenged each other to see who could contribute the most cans and, of course, get their names in the paper or on the local news. Banks, doctors' office employees, the Chamber of Commerce and the local markets were all turning out for this event. There wasn't a parking spot in sight. She sighed.

'Thanks, Evan. I'll take you up on that. Kids, let's go. I'm supposed to lay the first can and, at this rate, I'll be the last one there.'

After Evan had loaded his hand truck, Mary hustled them all across the park toward the library/city hall building, her purse and the shopping bag with the dog dishes in it slapping her leg

the entire way. She was puffing when they got to the steps. So
was Evan, but the cartons were all still on the hand truck.

'What do you want me to do with them?'

Mary looked at the steps then down at the heavily laden hand
truck. 'Take them up the handicap ramp and into the building.
We're going to build the tree right in the middle, between the
library and the city offices. I've got to get up there and see
what damage all those people are doing to my plan. Kids, stay
with me.'

Telling each child not to dare leave her side, she forged up
the stairs and through the doors.

'Here she is now!' A TV camera appeared in front of her.
'Mrs McGill, can you tell us how many cans you expect to get
this year?'

Another voice and another microphone came at her from the
left. 'Mrs McGill, are you only collecting cans? What about fresh
fruit and vegetables? Turkeys?'

Someone out of sight commented, 'They can't collect fresh
stuff now and keep it in the lobby for two weeks.'

Mary stretched her neck to try and see who it was making the
first sensible comment she'd heard. 'All fresh food donations go
directly to the food bank, as do all donations of money. We're
here to collect canned goods or boxes of things like cereal or
rice.'

'We were told you're collecting dog and cat food this year
too. Is that right?' It was the roving reporter for Channel Two,
the one who always looked like she disapproved. True to form,
she looked like she disapproved right now. Maybe she didn't like
dogs and cats. Or children. Or poor people.

'That's right. Pets are important for children. All the experts
say so.' There. Let her disapprove of that. 'So, with the help of
the Pure Breed Dog Club of Santa Louisa, we're collecting pet
food so families who can't otherwise afford to have a pet, or
have one and can't afford to keep it will get some help. Furry
Friends pet shop has kindly donated some pet food bowls, leashes
and collars, as well as some other things. There's Evan Wilson,
the owner, bringing in the food.'

The TV cameras and the reporters turned as one to focus on
Evan, who struggled to get his hand truck through the glass doors.

He turned beet red as they gathered around him, peppering him with questions, flashbulbs going off in his face. He didn't object, however, when the questions centered on his store. Mary sighed in relief, checked to make sure she had each child safely secured and headed for the middle of the vestibule.

'Are we all set?'

'Hey. I thought you'd gotten lost. We're ready to go when you are.' A young man with long blond hair swept back in a ponytail knelt on the floor doing something with chalk. 'I've got our circle drawn out so all your people have to do is fill it in.' He stood up, stretched and looked at Dalia and Ronaldo. They looked back at him, mouths slightly open, as they stared at the diamond he wore in one ear. He grinned at them. 'Who are you guys?'

'I'm Dalia. This is Ronaldo. He's my brother.'

The young man nodded. 'I'm Luke, from the library. Nice to meet you. Why does Mrs McGill have you so tight by the hands? She afraid you'll get away?'

Ronaldo laughed but Dalia answered in her most serious tone. 'No. There are lots of people here. She doesn't want us to get lost.'

'In that case, you'd better help her lay the first can. As chairperson, she's going to do the honors.' He looked at Mary, smiled and nodded. 'You look really nice.'

Heat climbed up Mary's cheeks. She'd taken extra pains because she knew the newspaper and TV people would be here. She tucked her cranberry blouse a little tighter into the waistband of her best black pants. She'd hesitated before she'd bought it. It was only two dollars at the last St Mark's rummage sale, but it fit and didn't look used. She smiled her thanks at Luke, who grinned back and picked up a microphone that lay on an amplifier box with speakers next to a large pile of food cartons. 'Let's do this thing.'

Mary put up a hand to stop him. She suddenly doubted she wanted the children out in the open where everyone could see them, or that she wanted their pictures spread all over the local news, but she was too late.

'Ladies and gentlemen, we want to thank you for coming this morning and for all of the wonderful contributions you've made.' Luke was the master of ceremonies. The microphone squeaked but immediately settled down, throwing his voice all around the vestibule. People stopped talking and started toward the large chalk circle. 'This year we especially need to make our can tree the biggest and best it's ever been. The food bank is almost empty, and we have more families that need help than we've had in years. Your generosity is going to make a huge difference. The first layer of our Christmas Can Tree will be laid by the people in this community who have been instrumental in getting our food drive organized, along with our beloved city officials. So, gather round while I introduce them. Our mayor, ladies and gentlemen, Harlan Campbell.'

There was the appropriate applause, accompanied by laughter when the mayor started pulling cartons of Campbell's soup into the center. He waved at the TV cameras and the newspaper flashbulbs.

'That your company, Harlan?' quipped one of the reporters.

'Closest thing my side of the clan ever got to this soup was eating it.' The mayor beamed a practiced smile while he unloaded the first carton.

The rest of the city council was introduced, then the head of the food bank and the president of the Chamber of Commerce. The children were starting to fidget when it was finally Mary's turn.

'And now, ladies and gentlemen, I'd like to introduce the person who made all this happen. The person who organized it all, who personally coordinated all of the committees, and without whom this Christmas Can Tree Food Drive would never have happened; the person who will chair our next Friends of the Library fundraiser, the person who is always there when help is needed, let's have a cheer for Mrs Mary McGill, ladies and gentlemen, and her two elves.'

Mary stepped into the circle, holding tight to Dalia and Ronaldo's hands.

'Where are the elves?' Ronaldo looked around the edges of the crowd, flashbulbs going off in his face.

'He means us, silly,' Dalia whispered loudly. She didn't ignore the cameras or the flashbulbs. Her smile was bright and broad as she faced them.

'Now, ladies and gentlemen, our dignitaries, led by Mrs McGill, will lay the bottom layer of cans for our tree, and we hope it grows as high as the ceiling. Drop by every day with your contributions and watch it grow.' He motioned for the children to come to him. Mary let go of their hands and they both sprinted toward Luke. He handed them each a couple of cans. 'Set them upright along the chalk line and come back for more.'

It didn't take long for the children to get the hang of it and they were soon lying cans around the edge – Ronaldo going one way, Dalia the other.

When the entire perimeter of the large chalk circle was covered with cans, the mayor took over. 'We'll get ourselves locked in the middle if we do it this way. Let's fill in as we go and work ourselves through the middle toward the doors.' He pointed toward the large glass doors that led to the steps. Everybody grabbed cans and started laying them out, Dalia and Ronaldo in the thick of things. Mary pushed herself up off her knees, a hand on the small of her back. Kneeling on the hard floor was not as easy as it had once been. She backed up toward the edge of the circle and stepped over the outer layer to join the crowd of watchers. She wouldn't be missed. There were too many hands in there anyway, and she could still keep an eye on the children. She stood beside Alma Maxwell.

'Mary, I see you've done your usual wonderful job.'

'My goodness, Alma. I haven't seen you in ages. How are you?'

Alma gave a small, sad smile. 'Feeling my age. As a matter of fact, Mary, I've decided to move down south with my sister. Your niece, Ellen, is coming over next week to talk about listing my house. I'm putting it on the market right after Christmas.'

Mary was rarely stunned, but she was this time. Alma moving away from Santa Louisa? Why, she'd always lived here. They'd gone to high school together. They'd married within a year of each other and lost their husbands within two. They'd never been close friends, but they'd known each other. Always. Why would Alma leave? 'Why?'

Alma sighed. 'You know my sister, Eva, moved to Atlanta.'

Mary nodded. Eva moved thirty years ago.

'Her husband died recently, she has a big house and she's invited me to come live with her. I don't have any family here, what with both my girls married and moved away, so I thought, well, this seems best.'

'What are you going to do with your dogs?'

Alma had raised cocker spaniels for as long as Mary could remember. She was a junior handler when they were growing up, had dogs during her marriage and delivered puppies right along with her two girls. Mary couldn't envision her without her dogs. Alma's dogs weren't as 'good' as Bonnie's, which she thought meant they hadn't won as many ribbons, but then, she didn't think Alma took them to as many shows either. There was that one dog, however. The one Cliff . . .

Alma sighed, a deep, heavy sigh. 'I sold the ones I had left to Bonnie.' Her eyes got misty and her hand shook ever so slightly. 'I'm taking Belle. She can't be bred and she's way too old to be shown. Besides, I love her and my sister likes dogs. The others . . . You know, Mary, after what Cliff did to Belle, I sort of lost heart. I've been thinking about this for a while and decided now is the time. Bonnie will be good to them, and she has that wonderful male. His bloodlines should blend nicely with my last two bitches.' Her chin had a determined, almost defiant set to it, but there was sadness in her eyes. 'Bonnie will be good to them.' She made a little choking sound before she went on: 'I'm going down to Atlanta to spend Christmas with Eva. Sort of a trial run. We'll work out the details then.'

Mary nodded slowly then reached over and gave Alma a hug. 'We'll miss you.' There wasn't much else to say. She understood how Alma felt. All of her hopes had been tied up in Belle, the best dog she'd ever had, and certainly the best one she'd ever bred. She'd paid a lot to breed her to some special black cocker and eagerly awaited the puppies. Only, instead of doing a pregnancy test, Cliff had got her mixed up with another cocker and spayed her, aborting the puppies and leaving her unable to have another litter. Alma had almost had a breakdown when she found out. She'd never totally recovered, and her interest in her dogs gradually diminished. She must also be feeling her seventy-some years, a feeling Mary understood, and no longer wanted to work so hard or go through the stress breeding and showing dogs put on you. Mary could only wish her friend well.

'Is it true Cliff was murdered?' Alma lowered her voice as

she pulled Mary back through the small crowd so they could talk more privately. 'I heard you found him. How awful. Do you have any idea what happened?'

Mary shook her head. 'I'm having a hard time making myself believe it's true, even though I saw him there. It was awful. Poor old Cliff. I can't imagine anyone doing such an awful thing.'

Alma didn't say anything. Instead, she looked at Mary, her usually soft gray eyes hardening to the color of steel. The lines around her mouth tightened and the words she spoke were equally as hard. 'I can.'

TEN

Karl Bennington's Five Oaks Small Animal Veterinary Hospital was in the north end of town, tucked away behind the Almond Tree Motel and Café. Mary had made the drive many times and drove it now on autopilot. Her conversation with Alma had shaken her more than she liked to admit.

The children sat in the backseats, faces still encased in smiles. They had had a wonderful time, placed cans with unbridled enthusiasm and took over from adults who no longer wanted to bend down. Now they sipped chocolate milk and argued over who laid out the most cans and who was going to pick the game they were going to play with Sampson. Mary ignored them. Her thoughts were consumed with Alma and the grudge she'd carried against Cliff all these years. She'd blamed him not only for the monetary loss she suffered when he spayed her prize bitch, but for the mental anguish she'd suffered and the loss of interest she'd had in rebuilding her kennels. Alma had let her hurt fester until it was like a boil under her skin. If she was younger, stronger, and a man, Mary would have considered her a suspect, but it made her realize how deep a hurt like that could go and how long it sometimes took to heal. Who else was out there, holding onto a grudge against poor old Cliff? He'd made some pretty awful 'mistakes' during those years when he'd systematically drowned his career in alcohol. In the process, he'd inflicted pain on a lot more people than himself. She hoped Dan found out who murdered him quickly. This was reopening old wounds she had hoped were closed for good. Alma's weren't. She wondered who else had an open wound.

She swung into Karl's parking lot. There was only one car other than Karl's SUV with the dog crate in the back. The office closed at noon and reopened at two, so their timing should be great.

'Don't you dare open the car doors until I'm parked and say you can.' She didn't care how empty the parking lot was, she didn't want the kids running across it. True to her expectations, the office door opened and a woman Mary didn't know walked out with a cat carrier. She barely glanced at Mary, who had pulled in beside her, but took a good look at the kids before she opened the back door and set the carrier on the seat. The cat yowled.

The woman walked around and got in the driver's seat. When she was clear of the parking lot, Mary spoke. 'Now you can . . .' That was as far as she got. Both children shed their seat belts, had doors opened and were at the front door before Mary had the keys out of the ignition. They didn't have to open the door. Karl did that for them.

'Perfect timing. Sampson's in the puppy pen, waiting for you.'

Karl's bald head shone pink in the sunlight, the little freckles on it almost glowing through the few thin strands of hair. He smiled as he pushed the door open wider. 'Pat's inside. She's got sandwiches made and some apple slices. You two hungry?'

Mary started to follow the children into the building but Karl stopped her. 'Wait. I need to talk to you.'

She turned to face him, surprised the smile was gone. The look on his face was serious. No. Worried. Karl never looked like that unless he was worried about one of the animals. Mostly, he looked mildly pleased with life, which, Mary was sure, was how he felt. But he didn't look pleased right now.

'What's the matter?'

'Do you know where Dan is? I have . . . something happened . . . I think he needs to know.'

'I have no idea where he is. What is it you think he needs to know?'

Karl looked at her for what Mary felt was a long time. 'I don't know if this is important or not, but . . .' He stopped, evidently mulling something over in his mind, trying to decide. His expression changed. 'Come into the office. I want to show you something.'

It was with more curiosity than dread that Mary followed him. The office smelled faintly of dog. That wasn't surprising. There were two dog beds in one corner, both currently empty. Bookshelves were crammed with veterinary books. Framed diplomas filled the space between two of them, along with pictures of dogs, cats and one horse. Mary looked twice at that one. Karl made no secret of the fact that he only took small animals as patients. A large glass tank held— No, she wasn't going to look. She didn't like reptiles and was sure they didn't like her. Instead, she took the only chair in front of Karl's freestanding-and-totally-loaded-with-papers desk.

'Well?'

Karl pulled out his desk chair and sank into it. He looked as if he was having a hard time finding a place to begin. 'A few weeks ago, Cliff came by to see me.'

That surprised Mary. Karl and Cliff had never been friends. Karl had been openly critical of Cliff's actions in the years before he lost his license. Cliff knew it and resented it. They'd never argued that Mary knew about, and she was sure she would have known if they had, but there was a coolness – no, more like a winter frost between them. 'What did he want?'

'He wanted a favor.'

'Really.' Now, that was a surprise. 'What kind?'

'He wanted me to send a DNA sample to the American Kennel Club to verify parenthood.'

'To do what? Parenthood? For a dog?'

Karl smiled his mildly amused smile, but there was worry underneath it. 'Most purebred dogs that are registered sires have their DNA on file with the AKC. It's required for most breeds, especially if the dog sires more than a couple of litters a year. Keeps things honest. If someone buys a purebred puppy and suspects the sire on the papers isn't the real one, they can request the puppy's DNA be checked. There are other reasons – verifying the identity of a dog when it's sold, things like that. Anyway, Cliff asked me if I'd send in his sample.'

'Why didn't he do it?' Mary tried to absorb all of this. She'd never heard of DNA testing for dogs, or for any animal, but then she knew next to nothing about dog breeding or showing. Why would Cliff want a dog's DNA tested? He no longer had anything to do with dogs of any kind, or did he? He'd been, when he was a young and eager vet, the doctor of choice for all the purebred breeders in this part of California; at least that was what she was told. No longer. So, what would he want with this test? Why didn't he send it in himself? The last two questions she asked aloud.

'He said,' Karl's words came out slowly, 'that he didn't think the AKC would let him send in a request because he lost his license and wasn't practicing anymore.'

'Is that true?'

'I think he just didn't want anyone to know what he was doing.'

'Why? Do you think it could have something to do with why he was killed?'

'Mary, I have no idea. I don't know what Cliff was after, who the dog was, anything. He didn't tell me and, honestly, I didn't ask. Just told him sure, I'd do it. A few days later he brought the sample, had all the paperwork filled out, gave me a check made out to me and asked me to send mine in with the package and to please call him when the results came back. They came back yesterday.'

Of all the odd things. 'Did you call him?'

Karl shook his head. 'Didn't have a chance. It was a busy day and we wanted to end early so we could see the *posada*. Besides, I was the vet on call for the extravaganza.'

Mary nodded. She knew that. She'd arranged it. 'You never talked to him?'

'No.'

'Have you looked at the results?'

'I didn't yesterday. It was Cliff's test and his business. I had no intention of opening it. However—'

'You opened it today?'

Karl nodded.

'For heaven's sake, Karl, do you know the dog? Or the owners? Don't sit there, looking mysterious. Tell me what's bothering you about this.'

Karl took a deep breath and let it out slowly. 'Do you remember last year when the Blisses' poodle got stolen?'

'The little black dog Naomi took everywhere? Yes, I do. They looked all over and finally concluded someone who visited the winery took him. Why?'

'That dog was a finished champion and was much in demand as a sire for poodles that size.'

'What does that have to do with— No. It isn't.'

'It is. Only, there's been no trace of that dog for almost a year. He can't be shown, and if whoever took him tried to stand him at stud . . .' Karl smiled at the puzzled look on Mary's face and explained, 'Used him to breed to other dogs, especially poodles . . . He's hidden someplace around here. He must be and somehow Cliff found him. I think he wanted the DNA test to make sure he was right.'

Mary sat stunned. Had Cliff stumbled onto something that got him killed? But, what? The puppy. Could he somehow . . .

'Sampson. The puppy. Is he a poodle?'

There was no longer even a trace of a smile on Karl's face. 'I think Sampson may be a very cute cockapoo.'

'A what?' Mary sat up straight and stared at Karl. Maybe she hadn't heard him right.

Karl smiled faintly. 'I can see you don't keep up with the latest "designer" dogs. A cockapoo has one parent who's a poodle and the other a cocker spaniel. They're becoming pretty popular. At least with everybody but those who don't believe in mixing purebred bloodlines.'

Mary tried to make sense of that but couldn't. However, it wasn't what she wanted to know. 'You think Sampson is a cockapoo? Is that what you said?'

'It's hard to tell with a puppy Sampson's age, but he sure looks like one to me.'

A picture swam into Mary's mind. Black puppies, black and white puppies. 'Evan has puppies in his shop. Black and white furry puppies. Is it possible Sampson is one of those?'

'The world is full of black and white furry puppies. If you're asking me if Sampson could be related to Evan's puppies, I couldn't begin to tell you. I don't know where Evan gets his puppies and have no idea where Sampson came from. All I can tell you is he's cute and appears healthy. However, I've started him on his shots. Just in case.'

Mary tried to hide her smile. Just like Karl, always thinking about the animals first. 'What are you going to do with him?'

Karl sighed. 'Hold onto him for a while, I guess. At least until Dan's satisfied he's not evidence of something. Then I suppose we'll try to find him a home.'

'Karl, do you think either of those dogs, the Blisses' poodle or Sampson, have something to do with Cliff's murder?'

Karl leaned forward on his desk. Mary had never seen him look so troubled.

'I have no idea. It seems too much of a coincidence for there not to be a connection, but I can't think what. I'll tell Dan about this test as soon as I find him and then bow out.' He looked directly at her. 'I think we need to keep this to ourselves. That sample is from Naomi's dog, but it doesn't tell us where the dog is or who has him, and it certainly doesn't tell us why Cliff was killed or by whom. Let Dan sort this out. All right?'

Mary nodded but slowly, and without conviction.

He got up and headed toward the door. 'I need to get back to work. It's after two and I have patients in the waiting room.'

Mary nodded again and followed him out the door. She needed to pry the kids away from Sampson, and she wanted another look at the puppy. Why, she had no idea. He could be part Beagle for all she knew, but she'd promised Dan she'd find out what she could. She wasn't going to do that by looking at him, though. There had to be another way.

ELEVEN

The phone rang as Mary pushed open her back door, her arms full of groceries. She set her full cloth bags on the floor and stared at the phone. She didn't want to talk to anyone. She was tired. It was after three and she'd been talking to people all day. The children were safely deposited with their mother and right now all she wanted was a cup of tea.

The phone kept ringing. She must have forgotten to set the answering machine again. With a snort of disgust, she picked it up.

'Mary, thank goodness. I've been trying to get you for hours.'

'Isabel. What's wrong?'

She sounded rattled. Pastor's wives weren't supposed to sound rattled. They had to deal with everything from committee women with their noses out of joint to distraught parents of a sick or dying child. Isabel usually handled her role with calm dignity that Mary found admirable. There was nothing calm about her now. 'Cliff and what we're supposed to do about him, that's what's wrong.'

Mary felt herself stiffen. Do? About Cliff? What was Isabel talking about? She set her handbag on the kitchen table and walked over to the stove. She checked the teakettle. It was full. She turned the fire under it full on blast and headed for the cupboard for a mug. 'What are you talking about?'

'I'm talking about Cliff Mathews. Everybody's asking me about the funeral. I called Dan's people and they said as soon as the autopsy was finished, so were they. Someone has to claim the body and arrange for burial. They won't. What are we going to do?'

Cliff's funeral. It'd never occurred to her. Her hand didn't get any farther than the cupboard door. It seemed frozen on the knob, incapable of pulling it open. Surely his family – only, she couldn't think of any family. His wife was dead, had been for over ten years. They had one daughter, but Mary didn't think she'd seen her since her mother's funeral. She'd had some kind of falling out with her father and Cliff hadn't mentioned her since. She'd almost forgotten about her, couldn't even remember her name. Where was she now? Mary had no idea. Had Cliff any siblings? She couldn't remember him mentioning any. Cliff wasn't a native of Santa Louisa but had bought his practice after he'd graduated from vet school. He'd moved here from . . . Where? They'd have to find out and find his next of kin as well. Everybody had someone. Surely it was just a matter of locating them. 'What about his family?'

'Don't know. Les is working on it. There's a daughter, but where she is . . . Anyway, the autopsy is scheduled for Monday and it won't be long after that before the body's released. We have to do something.'

'What do you mean by "we"? Cliff wasn't a member of St Mark's, and if you mean you and me, I'm sure he had closer friends.'

'Cliff didn't officially belong to St Mark's, but Les said he'd do the service. Eloise, his wife, was a member for years and Les officiated at her funeral. If memory serves, you and your committee did the food for the reception after her burial.'

Isabel was right. Mary remembered that day. Cliff had looked like a lost child, dazed, uncomprehending. A vague picture of the daughter came up. A thin woman, boney actually. Her hair was pulled back in a severe ponytail, her black dress a little too large through the hips, as if she'd lost weight and hadn't bothered to replace the dress, or even take it in. Only, she couldn't remember anything else. Nothing she said, no one she talked to, not even her father. Her memory put the woman at the grave site. She couldn't remember if she'd even been at the reception. So sad.

'They bought two plots and Les says we're going to bury Cliff beside her. Unless, of course, someone comes along and says different.'

If Mary's memory of the daughter was correct, she thought that highly unlikely. That Reverend Lestor McIntyre was going to give Cliff a proper send-off wasn't. It solved one problem, one she hadn't thought about. There were plenty of others. 'What does Les want us to do? Provide food for the gathering afterward? Flowers?'

'Well, a little more, I'm afraid. He wants you to contact the funeral home and make the arrangements. Dan wants you to meet him at Cliff's. He needs to look through the house. While he's there he thought you could collect the, you know, clothes and things like that, for the burial.'

The teakettle started to scream. Mary removed it, took a mug from the cupboard and a tea bag from the canister, plopped the bag into the mug and filled it with hot water. It started to turn a rich brown almost immediately. This was going to take a few minutes, though. She pulled out one of the chairs by the old white table that sat under her kitchen window, sank down onto it and tried to push the shoe on her left foot off with her right one. She almost groaned with relief when it slipped to the floor. Now for the other one. 'Why me? I knew Cliff, of course, but not that well. It was Eloise I knew. After she died I didn't see Cliff all that often.'

'You're the chairperson for St Mark's Hospitality Committee.'

'Arranging other people's funerals doesn't come under the heading of Hospitality.'

'Visiting people in the hospital. Sending people cards and flowers. Making sure people have food after a funeral – that kind of thing does. It's the closest committee we could think of to do this. You will, won't you, Mary?'

Oh, for heaven's sake. Mary took a deep breath, willing herself not to be huffy. She'd had a long, exhausting day and she wanted to sit here, sipping her tea, alone, letting the day just slip away . . . There wasn't one thing about any of this she liked or wanted any part of.

'First, I'm the co-chairman of that committee. Naomi Bliss is the other one and all she does are the cards and flowers. I do the food and all the organizing. Neither of us signed on to arrange funerals.'

'Well, if you don't want to do it, tell Les and Dan. Not me. But, Mary, I'm a little surprised. You're always the one we can count on when we need help.' Isabel sounded surprised and more than a little hurt.

Mary sighed and got up to get her tea. It looked black and strong. She fished the teabag out and put it in the sink before gingerly taking a sip. Too hot. It would be another couple of minutes. Drat. She needed that tea. 'I'm sorry, Isabel. I guess I'm a little tired. The extravaganza and the can tree thing have worn me out. Then all this with Cliff. I suppose Les wants to use O'Dell's Mortuary.'

'Who else?'

Who else, indeed. The O'Dells had been members of St Mark's for three generations and took care of all the funerals for the congregation. They'd also volunteered their services in cases like this before. Not in murder cases – at least, Mary couldn't think of one, but in cases when someone died without the necessary funds or if there was no family. They'd waived their fee when the Ryans' little boy died. Pat Ryan had been out of work for almost a year and the child's hospital bills had gotten out of hand. The Ryans were in danger of losing their home as well as their child. Mary sighed. If the O'Dells were willing to help, she guessed she was too. That didn't make her feel any better, though. There was something creepy about arranging a funeral for someone who wasn't a relative, someone who you knew only casually, whose wishes you could only guess at. Was she supposed to pick out the casket as well as Cliff's last outfit?

She shuddered and tried a sip of tea. 'All right. I don't like this one bit, but I'll do it. When am I supposed to meet Dan?'

'He said he's at Cliff's right now and could you come there. I have the address. It seems there's a problem with the landlady and Cliff's things need to be taken care of by tonight.'

'Tonight!'

'That's what he said. He's called Ellen as well.'

'Oh, all right. I'll see what I can do. But, I'm finishing my tea before I do another thing.'

Isabel laughed and hung up.

Mary looked at the clock and at the groceries she hadn't unpacked and groaned. The last thing she wanted was to go out again. Her back hurt, so did her feet, and she wanted to put on her slippers, sip her tea and watch the local news. Well, maybe she still could. It wasn't quite four. If she left now she could run by and see what it was that Dan needed. Maybe most of it could be done tomorrow. With a deep sigh, she opened the cupboard that held vitamins and other everyday medications, shook two Tylenol out and popped them into her mouth, picked up her mug, drained it and put it in the sink. She pulled the orange juice, butter and fish out of the sack and put them in the refrigerator. She'd do the rest later. She had to make a phone call before she left. No, two. O'Dells needed to be put on alert. And Naomi. She wasn't doing this one alone.

Mary followed Dan. She caught only a glimpse of a small poodle before Naomi clutched the picture to her breast. That it was of a dog wasn't a surprise. Naomi's reaction was. She looked over at the buffet. The top was covered with pictures of dogs. Mary didn't recognize any of the animals, but she knew a lot of the people.

'Why, that's Ray Blackburn. I'd forgotten he had a police dog.' A beautiful German shepherd sat beside a slender young man with bushy black hair, almost dwarfed by his police equipment. He grinned from ear to ear. His dog looked equally happy. 'That was taken the day Ray and Spike graduated from the canine academy. I've never seen Ray so happy. Before or since.' Dan paused to stare at the picture. 'Where did . . . Ray must have given it to him. Cliff took care of Spike.'

Mary nodded, but her attention had been caught by another picture, obviously taken in a show ring. 'Isn't that Luke? Luke from the library? My goodness, he looks so young.'

Naomi, her picture still clutched tightly to her breast, glanced up. 'Why – yes. That's Luke when he was a junior handler. That was years ago. Why would Cliff . . . He was the one who ruined Luke's chances for a scholarship. Neither Luke nor his parents ever forgave him. What's he doing with that picture?'

Luke must have been in middle school when it was taken. There was no mistaking that slightly awkward look so many of them, especially the boys, had at that age. Luke looked more put together than most. He also looked happy. Happy and about to burst with pride. He held a huge blue ribbon in one hand, a dog lead attached to a large and elaborately groomed poodle in the other. A scholarship? At that age? What was Naomi talking about? She didn't get a chance to ask.

'What's that picture you're holding, Naomi? You'll have to put back. We'll have to do an inventory of all this stuff and . . .'

Naomi turned the picture over and held it out for them to see. A small black poodle stood proudly in front of an elaborate sign bearing the words, 'Best in Show.' A woman in a black and silver pantsuit knelt beside him, holding his lead. A distinguished white-haired man holding a large silver cup stood next to them. 'It's Merlot,' Naomi whispered. 'This was him winning the West Coast Specialty last year. It was the last show he went to before

TWELVE

Mary pulled up to the curb and stared at the row of townhouses. She looked down at the address written on the back of her grocery list then again at the tired-looking building. So this was where poor old Cliff lived after he lost his wife, his house and his practice. She sighed, unsnapped her seat belt and climbed out of the car.

'There you are. Dan's inside.'

Naomi came down the stairs of the middle townhouse, the one with the dead bush in the pot on the front porch. Mary shook her head in wonder. Naomi was the only woman she knew that still wore high heels. High, high heels. She wasn't much taller than Mary, at least Mary didn't think so. It was hard to tell because she wore those torture chamber shoes all the time. How she stayed on her feet all day in those things, Mary couldn't begin to fathom. But then, she was younger than Mary and didn't have her soft curves. In fact, she had no curves at all. Naomi was practically straight up and down. Mary sighed. *She* wasn't. She ran her hand down the side of her sweatpants, the ones that fit snugly over her hips. Why was Naomi the only person she knew who made her feel self-conscious? She'd put on her new – to her – Santa Claus sweatshirt before she left, thinking it was nice and warm and would wash easily. Perfect for packing up someone's belongings. Naomi wore knit pants that wouldn't dare bag at the knee, a silk shirt Mary was sure wouldn't wrinkle, and her makeup wasn't mussed. Mary wore no makeup. Was the fifty cents she paid for her sweatshirt at St Mark's rummage sale such a good deal after all? Deciding this wasn't the moment to worry about her wardrobe, she climbed the stairs.

'Have you already been in there?'

Naomi nodded. 'Did you call O'Dells?'

'Yes. They're going to take care of everything but the casket. We have to pay for that, so we'll have to go over tomorrow after we find out how much we have to work with and pick one out. I have a budget from the church charity fund but it's not much. I hope Cliff left something.'

'I don't imagine he did.' Naomi sighed deeply, turned on her spiked heel and headed for the front door. 'I still can't believe . . .' The rest of her sentence was lost in the squeak it made as she wrenched open the door.

Mary followed her inside with reluctance. She couldn't shake the feeling she was intruding, walking into someplace she had no business being. However, there didn't seem to be an alternative, so she continued on into the middle of the room, stopped and looked around. There was only one way to describe it. Depressing. A sofa, whose flowered pattern had long since faded into nothingness, sat against a long wall. A square end table of no particular design sat beside it and a matching coffee table in front of it. The end table held a wooden lamp that looked like a Walmart special and a collection of magazines. Dog faces looked up from the front covers. The coffee table was equally sparse. Aside from dust, it held nothing but a TV remote and a plate with what were probably the remains of Cliff's last meal. No pictures graced the wall behind the sofa, no pillows softened it. A recliner, its vinyl worn through on the arms, sat at an angle facing the small TV. It was a flat screen, the only new thing in the room, and easily fit on the small table that separated the two bookcases on the wall opposite the sofa. A small dining set that also looked suspiciously like Walmart almost filled the tiny dining area. A lovely old mahogany buffet was wedged along the back wall. There was nothing about it that suggested Walmart. It was the only piece, and the only wall, that held anything personal or decorative. The top was covered with pictures. So was the wall above it. The only other available space in the room held a battered rolltop desk and an elderly swivel chair. In the chair sat Dan.

'You finally got here. Good.' Dan turned from the scarred old desk he'd evidently been searching through and smiled at her. 'Did you talk to O'Dell's?'

Mary nodded. 'All I have to do is find a casket that fits the church budget. I don't suppose Cliff left any money we can use?' She looked at the piles of bank statements, bills and letters and

blanched. 'Dan, should we really do this? Go through Cliff's things?'

His voice was grim. 'I got a warrant. The courts might on us if we didn't follow all the legal steps.'

'Oh.' Mary wasn't sure being legal made her feel any le a snoop, but there didn't seem to be anyone else to do this. B there might be a clue as to who killed him and the other q that plagued her: why? 'Do you think there's enough to bur

'Doesn't look like it.' Dan put a checkbook down on pile of bank statements. 'Cliff's landlady paid me anotl before you got here. Seems he was about three months on his rent and she had served him eviction papers.' He pi an official-looking sheet of paper with a heading in red sc 'Notice to Pay or Quit.' 'She wants his stuff out and wai now. I think she feels bad, but she says these apartment only income and she needs to get this one rented. I ti into giving us until sometime tomorrow. Les says we all his things in the storage room at St Mark's until we his daughter. We're going to have to pack up all of Cliff' ings and get them over there by tomorrow afternoon put them out on the curb.'

Mary looked around the apartment once more. It take long. But the storage room? She knew it well. S for many of the events that went on and had plant it again to store the donations they would soon be col the annual rummage sale. She groaned inwardly, wonc they were going to manage. That they would, someho no doubt, but hoped Dan found the daughter soon. 'D a will?'

'Not that I've found.' He frowned and waved a piles of paper stacked on the desk.

'I haven't found an address book either, and no on to can remember the daughter's married name or eve she lives in.'

He was stopped by a sharp intake of breath. They Naomi held a picture in her hands, staring at it.

'Did you find something?' Dan pushed his ch started toward her.

She didn't answer, just kept staring at the pictu

he was stolen.' Her eyes clouded over with tears, her words almost buried in the sobs she tried to suppress. 'I had it at the winery, up on the wall in the tasting room. One day, a couple of weeks ago, it was gone. We looked everywhere but couldn't find it. Cliff must have taken it. Only, why? Why?' Her voice became stronger. Her eyes no longer threatened tears. Instead, they radiated anger. 'Bill was sure I'd lost it. He was sure I lost Merlot too. As if I could. He kept asking why would anyone take his picture, or him, for that matter? The dog was famous. No one would dare. But someone did. Todd Blankenship saw him in the backseat of a car. He said he didn't realize what dog it was until later. Cliff didn't steal the dog. So why did he take the picture?'

Mary looked from Naomi's angry eyes to the picture of the lovely little dog to Dan.

He didn't look any happier than Naomi, but his voice was soft. 'I have no idea, Naomi, but I'd like to find out.'

THIRTEEN

'Ellen, I can't thank you enough for doing this. I simply couldn't face it last night. I know it's early, but Dan's arranged for Ricker to bring his truck by at two, and I would never have finished by myself.'

Mary turned from the pile of clothes she had spread over the bed, sorting them into two piles. She and her niece had easily chosen the clothes Cliff would be buried in. There was only one dress shirt that had all of its buttons and one pair of pants that didn't have stains of some sort. It seemed a shame to bury the only halfway nice things Cliff had left, but then he deserved to be dressed this one last time in something decent. Mary packed them carefully in an old suitcase she'd found and started sorting the remaining clothes into a pile to throw away and another that could potentially go to St Mark's next rummage sale. The throw away pile was growing faster than the one for St Mark's.

'I know this isn't much fun, going through a murdered man's

clothes and things, but there doesn't seem to be much choice. After Naomi found that picture, she announced she was going home and couldn't come back this morning. Dan sent Agnes over to help but . . .'

Her niece interrupted. 'Will you look at this?'

'What?' Mary dropped the shirt she'd folded into the carton box packed with the clothes going to St Mark's. She ran her hands down the sides of her pant legs and walked over to see what her niece had found.

'It's a diary.' Ellen thumbed through the well-worn brown leather-bound book. 'It dates back' – she flipped back to the front page – 'about five years ago.' She handed it to Mary. 'Go to the end.'

Mary took the book but made no move to open it. She didn't want to know Cliff's thoughts, what made him happy or, more likely, what saddened him. She felt she had intruded enough cleaning out his closet and packing up his meager kitchen supplies. Something as private as a diary . . . 'Can't we give this to Dan?'

Ellen picked up a pile of sheets, towels and pillowcases off the end of the bed and put them into a carton box. 'Just a sec.' She wrote what she had packed on the inventory sheet they would attach to the box when it was full. 'Yes, but you need to read the last few pages.' She left her box, walked over and gave Mary a squeeze. 'I know. It feels creepy. Like we're spying on him, or something. But I think you need to read some of that. I want to know what you think.'

Mary looked at Ellen, who nodded, then down at the book. Its soft cover appeared like it had been held, opened and read a lot. She sighed. There was a purple ribbon attached to mark the owner's place. She let the book fall open to where the ribbon separated the pages. The date was 27 November this year, the weekend after Thanksgiving. The day Cliff's landlady had handed him his eviction notice? Mary counted quickly. Yes, the number of days allowed on the notice had passed. Cliff had to be out. Mary's hand shook as she read the entry.

'Just got an early Christmas present. Only, if I don't come up with some money, I won't be here for Christmas. Where I'll go, I have no idea. Don't know how I'm going to get money, either.

Or, do I? I've been wondering about this for some time. If I'm right . . . I know I'm right. Now, if I can prove it, Christmas might turn out merry after all.'

Mary almost dropped the book. She looked at Ellen then flipped the page and read the next entry. And the next. 'What's he talking about?'

'I have no idea. That's why I wanted you to read it.' Ellen held out her hand.

Mary put the book in it.

'He didn't post every day and most of them are just short sentences. They don't make much sense. Look. *"Father D'Angelo's got a new cat."* Why should Cliff care? And here. *"Alma's bitch had a litter. Does she know?"* Who's Alma, and if it's her dog, how could she not know?'

'I think I can answer that one. Alma Maxwell. She bred cocker spaniels for years, probably before Bonnie Blankenship started, but Cliff . . .'

'Oh, no. She isn't the one who had the dog Cliff spayed, is she?'

Mary nodded. 'She held on for a long time but told me yesterday she sold all the dogs she had left, except for that one, and is moving to Atlanta to live with her sister. She might not know one had puppies, but Cliff makes it sound like it's a big deal. I'm not sure why it should be.'

Ellen frowned. 'I know about her move. I'm going over this afternoon to talk about listing it. I didn't know about the dogs, though.' She looked at the book and flipped to another page. 'Listen to this. *"Should I do something about Luke?"* What does that mean? Then he has one about Evan. He owns Furry Friends, doesn't he? He wonders if Evan knows. Knows what? They're all like that. There's even one about those people who own the winery. Bliss – Bill and Naomi, right? He's got this one liner about them. *"Don't think Naomi is in this, but Bill? I don't know."* In what?'

'The Blisses are the ones who lost the little poodle. He was a champion and, I guess, very valuable. Naomi was devastated.' Mary thought of Naomi holding the picture of the little dog to her breast, her eyes filled with tears.

'I heard' – Ellen held up her hand to stop Mary's protest – 'I

know, no gossip, but this might be important.' Ellen looked from
Mary to the book and then waited.

After a second, Mary nodded.

'I heard Bill Bliss wasn't nearly as devastated as Naomi and
the dog was insured to the hilt. I don't know what "this" is or
what Cliff's talking about, but he seems to think Bill could be
implicated.'

Mary felt a little lightheaded and the notion to sit down was
suddenly strong. The edge of Cliff's bed was all that was available and she took it. 'Implicated in whatever it was that got Cliff
killed. That's what you mean, isn't it?'

Ellen nodded. 'Cliff's got a lot of comments in here that could
mean nothing, just him rambling, or that he found out something.
Something someone didn't want known. He mentioned money.'
Ellen paused and took a deep breath. The look on her face plainly
told Mary she didn't like what she was about to say. 'Do you
suppose Cliff tried to blackmail one of these people and it
backfired?'

'What?' Mary thought of all the people mentioned in Cliff's
diary. She knew them all, had known them for years. 'What could
any of those people possibly have done that would result in
blackmail?' She paused and shook her head empathically. 'Or
murder?'

'I have no idea. Cliff must have been pretty desperate to have
tried blackmail.'

'Who's blackmailing who?' A large carton box appeared in
the bedroom door. It almost totally obscured the person who
carried it. 'I've got everything packed, sealed and inventoried in
the living room and had a box left over.' The box fell to the floor,
revealing a short, rather round gray-haired woman tightly encased
in dark blue police pants, a wide black belt and a light blue
long-sleeved shirt tightly buttoned around a dark blue tie. 'Now,
what's all this about blackmail?'

'We found Cliff's diary. It sounds – odd.'

'Like he was blackmailing someone?' Agnes stopped in the
middle of the room, spread her feet apart slightly, hooked her
thumbs in her belt and stared at Mary.

Mary inwardly sighed. Agnes had recently been hired by the
police department to do office work. She answered the phones,

had learned how to contact the few squad cars Santa Louisa owned, took messages, handed out forms and did everything that wasn't an emergency or had to do with actual crime. Today she was here helping Mary and Ellen at Dan's request, but she'd somehow turned it into official police business. She checked everything Mary and Ellen packed as if she thought they might run off with something, a thought that made Mary shiver. She'd insisted they put the contents of each box down on an inventory list and sign each one before it was pasted on top. The inventory would come in handy when they needed to make a final disposal of Cliff's things, but Agnes' attitude was beginning to wear thin. She was not now, and never would be, law enforcement, a fact that seemed lost on her. More and more, Agnes reminded Mary of Barney Fife from *The Andy Griffith Show*.

'Who was he blackmailing?'

'We don't know that's what he did.' Mary looked at the book Ellen still held and shuddered. 'How much more did you read?'

'Not much. I didn't want to go any farther.' Ellen put the book down on Cliff's dresser and stepped back from it.

Agnes walked over and picked it up. 'Where does it say he was blackmailing someone?'

Mary's fists clenched. 'It doesn't. He says, toward the end, that he needs money and maybe knows how to get some.'

Agnes blinked. She stared at Mary, then down at the book. 'How?'

Ellen snorted with what Mary thought was an interrupted laugh. 'How was he going to get money? He doesn't say. Agnes, it's all innuendos. We don't have any idea what Cliff meant. Except, he seems to be sorry for all the things he did while he was drinking. Talks about how he wants to make up for what he did.'

It was Agnes' turn to snort. 'That's hard to believe. I've known Cliff Mathews ever since he set foot in this town, and I'm here to tell you, he was a much nicer man drunk than he ever was sober, and that's a fact.'

Mary glanced over at Ellen, who reached out and took the book back. She looked confused, exactly how Mary felt.

'Agnes, what are you talking about? Everything we read in that book says Cliff regretted all those things he did when he was drinking. Why, he even talks about Luke and how he should do something. He got Father D'Angelo a new cat. I don't know what he did to the old one, but he seemed to feel responsible.'

Agnes laughed. A loud and not very mirth-filled laugh. 'He got him a cat all right. The meanest, most cantankerous cat I've ever seen. I think Cliff did it on purpose. Blasted thing attacks Father every time he comes in the room. The cat's taken over Father's favorite reading chair, and the good man lets him. He – the cat – rules the house.' She paused for breath.

Mary and Ellen stared at her then at each other.

'Why does Father let him?' Ellen asked.

Agnes shrugged.

Mary's question was more direct. 'Did Cliff know what the cat was like?'

'He must have.'

This was not the Cliff Bonnie talked about. But Cliff had taken Naomi's picture of her poodle. Why? He'd brought Karl a DNA sample of that same dog to identify. What was that all about? Had he hidden the dog? No. He couldn't. Only . . . 'You make him sound mean.'

Agnes reached out and touched the diary, then withdrew her hand and let it drop to her side. 'Cliff was a nice man when he came here. He was nice when he started drinking. Even when all those things happened, all those "mistakes," he seemed sorry. He seemed kind. Then his wife died, his daughter left, he lost his practice and he got sober. I don't think he liked being sober. He got morose. He blamed everyone but himself for all the bad things that happened, and every year he got angrier. What're you going to do with that book? It should go in with the other books.' She reached out her hand.

Mary withdrew hers. 'No. I don't think so.' She looked over at Ellen, who nodded.

'What are you going to do?'

'There's only one thing to do.'

As one, Mary and Ellen said, 'Give it to Dan.'

FOURTEEN

Mary sat in a straight-backed chair opposite Dan's desk, trying not to fidget. Ellen wasn't doing as well. She shifted her weight in her chair beside Mary, picked up her Styrofoam coffee cup, put it back on the corner of Dan's desk and sighed heavily.

'All that isn't going to help me read faster.' Dan didn't take his eyes off the page he was reading.

'First-graders read faster than you.' Ellen squirmed again.

Dan closed the diary and surveyed them both before reaching for his coffee.

'Well?' Mary leaned forward, almost not noticing the toll the chair's hard surface had taken on her behind.

'What do you think?' Ellen leaned her elbows on the edge of Dan's desk and stared at him intently.

'What do you want me to say?' He took a sip of the coffee, made a face and put it back on his desk. 'That after reading a month's worth of Cliff's ramblings I now know who murdered him and why?'

'Yes.'

Dan smiled at his wife. 'I appreciate your faith in me, but it doesn't usually work that way. Wish it did.'

'Dan, you must have some idea what Cliff was thinking. We only read a few pages. They weren't very clear, but it sounded . . .'

'As if Cliff was contemplating blackmail?' He picked the book back up and held it as if he could squeeze more information out of it. 'He may have. However, he never comes right out and says so. He rambles. Talks about how sorry he is for some of the things he did, how Alma Maxwell still, after all these years, won't speak to him. He says he can't blame her, only he doesn't know how to fix it for her. He talks about how he knows Father D'Angelo felt terrible about losing his cat and he guesses he's responsible. So he found him another one.'

'He found him another one, all right.' Mary paused, coffee

cup halfway to her mouth. 'According to Agnes, he got Father
D'Angelo another cat without even talking to him.'

'That seems a little high-handed, but at least it was well
meant.'

'Not the way Agnes tells it.' Ellen stretched out her legs and
sat back. 'She says it's meaner than a bobcat. Says he gave Father
D'Angelo the cat on purpose. I guess Father doesn't know what
to do with it, but its terrorizing him and Mrs Farrell.'

'Who's Mrs Farrell?'

'His housekeeper.'

'Oh.' Dan shook his head a little. 'Most of what's in here are
lamentations on the hurt he caused people and what he can do
to make it up for them. Doesn't sound as if there was much.'

Ellen and Mary looked at each other. 'Who else?'

'Who else what?'

'You know very well what I'm talking about.' Mary used her
best middle-schoolteacher voice.

Dan grinned. 'Who else did he think he'd hurt and what did
he plan to do about it?'

'Luke, for one.'

'Luke who?' Ellen looked mystified. 'Do we know a Luke?'

'Luke from the library.' Mary turned toward her. 'You
remember him. Young, ponytail, diamond earring.'

'Oh. That Luke. What did Cliff do to him?'

'I'll read it to you. It's one of the most poignant.' Dan opened
the diary and flipped through pages, pausing at a couple before
stopping. 'This is it.' He glanced up at the two of them, both
waiting, sighed a little and started.

'"*Every time I think of young Luke, I want to cry. It's hard to
realize what I'd do for a drink back then. I don't think Liam
MacDougle really asked me to rig that junior handler class. I
remember him telling me he'd spot me a bottle if I helped his
kid, Ronnie. He meant coach him. I used to be a good coach.
There was just about nothing I couldn't get a dog to do and I
could teach the kids how to handle the dog too. The kids I coached
won a lot. Liam is an honorable man. That day – it's still foggy.
Why I thought . . . Then, after it was all over and Luke got thrown
out for trying to show a drugged dog, the look Liam gave me,
I'll never forget that. Ever. I don't remember if his kid won or*

not. I sure remember Luke not winning. Why, oh why, did I do those things?"'

Mary sucked in her breath, hard. It made her stomach hurt. So that was what happened. 'I wonder if Luke knows how Cliff felt.'

'Not if Cliff hadn't approached him yet.' The look on Dan's face was speculative, as if he, too, was mulling a possibility over in his mind.

'Cliff seems to have tried to make amends to everyone else he could think of.'

'Or at least have thought about it. His writing about it in his diary doesn't necessarily translate into action.'

Mary nodded. Ellen was right. There was nowhere in the part of the diary she read that mentioned any overtures Cliff had made to anyone. 'That's true. He talks about making amends but doesn't say how. Except for Father D'Angelo's cat.'

'That doesn't sound much like making amends.' Ellen bent down to pick up her purse, took out her cell phone and checked the time.

'You know, the more I think about it, the more his comments sound speculative.' Mary spoke slowly, as she tried to remember how Cliff phrased his cryptic sentences.

'As if he was assessing his chances for blackmail?' Ellen looked over at Dan, who shrugged. 'All those people he mentions, they were all victims, them and their animals. He may have been sorry, but he doesn't say he did anything to ask for their forgiveness. People like Alma, like Father D'Angelo, don't seem like potential blackmail victims. To the best of my knowledge, they're both squeaky clean and neither of them has any money. He could hardly blackmail Luke. He mentions the Blankenships but they were good friends and no comment he makes refutes that. He talks about the Blisses being involved in something, but he doesn't say what and it doesn't sound ominous. So, who was he thinking about?'

'I have no idea. If he had decided to try to blackmail someone, I can't see who from his diary.' Dan shut the little book and laid it on his deck. 'Where did you find it? Sergeant Ricker and I searched that place pretty thoroughly yesterday afternoon. I got all his papers and personal things from his desk and brought them back here. We went through everything, I thought.'

'It was in his pillowcase.'

Dan stared at his wife then burst out laughing. 'His pillowcase?'

Ellen nodded. 'I was stripping the bed, packing up all the linens and it fell out. I picked it up to see what it was and it fell open. I read some and then called to Aunt Mary. It sure sounded as if he planned to blackmail someone.'

Dan nodded. 'It does. Only, who?'

Mary shrugged. 'That's why we brought it over. We thought you needed to see it right away.'

Dan leaned forward, resting his chin on his hands.

Mary and Ellen waited.

Finally, he sat up straight. 'Have you finished packing up all his stuff?'

Mary shook her head. 'Almost. We've finished the kitchen, and Agnes did the living room. We were working on his bedroom when we found the book.'

'OK. Are you going back? Cliff's landlady wants everything out this afternoon, and Ricker will be there . . .' he glanced at the digital clock on his desk . . . 'in a little more than an hour. Is Agnes still there?'

'I can't go back. I have an appointment to list Alma's house and I need to go home and change.' Ellen pulled out her cell phone and glanced at the time. 'I really need to get going.'

'I can for a little while, but I promised Luanne I'd pick up the children after school. She does the bookkeeping out at Golden Hills winery. It's Friday and she has to close out the books and can't get away until about five. I want to be there when they come out of their classes.' She paused and took a deep breath. 'Dan, do you really think the children are in danger? Luanne is worried sick. So is Tony, and they're trying so hard not to let the children feel it. Today is Renaldo's soccer practice and he pitched a fit when they told him he couldn't go. I said I'd take him, but they both felt that – well, the field is big and the kids are all over the place. Hard to keep them in sight, so they decided he needed to skip it. I have errands to run, and they can tag along until I can deliver them to Luanne at the winery.'

It was as if a cloud settled on Dan's face. 'I don't know much of anything yet, and I don't want to take a chance they've spooked this guy. We know the kids saw him. He's got to be wondering if they can identify him. I'd rather have Ronaldo mad at all of us for making him miss soccer practice than see him hurt, or worse.'

A shiver ran through Mary, from her head to her toes. The very thought of anything happening to those children . . . 'Ronaldo will have to deal with it. How long do you think we're going to have to keep this up?' She ran her calendar through her head, wondering how much Luanne would need her and which committee meetings wouldn't bore them to tears. All of them would.

'Dan,' Ellen was on her feet, her tote bag slung over her shoulder, 'have they done the autopsy yet?'

'As we speak.' He paused, as if trying to decide what to say next. 'Doc did tell me one thing.'

Ellen stood still; so did Mary.

Dan smiled. 'You two watch too many crime shows. He says he was stabbed with something long, thin and pointed. It went in through the rib cage and he's pretty sure right into his heart. He'll know more when he gets in there.' He leaned over his desk, pushed some buttons on his desk phone and picked up the receiver. 'How long will it take to finish boxing up all his things? I have to get them out of there and over to St Mark's this afternoon. It was nice of Les to say he'd store them. When we locate the daughter, we'll know what to do with them. I wouldn't be surprised if most of his things end up in your next rummage sale, Mary.'

Mary had a little trouble making the shift from long, sharp murder weapons and possible harm to the children back to Cliff's old dishtowels. 'Oh. An hour or so. Agnes may be finished by now.' She thought about the lovely old buffet and hoped Dan found the daughter soon. She got to her feet and steadied herself. 'You'd better get this solved, and fast. We're not going to be able to keep those kids under wraps for forever.'

FIFTEEN

Mary parked the car as close to the school as she could. Cars were parked two deep in front of it. She had no idea that many parents picked up their children. Then again, this was St Theresa's, a Catholic school. No school buses. She wondered what the mothers did who worked. She didn't think St Theresa's had an after-school program. She shook her head as she made her way through the parked cars and the chattering mothers. They must have quite a car pool system worked out. She pushed the front glass doors open and headed for the office. She hoped Luanne hadn't forgotten to send a note to the secretary authorizing her to sign out the children. The school would never hand them over to anyone who didn't have written permission from the parent, no matter how well they knew them.

The school secretary was on the phone. She wiggled her fingers at Mary while she agreed with whatever the caller had said. Mary found a chair, sank into it gratefully and waited.

She didn't wait long.

'Mary.' Sister Margaret Anne poked her head out of her office and waved at Mary. 'Can you come in for a moment?'

Mary nodded. She'd expected this. 'Good afternoon, Sister. It's been a while. Wasn't it the fundraiser for the new children's wing at the hospital we helped organize?'

Sister Margaret Anne nodded absently, obviously not interested in what happened since she'd seen Mary last. Her only interest was in what happened today. 'What's going on with the Mendosa children?'

She closed the door, walked behind her desk and sat, motioning for Mary to do the same. 'Luanne called here, her voice practically shaking, saying you'd pick them up and no one, emphasizing no one but you, Mr Mendosa or her was to come near them. Oh. Dan Dunham could. Mary, he's the chief of police!'

Mary tried to swallow her sigh. She didn't blame Luanne one bit for being upset, but falling apart wasn't going to help.

However, Sister Margaret Anne needed to know what happened. They needed her to help keep the children safe.

'It's about Cliff Mathews. I'm sure you've heard.'

Sister Margaret Anne nodded, but she didn't smile. 'He was murdered. In the manger scene on St Theresa's lawn, of all places. What a wicked thing to do.'

She sounded more outraged than scared. That might change, soon.

'The Mendosa children saw the person who did it.'

Sister Margaret Anne didn't say a word. She stared at Mary, her mouth slightly open, her eyes wide. Finally, she blinked. 'Good Lord.'

Mary nodded. 'No one knows this, except whoever killed Cliff. It has to stay that way.' Mary relayed the events of Wednesday night.

Sister Margaret Anne sat rigid, her clasped hands increasingly tightening. 'You really think the children might be in danger from this man?'

'We have no idea. We don't know who he is. If he thinks they recognized him, well, I can't say what he might do. We just don't know.'

Sister Margaret Anne nodded but her hands didn't relax. 'You can't rule out the possibility he might do something here, on the school grounds. Shoot them, perhaps.'

'Oh, I don't think so.' Mary shook her head vigorously. 'I really don't think so.' But she did think he might do *something*. Wasn't that why she was here? 'It's more likely he'd try to take them – grab them. Or something.' Her voice got weaker as she wound down.

'You have no idea what might happen.' Sorrow and fear were in Sister Margaret Anne's voice and in her eyes. 'I'm responsible for all these children. If there is even a remote possibility of danger . . . I'd better call Chief Dunham.'

Mary wished she'd never opened her mouth, but she'd had to, just as Sister Margaret Anne had to call Dan. That was one phone call he wasn't going to enjoy.

The bell rang, announcing the end of the school day with enough noise to send shock waves through Mary. Sister Margaret Anne almost seemed not to have heard it. But she had. She got to her feet. 'I need to help make sure the kids get in the right cars. It's hard to keep track, and sometimes the older ones don't tell us when plans change. Come on. I'll help you find the Mendosa children.' She paused as they got to the door. 'Tell Luanne I'll talk to her this evening.' She took a step but turned once more, this time with anger in her eyes. 'This is outrageous. Those innocent children and poor old Cliff.' She paused and her voice softened. 'We had a dog at the convent once, a wonderful little dog we found one morning on the front porch. Cliff took care of that dog for years and did it with kindness and patience. Well, until those last few years. He didn't deserve this, though. And the children! They must be terrified. The police had better catch that man, and fast. This is just too much.' She wheeled around, her skirt and short veil flying, and left the room.

Mary followed. It didn't sound like Sister Margaret Anne had any recent memories. If she had, would she be as sympathetic? Probably. She was a kind woman. One thing they could agree on, the police had better catch whoever killed Cliff, and fast. As for the children being terrified, she wasn't so sure. They'd been pretty scared at first, but now she thought they were beginning to enjoy all the excitement. Which was not a good thing, not a good thing at all.

SIXTEEN

'Why are we going here?' Dalia sounded confused and not too pleased.

Ronaldo already had his seat belt off and his door half open.

'You said we were going to the pet shop.'

'We are.' Mary glanced in her rearview mirror. 'Ronaldo, don't you put one foot in the street until I tell you.'

The boy stopped, his foot half in and half out of the car. He looked like a runner ready to take off as soon as the gun fired.

Mary sighed, released her seat belt, reached over to the passenger seat and picked up a folder. She found the paper she wanted, extracted it and opened her door. 'Stay with me, both of you.'

Ronaldo pushed open the door to the Village Hardware store and the three of them entered. The store appeared to be empty.

'Mary McGill. I haven't seen you in here in ages.' The man seemed to appear out of nowhere, grinning from ear to ear. He looked like a lumberjack in his blue jeans, lace-up tan boots and plaid flannel shirt, sleeves rolled up to the elbows. His head was covered with thick black curls and his deeply muscled forearms with black hair that extended down to the knuckles of his stubby fingers. 'Hope that sink isn't blocked again.'

'No, Todd. The sink is working fine. I hoped you could take this home to Bonnie. It's a receipt for the donation the Pure Breed Dog Club made to the Christmas Can Tree. They'll need it for their taxes.'

Todd Blankenship glanced at it but made no move to take it. 'I don't suppose you'd consider driving this out to Bonnie.' He looked at Mary forlornly. 'Bonnie needs some company right about now, some cheering up. She's taking Cliff's death pretty hard.'

'Oh.' She didn't know what to say. Stopping at Bonnie's wasn't on her schedule, but she'd wondered if she was all right. Cliff had been Bonnie's vet and friend for many years. 'I have to go to Evan's then drop the children off at the winery – I can stop by your place on the way back.' She glanced at her watch and tried not to let Todd see her reluctance. She'd planned on going home early, taking off her shoes and doing nothing harder for dinner than heating up the chicken and rice soup she took out of the freezer this morning. But if she could help Bonnie . . . 'She's taking it hard?'

'Very hard.' Todd didn't look too happy. He shook his head in bewilderment. 'How could anyone do such a thing?'

'I don't know.' Mary tucked the paper back in her carryall and looked around for the children. They were by a large bin filled with sale items and were intently examining something that looked like barbeque tools. 'What are you two doing?'

'Looking for a Christmas present for Tony. We want to get him something with our own money. Mom too.' Ronaldo returned his attention to the bin.

'Do you think Tony would like this? He loves doing barbeques.'
Dalia held up a barbeque apron embossed with a chef's hat, a
whiskey bottle and a saying Mary didn't think appropriate for
a gift given by two small children.

'It has a broken apron string.' She removed the apron from
Dalia's hand.

'It's only two dollars.'

'It's still overpriced.'

Ronaldo dug a long-handled spatula out of the jumble of things
in the bin. 'I'll bet he'd like this. Where's the fork thing?'

Todd removed the spatula from Ronaldo's hand. 'It's gone.
I've priced these things so low because parts are missing or the
packages are torn, or something. I'm not sure this is where you
want to shop for a Christmas present.'

Dalia looked at him then down at his boots. A slight frown
passed over her face. 'We only have five dollars and we don't
want to get any money from Mom if we can help it.' She turned
back to the bin, moved stuff around and came up with a package
of barbeque skewers, long, thin ones with heavy wooden
handles. 'Look! These are nicer than the ones Mom and Tony
have and they're only three dollars.' She held the package aloft,
grinning.

'Oh. That package is torn and one's missing.' Todd reached
for it but Dalia clutched it to her chest.

'Mom can find a box.'

'Aunt Mary will find one.' There was no doubt in Ronaldo's
voice. 'We'll give it to both of them.'

'Would you?' Dalia's expression was hopeful as she looked
at Mary. 'They're only three dollars. We can get something for
the baby with what's left.'

'Of course I will.' Mary's thoughts whirled. How was she
going to wrap those wicked-looking things? The ends were sharp.
They'd go through any wrapping paper . . . The long, awkward
box under her bed. She'd been certain it would come in handy
someday. She examined the skewers. Five of them. Should be
six but Tony and Luanne wouldn't mind. That was more than
enough for their family and the baby wouldn't be eating barbeque
food for some time. 'Ring them up, Todd.'

Todd looked at Mary then down at the children, reluctance

evident in his furrowed brow and his tight shoulders. 'That's mighty thoughtful of you kids, but are you sure? Someone destroyed the package and there are only five skewers.' His voice trailed away as the children said nothing but showed no signs of replacing their prize in the sale bin.

Mary glanced at her watch. 'They'll do fine. Ring them up, Todd. Dalia, where's your money?'

Distress passed over the little girl's face. 'My wallet's in my backpack in the car.'

'I'll go.' Ronaldo beamed at Mary. 'The car's right outside. Can I?'

Mary's car was parked outside the store window in plain sight. Nothing could possibly happen to the boy with her eye firmly glued on him. Had she locked it? No. She never did, not in this town. She nodded and he was off.

'We're going to the pet shop next. They have the cutest puppies.'

Ronaldo was half in and half out of the car and Mary gave Dalia's statement only half her attention.

'You like puppies?'

Mary turned quickly away from the window.

Dalia nodded. 'We found one, Ronaldo and me. We're trying to get Mom and Tony to let us keep him.'

Todd's next question was sharp with surprise. 'Where?'

Mary quickly intervened. 'Over by the church. They found it over by St Theresa's. A stray, I guess.'

'Where is it now? Is it OK?'

Another dog person. Mary wondered if he'd act this concerned if the kids had found a newborn baby. That wasn't fair. There were more stray dogs than lost babies, and it was a good thing people cared about them. 'It's at the Benningtons' clinic.'

That wasn't enough for Dalia. 'Doctor Bennington's going to keep him until he's bigger and learns to – you know – go to the bathroom outside. He's real cute. He's got one white foot and white down his front and all his toenails are white and his ears are curly. He looks like the puppies over at the pet shop. You can go look at them, if you want, and you'll know just what Sampson looks like.'

Todd might be a dog person, but he didn't seem to have any

interest in Evan's puppies. He opened his mouth ready to ask another question, but Ronaldo burst in the door, panting slightly but proudly waving Dalia's wallet over his head. 'Got it.'

Dalia handed Todd a five-dollar bill. He rang up the sale, gave Ronaldo the package and Dalia the change. She gravely counted it and put it in her wallet.

Mary hid her smile. 'We've got to get going if we're going to meet your mom at the winery.'

The children beamed as they carried their treasure out to the car. Mary put the skewers in the trunk and took both their hands, and they walked across the street to Furry Friends pet shop. She glanced back. Todd Blankenship watched them from the door of his shop. Mary waved. He waved back, turned and walked back into the store.

SEVENTEEN

The children skipped as they crossed the street, at least Dalia did. Mary could hardly keep up with them. She didn't drop their hands, however, until they were inside. They immediately headed for the puppy pen.

'Where's the one who looks like Sampson?' Dalia turned toward Evan, who approached at almost a trot, followed by two men who couldn't have looked more unalike. 'Is he all right?'

'That puppy sold. He's going to be a little girl's Christmas present from her grandma.'

He smiled at her. So did the two men who stood behind him. Mary watched relief flood Dalia's face. Ronaldo knelt beside the pen and put his hand over the top, ready to scratch the ears of any puppy who came close. They all did.

Mary finally looked closer at the two men. 'Why, Glen Manning. John Lavorino. I haven't seen you two in ages. Where have you been and what are you doing here?'

John, short and swarthy, with what Mary thought an unfortunately large nose, looked across at Glen. John fiddled with the gold chain that hung around his neck, clearly seen through his unbuttoned lavender Henley. Today his jeans were black and very tight. John's jeans were always tight. He glanced back at Mary, then at Evan and back at Glen, but he didn't say anything. Instead, he knelt down beside Ronaldo, reached into the puppy pen, picked one up and handed it to him. The puppy immediately started to lick Ronaldo's nose. The boy giggled and sat on the floor, Indian style, the puppy wiggling in his lap.

John looked over at Dalia. 'You're the Mendosa children, aren't you?'

Dalia nodded, her eyes glued on the remaining puppies.

'You want to hold one too?'

She nodded again, a smile playing around the corners of her mouth.

'Sit down.' John reached into the pen and pulled out the smallest puppy, almost equally black and white, with a pink nose. She had white feet and shiny clear toenails.

'She looks like she had her nails done.' Dalia laughed and held the puppy close to her face, where she also got a kiss on the nose. She laughed again, lowered the puppy into her arms and started to rock it back and forth, humming under her breath.

'Starts early, doesn't it?' Glen was tall, thin and dressed in well-pressed chinos and a blue button-down collar shirt, cuffs turned back once over the sleeves of his navy blue pullover. Brown leather sandals over white socks completed the picture. Mary blinked at the sight of him. She'd never seen Glen in anything but the carefully tailored suits he wore at the bank. Shouldn't he be at the bank? Evidently he was starting his weekend early.

He smiled at the picture the girl and dog made. Mary didn't. It was appealing, but she couldn't help think the child was growing up too fast and fear for her made her throat close. The fear wasn't for her growing up but that something might happen so she didn't. Whoever killed Cliff would have to get by Mary first before he harmed one hair on the head of either of these children. She shifted slightly and saw Evan out of the corner of her eye. He wasn't smiling. Glen saw him as well.

'Lighten up, Evan. It's good for the puppies to be held and good for the kids to hold them. They're not going to hurt them.'

Evan almost wrung his hands and his face was contorted with anguish. Little beads of sweat appeared on the edges of what hair was left on his scalp. He kept glancing at the door as if he expected someone to burst in any minute. What was the matter with him? Almost as if he'd read her mind, he said, 'Those aren't my puppies. They're here for sale. I'm responsible for them. The' – he paused, as if he'd caught himself just in time – 'owners might not like them being held.'

Ronaldo looked up, alarm in his eyes. 'Do we have to put them back?'

'No.' John was emphatic. 'Evan gets nervous. You can hold them for another couple of minutes.' He looked at the crestfallen faces and knelt down once more between the children. 'Tell you what. When Glen's and my next litter of cockapoos are ready for Evan to sell, we'll let you know and you can come hold them as much as you want.'

Ronaldo grinned but Dalia held her puppy up and examined it closely. 'Is that what these puppies are? Cockapoos? What does that mean?'

'It means they have a cocker spaniel for one parent and a poodle for the other. Cockapoos.' Glen bent down and took the puppy out of her hands. 'Evan is right. It's time to put them back.'

The children groaned but handed over the puppies. Evan leaned against the counter and ran a hand over his damp scalp.

Mary looked at her watch. 'It's after four. I told your mother I'd have you out at the winery before five. We'd better get going.' She looked at them. 'If she sees you looking like that she'll never trust me with you again. You need to wash, and Dalia, you have to comb your hair. Do you have one?'

Dalia cheerfully shook her head.

'You're in luck. I do. Evan, do you have a bathroom where the children can wash up?'

Evan pointed toward the back of the store. Mary handed Dalia the small brush she always carried and the two dejectedly walked in the direction of the bathroom.

'Don't dawdle, either. We have to get going.'

She dived into her carryall and pulled out the receipt for the donations Evan had made and handed it to him. 'This is why I came in. You'll need this for your taxes, and I want you to know the entire can tree committee thanks you.'

Evan smiled a weak smile and took the paper. Mary didn't smile back. Two questions had occurred to her and she wanted answers before the children came back.

'Evan, where do you get the puppies you sell?'

'What do you mean?' Evan's eyes shifted and he ducked his head. She'd seen that look on every seventh-grader she'd ever taught when they were trying to avoid answering a question.

'Where do the puppies come from? Who owns them? What do you know about them?'

'Why?' The reptile tank suddenly seemed of supreme importance. Evan walked over, put his hand in and moved a fake green tree a little to the left, much to the annoyance of the lizard asleep under it.

'She wants to know if you buy puppies from a puppy mill.' John propped himself up by leaning on the counter next to Evan. He lounged back against the counter, letting his elbows hold him, and looked at Evan over the top of his sunglasses, which he let fall from the top of his head where he'd pushed them.

'Straighten up, John.' It sounded like something Glen said often.

John grinned but straightened up. When he looked at Mary, all trace of a smile was gone. 'He doesn't, you know. He knows every breeder who brings dogs, cats or anything else in here to sell. He makes sure every animal has its shots, or whatever they need, and demands a vet certificate to prove it. I think he'd shoot anyone who tried to bring an endangered animal in the door. Our Evan is a good man. We wouldn't bring our puppies to him if he wasn't. We wouldn't keep bugging him to sell us part ownership in the shop, either.' He looked over at Glen, who stood, not moving, smiling or talking, next to a tank that held small turtles. 'Would we?'

Glen shook his head. 'No, we wouldn't.'

Mary glanced toward the bathroom, but there was no sign of the children. No screams came from that direction, either, so she decided it was safe to ask her next question.

'I haven't seen any of you in church for, oh, several weeks. I heard – I haven't talked to Reverend McIntyre but . . . I hope I'm wrong.'

Glen, John and Evan exchanged glances. Evan left the lizard alone and turned back toward the puppies. Tension was evident in his back muscles, even through his blue long-sleeved polo. John's face seemed to turn black. His eyes snapped and his nostrils flared. He appeared about to say something when Glen laid a hand on his arm. 'You're not wrong. There was a little . . . unpleasantness. We didn't want it to get out of hand and didn't want the congregation to start choosing up sides, so we thought – we decided – to start attending services at a church in San Luis Obispo. We're going down there tonight. They're having a potluck, with music and dancing after.' He paused and glanced at the other two men before going on. 'Attending the dances at St Mark's is a little awkward.'

Mary couldn't remember when she'd felt as sick, as humiliated for her friends. Where had Les – Reverend McIntyre – been in all this? How much did he know? Should she do something? Say something? She should, and would. 'I can't tell you how sorry I am and how appalled. What can I do to help?'

'Nothing, Mary.' Evan tried to smile but it didn't work very well. 'Some things are just the way they are.'

'Surely we can do something. Who is it that's acting this way? I'll talk to them; I'll get Les, Reverend McIntyre, to talk to them also. You must know that most of us don't . . . What is it?'

The three of them looked at her with almost identical expressions of wry amusement, sorrow and fury.

Finally, it was Glen who spoke. 'You want to know who stirred up some of the congregation against us.'

Mary nodded, a feeling of dread creeping up her throat.

'Cliff.'

EIGHTEEN

Mary drove almost on autopilot. The children sat in the back, discussing the merits of the puppies they'd held, the other critters offered in Evan's pet shop and what they could get for the baby for two dollars. Mary barely heard them. Her thoughts were on Cliff. What had he done, and why? John and Glen had been members of St Mark's for years. Everyone knew them, knew they were a couple. No one cared. At least, Mary didn't think anyone cared. Evidently, she was wrong. But what could Cliff have done to make them change churches? He wasn't even a member. Well, not an active member. It must have been something pretty uncomfortable. What that was, Mary silently vowed to find out.

The light changed, she made her left-hand turn and entered the winery parking lot. It was after four, but the lot was still half full. Mary stepped out of the car and waited for the children, who joined her almost immediately. She took each by the hand but didn't move. Instead, she looked around. She'd heard the winery was impressive but still wasn't quite prepared for what lay before her. The building sprawled out on top of a knoll, covering most of it. The stucco was painted a pale creamy yellow, the shutters on the long windows were a bright blue and the door leading into the building from the cobblestone courtyard was massive oak, its handles hammered wrought iron. A tiled terrace was to the right of the building, iron tables and chairs scattered over it. The umbrellas were tied down, the tables empty. Why, wasn't hard to guess. The early winter breeze made sitting outside uncomfortable. Mary let go of the children and pulled her jacket tighter around her, took each child's hand again and started toward the doors.

Dalia pulled away and stared at the vineyard that trailed down the hill toward the highway. Houses could just be glimpsed between the highway and where the vines ended. 'Look. There's Tony's truck.' She pointed toward a dirt road that ran between the vines. A group of men piled into the back of a dirty brown pickup. Another group stacked branches at the end of a row of vines. 'They must be done pruning for the day.'

They watched for a moment as the truck slowly made its way up the hill. It turned off, headed for what looked like an equipment barn about halfway up the slope. It disappeared through blue double doors.

'Come on.' Mary tugged at the children. 'Tony will be up here soon enough. Let's go find your mother.'

Mary had been in half the wineries in Santa Louisa but she'd never seen one like this. The room they entered was huge and filled with light. The wall that overlooked the terrace held a series of French doors, showcasing the panoramic views of Santa Louisa and the hills beyond. There were brightly striped canvas roll-up canopies on the outside to protect the room, and those who sat on the patio, from the hot summer sun. This afternoon they were pulled up to show the beginnings of what promised to be a beautiful winter sunset.

A large round display table stood just inside the windows, piled with majolica pottery and pewter platters, all in some sort of grape pattern. Books were featured on another, and there was one full of crystal wineglasses. The one closest to the door where Mary stood offered cookbooks. Main courses made with wine, pasta dishes from Tuscany, artisan bread recipes, straight from the grill delights. There was a book for every taste. There was also a goodly display of barbeque tools, baking dishes, kitchen implements and cork pullers. Mary looked at the barbeque skewers and wondered if she should try to talk the children into another choice. She strained to read the price tag and gave a gasp. What they had already purchased would do just fine. She turned as the children tugged her toward a hallway that opened up on the far side of the long and very crowded tasting room bar. People stood against it, resting their feet on the brass rail, making notes in small booklets with stubby pencils as they sipped tiny amounts of wine from long-stemmed glasses. For many folks it would not be a dry Christmas.

'Mom's down this way.'

She was being tugged down the hallway toward what looked like offices. She'd seen people tasting wine before. That wasn't what held her attention, or caused her to drag her feet. It was the cookbooks. She wanted to look at them. Maybe later.

'Mary.'

Naomi stood in an open doorway of a spacious room that held two large desks, back to back, in the middle. Bookshelves lined the far wall, loaded with bottles of wine, pictures, plaques and long-stemmed glasses. There were a couple of upholstered tub chairs, a credenza and a load of electronic equipment. The Blisses' office.

'What are you doing here?' She looked down the hall past

Mary to where cries of 'Mom' and soft laughter sounded. 'Oh. You had the Mendosa children.'

Mary nodded. 'Glad you're here. It'll save me a trip.'

'A trip?' Naomi looked blank.

'Yes. Cliff's memorial. We talked about it yesterday.' Mary was beginning to feel tired and faintly irritated. 'We've finished packing all of his things and some of the church people are picking them up to take to St Mark's. Les has agreed to store them temporarily. Now, we need to decide what we're going to do about the service.'

'Nothing.'

'What?' Mary wasn't sure she'd heard right. Nothing? 'What are you talking about? Les, Reverend McIntyre, asked us to – well, Isabel asked us.'

'I talked to Bill about this. He thinks, and he's right – Mary, I can't do it.'

The words weren't making any sense. 'I don't understand.'

'Come in the office.' Naomi turned her back on Mary and walked into the room.

Mary glanced down the hall, nervous she hadn't personally delivered the children to their mother, but another burst of laughter reassured her. They were with Luanne. Mary followed Naomi and sat herself in one of the chairs. 'Now. What's all this about?'

Naomi sat behind her desk, a gold pen in her hand. She didn't look at Mary but stared at a yellow legal pad set squarely in the middle of her desk. 'I can't do it. Memorials mean saying nice things about the dead person. Friends gather, console the family and each other and remember things they'd done together, good things.' She made some marks on the legal pad, drew a figure of what Mary thought might be a dog, then a bottle, then a stick man. Finally she let the pen go slack in her hand and looked up. 'There aren't any good memories.'

Mary had no idea what to say. She didn't need to. Now the difficult words were out, Naomi seemed eager to explain.

'We've only been here about four years. We never saw the Cliff so many of you remember. The kind one, the one who was a good vet. The sober one.' She picked the pen back up and started rolling it around in her fingers, keeping her eyes resolutely fixed on it. 'The first time we met Cliff he showed up here, drunk. It was our grand opening. Bill was all for throwing him out, but the mayor was here and a couple of other people who knew him. They got him out before he caused a disturbance. He kept coming back. Sometimes he was sober, sometimes not, but always he came because he wanted to see Merlot, the little poodle who . . . disappeared. It got to the point where I'd lock the dog in my office when I saw him coming.' She laid the pen on the paper and looked straight at Mary for the first time. 'It wasn't any better after he got sober. He didn't come as much, but when he did he hung around, not saying anything, just picking up bottles, putting them down, looking for the dog. Mary, he was weird. He wasn't very good for business, either.' This last she said with a rueful little laugh well mixed with bitterness. 'I got to the point where I almost hated him. I hated seeing that old car of his drive into the parking lot.' She paused again and this time sighed deeply. 'Bill thought I was overreacting. Maybe I was, but I'll tell you something . . .' She paused again, as if choosing her words carefully. 'I've wondered if Cliff had something to do with Merlot's disappearance.'

Mary sucked in her breath quickly. 'Oh. Oh, no. Why would he?'

Naomi shook her head. 'I don't know, but he was here that day.' Her eyes filled with tears. She pulled her desk drawer open, pulled a couple of tissues out of a box Mary couldn't see and slammed it shut. 'He was so damn weird about the dog, always telling Bill we should breed him, even. I've always wondered, and when I saw that picture yesterday, it all came back. Mary, there is no way I can help put on a memorial for that man. I don't have even one good memory to share.' She dabbed both eyes, blinked away any remaining tears, straightened herself and laid her folded hands on the desk. 'I'm sorry.'

The person Naomi described wasn't the one Mary knew. Or thought she knew. Why would Cliff act like that? But then, why would he complain to Reverend McIntyre about John and Glen? Why would he give a half-wild cat to Father D'Angelo? The cryptic sentences in his diary – what did they mean? A throbbing started in her temples. 'I'm sorry, also. Of course you don't have to do anything. I had no idea – I'll talk to Les.' She had a lot to talk about with Les.

'Oh. I didn't realize you had someone – hello, Mrs McGill.'

Mary twisted in her chair at the sound of the man's voice. The sun was almost finished for the day and a shadow obscured the doorway. At first, she didn't recognize the man who stood there. He walked into the room and she knew him immediately. Bill Bliss. Naomi's husband. He wasn't a man you easily forgot. Tall, solidly built, he wore his gray wool slacks, open-necked blue dress shirt and soft navy jacket with an easy confidence. Mary was surprised he remembered her. They had been introduced once at church and had nodded at each other a few times, but she'd always felt it was cursory. Maybe she'd been wrong.

She smiled and nodded. 'Nice to see you, Bill.' She would have sworn he blinked at the 'Bill' but covered it quickly. Her smile widened.

'We're leaving now.' Dalia skipped into the room and skidded to a stop when she saw Bill Bliss. 'Oh.'

He turned to look at the child, a frown narrowing his eyebrows. They looked like brown and gray caterpillars.

Dalia looked back, her mouth still forming a small 'Oh.'

Ronaldo almost ran into her as he entered. 'Why are you standing— Oh.' He, too, stared at Bill before he glanced at his sister.

Their eyes met, then they looked at Mary, soundless. Soundless, for them, was not a normal occurrence. The moment didn't last.

Luanne walked into the room, carrying a briefcase. 'I'm going now. Oh, Bill. I didn't know you were back.' She nodded, but it was Naomi she addressed. She looked tired and didn't seem to notice as the children backed up to stand close, one on each side of her.

Ronaldo reached for the briefcase. 'I'll carry that for you, Mom.'

She squeezed him with her free arm. 'That's all right, sweetie. That's my laptop. I think I'd better hold it, but I forgot my tote bag in my office. Can you carry that?'

Ronaldo beamed and headed out the door. Dalia gave Bill Bliss one more look, ducked out from under her mother's arm and followed. Mary watched them go. So did Bill.

'Brenda's closing out tonight. I'll make the bank deposit Monday. The payroll's ready, all except the hourly people, and the inventory is up to date. I'll go over that with Brenda on Monday. She's going to be fine.'

Naomi nodded. Bill frowned. Mary heaved a silent sigh of

relief. She hadn't known if Luanne and Tony worked weekends or not. The first committee meeting for St Mark's spring rummage sale was tomorrow. She wouldn't mind missing it. She'd attended more than her share. However, try as hard as she might, she'd once again been elected chairman. She needed to show up. 'What about Monday? Do you want me to pick up the children?'

Luanne glanced at Bill then over at Naomi. 'Let's see what happens. Can you drop by the house after church on Sunday? Tony should know his schedule by then. And Mary, thank you.'

Mary smiled and nodded. She was happy she could help but secretly relieved she wouldn't be needed until Monday. There were things she had to do besides the committee meeting. At some point in the next couple of days she wanted to talk with Les. She wanted to know what to do about Cliff's memorial. If a lot of others felt the same way Naomi did John and Glen wouldn't be coming, and she didn't think Evan would either. What had happened with them? What had Cliff done? Yes, she had to talk to Les. Right now, however, she had to go see Bonnie, and then she was going home. Did she have a bottle of wine in the refrigerator? She couldn't remember. Well, she was in a winery.

'I need to go as well. However, I hear your Chardonnay is exceptional. May I buy a bottle?'

Bill Bliss smiled for the first time since he'd come in. 'You may indeed. Let me get one for you.' He took her by the arm and they headed toward the tasting room. Mary looked back. Luanne was right behind them, but she turned the other way down the hall.

'Mary, thank you again. We'll see you Sunday.'

NINETEEN

The drive to Bonnie's was too short for Mary to sort out all of her thoughts. Why had the Mendosa children fallen quiet when they saw Bill Bliss? The children were many things, bright and fun, but never quiet. Had they recognized him? Or thought they did? No, not possible. They hadn't looked scared.

Wary perhaps, but not scared. Well, he was their mother's boss, and their stepfather's as well. Could that account for it? Someone had said something, though. What was it? Something . . . insurance. That was it. Ellen said the little poodle the Blisses had was insured to the hilt. Could Bill really have done something to the dog, made it disappear somehow, and collected the insurance? Could Cliff have found out and decided to blackmail him? She shook her head. This was beginning to sound like a made-for-TV movie.

She turned into Bonnie's driveway and paused. The big gate was open. She drove through.

No one seemed to be around. Bonnie's car was parked by the kennel building. Her van wasn't, but that didn't mean anything. Some people actually kept cars in their garage. She got out, stretched and let the car door slam. Immediately dogs barked. Yelped. Demanded to know who was on their property. If Bonnie was here, she knew that Mary, or someone, was also.

She'd heard. She appeared in the doorway of the kennel bulding, peering into the dim light of the yard. 'Mary! I didn't know you were coming.'

'I was at the winery and thought I'd stop off and give you the receipt for the donations. I didn't know if you were a nonprofit or not but thought you should have it. The Christmas Can Tree Drive is very grateful for your help.'

'Nonprofit?' Bonnie looked a little surprised then laughed and nodded. 'There are times.'

Mary held out the paper she'd carried out of the car with her, but Bonnie shook her head again. 'Can you put it on my desk inside? My hands – I've got gloves on.'

For the first time, Mary noticed the thin gloves Bonnie had on. They were the same kind the nurse and doctor wore when she went in for a check-up. The ones the dentist and his assistant wore – even the people at the bakery wore them when they filled your order. What was Bonnie doing with them? Mary looked closer. The knees of her jeans were damp, as if she'd been kneeling in something wet, her T-shirt was stained and there were streaks of dirt on her face. What was she doing?

'Whelping.' Bonnie smiled as if Mary had spoken out loud. 'Mindy is having her babies. You're just in time to see. Come on in.'

She headed back through the kennels' doorway, Mary close behind. She'd only seen puppies born one other time, years ago when one of her sister's dogs had produced a litter. She had obligingly let the entire neighborhood watch. It had been fascinating; she remembered that but not much else. She hurried a little faster.

'Put that down on my desk then come in the last kennel. Try to be quiet. She's a first timer and is doing well, but she's a little nervous.'

Tiredness forgotten, Mary placed the tax statement on Bonnie's cluttered desk, hesitated as she wondered how to keep it from getting lost in the pile of papers already there, placed a clear glass paperweight with a cocker spaniel etched on one corner of it and tiptoed down the aisle to the open kennel. Bonnie knelt in the dirt beside a large slat-sided box filled with shredded newspaper.

'Is she all right?'

'She's fine. So are the pups. Come look. She's got three already. She's taking a little rest before she does it again.'

Bonnie sat back on her heels. Mary looked at her, sighed, then lowered herself down on one knee, placed a hand on the ground and got down on both of them. This was only going to last a short time. She hoped she'd be able to get back up.

However, while she was here, there were three puppies laying, wiggling by their mother. One was already sniffing the air, pulling itself around while making soft mewing sounds. 'Where is he going?'

'He's trying to find his mother's nipple. He can't see yet, that will take a while, and can't really get up on his feet, but he can smell and he knows he's hungry.'

They watched the pup in silence while it tried to find its first meal.

Finally, Mary asked, 'How many more will she have?'

'One. At least, if that ultrasound we took is right. Probably is. Cliff said she had four and I've never known him to be wrong. She'll lick these guys a little more, let them try to find a nipple then go back into labor. She'll kind of shake off anyone who's figured out how to latch on, break the sack on the new one, break the cord and lick the pup until its breathing on its own and starts to wiggle around. I never tire of watching this. It's like a miracle, each time.'

Mary had no trouble agreeing with that. So tiny, so perfect, and both mother and babies seemed to know just what to do. 'Who's the father?'

'The dog you saw the other day. This is his first litter, for me, that is, and I already have all of them sold.' There was great satisfaction in Bonnie's voice and obvious pride.

Mary thought back to the puppies she had seen at Evan's pet shop earlier that day. Those puppies looked a little like these and the older pups she'd seen here when she'd collected the dog food for the Christmas Can Tree. That honey-colored one still stuck in her mind. So sweet, such long, silky ears, so . . . 'Are these purebred cocker spaniels?'

From the expression on Bonnie's face, Mary thought she'd just said something blasphemous. 'Of course. That's what we do. Breed cockers. I'm known for my cockers. Why would you think they would be something else?'

Mary was taken aback by how upset Bonnie seemed to be. 'I didn't mean – only I don't know much about dogs and the puppies we saw at Evan's shop look a little like these and they were only part cocker. So, I wondered if you ever did that.'

'No.'

Mary had never heard a more emphatic one.

'The dogs you saw at Evan's are cockapoos. Part poodle, part cocker. People pay huge amounts for them but I wouldn't consider breeding them. When people buy my dogs, they know they're getting the best pure cocker spaniel bloodlines they can find anywhere.'

That seemed to be the end of that subject, and it was just as well. Mary could feel her knees protesting. The dirt was hard, her knees were used to a soft garden kneeler when she worked in the yard, and they were not happy. Neither was her back. It was time to go. She put her hand on the ground and started to position one leg under her, hoping she could get up in one movement, when Bonnie grabbed her arm. 'Look. She's getting ready.'

The little dog contracted. She lay on one side and pushed. A small, greenish sack appeared from under her tail. The dog paused, panted a couple of times, looked back at the sack, laid her head back down on the newspaper and pushed again. The sack slid out a little farther, enough so Mary could see a nose. A little black nose. With a groan, the dog pushed one more time and the sack was almost out. The puppy it contained didn't move. Neither did the mother. Mary forgot her knees, her back and how to breathe. Were they dead? The beautiful mother, her head limp on the damp newspaper, and the puppy entrapped in the thick membrane sack would surely die as well. They had to do something. Why was Bonnie not . . .

She was. 'Tired, aren't you.' She reached under the dog's stub of a tail, gently pulled the sack all the way out and broke it open. Liquid poured out along with a puppy. A black puppy with white feet, with white across its shoulders, its flanks and a white diamond mark on its chest. 'Will you look at that. A parti-color. I wasn't expecting that.'

The puppy started to shudder. At least, that's what it looked like to Mary. The mother picked up her head, looked back at her baby, turned so she could reach it and started to lick. The sack was off completely, the cord disappeared and the puppy started to wiggle.

Mary breathed again. 'How many times a year do you do this?'

Bonnie laughed. 'I have three bitches and I only breed them once a year. She's got four beauties. Time to leave her alone. Come on, I'll help you up.' She stood, reached out to Mary and helped her to her feet. They stood for a moment, looking at the mother dog as she let the first puppy nurse while she licked the newest one. The other two sniffed the air and headed for their first supper.

'Even three times would be a little too much drama for me. I'm wrung out.' Mary stretched and flexed her knees. They were fine. 'Does that include the dogs you bought from Alma?'

It was almost as if Bonnie hadn't heard her. 'Cliff used to be with me when I had a litter born. The first time I thought I was going to pass out, but he walked me through the whole thing. The dog was fine. I almost didn't make it. He taught me so much, not just about whelping but about breeding, about caring. He knew what to look for in a dog. He was the one who taught me how to judge. He went to dog shows with me. Even after . . . He would have been here with me today. It's hard to believe he's gone.'

Bonnie wiped her eyes with the back of her hands, seemed to realize she had on gloves, stripped them off, threw them in a close-by trash can and headed out the kennel building's doors into the now-dark yard.

Mary followed. 'Alma's dogs. You have three including hers?'

Bonnie stopped and looked around. 'Oh. Alma's dogs. No. I haven't bred them yet. I'm not sure what I'll do. They're nice but not quite . . .' She seemed a little lost once more. Grief. Grief and strain.

Only, from what she had read in Cliff's diary . . . She must have misunderstood. Or Bonnie had. Anyway, it wasn't important. What was important was that she went home and took off her shoes.

'Is there anything I can do for you?' She fervently hoped not and immediately felt guilty. Bonnie was grieving. If she needed help, Mary would give it, but she really wanted to go home.

Bonnie shook her head. 'No. Thank you for asking, and thanks for coming by. Actually, it helped just having someone else here. Todd will be home soon, and even though he doesn't know it yet, he's taking me out to dinner.' She pushed back a strand of hair and left a grayish streak on her cheek.

Mary got in her car and rolled the window down. Bonnie rested her elbows on the door and leaned on them. 'You're close to the Mendosa family, aren't you?'

Mary nodded. What had brought that on?

'I heard the Mendosa children were in the manger when Cliff . . .' She shuddered. 'I heard they saw the man who killed him and that's where they found the puppy. Is that true?'

Mary felt as if she'd been hit in the chest with a meat mallet. 'Who told you that?' She could barely get the words out.

'It's all over town. Do they know who the man was?'

Mary wasn't sure what to say. All over town? No. It couldn't be. If the murderer heard that, if he thought those children really knew who he was . . . She had to stop this rumor, right now. Starting with Bonnie. 'They don't know anything. They did go out to the manger. They wanted to see their mother ride in on the donkey, and that's when they found Cliff's body. They have no idea – they saw a shadow. It might not even have been a man. Dalia thought it was a cow.' She tried to laugh a little. It came out as a giggle. 'The only ones who might know anything are the police, and so far they haven't said much. As for the puppy, no one seems to know where it came from. I don't see how it can be connected.' Mary was babbling. She didn't approve of lying and wasn't very good at it. 'You tell whoever's spreading this they're wrong. Dead wrong.' Oh, that wasn't good. Never mind. Was she convincing? She hoped so. She needed Bonnie to spread the word that the children knew nothing. If whoever did that to Cliff thought they could identify him . . . Goose bumps broke out on her arms. It was a long shot, but the best she could do right now. She smiled. 'You're sure there's nothing I can do for you?'

Bonnie stepped away from the window and shook her head. 'No. Thanks, Mary. I'm fine. I'll go feed the dogs and wait for Todd.'

Mary nodded. She tried to read the expression on Bonnie's face but couldn't. Did she believe her? Would she tell whoever was spreading the rumor they were wrong? Would she even talk to that person? Mary ground her teeth, slipped the car into gear and drove out through the gate opening.

She turned into the street with one hand and fished in her tote bag for her cell phone with the other. She knew she shouldn't drive and talk, but this was important. There was one person who needed to know about this rumor going around and needed to know right now. She dialed the police station.

'Hello, Agnes? Did they get the apartment cleaned out? Good. Agnes, I need to talk to Dan. Now.'

TWENTY

'Tell me that again. Bonnie says it's all over town the kids saw a man in the manger? That they know who he is?'

Mary picked up her water glass, looked at it and held it in front of her. 'That they saw someone, yes. That they know who it is I'm not sure. However, the way rumors work, by tomorrow the story will be they not only knew him but shook his hand on his way out.' She put it down and picked up her wineglass. 'What are we going to do?'

Mary sat at Ellen and Dan's dinner table, along with Pat and Karl Bennington. She had no more than walked in her door when the phone rang. It was Ellen. Dan was home, had gotten her message and wanted to talk to her. Since she was coming over, she might as well stay and have dinner with them.

Mary thought about her feet for a moment, but she wanted to talk to Dan as well. She accepted and offered to contribute the bottle of wine she'd just purchased. So, here she was, sipping wine and waiting for someone else to bring in dinner. Somehow, that didn't feel right. However, she was tired. Ellen was a good cook. She'd taught her, and it would be fun to see what she produced. But she felt uneasy. She should be standing over the stove, supervising, stirring, mashing, not just sitting here doing nothing. *Get over it.* She'd try. She took a small sip of the wine.

'I guess it was inevitable.' Dan sipped his wine absently. He looked directly at Mary but she didn't think he really saw her. He was probably going over the night of Cliff's death, wondering if there was anything they could have done better to protect the children. What it could have been, she didn't know. Father D'Angelo had taken them directly to St Mark's, where they waited in front of the manger for their mother to arrive. It had taken the crowd a little while to realize the *posada* was going to St Mark's, that something unexpected had happened at St Theresa's. She'd spent some time pointing toward the corner and making shooing motions, but finally the crowd had mostly turned the corner. It had evidently taken no time at all for them to see Ronaldo held a puppy. Coos and goos had apparently come from all sides, accompanied by 'Where did you get him?' She'd been told the children only said they found him, but somehow where they found him had quickly become public knowledge. So did the fact all those police cars and all that yellow tape was because Cliff Mathews was dead and the children had found him as well. Murdered. Mary fervently hoped none of them knew they'd not only found the body but had actually seen the murderer. It seemed she'd hoped in vain.

'How did that piece of information seep out?' Evidently Dan was struggling with the same puzzle.

She shook her head.

The swinging kitchen door opened and Ellen and Pat appeared, bearing plates. Ellen put one in front of Mary. Pat sat one in front of Dan and another in front of Karl.

'What is this?' Mary looked at her plate. It held a small piece of chicken breast topped with prosciutto and covered with a sauce that gave off a slight tangy fragrance. Mary had never seen chicken done that way and it smelled delicious. Whipped sweet potatoes and fresh green beans completed the picture. A basket of crunchy French rolls appeared along with a bowl of spinach salad. She'd come to talk to Dan. This was an unexpected bonus.

'It's Balsamic chicken.' Ellen stood back a little and surveyed the plates with satisfaction. 'It's a new recipe I got off Williams-Sonoma's website. It sounded wonderful and it was easy. So, you're my guinea pigs. Tell me what you think.'

The rapidly emptied plates spoke louder than any words. Mary pushed back her chair and started to clear the table, but Pat took the plates out of her hands before she could make for the kitchen. 'You're off duty. I think both Dan and Karl want to talk to you. I only hope the conversation doesn't spoil your appetite for dessert. I brought over Brownie pudding.'

'Oh, goodness. I haven't had that in ages. It's a perfect winter's night dessert. Can I make the coffee?'

'You can sit right there and help these two try to figure out what's going on.'

Ellen and Pat disappeared through the swinging doors. Dan poured Mary a little more wine and offered the bottle to Karl, who nodded. Dan topped off his glass then poured the last few drops into his own.

'There was no useful forensic evidence in that whole damn manger scene. Lots of people had been in and out, but we did find one whole footprint.'

'Whose?'

Dan didn't answer Mary right away. He seemed to weigh how he wanted to answer. 'It was a sandal. A man's sandal.'

'Where was it?'

Dan actually smiled. 'In a cow pat.'

'In a . . . oh.'

'Father D'Angelo?' There was no smile on Karl's face. 'No one else wears sandals this time of year. That can't mean much. He's been in and out of the manger for days.'

Dan nodded. 'It doesn't implicate him, but it doesn't eliminate him, either.' He held up a hand before Mary could say anything. 'Whoever stabbed poor old Cliff didn't leave right away, which might. Father was pretty much in evidence all evening. Our murderer was by the animals, the darkest part of the manger scene, when the kids saw him. Well away from the manger and the body. Logic would say he would have left immediately. Why did he stay? There's only one answer.'

'And that is?' Karl looked as if he knew the answer.

Mary thought she did also.

'He wanted the puppy. The kids interrupted him, probably startled him pretty bad. We're just lucky he didn't do anything when he saw them.'

Mary looked into her wineglass, shuddered and picked it up. Her hand started to shake at the thought of what might have happened and she set it back down. She ran her fingers up and down the stem instead. 'There's one other person I know who wears sandals.'

Both men turned to stare at her.

'Who?' Dan said.

'Evan Wilson.' She thought back. Wasn't there someone else? Was it Glen? She wasn't sure. 'He helped me take the dog food to the library the day we started the food drive. He wore sandals and white socks. Only, why would he kill Cliff and what would he want with the puppy?'

'I have an idea about that.'

Dan and Mary turned their attention to Karl. He had been quiet through most of dinner, through all the conversation, contributing almost nothing. Now he pushed his glass aside, clasped his hands on the table and leaned forward.

'Mary knows this but I haven't been able to catch you. Remember that little poodle stolen from Golden Hills winery last summer? Belonged to Naomi and Bill Bliss?'

Dan nodded. 'Cliff had a picture of it. Naomi had broken down when she saw it, claimed he took it from the winery. Why is another mystery. I'm afraid that dog is long gone.'

'No. He's not.' Karl raised his head and looked directly at Dan. 'He's very much alive and I think someone close is using him for breeding. That puppy the kids found? I think that poodle is its father.'

The room was so quiet the faint clink of dishes in the kitchen could be heard. A laugh from Pat broke the stillness, but Dan didn't say anything. He simply stared at Karl. A loud meow from Jake, Ellen's yellow Tom, announcing his presence as he passed through the dining room on his way to the living-room bookshelves finally seemed to restore Dan's speech.

'How do you know that?'

'Two things. Cliff brought me a saliva sample from a dog he wanted the AKC to test for DNA. He asked me to send it in. I did. The results came back the day he died, so he never saw them. The dog was the Blisses' poodle, so he's alive. At least, he was when Cliff took the sample. Alive and close.'

'What's the second?'

Mary didn't think she'd ever seen Dan look so intent.

'I got to looking at Sampson a little more closely. I'm sure he's a cockapoo. And his toenails aren't right.'

'His what?' Mary wasn't sure she'd heard right. 'His toenails?'

Karl nodded. 'Dogs have either clear or black nails. A black dog will have black nails. A black dog who has a white paw will have clear nails on his white paw, black ones on his black paws. If the paw is only partly white, the nails will probably be mixed as well. There are a few poodles who have a recessive gene for clear nails. Merlot, the Blisses' poodle, has that gene. He's passed it on to several of his pups. He's the only dog I know, personally, who does. Sampson has clear nails on all four paws even though two of his paws are black.'

Dan didn't say anything. Mary found she couldn't.

Dan found his voice first. 'You think Cliff found the poodle and took a puppy from whoever has him to do . . . what?'

'Blackmail somebody.'

Mary almost dumped what was left of her wine on the tablecloth. She hadn't heard Ellen and Pat come back into the dining room, but they must have been there a few minutes, long enough to hear what Karl had said. 'Oh, you startled me.'

Ellen grinned, pulled out her chair and sat. 'I could tell. You jumped a mile. Coffee's brewing.' She turned toward Karl. 'You think Cliff found the Blisses' poodle?'

'No doubt about that.' Karl gave one decisive nod. 'The question is, where?'

'I hope not in a puppy mill.' Dread filled Pat's voice.

'We've had no reports of one for some time.' Dan looked over at Karl as if for corroboration. 'That dog has been missing for over six months. Usually we hear when the first pups show up.' He paused, as if thinking it through. 'What's the gestation period for a dog?'

'About twelve weeks. Add six weeks for the pups to be weaned and Sampson could be Merlot's.'

'I'll put out feelers.'

'What's a puppy mill?' Visions of a stream, water wheel and sacks of grain filled Mary's head. She didn't think that's what they were talking about.

Karl voice was heavy with disgust. 'It's a place that turns out puppies like a factory. They vary in awfulness. Some buy second-rate pure breeds, but some don't care how they get their breeding dogs. They're interested in one thing only: puppies. Little things like health, clean conditions and the quality of the dog don't matter. If it can pass for a purebred, they can sell it for one. Papers aren't included, but lots of folks don't care.' He paused, looked over at Dan and shook his head slightly. 'But I think it's more likely he's local, servicing some backyard breeder's dogs and possibly producing cockapoos.'

Dan nodded. 'It makes sense. Keep Merlot under wraps, bring just one or two bitches to him and sell the puppies out of the area.'

'Sampson wasn't out of the area.' Ellen pushed back her chair and headed for the kitchen. 'I'll bring in the coffee. Don't solve this thing until I get back.'

'She's got nothing to worry about.' Dan sounded glum. He picked up his teaspoon and started to tap it on the table.

Mary reached over and took it away. 'We're on edge enough.'

He smiled and let her. 'The rest of Sampson's litter could be in Southern California, for all we know. Maybe they kept him back for some reason.'

'Or the rest of them could be right here.' Mary became light-headed. Sampson and the puppies in Evan's shop were about the same size, and they looked alike. Could Cliff have stolen him to blackmail . . . who? Evan hadn't said who the puppies belonged to, but he knew. He had to. He'd looked nervous when the children were handling them. Why? If Merlot was the father, then the mother had to be a cocker. Did Evan have a cocker? Mary had no idea. He lived just about a block from her, but she'd never been to his house. Evan, mild-mannered Evan, who ran an immaculate and seemingly honest store, a man who wouldn't steal a dog or condone anyone else's doing it. A man who enjoyed playing Scrooge at the Christmas extravaganza during which he wore a long bathrobe, tied at the waist, a bathrobe that had a hood, and sandals. No. It couldn't be. Who else had cockers? Half the people in Santa Louisa. Maybe not half, but they were a popular breed. Glen Manning and John Lavorino. They had at least one female cocker. Maybe Cliff making trouble for them at St Mark's had nothing to do with lifestyle. Maybe it was about dogs. Could that be? Should she say something?

'What do you mean, they might be here?' Dan set down his spoon and looked at her suspiciously.

'I mean – well . . .'

'She means Evan has puppies for sale that look like Sampson,' Pat answered for her. 'I saw them when I was in there a few days ago.'

'He does, does he?' Unfortunately, Dan looked interested.

Mary nodded.

'Are they cockapoos?'

'Evan says so.'

'Who owns them?' Ellen seemed as interested as her husband.

Mary shrugged. 'Evan didn't say.' She didn't add Evan seemed determined not to say.

'Odd.' Karl pushed his dish away. 'Evan usually gets me to check out any of the animals he sells. He doesn't care about papers and breeds, and if the dogs don't have papers, he'll say so. However, he's careful about shots and health. He doesn't want anyone to buy an animal from him that's going to go home and die.'

'How about goldfish? Susannah won some at the fair a couple of summers ago. They only lived a day.'

'Fish are tricky, especially fair fish. Still, Evan wants everything alive and healthy when they leave him. I wonder why he didn't call me.'

'Hmm.' Dan attacked his pudding with gusto. 'Maybe I'll drop in on Evan tomorrow. Take a look at those puppies.'

Should she say something about John and Glen? No. Those two had been through enough. She'd corner Evan tomorrow, right after her committee meeting, and make him tell her who owns the puppies. If he wouldn't tell her, she'd have to investigate further. If it turned out they belonged to John and Glen, she'd . . . she'd decide what to do then. Right now, saying anything would be the same as idle gossip. She looked at the brownie pudding Pat put before her and her stomach lurched. She reached for her coffee instead.

TWENTY-ONE

It had not been a good night. She had fallen into bed almost as soon as she closed the door. She hadn't paused to admire anyone's Christmas decorations as she drove home, hadn't even bothered to put her car in the garage. She'd staggered into the kitchen, thrown her coat over a chair, her purse on the table and gone to bed. But not to sleep. Every time she started to doze off, a dog barked. All night. As the night wore on, the dog became more frantic. She'd gotten up a couple of times, worried it might be in trouble, but she had no idea where it was. Down the block somewhere, probably. She wasn't the only one who couldn't sleep. Lights went on and off in several houses. On toward morning, it stopped. Either its owner had come back or it was exhausted. She hoped the owners had gotten it. She'd never heard it before and fervently hoped she wouldn't again.

Mary watched the coffeepot drip out enough for one cup. Thanking Ellen, who had given her this pause and pour coffeemaker, she poured. The coffeemaker paused. She reached for the Tylenol and washed down two of them with a small mouthful of way-too-hot coffee.

As she sipped, she reviewed the schedule she'd mapped out during those wide-awake hours. The first meeting for the annual St Mark's Spring Rummage sale was at nine. Evan's shop wouldn't be open yet. What time had he gotten home last night and had the blasted dog kept him up? She hadn't been by the can tree in at least two days. Her committee was great, but she needed to check in. The volunteers with pickup trucks would arrive midweek, dismantle the tree and take all the food to the food bank. In the meantime, she needed to make sure the stacking volunteers arrived daily, making the tree grow. The press would return right before they started tearing it down and hopefully those people who hadn't donated or had somehow not been aware of the food drive would come through. Then she would visit Evan. First, a little breakfast and a shower. Where had she put those folders? On the kitchen table. One folder for each committee with a to-do list and a timeline for completion. Each sub-committee head would get one. She'd keep the master list. Things should go smoothly. She drained the last of the coffee and headed for her shower.

The morning was chilly, the meeting informal. Gray sweatpants and the green sweater with Mrs Claus appliquéd on the front would do fine. The sweater had been a gift. Why, she wasn't sure, but it seemed appropriate for today and was soft and warm.

She slowed as she passed Evan's house. No car in the driveway. Had he already left for the shop? Probably. There were a lot of animals and she supposed cleaning before the shop opened was the best time. She noted, with satisfaction, the street in front of St Mark's contained nothing. No trash, no animal droppings, nothing to show that hundreds of people had been tromping through the streets and on the lawn only a few days ago. She must remember to drop the city maintenance people a thank-you note.

The meeting was in the small room off the main hall called, appropriately enough, the all-purpose room. It was used for Bible study, Sunday school, the breakfast prayer group and a meeting place for a variety of committees and clubs. Today a round table took up the center, with folding chairs around it. A large coffeemaker gave off gurgling noises, along with an inviting smell; thick white mugs were stacked beside it. Mary laid her folders on the table and headed its way.

'Guess we're a little early.'

Mary nodded and filled her cup. 'Good morning, Joy. Glad to see you. Which committee do you want?'

'Same as always. I'll take charge of the pricin', sortin' and settin' out.'

Mary nodded once more. Joy had been doing that for years. She knew how much to charge for just about anything. Antique brooches, slightly used high chairs, an out-of-date suit donated by a still-grieving widow who claimed it had 'plenty of good wear in it,' baby clothes stained with God alone knew what, really nice lamps and not-so-nice end tables, even wedding and prom dresses. Joy put a price on them that would see them out the door and still make their cash box rattle pleasantly at the end of the day. She smiled at her over the top of her coffee mug. She didn't get one back, but then, she hadn't expected one. Joy didn't live up to her name. She looked to be about Mary's age, early seventies. That she was only fifty-seven, Mary knew for a fact. Joy seemed to take a perverse satisfaction in presenting herself as a neat, clean, plain no-nonsense homebody. Her haircut certainly looked home done, her nails were chewed off, not cut, and her hands were always a little red and chapped. Today she had on a shapeless plaid dress covered with a sweater that had been washed so many times Mary couldn't guess its original color. Her stockings were thick, and so were her lace-up brown oxfords. She could, however, make an angel food cake from scratch that was so light it almost floated away. Her buttermilk fried chicken was second only to Mary's and her biscuits were incredible. How such good food came out of a home so dour, made by a person who seemed to find no pleasure in its creation, Mary wasn't sure. However, Joy was a person you could count on, and Mary did. Often.

'Heard you were there when they found Cliff Mathews.' Joy pushed her plastic glasses back on her nose and blew into her coffee mug. The steam immediately fogged her glasses. She set the mug down on the table and cleaned them with a paper napkin. 'I was no fan of his, but he didn't deserve to die that way.'

Mary felt a little start of surprise. Somehow, she hadn't associated Joy with a pet. 'You knew Cliff?'

Joy's expression didn't change. She took a sip of her coffee, set it back down and put her glasses back on. 'You could say that. Not well, but I knew him. I got a little black cocker from Bonnie. She said she wasn't show quality and if I wanted her for my granddaughter, who was sick a lot back then, I could but I'd have to pay to have her spayed. I agreed and took her to Cliff.'

A jolt made Mary's hand shake. She knew about Alma's bitch, but she hadn't given any thought to who owned the other dog. 'It was your dog Cliff was supposed to spay? But he did Alma's?'

Joy's face looked even more disapproving, if that was possible. 'After that I took the dog to Karl Bennington. You know Karl, don't you?'

Mary nodded.

'Good man, Karl. He's taken real good care of that little dog. I don't hold with dogs in the house but have to admit, it sure helped my granddaughter. Perked her right up. Never saw much of Cliff after that, but I heard plenty.'

'Are you talking about Cliff? That was the most horrible thing. The manger! How could anybody do such a thing? Hello, Mary, Joy.'

Annie Wilkes shed her coat and dropped it on a chair and reached out for a mug. 'It's getting chilly out there. Amelia couldn't come. She's got a cold. I'll take her folder to her.'

It didn't matter. Amelia had headed up the donations committee, along with Annie, for the last five years. Mary knew there'd be no lack of items donated to sell. 'Tell her I hope she feels better. This is no time to get sick.'

'I know. I'm so far behind. We haven't even put up the tree yet. It's sitting in the backyard in a tub of water. I don't want to do it unless we can all be there, but the kids are going in different directions and we can't seem to all get together. This teenage stuff is for the birds.' Annie filled her mug, added a generous amount of sugar and looked around for a spoon. 'Don't we have any— Thanks.'

Joy produced a white plastic one and silently handed it over.

Mary watched the small interplay. She'd known both these women for years. Neither had changed much. Joy had always been dourly competent, her household run with the rigidity of Mussolini's train schedule. Annie's house was filled with kids, dogs, activity and laughter, but she always got the job done. People were, indeed, interesting. 'Before I forget, we have all of Cliff's stuff for the sale. Well, all his furniture and some of his kitchen stuff.'

Annie lowered her mug and stared. 'How'd we get that?'

Joy said nothing but her frown deepened.

'He was being evicted. His landlady had filed the papers and it was past time for him to be out. She was going to put all his stuff out on the street but said if we wanted it for the sale we had to come get it. Agnes, from Dan's office, helped, so did Ellen, and we got it all packed. It's all here, somewhere.' Mary looked around but no boxes, TVs, toasters or really bad pictures were in evidence. 'Maybe they're in the storage room. It's a start.'

'I thought he had a daughter. Wouldn't she want some of it?' Disapproval deepened the wrinkles across Joy's forehead.

'No one knows where she is. Dan's trying to locate her.'

'She lives in Charlotte, NC.'

Annie and Mary stared at Joy.

'She does?'

'How do you know?'

'She and my daughter were friends. They still keep in touch.'

'Does she know about her father?'

'Don't know. I don't pry into other folks' business.'

Mary tried to bury her sigh. No, Joy wouldn't pry, but this hardly qualified. 'Do you know her married name or how we can contact her?'

'No.' That came out of pursed lips which relaxed just enough for the next sentence to arrive. 'I guess I could ask Charity, though.'

'Better yet, ask Charity to contact Dan.' Mary barely remembered Joy's daughter, although she usually remembered the children in her middle-school classes. However, if she grew up anything like her mother, Dan was better equipped to get the information than Mary was. She wondered if this let her off the hook for organizing Cliff's memorial. She fervently hoped so. Packing up his meager possessions had been bad enough. 'I'll tell Les to hang on to his things. If she wants to donate any of them, fine. I'll feel a lot better taking them from her instead of Cliff's landlady.'

Annie glanced at her cell phone. 'Mary, it's almost nine thirty. Can we get started? I have to pick up my kids from band practice in an hour and I need to go to the grocery store first.'

'Where's Leigh Cameron? She said she'd . . .'

The door flew open and a rather shapeless woman with a nervous expression rushed in. Her hair was the color of goldenrod and was almost as stiff. It fell, without moving, just above her shoulders. Her pink and mauve track suit didn't appear to have ever been near a track, or a gym. Neither did her running shoes. However, her panting sounded as if she'd just come in from a brisk run. Mary knew it was nervous energy, not exercise that caused the stitch in her side she now dramatically covered with her hand.

'I'm sorry I'm late. I had to pack Dave's lunch – he's going on some kind of hike with the boy scouts and Emily has dance class this morning, so I was rushed and then the dog threw up. The kids wouldn't clean it up so I stopped by Evan's Furry Friends, but it's closed. He has that special food – I was going to get some last night but that stuck-up Bill Bliss went in the store and I didn't want to talk to him so I bought food at the grocery store. Do you think that's why she threw up? Maybe I should take her to Karl. Are you all done already?'

Leigh had been the head of the advertisement committee last year and had done a terrible job. Press releases had never made the paper, flyers hadn't been distributed and promised radio spots hadn't gotten their copy; Mary had ended up doing it all. She vowed then that if Leigh volunteered again, things would be different.

'Actually, we were just getting started. The folders are over on the table. Leigh, I have a special favor to ask. I don't have anyone to organize the volunteers the day of the sale. Could you do that? I'll give you a list of them, with all of their assignments. You'll just need to make sure they know where to go.' All of the volunteers already knew their jobs and they all knew Leigh.

'As well as the publicity?' Worry creased the pancake makeup on Leigh's face.

Mary was briefly distracted. *Where does she get that? I didn't think anyone made that thick stuff anymore.*

'Oh, no. Kay Epstein, over at the newspaper, offered to do the publicity. She deals with it all the time.' *And gets the job done on time, and well.* 'You'll be so much more valuable handling the volunteers.' Mary held her breath. She didn't want to insult Leigh, but she couldn't go through another year like the last one.

Different expressions crossed Leigh's face until finally she smiled. 'That's a great idea. I have so many other committees that this will fit in easily.'

Relieved, Mary headed for the table and the folders. 'OK, let's see where we are so we can all get out of here.'

She spread out her lists. What was Bill Bliss doing in a pet store? Naomi hadn't said anything about another dog. She forgot about him in a blur of who was going to be in charge of what, and when.

TWENTY-TWO

Mary stood in the doorway of the atrium between the library and the civic offices and gasped. The can tree had grown to at least twice the height it had been the last time she saw it but it wasn't going any higher. It ended at the ceiling with one large can of beans topped with a red velvet bow. There were paper streamers, obviously made by small hands, draped over the tiers of cans, interspersed with lopsided green and red, as well as blue and white, bows. The local grade school children had been busy. Boxes of cans were placed around the perimeter of the tree that could hold nothing more. Mary's smile beamed satisfaction as she looked at the food they'd collected. It would make the difference between a full belly on Christmas Day and beyond for many families who would otherwise go hungry. Hungry! In this country! In her own county, town! The thought filled her with rage, but the sight of the tree made her smile grow broader. They'd done good work, but it wasn't finished. The press was scheduled to take pictures of the tree and do a follow-up article on Tuesday, after which it would be dismantled and everything moved to the food bank. Maybe the cases and sacks of cans piled around the tree could be moved now. She needed someone with a pickup. Todd Blankenship had one. Would he help? He never had before. Who else? Bob MacIntosh ran the food bank. He had a van. Maybe he could take some of it, and he must know someone with a truck. The town was full of trucks.

The door to the library opened and Luke walked out. 'Mrs McGill. I was going to call you. What do you think?'

'I'm overwhelmed. I hope Toys for Tots is having as much luck. It's going to be a Merry Christmas for a lot of families.'

Luke grinned, a wide, expansive grin. 'I know. Half the real estate offices in town have been here, piling up cans. A lot of them got on the phone and called their clients. They collected money too. There'll be turkeys and a lot of fresh produce this Christmas. Some of the money is going to the Meals on Wheels people to pay the hospital for some special meals for those old folks who can't get out.'

Mary stood in front of the tree, examining it and the boxes of food in front of it. Luke stood beside her.

'Are all those cartons all right with you? I don't want anyone tripping, trying to get into the library.' There were cartons stacked behind the tree, more behind the library doors and some over by the elevator.

'Should we get someone to take these over to the food bank right away? It doesn't look safe.'

'I thought so too. You want me to ask Bob? He's been over here almost every day, watching this thing grow. You can almost hear him purring, he's that pleased. He'll figure out how to get them over there. I'll get some pictures before he removes the extras.'

Mary nodded. 'That would be great. The newspaper will be out Tuesday to take pictures. Then we can start tearing it down. I'll try to get some of the children who made the decorations in the picture. Let's see. Harry Waters is head of the committee to get the cans moved. I'd better call him . . .'

She stopped as Luke's smile grew. 'Harry and a bunch of other realtors have already been here, planning the dismantling. I'll take pictures of it coming down as well, and we'll post them in the library later.'

She laughed. 'This committee is the best I've ever worked with. I'm going to quit worrying about all of you.' She stopped, not sure how she should phrase what she wanted to say next. 'I – well, I wasn't over here yesterday because I helped pack up Cliff's things. He had a picture of you at a dog show, holding onto a poodle and a blue ribbon. I thought you might like to know where it is and how to get it back. If you want it back.'

Luke didn't say anything for so long Mary thought maybe he hadn't heard her. Or understood.

'It's in a box with a lot of other things at St Mark's. I can ask . . .'

'I heard. And thanks. It's just that . . . I gave Cliff that picture. It was my last showmanship win before the show where everything fell apart. The Pure Breed Dog Club of Santa Louisa gives a thousand-dollar scholarship every year to the junior handler who wins the most points in showmanship at California dog shows. Cliff was my coach. I needed just a few more points to win. I'd already planned what I'd do with it. I was going to be a vet, just like Cliff, and that money would have helped me pay for it. The poodle, Jester we called him, was a great dog, but a clown. He loved to show, but he sometimes got distracted and blew it for me. We practiced and practiced. If I won that show, the scholarship was mine. Then Cliff gave the dog tranquilizers. I guess he thought he was helping me, but I got blamed and kicked out of the club. Cliff never admitted he'd done it. I haven't been in a dog show ring since and, as you can see, I didn't go to vet school. I think I'll pass on that picture, Mrs McGill. The memories it brings back aren't exactly pleasant.'

There was no trace of a smile on Luke's usually cheerful face and the bitterness in his voice was deep and old. Another unsettled score Cliff had left behind.

After all these years, had Luke's bitterness erupted? Only, in Cliff's diary, he'd said . . . she couldn't remember exactly what he'd said. However, it seemed unlikely it was Luke Cliff had tried to blackmail, and that seemed the most logical motive for his murder. She shifted her purse to her other shoulder and surveyed the tree once more.

'Let me know if you can get the children over here for photos. What time is the press coming?'

'Don't know. I'll find out. I'll call you Monday.'

'Will you call Bob?'

He nodded.

Mary smiled at him. 'Thank you, Luke. You've been invaluable. I'd better run. I need to stop at Evan's for a minute.'

She could actually feel Luke wondering why she was stopping at Evan's. She didn't have a dog or a cat or even a bird, but all he said was, 'Tell him I'll be in later for some of the special dog food he carries. He knows what kind. Same as he feeds his little dog.'

Mary came to an abrupt halt, turned and faced Luke once more. 'Evan has a dog?'

He nodded and a trace of his smile was back. 'A cocker. Pretty little thing. Not show quality, but a sweet dog. He got her from Alma.'

'Alma? I thought she sold all of her dogs to Bonnie Blankenship.' Mary became a little lightheaded. Not only did everyone in this town seem to have a dog, they all seemed to be related.

'She sold the last two bitches, her best two, to Bonnie. Earlier, she sold one to Evan and the other two bitches to John and Glen.'

John and Glen again. They had two female cockers and they bred cockapoos. The same kind of dogs Evan had for sale. Sampson, whose sire was – might be – the missing winery dog, was also a cockapoo. 'Do you have one of Alma's dogs also?'

Luke shook his head. 'I'm still a poodle man. Actually, I have one of the Blisses' dogs. He was in the first litter Merlot sired. It was a real tragedy when that dog disappeared.'

Mary didn't say a word. She stared at Luke for a moment, turned on her heel and headed out the door. She was still shaking her head as she walked down the stairs and started across the park toward Furry Friends. It was time to have a long conversation with Evan.

TWENTY-THREE

The shop was closed. It said so on the sign that hung in the glass door and in the lowered blinds that covered the windows on each side of it. Inside, soft barks, a rustling noise, other stirrings, but no voices, sounded. Where was Evan?

She stood for a moment, trying to decide what to do. Evan's car hadn't been in his driveway when she passed. Of course, he could have put it in the garage. Just because hers was full of rummage sale boxes, her washing machine and other assorted things didn't mean others filled theirs the same way. Only, why wasn't he here? She checked her watch and double-checked that against her cell phone. Ten thirty. Past time for him to open. She rattled the door. The barking intensified, but no one came. Could he be sick? He could be hung over. She had no idea what the three of them did last night.

She briefly wondered if John and Glen were home. The bank was closed on Saturday, so she couldn't run over there to check with Glen, the branch manager. They must have come home last night, though. John was a surgical nurse at the hospital and was probably . . . no. He took a leave of absence. She knew where they lived. Should she stop by? Better to go back to Evan's house and see if he was there. See if his car was in the garage. Then, well, then she'd decide. This was bound to be something simple. Something easily explained and Evan wouldn't thank her if she went off half-cocked.

She walked back across the park, avoiding the vendors set up for the Saturday Farmers' Market, but turned to look back before she entered the parking lot beside the library. The closed sign still hung on the door and the blinds still covered the windows.

It was with a growing sense of urgency that Mary climbed into her car and headed for Evan's.

The driveway was still empty. She pulled her car in far enough to clear the sidewalk, stopped, got out and stood by it, staring at the house. Now what should she do? Go up and bang on the door? Tell Evan to get up, he was late? Ask if he was all right? That she was worried because the shop was closed? That would go over big. She wasn't his mother and, even if she was, he was beyond needing one to monitor his movements. It wasn't like him to be late, though.

Reluctantly, she walked up on his front porch and rang the bell. Noise exploded from the backyard, the same noise she'd listened to all night. Mary hurried down the steps, around the house and into the backyard. There, in a large chain-link dog run, was a small black cocker spaniel, running back and forth like an insane thing, barking the whole time. The dog stopped and stared at Mary. Mary stared back. She walked closer. So did the dog. There was a small doghouse in the run and also a stainless-steel, empty dog dish. Another one, upside down, lay close to the gate. The dog pawed at it and looked back at Mary. This must be the bitch Evan had bought from Alma. It was also the dog that had barked all night. Why was she out here, with no food or water, coat tangled, toys torn to shreds? The dog came toward the gate and jumped up on it, her paws pushing the wire, and whined. That she wanted Mary to do something was obvious, but what? Fill her water dish? Feed her? Let her out? Find Evan. That's what she needed to do, and right now. She started to back up. The dog whined more.

'Oh, don't.' Mary didn't know when she'd felt so helpless. She walked back and stuck her fingers through the wire. The dog put her nose against them and gave a gentle lick.

'You poor thing. Are you thirsty? Is that it? I can't believe Evan would – well, I'm sure he won't mind if I give you water. Only, I'm not sure . . .' The dog cocked her head as if listening to Mary then jumped on the gate again. The snap wiggled but held. Should she open the gate? What if the dog ran out? She couldn't catch it. Damn Evan anyway. She turned to look at the house once more. No sign of movement. Surely, if he was here he would have heard the dog barking, the doorbell ringing.

Where was he? She had no idea. She turned back toward the dog and spotted a hose. That solved one problem. She stuck the end of it through the wire fence. It just reached one empty bowl. Mary filled it with water. The dog drank greedily, her long ears dipping into the bowl along with her tongue. She came up for air and shook her head. Water drops sprayed everywhere. Mary laughed. The dog looked at her and seemed to smile. Mary stopped laughing. The dog sat down and stared at her again.

Now what? She'd check the garage for his car. The door was down and there was no handle. That meant an automatic opener. A window. There, on the side. Only, the window was higher than Mary, and she wasn't at all sure she could see over the sill. There must be something she could stand on. There was. A gardening kneeler, the kind you turned over and it became a seat. She dragged it under the garage window, turned it to the highest position and wiggled it. Unfortunately, one end wanted to sink into the slightly damp soil, but all she needed was one peek. She put one foot on the kneeler then looked over her shoulder. The dog sat in the corner of the run, watching her with what seemed to be great interest. Mary sighed, grabbed the windowsill, put her other foot on the kneeler and pulled herself up. The garage was empty. Gingerly, she let herself down and abandoned the kneeler. Evan truly wasn't here. Where was he?

She walked back to the dog run, where the dog waited for her. She once more jumped on the gate, making it clear she wanted out.

'I can't do that,' Mary told her.

The dog rattled the gate once more.

'Look, I'm going now. Maybe Evan's at the shop. Maybe he stayed down in San Luis Obispo for some reason and he's back at the shop right now, opening it up. I'll find him, I promise, and then we'll get you out of there.'

The dog whined. Mary sighed. She turned toward her car. The dog started to bark, loud, insistent barks, letting her know she didn't appreciate being abandoned.

'I'll be back,' Mary shouted, then started her car and backed out of the driveway. Evan had better be at the shop. If not, she was going to go to John and Glen's and bang on their door until they answered and helped her figure out what was going on.

TWENTY-FOUR

T he shop was still closed. Mary found a parking spot in front of it, a rare occasion on a busy Saturday, but she didn't get out. Nothing had changed. Now what? She pulled back out and her spot was immediately taken by a large SUV filled with laughing children and a flustered-looking woman. Mary turned the corner. She'd go down the alley. Furry Friends backed onto it. A car was parked out the back of Evan's shop. What type of car did Evan drive? Was that it? There was an open spot next to it. Mary pulled in and got out. She walked over to the car and looked at it as if it could tell her something. The car remained silent. She peered in the driver's window. Nothing. Not even a candy wrapper. She walked around the car, trying to look in the rear windows. This was an SUV of some type so there would be a storage area in the back. The windows were darkened but she could make out a shape – a dog crate. This had to be Evan's car. How long had it been here? What was it they did in mystery novels? Tested to see if the hood was warm. If it was, the car had recently arrived. She laid her hand on it. It was cold. She looked around, but there was nothing to see. The dumpster looked like a dumpster. Boxes stuck out of the top, sacks of something were barely visible, smells, definitely, but nothing you wouldn't expect of a dumpster.

The back door of Evan's shop looked undisturbed. Mary walked closer. She wasn't sure what she was looking for. There wasn't anything to see but a closed door with no window. There was, however, a window next to it. Bars. Probably practical on a shop, but not very helpful to her. Could she see into the back of the shop through the window? There probably wouldn't be anything to see, but that uneasy feeling had turned into out and out worry. Something was wrong. Very wrong. What, she didn't know, but she was certain she needed to find out.

This window wasn't any lower than the one in Evan's garage, and there was no garden kneeler in sight. However, there was a slatted box. It appeared to have contained lettuce or maybe flowers, but if she stood it on one end it might be tall enough. Not too sturdy, but then, she wasn't planning on standing on it very long. Besides, she could hold onto the bars to steady herself. All she needed was to make sure . . . Make sure what? She didn't know, only that she had to look.

The sense of urgency kept getting stronger. So was the urge to call Dan, but right now she had nothing to tell him. She dragged the box under the window and put one foot on the solid wood end. The side slats groaned but held. She grabbed the bars and slowly pulled herself up, put her other foot on the box and leaned forward, closer to the window. The back room was dim. She could make out a few shapes but not much more. Cartons of what were probably unpacked merchandise sat in one corner, an empty fish tank and a couple of chairs in the other. A half-open door must be the bathroom. Something lay on the floor in front of it. A bundle of rags? Dog blankets? No. That pile of cloth had a person inside it. It couldn't be. Surely it wasn't. She shifted her weight and leaned into the bars for a better look. It *was* a person. Wasn't it? Evan? Could it be? She didn't know, but she now had something to tell Dan. She needed to call him right now. Did she have her cell phone? She let go of the bars and slid her hand down into her jacket pocket. Yes. There it was. She'd better get down off this box before she tried to punch any buttons. She lifted one foot, letting it drift in midair as she shifted her weight. The slats in the box groaned alarmingly, followed with a resounding crack, and the box collapsed. It was the last thing Mary heard as she crashed to the ground, the box in splinters around her.

TWENTY-FIVE

'Don't move.'

The voice sounded familiar, but she couldn't place it. What did he mean, don't move? She needed to find Dan. She started to roll over but immediately stopped. A pain shot down her leg like a thunderbolt and another one tried to drill a hole in her head. Maybe she wouldn't move after all.

Mary opened her eyes, which for some reason were closed, and looked into the smiling face of a young man she remembered quite well. He was doing something to her leg, something that seemed to involve cutting her sweatpants and blood. She tried to repress the shudder that ran through her, but it wasn't a success.

'Almost done. Remember me?'

'Of course. Only, last I heard, you moved down south.'

'We did. My folks, I mean. I went to college in LA, got married and decided this was a better place to live. I took your advice, you see. Actually, your order, and got my act together. Stay still. I'm almost done.'

'Thank you, Randy, for helping me. My leg feels . . .'

'It's your head I'm more worried about, and as for helping you . . . I owe you. You spent plenty of time helping me.'

'What about her head?'

That voice she knew. Dan.

'I was going to call you. Something's wrong and I can't find Evan. No, that's not right. I think I saw him, only I can't remember. Where am I?'

'In the alley behind Furry Friends. Remind me to ask you later what you are doing back here. In the meantime, you've earned yourself a trip to the emergency room in an ambulance. If you're lucky, they may run the siren.'

'What?' Mary tried to sit up but was immediately pushed down.

'Don't move. You've got a nasty bump on your head as well as this cut on your leg. The nail that got your leg was huge and nicely rusted. Now, we're going to put you on this stretcher and lift you up into the ambulance. We can sound the siren if you want, but you don't really need it.'

'Randy Johnson, you'll do no such thing. I'm not going to any hospital, and furthermore . . .'

That was as far as Mary got. Pain from her leg shot through her, accompanied by a throbbing in her head and neck. Instead of finishing her protest, she groaned. Damn! 'Was it Evan?'

'Yes.' There was more than a trace of bitterness in Dan's tone.

'Why? Why would someone hurt Evan?' She tried to lift her

head to see Dan, but pain and the collar Randy was fastening around her neck made that impossible.

Dan's face, however, appeared above her, looking down as Randy tucked a blanket around her and fastened thick yellow straps to hold her in place. She wanted to protest but somehow couldn't.

'Just a minute, guys. Mary, how did this happen? Did someone attack you?'

Mary gasped. That thought hadn't occurred to her. Worry and anger showed in Dan's face.

She almost preferred his version to the truth, which, as she thought about it, was embarrassing. However . . . 'No. I was looking for Evan. I was worried, especially after I found his dog. So, as the shop wasn't open, I stood on the box to look in the window and, well, it sort of collapsed.'

Dan didn't say anything for a moment.

Randy, who stood beside him, blinked. 'Huh?'

'It all makes perfect sense,' Dan said finally. 'Take her away, guys. I'll meet you at the hospital as soon as I can get there.'

'On my count of three.' Randy and another man bumped the stretcher against the back of the ambulance, the legs collapsed and Mary rolled in.

Before the doors closed all the way, she managed to call out, 'Dan. Send someone over to Evan's place to get that little dog.' The doors shut firmly behind her.

TWENTY-SIX

Mary limped into her house by the back door, ignored the kitchen, for perhaps the first time in her life, and headed for the sofa in the living room. She sank down on it, raised her legs as she had been told in the hospital, and propped her head up on one of the sofa pillows. What an ordeal! They'd stitched her leg, given her shots, put IVs into her hand, pushed her through some kind of tunnel machine to take pictures of her head and finally told her she was fine and could go home. She knew she was fine. A couple of butterfly bandages would have taken care of the leg and two super strength Tylenols would take care of her head. That and an ice pack. Ellen brought the ice pack.

'Tea?'

Mary started to nod but thought better of it. 'Please.'

Ellen paused long enough to put another pillow under Mary's head and an afghan over her knees before returning to the kitchen. Mary lay still and fumed. If that stupid box had held together one more minute, none of this would have happened. She closed her eyes and let her drifting thoughts take over. Evan. Killed. Lying all night, dead, in his shop. She hoped he'd been dead. The thought of him lying there, no one to help him, perhaps in pain, was too much. The only possible good thing she could think of was it meant Evan hadn't killed Cliff. Didn't it? It must, but somehow that was no consolation.

She let her thoughts move on to what was now the most important question. Why? It had to have some connection to Cliff's death, didn't it? Something to do with the dogs, with the missing poodle. Only, what? Evan didn't have anything to do with the poodle. He sold cockapoos in his shop, though. He sold them for John and Glen. He sold his own puppies. Were they cockapoos? What a silly name for a dog. Why would anyone . . . ? The puppies were so cute. She thought about Sampson. Where had he come from? Was he part of the litter Evan had in his store? How did you go about finding out? Who owned those puppies, anyway? Poor Evan. What a terrible thing. This had to stop before anyone else – oh my God. The children. Mary sat up abruptly, holding the ice pack to her head. If the same person killed both Cliff and Evan, were the children next?

'What are you doing? You're supposed to be lying down.' Ellen set two mugs of tea on a magazine on the coffee table and walked over to her aunt. 'I'll help you.'

'I don't need any help, and I can't drink tea while I'm lying down. Quit fussing.' She took a deep breath and let it out slowly. 'Ellen, do you think the same person killed both Evan and Cliff?'

Ellen didn't say anything for a moment. She picked up both mugs of tea, handed one to Mary and sat down in the rocker. 'Ouch. This is hot.' She passed her mug back and forth between her hands. 'It seems likely. But why? Evan didn't have anything to do with Cliff. At least, I don't think so.'

'I don't know of any connection between them, either. Do you think whoever it is will try to harm the children?'

Ellen almost dropped her tea. 'Oh, my . . . twice. This person, whoever he is, has murdered twice. At least, we think so. But children?'

'They saw him.'

'They didn't recognize him, though.'

'The murderer doesn't know that.' Mary blew into her tea. She thought about the children and their reactions through all this. How much danger, if any, might they be in? They had to find the murderer, and fast, before something else terrible happened. The children's reactions. The Blisses' winery. 'Bill Bliss.'

'What?' Ellen looked at her aunt as if the bump might have done something more than cause a headache. 'What about him?'

'Reactions. I was thinking about Dalia and Ronaldo's reactions. When we were in the Bliss winery, they stopped short when they saw him. Just skidded to a halt and stared at him. I've been thinking about it. Maybe it was because of his size.'

The expression on Ellen's face clearly said that bump had done some damage. 'His size? Bill Bliss isn't fat.'

'No. But he's tall. They described the murderer as tall. Father D'Angelo is tall. So was Evan.'

'We can eliminate Evan as a murderer.' She seemed doubtful but willing to try to follow Mary's train of thought. She took a sip of her tea as she thought about what Mary said. 'That's not much to go on. There are a lot of tall men around. Dan, for one.'

Mary put down her ice pack and reached for her mug. 'I think we can eliminate him also. I know it's not much, but it's the only place I can think to start.'

'So, you think Bill Bliss could be the murderer? Why?'

'Insurance money. Maybe he didn't want to kill the dog so he handed it off to someone, claimed it was stolen and collected the insurance. Cliff found out, so he killed him. We know the dog is still alive somewhere.'

'OK. But how do you explain Evan?'

Mary couldn't. 'Bill Bliss went into Evan's shop right about closing yesterday. Why he might want to kill Evan, I don't know, but he had the opportunity.'

'He was probably going in to buy dog food. That's where I buy Jake's cat food.'

'They no longer have a dog. Naomi said so.'

Ellen started to shake her head but stopped when her tea sloshed. 'It seems so improbable. The Blisses have plenty of money. Why would he do such a thing?'

'I don't know. I wouldn't have even considered him if the children hadn't had such a strange reaction when they saw him.'

'The children. We have to talk to Luanne and Tony. It's obvious they can't be left alone, even for a moment. I have a hard time believing they could be in danger, but I wouldn't have believed Evan could be either.'

She didn't say it, but Mary knew what Ellen was thinking. She had the same thought. Evan was dead. It didn't matter what they believed, or had a hard time believing. What mattered was what they did, at least until they knew beyond any doubt the children were safe, and that wouldn't be until they knew who murdered both Cliff and Evan.

The front door opened and Pat appeared. 'Ellen, could you help me, please?'

'Sure. Help you do what?' Ellen set her mug down and walked toward the door. 'What's all this?'

Ellen backed up, her arms now full of a dog bed, a sack of dog food, a bowl and a leash draped over one of her arms. A large dog carrier followed her into the room, pushed by Pat Bennington.

'This thing is heavy.'

A whine emanated from the carrier in response.

What do you have? Mary was on her feet, staring at the dog crate. It couldn't be, could it?

Pat answered as if Mary had asked her question aloud. 'We'd better get this little girl out of there and in the backyard before we do another thing.'

A loud bark emanated from the crate, a bark Mary was sure she recognized.

'Is that . . .'

'Evan's dog? Yes.'

'Why did you bring her here?'

'Dan called. He told us what happened to Evan.' Pat stopped pushing the crate and ran the back of her hand over her eyes. It looked suspiciously as if she wiped away tears. Her voice broke. 'He said she was all alone and you were worried about her.'

'Well, yes, but I didn't think you'd bring her here.'

'It'll just be for a day or so. We're full up at the clinic, and I didn't know where else to take her.' Pat opened the door of the crate and waited.

The dog poked her head out and looked around. Evidently she didn't think any of them looked dangerous because she took a step into the room.

Pat immediately removed the leash from Ellen's arm and snapped it onto her collar. 'Come on, baby. There's a whole lot of nice grass out there, just waiting for you.' She started for the kitchen, the little dog trotting at her heels, when she stopped and looked back at Mary. 'You don't mind, do you? Dan said you got hurt, but not badly, so I thought it would be all right.' She looked more closely at Mary. 'I don't know. That's a pretty good-sized lump on your head. Can you handle this?'

Mary bristled. If she could handle just about every difficult woman in town, she could certainly handle one small dog. 'Of course I can. It's just that, well, I've never had a dog.'

'I'll teach you.' Pat smiled and walked on toward the back door.

Mary followed. If Pat was going to teach her, she'd better start to learn.

There wasn't much to it. Pat let the little dog loose and watched her wander around the yard, dragging her leash. The dog squatted, Pat picked up the leash and they both headed back toward the house. Mary stood aside as they came in then closed the door. She followed them into the living room and went back to her sofa and mug of tea. If that was all there was to dog ownership, why had she put it off so long?

Pat accepted the mug of tea Ellen handed her. The dog, no longer dragging the leash, curled up on the living-room rug and went to sleep. They all looked at her for a minute.

Pat looked at Mary. 'OK. What happened?'

'I don't know.'

'You must know something. You were in the alley getting yourself a cut leg and a goose egg on your head and poor Evan is dead. Something happened.'

Mary sighed. 'Something did. I just don't know exactly what.' She drained the last of her tea and sat back, resting her head on a pillow and stared at the dog, who snored. 'She barked all night.'

'Who did?' Ellen looked down at the dog.

So did Pat.

'That dog?'

Mary nodded. The dog slept on. 'I didn't know it was her. I had no idea where the dog was, but it was the first time I'd ever heard it. Anyway, in the morning I went to my rummage sale meeting then over to see how the Christmas Can Tree was coming along.' She paused and smiled. 'You wouldn't believe how much food we've collected.'

'Never mind that. What did you do then?' Ellen's tone left no doubt the Christmas Can Tree had lost all interest for her.

'Well, after I talked to Luke, I went over to Evan's shop. I wanted to know who owned the puppies he had for sale. Only, the shop was closed and it was after ten.'

'And?' Pat's tone said let's get to the point.

'I was worried, so I went to Evan's house. He and Glen Manning and John Lavorino were supposed to have gone to San Luis Obispo to some church function last night. I thought maybe something had happened.' She felt herself get a little shaky as she relived those anxious moments. She had been so certain something had happened and had been so right. 'His car wasn't there but the dog' – she nodded toward the still sleeping dog on her living-room rug – 'was. She had no food or water. That really got me worried. It wasn't like Evan to neglect an animal. I went back to his shop and found his car parked out the back.'

'That's when you got attacked?' Pat leaned forward in her chair, her hands clasped, her eyes anxious.

'I didn't get attacked.' Mary stopped. Her cheeks heated. It really was silly of her to climb on that box. She should have found something stronger. 'I found a packing crate and stood on it to look in the window. Poor Evan was lying on the floor right by the bathroom and then, well, the box collapsed. That's all I remember until I woke up and Randy was trying to put me on a stretcher to take me to the hospital. Totally unnecessary.'

Pat and Ellen looked at each other and grinned. The grins turned into giggles, which dissolved into gales of laughter.

'I fail to see anything funny in this.' Mary bristled.

Ellen grabbed a napkin and wiped her eyes. 'Debbie from the flower shop next door said she heard a loud crack. She thought it was a gunshot. She peeked out her back door and saw you lying in the alley, bleeding. She was sure you'd been shot so she called nine-one-one. Poor Hazel, our unflappable dispatcher, almost had a heart attack. She darn near gave Dan one too. By the time I heard about it, they knew you weren't dead.'

'Oh.' Mary couldn't think of anything else to say. She had no idea she'd caused so much fuss. Why on earth hadn't the silly girl come over and looked? She would have seen she was very much alive. Shot, indeed.

The dog lifted her head and stared at the front door. So did Mary. It opened and Dan appeared. He looked tired and profoundly irritated. He stopped when he saw the dog, glanced over at Pat, stepped over the dog and squatted down beside the sofa. 'How are you?'

Mary lowered her ice pack and smiled. 'I'm not shot.'

He smiled back. 'Glad to hear it. So far, neither is anyone else.' He patted her hand, nodded with what seemed to be approval and stood. 'I don't suppose there's any coffee?'

'We're having tea, but it won't take a minute.' Ellen headed for the kitchen. 'We've got about a thousand questions, so don't start until I get back.'

'Why am I not surprised.' Dan stood over the dog, looking down. The dog sat up and returned his stare.

'I see you got it.'

Pat nodded. 'She was glad to see me.'

'What are you going to do with her now?'

'Mary's going to keep her until we can find other accommodation.'

Dan turned toward Mary with a quizzical look. 'Are you sure you can handle that?'

Mary's hackles rose. If one more person asked her if she could handle something . . . 'It's a little dog. I think I can manage.'

A smile played around the corners of Dan's mouth. 'I imagine you can.'

'OK. Now, tell us what happened.' Ellen walked back into the living room, wiping her hands on a dishtowel. 'Coffee will be right up, but in the meantime, who killed Evan and why?'

Dan gave a little start then started to laugh. 'Nice to know you have that much faith in me, but I don't know yet. We know how he was killed, like Cliff. Stabbed with something long and sharp. I have no idea who did it. Well, I have some ideas but no proof.'

The three women all looked at him, puzzled. The dog just looked. 'That requires an explanation. Sit down and tell us.'

A lifetime of obeying Mary was not to be denied. Dan sat, seemingly gratefully. 'This is what we know so far.'

'Wait.' Ellen held up her hand. 'I don't want to miss a word of this. That coffee should be ready. If it's not . . .'

Dan settled himself in her large reading chair. Ellen would be back immediately. The pause and pour coffee machine was coming in handy. She was right. Ellen appeared with a mug filled with freshly brewed coffee which she handed to her husband. Mary sniffed. It smelled good. Maybe her next mug full would be coffee as well. In the meantime . . .

'Talk,' was all Ellen said.

'We think he was killed after he closed the shop.'

'What makes you think that?' Mary thought so as well, but she wanted to know why Dan did.

'We have reports of people seen leaving the shop after the closed sign was up and the blinds pulled down.'

'Oh.' Ellen and Pat looked at each other than at Mary. *We're all thinking the same thing.* 'Who?'

Dan's frown was deep and unhappy. 'Father D'Angelo for one.'

Ellen groaned.

'John Lavorino and Glen Manning came out carrying something, and John looked furious. Luke, from the library, was there as well.'

'How do you know all this?'

'Our little friend at the flower shop. She evidently wasn't very busy Friday afternoon.'

'Sounds like he was having open house.' Pat sounded as distraught as Ellen.

'Bill Bliss was there around closing time. Did anyone see him leave?'

'No. No one mentioned him. How do you know that?'

Mary thought Dan looked unusually interested in that piece of information. 'I heard it at the rummage sale committee meeting. Leigh Cameron told me. She needed dog food, but when she saw Bill Bliss, she went to the market instead. She doesn't like him – thinks he's stuck up.'

'Mmm.' Pat didn't offer a comment but from the muffled sound she made, Mary thought she agreed.

'Anyone else?' Ellen's remark sounded a little sarcastic.

Pat wasn't far off the mark when she said it seemed like open house. It sounded as if half the town had been in and out of Evan's store yesterday afternoon.

'Todd Blankenship, but he didn't get in. The door was locked by the time he went over,' Dan answered.

'Who saw all this?' Ellen made it sound as though someone had had the place staked out, watching all the comings and goings.

'I had someone asking questions in all the stores. Todd claimed he needed to buy dog food but the door was locked by the time he got there. He knocked but there was no answer. He assumed Evan had left, so he did also. Mary's savior, Debbie from the flower shop, saw Father D'Angelo go in but didn't see him come out. That was probably after John and Glen left. Luke says he went over right after he closed up the library, at five. He walked over so he'd get there before Evan closed. He says John and Glen were still there, talking to Evan rather heatedly. He didn't see Father D'Angelo so doesn't know if he came after him or before.'

'What were Evan and John and Glen talking about?'

'He doesn't know. We'd ask them, but we can't find them.'

Dan's tone when he said that was mild but the statement sent shockwaves through Mary.

They weren't home? Where were they? Surely not still in San Luis Obispo? They also had dogs to take care of.

'What is it?' Dan looked directly at Mary and his voice was a lot sharper. 'What do you know?'

'Nothing really.'

'Uhuh. Suppose you tell me about nothing.'

Mary sighed. It really was nothing. 'John and Glen were in Evan's shop on Friday. They said they were going to San Luis Obispo to a church function, Evan too. Did they stop by the shop to pick Evan up? Only, he didn't go. Where are they now?'

'Good questions.' Dan looked increasingly thoughtful.

'Wouldn't they have picked him up at home? He'd want to shower and change, wouldn't he?' Ellen walked around, picking up empty mugs and headed for the kitchen. 'I'm surprised they're not home now.'

'They may have gone somewhere else today and haven't heard the news yet.' Pat followed Ellen toward the kitchen. 'Mary, more tea? Coffee, Dan?'

They both shook their heads.

'If they haven't heard yet, they soon will. At least, they will if they're close to a radio. The local news will be all over this.'

Mary nodded but her thoughts weren't on John and Glen. At least, they weren't right that minute. 'Dan, why would anyone want to kill either Cliff or Evan? Well, I guess Cliff gave people reasons to hate him, but Evan . . . the most disagreeable I've ever seen him was when he played Scrooge in the Victorian Christmas Extravaganza and he wasn't too mean then. Why would anyone do such a thing?'

Dan sat very still then shook his head. 'I don't know. Yet. But I'd guess Evan knew something. Maybe something about why Cliff was killed.'

'Dogs. It's got to have something to do with dogs.'

'Maybe. Maybe not. But one thing is clear: whoever's doing this isn't shy. Cliff was killed in a place about to be invaded by literally hundreds of people. Evan was killed in his own shop, a busy shop. My team is going over the shop right now, hoping to find something, but it's not going to be easy.' He pushed himself to his feet. 'I came by to make sure you were all right, but also, Mary, I'm worried about the Mendosa children. I'm going to talk to Tony and Luanne, but until I know who's doing this, I want those kids with someone. Day and night. If you don't feel up to it, then I'll help the Mendosas cover them. Maybe Agnes can stand in when Luanne is at work or at the doctor. Sister Margaret Anne called and after she gave me an earful, we worked out something for the school. But—' He never got to finish.

'I'm just fine. When did a little scratch on the leg stop me? I will, of course, help with the children. Tell Tony to stop by here and we'll make a plan. Now, go back to finding out who's behind all this. I'll tell Ellen . . .'

'You'll tell Ellen what?'

'That I probably won't be home for dinner.' He put his arm around his wife and kissed her on the nose.

She smiled at him. 'I hadn't planned on you being. I figured you'd be a little busy. Just be careful, OK?'

'I think I can manage that.' He gave her one more squeeze, turned, gave Mary a very careful kiss on the cheek and headed for the door. 'I'll call the Mendosas when I get back.'

'Dan, wait.' Pat stood in the doorway to the kitchen, looking worried.

Dan stopped, looked at her and waited.

'The animals in the shop. The puppies, and I think there are still a couple of kittens. There are turtles, lizards and snakes. Who's taking care of them?'

'I called Karl. He sent someone over. Cute girl. Doesn't seem to be afraid of any of them, even that ugly lizard who hisses.'

'Pam. Thank goodness. She's a vet student. Works for Karl sometimes. That's perfect.'

'She also follows directions, which is helpful. My guys are trying to take fingerprints and look for anything that might give us a clue, and she keeps out of their way. Pretty hopeless job considering the number of people in and out of that store, but you never know.' He turned and was out the door.

The three of them watched him go. Even the dog raised her head, stood, stretched and looked around expectantly.

'Does she have to go out?' Mary suddenly found she was nervous watching her. She had no idea what the dog had in mind. She could tell by the way a child sat in class whether they were paying attention or planning mischief. She could tell by the gleam in an eleven-year-old boy's eyes if he was thinking about tripping his arch enemy as he walked down the aisle, or if a twelve-year-old girl hadn't heard a word Mary said but had gotten every nuance directed her way by the boy two seats in front of her.

Suddenly, she was afraid she was out of her element with a dog. 'Should I take her outside?'

'Feed her.' Pat grinned and started for the kitchen. 'Come on. I brought the food I found on Evan's back porch. I brought her dinner dish and water bowl as well. We'll set her up on your back porch. She'll feel right at home.'

Mary followed Pat into the kitchen. The stainless-steel bowls she'd seen earlier that morning were now on her counter beside a huge bag of dog food. Pat filled one bowl with water and carried it onto the back porch. The dog followed and started to lap. Mary watched her for a moment then picked up the other bowl.

'How much of that stuff does she get?'

'I don't know what Evan fed her, but for a dog this size one scoop should do it.' She produced a red plastic scoop out of the bag and handed it to Mary. 'Scoop away.'

Mary had to stand on tiptoe to get the scoop into the bag. 'We'll have to put that sack somewhere lower. Is this enough?' She poured the food into the other dish. There didn't seem to be very much. Mary was used to feeding people and did it with a generous hand. This didn't look very generous. It didn't look very appetizing, either.

'It's plenty. Just set it down beside the water.'

They spent the next few minutes getting both Mary and the dog settled in. The dog ate, went outside, came back in and looked around.

'What's she looking for?'

'Her bed if she's got any sense. She's likely tired after the night she put in.' Ellen pushed herself away from the doorjamb she'd been leaning against while she watched the dog-settling program. 'Where is she going to sleep?'

That caught Mary by surprise. She hadn't given it a thought. Where did dogs sleep? Some of her friends let their dogs sleep on their beds. She wasn't quite up to that.

'I brought her basket. It's on the front porch. Tell me where you want it. Where ever you start her off, that's where she'll stay, so decide.'

'Unless she changes her mind.'

'There's always that.' Pat headed for the front porch and almost immediately was back. 'Where do you want her to sleep?'

Mary felt a bit helpless, an unfamiliar feeling and one that was not welcome. 'I don't know. Where do dogs usually sleep?'

'Depends. You can put her bed beside yours or you can put it in the living room, or you can put her on the back porch and close the door. You can even put her bed out on the back steps.'

Horrified, Mary stared at her. 'On the back steps? She'd be lonely. Scared. Do you think she'd like her bed in the living room?'

'She'd like it better if you put her bed beside yours. She'd be less lonely that way.'

It took Mary a minute. 'You're setting me up. That damn dog doesn't care if she's next to me or the TV.'

'I don't think that's true, I really don't, but I think you'll feel better if she's right beside you. Try it tonight and see how it goes.'

Unconvinced, but also not sure what else to do, Mary agreed. It took no time at all until Pat had the dog's basket, with the dog bed in it, set up beside hers. The dog sniffed it, decided it was indeed hers, got in, curled up and promptly fell asleep.

Mary stood for some time after Ellen and Pat left, staring down at the sleeping dog, wondering how she'd gotten herself into this, wondering what 'this' was. Cliff dead, Evan dead, the children in danger, well, perhaps in danger. What was going on? She wasn't going to figure it out tonight. She was exhausted and she hurt. She also needed to eat, but the bowl of soup she ate while watching a rerun of *Antiques Roadshow* didn't help much. Tylenol was needed. She walked back to the kitchen, conscious she was moving slowly. She rinsed her bowl and put it in the dishwasher, poured a glass of water and swallowed two pain pills. She slipped off her, by now, very dirty sweater, examined it closely, decided it would recover from a good washing and laid it over a chair. She'd wash it in the morning. The same could not be said of her blood-stained and torn sweatpants. They went into the trash. Clad only in a bra and panties, she headed for the shower. That pleasure was denied her, at least for tonight. Don't get either bandage wet, she'd been warned. The hot washcloth she applied liberally to her body was a poor substitute for a hot shower, but it was better than nothing, and it got off a little of the hospital smell. Her nightgown warmed and soothed as it settled over her and, slowly and carefully, she crawled into bed. Her head still hurt, and so did her leg, but her brain refused to succumb to pain and exhaustion. What had happened to Evan? Where were John and Glen? Why wasn't Evan with them last night? Did they know he was dead? What was Bill Bliss doing at Evan's shop? What was Father D'Angelo doing there? Buying cat food? Maybe. Bill Bliss wasn't. And Luke. He'd said he needed dog food. What else did he need? Her thoughts went round and round until finally the painkillers worked and sleep wiped away all of her worrying thoughts. The last thing she remembered was her hand creeping over the side of the bed, reaching out, finding and stroking the silky black fur of her very new friend.

TWENTY-SEVEN

Her hand was wet. Something was licking her. Mary bolted upright and looked at her hand. Wet. What . . . The dog sat on the floor, looking up at her. She made a soft whine, stood up and headed for the bedroom door. She couldn't have made it plainer. Mary slid out of bed, thrust her feet into fur-lined moccasins, grabbed her robe off the end of the bed and followed. The kitchen clock said eight thirty, late for her. She yawned and opened the back door. The dog bolted out. Mary returned to the kitchen, looked at the coffeepot. Should she push the button or go back to bed? She pushed the button.

The dog returned to the kitchen, sat down and looked at Mary.

'It's too early for breakfast. I haven't had my coffee yet.'

The dog walked over to her empty bowl, looked inside and made a whining sound.

'Oh, all right.'

She bent over to pick up the bowl and immediately the room started to spin. 'Oh, that isn't good.' She dropped the bowl on the countertop and leaned against it until her head cleared. 'Why did that happen? I don't have a concussion.'

'Probably because you banged it hard on asphalt and have six stitches in your leg. Go back to bed.'

Mary's hold on the counter slipped as she swung around to face the owner of the voice. 'How did you get in here?'

'You didn't close the door after you let the dog in. Go sit down. I'll get your coffee and feed the dog.'

Ellen crossed the kitchen and put an arm under her aunt's and led her to the kitchen table. 'Sit.'

Mary did. Much to her annoyance, her leg was on fire and her head hurt. The dizziness was gone, but the side of her head, where the goose egg hadn't retreated, ached. 'Damn.'

'You can't expect to fall through boxes onto asphalt and come out unscathed.' Ellen put a full mug of coffee in front of her aunt, turned and set a bowl of food in front of the dog. The dog started to eat and Mary immediately picked up her mug. She put it down almost as fast as she picked it up. 'Hot.' She tried to smile but suddenly even that seemed too much of an effort. She needed pain pills. Two white pills and a glass of water appeared in front of her.

'What's this?'

'You look like you need them. Did you sleep?' Ellen set her mug on the table, pulled out a chair opposite Mary and settled into it.

'Better than the dog did. I heard her prowling around a couple of times. I had to get up to use the bathroom and offered her a chance, but she ignored it. She just prowled around.'

Ellen sighed. 'Looking for Evan. Poor little thing. Are you going to keep her?'

'I don't know.'

Mary had never had a dog. She'd never felt the need, even after Samuel died. Lots of her friends took comfort in their pets, treating them almost as they would, or had, their children. Mary had had all the children she needed while she taught middle school and, after she retired, her volunteer work and her closeness to her niece and her family and her many friends fulfilled her. She didn't need the added work of a dog. But this one . . . The dog left her now-empty bowl, pushed close to Mary's leg and sighed.

'Maybe.' Mary reached down and rubbed the dog's ears, soft and silky under her fingers. 'We'll see.' She glanced up just in time to see a smile hastily wiped off Ellen's face. 'What are you doing here at this time of morning, anyway? Church doesn't start for another hour.'

'I came to see how you are and to bring you a message from Les. He says he doesn't want to see you in church this morning and if you show up he will personally escort you back out the door and bring you home, even in the middle of a sermon. I'm to make sure you don't try.'

'You're all making a terrible fuss over a little accident. I'm fine.' She took another sip of coffee and hoped burying her face in her mug would hide her relief. As much as she wanted to talk to Les, she really didn't feel like getting dressed and going downtown.

'The hole in your leg isn't small but the knot on your head's bigger. What made you climb on that crate, anyway?'

Mary absently scratched the dog's ears. Why had she? 'I was worried about Evan. When I saw his car in the parking lot and realized the engine was cold . . .'

'You felt the engine?'

Mary nodded. 'I wanted to know how long the car had been there.'

Ellen shook her head. 'Dan's right. We've got to stop watching *CSI*. OK. The engine was cold. Then what did you do?'

'Tried to look in the back window of the shop but it was too high. I was beginning to get nervous, so when I saw the crate, I used it. It wasn't very sturdy.'

'No.' Ellen shook her head again. 'Why didn't you call one of us?'

'I didn't have anything to say. Just an uneasy feeling that something was wrong. This dog was barking all night. When I found her and realized Evan wasn't home, I was sure something was wrong. He's not – wasn't – the kind of person who'd neglect his dog. Do you think she misses him?'

'What? Who? Oh.' Ellen looked at the dog, who stared back. 'I don't know much about dogs, but she must be pretty confused. So am I. Why would anyone want to kill Evan? He wasn't victim material.'

Mary squelched the laugh that threatened to erupt. It was guaranteed to make her head hurt. She had to agree with Ellen, however. Evan was the last person she thought would be a murder victim. This was no random mugging, no bullet going astray and killing an innocent bystander. This was a deliberate act intended for Evan and him alone. Why? What could gentle, slightly nervous but always kind Evan have done that made someone angry enough to kill him? 'What does Dan say?'

'A lot, but none of it very useful.' Ellen grinned. 'He's furious. First poor old Cliff, now Evan, and he doesn't have a clue for either who or why. When he thought you were shot, that really sent him over the edge. I wouldn't want to be in the murderer's shoes when he catches him, and he will catch him.'

'I'm sure you're right.' Mary sighed deeply. She looked at the dog who hadn't moved from her side. 'This all seems so senseless. Unless . . .'

'Unless, what?' All traces of a smile were gone from Ellen's face. 'What are you thinking?'

'About dogs.' The vague thought forming disappeared under the insistent ringing of her front doorbell.

'Good grief. Who is that at this hour? Are they trying to push the bell through the wall? Ellen, will you go?'

Ellen was already halfway across the kitchen. 'Whoever it is, they better have a good reason for trying to push that bell through the wall.' The ringing turned into knocking. 'I'm coming. I'm coming.' Her step quickened with extreme irritation. If whoever that was didn't have a good reason for making all that noise Ellen was likely to make a little of her own.

'Where is she?' Mary was sure that breathless shout belonged to Glen Manning.

Ellen's exasperated 'what on earth' was loud enough to reach Mary in the kitchen. She was prepared when Glen appeared at her side. He was dressed in the same chinos he'd had on when she saw him late Friday afternoon, only now the sharp crease down the pant leg had disappeared. But the sandals he'd worn hadn't.

'Are you all right? Oh, your poor head.' He squatted down beside her and reached out his hand, but stopped before it made contact with the bump pushing up through the shaved part of Mary's scalp.

'Don't touch it.' John was right behind Glen, his voice sharp, almost as sharp as the welcoming barks the little dog gave as she circled the two men, her stub of a tail wagging her rear end. John knelt down and was immediately plied with wet kisses. 'Oh, Millie, oh, poor Millie. Are you all right? Have you been nice to Miss Mary? She got hurt too.' He gathered the little dog in his arms and looked at Mary. 'We came as soon as we heard.'

'Heard what?' Ellen leaned against the doorjamb leading from the dining room into the kitchen, her face devoid of expression.

'Why, about Evan's death, of course, and about poor Mary getting attacked by the murderer.' John, still on the floor, held the dog a little tighter as he looked from Mary to Ellen and back.

The dog yelped.

'We spent the night in San Luis Obispo. We'd been trying to reach Evan – he always feeds our dogs when we're gone – but he didn't respond to any of our messages, so we got an early start back. We walked in the door and our answering machine was blinking like crazy. We still can't believe it. Are you all right, Mary?' Glen once more leaned in toward Mary, this time touching her on the shoulder. 'Do you know who attacked you?'

Ellen smiled and pushed herself away from the door. 'She was attacked by a wooden box. Would you two like coffee?'

'What?' Glen stood and stared at Ellen.

'A box?' John let go of the dog and also got to his feet.

The dog went back to Mary, put her front legs in her lap and let her head drop down into it. Mary trailed her hand through the soft curls on one ear. 'I was worried about Evan. I thought he'd gone to San Luis with you two, but his dog barked all night. I didn't think he'd leave her out like that, without food or water, but I couldn't find him. It was after ten and he hadn't opened his shop, even though his car was there, so I tried to look through the window. I stood on the box and it collapsed.' Her face heated. 'It was a very flimsy box.'

'You two spent most of the weekend down there?' Ellen poured coffee into two mugs, her back to all of them. Her stance looked rigid and her voice unnaturally careful. Ellen liked John and Glen and thought John was funny in spite of his not-funny job as a surgery nurse. She banked at the local bank which Glen managed and had nothing but good things to say about how he ran it, so why, now, was she being so cautious? Or was it something else?

Ellen turned and handed Glen one of Mary's blue and white mugs. She walked across the room, avoided stepping on the dog still glued to Mary's side and handed John the other one. Then she picked up her cup and resumed her seat across from Mary.

John and Glen looked at each other over the tops of their mugs. John took a tentative sip.

Glen looked into his. 'Yes. We'd planned to come home Friday night, after the dance, but one thing led to another and, well, driving home wouldn't have been a good idea. A friend offered us a bed and we took it. We left Evan a voice message, asking him to take care of the girls.'

'That was Friday night, wasn't it?' Mary's tone left no doubt that she wanted to know where they were last night as well.

John shrugged. 'A bunch of our friends decided to go to the beach. It's nice over there this time of year. We called Evan, but no one answered. We thought he was still pouting but knew he'd take care of the girls, so we went along and ended up spending the night.'

'Pouting?' Ellen walked over to the sink and ran water in her coffee mug. 'What was he pouting about?'

'Evan was supposed to come with us but begged off at the last minute.' Glen didn't look at either Mary or Ellen but studied his mug intently. 'I think he had an attack of shyness. He didn't know any of the people we were going to be with. We put a little pressure on him – he'd never get to know them if he didn't try, but that sort of backfired. We stopped by one last time to persuade him to come, but he wouldn't, so we went without him. When he didn't answer, we thought he was . . .' There was a catch in his voice. He cleared his throat. 'I – we – couldn't believe it when we got home this morning and heard the messages on the machine.'

Neither Mary nor Ellen said anything while Glen cleared his throat again.

'I still can't. Why would anyone want to hurt Evan?'

John set his mug on the table, walked over and took Glen's hand. He squeezed it before he looked at them. 'Evan was our best friend.' A simple statement, but the emotion in it was raw. He blinked several times, dropped Glen's hand and walked over toward Mary and peered at her head. 'Did they put stitches in your scalp?'

Mary had to think about that. 'I think so, but not many. They shaved off my hair and put me in that awful machine to see if I had brain damage. I could have told them I didn't.'

'You did. Several times.' Ellen walked back over to the coffeemaker and turned her attention to the two men. 'So, you didn't know about Evan until you got home this morning?'

'Not exactly.' Glen joined Ellen at the sink. He took the empty pot out of her hands, rinsed it, filled it with water and handed it back to her. 'We went out for an early breakfast. There was a TV turned on to the local news. We couldn't believe it.'

'We left right away and came home. Our answering machine was full. Someone said you had Millie.' He paused and scratched his head as if thinking. 'Can't remember who. But they also said you were hurt. Or was that someone else?'

Glen interrupted. 'Anyway, we're here and so glad you weren't attacked. What happened was bad enough. Did you, ah, see anything before the box collapsed?'

'Evan's body on the floor right in front of the bathroom.'

John gave a visual shudder.

Glen's face paled. 'Do you know what happened?'

'Someone stabbed him, just like someone stabbed Cliff.' Ellen's tone wasn't quite as frosty but it wasn't especially friendly. Why?

Glen's face hadn't regained any color and he clutched his coffee mug closely to his chest, but his voice was steady. 'Any idea when?'

'The coroner thinks sometime between six and eight on Friday evening.'

Mary turned a little too quickly to look at Ellen. 'When did you learn that?'

'Dan talked to him this morning.'

'That means he was killed shortly after we left.' Glen's tone was soft and thoughtful.

John's wasn't. 'That's awful. I can't believe we no more than got out the door than someone stabbed poor Evan. Who would do such a thing?'

The dog looked up at the half-hysterical tone of John's voice then curled up as close to a ball as she could, one paw on Mary's foot.

'Who was in the shop when you left?' Mary looked at the dog. She, at least, looked peaceful. The rest of them didn't.

'Father D'Angelo came just as we left. Luke Bradshaw was there too, buying dog food.' Glen paused and finished off the coffee in his mug. He looked over at the coffeemaker, but it hadn't finished dripping coffee into the carafe.

'Evan and Luke were arguing.' John dropped that into the conversation as if it were a juicy bit of gossip he'd saved just for this moment.

'Arguing? What about?' Mary glanced at Ellen, who almost unperceptively nodded. Evidently Ellen was going to keep out of this conversation.

'About purebred dogs, as usual. Evan wanted Luke to let us breed one of our cockers to his poodle. Luke wasn't having any of that. He thinks cockapoo is a four-letter word.'

'I beg your pardon?' Mary felt this conversation was getting away from her. What was wrong with cockapoos? They were adorable. They reminded her of those cute stuffed animals all the teenage girls loved. What could be better than having a live one?

The look Glen shot John was razor sharp. 'Most breeders of purebred dogs don't like hybrids. They're interested in trying to improve the breed they've chosen and don't want to muddy up their precious bloodlines. Horse people aren't too much different. People who breed cockapoos are trying to get them recognized as a breed by the ACK, but so far that hasn't happened. So people like Naomi Bliss and Bonnie Blankenship never let their dogs cross bloodlines. Luke bred his dog to a cocker once. Evan thought he might again. He's not going to show the dog or stand him at stud, even though he's an especially nice one.'

Ellen held her coffee mug in both hands as if it might escape if she let it go. Her face had lost its stony look. Instead, it had the intense look of a bloodhound who had picked up the scent.

'Why did Evan think Luke might be willing to have his dog father puppies for you two?'

Glen and John exchanged looks again.

'Because he let Evan breed Millie to him.' Glen sounded as if each word was pulled out of his mouth against his will.

Mary's foot was going to sleep under the weight of the dog's head and she moved it a little. The dog looked at her, moved a little closer and let her head drop back down on the foot again.

Mary wiggled her toes. 'If Luke let his dog father one litter of cockapoos, why did he balk at doing it again?'

Both men shrugged.

'I always thought it had something to do with Cliff. He was so adamant about never crossing breeds. Some of that rubbed off on Luke when he was young.'

'Then how did Evan get Luke to let his dog father Millie's pups?' Mary looked at the still sleeping dog, trying to picture her as a mother. She was sure the puppies had been adorable.

'We never could get Evan to say,' John said, 'and Lord knows, we tried.'

'We have to go. Mary, we're so glad you aren't hurt any worse. This is all so terrible. I'm still in shock. It doesn't seem real, but it is.' Glen set the cup on the drain board, paused, his back to them, his shoulders rounded, his head slightly bowed before he turned. 'We have to meet with Les after this morning's services and plan Evan's funeral. Is it all right if we leave Millie here for a little longer? We'll be back to get her as soon as we can.'

Mary felt a jolt go through her. They were going to take the dog? 'Why?'

'Why, what?' John paused on his way to deposit his mug in the sink.

'Why take her? I like her and think I'd like to keep her.' Mary looked at the black head, still firmly planted on her foot. She trembled a little when she realized what she'd just said. A dog was a commitment. Taking responsibility for any pet was one she'd never been willing to make before. So, why now? What was there about this dog . . . she didn't know. But she wanted her. 'I'll take good care of her.'

'I don't know . . .' John began slowly.

'Is it up to you to say?' Ellen sounded a little short, as if she thought John had overstepped his bounds.

'Actually, yes.' There was something in Glen's tone . . . asperity? Impatience? Certainly a little sharpness. 'We are Evan's executors.'

Why Mary felt stunned, she didn't know, but somehow that wasn't expected. 'Executors? What about his family?'

'Evan was an only child,' Glen said. 'His father is dead and his mother has dementia and is in Shady Acres. She has no legal capacity over her affairs. Evan was worried about what might happen if he had an accident or something. We worked this out last year.'

'I'm taking over the shop.' John seemed, for the first time, serious. No gushing over the dog, no almost hysterics, no waving about of arms, just a short, simple statement. He and Glen again exchanged glances. Glen nodded slightly.

'I've wanted Evan to sell part ownership to me for ages. I was totally burnt out at the hospital and wanted something else to do. He wouldn't make up his mind, but he did make us the trustees of his estate. The shop will be open for business again very soon. We'll let you know about the dog.' He walked over to Mary and gave her a light pat on the shoulder, repeated the pat on Millie's head and nodded at Ellen.

Glen dropped a feathery kiss on Mary's cheek, patted Millie, smiled at Ellen and they were gone.

'Interesting.' Ellen stared at the empty kitchen doorway.

'I don't think they want me to keep the dog. Why?'

'I have no idea. I didn't know they were that close to Evan, either.'

'Neither did I.' Mary let her hand drift down the dog's ear, who had lifted her head as the men left. 'I'd heard John left the hospital but had no idea he wanted to run a pet shop.' She paused. 'I wonder how badly he wanted to.'

Ellen shrugged, picked up Mary's now-empty cup and headed for the sink. She stopped midway; turned to face Mary again. 'Wasn't John a surgical nurse?'

Mary nodded. 'Yes. Why?'

'Just thinking. He'd certainly know where to insert something long and sharp that would penetrate the heart, now, wouldn't he?' The look on Ellen's face was more troubled than Mary thought she had ever seen. 'They were at Evan's around five thirty or so. Right?'

Mary thought about it and nodded.

'Most dances for adults start sometime between seven and

eight. San Luis Obispo is just a little over thirty minutes away. I'd like to know why they left so early and what they did for that couple of hours.' Ellen dropped a kiss on her aunt's forehead and turned toward the kitchen door. 'Dan and I'll be back later this afternoon to check on you. For heaven's sake, try to rest.'

Mary could think of nothing to say as the door closed firmly behind Ellen.

TWENTY-EIGHT

Mary sat for quite a long time after Ellen left, thinking. A long, thin, sharp instrument slid into someone's chest between their ribs and into their heart. She didn't think she could do that and doubted many people could. What kind of skill would someone need? Ellen was right. John would have it, but why would he want to kill Cliff? And Evan? He and Glen had been close friends of Evan's, if not of Cliff's, so, why? Could it have something to do with the pet shop? She shook her head but immediately stopped. It felt better but still wasn't up to shaking. She needed food. The dog had eaten, but she hadn't. Two cups of coffee were having an effect on her empty stomach. The thought of an egg, or anything else she had to cook, overtook her hunger pangs. With a sigh, she pushed herself to her feet and headed to the refrigerator. The dog raised her head from her position beside Mary's chair and looked hopeful.

'You already ate.' Mary opened the refrigerator door and looked in. 'Besides, mocha yogurt isn't on your dietary program.' She took out the yogurt and looked at it. She'd bought it last week at Trader Joe's but hadn't yet tried it. Was she up for a new adventure this morning? Even one as mundane as yogurt? She peered again at the contents of the refrigerator. There was nothing else that she didn't have to fix. Even toast seemed like too much effort. There was one rather tired-looking orange in the hydrator. She sighed, closed the door and took the yogurt back to the table.

The dog hadn't taken its eyes off her.

'Not a chance.' She took a small mouthful. 'I wish you could talk. I'd love to know what happened between your other owner and John and Glen.'

Other owner? She had to smile. 'I guess you're going to stay. At least, I hope so. I sort of like having someone to talk to.'

The dog cocked her head.

'Did Evan really leave everything to John and Glen?'

The dog said nothing but saliva built up at the corners of her mouth.

'How about the house? Do they get that too? Or are they just the executors?'

The dog whined softly, her eyes watching every spoonful Mary put in her mouth.

'Did you go to the shop much? Did Bill Bliss come in often? I can't think why he was there. They don't have a dog. I'm pretty sure they don't.' She thought about that.

Millie seemed to be thinking as well, but not about Bill Bliss. Tiny drops of saliva hit the floor as she stared at Mary's yogurt carton.

'Maybe they have a cat. That would be a sensible animal for a winery.'

The dog whined softly.

'Luke was there last evening. I don't understand all this about using his poodle. Why wouldn't he let John and Glen use his poodle? People generally pay to do that, don't they?' She took another spoonful. How much could one charge for such a service? 'As for Cliff influencing Luke, I doubt if he's been able to do that in years.' She took another spoonful and looked into the carton. It was empty. 'You didn't mind having pups with a poodle, did you? Cocker spaniels and poodles, they're both darling dogs.'

Millie looked crestfallen as Mary put the empty carton on the table. She stood, staring at the yogurt cup, as if daring it to move her way, and gave one sharp bark.

'You want the empty yogurt cup? I'm pretty sure I heard dogs aren't supposed to have chocolate. Besides . . .'

The dog barked once more and scratched at Mary's knee.

'Oh, well. There's not enough left in there to hurt you.' Mary put the cup on the floor. The dog picked it up and headed for Mary's bedroom. Mary hoped she planned to take it to her basket in her bedroom and not her living-room sofa. She pushed herself up to follow and the doorbell rang. And rang again. And again. 'What is there about this morning that makes everyone so insistent?' She hobbled toward the front door. No sign of the dog on the sofa. She pulled the door open.

Dalia and Ronaldo stood there, their faces beaming. Tony and Luanne stood right behind them, holding a large donut box.

'We came to bring you a donut so you'd feel better.' Ronaldo's grin seemed to go from ear to ear.

Dalia's face was more serious. 'Are you all right? Mrs Dunham said you had a knot on your head and stitches in your leg but were OK. Are you?'

'I'm fine. What are you doing standing on the porch? Come in. Come in. Coffee's hot and I'll bet I can find some hot chocolate. It's a cold morning. Something hot will go good with donuts, won't it?'

A black bomb exploded out of the bedroom, barking and wagging at the same time. She skidded to a stop behind Mary, making a huge fuss as the children drew back. Then she stopped, looked up at Mary as if for approval, and sat down.

'This is Millie.' Mary wasn't sure if she should laugh or be alarmed. She'd never seen the dog act like that. Should she put her outside? Would she bite the children?

'Millie.' Dalia was already cooing at the dog, calling her name softly, squatting down and holding out her hand.

The dog stood and inched toward her, sniffing at the open hand, wagging her stump of a tail harder as Dalia rubbed her ears.

'I want to pet her too.' Ronaldo knelt down beside his sister and reached out for the dog.

Mary held her breath. Luanne grabbed Ronaldo by the arm.

Tony smiled. 'She's fine. That's Evan's dog, isn't it? She makes a lot of noise but she's never bitten anyone I've heard of.'

As if to prove his point, the dog planted a wet kiss on Ronaldo's face. He laughed. Dalia scowled.

The children played with the dog for a moment before Mary looked at Tony and Luanne. They also watched the children but with no joy on either face. Stress lines framed both of their eyes.

'Why don't you kids take Millie outside to play? Just in the backyard. I don't know how well she does on a leash yet. Ronaldo,

I think there's an old tennis ball on the shelf above the washing machine. Why don't you see if she likes to play fetch?'

Both children were on their feet, calling Millie and heading for the back door.

Dalia paused to look at her mother. 'Can we?'

Luanne nodded.

No hesitation there. She'd been right. Luanne and Tony wanted to talk and she didn't think it was about her failed encounter with the slated box.

TWENTY-NINE

I t took a few minutes. Ronaldo couldn't reach the ball and implored Tony to help him. Dalia pronounced the grass too wet for her shoes then assured them all that the dog didn't want to play ball. It took the promise of hot chocolate and another donut to finally get all three of them into the backyard. They promptly started a loud game of fetch in which Millie gleefully participated.

The three adults watched for a few minutes.

Finally Tony turned to Mary. 'We've got to talk.'

Mary nodded and gestured toward the kitchen table. 'Let's sit in here so we can see the yard.'

Tony pulled out a chair for Luanne, who lowered herself slowly onto it.

Mary headed for the coffeepot, rinsed out the remaining few drops and filled it with water. 'Luanne, can you drink regular?'

'It's the only caffeine I allow myself. I had half a cup with breakfast so I'm ready for more.'

She looked as if she needed it. There were black circles under her eyes and her mouth was pinched and worried. Mary glanced over at Tony. He didn't look much better. His usually immaculately groomed black hair stuck up in the back and a five o'clock shadow had advanced to ten o'clock stubble.

Mary poured the last tablespoon of coffee into the filter, flipped the switch and turned back to face them. 'OK, what's happened?'

Tony managed a small smile as he tore his eyes away from Luanne to look back at Mary. 'How did you know?'

'All I had to do was look at you. Besides, you didn't come bearing donuts so you could examine my stitches. What's wrong?'

Tony sighed. Luanne swallowed a sob.

'I'm not sure,' Tony finally said, 'but we think someone tried to break in last night.'

Mary almost dropped the mug she'd reached for. Clutching it tightly, she whirled around to face him. 'Someone tried to do what?'

'Tony found footprints under Ronaldo's window.' Luanne looked as if she was going to break down or have hysterics, or both, and soon.

'Footprints? Under his window? How did you . . . ?' Mary took a deep breath to quell the panic that was beginning to rise, took down another mug, filled them both and set one in front of each of them before refilling her own. 'Tell me what happened.'

Tony put his hand around the mug but made no attempt to pick it up. He glanced over at Luanne, who held hers halfway to her mouth, staring at the steam that rose lazily toward her pale cheeks.

'I'm not sleeping too well. It's hard to get comfortable.'

Mary nodded. She certainly didn't look too comfortable.

'It must have been around midnight. I'd gotten up to use the bathroom and was having trouble getting back to sleep when I heard a noise.'

'What kind of noise?' Mary envisioned scratching at the window, glass breaking, something dramatic.

'A sort of rustling noise. Like someone or something was in the bushes by the side of the house.'

'Most likely a cat.' Mary heaved a silent sigh of relief. Their nerves were all on edge. This was sure to have been a false alarm. But hadn't Tony mentioned a footprint?

'That's what I thought. I was sure I heard it meow. Only, cats don't whisper or break branches off bushes.'

Mary made a soft 'oh' with her mouth. 'You heard someone whispering?'

The sound Luanne made was somewhere between a sigh

and a sob. 'It sounded like a whisper. It sounded like someone said "damn it." Then a branch broke. That's when I woke up Tony.'

He nodded. 'It's funny how fast you can wake up. One minute I was sound asleep, the next wide awake. I heard the rustling too. I told Luanne to go into Ronaldo's room but not to turn on the light and I'd see what was happening.'

'Why Ronaldo's room?'

'The sound seemed to be coming from outside his room. I started for the back door, but it was dark and I bumped into a chair in the kitchen – one the kids hadn't put back where it belonged, and knocked it over. By the time I got the door open and turned on the light, no one was in sight. I looked around but couldn't see anything. I decided it was a cat, that we were all getting paranoid and went back to bed. But I didn't sleep very well. This morning I went out to look. I found the broken bush and a footprint.'

'How could someone leave a footprint? The rain the other night was barely enough to dampen the sidewalk.'

'I'd just mulched the beds.' Tony smiled. 'Loose compost takes a good footprint.'

Mary's scalp tingled. Another footprint. She had to ask. She didn't want to. She didn't want him to have anything to do with this, but she had no choice. 'Could you tell anything from it?'

'It was a sandal.' Tony seemed to stumble over the words. 'What was he doing in our bushes in the middle of the night? Priests don't prowl around in bushes. They don't – I can't believe – but I don't know anyone else who wears sandals in the middle of winter.'

'Luke does.'

Almost as one, the adults wheeled around to stare at Dalia, who stood in the doorway, watching them, her brow furrowed, her eyes wide with anxiety.

'Who's Luke?' Tony sounded a little taken back but also a little hopeful.

'Luke from the library. He had them on the day we built the can tree. Only he wasn't barefoot, like Father D'Angelo. He had on white socks. Ask Ronaldo. He saw them too.'

They didn't have to ask him. He stood behind his sister, Millie at his heels, and nodded. 'Dalia's right. Luke wears sandals. I'd like to wear my sandals like that. With socks.'

Tony looked over at Mary. 'Is that right? This Luke, does he wear sandals?'

Mary shook her head. 'I don't know. I've never looked at his feet. Why would Luke be rummaging through your bushes?'

Tony's face was grim, his eyes large and angry. 'Why would anyone? There's only one answer I can think of.'

The stillness in the room was oppressive, as if Tony's remark had somehow sucked all of the air out of it. Then, suddenly, they all started to talk at once.

'Why are you talking about sandals?' Dalia's voice held deep uncertainty, her eyes more than a little frightened.

'No reason. We were just talking.' Luanne made what Mary thought a valiant attempt to be casual. But it didn't appear to fool Dalia.

'Actually, we were talking about Mrs McGill's accident. Good thing she had on running shoes. If she'd had on sandals . . .' Tony smiled at Dalia.

She just stared. She appeared to be buying none of it.

'Millie's real good at catching a ball.' Ronaldo's interest in sandals ended when the conversation didn't include him. 'Aunt Mary, are you picking us up from school tomorrow?'

'She can't.' Luanne made that statement emphatic.

Did Mary hear a little wistfulness in there?

'Of course I can. You don't think I'd let a little cut on my leg stop me from collecting you two, do you? We'll go see how the can tree looks before it gets torn down. I want a picture of you both in front of it. After all, you helped build it.'

The children looked at each other and giggled. 'Can we get Sampson and have him in the picture?'

That, of course, came from Dalia.

'No.' Tony and Luanne gave one horrified gasp together.

Mary didn't say a word but thought that wasn't a bad idea. Someone might see it and identify him. She'd suggest it to Dan. In the meantime . . .

'How long before Christmas break?'

'Next week.' Luanne sighed. 'Christmas is coming fast and

I'm not ready. So much has happened . . .' She looked at the children, then at Tony.

'My mom is coming out next week. She's going to stay until after the baby is born.' He looked at the children with an uncertainty Mary hadn't seen before. 'It'll give the kids a chance to get to know her. However, if you can help out until she gets here . . .'

A surge of different emotions ran through Mary. She, too, was worried about the children and if she could help keep them safe, she would. However, she wasn't ready for Christmas either. She hadn't even dragged out her decorations. Maybe she could get the kids to help. That would keep them busy and under her watchful eyes. As for this latest development, she wasn't sure what to think. Had someone really been under Ronaldo's window with the idea of breaking in? Tony seemed to think so, but Mary thought it seemed a foolhardy thing to do. Whoever killed Cliff and Evan could hardly think he could sneak into their house and . . . do what? Kidnap the children? That wouldn't have been successful. Harm them? That was a thought too awful to be considered. Besides, he couldn't realistically have expected to get away with it. However, the other two murders had been pretty brazen. A shudder ran through her. She needed to talk to Dan. Tony had called him, hadn't he?

'You did call Dan?'

Tony nodded his head slightly.

Luanne looked stricken. She turned toward the children, who were listening intently to every word. 'What are you two doing back in here? I thought you were out playing with the dog.'

'We were, but we thought we'd better tell you.'

Dalia's tone was matter-of-fact but there was a spark of something in her eyes that Mary couldn't quite identify. Fear? Certainly uneasiness. 'Tell us what?'

Dalia took a deep breath and turned her gaze on Ronaldo as she slowly let it out. 'There's a man in our bushes. I think he's looking for something.'

Luanne put her hand on her stomach. 'What makes you think that?'

'He's behind the bush outside my window, and he's bending down doing something. I don't like having someone outside my window.' Ronaldo looked as if he was torn between anger and fright. Anger was winning. 'Who is he?' The look he gave Tony was almost a glare.

Tony didn't answer. 'We have to go if we're going to make ten o'clock Mass.'

Luanne pushed herself forward in her chair in preparation to pushing herself to her feet. Tony was there ahead of her, holding out a hand, pulling her up. The smile he gave her and the hand carefully holding onto her elbow as she steadied herself were tender, caring. No trace of the impatience and the sometimes quick anger he was capable of.

He motioned to the children. 'Let's go. We'll walk, so if you have to go to the bathroom, do it now.'

'Good heavens, look at you.' Luanne held Ronaldo at arm's length, examining the dirt on the child's cheeks and the hair that had escaped whatever she'd combed it with earlier. 'How do you do it? You were clean when we came over here.' She turned to Mary, who had no trouble anticipating Luanne's request.

'Of course you can use the bathroom. Dalia, go with your mother. You don't look much better.'

She and Tony watched Luanne herd the children down the hall.

When the door closed, Mary turned toward him. 'OK. What's that man doing in your bushes?'

'Taking a cast of the footprint, I suppose.'

Mary nodded. Forensics. That made sense. 'Does Dan really believe someone tried to get in last night?'

Tony ran a hand through his hair. 'I don't know. He didn't say much when I told him. Just that he'd investigate.' He paused, shook his head and seemed to stare through Mary. 'Someone was there. Who it was and what he wanted, I don't know. The thought he may have tried to get in, to do . . .' He broke off, looking a little sick. 'This whole thing is unreal. Luanne is trying hard not to show it, but she's worried sick. That's not good for her or the baby. I'm not much better.'

He was probably worse.

'I can't concentrate on anything. I keep thinking about Cliff and wondering why . . . and Evan. Why would anyone . . . Do you think someone would really try to hurt my kids?'

His kids. Mary was sure Tony thought of them that way. He

wanted this baby, badly, but he'd been a close friend of Cruz, the children's father, and had known both since they were born. He was the only father they could remember. Mary was positive he loved them deeply.

'I don't know, but with you, Luanne, Dan and me on the job, he's going to have a hard time getting near them.'

'We can't even begin to thank you enough for what you've done, but I – we – feel so guilty. Are you sure you're up to picking up the kids tomorrow?'

Mary thought if one more person asked her if she was up for something she'd scream. Or attack someone with a rolling pin. She was fine. Almost fine. She hurt, but then, when you got to be her age, hurting was nothing new.

'Of course I am. I'm certainly not going to let a couple of stitches hold me down. Now, about tomorrow. I'll pick them up from school. Then what? Do you want me to bring them to the winery or do you want me to bring them here?'

Tony looked blank. 'We'll have to ask Luanne. I'm not sure what her schedule is. It's probably better if you drop them off at the winery, even though I'm sure they'd love to help you, take the dog for a walk and feed it, that kind of thing.'

Feed it. Something stirred in Mary's head. Someone had said something – Bill Bliss. He'd gone into the pet store. At least he had if Leigh was right. 'When did the Blisses get another dog?'

Tony looked blank then totally confused. 'A dog? What gave you the idea they have another dog?'

'A cat then?'

Tony shook his head emphatically. 'Not even a hamster. Why?'

'No reason. Someone said . . . I must have heard them wrong.'

Tony's eyebrows narrowed as he looked at Mary. 'I hope they never get another dog. At least, not a little one like Merlot. I'm surprised he lasted as long as he did.'

'What are you talking about?'

'Naomi let him run loose. That wasn't so bad when he stayed up by the winery, but he'd taken to roaming the vineyard. We have machinery in the vineyard. Tractors, cultivators, sprayers, all kinds of things. That dog was little. No way could someone on a tractor see him. Or stop the sprayer from spewing insecticide on him. I told them both, he had to stay out of the vineyard, but neither Bill nor Naomi listened. She thought it was cute that he roamed all over. Bill just couldn't be bothered. When he went missing, I was sure we'd somehow killed him and we'd find his body down by that damn fence he patrolled. Instead, he was stolen. I feel sorry for the dog, but I'm glad my crew had nothing to do with it.'

Before Mary could make a comment, Luanne appeared, towing the children behind her. They looked much better. Sticky donut sugar mixed with backyard dirt was gone from both faces and hands and both heads were damp from the water Luanne had liberally used on the comb.

'We're ready whenever you are.'

Tony smiled at her and at the children. 'You look a lot better.'

From the scowl on both faces, Mary doubted they thought so.

'Let's go.' Tony headed for the door, the reluctant children slowly following.

Luanne paused to give Mary a kiss on the cheek. 'If you don't feel up to dealing with them tomorrow, give me a call. I might be able to tuck them away in my office for a couple of hours. You've done so much, and been through so much, I'd certainly understand. I'm sure Naomi wouldn't mind.'

Mary doubted that. Naomi might not have minded if her little dog wandered all over the winery and vineyard, but Mary was pretty sure that indulgence didn't extend to children. 'I'll be fine. I'm going in right now to shower and get dressed. And I'm going to try to get into the beauty shop in the morning. I'd feel a lot better if I can get some of this sticky blood out of my hair.'

Luanne was on her way to the open front door but stopped and turned back to face Mary. 'I thought you couldn't get stitches wet for a few days.'

'Irene can at least see where they are and wash around them.'

Luanne looked doubtful. 'Just be careful, won't you?' She sighed. 'You won't, though. You're going to do whatever you want. OK. Call if you need anything. Otherwise, I'll see you at the winery tomorrow afternoon.' She blew Mary another kiss and was out the door.

'"Need anything."' Mary addressed Millie, who looked at her as if to say, *What?*

'Exactly what I was thinking. What could I possibly want her to do? I'm fine. Just fine.'

Only she didn't feel too fine. In spite of the Tylenol, her leg hurt – burned would be a better way to describe it – and her head still throbbed. She wished she could stand under the shower and see if it could wash away any remaining blood from her hair. But, since she couldn't, she was going to find out more about that footprint. Maybe Dan was still there, looking for more. If she hurried, she could catch him.

'Stay here,' she instructed Millie. Limping only slightly, she walked out her front door and headed for the Mendosa house.

THIRTY

'Mrs McGill! What are you doing here?'

Mary had known Gary Roberts all his life, had applauded his choice when he joined the Santa Louisa police department, had seen him in action during several police investigations but had never seen him look so stricken.

'Why? Is there something I shouldn't be seeing?'

'No. Not at all. It's just that . . . You shouldn't be out of bed. Should you?'

Mary stopped herself from saying something she'd regret. She didn't want to snap Gary's head off. She wanted information and he wouldn't give it to her if she got his back up. She took another look at his closed face and sighed. He probably wasn't going to give her any no matter what she said. Or didn't say.

Luckily, Dan appeared. 'What are you doing here?'

'He already asked me that. I want to know about that footprint.'

'So badly you couldn't wait to get dressed?'

Mary looked down. Her pajama bottoms peeked out from underneath the bottom of her heavy bathrobe, the one with the reindeer romping around on it. She'd gotten it at St Mark's semi-annual rummage sale for less than a dollar several years ago and had been wearing it ever since. She'd actually forgotten she had it on, so many things had happened.

She shrugged.

Dan smiled. 'Come on. I'll walk you home.

'I don't want to go home. I want to know—'

'About the footprint. I'll tell you what we know while we walk.' He took her by the arm and gently but firmly turned her around. 'This wasn't exactly the way I wanted to spend my Sunday, tromping through bushes looking at footprints.'

'Did you find one?'

'We did. Also some freshly broken branches. Someone was there, in front of Ronaldo's bedroom.'

Mary's breath caught in her throat. Tony was right. 'Was it a sandal?'

Dan nodded. 'A big one. Belonged to a tall man.'

'Oh, no.' She stopped and clutched Dan's arm. 'Do you know whose it was?'

'If you mean, have we matched it with Father D'Angelo's, no, not yet.' He gently removed her arm from his sleeve and propelled her up her front walk.

'Why ever not?' Mary didn't want Father D'Angelo implicated, but the thought that someone had been outside the children's windows, trying to get in, made her sick to her stomach. She couldn't believe Dan wasn't going to do something to find out who had been prowling around.

'We're taking a cast of the footprint and pictures, besides examining the branches broken off the bush. We'll compare the footprint with the one we took in the manger. If they match, we'll have a little talk with Father D'Angelo. Until then . . .'

They were on the porch.

Dan opened the door. A small, yelping whirlwind immediately descended on them, barking, whining and welcoming them home.

Dan caught Millie just as she tried to jump into Mary's arms. 'Here, stop that. You're going to knock her down.' He held onto the wiggling dog while closing the front door with his foot. 'For Pete's sake, go sit down so I can let go of this thing. You'd think you'd been gone a month.'

Mary sank down on the sofa with more than a little gratitude. She hurt more than she'd thought.

Dan let go of the dog, who immediately jumped up on the sofa, buried her head in Mary's lap and sighed.

'She gets upset. I think she misses Evan.' Mary stroked the

silky ears and gave a small sigh of her own. 'All right. What happens if the footprints don't match? Even if they do, how do you know the sandal is Father's? How do you know it's a sandal?'

Dan looked around, grabbed the back of the rocking chair, pulled it closer to the coffee table and sat down. He leaned forward but didn't let it rock. 'We know it's a sandal because of the tread and shape of the sole. We also know whoever was outside didn't try to get into the house. Never touched the window.'

Mary stopped stroking the dog's ears and stared at him. 'How do you know that?'

'We dusted both Ronaldo's and Dalia's windowsills for prints. Nada. Nothing.'

'None at all?'

'Remnants of old ones, half washed away. We had rain the night of the Victorian Christmas Extravaganza. Not much, but enough to leave nice fresh dirt on the windowsill but no fresh prints.'

'Then why . . . ?'

'Don't know. Someone was there, behind the bushes all right, but whatever he was doing it wasn't trying to break into the house.'

The dog nudged Mary's hand with her nose. Absently, Mary resumed stroking. 'Luanne said she thought she heard a cat. Could it have been . . . ?'

Dan shook his head. 'It was a man out there. A fairly big man. He wears about the same size shoe I do. I don't know any man who would wander around in the bushes looking for a cat. Most would figure the cat could get along fine without them. I doubt I'd go out looking for Jake, and I'm pretty fond of him.'

Mary buried her smile by looking at Millie. If Jake was outside when Ellen didn't want him outside, Dan would go looking. Of that, she was certain. However . . .

'If whoever it was wasn't trying to break in or look for his cat, what was he doing? Wandering around in someone's bushes in the middle of the night isn't a normal pastime.'

All traces of amusement left Dan's face. 'You're right. We don't know what he wanted.'

'Do you think it was the murderer?' Mary could hardly get the words out around the tightness in her throat. 'Did Tony scare him off before he could do anything?'

Dan shook his head. 'Don't know. That's certainly a possibility but since nothing happened . . .'

'You have the footprint.'

'We do, but we can hardly go house-to-house asking every man over six foot tall if he has a sandal and can we see if it matches our casting. This isn't Cinderella. Even if we found the right person, which is more than doubtful, what do we do then?'

'Ask him what he thought he was doing prowling around under the windows of small children.' Mary sat up as straight as the soft sofa cushions would allow. Worry and indignation made her forget the pain in her leg.

'I don't think we'd get an answer. Right now we'll just keep as close an eye on them as we can and keep working on finding whoever killed Cliff and Evan.'

'Are you making any progress?' Suddenly, tiredness overtook Mary. The sight of the bundle of blood-soaked rags that had been Cliff swam into her memory, followed closely by the crumpled body of poor Evan laying half in and half out of the tiny shop bathroom. A shudder ran through her, one strong enough to make her head ache.

The look on Dan's face didn't help any. 'Not much. Half the people in town were in and out of Evan's shop. Trying to sort out all those prints is impossible.'

'How about the people who were there yesterday?'

'Yesterday was Saturday. Evan was killed Friday late afternoon or early evening.'

Mary nodded. Dan was right. Yesterday was Saturday. She'd found Evan mid-morning and had fallen off the crate around then as well. It hadn't been her best day.

Dan grinned. 'Town was full of people. We're interested in the ones who were there in Evan's shop last, but that's proving a little confusing as well.'

Mary let her hand drop off the dog's ears as she concentrated on what Dan said. 'What do you mean?'

Dan shrugged. 'We've talked to most of the shop owners and, of course, to Luke. The flower shop girl – what's her name – Debbie? Anyway, business was slow and she evidently spent part of her time looking out the front door. She remembers seeing Luke go in, also John and Glen, but not exactly what time and can't remember who came out first. She didn't see Father D'Angelo coming out but remembers him going in.'

'How about Bill Bliss? We know he went in, but I can't for the life of me figure out why. They don't have a dog. They don't even have a cat.'

Dan looked at her curiously. 'You mentioned him before. How do you know they don't?'

'I asked Tony. He said he was glad they didn't. The little dog that disappeared, Merlot, was always running through the vineyard and he was scared he'd get hurt, or killed, because they couldn't see him. He said he didn't want to go through that again.'

Dan sat back and ran his fingers through his hair as he stared at Mary. 'Sometimes I wonder why I have detectives on staff. What about Luke? From the library Luke. What do you know about him?'

'Other than what we found out the other day? He has a poodle but doesn't show him. However, he does breed him. Or did once. He let Evan use the dog on his cocker to have puppies . . .' Mary looked at the little dog then back at Dan. 'It was Millie who had the puppies.' She ran her hand through the curly hair on the back of Millie's neck. 'Wasn't it?'

The dog didn't answer.

'I know it was her. Luke said it was, and she is the only dog Evan had.' Mary felt stricken for no good reason she could understand. Dogs had puppies all the time. Millie looked perfectly healthy and she certainly looked happy. At least, she did right now.

'What's the matter?'

Mary could feel Dan's eyes on her, curious about her sudden change of mood. 'I don't know exactly.' Her words came out slowly as she tried to sort out her thoughts. No. More like emotions. 'It's just that, well, John and Glen were here earlier. I guess they're Evan's heirs, if that's the word, and they intimated they wanted to take Millie. They said they thought she might be too much for me.' Mary snorted.

Dan laughed.

Mary shot him a look. 'They breed little dogs called cockapoos.'

Dan looked blank. 'Why does that matter?'

'I don't know that it does. Only, Millie—' Mary let her hand once more caress the dog's ears, who sighed with pleasure and wiggled deeper into Mary's lap. 'Millie had puppies and Luke's poodle was the father. John and Glen wanted to use him on their dog but he refused. Evidently Cliff had something to do with that, but I'm not sure what.'

'And your point?' Dan watched her, his head slightly cocked to one side, his expression dubious.

'I'm not sure, but everything about Cliff and Evan seems to revolve around dogs in some way. I can't help but feel . . .'

'I can't say we're coming up with anything any better, but somehow dogs don't seem a very good reason for murder.' The expression on his face changed as he, too, seemed to follow a thought. 'However, financial gain might. From what Les says, John and Glen are the heirs to whatever Evan had, and that was more than appeared on the surface. The house is free and clear. He also owned the building where his shop is. The only stipulation is that they keep his mother in Shady Acres.'

'How do you know that?' John and Glen had told Mary they would take over the shop, but they hadn't mentioned any of the financial arrangements. Not that they should have. It was none of her business. But now she wondered. Was she wrong about the dogs? No. She didn't think so, and she refused to believe that either John or Glen would murder someone. They might have a motive, of sorts, but what about Cliff? Surely the same person was responsible for both murders. However . . . 'Oh.' She gasped.

'What?' Now Dan leaned forward, his hands resting on the arms of the chair, ready to push himself up. 'What have you remembered?'

'John and Glen. They were here this morning.'

'So you said. What about it?'

'Glen. He had on . . . he's usually so carefully dressed.'

'Mary, get to the point.'

She could hardly get the words out, but she had no choice. 'Dan, Glen had on a sweatshirt over some kind of workout pants.'

'I don't think workout pants made you go white. What else did he have on?'

'White socks.'
Dan raised one eyebrow. 'And?'
'Sandals.'

THIRTY-ONE

Mary sat for a long time after Dan left, running dozens of thoughts through her mind. It seemed as if there were a whole lot of different threads running through this story and she couldn't untangle them. She was convinced the same person had murdered both Evan and Cliff. There were several people who might have wished one of them dead, but she couldn't think of anyone who might want both of them out of the way. There had to be something that connected them, but what! She needed more information. She also needed a shower. She still smelled like a hospital, despite using the washcloth.

'Down you go.' She tried to pick up Millie, but she was heavy. However, the dog took the hint, jumped down and headed into the kitchen where she stood beside her dish and looked hopeful.

Mary followed. 'It's only three thirty. Are you sure you eat this early?'

The dog wagged her stub of a tail.

Still dubious, Mary picked up the dish, pulled out the dog food sack from the broom closet where Ellen had stashed it and scooped some into the dish. The dog drooled on the floor.

'Shades of Pavlov.' Mary set the dish in front of Millie, who evidently didn't care about Russian scientists. She buried her head in it and proceeded to devour the food. Mary watched her for a moment, returned to the closet and stuffed the sack back in. She rummaged through the boxes on the floor and brought out a large black trash sack. 'Just the thing to put over the bandage on my leg, don't you think?' She got no answer, but then, she hadn't really expected one. She started to close the door but stopped. Dog food. What kind was it? She pulled the sack back out. It didn't seem to be one of the commercial dog foods they sold in the grocery. This food was in a large, tough brown paper sack stamped the same way as the bags in Bonnie's feed room. She wasn't sure but thought the name of the company was also the same of a company in Los Angeles.

'Bonnie has these kinds of sacks in her feed room.'

The dog paid no attention. She put one foot in the empty bowl and started licking the edges.

'Do you suppose she bought all that special food she talked about from Evan?'

The dog gave up licking the immaculate bowl, sat down and yawned.

Mary continued to stare at the dog food sack. 'Half the dog owners in town seem to have bought their food from Evan. Is it really so much better?'

The dog got up and walked to the back door. She looked back at Mary and gave a sharp bark. Mary hurried to open it. The dog walked through it and down the stairs without a look back.

'You've adjusted well.'

She sniffed around the grass, evidently looking for a perfect spot, but Mary's mind wasn't really on the dog. At least, not Millie. It was occupied trying to figure out what Cliff and Evan had in common that could have gotten them killed. She wasn't coming up with anything. Except dogs. Cliff was a vet. He cured sick dogs. Evan ran a pet store. He sold dogs and the things people needed to take care of them. There had to be more to it than that. In a way, Evan also took care of dogs. Bonnie had been adamant about what she fed her dogs, a food Evan evidently supplied. Luke, from the library, fed his dog the same food. So did John and Glen and Leigh, spacy as she was. A lot of people did. However, Evan could hardly have been killed over dog food. She sighed, watched Millie come in, closed the door and headed back into the kitchen to tie the trash bag over the bandage on her leg. Sponge baths were well and good but she didn't feel clean. She wouldn't until her hair was washed, but she'd leave that to Irene.

'I'm taking a shower, but I need to make a phone call first.'

Millie looked at her and stared with apparent interest at the sack but made no comment.

THIRTY-TWO

'**Y**ou heard me. Dog food. What's the difference between what Evan sells . . . sold . . . in his shop and the kind you buy in the market?'

Mary held the phone gingerly against her right ear. The wound on her scalp was a little more sensitive than she'd thought. Maybe she shouldn't have dabbed at it with that washcloth, but the dried blood around the bandage was sticking to her hair and driving her crazy.

The question seemed to have left Karl speechless for a moment and his reply wasn't helpful. 'Why?'

Mary carried the phone into the living room and sat down in her oversized reading chair. She felt the need to get off her feet, but she wanted an answer. Not for the first time, she was grateful for the cordless phone. The dog jumped up and sat beside her. 'I'm trying to find some connection between Cliff and Evan, something that might have resulted in their murders.'

'I doubt you'll find it in dog food.'

'Maybe not, but lots of people around here bought their dog food from Evan. Is it so much better than the commercial ones?'

Karl's voice had lost its faintly amused sound. 'Depends.'

'That helps.'

'There are some excellent foods out and there are some full of fillers.'

'Fillers?'

'Yes. Stuff that takes up volume but is hard for dogs to digest. There are some that sneak by the government inspectors and are made from ground-up dead animals. That kind of thing.'

'Yuck. Really?'

'Most kinds you buy at the store are just fine, but Evan was a fanatic about food. There's a company in Los Angeles that makes several special mixes. Evan carried four kinds: one for puppies, another for pregnant and lactating dogs, one for most dogs and the last for seniors. He praised the nutritional value in those mixtures to the hilt and sold a lot of people on their benefits. It's probably the only food Millie has ever had.'

'So I should continue to feed it to her?'

'You could switch her over to something else, but slowly. However, if John and Glen continue to stock it, yes, stick with it. She looks great.'

Mary switched the phone to her other ear and scratched behind Millie's ear. The dog sighed and laid her head on Mary's lap. 'You said Evan was a fanatic about feeding. John and Glen said he was very selective about the animals he took into his shop. Made sure they had their shots and whatever else they needed to be healthy. He must have really cared about them.'

'He did. Evan was a kind man. He even took good care of that blasted lizard, who'd just as soon bite your finger off as look at you.'

'What lizard?' Mary couldn't remember any lizard large enough to put a finger at risk. Only the one who'd been napping under the plastic tree and it didn't look dangerous to anything larger than a fly.

'He had him in a glass cage in the back of the store. Evan was afraid a child would get hurt if he put it out front. Nasty creature. Should be in a zoo somewhere, but Evan took good care of it. All God's Creatures, Great and Small, that was his motto. It wasn't Cliff's.'

'What do you mean?' Mary's hand slipped off the dog's ear as she sat up straighter. The dog raised her head and looked at Mary with reproachful eyes. Her hand dropped once more onto the dog's head. 'I thought Cliff loved animals, especially dogs. Bonnie had nothing but praise for how he helped her. Even Luke said how good he was at coaching . . .' Somehow those incidents didn't really translate into universal love of animals.

'Cliff loved to win. He helped Bonnie because she had good dogs who won. Luke was a talented kid with an excellent poodle who also won. Cliff believed in purebred dogs and the people who bred or owned them. He was nice to his patients and their owners, but he only really cared about the prestigious ones. I don't approve of his attitude but I have to give him credit. He knew his dogs. Naomi should have listened to him.'

'What?' Surprise almost brought Mary to her feet. The dog raised her head and waited for Mary to settle back down. 'What are you talking about? Listened to Cliff about what?'

'He wanted her to stand her little dog, Merlot, at stud. He was a finished champion and, according to Cliff, an especially fine dog. He told Naomi she could make a lot of money standing him and if she didn't want all of the hassle, boarding the bitches, paperwork, all that kind of thing, he'd manage it all.' Karl paused. 'I think Bill was for it, but not Naomi.'

Mary thought back to Naomi's description of Cliff, his old car, his showing up half drunk, his many 'mistakes' as a vet and didn't blame Naomi one bit. Cliff had proved over and over again he wasn't capable of accepting responsibility for getting his own dinner. He certainly wasn't capable of running a dog-breeding business. At least, Mary didn't think so and, evidently, neither did Naomi. Only, why hadn't she said that was why Cliff kept coming around? Karl's next sentence brought her back to their conversation.

'Both Cliff and Evan were involved with dogs but from an entirely different direction. I don't see any common motive for murder.' Karl sighed deeply. 'I don't see any motive at all. Cliff – maybe. He made some horrific mistakes and upset some people pretty badly. But Evan, I can't imagine who'd want to kill him. He was a truly kind person.' There was a pause. Mary thought she could hear a catch in Karl's voice before he went on. 'We'll miss him a lot.'

'Yes.' She looked at Millie, who had gone to sleep on her lap, and vowed to give her the best life possible. Another thought struck her. 'Karl, is Millie spayed?'

'No.' Another pause. 'I talked to Evan after her puppies were born and asked if he wanted to, but he said no. I think he was going to breed her again.'

'To who?'

'I don't know.'

'Luke's poodle again?'

'Evan never said. Only that he was thinking about breeding her.'

'I wonder if Luke would have agreed.'

'He did once and I heard he made out pretty well on that deal. Why wouldn't he do it again?'

'I heard . . . someone said . . . Cliff gave him grief because of it.'

Karl heaved a heavy sigh. 'I doubt if Luke paid any attention to anything Cliff said.' There was a pause and Mary heard a voice in the background. 'Mary, I've got to go but Pat wants to talk to you. Hold on.'

She moved the dog's head off her leg, which had gone to sleep. Millie opened her eyes and gave her another reproachful look. She wiggled closer and put her head back where she evidently thought it belonged. Mary gave up and moved the phone to her other hand.

'Are you there?' Pat spoke into the phone.

'Yes. I was trying to move the dog's head off my leg. She seems to think that if I sit down she gets to sit on me.'

Pat laughed. 'You can make her get down.'

'I suppose so, but I keep thinking if it gives her comfort . . . she must be so confused, wondering where Evan is, when he's coming back, when she's going home. It just breaks my heart.'

'It doesn't sound as if she's falling apart too badly. How are you? I'm sorry I didn't get over there this morning, but I went to church and got sidetracked.'

'I'm fine. A little headache but other than that . . . did you by any chance talk to Les?'

'That's why I wanted to talk to you. They found Cliff's daughter.'

Mary heaved a sigh of relief. 'And?'

'Oh, Mary, it's so sad. She's not coming. She has children, says she can't afford the airfare, every excuse she could think of. She said a graveside service would be fine. No one will come to a funeral. All he left behind was bad memories and, by all means, put his stuff in the rummage sale. Except the buffet. She has enough money to ship that to North Carolina.'

There was no lack of bitterness in Pat's voice as she relayed the sad tale. Poor Cliff. He hadn't left much of a legacy.

'Did Les mention Evan? I guess John and Glen are in charge of those arrangements, but I'll bet we get called in to do the food.'

'Count on it. Evan will fill the church. He was as popular in this town as Cliff was not.'

'John and Glen stopped by. They were in San Luis Obispo. Returned this morning when they heard the news about Evan. Glen says they're going to run the pet shop. I guess Evan left them everything.'

'Including his mother.'

'What do you mean by that?'

'Evan was an only child. His mother was over forty when he was born. Sometimes older mothers dote on their child to the point of ruining them. Not her. Anyway, she's in Shady Acres Alzheimer unit. From what I hear, they get the shop, the house and whatever money there is but have to take care of her until she dies. They'll earn every bit of it. She's not an easy woman. Wasn't when she was younger and now she's a real terror. Didn't recognize Evan the last few months when he came to visit. Doesn't know much of anything anymore except how to make life miserable for everybody around her.'

'How do you know all that?' This time Mary pushed the dog off her lap and onto the floor and stood. Her leg felt like it was being stuck with pins. She stomped on it.

'What's that noise?' Pat sounded alarmed.

'Me trying to wake up my foot.' She stomped on it again.

'The hurt one?'

'No, the other one. How do you know all that about Evan?'

'Irene – you know Irene. At the Beauty Spot?'

'Of course. She cuts my hair.'

'She cuts mine also. And, she cuts both John's and Glen's. I doubt she gets much information out of Glen, but John has loose lips and Irene loves to gossip.'

Mary didn't. She knew almost everyone in town and knew quite a lot about most of them. After all, it was a small town. She didn't, however, deal in speculation about them or spread rumors. Mary approved of facts. And facts were what she wanted right now.

'I assume that includes Millie?' For some reason the words were hard to get out. Why, for heaven's sake? She'd only had the dog one day and dogs were a lot of work. Hair everywhere, yards to clean up, all kinds of things. She wouldn't miss the little thing one bit. But, looking into the soft brown eyes, a pang of loss she hadn't experienced in a long time went through her.

'Millie? I guess. I don't know why they'd want her, especially. They have two of Alma's other dogs and one they bought from Bonnie a couple of years ago. Millie's sweet but not near the quality of the other dogs. Her cockapoo pups were cute, but I can't imagine anyone feeling bereft because she wasn't in their cocker breeding program.'

'Is that what John and Glen do with all their dogs? Breed them?'

There was a pause so long Mary thought Pat hadn't heard. She continued, 'I mean . . .'

'I know what you mean and I don't really know. They only breed one dog each time so they have two litters a year. I know they love them and certainly don't keep them in kennels all the time – are they pets the same way you'd make Millie one? I'm not sure. However, if they keep Millie and breed her, it will have to be for cockapoo pups, and that's how they got into disfavor with so many purebred dog people in the first place.'

Mary blinked. 'What are you talking about?'

'The fuss the purebred dog people made when they bred one of Alma's bitches to a poodle. Some of them, led by Cliff, think if you breed a purebred dog to one of another breed, you are bastardizing the pups. Not only do they not have AKC papers, the offspring can't be bred back into either the cocker or poodle registries. There are no AKC specialty shows for them, so what do you do with them?'

'Love them.'

Pat laughed. 'That's what most of us do with our dogs.' Her voice got serious. 'That's not what I wanted to talk to you about. Do you have your tree yet?'

It took Mary a minute. 'What tree?'

'Your Christmas tree, of course. The Humane Society people decided to sell them this year as a fundraiser. So far they haven't raised many funds. In fact, they're in danger of going in the red, so, of course, Karl bought what looks like half a truckload.'

'What are you going to do with all those trees?' Mary's voice sounded a little faint even to her. Did Pat want her to help sell them? It was a good cause, but . . .

'We're giving them away. We took some down to the food bank, we're giving some to the various homeless shelters, one to the hospital and another to Shady Acres, but we're giving most of them to clients and friends. Can we bring one over to you this afternoon? I'm making chili and I'll bring you some of that as well. That way you won't have to cook.'

'Why, that would be wonderful.' Mary was a little out of breath. She usually had her tree up by now, but this year, for some reason, or maybe for several reasons, time had gotten away from her. A tree would be most welcome. 'Do you think Karl would mind putting it up? Not the lights or anything, just in the stand?' That was the part that always flummoxed her. The blasted thing never stood up straight when she did it.

'He's counting on it. About four?'

'That would be fine.'

'See you then.' The line went dead.

A smile spread. Her Christmas tree was coming. She hadn't planned to do much decorating. There wouldn't be nearly as many people around as there had been last year when Ellen and Dan were married, but she had wanted a tree. It was a long-standing tradition that everyone came to her place for Christmas breakfast, and it wouldn't feel right without one. She needed to get out her decorations. She'd bought a set of beautiful cardinal ornaments when she was in Colonial Williamsburg last spring. They were too big to go on a tree, so she'd planned to put them on the mantle after she draped it in fresh branches. She'd put them away . . . where? The cranberry wreath she purchased years ago would go on her front door. She put her hand up to touch the bloody bandage on her head. It would have to wait until morning. However, she could get in a shower. She'd better hurry, though, if she didn't want to get caught in her nightgown. Maybe Karl would pull all those cartons of Christmas decorations out of the spare room closet. The tree lights were in the garage. So was the tree stand. She patted Millie on the head. Where was that trash sack she planned to use to keep her leg dry? In the kitchen. She headed that way, but the dog stayed where she was, watching her.

THIRTY-THREE

Mary put her hands on her hips and turned slowly in a circle, surveying her living room. One of the prettiest trees she'd ever had, blazing with light and covered with ornaments, sat in her living-room window, also outlined with lights. The cardinals sat on the mantle, their little feet buried in fresh pine branches interspersed with tall white candles in small crystal candleholders. Her crèche, the one Samuel bought for her the year they married, sat on her round table by the front door; her cranberry wreath, complete with a fresh bow, adorned the outside of it. All of the other decorations she'd collected over the years were scattered around the room in the spots they occupied every Christmas, put there by people who had been in her house every Christmas for most, if not all, of their lives. She looked around at them and smiled. It had been a hard week, but this afternoon had turned out special.

Ellen walked over and slipped her arm around her waist. 'It looks pretty good, don't you think?'

'It's beautiful. The whole room is just beautiful.'

Pat walked in carrying three wineglasses and an open bottle. 'I love this room. It looks just the same – well, almost the same – as it did when I was a little girl. The only thing missing is the smell of gingerbread men baking.'

Mary beamed. 'I can take care of that.'

'Not tonight you can't.' Pat and Ellen spoke together then laughed.

'Tonight you're doing nothing,' Ellen continued.

Pat nodded.

'We've brought everything. Even cornbread. You're going to sit, relax and enjoy all this.'

Mary obediently dropped into her large armchair and accepted the glass Pat handed her. 'Oh.' She lifted her glass high over the head of the little dog who followed her into the chair. 'You almost had this dumped on your head. You can sit here, but we're going to have to work on letting me get settled first.'

Dan and Karl walked into the room, both carrying beer cans. 'Outside lights are up and your lamp table, the lamp and all the other stuff you had on it is in the garage, covered with the old sheet like you wanted. You're now officially ready for Christmas. What's for breakfast Christmas morning?'

'I can taste it already.' Karl took a healthy swallow of his beer and went on. 'If we get a vote, I'll cast mine for that strata thing you make, the one with the chilies and the cheese. And those sticky buns. I do love Christmas.'

'You love the food.' Pat smiled and took a small sip.

'Speaking of which . . .' Dan looked at the women expectantly before he tilted his can and took a drink. 'All this Christmas stuff makes me hungry.'

'Everything's ready. We were waiting for you two to finish.' Pat nodded toward the table, set with Mary's outdoor tablecloth in deference to the casual menu. 'I thought we'd eat early since you each have another tree to put up tonight.'

Dan and Karl looked at each other and groaned.

'You want our trees up tonight?' Karl asked.

Dan sighed, tilted his can again and took another drink.

'I think we'd better,' Ellen said. 'You both get a lot of unex- pected calls but so far tonight you're free. Pat and I thought we'd better get this done while you're available.'

'I thought you wanted to wait until Susannah was home.' Dan addressed this to Ellen's back as she disappeared into the kitchen.

'I thought you wanted Neil home too. That tree will keep another week if we put it in a pail of water.' Karl watched as Pat sat a large soup tureen on the table.

Ellen followed with a bowl of salad in one hand and a basket loaded down with cornbread squares in the other.

'I do, but that's not going to work. Neil has midterm exams and so does Susannah. We don't know when either of them will make it home. I'll keep a few ornaments back for Neil to put on.'

'I'll keep the ones Susannah used to do when she was little. The rest of them need to go on,' Ellen said. 'Let's eat, everyone.'

Mary thought Ellen sounded a little wistful. Families had their

traditions and they were especially important this time of the
year. However, this was Ellen and Dan's first Christmas as a
family and they were sure to start some traditions of their own.
Susannah would be a part of it, but only a part. It wouldn't be
long before she would be setting up traditions of her own. The
years went too fast. However, Mary would make sure Christmas
morning followed tradition. She looked around once more and
smiled. It would be a beautiful Christmas. A slight frown replaced
the smile. At least, it would be if they could find out who had
killed both Clint and Evan. With a small groan, she started to
push herself up. Dan beat her to it.

'Give you a hand?' He smiled at her.

Mary smiled back and accepted Dan's offered hand to help
her to her feet. Millie immediately looked up and jumped down
from the chair before Mary could move, ready to follow her
wherever she was going.

'You've already eaten,' Mary told her and headed for the table.
She couldn't blame the dog for being hopeful, however. The
spicy aroma of chili underlay the aroma of fresh baked cornbread
and, suddenly, she was also famished.

Bowls were filled, salad passed and cornbread buttered before
the conversation started again.

Something had been trying to get to the front of Mary's mind
for a while and suddenly it was there. She put down her spoon
and addressed Karl. 'Didn't you say Cliff knew where that little
dog, Merlot, was?'

Karl nodded. 'He had the DNA sample. He had to have
known.'

She turned to look at Ellen. 'Cliff's diary made it sound as if
he planned to blackmail someone. Probably whoever has Merlot.
Right?'

It was Ellen's turn to nod.

'So that would be the motive for murdering Cliff.' This time
she addressed Dan, who nodded.

'It's a possibility.'

'OK. Let's say, for the sake of argument, it's more than that.
Let's say someone stole Merlot and is breeding him. Cliff found
out somehow and it meant so much to that person not to be
exposed, they killed him.'

'It would mean more than being exposed. Whoever stole him could go to jail.'

There was a hard edge in Dan's voice Mary rarely heard. She hadn't thought of that, but, of course, Dan was right. Cliff's attempt at blackmail would destroy someone's life in more ways than one. So they destroyed his. But, for the hundredth time, why Evan? She went on more slowly, feeling her way.

'Let's say Evan also knew who had Merlot. Either Cliff told him or he found out accidently. I doubt Evan would try blackmail, but he'd tell someone, probably Dan, about his suspicions. Evan was an honest man. He wouldn't have tolerated either the stealing or breeding the dog.'

Pat leaned forward a little and pushed her plate to the side. 'He wouldn't have tolerated murder, either. How could Evan have found out? Cliff wouldn't have told him.'

Karl listened and finally jumped in. 'The toenails.'

'Exactly. The toenails.' Mary reached for her glass of wine and took a small sip. 'I'll bet you anything Sampson is from the litter Evan has for sale in his shop. He's about the right size. Maybe Cliff saw him, noticed his toenails were the wrong color and asked Evan about him. Then the puppy disappeared and Cliff died. Evan had to have been pretty upset. The person who owns the pups would have been also. He had to make sure Evan didn't talk to anyone, especially the police, so he killed Evan as well.' She leaned back and looked around the table to see how her theory was going over. The expression on each face was a little different, but everyone seemed to consider it.

'How do we know Sampson is from the same litter in Evan's store?' Ellen asked.

'We don't.' Dan looked over at Karl. 'Is there any way to find out?'

'Blood tests, DNA. That will tell us, but it takes time. We can go look at them. If any of the rest have clear nails on a black paw, that's almost a certainty they were all sired by the same dog.'

'Merlot?' Ellen asked.

'Merlot.' Karl replied, somewhat sadly.

'So, what do we do now?' Mary sat up straighter. Maybe, finally, they were getting someplace.

'I guess we could go look at the pups.' Pat seemed a little hesitant. 'We'd have to ask John and Glen, of course.'

Mary wasn't sure that was a good idea. 'Couldn't we just go to the store and look at them?' She studied Pat for a second. 'Is that where you buy your dog food?'

'Actually, no.' Pat seemed embarrassed. 'We carry a line of special food for dogs with specific problems, but for dogs and cats that board with us, we just feed a general good quality kibble.'

'I could do it.' Ellen was swirling the wine left in the bottom of her glass around and around, not looking at her husband. 'I buy Jake's food there, and we're getting sort of low. I could drop in tomorrow and just, you know, admire the puppies. I'll bet everyone who comes in the store stops to visit them.' She stole a glance sideways at Dan.

'Are you seriously thinking of skulking around that store looking at the puppies' toenails? Why? What do you think you're going to find out?'

'If one of the black ones has white toenails.'

'Then what are you going to do?'

'Come back and tell you, of course.'

'What am I supposed to do? Run out and arrest John and Glen? Last I heard it wasn't against the law for puppies to have different colored toenails.'

'That's not why you'd arrest them. It would be because . . .' Ellen stopped and shook her head.

Dan smiled. 'Exactly. Even if we think that litter might – and I repeat, might – have been sired by Merlot, that doesn't tell us much. It doesn't tell us who has the dog or who owns the puppies, and it sure doesn't tell us who killed either Cliff or Evan. Go, if you want. But don't expect much.'

Everyone went quiet. Ellen swirled her wine some more and Pat ran her fingers up and down the stem of hers. Karl stared at his beer. Dan took what seemed to be the last swallow of his.

Mary sat still and thought. 'Evan must have records.'

'What?' Dan put his can down and looked at her. 'What are you talking about?'

'Records. You know, who owned the pups, how much they wanted for them, what Evan's cut was, some kind of contract or bill of sale. I don't know. Something.'

Dan nodded slowly. 'You're right. He must have had something.'

'How do we go about finding out?' Ellen looked dubious. 'Ask John and Glen?'

Mary had a number of questions she'd like John and Glen to answer but didn't think she wanted to start with that one. She couldn't believe either of them was a murderer, but there were a few things that made her uneasy. However, she couldn't think of any other way to find out who owned the pups. 'Can you get a subpoena or something?'

Dan didn't say anything for a moment but the look he gave her was a little more than thoughtful. 'I've already requested a court order to go through Evan's effects, looking for clues to his murder. Why don't you want to ask John and Glen?'

She didn't want to tell Dan her suspicions. That's all they were, suspicions, but she couldn't come up with a way to avoid it.

Dan watched her, saying nothing, waiting.

She sighed. 'I just . . . there are some things . . . John was a surgical nurse. He'd know how to stab someone through the heart. At least, I suppose he'd know.'

'Go on.' Dan looked interested. 'There must be more than that.'

'Well, they inherited everything, including Millie.'

The dog pricked up her ears at the sound of her name.

Dan simply said, 'And?'

'I think they might be the owners of the puppies at Evan's shop. If they are, then they have Merlot.'

Dan looked startled. Apparently he hadn't been expecting that. Ellen sucked in her breath and Pat's mouth made a small 'o.' Karl looked as if he was going to say something but stopped when Dan held up his hand.

'That's a pretty serious accusation. What makes you think they might own them?'

'They were pretty free letting the children hold them. Evan didn't like it, but when John said it was all right, he backed off. I thought that was strange.'

'There's got to be more than that.' Dan's brow furrowed as he watched her.

'They have a couple of litters of cockapoos every year. Their dogs are cockers and they always breed to poodles. That's what got them in so much trouble with the purebred dog people. I think they didn't want anyone to know they bred another litter of cockapoos, especially since they bought two of Alma's cockers. No, bitches – that's right, isn't it? Girls are bitches?'

Pat started to laugh and Ellen joined her. The corners of Dan's mouth twitched.

'Not all of them,' Karl said. 'However, technically, you're right. Female dogs are bitches.'

Heat crawled up the sides of her face. 'Thank you.' She turned toward Dan. 'Glen evidently wears sandals with white socks on his days off from the bank. He's about the same size as Father D'Angelo. And, according to the very observant children, so does Luke.'

'Are you still trying to identify the footprints you found around the manger where Cliff died?' Karl asked.

Dan hesitated for a moment. 'Yes, but that's not what Mary is talking about.'

'Oh, oh. Something more has happened. What?' Pat's expression lost its amused look. Foreboding took its place.

'Someone was prowling around in the Mendosas' bushes the night before last. Whoever it was didn't try to get in the house but was under Ronaldo's bedroom window. We found a print.'

'Let me guess.' Karl looked a little pale and there was anger in his voice. 'A large sandal print.'

Dan nodded.

'What you and Mary are saying is that Glen and John, or one of them, could be implicated in all this, so you don't want them to know what we're thinking?' Pat looked as if she was having a hard time swallowing something.

'It's always a good idea not to let anyone know what you're thinking in a murder investigation.' Dan yawned.

'Then why are you telling us?' Ellen stood and started clearing the table.

'Because, for some reason, I always seem to. Need help?'

'No.' She smiled and picked up his beer can, shook it gently and put it on the pile of dishes she held. 'Why don't you and Karl run our Christmas tree over to our house, find the stand and get it up? Pat and I will clean up all this and we'll be right behind you. If we don't get it done soon you'll fall asleep and it'll be New Year's Eve before the trees are finished.'

'I have something other than decorating a Christmas tree planned for that evening.' The smile Dan gave her was amazingly tender for a man whose job did nothing to reward tenderness. New Year's Eve would be their one-year anniversary. Dan's plans didn't seem to include anyone else but the two of them. That was as it should be.

'You go along.' Mary told Pat and Ellen. 'I can manage all this just fine.' She pushed herself out of her chair but didn't move. Her leg was stiff and sore and her head ached. She reached for the empty cornbread basket, only to have it taken from her hands.

'You're supposed to rest. We're doing this.' Pat took the basket, stacked the rest of the bowls on top of it and followed Ellen into the kitchen.

Dan walked over beside her. 'Want an arm over to your chair?'

Mary shook her head. Big mistake. The room swam a little. Dan caught her under her elbow and walked her to the chair. 'Falling off boxes, slicing open your leg and getting bashed in the head would take its toll on someone far younger than you. Do us a favor. Rest a little.' He placed a small kiss on her cheek. Karl, who was right behind him, gave her arm a soft squeeze, and they both turned to go.

'Mary, forget murder, at least for tonight. OK? Your valiant police department is on the job. We'll find out who did this. I promise.' They headed for the kitchen.

Dan asked Ellen if she had her car keys. She murmured an answer, then the back door opened and shut.

Suddenly, Mary was very tired. Maybe she'd close her eyes for a minute. She let her hand rest on the dog, who had joined her. So soft. Why had she never had a dog before? She couldn't remember. Maybe because . . . she didn't remember anything else until a hand gently shook her and a quiet voice spoke into her ear.

'I'm sorry to wake you, but we're going and you really should go to bed. Do you want me to help you?'

Ellen leaned over her, amusement and concern equally mixed.

Irritation filled Mary, not for Ellen but for herself. Surely she hadn't dropped off to sleep? She never did that. But she had.

'The day I can't put myself to bed will be a sorry one, indeed.' Mary sat up straight, waking the dog, who seemed to feel no embarrassment about dropping off. 'You both run off and get your trees up. I'll be just fine. Go.'

Ellen hesitated for a minute.

Pat joined her. 'You're sure? Yes. I see you are. Promise you'll call if you feel . . . All right. All right. We're going. Do you want us to let Millie out one more time?'

'No. I'll do that before I go to bed.'

'Well, make it soon.' Ellen followed Pat toward the kitchen.

Mary listened for the sound of the old screen closing and looked around at her living room. It looked, and smelled, wonderful. She loved Christmas. Such a happy time of the year. Maybe she should take inventory of the presents she'd already bought. Or get the box of gift wrap out of the closet. She had some left, but how much? She wasn't ready for bed. That few minutes of sleep had left her wide awake, but not energetic. 'How do you feel about *Masterpiece Mystery*?'

Millie's snore was her only answer.

Mary took it as assent. 'I'll go get some Tylenol and a glass of water and we'll watch it before we go to bed. Who knows, maybe it will give me an idea as to who killed Evan.' She sighed, pushed the dog over and went in search of the remote.

THIRTY-FOUR

Mary's eyes popped open. She'd been dreaming, something . . . it had gone. It had something to do with murder. Something on *Masterpiece Mystery*? No. Something to do with Cliff and Evan. She'd been thinking about them, about what had happened, about the children . . . That was it. The children. She dreamed something had happened, only she couldn't remember what. What time was it, anyway? Three. Why was it always at three a.m. when she was worried? She sighed and pushed back the covers. There would be no more sleep for a while, so she might as well do something constructive.

Millie raised her head and looked at her questioningly.

'I'm going to use the bathroom. Do you want to go outside?'

Millie dropped her head back down on her bed and closed her eyes. Evidently she didn't suffer from bad dreams. Mary yawned. If she went back to bed, would she sleep? No. She'd only stare at the ceiling, letting a lot of questions roll around in her head. If that was going to happen, she might as well put them in some kind of logical order. She'd always found putting things on paper helped her to think. Maybe, since she had to get up anyway . . . She felt around for her slippers, made it to the bathroom then headed for the kitchen to find pen and paper and heat up any leftover coffee.

Mary stared at the paper, steam from her coffee mug rising silently toward the ceiling. In lots of the mystery novels she read people made a list and it helped them understand what happened and often made clear who the killer was. Only, she'd never done this before and wasn't sure how to go about organizing it. She had to start somewhere, so she divided the paper into three equal columns. At the top, she labeled one column 'suspects.' That seemed logical. The next column she labeled 'motive.' She sat back, took a sip, gasped and immediately set the mug down on the saucer. Even McDonald's didn't serve coffee that hot. She'd go back to her list while it cooled. She gave a small nod and stared at the third column. What should she put there? Connection to Merlot? There had to be one. Somehow, the disappearance and reappearance of that little dog figured strongly in all this. How did she go about finding out how?

She'd start with all the people who visited Evan's pet shop the evening of his death. Reluctantly, she wrote John and Glen's names as number one under suspects. They certainly had a motive. That is, they had if obtaining the pet shop was that important. Or was there something else? Were those puppies theirs? Had they stolen Merlot to breed to their cockers? The purebred people in town made their position clear on mixed breeds, but Mary doubted if either Glen or John cared much. They would, however, care a lot about going to jail and she was equally sure Dan was right: stealing a dog like Merlot would mean that's where they'd go. That changed things. Was that why they wanted to use Luke's dog? So any new puppies would carry the same genes? How did that work, anyway? John would know. Cliff had never liked them. If he found out they had Merlot, she didn't think he'd hesitate to threaten blackmail. But Evan. Would they . . . Evan wouldn't tolerate stealing a dog, and he certainly wouldn't ignore murder. Shutting him up would make them safe and also give them the pet shop. They'd been there, in the shop, right about the time Evan closed and they'd had more than enough time to murder Evan and get to San Luis Obispo to set up an alibi. As much as she couldn't bring herself to believe they were guilty, she had to leave them on her list.

Who else? Father D'Angelo. Should she even consider him? He had no connection to Merlot that she knew of, but he had one to Cliff. Had he ever forgiven Cliff for whatever he did to his cat? He must have. He was a priest. But Father D'Angelo had a temper. She'd worked with him on too many committees not to know he sometimes struggled not to lose it. She'd watched him turn beet red, seen his eyes flash and almost physically felt him swallow the words he so desperately wanted to say. But he'd never lost it, at least in public, and he would never hurt the children. Or did that keep him on the list? The murderer had brushed by the children, hiding his face with a hood. He'd made no attempt to hurt them. The sandal print under the children's window could have been his. So could, and probably was, the one in the crib scene. Did that prove anything? Probably not, but the children saw someone in a robe like the one he wore, and he was the victim of one of Cliff's mistakes. That alone had to keep him on the list. She finished filling in his name with sadness.

That brought up another thought. Had any of the other people she needed to put on this list worn a costume to the extravaganza? She didn't know and wasn't sure how to go about finding out. Bill Bliss, for instance. She couldn't picture him traipsing around in a medieval robe. However, he had been seen going into Evan's shop at about the right time on the day of Evan's murder. Why? He and Naomi didn't have any animals but he had a connection to Merlot. He once owned him. Insurance. Had he done something with the dog to collect the insurance? Had Cliff found out? Cliff found the dog. Was it Bill Bliss Cliff planned to blackmail? Mary didn't think she'd want to. There was something cold – almost, but not quite, menacing about the man. She'd be less surprised if he turned out to be the killer than any of the other people she'd been considering. But why Evan? The telltale toenails. That had to be it. Evan knew about dogs and evidently that recessive gene wasn't common. Had Evan guessed? If he had, he wouldn't have let it go. He'd have investigated and, if he thought something illegal was going on, he would have done something about it. Mary sighed. It was an idea, nothing more. She had lots of ideas, but nothing that came close to proof. She wrote down Bliss's name but left the other two columns blank. She needed to find out more. Lots more.

Who else was in the store that afternoon? Luke Bradshaw. No. Luke was the last person to have done something so brutal, surely. He was . . . Mary paused. What was he? Who was he? She barely knew him. A pleasant, helpful young man who seemed to like the children. A young man who had chosen to work in the library. Hardly a job for a vicious killer. A young man whose chosen career was sidetracked by Cliff. A young man who owned a son of Merlot. Was that a connection somehow? Cliff mentioned Luke in his diary that he wanted to make amends. He must have contacted Luke. Had he found out things he wasn't meant to know? What did this 'son of Merlot' look like? Did he resemble his father? If so, how much? Could this be a purloined letter affair? She threw down her pen. This was doing nothing but giving her a huge headache. There was someone else who was seen going in the shop that afternoon, but she couldn't remember who, and she wasn't going to try. She was going to take two Tylenol and go back to bed. First, she was going to give Millie one last chance to go outside.

The air was cold. The first frost of the season had been forecast, for once correctly. She shivered, pulled her bathrobe closer around her and hoped Millie would be quick. She was. Mary shut the door and hurried back to the bedroom without another look at the paper sitting on her kitchen table. It had done nothing but confuse her more. She was going to leave all this up to Dan. She had more than enough on her plate. Tomorrow she'd try to get into the beauty shop for a shampoo before she picked up the children. She had some shopping to do and had to see if dismantling the can tree was on schedule and the press would be there. She also needed to . . . she couldn't remember what else. There was something . . . It would come to her in the morning. Her eyes closed, but they jerked back open. There was something on her bed. What on earth . . . a wet nose nudged her arm and a small body curled up next to her. Millie. She'd jumped up on her bed. She'd have to get off. Mary didn't approve of dogs on beds. At least, she didn't think she did. But she was tired, tired and upset. The dog must be also. She seemed to take comfort lying so close to Mary. Maybe she wouldn't push her off. Having the dog nestled next to her this way was warm and comforting somehow. Maybe she'd let her stay, just this once. Tomorrow she'd be stricter. Her eyes closed again and she drifted into a deep and dream-free sleep.

THIRTY-FIVE

The beauty shop was packed. That meant, for this tiny two-chair shop, there was one person in Gloria's chair and one other waiting. Irene had been more than willing to squeeze Mary in, provided she could come right away. Mary could and, at this hour, she wouldn't be inconveniencing anyone. Irene and Gloria were the only stylists in the small shop. The two stylists and their two early clients gathered around Mary.

'What happened to you?' Gloria Hugger, blunt and to the point, stood in front of Mary, curling iron in one hand.

'Were you really mugged?' There was horror and Mary thought a little thrill in Alice Ives's voice.

'Is it true you found poor Evan?' This from Leigh. She had on another workout pantsuit that had never visited a gym. Today she clutched something that looked like an old burlap sack. Mary didn't have time to satisfy her curiosity.

'Does Dan know who killed them?' Irene asked.

'If he does, he hasn't told me.'

'Are you all right?' This time Mary only nodded, but Irene

didn't look convinced. She took her by the arm and guided Mary over to the empty chair in front of the basin. She carefully draped the protective cape around Mary's shoulders, gently wound a cloth around her neck, tucked in the collar of her blouse, leaned her back in the chair and gasped. So did the other women who gathered around the shampoo chair.

'What did he hit you with?' Irene gently touched the blood-soaked bandage that hung entangled in Mary's hair. 'I'm going to have to get this off. It's not doing you any good, anyway.'

'No one hit me with anything. I fell off a box.'

That stopped Irene in mid-yank. 'What were you doing on a box?' She finished the yank. The bandage that had been stuck on nothing but Mary's hair came away, but not without a sharp intake of breath from Mary.

'Looking for Evan. His car was parked out the back but the shop wasn't open. I was worried about him.'

'Turns out you had something to be worried about.' Irene ran her fingers gently through the hair around the stitches, pulling it this way and that, separating the blood-soaked strands. At least, Mary thought they were blood-soaked. She couldn't see them. They might be stained with butadiene. They used that with a more-than-liberal hand.

'Do I have any hair left there?'

'Some. After they take the stitches out, I can sort of comb what's left over this spot until it grows back. You'll hardly notice it. Right now, I'm just going to rinse around it and get the worst of the sticky stuff out.'

Lovely warm water gently washed away dried blood and grime. It effectively shut out the questions from everyone else. Alice returned to her chair, where Gloria resumed twisting her wispy hair into little curlers before setting her under the dryer. Leigh picked up a magazine, featuring a beautiful woman with a haircut that was never meant to be worn by anyone who took care of children, cooked meals for a family or attempted sleep.

Mary's eyes closed; the soothing warm water and Irene's fingers gently running through her hair. The familiar voice barely penetrated but it made Mary open her eyes. It was the sight of Leigh, magazine abandoned, wrapped in what appeared to be a burlap sack that made her sit straight up. 'What on earth is that?'

'Mary, lean back. You're dripping water all over. It's just Leigh in her choir robe.'

'It's too long, isn't it?' Leigh turned around with a swish, but if she thought the robe would swish with her, she was mistaken. The brown material hung heavy and limp from her shoulders, held in place at the waist by a coarse rope. It looked much like the one Father D'Angelo wore, only he never wore high heels. Leigh pulled the hood of the robe up over her metallic gold curls and fluffed it out so it framed her face. She was right. The thing was too long and the hood was too big.

'That's a choir robe?' Water dripped down the back of her neck, but she ignored it. Leigh looked ridiculous. She must have agreed with Mary because she squirmed inside the enveloping robe.

'Yes. We had them made special for the Victorian extravaganza and the Christmas parade. We wore them for the first time when we followed the *posada* the other night. You must have seen us.'

If she had, she didn't remember. If they all looked like Leigh, she was sure she would have. The only thing, other than murder, that stood out in her mind about the *posada* procession was the cow.

Leigh went on: 'I had to wear high heels to keep this thing from dragging and almost killed myself. I can't do that again for the Christmas parade and I don't know what to do.'

'Shorten it.'

Irene giggled, or at least Mary thought she did.

'Oh, Mary. I couldn't do that. I can't sew a stitch.' Leigh sounded distraught but maybe just a little smug as well. Surely she wasn't proud of not being able to take up a hem? Well, maybe she was.

'Get Bonnie to do it.' Irene put her hand on Mary's breast bone and lowered her back into place over the shampoo bowl. 'She made it for you, didn't she?'

'She made half the robes in the choir and got rich doing it. Why, she charged fifty dollars a robe!' Leigh sounded incensed, but Mary thought she wouldn't have done it for that. Those hood things looked tricky.

Irene finished rinsing. She sat Mary up and wrapped her head in a towel. 'I'd hardly say she got rich, but I'm sure she was glad for the extra money. It costs a small fortune to feed all those dogs and run that kennel building, especially as Todd's business has fallen off.'

A start ran through Mary. She'd never thought about that but, of course, Irene was right. Keeping up kennels must be expensive. She'd heard Todd was having a hard time competing with the big box store that had recently moved into town. Several downtown merchants were. However, she hadn't thought about it in conjunction with Bonnie's kennels. So, Bonnie was drumming up business of a different kind. Good for her. 'I didn't know Bonnie could sew.' She knew very little about Bonnie.

'She made a bunch of the robes. We'd been talking about what we could do that would be different for the *posada* and the parade. She suggested we dress sort of medieval and brought in hers to show us. They looked about right and they weren't that expensive, so we voted to go with it, especially when Bonnie said she'd make one for anyone who wanted her to, but it'd be fifty dollars and we would buy the material. Cheap at the price, in my opinion. She did mine.' Irene threw a look at Leigh that said plainly she thought Bonnie had treated them fairly.

'Do you think she'll charge me to take up the hem?'

Leigh eyed Mary as if she might ask her to do it. A retired home economics teacher should have no trouble putting up a hem and certainly had a sewing machine. Mary silently vowed this was one time she wasn't volunteering. She didn't mind helping. She went out of her way to help organizations and people, but she didn't care one bit for being taken advantage of, and that's just what Leigh had in mind.

'Call Bonnie and ask her.' Irene looked at Leigh, then down at her shoes and sighed. 'You'd better do it soon. That parade is coming up and you'll kill yourself in those things.' She stood in front of Mary, blow dryer in her hand, studying Mary's hair. 'I won't be able to do a very good job with this. I'm afraid of hurting your stitches.'

'They're already hurt. Do what you can.'

'I think we need to put a bandage of some kind back on.' Irene walked closer and examined Mary's head again. 'I've got a first-aid kit in the back. I'll go see what I can find.'

She laid her dryer on the stand and left.

Leigh moved in closer. 'Do you think I should ask Bonnie to take up the hem?'

'She made it. I'm sure she'll take it up.'

'Yes, but will she charge me?'

'Leigh, I don't know.' She paused as she looked at her. 'It seems a little big everywhere.'

Leigh looked down at herself and ran her hands down the sides of the garment. 'My James has mentioned he might like to join. He's in the choir at school. I thought I'd get it a little big so he could wear it too. That way I wouldn't have to pay for two of them.' She pulled the material out around her hips. There was quite a lot of it. 'Maybe I shouldn't have had it made so . . . big.'

Mary stared at her. 'How are you going to work that if you're both still in the choir?'

'I hadn't thought of that.' Leigh looked a little taken back.

'How long have you been a member?' Mary put her hand up to her head and gingerly touched the shaved spot. It felt bigger than she'd thought. Drat. How long would it take for her hair to grow back?

'Not too long. I joined about the time John Lavorino left. Too bad. Everyone said he was one of the best tenors they'd had in years. Dog people certainly do get upset.'

Mary abandoned the problem of her hair, or lack of it, to give Leigh her full attention. She'd forgotten John was in the choir. She listened to them on Sundays, sometimes with appreciation, sometimes with a cringe, but she'd paid little attention to who was involved. 'When did he quit? Before or after you all ordered your robes?'

Her tone must have sounded a bit sharp because Leigh took a step backward and opened her eyes wide. 'Why, let me see, it must have been after. I remember thinking there went one hundred perfectly good dollars down the drain. It's not like we can wear these things for anything other than choir, and not very often then.' She stopped and the expression on her face changed. 'Why?'

'Was Glen a member as well? I don't remember that.'

'Probably because they buried him in the back row. Glen can't carry a tune in a bucket.'

Ignoring the cliché, Mary tried to remember who else was in
the choir. She saw them every Sunday. Why was nothing coming?
Bonnie played the piano for them, and she remembered Naomi
. . . Naomi. 'Is Bill Bliss . . .'

'Of course not. Can you imagine that stuck-up man wearing
a robe like this? Parading through the streets, following some
woman on a donkey, singing "We Three Kings"? Hummp. Mr
Bliss thinks he's the king and we're the servants. He wouldn't
stoop so low as to mingle among us.'

Mary briefly wondered what Bill had done to engender so
much dislike from Leigh, but her mind was going in a different
direction and she pushed Bill aside. A mental picture of the choir
was starting to form. 'Luke. From the library Luke. He's in the
choir, isn't he?'

'He is. Nice boy.' She gave a little laugh. 'Can't help thinking
of him as a boy, but he's a man now.'

'And Todd? Todd Blankenship? Bonnie's husband? Is he in
the choir?' This came out a little faint. Mary felt a little faint. It
seemed there were medieval robes everywhere.

'Mary, why all this interest in the choir? If you want a list of
the members, ask Bonnie. Actually, ask Misha Turner. She's the
adult choir director. Or, if you want to get the contract to make
the next robes, well, I'm not sure Bonnie . . .'

Mary didn't let her finish. 'I have no interest in making
anything. No. I only wondered . . . such an interesting idea . . .
it seemed there are a lot of new people in the choir . . .'

Leigh still stared at her, almost willing her to say more.

Saved by Irene. 'Found this gauze and tape. Let me put this
bandage on before I try to fix your hair.'

Mary watched Leigh out of the corner of her eye while Irene
tried to make the bandage stick. She seemed undecided whether
she should continue to question Mary or not. However, she wasn't
going to get the chance. Irene was asking the questions: exactly
how had Mary fallen, what made her think Evan might be in
trouble and did she have any idea why Cliff was in the manger,
let alone at St Theresa's. Mary had no answers. Leigh listened
intently for a few minutes then gathered up her robe and, wobbling
a little on her high heels, left. Was she going to call Bonnie?
She thought about all the choir robes. Too many robes. Too many

people connected to these terrible events seemed to have one. It must all mean something, but for the life of her she couldn't figure out what.

THIRTY-SIX

Mary sat in her car in the library parking lot. After turning the car off, she leaned forward on her steering wheel and thought about what she'd just learned. Had she, though, learned anything of significance? The choir had robes that looked a lot like the one Father D'Angelo wore. Enough so two small children, in the dark and already scared half to death, might mistake someone wearing one for him? Mary thought it possible.

Luanne said half the town was dressed up for the extravaganza, but they didn't all wear robes like a Franciscan friar. There were Dickinson-era carolers, elves and reindeer, Maids a-Milking, who had ruffles everywhere except where they were needed most. None of them would be mistaken for a monk. The Morris dancers with their ballet slippers, white pants and full-sleeved blouses and the lady who read stories out of a very large story book were out. So were the people who gathered around the Charlie Brown Christmas tree portraying the Peanuts gang.

There weren't a lot of monk robes she could think of. That narrowed the field of possible suspects but didn't mean the murderer had to be a member of the choir. She had no idea how many of them had anything to do with dogs. Mary was certain dogs came into this. They had to. Cliff had found the Blisses' poodle, Merlot, who she was sure someone didn't want found. Why was easy: they faced jail. Who wasn't so clear. She sighed deeply and got out of the car. She didn't know if Luke would be at the library today, but she had to make sure the cans that hadn't been used to make the tree had been picked up and the volunteers who would dismantle the tree were on track. If Luke was there, perhaps he could answer a few questions. If, that was, she could think of a tactful way to ask them.

'Oh, boy.' Luke slumped in his chair and ran his hand over his hair, pulling strands out of its ponytail. It gave him, Mary thought, a somewhat frazzled look.

'You just asked for the half-hour lecture, and if you really want to understand it, plan on an hour.'

'Don't you have a five-minute version?'

'I'll try. OK. There are several things that determine the amount a breeder can ask for a stud fee. First, bloodlines. Does the dog have a lot of champions in his background and did they, in turn, produce a lot of champions? Then, has he been shown and how did he do? Is he a finished champion and, most importantly, has he produced champions? If you have all of those things, the stud fee can be in the thousands.'

Mary's mouth dropped open, but she didn't care. Thousands? Surely she'd heard wrong. 'Did you say thousands? Why would anyone pay thousands?'

'Let's say you have a really good bitch and you want top-quality puppies. You'd expect to pay what Bonnie's asking for that new dog of hers – twenty-five hundred dollars. The pups that were just born were his.' The expression on Luke's face was unreadable. 'She says she has them all sold for between two and three thousand each. Do the math. Take off a couple thousand for vet bills, food and running her kennel, and she's still ahead. Nicely ahead. But, of course, it's not that easy. You're not always going to have a whole litter that's show quality, no matter how illustrious the parents. There will be some litters where no pup is show quality. Then you're looking at maybe breaking even. Not all litters will have five puppies. There are lots of variables.'

'Has she had many people pay that?' Mary's voice was faint.

'I haven't heard of anyone, so far. But maybe in the spring . . . I hope so, for her sake. She paid a lot for that dog.'

'What's a lot?'

'I don't know the exact amount, but if what I've heard is true . . . it could be upward of twenty thousand.'

A cold chill ran through Mary. She felt like one of those people on the *Antiques Roadshow* who had just been told their Aunt Bessie's ugly parlor lamp was a rare Tiffany Lamp worth more than their house. 'How much?'

Luke was at the counter, smiling at a little girl who labored to sign her name on a library card application. Her mother stood beside her, beaming. 'Your first library card. I remember when I got mine. It was a special day.'

'Did you get ice cream?' The child looked up with a hopeful expression.

Her mother looked a little taken back but recovered quickly. 'I believe I did. Would you like to celebrate with an ice-cream cone?'

The child nodded, a small smile starting to form.

'Finish your name then. Have you picked out your books?'

The child nodded and pushed two books that lay on the counter closer to Luke, who picked up the card and looked at the slightly smudged signature. 'Good job, Clarisse.' He handed her a new card with a bar code on it. 'Keep this somewhere safe and bring it every time you want a new book.' He swiped the books under the scanner then gave them back to the child, who solemnly picked them up and tucked them in her book bag.

'Ready?' her mother asked.

Clarisse smiled broadly, because of pride in her new library card or the thought of ice cream, Mary wasn't sure, but she smiled as well as they walked out the door.

Luke leaned on the counter as he watched them, then straightened and nodded at Mary. 'It's that kind of thing that makes me stay at this job. Kids learning to love books, old people who come to get ones they can't afford to buy, young people who don't have a computer but come in here to do research papers . . .' He gave a rather rueful laugh. 'It sure as blazes isn't the money.'

'No,' Mary said a bit slowly. 'I don't imagine it is. There have been so many cutbacks and it always seems the library and anything connected with music or literature are the first to go.'

Luke laughed, but there was more than a trace of bitterness in it. 'When I decided not to try for vet school, I thought I was making such a sensible choice. A degree in English Lit and a Masters in Library Science. Sort of a nerdy field, but one I loved and I'd always be able to find a job. I wouldn't get rich, but I'd have stability.' He shook his head, his earring sparkling. 'Didn't quite work out that way.'

There had been a lot of talk about money the last few days. The shortage of it, or the possibility of a shortage. She wondered . . . she'd never find out if she didn't ask. After all, he didn't have to answer. 'Is that why you bred your little poodle to Millie? Did Evan pay you?'

Luke's head jerked up and he stared at Mary for a moment, expressions coming and going like a kaleidoscope across his face. 'How did you . . . ?'

'I have Millie, at least for right now. John and Glen have inherited her along with everything else Evan had, and they might want her back. I guess her puppies were pretty cute. So, I wondered, if you made some money by . . . what do they call it? Standing your dog at stud? Why you turned down John and Glen. Don't you approve of breeding to anything other than another poodle?'

Luke's mouth was slightly open as he stared at her. It seemed he'd forgotten to breathe for a moment, then he let it all out with a whoosh and a small laugh. 'Who have you been talking to? Whoever it is, they have it wrong. I love poodles, but I also love dogs and was happy to work out something with Evan. I don't want it advertised, but that's because I really don't want to get back into the dog business. Fred's a pet. He's pedigreed, and he's a really good dog, but I don't plan on showing him or standing him.'

'Then why didn't you let John and Glen use him?'

'Mrs McGill, it's very simple. They don't want to pay me. At least, they didn't want to pay what I asked. Evan only paid me one hundred dollars, but he gave me a year's worth of dog food for free, much of which I will now not be able to collect. Evan sold those pups for between three and five hundred dollars each. There were five of them. A lot for a little cocker like Millie. But, think about it. He did just fine on that deal, but so did I. Dog food is expensive, at least the special kind I feed. When John and Glen approached me, I said I wanted pay equal to the sale of at least one pup. They didn't want to do that, so – we didn't. Simple as that. Now, are you all right?' He peered at her closely, especially her bandaged head. 'I heard you got mugged, and your head looks pretty sore. Should you be up and around?'

'I'm a little bruised but fine,' she answered throug[h] clenched teeth. 'And I wasn't mugged. I fell off a box [to] see through the back windows of the pet shop.'

'The back window of Evan's shop? Why?'

Mary didn't want to answer. She'd told this story one t[oo many] times, but Luke looked genuinely upset. Repressing a s[igh, she] told it again. Millie barking all night, discovering Evan['s] home and the shop still locked long after opening tim[e even] though Evan's car was parked out back . . . 'So I decided [to look] in the window. The crate I found wasn't very strong and [broke] when I tried to get down.' She paused, remembering th[e horror] she'd felt when she saw Evan's crumpled body. If she'd ju[st been] a little more careful . . .

Luke appeared beside her, placed his hand under her a[rm and] lowered her into a chair beside a table opposite the ch[eckout] counter. He pulled another up beside her.

'You haven't had such a great week, have you? First [this,] then Evan.' He sighed deeply. 'It hasn't been much of a [week] for any of us.'

'Luke, you knew Evan well, didn't you?'

He nodded. 'I guess you could say that. I've bought a[ll my] dog supplies from him since he opened.'

'Did you know he had cockapoo puppies for sale in his s[hop?]'

'Yes, I've seen them. Why?'

'Do you know who owns them?'

Luke's eyes widened slightly, apparently in surprise. 'I [guess I] never asked, although I was a little curious. Since Millie [and] Fred had theirs, I've been more interested . . . but, no, I [don't] know.' He paused and looked at Mary intently. 'Where are [you] going with this? You wouldn't be asking unless you had a rea[son.] A good one.'

Mary leaned back a little in the hard chair, winced an[d sat] forward again, using the table to rest her arms on. She ope[ned] her fingers and let them spread out across the worn wood. [I'll] get to that in a minute. First, tell me a little more about [dog] breeding. You said you only got one hundred dollars to br[eed] your little poodle . . . Fred . . . to Millie. Is there a standard f[ee?] What would you expect to pay to get dogs like Bonnie's, [for] instance?'

'Again, I don't know the exact number, but a dog like that, with his bloodlines, his show wins, has to be worth a whole lot of money.'

Mary did a quick calculation. 'You'd have to breed about eight bitches a year to pay for him, and that doesn't take into account all the other variables and expenses. Could you do that?'

'There are some kennels that can, but I'm not sure Bonnie's is one of them. She has good dogs and is fairly well-known around the central coast, but I'm not sure she's going to get out-of-state dogs to breed. Of course, if she starts getting really good pups from her dogs she can make a lot of his purchase price back selling them, but it's not going to be easy.'

Mary barely heard it when Luke changed the subject. 'Come look at the can tree. Most of the overflow cans have been moved, but we've gotten more. Did you contact the press? What time will they be here?'

'What?'

'What time tomorrow will the press be here? The real estate guys want to start pulling this down right after lunch.'

'Oh. Yes.' She shook off thoughts of dogs and murder and tried to concentrate on soup cans and newspaper people. 'I haven't called them yet. I wanted to talk to you.' She turned toward the tree, thinking how many people would have full tummies on Christmas day because of the generosity of the town and had a rush of pride. It didn't last long. The leashes Evan had given hung from dog food cans somewhere in the middle of the tree; dog bowls and squeaky toys lay on the floor in front of it. She became a little sick looking at them. 'I'll see if I can get some of the school kids who made those decorations over here around noon. I'm pretty sure I can get Ben to send a reporter over then, and I'll see if the local TV people can come.'

Luke nodded. 'Let me know. And, Mrs McGill, I heard you were heading up the Friends of the Library fundraiser again. Is that true?'

Mary nodded.

Luke beamed. 'Then it will be a huge success. Oh, oh.' He turned to look through the glass doors into the library. A woman stood at the checkout counter, looking around, fingers drumming on the counter. 'I've got to go. Talk to you later today?'

Mary waved her hand at him as he went through the glass doors into the library. She pushed through the vestibule doors out onto the street. The pet shop was directly opposite. She stopped for a moment, staring at it. The drawn blinds over the plate glass windows gave it a mournful look. Admonishing herself not to be morbid, she started for the corner and the parking lot, but stopped. A notice with a wide black boarder was pinned prominently onto the front door. How Victorian. She crossed the street to read it.

Due to the sudden and tragic death of Evan Wilson, this shop will be closed until after the funeral and memorial service. The shop will re-open under new ownership in time for all your Christmas shopping needs and with the same policies and standards held by our beloved Evan.

John Lavorino and Glen Manning

Mary stared at the notice for what she felt was a long time. She wasn't sure what she thought. There was no practical reason why John and Glen should lose Evan's customers, nor should the customers be left in limbo, wondering if they should find another place to buy their Christmas supplies. But there was something about the promptness of all this, the quickness with which the funeral was planned, with which the turnover of the shop was being accomplished, that made her a little . . . nervous. That was it, nervous. She supposed it made sense. Christmas sales were important to any store. It certainly didn't mean John and Glen weren't grieving for their supposedly best friend, but still . . . It was good business. Wasn't that what Luke had talked about? Breeding dogs? Running pet shops? It was all about business. Wasn't it?

She turned and, more slowly, walked around the corner, got into her car and headed for home. A glance at her watch told her she had a little over two hours before she had to pick up the children. Plenty of time to call the newspaper and the TV station to see if she could arrange coverage for the grand dismantling of the can tree. But her talk with Luke wouldn't leave her alone. Dog breeding was big business, with at least relatively big money involved. Was that what was behind Cliff's and Evan's deaths? Money? If so, it let out Luke. Or, did it? She wasn't sure. However, she was sure, it let in Bill Bliss and John and Glen. Who else?

She put her foot down a little harder on the accelerator and almost skidded as she turned onto her cracked cement driveway. She needed to take another good, long look at her list of possible suspects and their motives. She had some revisions to make, and she needed to make them now.

THIRTY-SEVEN

Mary laid her purse and keys down on the kitchen table and knelt to stroke the wiggling, whining black bundle of fur that wound in and out of her legs. 'My goodness, I was only gone a couple of hours. Are you always this glad to see someone when they come home?'

She glanced at the clock on the opposite wall. One thirty. She had time for a cup of tea and a quick sandwich before she picked up the children. She'd swallow a couple of Tylenol with the tea. She'd put up a brave front for Luke and the women at the beauty shop, but her leg was aching something fierce and the back of her head and neck was beginning to throb. She was definitely too old to be falling off boxes. She suspected she was getting too old for a lot of things.

She opened the back door for the dog, who shot out gleefully. Mary watched for a minute then crossed to put on the teakettle. One eye on the back door, she rummaged in the refrigerator for something to eat that she didn't have to cook. Leftover chicken and rice soup. It would go beautifully with tea and all she had to do was heat it.

She absently finished the last bite, swallowed another mouthful of tea and leaned back, getting a small protest from Millie, who lay under the table, her head on Mary's foot. Mary shifted it slightly, wiggled her toes and once more picked up her list which she'd updated, adding every possible name to it, while she ate her soup. Even Alma had a column. Mary thought that was a stretch but she didn't want to overlook even as remote a possibility as Alma. She had been in the dog breeding business and she'd hated Cliff. Mary entered a 'w' against her name. She had placed one next to the name of all those who were or had been in the breeding business. The only one it left out was Father D'Angelo. He was also the only one who didn't have a dog. He had an old grudge against Cliff, though. The children had seen a man, a tall man, dressed in a robe, wearing sandals. No. That wasn't right. They hadn't said a word about footwear. Only that the man they saw wore a robe of some sort and carried a stick. A long, pointed stick? Mary shuddered. That left out Alma. She wasn't a man, she wasn't tall and Mary didn't think she had enough strength to push even the sharpest of sticks through someone's front. She set her tea down and pushed away the mug. This was getting her nowhere. She shoved back her chair, picked up her dishes and headed for the sink, the dog right behind her.

'You're going to get stepped on, or trip me and, if I fall on you, you won't like it.'

The dog paid her no heed. She sat by Mary's ankle, watching while she washed out her soup bowl and put it in the dishwasher. Mary turned, dried her hands on a dishtowel and stared down at the dog, who stared right back.

'I have to leave here in fifteen minutes. What am I going to do with you?'

The dog whined.

'I can't take you. I have to pick up the children and deliver them to the winery.'

The dog cocked her head on one side, pricked up her ears and let her tongue roll out the other side.

She looks as if she's smiling. Only, dogs can't smile. Can they?

'Well, I do have a leash and the children love you.' She drained the last of her tea and put the mug in the dishwasher as well. 'I guess it wouldn't hurt if you came. The winery has had dogs visit before, but you have to be good. You can't . . . drat.'

The red light on her answering machine was blinking. Why hadn't she noticed that before? She walked closer and pushed the button. Father D'Angelo.

'Mary, I just hung up with Sister Margaret Anne. She says you'll be here this afternoon, picking up the Mendosa children. I have something I want to ask you. Would it be possible for you to come a little early and stop by the rectory? If you're feeling

all right, I mean. I heard about your . . . accident and don't want
you . . . If you can. I'd appreciate it. Thank you.'

What was that all about? Mary had never heard him sound so
hesitant, so, well, distraught.

She stood for a moment, undecided, wondering what she should
do. It settled one thing.

Millie couldn't go. She didn't want to leave her in the car,
alone, but she wouldn't be very long at the rectory. What could
he possibly want? Was it about the children? He knew they'd
seen Cliff in the manger. He'd been there. He'd taken them to
St Mark's. They hadn't wanted to go with him. Could that be
because . . . they'd said they thought it might be him they saw.
Oh, dear lord. Was he trying to find out if they'd seen . . . if they
recognized . . .

Could that be why he seemed so nervous on the phone? Only,
how did the puppy fit in? It couldn't be him, but still . . . just
the idea he might be involved made her a little queasy. She had
no choice. She'd go. One glance at the clock said she'd better
get moving if she was going to see the good Father and pick up
the kids on time.

Millie whined, ran to the back door and gave a sharp bark,
then ran back to Mary.

'Are you telling me you want to go for a ride or that you have
another need?'

The small stub of a tail wagged her whole rear end.

'OK, we'll do both.' Mary picked up her purse, checked to
make sure she had her keys then opened the back door. 'Go on.
I'll be right behind you. I think your leash is on the washer.'

The dog bolted out the back door. Mary followed, carrying
her purse, the dog leash and a full load of anxiety. What if he
was trying to find out if the children recognized him in the
manger? Could he have been the person in the bushes under
Ronaldo's window? Surely he didn't think she'd tell him . . .

Should she call Dan? And tell him what? No, she'd see what
the Father wanted and go from there.

Hopefully, she'd get answers to a few questions of her own.
Maybe she'd even get a glimpse of the devil cat.

Mary went down her back-door stairs a lot more slowly than
Millie had and she didn't get into her car with anything like the

enthusiasm the little dog expressed as she jumped into the back-seat. She just might be on the way to unravel one more strand in this very tangled mess, and she wasn't one bit sure she wanted to. She backed slowly out of the garage, hit the garage door opener and, with very mixed emotions, turned toward St Theresa's.

THIRTY-EIGHT

Mary found a spot under an old elm that still had some leaves. The afternoon wasn't hot, quite the opposite, but she wanted to make sure Millie would be comfortable so she rolled each window down just enough so she could get her nose through, but not her head. Hoping she wasn't the kind of dog who chewed on upholstery when left alone, she walked to the rectory door and rang the bell.

It was answered promptly, as if the woman who stood there, examining Mary, had been waiting for it to ring.

'Good afternoon, Mrs Farrell.' Mary smiled.

The woman didn't smile back.

Mary gave up. Getting a smile out of this woman would take more work than she was prepared to give. She knew Margaret Farrell only slightly and had never seen her smile. She'd never seen any expression except the one she wore today. Neutral, with just a hint of suspicion. She'd never seen her in any kind of dress but the one she had on. A black dress of some kind of shiny material, buttoned down the front, with a white lace fissure around the neck, black stockings, black sensible lace-up shoes and a cover-all apron. The pattern on the apron changed, but not the style. A high bib with straps over the shoulders crossed in the back and wrapped around the waist to tie in front. The skirt had two large pockets in front, always bulging. Mary wondered what was in there but never found the right moment to ask. Today the apron was made of bright blue, pink and white dots on a field of pale yellow. It was an incongruous sight over the severe black of the dress.

'I got a phone call from Father, asking me to drop by.' Mary waited.

Margaret Farrell turned her head slowly to look back into the dim interior of the house. Two hairpins fell out, landed on her shoulder then slid to the floor. Iron-gray strands fell from the bun that hung loosely on the back of her head. Mary suspected the bun had been tight early this morning but had loosened as the day progressed. Would it completely escape its confinement by bedtime?

'He did, did he?' Suspicion deepened on Mrs Farrell's face. Mary nodded.

'Hmmm. Well, I guess I could call him. Tell him you're here.' She made no move to do so. 'He's due in the confessional in . . . let's see . . . about thirty minutes.' She paused and looked at Mary as if she expected her to respond to that statement.

Mary wasn't sure what was expected, so she smiled instead. 'Hump.'

There was more disgust in that 'hump' than Mary thought possible, and Mrs Farrell still hadn't moved. Finally, she sighed loud enough for it to be heard in the church next door. 'I'll tell him. Come on in.' She held the door a little wider and let Mary pass by her. 'Go on in there.'

'There' was what the builder had long ago dubbed the formal living room. It was small with one window exactly in the middle of the wall that looked out onto the street. Mary walked in and looked around.

'Take a seat, if you've a mind to.' Mrs Farrell followed Mary into the room and gestured vaguely at the celery green plush-covered sofa that screamed it belonged in the seventies. Mary hesitated but sat. Mrs Farrell nodded with the first thing that looked like approval and left the room, closing the door behind her.

Mary took a deep breath in and slowly let it out. Why that woman exasperated her so, she couldn't imagine. She hoped she didn't have that effect on Father D'Angelo. If so, he must lead a very uncomfortable life. She sat up straighter on the elderly but immaculate sofa and looked around. It wasn't a very hospitable room. Mary had been in several homes of this floor plan over the years and was familiar with the layout. This room was designed for guests, or adults only. Off the entryway was a hall that led to two bedrooms that also faced the front. The master bed and bath, the kitchen and large family room were at the back.

In most houses this small room didn't get used much, but she supposed it served the rectory well. It was furnished as a cross between an office and a reception room, both a bit shabby but hospital clean. Nothing matched. The two wing-backed chairs were covered in a red, white and blue print much too bold for that type of chair and the pseudo-early American end tables held wrought-iron lamps in a vaguely Spanish style. The coffee table was blond modern, or what had passed for modern in the sixties. A desk sat in a corner at an angle so as to face the rest of the room, but it held no computer or much of anything else. A maroon swivel chair sat behind it. The bookshelves were filled with religious books and the wall decorations were either depictions of Jesus on the cross or paintings of The Blessed Virgin holding the dead body of Christ. There was one rather large picture of a nun in a brown habit and black veil. St Theresa, she supposed. She stood up to take a closer look but a click brought her attention back to the door, which opened and a smiling Father D'Angelo appeared. He was followed closely by a huge black-and-white cat.

'Mrs McGill, so good of you to come.' He walked quickly across the room and reached out a hand. Mary offered hers, which he gave a single shake before dropping it. 'I hope you're getting along . . . ah . . . feeling better. I heard you had an accident but were doing all right.' He paused to stare at the white patch Mary was painfully aware showed on the side of her head. At least her pants covered the blue wrap stretched tightly around her calf.

'You are, aren't you? All right?'

'I'm fine, thank you. Just fine.' She paused, giving him a chance to say something, offer her a chair or tell her why he'd called, but he seemed not to know how to start. Maybe she could help him.

'That's a handsome cat. Is he . . .' The cat had to be a 'he.' No female would have those heavy jowls, that broad front, the muscled hindquarter, '. . . the one Cliff gave you?'

The priest looked at the cat, who sat at his ankle, staring at Mary. She had little experience with cats, only with Ellen and Dan's yellow Tom, Jake, but she knew instinctively this was no ordinary cat. At least, he didn't consider himself ordinary. The stare he aimed at her was unblinking and the low rumbling in his throat was no purr. He was letting her know something . . . what, she wasn't sure.

The priest seemed oblivious to the cat's threats. 'Yes. Isn't he magnificent?'

'Yes.' Mary didn't know what else to say. The cat was, indeed, magnificent. And threatening. 'I thought . . . I was told . . . everyone said he's a holy terror. I wondered why Cliff would give you a cat . . .' She wasn't sure how to go on, especially as the priest seemed to regard the cat with genuine fondness.

'We had a few problems getting started, but he's really come around.' He paused, looked at the cat and a slight blush stained his cheeks. 'I must admit, I wasn't too sure at first. I even named him Lucifer. I'd change it now, but he doesn't seem to mind and he comes when I call.' He paused and smiled at Mary. 'When the cat first arrived, I wasn't sure if Cliff thought bringing him was some kind of joke or what, but then, I realized he knew the cat needed me. It was really an act of kindness.'

Mary tore her eyes off the cat to examine Father D'Angelo's face. Was he kidding? Everyone, well, almost everyone said the cat was awful. 'How long have you . . . has the cat lived here?'

'About six months, I think. I took him over to Karl . . . for an operation. You know.' The red got brighter and crept higher on his face. The look he gave the cat was almost apologetic. 'It took him a few days, but he started to get better. He's quit biting me, doesn't hiss when I feed him or tries to sit on the sofa. He even sleeps on the end of my bed sometimes.'

Mary couldn't quite control the little gasp she gave nor the immediate need to sit down. She sank down on the sofa. As if he'd been waiting for her to sit first, Father D'Angelo folded himself into one of the wingbacks. The cat immediately jumped into his lap and began to purr, loudly. The priest smiled and started to stroke his ears.

'He bit you?' Mary was pretty sure he'd bite her if she offered a hand to stroke him. It wasn't something she'd try.

The priest's smile got broader. 'He was scared. I knew that and was determined to make friends. I've always had animals. It was the hardest thing for me to give up when I became a Franciscan. Parish work let me have one again, and I chose a cat because . . . lots of reasons. I was determined to win this one's confidence. We're making progress. He still wants to wander at night sometimes and then I have to go after him, but he lets me catch him now and doesn't hiss or claw me. He curls up next to me on the sofa and I think he actually enjoys sitting with me while we watch TV.' He paused and laughed a little self-consciously. 'We both like the PBS stations.'

Mary felt as if she'd just heard Father D'Angelo's confession, a very unreasonable feeling given the nature of his 'sin.' Keeping a cat, being nice to it, rescuing it from a life on the streets was hardly something to condemn yourself for. It wasn't weakness to be kind, but maybe that wasn't what he felt. She wasn't sure, but she'd been given a glimpse into his life that she didn't want. However, he'd just given her the perfect opening to ask for information she wanted. 'Is that why you were at Evan's shop the night he died? To get . . .' She looked into the cat's eyes, where he sat perched on Father D'Angelo's lap, almost level with her . . . 'Lucifer's cat food?'

Father D'Angelo nodded. 'I was just in time. I'd been trying to get there all day but things kept coming up . . . I don't like changing his food. He gets . . . you know . . . the runs if things change.'

Mary didn't know and didn't want to imagine. 'That was about five?'

The priest nodded. 'I snuck in just as Evan was pulling down the window shades. John Lavorino and Glen Manning were going out the door. Do you know them?'

Mary nodded. 'Was anyone else there?'

'Luke, I can't remember his last name, but the young man who runs the library . . .' He paused, as if waiting for Mary to acknowledge she knew who Luke was. She nodded. '. . . rushed in as I was grabbing the cat food. Evan seemed irritated and said he was closed, but Luke laughed and said he wouldn't want his dog to starve now, would he, and he'd only eat Evan's brand.' Father D'Angelo took a deep breath and let his hand rest on top of the cat's head. The cat started to purr. 'Evan muttered a rather crude word, then said, "Oh, all right" and went in the back. That's when I left.' Father D'Angelo didn't say anything for a moment, just stroked the cat's ears and seemed to listen as the purring got louder.

Mary didn't say anything either. She wanted to hear whatever it was the priest was trying to decide if he should mention.

Evidently, he made up his mind because he raised his head and looked straight into Mary's eyes. 'Evan was a nervous wreck that afternoon.'

Whatever Mary had been expecting, it wasn't that. 'What?'

'Evan. He was . . . not himself. Evan was a nice man, never snapped at anyone, never neglected his animals, but that afternoon . . . it wasn't only Luke's head he almost snapped off. Bill Bliss . . .' he paused at Mary's look of surprise, '. . . you know, the man who owns Golden Hills Winery? He came in and Evan told him he couldn't talk right then, to go talk to the florist.'

'Yes, I know Bill. The florist? Why would he send him to the florist shop?'

'I have no idea, but Bill went.'

'He did?' The thought that Evan had the nerve to send Bill Bliss anywhere was surprising, but that Bill went wasn't processing.

Father D'Angelo looked as if he was as puzzled as Mary. 'He seemed unhappy when Todd Blankenship said he'd be back with his truck to load the dog food he ordered. Evan said "Tonight?" as if it was the last think he wanted to do, but Todd only nodded and left. I took my purchase and left as well. Evan was drawing the blinds on the front windows as I walked away.'

There was something wrong here. Something didn't fit.

'I feel terrible about all that's happened, and maybe this isn't the time to ask, but we're right up against winter and I don't know who else to approach . . .'

What was the man talking about? Not Evan any longer. It took an effort for Mary to bring her attention back to the shift in the conversation. 'Ask me what?'

'How I go about setting up the church hall as a shelter this winter for some of the homeless people who live under the bridge.'

'What? You want to do what?' Now he had her attention. The homeless population was growing. They would be among the first to have access to the food from the Christmas Can Tree. Only, it had never occurred to her this was what Father D'Angelo wanted to talk about. Why, she didn't know. Catholic charities were famous for the good work they did. It wasn't always reflected in individual parishes, however. 'Are you sure?'

'Oh, quite sure. I just don't know how to – well, organize . . .' His eyes shifted away from her and onto the cat, who hadn't moved from his side. 'We have the women's guild, of course, but they help plan activities for the school, raise money for textbooks and make sure they have funds available for our needy families, but to put up a whole bunch of homeless, well, none of them seem to know any more about how to do that than I do. However, someone needs to do something and . . .' The look he gave her was clearly tentative hope. Why her? She had more causes than she could possibly handle now. 'Have you talked to Bob at the food bank?'

The priest shook his head. 'No. I thought I'd talk to you first. Everything you organize runs so smoothly. I thought if you couldn't help, you might be able to tell me who to contact and how to . . .' The worried, helpless look in his eyes intensified.

Mary sighed. No wonder his women's guild shied away from this. She knew most of them and, while they had good intentions, none of them had much experience organizing anything larger than an eighth-grade dance. 'What do you have in mind? Shelter when it rains? Every night? Just for families with children? Are you going to serve food? Have you talked to the city about permits?'

The priest held up his hand and drew back into his seat, as if the onslaught of questions had pushed him into it. 'I have no idea. I don't think we could open it every night. There are a lot of church functions that go on there, so maybe just in emergencies. Like, when we have a storm. I hadn't thought about food, but I guess . . . do we need a permit?'

Mary sighed again. 'Call Bob. He has contact with the homeless all the time. Did you know St Mark's serves a hot meal to the homeless once a week in the evening? Maybe we could work out something with them. If you plan to put people up for the night, you'll need cots and blankets and we'll have to see if the bathrooms are compliant. Do you know what the occupancy rate is on the hall?'

Father D'Angelo shook his head. 'It's posted, but I can't remember what it is.'

'Hmmm. We'll have to find out.'

For the first time, Father D'Angelo smiled. A somewhat tentative smile, but a real one. 'Does that mean you'll help?'

Mumbling things to herself like, *You're an idiot, you don't have time to do all you've signed on for, Christmas is coming, you have a houseful of people arriving for Christmas breakfast and you haven't wrapped even one present . . . You'd never forgive yourself if you'd done nothing to help those people living under a bridge. And in the rain!* 'Yes, I'll try, but I'm not promising anything and I won't chair any committee. Call Bob, tell him what you're thinking and have him call me. We'll set up a meeting. We'd better get going if you want to get anything done this winter.' She glanced at the digital clock on the desk and started to her feet. 'I'd better move if I'm going to get those children on time. School is about to let out, isn't it?'

Father D'Angelo nodded. 'The bell will go off any minute now.'

Mary had heard that bell and had no doubt everyone on this block knew when school was out.

'Call Bob as soon as you can. Let's try to get together next week. You have his number, don't you?'

Again Father D'Angelo nodded, but this time with enthusiasm. 'I can't thank you enough for offering to help. Every time I think of those children, the only roof over their heads the underpass of a bridge, no heat, no bathroom, no lights to read by or . . .'

Mary waved her hand, as if she could wave away the image he had so inexpertly but vividly painted. She hadn't offered. She'd been shanghaied. However, first things first. It was time to pick up the Mendosa children. Telling him once more to have Bob call her, she headed out the door and over to the schoolyard, accompanied by the clanging of the school bell.

THIRTY-NINE

M ary made the now-familiar turn off the highway onto the road that led to the winery and to Bonnie's house almost on auto-pilot. The children sat in the backseat, talking about their plans for Christmas break and what Santa might bring, but Mary barely heard them. Her mind was full of her discussions with Luke and Father D'Angelo. She slowed, however, as she passed Bonnie's street. The house had the blinds drawn, giving it a solitary, almost sullen look. The big gate was closed and, for the first time, she noticed there was no sign proclaiming it as a dog-breeding business. Why? Wouldn't Bonnie want the world to know where her beloved dogs lived and wouldn't she welcome visitors? Perhaps it was some sort of zoning thing. No. The house next to Bonnie's proudly displayed the picture of a paint horse, Warrior something, loudly advertising his services. If they could, so could Bonnie. She drove into the parking lot of the winery, lost in thought.

Naomi was in the parking lot watching a young man place a case of wine in the trunk of a silver Lexus. She was flanked by an older couple, both with clouds of expertly cut white hair, both expensively dressed, both beaming at Naomi as they climbed into their car. It wasn't until they disappeared down the long drive that Naomi turned toward Mary and the children.

'Kids. You can't go in to see your mother for a while. She and Mr Bliss are busy.'

'What are they doing?' Ronaldo stopped trying to untangle Millie from the leash she'd managed to get caught around her legs in her rush to get out of the car.

'Going over the books. Your mother will have to take some time off, and we need to make sure everything is in order.'

Dalia took the leash from Ronaldo and unwound the little dog, who immediately sat and stared at Naomi. 'Of course things are in order. Mom doesn't like it any other way.'

A flush spread across Naomi's cheeks. 'I'm sure they are. However, it's always a good thing to double-check.'

Mary nodded. She'd spent more than one day cleaning up a mess someone had assumed was fine instead of checking. 'How long do you think they'll be?'

'Oh, a half hour or so. I have some soft drinks. Would the children like one?'

The children looked at Mary with hopeful smiles that turned into bright beams as she nodded.

'What may I offer you, Mary? Glass of wine? Coffee?'

'Coffee sounds wonderful. Thank you.'

They followed Naomi into the tasting room and down the hall to her office. 'Sit down.' She motioned Mary to the chair beside her desk, and pointed the children to a small sofa on one side of the room. Millie she stared at for a moment. 'I think I have one of Merlot's dishes in this closet. I'll get her some water.'

It was no time at all before everyone had a drink of some sort in front of them and had settled down to wait. Naomi handed the children a copy of a dog magazine and it took only a moment before they were engrossed in it, comparing Millie to other cockers and Sampson to other puppies. Naomi watched them for a few minutes, an expression on her face Mary found unreadable.

Finally, she pushed her coffee aside and leaned over the desk and stared at Mary, her voice low. 'Are you all right?'

Mary nodded. 'Still a little sore, but fine.' News certainly did fly fast in this town. She wasn't sure she liked it, but Naomi had given her an opening. She didn't get a chance to use it. Naomi was in a talkative mood. Or was it nerves?

'It's terrible, what happened to Evan. He was a good person. I can't believe someone would do something like that.' She paused. There was the tiniest hint of a smile in her voice as she asked her next question. 'Did you really fall off a box, looking for him?'

Try as hard as she might, Mary couldn't repress the snort of disgust that escaped. Was there no one in this town who didn't know about that dratted box? 'Yes. I got worried when I found he wasn't home or at his shop, but his car was in the parking lot behind it. I stood on the box to look in the window. I only had time to see him lying on the floor before it broke.'

Naomi's mouth formed a soft 'oh,' as her eyes drifted up to the bandage on Mary's head. 'I just can't believe it. Why would anyone want to . . . Cliff had enemies.' She paused. 'Maybe not exactly enemies, but he made a lot of people angry.' Deep furrows showed in her brow and around her mouth that Mary hadn't noticed before. The breath she took before she continued sounded a little ragged. 'Evan . . . they were opposites in every way. I can't see any connection.'

Mary thought she could. There were a couple of possibilities and one, the more she thought about it, seemed distressingly possible. Dogs could be big business, at least in some circles, and that business, or some kind of business, was at the heart of all of this. John and Glen wanted the pet shop. Bad enough to kill Evan? She couldn't make herself believe that, but someone had killed them both, and dogs and the business of dogs seemed to be at the heart of it. There was one question Naomi could answer that might help. Mary wasn't in the least bit sure she would, but at least Mary could try. She stole a quick look at the children, who seemed absorbed in the dog magazine, put down her coffee cup and leaned across the desk, keeping her voice low.

'I heard Bill was at the pet store right before it closed. Did he say anything to you?'

'About what?' The furrows across Naomi's brow seemed to deepen and her eyes narrowed.

'About Evan. I heard he seemed . . . nervous. Did Bill think he seemed all right?'

'He didn't say one way or the other. He wasn't in Evan's shop very long. We're trying to take over the lease the flower shop has and, since Evan owns the building, we had to make sure he'd let us.' She gave a soft laugh, probably at the look of surprise Mary was sure was on her face.

'What do you want with a flower shop?'

'Nothing.'

The laugh disappeared, replaced with a look of faint irritation. Why? Did Naomi dislike the idea that where Bill was and why he was there was a subject of discussion in town? If that was so, Mary could sympathize. However, it seemed a legitimate question.

'It's not the flower shop we want, it's their space. We want to open a tasting room in town but haven't openly talked about it because we're not sure we can get the shop. It's a great location. Right on the town square, facing the library. Everyone passes there. It should do very well. The flower shop, for whatever reason, isn't. Bill's been talking to Evan about taking over their lease. Evan wasn't too excited about it. I don't know why. He's had some trouble getting his rent paid and if we went in, he knows . . . knew . . . oh, dear. I don't know what's going to happen now.'

'Do you know that John Lavorino and Glen Manning are Evan's only heirs? They've got everything, including Evan's mother, so probably they're the ones you need to talk to. You might want to wait a little, though. They have a lot of things to sort through.'

Naomi's face said she hadn't known. Her eyes widened, her chin lifted and something that might have been a smile grew. 'John and Glen? From St Mark's choir?'

Mary nodded.

'Well.' There was a speculative look on Naomi's face, a smoothing of the worry wrinkles that had creased her brow. Worry, however, soon came back. 'Are you sure?'

'That's what they told me. I think they were at the shop this morning. Someone put a note on the door, one bordered in black, saying the shop would re-open after the service, in time for Christmas shopping. I rather think John did that.'

Naomi laughed. Really laughed.

Mary wasn't amused. 'Is that good for you? Having John and Glen to deal with, I mean.'

'Glen has always thought our opening a tasting room in town a good idea, and I don't think he'd put up with consistently late rent payments for a minute.' Her smile spread. 'Yes, I think we can work out something with Glen.' Again, her face changed, but this time the distress was different. 'It sounds so callous to talk about our concerns when poor Evan . . .'

Mary nodded. 'I know how you feel. It's been a horrible week. First Cliff, then Evan.'

Naomi gave Mary one of the saddest smiles she'd ever seen. 'But I'll grieve for Evan.'

That was probably true. Naomi and a lot of other people. Evan had been well liked and respected, whereas Cliff . . . 'Luke, from the library Luke . . .' she paused and Naomi nodded, '. . . said he had one of your little poodle's sons. Did you breed him, Merlot, a lot?'

'Not as much as Bill would have liked. He sired two litters and, yes, Luke has one of the pups. He's a good dog and looks a lot like his father.' Her left eye twitched and her mouth pursed. 'Luke calls him Fred.'

Mary wanted badly to laugh but thought she'd better not.

Naomi might not appreciate that and she needed an answer to her next question. 'How did you pick the females to breed with?'

Naomi's eyes widened in surprise and the hint of a smile returned. 'I didn't. They picked us.'

'I don't understand.'

'Merlot was in a lot of local shows. He was a finished champion and had three Best in Show wins. His pedigree was impeccable. People with female poodles contacted us and inquired about breeding.' She looked around the room, seemingly lost until her eyes stopped on the picture of the little dog she'd taken from Cliff's apartment. 'Cliff had been badgering me to stand him, but this place takes all my time and energy. Standing a dog like Merlot takes a facility, a lot of time and a whole lot of paperwork. I didn't want to get into it.'

'Then, why did you?'

'Bill, of course.'

There was more than a trace of bitterness in Naomi's voice.

Sympathy and a deep sadness, but no surprise filled Mary at Naomi's statement. 'What did you do?'

'I didn't do anything. Bill and Cliff worked out a deal with Bonnie. Well, with Todd. Bonnie, of course, did all the work. It didn't last long.'

A start went through Mary. She hadn't expected that. 'What kind of a deal?'

'We rented her barn. You know, the old one at the back of her property. Cliff was supposed to take care of the bitches who came in for breeding and do all the paperwork. We paid for the improvements, such as they were, and we put in the gate between the vineyard and their yard. That was so one of us could get over there without having to go around, but I don't think it was ever used. We bred him with exactly two bitches and the whole thing came to an end.'

'Why?'

'For the reason I wanted nothing to do with it. I told Bill, but would he listen? Bonnie was busy with her dogs. She hadn't bought that new stud dog yet, but she was looking around. I think the only reason she agreed was because she got all those kennels and things for free. Cliff, of course, made a mess of everything he touched. He never helped clean or feed. He was

only there when the female dogs were brought in, but so was I.
The only reason I let Merlot stay while the females were there
was because of Bonnie. I wouldn't have trusted him to Cliff's
care for one minute. He didn't do one thing right. It didn't take
long before Bonnie got fed up and put an end to it, much to my
relief and Bill's fury. That happened shortly before Merlot was
stolen. We didn't make a dime on that deal, but Cliff made a
couple of months' rent. I didn't even get a puppy.' The bitterness
in her voice intensified and a tear appeared in the corner of one
eye. Naomi roughly rubbed it away.

'What do Bonnie and Todd use the barn for now?' Mary's
mind whirled. Could it be . . . evidently not. Naomi's next statement knocked her burgeoning idea to pieces.

'I was told they dismantled all the kennels we built and use
the barn for storage for the hardware store. When Bonnie bought
that new dog, I thought she might use the barn for visiting
females. Her kennel building isn't very big, but no. She always
said it was too far from the house.' Naomi shrugged as if she
didn't agree. Mary thought she didn't care, either. 'I guess it
hasn't been a problem. I don't think she's had a booking so far.
She wants a lot of money to stud that dog.'

Mary had a lot more questions formulating, twisting and
turning around in her brain, but they weren't going to get asked
right now.

Millie started to whine.

'I think she has to go outside.' Dalia picked up the little dog's
leash and started to her feet. 'I'll take her.'

'I'll take her.' Ronaldo got up as well and reached toward his
sister's hand.

'We'll all take her.' Mary pushed back her chair and stood for
a moment, making sure her leg was securely under her. 'Give
me her leash while you two pick up your cans and put that
magazine back where it belongs.' Millie's whine got louder. She
started to dance a little and looked at Mary as if to say, 'I need
to go *now*.'

Naomi scooped up the empty cans and grabbed the magazine.
'Go ahead. Take her out the big French doors and turn to the
right. Go down the hill a little way and you'll see a sign that
says "Visiting dogs." She can go there.'

Mary nodded, tightened up on the dog's leash and told the children in her strictest middle-schoolteacher's voice, 'Don't leave my side,' and started down the hall toward the spot the dog needed fairly urgently.

'Thank you,' she threw over her shoulder toward Naomi, but she had already gone back into her office. Mary heard the click of the door as she followed the dog toward the grass and relief.

FORTY

M ary stood on the top of the slight incline, watching Dalia follow Millie up and down the slope, sniffing, stopping, trying to find the perfect spot. Finally, she decided on one and squatted. Mary's attention moved to the flat board fence at the bottom of the hill. Rows of young grapevines were the only thing between where she stood and the dirt farm road that ran along the fence and continued in both directions. That fence had to be the back line of the Blankenship property. She'd never seen it from this angle before. She could make out the roofline of the old barn, the door leading into the hay loft and the rooster weathervane, but she couldn't see into the yard. She backed up the hill to get a better view.

The kennel building, or the roof of it, came into view. So did the roof of the house, but the kennel runs, the driveway and the large gate leading from the road into the back of Bonnie's property were hidden. She let her gaze drift back down to the fence. It looked just as high and impenetrable on this side as it had on the Blankenships. Where was the gate Naomi talked about? Her eyes traveled the length of the fence and finally stopped. There it was. Close to where the old barn was located. It blended in beautifully and she would have missed it, but a little light showed through a gap . . . a gap? Was the gate open? Should it be? That didn't seem right. Naomi said no one ever used it, even when they had a need to. They didn't now. Merlot was gone. There was no reason for anyone from the winery to go onto the Blankenship property, and no reason Mary could think of for the Blankenships to come onto the vineyard. Had one of the workmen . . .

'Mrs McGill, Millie's finished. Can we go in now?'

Dalia stood beside Mary, looking at her, Millie sitting at her heels. Ronaldo was down the hill, staring at a grapevine.

Mary tore herself away from the mystery of the open gate but not from the mystery of the murders. She'd been thinking, had an idea she didn't like, but decided, before she went further, she had to eliminate other suspects. There was one question she didn't think anyone had thought to ask, and it seemed a good place to start.

'Ronaldo, can you come up here?'

The boy looked up then back at the grapevine. He started toward them, but slowly. When he got close enough not to shout, he gravely said, 'There are little dried-up grapes on those vines. They look like raisins. I thought about tasting one, but thought I'd better ask you first.'

'Very sensible of you, but that's what raisins are. Dried-up grapes. I think it would be all right to taste one, but first, I have a question for both of you.'

Neither of them looked happy. Dalia's shoulders tensed and the interested look in Ronaldo's eyes faded. A look of apprehension took its place.

'I don't want to upset you,' Mary said hurriedly, 'and if you don't want to answer, or don't remember, it's not something to worry about. I wondered . . .'

She'd better not drag this out. They seemed apprehensive enough, and Millie was on her feet, looking down the hill. They needed to get inside, but first . . . 'Remember the night you found the puppy and the man in the robe brushed past you?'

Both children nodded. The look on Dalia's face plainly said it wasn't something she'd forget anytime soon.

'Did either of you notice what kind of shoes the man wore?'

The expression on Ronaldo's face went blank and his mouth opened slightly as he stared at her. He didn't have to say a word. He clearly had no idea what she was talking about.

'Work boots.'

'What?' Mary wheeled around to look at Dalia. The little girl's face was expressionless, but there was plenty of expression in the word she'd uttered.

'Work boots. You know, the kind Tony wears when he goes into the vineyard. They lace up around your ankle. That kind.'

'Are you sure?' The moment the words came out, she knew they were unnecessary. The child was very sure.

Dalia nodded.

Mary felt a little sick. This was not the way she wanted this to end. Admittedly, she'd wondered.

Enough of the ends fit. In a bizarre way, it made sense. At least, she guessed it did, but it all seemed so sad. Now what did she do? Did she have enough evidence to call Dan? Of course she didn't. All she had were a few threads and a gut feeling she was right.

'Hey.' Alarm sounded in Ronaldo's voice. 'What's she doing?'

Millie stood straight and tense, staring down the hill at the high wooden fence. Mary could hear dogs barking, faintly but barking. Suddenly, Millie gave one sharp bark of her own and took off, tearing the leash out of Dalia's hand, flying down the hill through grapevine wires, her leash whipping behind her.

'She's going to get caught.' Distress rang out in every word Dalia shouted as she, too, headed down the hill, but not through the wires.

'I'll get her.' Ronaldo was right behind his sister, trying his best to outdistance her.

Dalia ran through the rows until she got to a farm road leading down the hill toward the fence and the slightly open gate.

Millie outran them both.

'Don't!' Mary screamed. 'Come back.'

No one listened. The race was on and there was no turning back. There was only one thing Mary could think to do. She started after them. Trying not to turn an ankle in the uneven soil between the vines, she hurried as fast as she could and still see where everyone was headed. The gate was Millie's goal and the children seemed determined to follow her. Mary stopped for a second when she reached the downward sloping road, as much to catch her breath as to see where everyone was. Ronaldo stood by the gate, trying to pull it open a little more; Dalia was halfway through it.

'Don't go in there!' Mary shouted as loud as she could, but she had little breath left. 'Wait for me.'

Either she wasn't loud enough or the thrill of the chase had left the children oblivious to anything else.

'She went in there,' Ronaldo shouted. 'Don't worry. We'll get her.' He disappeared through the gate right behind his sister, who was already out of sight.

'Oh, Lord.' Mary headed for the gate as fast as the steep terrain and her elderly legs would allow her. 'Let's hope I'm not too late.'

FORTY-ONE

The yard was quiet. No dogs barked. No children spoke. No one in sight. What should she do next? She was on the road that wound around the Blankenship property, the one that ran past the front of the old barn. The doors were tall and looked new. So did the metal rails they rolled on. One of the doors was rolled back slightly, but no light came through and no sound. She looked toward the kennel building and the house. There was no car in the carport and no activity in the kennels. The front door was closed and no sign of dogs in the runs. Where had Millie gone? Where had the children gone? There was only one answer. Mary walked over to the barn, pushed the door back all the way and stepped in. She was greeted by an explosion of noise.

'Oh, Aunt Mary, look what we found.' That, of course, was Dalia, squatting beside an open kennel door, a puppy in her lap. A black-and-white cocker, obviously the mother, sat beside her, nuzzling the puppy then worriedly looking back through the open gate at the remaining puppies, who hadn't yet realized the gate was open. They would soon.

Mary looked at Dalia only long enough to be sure she was in no danger from the mother. Her eyes were drawn like a magnet to metal around the rest of the barn. It had originally been a horse barn, divided off into four large box stalls, the rest of the area probably given over to feed storage, tack and other supplies. The board fronts of the stalls had been removed and replaced with heavy duty chain-link fencing, a gate at one side of each stall. Three of them each contained a cocker bitch, the two whose gates were still shut barked in sharp warning at the interlopers, especially the one who had a pup by her side. One curled her lips in warning before she let loose another explosion of barks. Mary watched her for a moment but was immediately distracted by the dog in the fourth pen. A dog who watched her every move but made no sound. A small black dog, overgrown with hair, his long, pointed nose and straight tail gave evidence he was no cocker. He was unmistakably, even to Mary's eyes, a male poodle, and she was certain she knew who he was and where he'd come from.

'Merlot?' she asked as she approached his stall.

The dog didn't move. The look he gave her wasn't filled with suspicion so much as apprehension, as if he waited for her to do something he might not like. Fear? She didn't think so. Watchful, guarded, he stood his ground as she moved closer. 'Merlot?'

'Is that his name?' Ronaldo suddenly appeared at her side, causing Mary to startle.

'Yes, I think so.'

'How do you know that?'

Mary wasn't sure how to answer him, but she'd found the missing poodle, just as Cliff probably had. Who owned the puppies in Evan's store, or why he had been killed as well, was no longer in doubt.

'Where's Millie?' she asked him.

'Over there. Making friends with that dog. Why are all these dogs here?'

Good question, but one she wasn't prepared to answer. Instead, she took Ronaldo by the hand and hurried over to where Dalia sat with the puppy on her lap. There was one more thing she needed to see before she and the children got out of here, and that had better be soon.

'Dalia, may I hold the puppy for a moment?' She bent down and held out her hand.

The child hesitated but handed over the puppy. The mother dog looked up in alarm and started to get to her feet. Another reason for Mary to hurry. She turned the puppy upside down and pushed the hair back on one front paw. An all-black paw and all black toenails. She checked all four black feet. All of them had black toenails. She handed the puppy back to Dalia and started to edge past the mother into the box stall where the remaining three puppies squirmed and whimpered, protesting the absence of their mother. One was all black, one had one white spot on its chin and the third was what Bonnie had called parti-colored. She started with that one, keeping a close eye on the mother, who started into the box with an unhappy curl to her lips.

'Dalia, bring that puppy in here, please. I think it's hungry.'

The child looked down at the puppy. 'Are you hungry, little thing? OK. Let's go find your mother.' She walked into the box and put the puppy down under its mother's nose, who immediately lay down and started licking it. The pup ignored its mother's ablutions and headed instead toward lunch. At least, for the moment, the mother seemed to have forgotten Mary, who held the parti-colored puppy up toward the light. All the toenails seemed to be the appropriate color for the hair on the foot. She put it down close to the mother, who immediately started to lick it as well.

'Why don't you go stand by Ronaldo?'

The mother dog was occupied for now, but she still had her eye on Mary and the other pups on the far side of the box stall. If she got nervous, it would only take one lunge for her to get between them and whoever she thought threatened them. If anyone got bit, Mary didn't want it to be Dalia. She started edging around the side of the stall toward the last two pups, making shooing gestures toward the child while she moved.

At first, Mary didn't think Dalia was going to leave the box. It was obvious she didn't want to. Finally, slowly, she backed out to stand beside her brother. Neither child took their eyes off Mary.

'What are you looking for?' Ronaldo's voice registered confusion but not concern.

Thank goodness. They'd been scared enough. She wanted to get this done and get them out of there before they found out that, right about now, they should be petrified.

'Why are you looking at the puppies' feet?' Dalia seemed less confused, but more concerned. Not good.

'I'm looking at their toenails. As soon as I'm finished, we're leaving. Get Millie away from that other dog and make sure her leash is secure. I'll just be a minute.'

Millie protested as Dalia dragged her away but the girl took no notice. 'I don't like it here. Can we go now?'

'Yes.' Mary put the last puppy back down beside the mother dog and stood. She'd started to think she'd been wrong, that the poodle wasn't Merlot, but he had to be. It was the only thing that made sense. Then the fourth puppy had clear nails on a very black paw. Time to get the children, Millie and herself out of there. 'Let me go first. I'll just make sure the coast is clear. Stay right behind me.'

The children did as instructed, but it didn't matter. The coast was anything but clear. Horror closed down Mary's throat. The back door of the house open and Todd appeared. He stood, staring right at the open barn door.

FORTY-TWO

'Get back,' Mary hissed at the children, who had appeared, one on each side of her. Millie squeezed in between her legs. 'He'll see you.'

'Who will?' Ronaldo pushed forward a little, trying to peer around Mary.

'The man from the hardware store, that's who.' Dalia's voice quivered and her hand went up to clutch Mary's. 'I didn't know he lived here.'

'The hardware-store man? Isn't he the one you thought . . .' Fear began to creep into Ronaldo's voice as well.

'Yes,' Dalia whispered. 'I wasn't sure, but his boots looked the same.'

The child didn't say the same as what, but she didn't have to. What did they do now? If Todd saw the children here, he'd be sure they'd recognized him. There was nothing she could say or do to convince him otherwise. She had to think of something, and quick. Her cell phone. Of course. She'd call

Dan, or at least Hazel. He'd come . . . her cell was in her purse, which sat beside a chair in Naomi's office. She looked over the hillside behind the fence, up toward the winery. Maybe someone was in the vineyard and she could scream . . . No one was in sight.

Grabbing each child by the arm while trying not to get caught up in Millie's leash, she backed away from the door. 'You have to hide.'

'Where?' Dalia didn't ask why. She seemed more than willing to hide and started looking around. 'In there?' She pointed to a door that led into what might once have been a tack room.

'No. That's the first place he'd look.' Mary's eyes scoured the room, looking for some corner, some safe place, something. They stopped at a set of stairs that led to the hayloft. It would have to do.

'Go up there. Now. Hurry. And, kids, don't make a sound. No matter what happens, no matter what he says or I do, keep quiet. Do you hear me?'

'What are you going to do?' Ronaldo's eyes were wide with worry and Mary thought she detected a tear.

'Fool him.'

'Shall we take Millie?' Dalia bent down and tried to pick up the little dog. 'Oh, she's heavy.'

'Leave her. She can help me fool Todd. Now, get up that ladder.'

'It's a stairway.'

Mary glowered at Ronaldo. 'I don't care what it is, get up it.'

They did and quickly disappeared over the edge. Mary took a second to let out her breath. 'What's up there?'

'Just a bunch of old junk.' Dalia's face appeared in the square opening above the staircase.

'Go hide behind it and don't make a sound.'

Dalia's face was gone just in time. Footsteps sounded on the road. She grabbed Millie's leash and pulled her over to stand beside her in front of the little poodle's pen. The gate on it worked with a latch. Hurriedly, she slid it loose and pushed the gate open just enough so it no longer locked. She had no idea if what she planned to do would work, but it was the only thing she could think of, and if the children stayed quiet no matter what happened to her, they, at least, should be safe. Todd couldn't know they were with her.

A shadow passed across the partly open barn door and Todd stepped through it. An immediate explosion of barking greeted him. Even Millie joined the chorus.

'Hush.' Todd shouted the word with impressive lung power. Silence fell instantly. He looked around at the dogs, staring at each one in turn. They stared back, but not one uttered a sound. Seemingly satisfied, he turned to Mary. 'Why, Mrs McGill. I didn't expect to see you here.'

His tone seemed pleasant enough and, at another time, in another place, Mary might not have noticed the hint of anger that underlay it. She did now, and the dogs seemed to have as well. What had he done to get them to quiet down so quickly? Right now, however, she had more important things to think about, like keeping the children safe and herself alive. She had no doubt Todd had killed both Cliff and Evan and had no reason to suspect he'd spare her. Unless, of course, she actually could fool him.

'Todd. Goodness. I didn't expect to be here, either. It was Millie. You remember Millie, don't you?' She had to stop babbling. There was no way he'd believe her if she seemed nervous.

Todd's eyes had fastened onto Mary when he walked in. He briefly dropped them to take in Millie before returning to Mary. 'Millie. Evan's Millie? How did you end up with her?'

The slightly disparaging tone he used made Mary stiffen. She almost said something but didn't have to. A low growl from Millie said more than Mary could have. Todd ignored it. The narrowing of his eyes, the faint menace in his voice told Mary he wouldn't be denied an answer. 'What are you and that dog doing in my barn?'

Crossing her fingers, Mary replied in what she hoped was her most convincing voice. 'I was visiting the winery, buying some wine for Christmas, you know . . .'

His weight shifted from one booted foot to the other. Lace-up work boots. The same ones he had on that day in the hardware store. It seemed a lifetime ago. Oh, Lord.

'Millie needed to go out . . .' at least that much was true, '. . .

so I took her to that spot up on the hill. She kept looking down this way and suddenly she just ran. I followed her through that gate over there . . .' The look on Todd's face stopped her.

'The gate was open?'

Mary nodded.

'Who opened it?'

'I have no idea. I didn't even know there was a gate until Millie ran through it. Can you imagine my surprise when I found her in here?'

Mary uncrossed her fingers. She decided that was close enough to the truth to pass.

Unfortunately, Todd didn't seem convinced. 'You're saying your dog ran through the gate and into my barn? Why?'

'I don't know that either, but she seems to like this little black dog. He is pretty cute. He's not a cocker, though, is he?' Mary thought she could easily play the ingénue in the next production of the Little Playhouse if her performance today was one to judge by. Just to make sure Todd knew how innocent she was, she smiled.

Todd's expression changed from angry to confused to cunning. He glanced over at the dog then back at Mary and smiled. 'Ah, no. He's, ah, boarding here for a while.'

'Oh. Well, he's pretty cute. Millie thought so too.' She chuckled. She couldn't believe it. She hadn't known she could pull it off. Should she try it again? No. What she needed to try was getting out of there. Fervently hoping the children would stay quiet until she could get help, she raised her voice so it could be heard in the back row of a theater. Or the top of a hayloft. 'Well, I guess we'd better be going. Millie is a naughty dog to go running off like that, but no harm. I'll go back to the winery through the gate, if you don't mind. Do you want me to close it?'

Todd didn't answer. Instead, he seemed to be listening. A car engine turned off and a car door slammed. Who . . . not help. Of that Mary was sure. If she could just ease out of there before . . . Footsteps crunched on the driveway then hurried footsteps drew closer. She gathered up Millie's leash, ready to make a dash for the barn door when another shadow passed over it. Bonnie.

A chorus of barking broke out as the dogs caught sight of her.

Only this time it sounded different. Joyous barking, welcome home barking. Dogs ran around in their pens and jumped up on the wire gates, begging to be recognized.

'Quiet!' The noise immediately stopped as Todd's voice overrode theirs.

Bonnie ignored the dogs, but she glanced over at Todd and looked hard at Millie and Mary, who still stood in front of the pen that contained the little dog Mary was certain was Merlot.

A look of sadness seemed to pass over Bonnie's face, but it was quickly erased. She sucked in her breath and let it out with a sigh. 'Hello, Mary. Just dropped in to say hello?'

'Actually, as much as I'd like to stop and visit, it was my dog I came to collect. I was telling Todd I was up at the winery and I took her outside to . . . you know . . . only she took off down here . . .'

'Really? How did she get over the fence?' There was no longer any trace of sadness in Bonnie's voice. Only sarcasm and the beginnings of anger.

'The gate was open.'

Bonnie wheeled around to stare at Todd. 'How did the gate happen to be open?'

He shrugged.

'I thought you were going to padlock it.'

'Yeah, well, I didn't. Must have been one of those tourists who keep wandering through the vineyard. I'll get to it this afternoon.'

'It's a little late, don't you think?' Bonnie's voice dripped with sarcasm. 'She's here and she knows. She's many things, but none of them stupid.' Bonnie looked around the barn, at the cockers in their pens, at Merlot then at Mary, anger building. 'One of the things you are is a pain in the rear. Why did you have to come snooping?'

'I didn't. The dog really did run down here. I just followed.' She paused slightly, wondering if she should go on, but it no longer mattered. 'I did wonder, though. You said you hadn't bred Alma's dogs, but you have them and they aren't in your kennels. Plus the toenails. Merlot has that recessive gene for clear toenails. One of the puppies for sale at Evan's shop did also. The one Cliff brought to the manger before he was killed. There were other things. You didn't want anyone to think you ever bred any other dogs than cockers but cockapoos bring in good money, and you needed money. I started putting things together and wondered.'

'Then you followed that miserable little dog and no longer wondered.'

Mary decided that was more of a statement than a question and didn't require an answer. Besides, she didn't trust her voice to come out without a squeak.

Bonnie looked around the barn, as if seeing it for the first time, and shook her head. 'I knew we should have done all this someplace else.'

'Where?' Todd's voice held a weariness that suggested it wasn't the first time the subject had been discussed.

'I don't know. If I did, we wouldn't be here.' Bonnie paused and looked back at Mary. 'You know, Mary, I've always admired you. So efficient, so willing to help, and so smart. This town will miss you.' She turned toward Todd, who looked a little pale but seemed attentive to whatever Bonnie was about to say.

So was Mary.

'I don't know how you want to do this, but you can't leave her alive, and you can't leave her body here. You'll have to dump her somewhere, and try to think of how to blame this on someone else. How about John and Glen? They had the most to gain from Evan's death.'

Mary had the most to lose by what Bonnie was obviously expecting Todd to do, but she wasn't going down without a fight. She reached behind and felt the gate. It swung backward under the pressure of her hand. She glanced back. The little dog was on his feet, watching it. Millie watched the poodle. Mary reached her hand down to touch her on the head.

'What are you doing?' Bonnie's voice was sharp and filled with alarm.

'She's getting nervous. I'm just reassuring her.' Mary's hand came off Millie's head and landed on the gate. With one hard push, it flew open. She twisted to grab Millie and the poodle took a tentative step forward.

'Run, it's your only chance. She'll kill you too. Run, Merlot.'

The dog paused to look at Mary as if in wonder, but he saw the wide open gate and headed for it. Bonnie saw it as well and threw herself forward in an effort to pull it shut. Too late. The dog dashed right between her legs, detoured around Todd, whose dive for him was interrupted as Bonnie staggered into him. The dog dashed out the door, silently intent on escape. Millie twisted out of Mary's grasp and followed, barking hard enough to wake the entire town, her leash flying behind her. Mary had time for one quick prayer they'd head for the winery before she was faced with a furious Bonnie.

'Why did you do that?'

'Do what?'

'Don't be cute, Mary. Letting that dog go wasn't a bright move. Now we've really got to do something about you.'

'What?' Todd's voice was scathing. 'You jumped all over me for getting rid of Cliff and Evan, even though you knew I didn't have any choice. Now you want me to get rid of the old lady?'

Bonnie's eyes shifted toward him. The look she gave him was filled with contempt. 'Cliff was my friend. You didn't have to kill him. He wouldn't have given me – us – up, as much as he hated the idea of producing all these half-breed puppies.'

'Is that why he demanded money? He was so worried about your precious reputation in the cocker spaniel world he wanted us to pay him not to wreck it? Is that why he took the puppy from Evan's shop? Is that why he said he could prove it was sired by that blasted poodle and if we didn't pay him, he'd have me arrested for stealing it? He may have hated the puppies, but he sure didn't mind the money he wanted from breeding them. Some friend he was.'

She'd been right. It had all been about dogs and Cliff had been trying to blackmail someone. However, being right wasn't going to save her from ending up in a grave next door to him. Unless, of course, she could think of something . . .

'We can't let her go. She'd be yelling "you murdered both of them" before she got to the gate . . . the gate. Oh, Lord. The gate is open. Those dogs will have everyone out looking for her any minute. You'd better go close it and, this time, lock it.' Bonnie stopped. She seemed to assess Mary, looking for what, Mary wasn't sure.

'Never mind. I'll lock the gate. You get on with it. And don't mess this up. She could send us both to jail for life.'

Without a backward glance, Bonnie hurried out of the barn. Todd turned toward Mary, and his body seemed to go very still. There was nothing in the studied look he gave her that spoke of hesitation, only deliberation. What was he planning? Before she could move, he grabbed her by the arm and was dragging her . . . where? Toward a familiar pile of dog food sacks.

He threw her at them and bent over, seemingly searching for something stashed in between the piles. He straightened, smiling, the missing barbeque skewer in his hand. 'Bonnie wanted me to get rid of this, but I knew I might need it again. Don't shake so. It'll hurt a whole lot less if you stand still.'

He had her by the arm, twisting it behind her, forcing it up between her shoulder blades. Did he really think she would just stand there and let him stab her? Besides, it hurt. Mary ducked, trying to twist around to free her arm, kicking out with her good leg.

'Quit it! Stop kicking. God damn it, stop . . .' Todd's hand went slack, the eyes that had bored with fury into hers went blank and he slumped to the ground, blood pouring from the side of his head. The loud thump she'd barely heard must have come from the ancient metal pail that now lay on the pile of dog food, blood staining the jagged rip on one side.

Surprise and shock kept Mary from moving as she stared at the unconscious Todd. At first, even the small voice coming from above didn't penetrate. When it did, she looked up to see two small faces peering down through the hole at the top of the stairs.

'Did we kill him?' There was a distinct quiver in Dalia's voice.

'No.' A twitch seemed to run through Todd and his eyelids fluttered. He wasn't dead, and he would soon be very much awake. They had to get out of there. 'Come down and hurry.'

'Are you mad at us?' Ronaldo seemed more worried about her reaction to their disobedience than how much damage they'd inflicted on Todd.

'For saving my life? I don't think so. But now I need to save yours, so hurry.'

The children exchanged glances and scurried down the ladder. 'What are we going to do?'

'Leave.' Mary took each one by the arm and started for the barn door. The dogs started to bark again, which was sure to bring

Bonnie running back. She had to get them out of the barn, but she also had to know if Bonnie had padlocked the gate. If so, that avenue of escape was gone. How she'd get by her and out onto the road leading onto the winery property, she didn't know. She did know they wouldn't be safe until they got somewhere more populated. She was no match for Bonnie in any kind of fight. She couldn't outrun her, either. Bonnie was going to be a problem.

She was right. Bonnie walked through the barn door, stopped and blinked as she spotted the children. 'Where did they come from?'

'Up there.' Ronaldo pointed up the stairs toward the hayloft.

'Hush.' Bonnie's voice didn't have the force Todd's had, but it served to silence the dogs. 'You were hiding up there, were you?' She turned to look at Mary. 'Very clever, but you're not going anywhere and neither are they. Too bad you had to turn up when you did, but sometimes . . . well, sometimes things don't turn out the way you want them to.'

Mary thought Bonnie looked very unhappy, like she didn't really want to kill Mary and the children. Maybe not, but Mary didn't think it would deter Bonnie. As long as Mary and the children were alive, neither Bonnie nor Todd was safe.

Dalia's face flushed with fear and she trembled under Mary's hand. Or was that her trembling? Not only did Bonnie block the door, but she'd pulled it almost all the way closed. Mary'd better think of something, and fast.

Todd groaned.

'What's that?' Bonnie looked around the barn and took another couple of quick steps toward them. 'Where's Todd?'

As if in answer, he gave another groan and started to stir. Bonnie was close enough now to see him, or at least one leg. She pushed past Mary to stare at him. 'He's bleeding. What happened in here?' She wheeled around toward Mary and the children, who started backing up, demanding an answer, but she didn't wait for it. She dropped to one knee beside Todd and started to touch him all over as if to make sure nothing was broken or missing, crooning to him, tears threatening to cascading down her face. 'Are you all right? You've got to be all right. Oh, your poor head. Todd, say something. I didn't mean to yell. Todd . . .'

Todd only groaned but his eyelids fluttered again. This was their chance, their only chance, as far as Mary could see. She mouthed at Dalia, *Pail.*

Dalia grabbed it off the top of the pile of dog food sacks as they quietly backed up more.

'Get the door,' she whispered to Ronaldo, who immediately turned toward it. One quick pull had it open wide enough for the children to slip through. It needed one more for Mary to get through too and that was enough to jerk Bonnie's attention away from Todd and back to them.

'Close the door,' Mary called to Ronaldo. He was way ahead of her. He stood ready to roll it shut just as Mary slid through.

'Does it lock?'

Ronaldo shook his head.

Mary grabbed the pail from Dalia. 'Run,' she told the children.

'Where to?' Dalia looked around. 'The gate's closed.'

'Is it locked?'

'Can't tell.'

'That way.' She pointed toward the kennel building. 'There's a gate just past that building. Run for it and head for the winery. Get help. Don't wait for me.'

They ran.

Mary knew she couldn't keep up with them. She could only hope they got the gate open and headed up the main road to the winery. With a little luck, they could raise the alarm before she had to fend off Bonnie. *What did Bonnie have in mind?* Mary hadn't seen any sign of a weapon, but she was absolutely sure Bonnie didn't plan on letting her leave this property alive. Should she try and hide or head for the gate and hope she made it out before Bonnie quit moaning over Todd and realized they were no longer in the barn? The gate into the vineyard. It was worth taking the chance, and she didn't want to get trapped anywhere inside this fence. She started toward it, clutching the old pail, surprised by how heavy it was, and turned to check the barn door. It was open and someone stood in it, shielding his eyes from the rapidly setting sun. Todd. Blood still dripped along one side of his face and down his shirt collar, and he held onto the barn door for support, but the fury evident in the scowl on his

face and the tight way he held the barbeque skewer at the side
of his leg lent him strength. He seemed to spot Mary at about
the same time she saw him and a small, mean smile replaced the
scowl. Slowly, he started toward her.

Clutching the pail, Mary backed up, turned and ran, faster than
she would have believed possible, away from the vineyard. She'd
never make it past Todd. She wouldn't make the gate by the
road, either. There was only one choice. The kennel building. If
there was a lock on the door, maybe she could keep him at bay
until help arrived. If it did.

She slid inside the door and slammed it shut. Was there a
lock? There was, but it was only a thumb latch. That wouldn't
keep Todd out very long, but long enough? How long was that?
A tremor ran through her so strong she had to hold onto the door
handle to keep upright. The dogs had started barking as soon as
she slammed the door, and she almost missed the voice, high
pitched and very distressed.

'Let me in. Hurry. He's coming.'

Dalia? Mary had the door open almost before the child finished
speaking. She grabbed her by the arm, pulled her through the
door then slammed it shut again, engaging the lock before she
turned to face the little girl.

'What are you doing here? I told you to run for the . . . where's
Ronaldo?'

Dalia seemed out of breath but, after she bent over, hands on
her knees, and had taken a couple of deep breaths, she put her
head up, looked at Mary and smiled. 'He's out by the gate,
waiting for the police.'

Mary could barely hear Dalia over the frantic yelps of the
dogs. 'Quiet!' she yelled at the top of her voice. She had no idea
if this would work, but it wouldn't hurt to try. Silence descended,
immediately broken by the high-pitched wail of police sirens
getting louder and more persistent by the second.

'The police?' The dogs started again, this time seemingly
protesting the screaming sirens.

'Here?' She had to mouth this last. Dalia couldn't possibly
hear her, but she seemed to understand because she nodded her
head and smiled – a smile that disappeared rapidly.

The door to the kennels shook on its hinges as someone tried to get in. Mary had no doubt as to who that someone was. She grabbed Dalia again by the arm and this time headed for the room where Bonnie kept the feed. Please, God, let it have a lock. She hoped Dalia was right and the sirens were, in fact, police cars coming to the rescue, but they'd have to be fast. The front door had just given way with an ear-splitting crash.

The feed room door had a lock, another thumb latch, but a lock. It wouldn't stop Todd, but it might slow him down. If Dalia was right, it would give Dan, or whoever was in those police cars, time to get in here.

'Help me drag this sack over there.'

Dalia grabbed one end of a dog food sack and looked around. 'Where?'

'In front of the door. We'll stack a bunch there.'

'Why?'

'Just do it.'

The sacks were heavy and unwieldy, but between the two of them, they managed to stack three before the door started to shake.

'You've trapped yourself nicely, Mary, and those kids as well. See you in a few minutes.' Todd's voice sounded faintly amused, but Mary knew it was because he thought he'd won, that there was no escape. Hadn't he heard the sirens?

Where was Ronaldo? Where were the police? The sirens had stopped. Did that mean they'd turned them off or that they weren't coming here? Police cars and ambulances weren't uncommon on Hwy 46. 'Keep stacking.' It was all she could think to do. That and pray like crazy. Todd was still holding the barbeque skewer last time she saw him and she had every reason to believe he still held it. The thought of it sticking into her, or worse, Dalia, made her break out in a cold sweat. Another crash on a door that didn't look as if it would hold much longer didn't help.

'Another one,' she told a panting Dalia. 'Heave.'

'How many more?' The child looked as if she was ready to give out, but keeping the door from caving in was their only chance.

'At least two.'

Mary had just grabbed the end of another sack when a commotion broke out in the hallway. Scuffles, yells, protests, Todd's voice above the others, shouting in rage, and another, familiar voice saying, 'Watch out for that skewer.' Someone else shouted something about handcuffs. The dogs were barking so loudly she wasn't sure about anything except the incessant attacks on the door had stopped. She and Dalia looked at each other.

'Is that the police?'

Mary let a smile spread, sank down on what was left of the pile of sacks and nodded. 'I think it is.'

Dalia took a deep breath and sat down beside Mary. She let it out then smiled at her. 'Good thing I finally remembered I had my cell phone in my pocket, huh.'

So that's what happened. Mary could do nothing more than nod, but that she did with gratitude.

'Dalia, Mary, are you in there? Are you all right?'

Mary found enough strength to answer. 'We're here and we're fine.'

Dalia found her voice as well. 'Where's Ronaldo?'

'I'm here. I opened the gate for them to get in.'

Pride was ripe in the boy's voice and Mary couldn't think of anyone who deserved to feel pride more. Unless it was Dalia, for staying cool and thinking enough to use her cell phone. Actually, for remembering to bring it. Looked like she had a lot of cookies to make for those two, but first . . .

'We can't get the door open.' Dan's voice. 'We want to get you out, but we'll need you to move whatever you barricaded it with.'

'We used dog food sacks. They're heavy. You'll have to wait a minute.' She pushed herself to her feet and stared at the pile, ten sacks high, each weighing fifty pounds. That last one felt more like a ton. How had they managed to pile so many? Adrenaline, which seemed to have deserted her. She looked back at Dalia, who hadn't moved from the sacks.

Her eyes were fastened on the door, still filled with fear. 'Is he gone?' she whispered.

'Yes. They have him. He can't hurt you, or anyone else, any more.' Mary sat beside her and reached out, but the child wrapped her arms around herself and seemed to shrink into them, as if burying herself in a cocoon. 'I know.' The words came out softly and she shook her head a little. She seemed to shake all over. 'I know they won't let him hurt me, or Ronaldo, it's just that I . . .' She couldn't seem to go on.

'It's that you don't want to see him?' Fear mixed with adrenaline had carried the child just so far, but now it was almost over, there was nothing left of the adrenaline, but the fear remained.

Dalia looked at Mary, her eyes clouded with tears, and nodded. 'He's a bad man. He hurt people something terrible and he tried to hurt you and Ronaldo. And me. I don't ever want to see him again.'

'We won't open the door until I'm sure he's gone. I promise. You stay right where you are and I'll go ask Dan where he is.'

Mary walked close to the door and called. 'Dan? Where's Todd?'

'Standing beside the car in handcuffs, alternating between using some of the most inventive cursing I've heard in a while and proclaiming his innocence. Why? Is there a problem?'

'Dalia doesn't want to come out until he's gone. She doesn't want to see him.'

There was a pause and she thought she heard Dan leave but soon he was back. 'He's in the back of a patrol car headed out the gate.'

'And Bonnie?'

'In another car, on her way to the station.'

'Did you hear? They're both gone.' Mary turned toward the little girl, who had already started to unwind herself. She wasn't smiling, but the tears were gone and resolve seemed to have taken their place as she joined Mary at the blocked door.

'Let's get out of here.' Dalia grabbed the end of the top bag and pulled.

FORTY-THREE

Mary sat in her rocking chair, an almost-empty mug of tea held tight against her, listening to the quiet in her living room. It had been a tumultuous afternoon and evening, starting with an unwanted and unnecessary trip to the hospital where she and the children were thoroughly checked and pronounced fine. Mary could have told them that. None of them had been hurt, just seriously terrified. It was going to take some time for the children to get over that, but they would. Their mother and Tony had already started the process. After the hospital and Dan were done with them and they were ready to start for home, they told the children Sampson would be coming for Christmas and he'd stay. Their excitement almost overrode the terror of this terrible day. Almost.

It had been after eight when Dan and Ellen brought her home. They had picked up In-N-Out Burgers on the way, a treat Mary rarely allowed herself, and Dan had pressed her with questions in between bites. Why had they gone through the gate? When did she realize Bonnie and Todd were responsible for all that had gone on? Why hadn't she left sooner? Why hadn't she called him as soon as she went into the barn? Those last questions came with an undertone of both relief and irritation – relief they were all alive and irritation she and the children had ever been in danger.

She swallowed the last onion ring and held up her hand. 'If you'll hush, I'll tell you everything.'

Dan looked a bit taken back; Ellen laughed. 'All right. Tell.'

Dan fidgeted while she took a sip of her coffee. She wasn't sure where to begin; her suspicions, then her certainty, had grown gradually. She'd start with the dogs.

'From almost the beginning, it seemed to me this had to be about dogs, not as pets, but as a business. It was the only connection I could see between Cliff and Evan.'

Dan said, 'What connection was that? Cliff took care of them, at least while he was still practicing. Evan sold them.'

Mary nodded. 'Evan did, but Cliff also worked with the people who bred them and showed them and made money doing it. Cliff's passion wasn't dogs for pets, but purebred dogs. He hated cross-breeding. He berated Glen and John for breeding their cockers with a poodle and he tried to bad-mouth Luke for breeding his little dog with Millie.'

The dog looked at Mary from where she had squeezed in beside her then let her head drop back into Mary's lap. Mary stroked her ears.

'Luke didn't care. Neither did John or Glen, which made them unlikely candidates for blackmail. Then Karl said the DNA test Cliff wanted proved Merlot was alive and close by, and so was whoever took him. Todd said he'd seen the dog go off in a car, but I started to wonder. They bred cockers and Bonnie was a fanatic about her purebred dogs and the reputation of her kennels, but she needed money to keep it going. Todd's hardware store wasn't helping. She bought Alma's dogs, even though they, like Millie, aren't show quality. I didn't realize that until Pat said Millie wouldn't fit in a top-notch cocker breeding program. Neither would Alma's dogs. She only had one that good, and Cliff ruined her. So what did Bonnie want them for? She didn't have them in her kennel building. It was when I learned how much cockapoos sell for that I started to wonder. She might be willing to breed Alma's dogs to a poodle, but that would mean finding one, arranging the breeding, all things that might get out and ruin her reputation as a cocker spaniel breeder and judge. I think that was more important to her than not paying a stud fee. But stealing a dog like Merlot could mean jail time. I didn't think she'd risk either so started to look elsewhere. Then Evan was killed. That started me thinking about John and Glen, but they had no reason to kill Cliff. Father D'Angelo did, and there were all those footprints, but he had no reason to kill Evan that I could see. By the way, I think he was the one in the Mendosas' bushes. He told me his new cat, who he named Lucifer, likes to get out at night and he goes looking for him.'

Dan gave a soft laugh. Ellen grinned at Mary, who smiled.

'The only thing that made sense, the only reason for Cliff to have the puppy with him, was blackmail. He wanted to prove to someone he knew about Merlot. Sampson has the telltale toenail. So do the puppies in the barn. At least one of them does. I didn't know that then, but things kept coming back to Bonnie. She made those dreadful robes for the choir. Todd could easily have gotten one. He knew the route the *posada* would take and that the lean-to would be unlit until they got there. He had plenty of time to arrange to meet Cliff and kill him. Bad luck for him, he lost the puppy, but even worse luck, the children found the rest of the barbeque skewer set and insisted on buying it. No one else would have connected it with a murder. I didn't – not at

first, anyway. Then Evan was evasive about who owned the
puppies he had for sale. Why? Because the breeder was someone
who didn't want it known they bred cockapoos. Someone Evan
trusted, at least where the health of the dogs was concerned. He
trusted John and Glen, but they'd already produced cockapoos
and openly planned to have more. Who else had been in that
shop Friday afternoon? Todd. According to Luke, Todd said he'd
be back to pick up dog food. Only, I remembered seeing a large
stack of dog food sacks when I picked up the donations for the
can tree. Why would Todd need food so urgently? Then Naomi
told me Bill and Todd had worked out a deal to stand Merlot.
It'd failed but Bonnie and Todd got all the improvements the
Blisses had made to the barn. I wondered if that's where Alma's
dogs were. When Dalia stated the man she saw wore work boots,
the kind Tony wears in the vineyard, the kind Todd wears, I was
certain, but before I could act, Millie ran off, the kids followed
and you know the rest.'

Dan looked stricken. 'Work boots, not sandals. We asked those
kids everything about that man but what he had on his feet. I
can't believe it.'

That was when the doorbell rang. A subdued Glen and John
walked in.

'We're only going to stay a moment.' John dropped a kiss on
Mary's check and scratched behind Millie's ear.

She looked up and wagged her behind but made no move away
from Mary. John sighed and glanced at Glen.

'What a terrible day.' Glen addressed them all with a wave of
his hand. 'We just can't believe it.'

'Yes, we can.' John's hand rested on Mary's shoulder and he
gave her a small pat. 'Bonnie was a fanatic about her dogs. She
got all that from listening to Cliff all those years, I'll bet. As
for Todd, he'd do anything Bonnie said. I think he adored her
as much as she adored her dogs.' He shook his head. 'What a
waste.'

'So tragic.' Glen waved away the offer of coffee Ellen started
to make. 'We're not staying but wanted you all to know we're
going to take their dogs, at least for now. The owners of the
black dog are coming to get him, but we'll take care of the girls.
So, Mary, we thought you'd like to know, since you seem to

want to keep Millie, and she seems to like it here, we're going to give you an early Christmas present.'

He dropped an envelope in her lap. Mary opened it. 'What's this?' She pulled out what looked like a certificate of some kind.

'Millie's papers. We've signed them over to you.' They grinned at each other. 'You'd better take good care of her now. We'll be watching.' John laughed.

Glen joined in but immediately turned serious. 'This is probably the only good thing that's come out of today. When I think what could have happened to you, or to those delightful children . . .'

Mary wasn't sure what to say. She hadn't expected this, nor the feeling of relief and happiness she felt. 'Oh,' was about all she could manage. 'Oh, thank you.'

'You're most welcome.' John followed Glen toward the door. 'See you next time you need dog food.'

Dan and Ellen left soon after, Dan assuring her he'd have more questions in the days to come.

That was fine, but right now . . .

'Are you sure you'll be all right here, all alone?' Ellen asked.

This time Mary didn't bristle. She let her hand drop once more onto the little dog's head. 'I won't be alone.'

'I guess you won't be at that.' And they left.

She and Millie sat there, warm and comfortable, enjoying the lights on the Christmas tree and the silence in the house. The mess Bonnie and Todd had made of their lives and the damage they had done to others weighed heavily on Mary, but there were a few bright spots. The children were safe, largely because of their own bravery. Furry Friends would continue to sell the supplies the local pet owners needed and she was sure John and Glen would follow Evan's high standard of pet care. Father D'Angelo had befriended a cat who appeared to be incorrigible and was on his way, with her help, to provide shelter for a lot of people who desperately needed it. Luke, from the library, would continue to take pleasure in his dog, his job and his help in making sure, through the can tree, no one in this town would go hungry, at least for a little while. Her job of protector had ended, mercifully, happily, and the Mendosa family would soon have two new members. Tomorrow she'd start organizing the reception to be held after Evan's graveside service and make sure they had room to put the first donations to St Mark's annual rummage sale in the church store room. She needed to make sure the children's ornaments with their Christmas wishes on them were all being taken from the Secret Santa tree in the church lobby and she'd better get busy on her package wrapping. After the New Year she had the library event, then the dedication of the new playground her parks and recreation committee had been planning and . . .

She sighed and Millie looked at her. 'It's not been the best day we've ever spent, has it, but it's over. All of it, and we have new things that need doing tomorrow. Are you ready?' Mary pushed herself to her feet. Millie jumped down and waited while Mary turned off the tree lights, then trotted beside her as they headed for bed.